GAMMA

GAMMA

M. SUSANNE WIGGINS

GAMMA

a novel

by M. Susanne Wiggins

This is a work of fiction. Names, places, characters, and incidents are either a product of the author's imagination or are used fictitiously. Any resemblance to actual persons, living or dead, locales, or historical events is entirely coincidental.

GAMMA, Book 1.

Printed in the United States of America.

ISBN 978-0-9970736-3-8

eBook ISBN 978-0-9970736-4-5

Library of Congress Control Number 2016919730

Data available upon request.

Contact information:

MSusanneWiggins.com

For Anna

To see a World in a Grain of Sand
And a Heaven in a Wild Flower
Hold Infinity in the palm of your hand
And Eternity in an hour
~ *Auguries of Innocence* by William Blake

1

Shadows

Some argue that Gamma's end came with its beginning;
...and so begins the end.

~

There was no trepidation lurking in Meg Arcana's expression, nor in her thoughts. Alec looked at the branch in question and worked on a strategy of how best to arrive there. It was positioned in such a way that they could climb to it like they did the first one.

"We'll go up like before, but that's it," he said. "We won't go any higher 'cause it gets trickier and we could fall and die and then our moms will kill us. Okay?"

"Okay."

Alec went first, grabbing the branch then pulling himself up. Secure on the higher limb, he held his hands down to reach for hers. Once her hands were in his, he began the upward tugging. It was a little harder this time, as they weren't on solid ground and he watched her face for panic.

At first there was none, but when she was halfway up to the second branch primitive fear evolved on her face. Her eyes widened, her mouth opened in what looked like the beginning of a scream, though she made no sound at all. Fearing she'd fall, he gripped her hands tight. She seemed frozen, and her eyes were fixed on a single point where a limb branched from the tree trunk.

He leaned forward and saw what garnered her attention—a spider. Alec figured he must have disturbed it when he went up. The fact that the spider was moving made matters worse, as he could feel the increasing tension in her hands.

"Ignore it, Meg. Let me pull you up."

"I can't, Alec," she whispered. "I think it's about to jump on me. I know it is, it's a jumping spider."

Alec sensed her working out a plan while he tried sorting out one of his own. Suddenly, it didn't matter. A well-formed sphere encapsulated the spider, its legs now walking along the sphere's inner surface. Meg waited for it to move farther down the limb, but when it took too long she inhaled a deep breath and blew the sphere away.

He realized all at once that it had been *her*. Meg had cloaked the spider; he hadn't even considered the idea yet when the sphere formed. He recognized the concentration on her face and it was strange seeing it on someone else. Then it dawned on him—Meg was different, she was like him. His heart beat a faster pace and seemed overly loud to him; he wondered if she could hear it.

With the spider far enough away now, she allowed the sphere surrounding it to dissolve. Eight legs on solid branch again, it skittered away. Her hands relaxed, like nothing had happened—like the hiccup in time never happened. She simply finished her climb and sat on the limb next to him.

Did she think it was normal for spiders to fly through the air just to suit her? He scrutinized her, searching for some kind of knowledge, some sense of awareness, but found none. Meg was too young to understand that what she did made her different.

He wasn't sure what it was all supposed to be for, but he knew she was the only other child on the island that could do what he was able to do. Alec remembered how scared his mother was, and her warnings echoed again in his thoughts: '*Keep what you can do a secret.*' He thought of Ila, Meg's mother—there was no way she could handle Meg being so different from everyone else.

His gaze swept over the landscape. Unsure of why, Alec knew he was always being watched. Though he never saw anyone, he could feel their presence and the hefty weight of their inquisitive stares, and sometimes he heard their whispers in the wind. He made a quick decision, a brash decision, but he'd prefer a more secluded place to do it. Time to coax Meg out of the tree.

"What's that building?"

Meg looked at where he pointed and giggled. "It's a barn, Alec."

"I know it's a barn, I have one, too. I was just curious about what's in *your* barn. Do you have any animals in there?"

"We have chickens and two horses in there. You want to see them?"

"Yeah, come on."

They worked their way down the tree. Once four feet hit the ground, they took off toward the barn. Alec bent down by the entrance and picked through several rocks until he found the kind he wanted: smooth and flat on one side; heavy, but small enough to conceal. He pocketed it and went inside to find her.

She introduced him to the horses first; their names were Antony and Cleopatra, even though they were both female and heavily pregnant. All eleven hens had names as well and Meg could tell them apart, but Alec insisted they all looked the same. She explained that some of the hens were incubating eggs and it wouldn't be much longer before they hatched.

Now's a good time, he thought to himself, but then she turned to him.

"I like watching them break open their shells," she said. "Have you ever seen that?"

"Nope. Do you think some have already started?"

Alec wanted her back to him. If he snuck up behind her, she'd never know what happened or that he threw the rock at her. Meg turned toward the nest boxes and crept up the ramp to keep from startling the hens.

Do it now, he told himself.

When she reached the entrance to the coop, just leaning over to poke her head in, Alec pulled the rock from his pocket and launched it. It made contact with the back of her head and landed nearby in the hay. He rushed forward to catch her before she fell; and, as though he was a bird swooping down on its prey, he opened his arms wide enveloped Meg like a cloak.

Other than the sound of crunching hay beneath his feet, the barn was silent. Alec lowered the unconscious Meg to the floor. He closed his eyes and concentrated harder than he ever had and soon a soft glow surrounded both the children, giving them the appearance of slumbering cherubs.

The sphere around them began to diminish, the opacity giving way to transparency and then the arc of energy vanished. Alec moved in a slow and cautious manner, unsure if he'd been successful. He lifted his arm off of Meg and waited to see what would happen, but still she remained motionless. He worried the rock hit her too hard and he found a sizeable lump on the back of her head. Alec leaned in and sighed with relief at hearing her steady breathing.

He brushed aside her mop of blonde ringlets to study her face, searching for anything different. Finding nothing, he closed his eyes and paid closer attention, blocking out the new sounds of horses munching on oats and the soft clucking of hens returning to the barn.

Alec felt it, something had changed. In one way, he felt bigger and stronger than ever. In another way, Meg seemed daintier and diminished in some new capacity. He opened his eyes again, but found nothing different about her physical appearance. Still, he couldn't be completely sure he'd succeeded in absorbing her abilities and this was the exact moment when Alec vowed to watch over Meg—forever if he had to.

He whispered in her ear, "I'll always protect you, Meg. I swear it."

She stirred a little and let out a small moan, worrying Alec as to whether or not she'd heard him.

"What the hell is going on in here?" came a thunderous shout from the barn door.

Alec's head snapped toward the sunlight filtering in to the barn's interior. His heart plummeted at seeing Ila's silhouette in the light.

"Meg wanted to show me the hatching eggs." Alec removed all panic from his face and voice. "But she tripped and hit her head on the ramp. I think she's starting to wake up now."

Ila's fierce glare softened, replaced by a concerned frown. She was by Meg's side in seconds, prodding her fully awake. Alec relaxed when Meg's eyes opened, but waited to hear what she'd say.

"Are you okay, sweetie?" Ila asked her.

Meg looked at her mother and blinked a few times, then she turned to Alec and the emerald-green eyes stared so long at him that Ila turned her gaze back to him. It took almost more power than Alec possessed to remain calm and indifferent.

"What happened?" Meg squeaked out.

Alec exhaled pure relief at hearing the question. Neither Meg nor Ila had any idea what he'd done to her and he would make sure it stayed that way.

Yet, there were those who saw. One, whose cloaked figure retreated to the shadows of the barn, glad she hadn't killed Alec after all. The other drifted away among the wood planks of the barn to prepare the way for a successor.

"Alec said you bumped your head," Ila told her, though it sounded more like a question.

"I was gonna show him the hatching eggs, and then I… I don't remember after that."

Ila scooped Meg up in her arms and hugged her. She thanked Alec for trying to help and reassured Meg that it wasn't the first bump on the head she'd ever had and probably wouldn't be the last.

~

A quiet decade had passed since that day in the barn, and Alec and Meg were walking along the same familiar beach they'd walked on countless times before. They called it Alaret Beach, a combination of their names; Alec and Margaret. They had coined the term when they were children and it became unofficially adopted thereafter by the rest of the islanders.

At nineteen years of age, Alec was almost three years older than Meg and he always reminded her that seniority rules. Throughout their childhood, Meg believed him when he told her that being older made him wiser. As she grew older, she grew wiser as well.

Though he made it his personal duty to protect her for as long as she could remember, it never bothered Meg, nor had she ever questioned why he felt it was necessary. At times, she thought it was nice having Alec look out for her. But life on the island was easy, certainly safe in her opinion, so there wasn't much to protect her from, and this day was no exception.

It was beautiful and sunny out—and typical, since it only ever rained at night when everyone on Gamma had retired to their homes. Meg leaned over, picked up a shell from the sand, and held it up in front of Alec. He guessed its name correctly, as he always did, and laughed when she tossed it over her shoulder.

Alec pointed out their shadows. "You've read, *Peter Pan*, right?"

"Yes. Why?"

"Remember when Peter was in the Darling nursery and he was trying to find his shadow so he could reattach it?"

"That's one of my favorite scenes. What about it?"

"Want to play with your shadow?"

Meg quizzed their shadows, each of which walked in step with their counterparts. "Hmm, I don't know, Alec. It kind of looks like they're glued to our feet. I'm not sure how much fun we could have with that. Are you bored, or just crazy?"

"Where's your sense of adventure? And I'm not crazy, by the way."

Meg laughed. "My sense of adventure lives in reality. Apparently, it lives alone at the moment."

"Fine, be that way." Alec sighed. "It could've been fun, though."

Meg scowled at him, but he stared straight ahead, as though bored now. His light-brown hair was messy, like he hadn't combed it since the day before and he had a bit of dirt on the front of his shirt. The blue of his irises were uncommon, different from the rest of the islanders. But they were beautiful, as the sunlight seemed to agree and reflected how blue could be made more perfect. The color reminded her of the ocean and sky together. To be sure, it was a color to envy and she always thought her green eyes must pale in comparison.

"All right. How does one play with one's own shadow?"

Alec smiled, exquisite dimples competing with inexplicable blue now. He knew she wouldn't be able to resist the challenge, not even the idea of it. "Pay attention to your shadow and try to concentrate on it."

Confused, but curious, Meg watched her shadow. Nothing happened at first, but then her shadow's arms lifted in a sort of signal for her to wait. Her eyes widened at the sight, as her physical arms hadn't left her side. She wanted to look at Alec, but couldn't tear her eyes away from the sand in front of her. Instead, she looked at Alec's shadow and saw it was near motionless and facing her animated shadow.

Her own began to inspect itself in a self-discovery sort of way, starting with its hands, then arms, and moving on to the legs. When it reached its feet, the shadow made a small hop and stood upright again. With hands on hips, the shadow shook its head, as though just as amazed as she was. After a shrug, it twirled in circles, then performed an odd version of an Irish jig. It continued for several minutes before coming to a full stop.

Slowly, with an apprehensive shyness, the shadow turned toward Alec's still motionless one. Little by little, the void between the two shadow heads closed. When there was only an inch between the shadow faces, and after a brief pause, hers quickly closed the gap between their lips.

It was a sweet kiss of youth; wherein the brief exchange, all of time squeezes itself into a sphere in which only two people exist. Nothing and no one would dare to interrupt, as it's simply understood to belong in the moment—a moment fixed in time.

Meg's shadow soon broke from Alec's and sunlight again divided them. Her shadow straightened, turned toward her physical self, and resumed its rightful place. Just as quickly as it began, it ended. Both shadows were normal ones again—

...bringing Meg and Alec, and us, back to our moment on Gamma's Alaret Beach.

"Are you okay?" he asked her. "Your face is red."

Her face burned all the more. Meg scrutinized him and saw his cheeks were also flushed. "I'm fine," she said, but was curious if he knew about the shadows kissing.

"What happened? What did you see?"

"You don't know?" she asked.

"No." Alec frowned. "I had to... go away for a bit." He smiled, but it was forced. "I had to give a little of me to you so you could have fun playing with your shadow. You know, like Peter Pan? Did it work?"

"Yeah." Meg shrugged, then nudged him. "It was the most amazing thing to ever happen to me. Or ever will, probably."

"You still haven't told me why your face is all red."

Turning redder still, partly from irritation now, she said, "My shadow danced, maybe that's why." Meg eyed him carefully. "Why's *your* face so red?"

"Is it? The sun, I guess," he said a little too quickly and stared at his feet as though he'd just discovered he had them. "What did my shadow do?"

Concerned he knew more than he was admitting to, but not wanting to quiz him about it because then it would be spoken aloud between them, Meg opted to drop the matter. "Your shadow just stood there looking at my shadow dance."

A few clouds formed, blocking the sun from providing further shadow viewing. They resumed their stroll along the beach, and were silent for a while before Meg gave in to asking the question that kept nagging her. "Where did you *go* exactly?"

"I don't know. Just forget about it, okay?"

As usual, she chose not to interrogate him about the strange things he was capable of doing. "Okay."

Silence fell on them again as they walked. Alec felt bad for lying to her, yet again, as he seemed to be doing more and more lately. He contemplated her question and was hit with even more guilt. He hadn't *gone away* while she played with her shadow, nor had he given part of himself to make it happen.

All he did was give back part of who *she* really was. Just a small bit so she could manipulate her own shadow. He hadn't been expecting her shadow to kiss his and was surprised by how weird it made him feel.

Alec chanced a peek at her. She was preoccupied, thinking about the kiss, he sensed from her thoughts. Though it embarrassed him, he'd rather she concern herself more with that instead of questioning how she was able to do what she did.

He'd been worried Meg may somehow sense her true self, the miniscule amount he gave back to her. It had been a risk, but he was sure she sensed nothing. He was happy she enjoyed herself, and it temporarily stayed his guilt.

"Race you back to the path," he said and took off running.

"Cheater," she yelled, running after him.

~

Later that same day, a man walked along a stretch of shoreline not far from Alaret Beach. Occasionally, he glanced at the island to make sure none of the residents had decided to go for an evening stroll.

Jack Cavanaugh had ulterior motives when he took the job as a researcher in weather analysis, but he couldn't figure out why he felt so drawn to Gamma. He looked back at the docks, checking that he hadn't wandered too far away from the boat he *borrowed* at the research station to get here.

He figured he could spend a few more minutes to recline on the sand and listen to the waves crashing onto the beach. It was a rare treat for him, to be in a wide open space instead of cooped up in that stuffy office with even stuffier businessmen. He closed his eyes and considered how far he'd gotten in his goal to expose them for what they did to his parents. Having worked there for almost a year, Jack had yet to find a shred of evidence that the Stone Davis Corporation was involved in their deaths.

Something in the wind shifted around him and when he opened his eyes, a man wearing sunglasses was sitting beside him, smiling down at him. "Hello, Jack," he said.

"Holy shit!" Jack panicked and tried to scramble away, but got nowhere as his wrist was soon clamped in a vise-like grip.

"Relax. You're not in trouble. I want to talk to you about something before you go back to your boring job on Digamma."

Jack frowned at him. He couldn't argue against how boring his work was, but it was insulting hearing someone else say it. "How do you know my name?"

"I've been watching you. Every time you come here I walk alongside you. Today's the first time I'm showing myself to you."

"Is that so?" Jack looked down the beach toward the docks and wondered if he could outrun the nut job. "Can I have my hand back?"

"Promise not to run?"

"Of course." Jack ignored the eerie feeling that the man had sensed the lie.

Soon as his wrist was free, Jack sprang to his feet and bolted. Halfway back to the docks he glanced over his shoulder, but no one was there. He stopped running and scanned the entire beach where he'd been. Maybe he'd only been dreaming. He shrugged it off and turned back toward the docks, finding himself face to face with the nut job.

"Oh, there you are," Jack grumbled.

"You said you wouldn't run."

"You said you were invisible. Who wouldn't run?" Jack scowled when a smile spread across the man's face. "Who are you?"

"My name's Drake."

"Why are you wearing sunglasses, Drake? Maybe you've been smoking something?"

"I'll take them off in a minute. First, I want to tell you why I'm so interested in you. You don't know it yet, but you're unique and I think we can help each other."

Jack backed away a little. "I'm flattered, but I'm not interested."

Drake ignored the misunderstanding. "I can help you, Jack. You want to know the truth about your parents. There's more truth there than you realize. I know your past. I know your future, too. Do you want to see it?"

"Who the hell are you?"

"Do you want to see what I see?" Drake asked.

"Sure, why not? Let's keep the weird and strange going, right?"

Jack resisted the temptation to run again when Drake moved closer to him. He watched Drake's hand go to the sunglasses and pull them down to the bridge of his nose, offering Jack a glimpse into the eyes that held everything.

He witnessed his future swirl with bits and pieces of the past, some of which remained just beyond recognition. Even the present moment worked its way into the fray of what was to happen. There were so many things he saw and wanted immediately, and was angry that he'd have to wait for them to unfold.

"I'm not done," Drake said. "Keep watching."

By the time Drake ended it, Jack was torn between hope and sadness.

"I don't want to believe any of it," Jack said, there lingered a wisp of doubt in his voice.

"But you know it's true." Drake pushed the sunglasses back into place. "You have to decide now, Jack. Will you help me?"

"I'd rather be dead than say no." Overwhelmed, Jack looked to the ocean as though it could provide him with guidance. "How am I supposed to get through it knowing what I know now?"

"That's not a problem for me. But you have to tell me, Jack, do you want what I showed you?"

"Yes."

Drake grabbed hold of him, an eye-blink second before Jack's instinct to escape kicked in. He lowered Jack's unconscious form to the ground and suppressed the memories of what he'd shown him.

Leaning in, Drake whispered, "You're a good man, Jack Cavanaugh. Thank you. *Remember*… but only when it's time to." Then he left in a blur of color and light.

He didn't worry about leaving him there; Drake knew Jack would wake soon, angry that he'd fallen asleep and hurry back to his job at the research station. There was so much more Drake needed to accomplish, and after he made his way through Gamma's forests to the mountain region, he settled down in his new home—waiting to discover who else on the island will be among those to help him shape the future and destroy a tyranny that had reigned for far too long.

2

Stolen Pearls

In the three years that had passed since the shadow incident on the beach, neither of them had ever broached the subject, nor did anything like it happen again. As their reality marched forward in time, Alec's vow to watch over Meg became more of a struggle. His easygoing watchfulness turned to aggressive guardianship the older she got, coinciding with her increasing rebellion against it.

~

They sat on two moss-carpeted boulders neighboring a small stream; their fishing gear and bait-crickets set on the ground nearby.

It was the middle of spring and the temperature was still mild. As they lazed in the forest, listening to the sounds that accompany this time of year, Meg closed her eyes to hear them with more clarity. The most prominent sounds came from all the birds singing their best spring songs. Right along with them, and for the same reasons, was a chorus of frogs and toads. Of course, their crickets had a lot to say as well. Meg wondered if they were also trying to attract a mate, or if they were chirping their swan song. The trickling stream provided the backdrop of the spring symphony.

"Guess what I found out the other day," Alec said, interrupting nature's musical.

Meg opened her eyes. "What?"

"Your name means pearl."

"Really?" She smiled when he nodded. "Not bad, I suppose. At least it's not something weird, like catfish whisker warrior."

"What?"

She shook her head. "I just made that up, silly."

"Anyway, Margaret's Greek for pearl. I thought it was kind of neat. Know how they're made?"

"Oysters, right?" she said, but her attention was now devoted to a toad hopping along the edge of the stream.

"Yep." Alec eyed the toad Meg stared at, knowing she wanted to pick it up. "Did you know pearls start off as an irritant to the oyster, and that it keeps adding layer upon layer on it until a pearl is formed?"

Meg watched the toad leap to the other side of the stream, as though it also knew Meg-handling was possible if it lingered too long. She turned her attention back to Alec. "Are you saying I'm irritating?"

"No." Teasing, he amended, "Well, maybe sometimes."

"Shut up."

"You're not irritating... much. I'd say you're more like the finished product, a rare pearl."

She gave him a sideways glance and it made him laugh.

"You're the one who's irritating." Meg thought about the process of an oyster making a pearl. "I guess that makes my mom an oyster."

"Maybe. What's that make me?"

"Oh, that's easy. You'd be the diver" –she held her hands up, making a snatching motion in the air– "who yanks the pearl from the oyster."

Though she'd only been joking, there was an instant shift in Alec's mood. His smile vanished first. Then he broke eye contact with her and stared at the ground, leaving her to guess at what could be the current cause of his increasing tendency to brood over nothing.

"What's wrong, Alec?" She sighed at his continued silence. "I was being silly. I don't really think you'd ever forcefully invoke your will and pluck me away from my mother oyster!" She'd let her voice boom theatrically, hoping to make him laugh again, but it only made him more sullen. "Hello, are you there?" She waved a hand in front of his face.

Alec looked into her eyes. "I don't want anything bad to happen to you." He leaned toward her. "I don't know what I'd do without you."

Meg leaned in closer still and whispered, "I don't know what I'd do without you either."

Her breath against his ear sent a shiver down his back and it didn't escape her notice. Meg backed up to see his expression and watched his gaze move to her lips. For a moment, she thought he might kiss her, but he sat up straight instead.

"You don't have to worry about that. I'll be right here, watching out for you like I always have for as long as I can remember." He stood, putting a comfortable distance between them.

Meg stared at the boulder where Alec had been sitting, frustrated and embarrassed now. She knew he wanted to kiss her, she'd felt it, and it wasn't the first time it had happened either. Many such moments had occurred, more so over the last few years, but they always ended the same way—with Alec pulling away and her never questioning him about it.

She hated admitting it to herself, but it became more annoying each time. As usual, she let it go and decided to ask him something else instead. She hopped down from the boulder and joined him by the stream. "How far back do you remember? The first memory I have of you is when you and Kyrie came over to my house on my birthday and I refused to come out of my room until you tempted me with tree-climbing."

"I remember that day," Alec said softly while staring at a school of small fish evade a hungrier, bigger fish.

"It's always been kind of fuzzy to me. Tell me what you remember."

"Come on, let's go." He finally looked at her again. "I'll tell you while we're fishing."

~

Three large freshwater lakes dotted the island and the one they settled down by was their favorite, mostly since it was the one closest to their homes. The second lake wasn't much farther away from where they were, though, and the two lakes situated side by side were often referred to as the twin lakes. A large waterfall accompanied the other, and it was beautiful, but Meg and Alec preferred to fish in the less turbulent water.

The third lake was high up in the mountainous area of the island. There were no shortcuts to get there and only one traveling lane provided accessibility to the remote area. A small population of islanders lived there and they had a smaller version of the main town center. They were sociable and friendly enough, but preferred living farther apart from one another than what the original layout of the residential areas had provided for.

At first, management had denied all requests from islanders seeking to build homes at the higher elevations, but they inexplicably changed their minds and allowed it. Their only stipulations were that all children attend the island's school, regardless of their residence, and that the parents were responsible for getting them there daily during the school year. Also, any and all medical care was to be provided by the island's sole physician.

"Have you ever seen the mountain lake?" Meg asked.

"A long time ago with my mom," Alec said. "Every now and then she has to take something to the other general store."

"What's it look like?"

"A big hole in the ground filled with water."

"Smartass." Meg picked up a small rock and threw it at him. "Seriously, what's it like there? I've never seen it, my mom refuses to go anywhere near it."

"It's creepy. Ila doesn't want to go up there because that's where Mors Cliff is. I don't particularly like that area either."

"Oh, yeah, I forgot about Mors Cliff." Meg fell silent for a moment and considered the cliff's tragic history. "I wouldn't mind seeing it for myself."

Alec snorted at the notion. "Forget about it. No way am I taking you to such an awful place."

Meg bristled at his presumption she'd need a chaperone, but chose not to challenge him this time since she wanted to ask for his help. "Hey, Alec?"

"*Hey, Meg?*" he mimicked her voice while baiting his hook.

"Will you help me with this?" She held out her own hook and the bait bucket.

Alec smiled at her reluctant patience. "What? You don't want to bait your own hook?"

"You didn't bring worms. You know I hate baiting with crickets."

"Yeah, I know, but there were crickets everywhere and it would've taken too long to dig for worms. Here, give it to me."

After much debate about how to bait a cricket onto a hook without being squeamish about it, they settled down on a log with their lines in the water. Twenty minutes passed and not a single nibble pulled on either of their lines.

"Think we'll catch anything?" she asked.

"Probably not, but you never know. Are you hoping to?"

"Well, Alec, let's see... I'm sitting on a log by a lake with a fishing rod in my hand, hoping something happens. I think it's safe to assume that catching fish is my objective. So, what are you hoping is gonna happen to the cricket at the end of your fishing line?"

"Okay, Madam Sarcastic. I was only hoping you won't be disappointed if we don't catch anything. It's getting dark and Ila will lecture me if we're out too late. You know how she gets, and it'll be all *my* fault, not yours."

"She's getting better about it." Meg sighed. "I'd like to catch one at least, even if I don't keep it. It's so exciting when you pull a fish out of the water."

"I guess," he said. "It's kind of weird, though."

"Weird in what way?"

"Well, here we are... you know, the fishermen, and there they are in the water, doing exactly what fish do, they live in the water and eat in the water. We come along and throw food in the lake that we know they like to eat, but it doesn't come without a price. We put a trap on the food. A fish comes along, falls for the ruse, and we yank him right out of his home without a care in the world. We never even consider what the fish thinks about it. And you know he doesn't like it because as soon as you pull him out, he starts flailing about in such a way that's obvious his only thought is to get back home."

When Alec finished his fish philosophy, Meg looked at him and asked, "How do you know the fish is a *he*?"

"It was just a thought, Meg. An idea, a way of looking at something from a different perspective."

"I know." She rolled her eyes. "I was being Madame Sarcastic again. Remember her? Besides, you're forgetting something."

"What?"

"You went on and on about the fish, but you didn't consider what it must be like for the pitiful cricket. From *my* perspective, the cricket has it worse. It's impaled on a hook, which is bad enough, but done in such a way that it still lives to be enticing. After that ordeal, it's forced to be prey to predators with no hope of escape. Then, it was all for nothing. The fish doesn't get to live either after its trick of a meal because of the strings attached to it. Pun intended, of course."

Alec chuckled. "Excellent point."

"Enough about fish and crickets, you said you'd tell me what you remember about my birthday."

"How much do you remember?" he asked.

"I remember bits and pieces. That was the first time you'd come over to my house to play with me, right?"

"It was the first time Ila had a birthday celebration for you. My mom told me Ila was kind of over-protective while you were a baby." Alec snorted. "Actually, my mom was probably worse than Ila."

"Yeah, she's mentioned how Kyrie was with you. She uses it as an excuse when I get angry at her for not letting me do what I want. I'll say how you get to do whatever you want, and she says it wasn't always like that. She told me Kyrie was a complete weirdo until after you went to school."

"I think it's because of management. You know how everyone here mistrusts them." Alec peeked over at Meg. He sensed her thoughts and found her still trying to sort through her memories. "What else do you remember?"

"Actually, I remember a lot of it." A crease formed on her forehead. "At least up until the part when we were in the barn."

Alec remembered this part clearly, like it had happened just yesterday. He'd spent much of his life struggling with the guilt of what he'd done, but relied on the standby of convincing himself that he did what was necessary to protect Meg from everything he and the entire island feared: management and the powerful influence they had over all of them.

Truthfully, he had no regrets about that day, not one. Meg had been different, like he was, until he absorbed it all. What shamed him was, what made her normal was what made him stronger. As much as he'd like to deny it, there was a bit of ego and superiority that came with absorbing what made Meg who she was. It also helped him go unnoticed and he relied on that, too, when the guilt threatened to keep him awake at night.

"Don't you remember the spider?" he asked.

"Absolutely! That part I remember well." Meg looked around the log. "You know how much I hate spiders."

"*Everyone* knows that," he said. "What about the barn?"

"Not much. I remember climbing the tree more than anything else."

"Best tree I ever climbed," Alec said, giving her a wink.

"What happened in the barn?"

Alec hid his discomfort by reeling in his line and saying, "You hit your head on the ramp."

"Yeah, that's what my mom told me," she said, sounding disappointed by the lack of new information.

~

It was early evening and after catching nothing, they released the crickets and headed back to their homes along one of the footpaths surrounded by vast tracts of forest trees.

Alec broke the awkward silence that had fallen on them. "Do you want to try fishing at Alaret Beach tomorrow?"

"I can't." Meg snapped out of her thoughts of wondering why Alec always lied to her, to an overwhelming sense of sadness. "I'm going to visit Frank and Lena tomorrow. I'll probably be there for a while."

Frank and Lena Doscher were an elderly couple who lived near both their homes. There was a small population of older people on the island and Meg had always gravitated toward them throughout her childhood. They were particularly fond of Meg, but none so much as Frank and Lena. They doted on her, fussed over her, gave her anything she wanted. They loved nothing better than when Meg came by to visit and she loved visiting them just as much.

However, she hated how their time was limited in their elderly years and it brought her fresh new pain every time one of the elders died. No matter how many times she experienced it, the loss never got any easier, and her heart broke in a hundred new ways. She loved them all and missed them terribly when they weren't there to visit anymore.

"I'm curious about something."

"Okay."

"I feel awful for wondering about it, but why do the elders like me so much? Sometimes, I can't stand it." Meg came to a stop. "That sounded really bad."

"I know how much it upsets you." Alec turned and faced her. "Don't beat yourself up for not liking death."

She frowned at him. "You know Lena's dying?"

Lena's declining health was common knowledge at this point, but Alec couldn't exactly blurt out to Meg that he'd been picking through her thoughts. "I just assumed that's what you meant. Is it certain?"

Meg nodded. "Frank told me a few days ago. Dr. Patrick said there's nothing that can be done, except make her comfortable. She'll die soon. Guess who she's asking for?"

"She loves you, Meg. Of course, she wants to see you." Alec took her hand, but when a warmth traveled up his arm and settled in his chest, he gave a gentle squeeze and let go.

"Right." Meg ignored the awkward step Alec took away from her. "I don't want her to die. I know it's inevitable, but I hate it. Lena and Frank are special to me, but it's not just them. Why do some of the dying latch on to some of the living at the end, and why does it always seem to be me?" She stared off at the nearest tree. "I swear, Alec, when Lena dies she's gonna take a little bit of me with her."

The tears that had been threatening her won and spilled onto her cheeks in a beautiful gracelessness. She wiped them away as they fell. Alec put his hand on her shoulder and the indescribable warmth greeted him again, but he ignored it this time. He wanted to comfort her, and at her continued silence, he pulled the length of his body closer to hers. As he stood just slightly behind her, Alec willed as much strength to her as he would allow.

He wanted her to know and see what he guessed the truth to be about the elders. Alec assumed they were drawn to Meg because of what they sensed about her. He thought they must see what he'd grown so accustomed to seeing that he hardly paid attention to it anymore. It was the unique light that always seemed to surround Meg, what he figured was the hollowed result of what he'd taken from her—the void left behind by thievery had filled with a light he constantly feared would tell on him one day.

Alec tried to find a way to impress this knowledge on to her without words, and especially without telling her the complete truth. He wrapped his arms around her, slowly at first, then with more purpose. Ideally, he'd like to transfer to her what he understood about the old and dying, though he barely comprehended it himself. He worried, though, how best to go about it without making irreversible mistakes.

He closed his eyes, trying to translate the knowledge for her. He put all the important parts into just a few feelings and thoughts so she would understand why they seek her out to accompany them in their last and final journey through life.

Just when Alec found the perfect thoughts, the tension in her muscles relaxed. She seemed to melt against his chest and he was suddenly cognizant of how close they were when Meg leaned her head back and rested it on his shoulder. His eyes opened and the first sight to greet him was her face leaning in toward his neck.

An all too familiar panic pulsed through his bloodstream. He wanted to look around to see if they were being watched, but he couldn't take his eyes away from the serene look on her face. She appeared to be at a strange kind of peace and he found it both captivating and bewildering.

A beautiful white light flowed all around her, it streamed away from her at times and thus encapsulated him as well. It felt more wonderful than anything he'd ever experienced before. Blue finger-like projections jutted out from the white glimmer and seemed to pet them both. Meg still had her eyes closed and he wondered if she was even aware of the animated light. He sensed her thoughts and knew she'd yet to see it.

What Alec saw was different from the soft light that always surrounded Meg, and he understood it was far greater than what set them both apart from the rest of the islanders. His mind raced to come up with an explanation to provide her with when she would open her eyes and see the odd enigma.

He relaxed a little at coming up with an idea that might make her feel better about Lena dying. Alec nudged her gently, coaxing her to open her eyes.

"Oh my God. What is that?" she asked in a whisper, staring wide-eyed at the strange lights and colors encasing them. They became more animated now. What had only been white with soft blues at first, burst into a myriad of colors.

"I'm not sure exactly." He frowned at how excited the entity appeared.

"It's so beautiful."

Refusing to give up on his idea, Alec contemplated his next words. However, he had trouble verbalizing anything as he continued to stare at the lights and colors, observing a distinct organization in its movements now. Alec detected a purpose, some intellect in its structure, and he desperately hoped it was only his imagination.

Less sure of himself, he said, "Maybe they're all the people who've come and gone. It wouldn't surprise me if some of the elders you cared about are in the more colorful parts."

"You really think it's possible?" The awe and hopefulness in her voice could've created new worlds.

He grew more uneasy about making up such an outlandish lie. Alec swallowed back the nervous lump in his throat and said, "Sure."

"Look at all the colors, Alec. Aren't they fantastic?" Meg still whispered, as if afraid speaking too loudly would make it all go away.

"Yeah," he said, mindful of a shift occurring in the enigma.

A stream of blue light came close to Meg's face and it seemed to be looking at her. It had no true shape at first, but slowly developed one and sent it forward. Alec suspected its intent was to make contact and he tensed to protect her.

The blue shape's projected arm paused at the change of atmosphere, as though having sensed Alec's concern, but then continued advancing toward Meg.

He felt powerless to stop it from gently caressing her cheek. It moved a little higher up her face, and appeared to place a loving kiss on her forehead. Alec worried it might scare her, but she didn't flinch. In fact, she appeared more at peace—happier and more perfect—than he'd ever known her to be.

It withdrew the blue appendage, back into itself, to rejoin the rest of the various colors of whites, pinks, and greens. Having resumed its initial form, Alec hoped it would leave now. Instead, it moved toward him and sent out a small tendril of white light so close to his face, he feared accidentally inhaling it.

Alec backed away, losing his hold on Meg, but it followed him and stayed within mere inches of his face. It occurred to him that the entity was searching for something. What it was determined to find he could only guess at, and now he worried it had done the same to Meg. Soon as the idea formed in his mind, the light conveyed a single thought: *'I have discovered her, and I know more about Meg than you ever have or ever will.'*

Though stunned, Alec only wanted to stop the light from studying him any further. The only plan that came to him was to whistle. He let out a loud, long monotone whistle, then switched it to the first melody that popped into his head. The light backed away from Alec a few feet, and moved in a way that, oddly enough, looked like dancing.

But it soon came to an eerie halt.

It gathered its many colors together in a more combined shape and turned around in the opposite direction. Alec stopped whistling, wondering why the light had lost interest in them. He scanned the trees, fearing something else was coming. In the distance, he saw two brilliant orbs of white light, both of enormous size, headed in their direction at a fast clip.

The mysterious enigma of color also saw the approaching orbs and compacted in on itself, forming a tight sphere of iridescence. It turned to Alec once more, imparting a final thought to him, *'I know what you did to her. It changes nothing.'*

It raced away from Alec in a blur and swirled around Meg before shooting off skyward. The two newly arrived white orbs chased after it with a speed that seemed immeasurable.

"What happened?" Meg asked. "Where did it go?"

"Where it should be, somewhere else," he said under his breath.

Alec had no idea where they went, what they were, or what had just happened. Finding himself with no way to decipher the strange events, he rushed over to Meg and grabbed her wrist. He wanted to get her as far away as possible, fearing the lights would return. Having tugged her along the forest footpath in silence for several minutes, he nearly jumped out of his skin when she spoke.

"Do you think she'll be with that… whatever it was we just saw?"

"What?" he asked, sounding annoyed as he searched the safety of the path and trees ahead of them while constantly scanning the sky for light anomalies. "Who are you talking about?"

"Lena."

He'd forgotten about their conversation prior to the lights showing up and scrambled to recall his last few words. What he remembered was how much he wanted to help Meg be at peace with accepting Lena's impending death.

"Probably." He shook his head at the creeping discomfort of trying to keep up the lie.

"I didn't see yellow in that light. Think Lena would be yellow since it's her favorite color?"

"If that's her favorite color, then I know she'll be yellow… if for no other reason than to make you happy. I'd be yellow for you." Shame and guilt nagged him for making it all up. Figuring everything had returned to normal in the forest, he slowed their pace. "Do you feel better about Lena now?" He hoped her answer would make him feel better.

It took a long time for Meg to answer him. "Yes, Alec, what we just saw has helped me more than you know."

He wasn't sure what that was supposed to mean. It really didn't sound like Meg at all. "Are you all right?"

"I'm fine."

Alec froze, but Meg had continued on a few steps before halting, then stood motionless with her back to him.

He made his way over to her and tried sensing what bothered her, but found that he was unable to. "What's wrong?" he had no choice but to ask.

Instead of answering him, she extended her arm and offered her hand out for him to take. He looked at it and wasted no time slipping it into his. Peacefulness began to find its way back to him at the contact. Meg turned to face him and the new look of defiance in her eyes surprised him.

"Did you make all those lights and colors happen?"

"No."

"Don't lie to me, Alec."

"I'm not. I have no idea what they were or where they came from."

"Then why did you say they were from all the people who died here?"

Alec frowned, wondering if she'd just tricked him, but decided to admit the truth anyway. "Because I didn't want you to be sad anymore. Before those lights showed up, I was going to tell you why I think the elderly are so drawn to you."

"Okay. Tell me now."

The birth of new confidence in her voice puzzled him as well. Had anything else changed about her? He stepped closer and leaned his face so near to hers that she started to inch forward as though he meant to kiss her. He smiled and said, "Meg, don't be silly."

Her eyes narrowed. "Are you going to answer me, or not?"

Alec grasped her shoulders to bring her nearer to his chest so he could whisper the answer in her ear.

"You're special, and the elders know it. I think they can sense things about people that others can't." He paused, worried that he'd been so caught up in sorting out what bothered her that he hadn't paid attention to their surroundings. "When I pull away from you, we can discuss how the elders see certain things, but I'm warning you now, don't question me out loud about why I think you're special. Nod if you understand me."

Meg nodded and moved her face closer to his ear. Her lips swept across his earlobe and it sent a shiver along his spine, forcing every hair he owned to stand on end.

"I understand, but why do we have to whisper?"

Still in a heightened state of awareness, more so by the fact that he could feel the weight of observation on both of them, he put his arms around her waist. Alec wanted the scene to look like two people sharing a private moment.

"Because they're listening," he said softly, and every muscle in her body contracted in fear. He ran his fingers along the base of her back. "Don't look so frightened, try to imagine what this looks like and go with it. We'll break apart in a minute and keep walking home like we normally do."

Meg relaxed and when she tilted her head back, her cheek brushed against his. Their lips were just inches apart and she pressed on until they touched. The initial contact felt glorious to her and she locked onto his fully.

A shockwave of energy shot through Alec's body, and he responded in a way neither of them had foreseen. His arms, still around her waist, tightened and his lips explored hers with increasing urgency. Alec felt a different sort of hunger, one that her lips failed to satisfy. When her body sensed the craving, she leaned against him and the intensity of her eager movements forced him to regain control of the moment.

He broke away from her. "Stop it, Meg."

The wildness in both their eyes seemed more easily tamed by Alec, leaving her with a feeling of frustration, yet again. Meg wanted to scream at him, but figured it would be more embarrassment than she could endure.

"You started it," she muttered. "It's getting late, I want to go home."

"Wait," he said when she walked away. "I'm—"

"Forget about it." The last thing she wanted to hear was a chivalrous apology. Trying to bring normalcy back to their conversation, she asked, "Do you want to come with me tomorrow to visit Lena?"

Alec hadn't paid a proper visit to Frank and Lena in quite a while, not since Lena started looking at him differently. Fearing Lena saw more about him than he'd prefer, he distanced himself from them. He made up excuses about having to work whenever he bumped into Frank.

"I can't. I told my mom I'd make deliveries tomorrow."

"If you had to work tomorrow, then why did you ask me to go fishing at the beach?"

"Well, maybe I would've put it off if you wanted to go."

Meg rolled her eyes at the sheepish glance he gave her, making it impossible for her to hold a grudge against him for long. She sighed and said, "Tell me about your opinions on the elders and why they like some people more than others."

"Do you remember Mr. Horton?"

"Yes."

"I noticed he could get around pretty well even though he was blind, so I asked him about it. He said after he lost his sight to that sea urchin, his other senses got better. He told me he could hear things better than anyone else on the island and he could sense things about them that he couldn't before. I think the elders are like that, too, even if they can still see."

"Why do you think that?"

"At their age, they've known people longer. They've seen more people born, and experienced more death than we have. They know more than we do because they've seen more. I think they pay closer attention to details we haven't got a clue about yet. I think when Frank and Lena look at you, and talk with you, they see a great person. They may even see you as a light or a color. That was what I really wanted to say to you earlier."

Meg smiled at the apology mixed in with his explanation. "A color, huh? What color would you say I am?"

"Oh, you're definitely a beautiful white." He perked up at what he considered to be an all-is-forgiven tone.

She contemplated the idea for a moment. It made sense that older people were better at understanding the world around them. It made even more sense that they would want certain kinds of people around them in the end, but the idea of people being a color perplexed her and she tried to imagine herself as a white in someone else's eyes.

"What do you mean? Why white?"

"You're a good person. The elders can sense that about you. To them, you represent everything that's right about the world. If they had to pick a color for that, they'd probably say white."

Meg stared off at the trees ahead of them, all the way up to where they met the skyline. "Do you think all things can be seen as a color?" she mused aloud.

Alec followed her gaze and chuckled. "Yes, Meg, trees are seen as green by most people, young or old."

She laughed. "What color would you say you are?"

Alec's gaze drifted from the trees to nowhere in particular. He'd already thought about this question and had pondered its answer. He considered his past, his present, and his uncertain future. He considered Meg's as well and guilt settled once again in his chest.

"I'd have to say my color would be black."

3

Drake

Frank met Meg at the door. "She's not doing very well." His voice sagged, much like his shoulders—his face more haggard than age alone would excuse. "Dr. Patrick said she won't hold out much longer."

She leaned her umbrella against the outside wall of the porch and stepped inside the eerily quiet house. It had been raining on and off since last night, unusual for Gamma's weather, and it was the sound of raindrops on her windowsill that woke her up this morning. She looked into his eyes, the sadness there made her own seem pointless.

"How're you doing?" she asked.

"I'm fine, but I don't know what I'll do without her."

Meg's heart broke at this and she put her hand on his. She also didn't know what life would be like without Lena in it. He seemed to understand, as he patted the top of her hand.

Frank then turned away and she suspected he was trying to hide his tears. For his sake, Meg headed toward the kitchen with the flowers she'd brought for Lena. "Are the vases still under the sink? I brought some of her favorite flowers. I'm gonna perk them up before I take them to her."

The flowers were perfectly fine, still wet from the rain, but she wanted to give him a moment to compose himself.

"They're still there, where she likes to keep them," he said. "You go ahead, child, I need to close the barn door before any more of this rain gets in and floods everything. I'll be right back."

The rain had lightened somewhat for more than an hour, and though danger of flooding was minimal, Meg understood Frank's need for solitude. As she opened the cabinet under the sink, Meg realized she needed a moment alone as well.

She wiped the errant tears from her cheeks and grabbed the prettiest of all the vases Lena had collected over the years on Gamma. With the flowers splayed out on the counter, she filled the vase with water and began the arrangement. One by one, she picked up the flowers and placed each one in the vase, coupling them with fond memories.

The first were the sunflowers, the giant sort with petals mimicking the color of the sun and a rich shade of brown in the center that reminded her of oak tree trunks. The next three flowers were musk roses; their alabaster white petals so like silk to the touch, their fuzzy stems like velvet, and their fragrance unchallenged from any other in Meg's opinion.

After the roses, Meg pulled four stems of lavender lilacs, the flower Lena referred to as the most stubborn and persnickety on all of Gamma. Then she reached for the last two flowers—edelweiss, and they were not only Lena's favorites, but coveted by everyone on the island. She wished there were more of them, but they were notoriously hard to find and she'd been lucky to have found any at all. Lacy green sprigs polished off the arrangement, along with slender pieces of driftwood she'd found washed up on the beach.

"That's beautiful, Meg," Frank said when he returned and joined her in the kitchen.

"Think she'll like them?"

"She'll love them. Let's go surprise her."

And so they went, down the hall to the door that would take Meg to her last moments with a dear friend. When they entered the quiet, soft-lit bedroom, Lena was sleeping. Frank sat on the quilt and waited a couple of seconds before putting his hand on top of Lena's. He gave it a gentle squeeze and her eyelids fluttered open. She looked at Frank and a smile spread across her face; he smiled back—there seemed a lifetime of conversations in their smiles.

"Look who came to visit you." Frank turned to reveal Meg standing in the doorway.

Lena's eyes illuminated. "What have you got there? Did you bring me flowers? You precious child. Bring them closer so I can get a proper look at them."

Meg put the vase on the nightstand and sat in a chair near the bed. "I hope you like them. I tried to find all your favorites."

"Of course I like them. You could've brought me dandelions and I would've loved them all the same. How've you been? I haven't seen you in a few days."

"Helping my mom with the horses," Meg said. "Three of the mares are pregnant and it won't be long before they foal. You know how anxious she gets when the mares are this far along."

"Imagine how the mares feel!" Lena tutted, but there was a playful twinkle in her eyes. "Tell Ila to stop worrying so much, mares have been foaling for eons. They'll do just fine."

"I'll tell her." Meg was happy to hear the frisky edge still intact in Lena's voice.

Lena turned to Frank. "I think I'll have some of that soup you tried forcing on me earlier. Give us girls a chance to talk. Thank you, Frank. You're too good to me and I don't deserve you." She gave him a wink when he chuckled at her.

He stood from the bed, too slowly, and Meg figured his knees were bothering him again. A pang of worry settled in her chest, but she pushed it aside so she could focus on Lena.

Frank walked to the doorway and turned to them before leaving. "You two have a nice visit."

When he left, Meg got up and sat on the bed. She picked up one of Lena's hands and held it in both of her own. "How're you feeling today?"

"Oh" –Lena grinned– "'bout the same as yesterday."

"Well, aren't you rather cheeky today?" They were having fun, teasing each other, but Meg wondered if Lena put on a brave face for her benefit. If so, then Meg was grateful. The thought of Lena in pain was more than she could stand.

"Margaret Arcana! I see you frowning. Don't you dare fret over me. I'm not in agony if that's what you're worrying about. Dr. Patrick gave me some wonderful pills and I have to say, I'm quite fond of them."

Meg only nodded and offered a weak smile.

"I've lived a very long life and it's time for it to end. I'm perfectly fine with it and I'm mostly happy with the life I've had. I had the best husband a woman could ask for, a lovely home, beautiful memories, and just as important as all the rest is you, Meg."

"Me?"

"Of course you, don't be an eejit. I remember when I first saw you. You were just a little baby, so precious and new. Why, I think I fell head over heels right then at the sight of you."

Lena pulled herself up higher onto her pillows to look at Meg fully. "Margaret, you were a beautiful child, you're a beautiful young lady, and you're a beautiful person. You've brought more joy to my life than you'll ever know. Understand me when I tell you, I'll die a happy woman. Does any of what I've said set your mind at ease?"

She stared at the beautiful pieced quilt Lena had made and fought back the urge to cry. She knew it was important to Lena that she accept the inevitable and be at peace with it. "Yes, Lena, I understand."

"Now, there's a good colleen."

Meg rolled her eyes and laughed at Lena's brogue. "You're impossible."

"I know. Frank's told me that since the day we met."

"Lena?" Meg's curiosity piqued. "Were you and Frank born on Gamma?"

There was a slight shift in Lena's demeanor. Her dependable look of always spunky transformed into a somewhat guarded expression, and it took a moment for her to answer. "No, we came here from somewhere else."

"Were you children when you came here?"

"No. We'd been married for about six years when we arrived, if memory serves me correctly.

Meg's mind was full of questions, but the one she settled on had always plagued her. "Why don't you and Frank have any children?"

The question was innocent enough, but the shock of it showed in Lena's unblinking stare.

"I'm sorry." Meg shook her head. "I shouldn't have asked that."

"It's okay, don't be embarrassed. You're just being curious and I don't mind talking to you about it." Lena turned her head toward the window panes. "We almost had a child once. We'd been married for four years and I suspected I might be pregnant. The doctor confirmed it and Frank and I started getting everything ready. The problems started halfway through, but I kept it to myself. The pain got so bad that Frank noticed and he talked me into going to the doctor."

"What happened?" Meg asked when Lena paused and closed her eyes for a moment.

"The doctor said the baby had died and that I needed surgery because infection had set in. I woke up later in the recovery room and Frank was there, holding my hand. He told me I'd be fine, but I knew he wasn't telling me everything. So, I demanded he tell me what he was hiding from me."

Lena paused again, as though going back in time to revisit a painful memory was about to get worse. "Complications came up during the operation and the surgeon had no choice but to save my life… I couldn't have children after that. I got so upset the nurse had to step in and sedate me. I lived in a terrible fog after I was released from the hospital, and for almost two years all I did was sit around the house and read books. Frank did everything, and sometimes he even had to remind me to take a shower.

"One day he came to me with a letter from the day's post, but I ignored it as usual and kept reading. For the first time since I'd met Frank, he lost his temper. He yanked the letter back up and yelled, 'Dammit, Lena, I've had enough of this. All you do is read and sit around this house like a ghost. If you don't snap out of it right this instant, I'm going to pack a suitcase and I'll leave you.'"

She chuckled at this memory, able to laugh about it now with the passage of time. "Well, that was enough for me. I loved Frank more than anything. A life without him would've been worse than a life without children. So, I got up from that ugly old armchair and asked him what he'd like for dinner. He said he didn't care about dinner, all he wanted was for me to read the damn letter."

"What was the letter about?" Meg asked, entrenched in the story.

"About coming here." The guarded expression and nervous tone returned. "It was an invitation, a sort of volunteer opportunity that management had offered to us. That's how Frank and I came to be here, and now you know why we have no children. However, I've grown so fond of you, Meg. If there could've ever been a substitute for me, you'd be it. I want to thank you for being part of our lives."

Lena let this be the end of her story and looked past the window panes again.

"Thank you for telling me about it, Lena."

"It's raining again," Lena said. "Did you know that rain on any important day is considered good luck?" She turned back to Meg. "Sweet child, please don't cry. I'm very happy. If you cry, it'll make me sad."

"I just don't want you to go." Meg looked up at the ceiling, trying to prevent gravity from pulling the tears down onto her cheeks.

"All right, enough of this sadness. Tell me more about how Ila's doing?"

Lena was wise to change the subject, it gave Meg something different to concentrate on, and some of the previous misery lifted off her shoulders.

"She's doing great. Management decided to make her the sole horse breeder on the island. The horses we're waiting on to foal have already been sold off to the mainland. It puts her under a lot of pressure, even more now since management keeps nagging her to increase breeding. Despite the stress, she's proud of herself and I'm happy for her."

"How's your flock doing?"

"I knew you were gonna ask me about them." Meg smiled; Lena was always ribbing her for having too many laying hens. "My hens are fat, happy, and sassy."

"That's good." Lena nodded and inhaled deeply. "I want to ask you about something else now."

"What?"

"What's going on between you and that boy?" Lena asked so matter-of-factly that it confused Meg.

"What boy?"

"That boy you're always going off with." Lena's voice took on a twinge of growing agitation.

"You mean Alec?"

"I think that's his name."

"You know his name perfectly well." Meg frowned at her.

"Fine. I know his name," Lena grumbled. "You haven't answered my question. What's going on between you and Alec?"

"He's my friend, you know that. We've known each other since we were kids."

"You're not kids anymore."

"Maybe not, but we're still friends."

"Are you sure about that?"

"Of course I'm sure about it. Alec's my best friend, he's the most amazing friend anyone could want. Are you implying he's not?"

"No, I'm asking you if he's more than just a friend."

Meg comprehended the meaning and blushed.

"The color on your face answers my question," Lena said and looked toward the window panes again. The rain had slowed, providing her a better view of the pretty colors she'd been seeing for days, swirling and dancing by the trees near her window. She considered asking Meg if she could see them, but was afraid she wouldn't and that it had been the medication causing her to hallucinate all along. Lena thought they were too beautiful to risk finding out they weren't real.

Meg remained silent, not sure how to respond, or even if she should.

While staring straight ahead at the window, Lena asked, "How far has your relationship with Alec progressed?"

She knew exactly what Lena wanted to know and heat blazed across her face. "Nothing like that!"

Lena turned to Meg, wearing a chastising expression. "Don't be so horrified and offended. You're not a little girl anymore, in case you haven't noticed. I'm quite certain Alec has."

Even when he pushed her away, Meg knew Alec was fully aware she wasn't the same little girl he'd grown up with. "I'm not comfortable talking about this kind of stuff with you," Meg said, shifting her gaze to the floor.

Lena ignored the hint and pressed on. "If you're telling me the truth that nothing's happened yet, I want you to make a promise to me. Will you do that?"

"What sort of promise?"

"That nothing will ever go beyond friendship. Even better, promise me you'll start distancing yourself from him. Make new friends. Find a boyfriend... or two. Whatever you do, just get as far away from Alec as possible. Promise me, Meg." Lena waited for the oath.

Though she feared it may break Lena's heart, Meg had no choice. "I'd sooner jump from Mors Cliff than make a promise I know I can't possibly keep. Why are you asking me to stay away from Alec?"

"Because I want what's best for you."

"Alec would never hurt me, he only wants to protect me and make sure I don't get into trouble."

"He's not good for you. He'll destroy you."

"Lena, that's ridiculous. Alec's not gonna destroy me. I don't understand why you're saying this."

"I suspect he already has destroyed part of you." There seemed a challenge in Lena's eyes as they narrowed to get her warning across.

Still, Meg defended him. "He's never hurt me in any way. I think maybe you're just being overprotective of me. Kind of like how Alec is sometimes. Could that be possible?" Meg affected light-heartedness in her voice, hoping to ease the increasing tension between them.

Lena snapped. "I'm not just being overprotective! Listen to me. I noticed something about him before he started avoiding me. I could see he was growing darker, like a blackness was taking over him. I'm scared that blackness will surround you, too, and drag you to the same place he'll end up. Promise me you'll stay away from him, Meg."

The admonishment seemed to have taken the last of her strength and Meg knew Lena would never regain the effort it took to get this emotional declaration out. Knowing this was why it was so hard for Meg to say what had to be said.

"I love you dearly, Lena, and I'll miss you more than you know. I'd give you some of my own years if that could make you live longer, but what I won't do is lie to you. Not even now, when I feel like you're giving me your dying request, I can't make a promise to you that I know I'll never keep."

Lena's face softened as she looked deep into Meg's eyes, and she held her hands out for Meg to take. They sat there for a short while, holding on to each other for the last time. The renewed rain pattering on the windowsill suggested a semblance of peace. Meg sensed Lena wanted to say something, so she leaned in closer to listen.

"Then I fear all you'll ever know is sadness and death."

Meg backed away from Lena, but held her gaze. Resolute defiance evolved on Meg's face before she responded to Lena's dying words. "You may be right, perhaps I will know sadness and death, but I have a feeling that'll be the only way I'll ever know about happiness and living."

~

Meg quietly slipped out of the bedroom when Lena fell asleep. From the hallway, she saw Frank seated at the kitchen table, reading a book and sipping his coffee. She took a moment to collect herself before announcing her presence.

Her visit with Lena had been emotionally exhausting, but it had also helped her gain a more placid acceptance of death. Meg was thankful for how Lena imparted the understanding that life, and the happiness there was to have, was what you made it.

It was only when the conversation turned to Alec did Meg feel a kind of loss that their last meaningful visit ended in such an unfulfilling way. It was unsettling to hear Lena prophesize such doom and gloom with the eventuality of her continued friendship with Alec. She shook off the oppressive feeling and headed down the hallway.

She put her hand on Frank's shoulder. "Lena fell asleep."

"It's the rain, it always makes her sleepy." He closed the book. "Did you have a nice visit?"

"Of course." Meg focused on the best parts of their conversation and remembered the story about Frank. "She said you're the best husband and that she's lucky to have you."

Frank laughed softly and stood. "Would you like some coffee?"

"No, but thank you. I told my mom I'd help her in the stables today," she lied, all she wanted was to be alone with her thoughts.

"Want me to drive you home?"

"I'd rather walk. Maybe I'll stomp a few puddles on my way home," Meg said, offering him a convincing grin.

It worked, and Frank teased her again about how when she was little, she'd go out of her way to find rain puddles perfect for stomping in.

After donning her galoshes and saying goodbye, Meg saw herself out. She grasped the umbrella, but decided not to use it. Considering her raw emotions, she thought the pounding rain would complement them rather nicely. She marched down the porch steps and resisted the urge to lower her head when the first pelting of raindrops stung her face.

She slogged through their front yard, aiming for the footpath that led to her house. When she reached the privacy of the trees, Meg allowed her tears to join the raindrops running down her face. She came to an abrupt halt at sensing she wasn't so alone anymore. Through the wall of rain, she couldn't be sure she hadn't seen a brilliant flash of colors before seeing the figure of a young man standing a few feet away from her.

Some odd eternity passed between them as they stared at each other in the middle of a downpour.

He wore a reticent expression under the wide umbrella perched over his head. Meg thought how strange she must appear to him, to be carrying her umbrella instead of using it. She considered nodding a polite hello to him and then continue on her way, but he stepped forward with his hand extended.

"Meg Arcana?" he asked.

"Yes." She lifted her hand and he shook it while giving her a warm smile.

"Hi, I'm Drake Quinlan." He released her hand and put his in his pocket.

"Hope I didn't startle you. I just came from your house and your mom said you were visiting the Doschers. I was just on my way over there."

"You know them?" She couldn't recall if they'd ever mentioned his name before.

"A little. Not as well as you do."

"Lena's asleep right now, but Frank's there."

"Actually, it's you I wanted to see. Ms. Elwin sent me to ask if you'd help get the school's auditorium ready for the children's art show this weekend. I'm already helping out, but there's still a lot of work to do."

"That's right, I forgot it was this weekend. I'd love to help. Tell her to call me whenever she needs me."

"Well…" Drake hesitated and looked at her sheepishly. "I think she's hoping you'll start today."

"Oh, of course." She shook her head. "I wasn't trying to blow it off, it just didn't register she needed help right away. You probably think I'm an idiot. I have a lot on my mind right now."

"I don't think you're an idiot." His tone took on a sympathetic understanding. "Your mom told me about Lena. I'm sorry for what you must be going through. Everyone on the island knows the Doschers. She'll be missed by all of us."

Meg was stunned by his compassionate words and turned toward the path again. She took a few slow steps, hoping he knew without her having to tell him that he was welcome to walk with her.

"Thank you for saying that," she said.

They walked along the path in silence the rest of the way to Meg's house. She saw an unfamiliar cart parked on the lane with a rain cover secured to it. In the back seat were several boxes filled with decorations: a few balloons already inflated, a rainbow of crepe paper rolls, and ribbons and streamers overflowed the sides. The bright colors made her smile again.

After telling Ila where she was going, Meg got into the cart with Drake. They were almost to the school when her curiosity got the better of her. "You live in the mountains, don't you?"

"Yes." He looked over at her. "Does that bother you?"

"No." Meg grinned at him.

~

As Ms. Elwin was in the middle of an art class, they went straight to the empty auditorium with the boxes of decorations. Meg set the box on the floor and looked around. She hadn't been in here since graduating, but it was the memory of being Ms. Elwin's student she tried to recall.

The auditorium was halfway set up for the art show and Meg chuckled when she remembered her own first-grade picture.

"What?" Drake asked.

"My first-grade picture hung on that partition." Meg went over to one of the several partitions used to hang the children's artwork on. "I was so proud to see it hanging here and how everyone on the island got to see what I considered to be a magnificent work of art."

"What was it a picture of?"

"A crayon drawing of a hen's nest full of eggs. Took me weeks to get it just right." Meg fell into a fit of laughter. "I wonder where it is now. I bet my mother saved it, even if it was hideous."

"Why would you call it hideous?"

She frowned at him. "Because I was six when I drew it."

"Hold on a minute," Drake said.

He rummaged through a large canvas bag and pulled out an artist sketchbook. Further searching produced sketching charcoal, and then he sat in one of the auditorium chairs. His hand raced across the page and when his brow knit in concentration, she took a few steps closer to him.

"Wait, it's not finished yet," he said in a soft voice.

She stopped and waited, but grew fidgety after a couple of agonizing minutes.

He looked up at her, wearing a tranquil expression. "Patience, Meg."

"Okay." She gave him a playful scowl and grabbed a decorations-filled box to begin readying the auditorium for excited first-graders.

She headed to the supply closet by the stage to get the ladder, tape, and thumbtacks she'd need to hang the streamers. After dragging the ladder out, she returned to retrieve the scissors. When she turned around, Drake stood in the doorway holding the sketchpad up for her to see. He had recreated her first-grade drawing.

"Is this what it looked like?"

"It's what it should've looked like," she said, staring in awe at the drawing. The shadows he'd created with the charcoal gave it such a lifelike quality, like she could almost pick up one of the eggs. "Wish I could draw like that."

"You can. Ms. Elwin mentioned to me she thought you had potential if only you would've spent more time working at it. I can teach you if you want."

Her eyes left the drawing and met his. Something promising, something fun and mischievous, swirled in his eyes, and it was intoxicating to her. She saw, or felt perhaps, something else as well—like a memory that hadn't happened yet.

"I do want that," Meg whispered. She lost her grip on the scissors and they clattered to the floor; the sound brought her back. "I mean, if you want to. I don't know how good of a student I'll be."

"You'll be a great student," he reassured her. "But first, we need to decorate this auditorium."

It took them the rest of the day to finish readying the auditorium. All that was left to do was hang the art, which Ms. Elwin would do herself. After returning the supplies back to the closet and clearing away the trash and boxes, they left to find the rain still coming down.

"Why are you stopping here?" she asked when Drake parked the cart in front of the general store.

"I need to pick up a few things for our art lessons."

A smile spread across his face and, for the first time since meeting him on the footpath, Meg noticed how beautiful he was. There was an infinite youthfulness about his facial features and curly brown hair.

"Then I should warn you now." She sighed. "I have an extremely over-protective best friend. His mom manages this store and if he's in there, you're probably gonna think he's the rudest person you've ever met."

"Why would I think that?"

"Because he's probably going to behave like the rudest person you've ever met. He's suspicious of people he doesn't know very well, especially anyone taking up too much interest where I'm concerned. Do you know Kyrie's son, Alec?" She hoped maybe they already knew each other.

"I've seen him around. Does that count?"

"Probably not, so I'm going to apologize in advance for the cold reception you're about to get."

"Are you two… *close*?"

She knew what he meant. "Yes, but not like that." Meg recalled the most recent fiasco of kissing Alec and it further embarrassed her. "No. He treats me more like I'm an annoying child that needs constant supervision, and he's the poor schmuck that got stuck with the task."

"Okay." He leaned over and peered into her troubled eyes. "I've been sufficiently warned."

Drake went to the art supplies area while Meg chatted with Kyrie, explaining that she and Drake had just finished decorating the auditorium for the children's art show. She also told her Drake had offered to give her art lessons.

"Lucky you, Nissa tells me he's quite good," Kyrie said. When Drake piled the supplies on the counter for Kyrie to sort through, she asked him, "How's Nissa doing? I haven't seen her in weeks."

"As witty and charming as an Irish woman can be." Drake gave Kyrie a warm smile. "How've you been?"

"I'm doing very well. Meg was just telling me you're going to be her new art teacher. I'm jealous."

"Care to join us?"

"Sounds nice, but I have a store to run."

"Alec could handle the store for you," Meg said.

"What about me?"

Alec had just returned to the store from making deliveries and heard his name mentioned. He saw his mother jotting down items in the ledger while Meg and a young man stood in front of the counter. Though they'd never been formally introduced, Alec recognized him as someone who lived in the mountains, and that he'd been spending more time recently at the island's school. Alec shrugged out of his raincoat and joined everyone at the counter.

"I was trying to convince Kyrie to take art lessons from me, but she's making up excuses for why she can't," he said to Alec and held out his hand. "I'm Drake Quinlan, and you must be Alec. I've seen you around."

Alec shook his hand. "You've been helping out at the school, for Ms. Elwin, right?"

"Yes. She's been having trouble with her arthritis lately and I'm substituting her art classes on the days she can't make it. Much as I hate the thought of her being in pain, I do enjoy teaching her art students."

"When she retires, I'm sure she'll give you a glowing recommendation to take over her job," Kyrie said while bagging Drake's supplies. "In the meantime, you can practice by being Meg's teacher. Ms. Elwin always said she had a natural talent, if only she'd stop climbing trees with Alec."

"Meg's teacher?" Alec asked, looking at each of their faces for an explanation.

"That's what we were talking about when you came in," Meg said. "Drake offered to teach me how to sketch."

"I'll turn her into a full-fledged artist in one week's time," Drake said.

"I can't wait to see her work," Kyrie said. "You think he can do it, Alec?"

Kyrie had seen the expression on her son's face change from a pleasant demeanor to something darker at hearing the news. She watched him appraise the two standing together in front of him and got a feeling he hated the idea.

"I guess we'll see," Alec said, eyeing Meg keenly. He sensed she'd already agreed to Drake's offer and that she looked forward to it. There was nothing he could do to prevent it, which angered him—even more so that he wanted to. It soured his mood and he suddenly wanted to share it. "Meg, how's Lena doing?"

The instant frown on her face brought him temporary pleasure, but he soon regretted it when he felt her sadness. He caught glimpses of her earlier conversation with Lena and he understood why she was hurting. Some of what he gleaned from her memories hurt him too.

"She's not doing very well," Meg said.

Only moments before, Meg was so at ease, and even happy, and now a gloominess flitted across her face. Alec hated himself for reminding her of Lena. An awkward silence had taken over, but the sound of thunder broke it—startling Kyrie and Meg, but Alec and Drake remained unfazed by it.

"Meg, I'm sorry." Alec took her hand, interlacing her fingers with his. He didn't care that his mother and Drake stood by watching. "Let me take you home."

She nodded, squeezing his hand before letting it go to turn to Drake. "I'll see you tomorrow?"

Drake smiled ever so slightly; they hadn't discussed when to start their lessons and he admired her determination.

"Let me check with Ms. Elwin first to see if she needs anything. I'll call you when I know more. Until then, I'll give you your first assignment." Drake handed Meg a sketchpad and several graphite pencils. "Pick an object, it can be anything, and work on drawing its outline. Don't worry about the details, just focus on the most prominent lines of the object."

Meg glimpsed an acknowledgement swirling in his irises for a brief second before they settled on a fixed color—a soft amber this time. A smile graced Meg's face again. "Thank you, Drake. Tell Ms. Elwin I'm sorry I missed her today, and tell her I'll start drawing the trees instead of climbing them."

"I will." Drake turned to Kyrie. "It was nice to see you again, and I'll tell Nissa you asked about her." He said to Alec, "Glad to finally meet you properly."

~

Meg told Alec about decorating the auditorium, then fell silent the rest of the drive to her house. She'd started thinking about Lena again, and by picking through her memories, Alec caught more of their conversation. It hurt him to know how badly Lena thought of him and he stopped trying to sense Meg's thoughts when he detected her turmoil and uncertainty. He didn't want to know if Meg gave more credence to Lena's warnings beyond what he'd already considered on his own.

The silence between them had become intolerable. Alec pulled the cart to the side of the lane, turned it off, and sat back against his seat. He waited. She remained silent, but eventually reached for his hand. The gesture comforted him, bringing relief that Lena's words hadn't completely turned Meg against him.

"Talk to me, Meg. I know there's something wrong."

"I'm just sad about Lena, and I'm worried about Frank losing her."

"I can't imagine it's gonna be easy for him, but he's got a lot of friends and we'll all be here for him." Alec hesitated for a moment. "Is that all that's bothering you?"

Rather than answer right away, Meg scooted closer to him and rested her head on his shoulder. He let go of her hand and draped his arm around her shoulder, hugging her close to him. Peacefulness returned to him at sensing some of her tension lift away, but then she sighed. Her breath on his neck created a tingling sensation that caused his body to stiffen.

Meg lifted her head to look into his eyes and then her gaze drifted to his lips. Her face inched forward and he leaned away. When he removed his arm from around her shoulder and sat up straight in his seat, Meg's mouth opened in shock. For more times than she cared to count, she'd been about to kiss him and he pulled away before she could. It was easier to count the times she'd actually made contact.

It was beyond embarrassing; it had become a shameful cat-and-mouse, chase-and-never-catch game between them. She'd had enough of the constant rejection, with just a hint of a reason to keep trying that he threw in occasionally. Even more humiliating was her consideration that he probably did care enough about her to stop himself from taking what she continued to keep throwing at him.

She scooted back to her seat and stared at the paved lane in front of them, refusing to look at him anymore. Meg loathed even sitting next to him any longer and desperately wanted to get out of the cart.

"Nothing else is wrong," she finally answered his earlier question, her voice cool and monotone. "I'm very tired, though. I'd like to go home now."

Alec noted a distinct shift in her emotions, as if she'd given herself over to a new resolve. Having refused to see more of her thoughts, fearful he'd hear more of Lena's unpleasant premonitions, he chose to let it go—figuring he could always sort it out later if need be.

"I'll see you later," she said after he parked as close as he could in front of her house so she could avoid the rain.

Meg gathered her things from the back seat, not once looking at him, not even when he suggested drawing one of Ila's horses for her first sketching assignment. As he watched her walk up the steps to her house, Alec began to regret not probing her thoughts. When she didn't turn around to wave goodbye before closing the front door, he felt the full brunt of her dismissal. He stared at the closed door for a moment before he left, confused by the overwhelming feeling of having just missed an opportunity to fix something before it was broken.

~

The phone rang early in the morning. It woke Ila first and while talking to Frank on her bedroom phone, Meg came in. Their eyes met and Meg knew what the call was about, Lena had died in the night.

Meg returned to her bedroom. She tried to go back to sleep, not wanting to think about Lena, but the attempt was useless—she kept remembering their last conversation. After giving up, she got dressed and went to the kitchen.

Ila was already there, sipping tea. When she heard Meg's footsteps, she prepared another teacup. Noticing the shoulder bag and sketchpad Meg had placed by the door, Ila said, "I think it's a good idea for you to immerse yourself into something new. I know you're sad about Lena's death and the best advice I can give you for how to handle the pain of losing someone you care about…" Ila frowned, remembering her own pain when Joseph died. "You just have to find something new to care about."

She figured Ila's thoughts had drifted to Joseph, Meg's father—a man Meg had only seen pictures of. Hoping to make her feel better, Meg said, "That's exactly what I intend to do. I'm going out for a while and I want to ask you for a favor. That is, if you don't mind fibbing a little for me."

"Fibbing? For you?" Ila raised her eyebrows. "I can't wait to hear this."

"If Alec… actually, *when* Alec comes by, tell him I'm not feeling well. I'm going to meet Drake for my first lesson and I don't feel like dealing with Alec today." Meg shook her head. "You know how he is."

Ila laughed. "I certainly do. I'll tell him you're not up for visitors if he stops by."

When Meg stood to take her teacup to the kitchen, the phone rang. She smiled and picked it up. "Hello?"

"Meg? Hey, it's Drake. I talked to Ms. Elwin and she doesn't need my help today. If you'd like, we can start our lessons."

"I'd like that. How about I meet you?" she suggested, not wanting to risk bumping into Alec.

"Sure. Meet me at the lake with the waterfall near your house. In about an hour?"

"Sounds perfect. I'll see you soon." She hung the phone up and turned to Ila. "I have to go now. I'll call you if I'm late for dinner."

Meg grabbed her bag and rushed out the front door, but had to turn around to get her umbrella since it was drizzling. Once she was facing the forest, she decided on the longer of the two shortcuts, just in case. The last thing she wanted was to run in to Alec, and she looked forward to a break from his ridiculous broodiness.

She ran the whole way and estimated she had at least half an hour to herself before Drake showed up. Meg wanted the time alone, she'd been waiting for it and savored it while she walked alongside the lake. The grief of Lena's death finally hit her and she sat on a flat rock by the water's edge.

Crying felt great, and when the tears ran dry, a sense of completion relaxed her. Lena was gone, she was never coming back except in fond memories, of which Meg decided to only remember the good things. She also decided to give up on whatever strained her friendship with Alec. He wasn't going to budge from his stance and he meant too much to her to keep testing him.

Meg caught sight of something white floating in the rippling water. She leaned over as far as she could to reach it. The paper was saturated and she laid it on the rock to examine it. Some of the lines had blurred, but it was clear enough to depict a drawing of a young woman sitting by a lake in the rain, staring out over the water. Beside her was a familiar shoulder bag and umbrella.

"What do you have against using an umbrella?"

Meg spun around. "Drake! You scared me."

"I'm sorry." He came closer and shared his umbrella.

Meg looked back at the drawing. "You drew this? How long have you been here?"

"I got here right after you did."

She was horrified he'd seen her crying, but supposed she should thank him for not including that spectacle in the drawing.

"Don't," he said. "Never be embarrassed to feel."

"Just the same, thank you for not drawing that part."

Drake stooped down to retrieve her umbrella and shoulder bag. "Ready to start our first lesson?"

"On one condition." A playful smile adorned her face.

An equal one spread on his. "I was already planning to take you there." The swirling in his irises intensified. "I'd prefer not to have any distractions."

~

Still early, they met no one on the lane while they drove past the town center and continued on to the mountain region. The higher up they drove, the softer the rain fell, and finally stopping altogether once they reached the place Meg wanted to see.

"Let me see the lines you drew," Drake said when they had settled down on the very tip of Mors Cliff.

Meg couldn't take her eyes away from the scene in front of her and she handed

Drake her shoulder bag so he could get the sketchpad himself. He opened it and studied the lines of the horse she'd worked on. She did exactly as he had instructed, drawing several examples of the same horse and focusing only on its most prominent lines.

"Very good. I'm impressed."

She took her attention away from the crashing waves below and glanced at her sketchpad resting on Drake's lap. "Are you sure? I was worried it looked strange without any details."

"Stop doubting yourself. You did what I asked, and did an excellent job at it. We'll work on adding a few details today."

She looked back at the waves slamming against the jagged rocks, awestruck by the explosions of white spray sent airborne for a time before returning to the sea. It was all so immensely powerful and violent, but it was also beautiful and she wondered why anyone would ever want to come here to die.

"Because it is so beautiful," Drake said of her thoughts. "Here, take your sketchpad and pencil."

She took them, saying in a playful daydreamer's voice, "What to draw, I wonder."

Drake looked out over the ocean and fixed his sight on an osprey just about to dive into the water. Instead of snatching up the fish the bird was hunting, it turned and flew in their direction. Meg's lips parted in surprise when it landed on the ledge next to Drake.

"He'll do." Drake smiled at the osprey. "He doesn't have a lot of time, though, he has a hungry chick to feed."

Immediately, Meg set her pencil to paper and worked on the outline of the osprey, who had jumped up into Drake's lap. Her pencil streaked across page after page, as she feared the raptor would leave at any moment.

'He has to go now. Make this your last sketch and add detail to his wings this time,' Drake instructed silently.

Meg's pencil paused on the paper. She looked at Drake, confused at hearing his unspoken instructions. The osprey grew restless, leaning and spreading its wings, its golden eyes searching seaward. She returned to her drawing and added details to the individual wing feathers. When she finished, the osprey took flight, going back to his previous task of hunting fish.

"Let's see how you did," Drake said, taking the sketchpad. He flipped through the pages and returned to the final drawing. "You're doing very well at seeing the important lines, and the details on the wings aren't bad. We'll work more on details tomorrow."

Ignoring his assessments, she asked, "How'd you do that?"

'You mean this? Talking to you without speaking aloud?'

"Yeah," she whispered.

'It's nothing. You can do it, too. Go ahead, try it.'

Meg wasn't sure what she was supposed to do. She stared into his eyes and saw the irises swirling in a beautiful array of colors. When she leaned closer to get a better look, she was happy he didn't back away as Alec so often did.

'Why do your eyes do that?'

'Because of who and what I am.'

'Our lessons are to be private, aren't they?'

"That's right, and I'm glad you brought that up," Drake said, returning their conversation to speaking aloud. "Our time together *is* to be private. To be sure of that, I'm going to shield your thoughts and memories of our lessons… particularly from Alec."

"So, you know Alec's different?"

"Yes, I know about Alec. You're different, too, Meg. You're very special, more so than Alec, and especially to me. I don't want to talk too much about that right now. I'll tell you later, on our last art lesson." Drake gave her a boyish smile. "Will you agree to wait till then?"

"I'll wait." She nodded, feeling more comfortably alive than she ever had.

They spent several more hours perched on the cliff. When lightning struck over the island's lower elevation, Drake knew Alec had just discovered where Meg was. Having returned a second time to Ila's house asking to see Meg, Ila told him she was out on her first art lesson.

This was when Alec's mood darkened, and the weather on Gamma fell in line to join his allegiance.

Drake decided to take advantage of the lightning and positioned his body behind Meg's so that he could put his arms around her. He took her right hand into his and guided her pencil across the pages of her sketchpad to draw out the lightning strikes—each strike appearing to slow down for him to capture its lines properly.

"You smell like trees," Meg said to him.

He had released her hand so she could draw the lightning on her own. However, he remained in the same position behind her, looking over her shoulder at her progress. His arms wrapped around her waist and his face turned in toward her neck. Meg's eyes widened at the tingling sensation occurring all over her body.

"And you smell like flowers," he whispered in her ear.

Her pencil ceased moving and she closed her eyes.

"Speaking of which," he continued, still speaking softly against her neck, "tomorrow we'll work on drawing flowers. They're great for learning detail."

"Any homework?" she asked.

"Go to bed early, that's all. I'll pick you up in the morning while it's still dark. Make sure you tell Ila tonight that you'll be gone before she wakes up."

"Okay."

~

Meg was asleep when the colorful stream of lights trailed in through her open bedroom window. It swirled above her for a moment before reaching out a blue tendril to caress her face. She sighed at the velvet touch and opened her eyes. She recognized the brilliant colors hovering over her as the same she'd seen in the forest with Alec.

'Good morning, Meg. It's almost dawn, time for our second lesson. I'll meet you outside.'

The blue tendril left her face and pulled the sheets down before gathering itself together and leaving out of the window. She smiled and rushed to the window to find Drake seated in the cart looking at her.

'I'll be right out. I need to brush my teeth and get dressed.'

Though still dark outside, the sun announced its forthcoming advent by casting orange and pink hues across the sky. Drake drove the cart through the forest along a barely discernable footpath that Meg wasn't familiar with. The trees grew denser and she wondered where he had in mind for their next lesson.

"It's a beautiful garden that none of the other islanders know about," he said and stopped the cart. "We're going to walk the rest of the way. It's just through the trees in front of us."

As they passed through a thick stand of tall evergreen trees, a magnificent garden came into view. It was unlike anything Meg had ever seen. Enough of the sun had risen to show her an explosion of color in the form of thousands of flowers.

"Whose garden is this?" Meg asked, astounded by its beauty.

"A very special woman, someone you'll get to know soon. She won't be here today, so we can have our lesson uninterrupted."

He took her hand and led her to a fountain. She sat on the bench beside it and marveled at how the water defied all she knew of gravity. Meg turned to Drake, thinking of asking how it was possible. His irises swirled again, reminding her of how she woke this morning.

"That was you I saw in the forest with Alec, wasn't it?" she asked.

'Yes.'

'And that was you in my bedroom earlier?'

'Yes.'

'Who were those other lights that came after you?'

'A couple of old friends who came by to visit me.'

"You'll tell me later, right?" Meg asked aloud, smiling at his refusal to share more information.

"That's right," he said, smiling back. "Ready to draw some flowers?"

They spent hours selecting and drawing various parts of different flower blooms. Meg grew weary of the process. "Can't we sketch a whole flower instead of butchering them?"

Drake laughed at her candor. "You're adorable, you know that? Okay, go find a rose you like and we'll sketch it."

Meg selected a deep-red rose and when she finished sketching it, she understood why Drake had made her spend hours drawing the individual parts of a flower. She attempted adding dimension, but he confiscated her pencil.

"I'll teach you about shading tomorrow. We've done enough for today and it's about to start raining again. Are you hungry?"

"Starving," she said.

"Let's have lunch at the café."

~

While sitting at a window-side table and waiting for their food to arrive, Drake pulled out her sketchbook to point out the progression of her work. She caught on to what he meant; it was the importance of knowing the definition of an object before trying to capture its nature.

"You're an excellent teacher," she said.

"You're an excellent student." Drake put his hand over hers on the tabletop. He knew Alec watched them through the window.

"Where will our lesson be tomorrow?" Meg asked after the waiter brought their food.

"Depends on the weather. I'll let you know in the morning." He winked at her and looked past the window at the increasing rain. Alec had just left, returning to the store to sort through his new feelings of jealousy. "I expect we'll have more rain, though."

4

The Future's Past

Meg was awoken again by Drake. As before, the blue tendril caressed her face and she decided to make sure her window was open every night from now on. Her bed sheet slid down from her body, and this time there was a long pause before she heard him speak.

'Are you ready for our third day of lessons?'

'Yes. I'll meet you outside.'

~

It was the day of the children's art show and they sat in the auditorium's top row. Drake had her sketch the backs of the chairs in front of them, coaching her to focus her attention on the shadows created by the auditorium lighting. They stifled their laughter at the increasing number of black smudges on their faces.

Meg liked the way the shading looked in her drawings, but wished she could go back to drawing the flowers again.

"It'll be trickier leaving, but I think I can manage it," he said.

When they stepped out of the auditorium, they were met with a wall of rain, forcing them to run to Drake's cart. Alec stood under the porch railing of the general store, staring at them while they laughed and drove away. Once they made the turn on the lane that led away from the town center, Alec jumped into his own cart to follow them. When he made the same turn, Drake's cart was nowhere in sight. Alec spent the next hour trying to find them before giving up.

~

'Wake up, Meg.'

She opened her eyes to discover the sheets already pulled back. Instead of the colorful lights hovering over her, Drake lay beside her on the bed, caressing her cheek with his fingertips.

'Fourth day of lessons?'

'Yes. Unfortunately, someone's waiting outside this morning. Alec seems determined to follow us. We'll have to leave out the back today.'

"I still need to get dressed and brush my teeth," she said, getting up to peek out the window. Alec sat in his cart on the other side of the lane in front of her house; Meg almost felt sorry for him.

She went to her closet and started to pull a pair of jeans off a hanger when a hand covered hers. Drake guided her hand to a different hanger, one with a white sundress.

"A dress?" She didn't bother hiding her disgust.

"Please."

"Turn around," she said, rolling her eyes.

He waited in her bedroom while she left to brush her teeth. When she returned, they crept down the hallway and left out the back door. As a precaution, Drake cloaked them both until they reached his cart, hidden in the woods behind Meg's house.

"We're going to the mountains today," Drake said after he maneuvered the cart through the trees and was back on the traveling lane farther away from Alec. "I want to show you the lake up there."

When they'd arrived at the mountain lake, Drake instructed her to sketch the waterfall. She'd been at it for over an hour while he occasionally offered suggestions. Each time Meg thought the sketch was finished, he told her it wasn't quite right and turned the page for her to start over. They sat on the blanket he'd brought and after a while, he lay back, continuing to watch her progress as she showed him one drawing after the next.

"I don't know what you mean by *capture the motion*," she said, exasperated.

"Take the lessons we've had so far and put them all together. Sketch the most prominent lines, add the details, and then add the shading. If you get it just right, you'll have created the illusion of the moving water."

She tried several more times, but still it didn't meet with his approval. She threw the charcoal and pad down on the blanket and lay back next to him. "My hand hurts, and I'm beginning to think I'll never get it right."

"Yes you will. Come with me."

Drake got up from the blanket and held out his hands to help her up. He led her to the edge of the lake and reached for the bottom of her sundress.

Meg had an idea of what he planned for her to do, so she allowed him to lift the dress and pull it off over her head. She stood there, clad only in her underwear, and watched him remove his shirt. She scowled at him for leaving his shorts on. They swam closer to the waterfall and waded under the cascading wall.

"Feel the way the water hits you," he said. "Watch how it splashes down into the lake and listen to how it sounds. Inhale the fresh scent of new morning. This is what you need to capture, a feeling of totality in your drawing."

Meg closed her eyes and listened to the water falling around her, visualizing how sound, scent, and touch could be drawn. She understood what he meant now and wanted to return to her sketchbook. When she opened her eyes again, she found herself already back on the blanket and Drake was offering her a towel.

"Dry yourself off and draw."

She was halfway through sketching the waterfall, knowing she got it right this time, when Drake slipped the sundress over her head. Meg stopped drawing long enough to slip her arms through the straps and resumed where she'd paused. When she was satisfied with it, she held it up for his approval.

"You did it!" He took the sketchbook to examine the details.

Meg stretched out on the blanket and stared at the sky. As had been the case for almost a week, there were only grey clouds to look at, but at least it wasn't raining where they were. She knew Alec was causing it, punishing the whole island for the time she spent with Drake, and she didn't care. It could rain forever; she was learning so much and enjoying herself too much to consider placating Alec's dark mood. The only thing on her mind was holding on to it for as long as she could.

"You said you could teach me how to be a better artist in a week's time. That only gives us three more days."

"I know," he said. "And I've been thinking about that. I have an idea I want to share with you."

Drake set the sketchbook aside and leaned over her, blocking her view of the clouds, their faces mere inches apart. Meg saw his irises swirling, but at a slower rate than she'd grown accustomed to seeing.

"You'll have to agree with my idea, though. It won't happen unless you accept it."

She turned away from his gaze. "Somehow, I think you already know my answer."

Drake hooked his finger under her chin and made her look into his eyes again. "Yes, I do, but you always have a choice. Never forget that." He smiled. "Actually, maybe I'm not so sure of your answer. In fact, right now, in this very moment, I feel stuck between two parallels because I said you can make your own choices."

"Then tell me your idea."

"I want you to tell Ila you're going to bed early tonight because you're tired and have to get up earlier than usual tomorrow."

"Why?"

"I want to come back to your house tonight and take you to where I live, to my house." Drake closed his eyes and took a deep breath. When they reopened, the irises had stilled. "I want you to stay with me for as much time as possible for the next three days, day and night."

"What if she checks on me?"

"She won't, not if you tell her tonight that you need to sleep for your early morning outing. Besides, I think she likes the idea of you spending time with me. Even if she did check on you and saw you weren't there, I don't think she'd ever mention it to you."

Meg nodded. "Yes, Drake, I want to see your house. I want to stay with you."

~

During dinner with Ila, Meg told her she was tired and going to bed. "I'm leaving early in the morning, probably before you get up. I'll call you if I'm gonna be late for dinner."

"Okay, sweetie. Get some rest." Ila yawned. "Those mares are about to run me into the ground. They're spoiled rotten. I think I'll turn in early, too."

Meg went to her room and looked at her bed. Truthfully, she was tired and hoped there was enough time to catch a quick nap before Drake showed up. She glanced at the window to make sure it was open and made her way over to the inviting sheets, welcoming the softness of her pillows. Within moments, she fell into a blissful sleep.

Her eyes opened again at the unfamiliar feel of someone else lying beside her. It was Drake, and he had fallen asleep. She looked at the clock on her bedside table; it was just past midnight. The quick nap lasted over three hours and she wondered how long he'd been here.

Meg studied his sleeping face. It was the same as when he was awake: youthful, boyish, and quite beautiful. Not how a woman is described, nor handsome like a man, but beautiful like light and color in its purest form. There was an element of nature in his features and it made her think of boundless expanses of forests with giant trees that couldn't be measured in any sense she knew of. She thought of plants, leaves, and flowers with creatures who visited them she didn't recognize, but loved just the same.

Yet, blended with all his beauty was an undercurrent of unrestrained power. It was almost like the sun, or how the forces of nature could sometimes be destructive. It reminded her of how the universe is destructive, but that it's forgiven since that's the only way to breathe new life in an otherwise hopeless and dismal end.

She reached out her hand to touch his cheek and it felt as equally beautiful to her as did his visual features. A series of images presented themselves in a neatly arranged collection, but then they occurred too rapidly and sometimes spiraled together, confusing her as to what they all meant and why they seemed so indecisive. One image in particular made her breath catch and the shock of it forced a gasp to escape past her lips.

Drake's eyes opened instantly and saw her flushed face, causing him to analyze every second that had just passed. A smile formed on his face and she smiled back despite what she'd seen.

"You've been studying me while I sleep." Drake cupped her hand, where it rested on his cheek, and brought it to his lips to kiss it. "The question now is will you politely ask me to leave, or will you come with me?"

"I only saw a little. The rest was too fast."

"You saw enough. Tell me, Meg—"

"I want to know more."

His irises, mirroring the emerald color of Meg's, swirled and shifted to the rest of his body. The stream of lights, green and white this time, left her bed and hovered at her door for a few seconds and then returned. Once again, Drake settled beside her and picked her hand back up—like he'd never left.

"What did you do to my door?"

"Gave it a reminder that you need your rest, just in case."

"How do you do that? How can you be lying here one minute and be those lights the next?"

'Because of who and what I am.'

'You'll tell me later, right?'

"Right." Drake laughed softly. "Actually, I'll explain it to you by showing you, but not yet. Are you ready? It's officially our fifth day of lessons."

"Are we going to your house?"

"Soon, but I want to show you another house first."

~

They left out of Meg's window and entered into a soft mist. The rain had stopped for hours, but clouds continued to loom over the island, ready to resume the deluge by morning. She followed Drake to the backside of the stables, where he'd hidden the cart before sneaking into her bedroom window.

He drove to Alaret Beach and parked the cart in the tallest of the sea oats. Once Meg got out of the passenger side, Drake gave the cart a brief glance and it vanished. He saw her eyes scan the sea oats, searching for it. "It's still there, only hidden." He tugged on her hand. "Come on, I want to show you something."

They walked quietly along the beach for a while, hand-in-hand. Finally, Meg was compelled to say, "I know this beach very well. I can't imagine what you want to show me that I wouldn't already know about."

"Is that so?" Drake was intrigued and surprised by her willfulness. "Besides teaching you how to sketch, and soon I want to show you how to add color, I want to also teach you how to be more confident. I want you to learn how to go after what you want. For now, you may *think* you know everything about Alaret Beach, but I assure you, there are some things you've yet to see."

"Ooh, don't you sound mysterious? All right then, lead on."

They continued down the beach, past a cliff wall, all the way to the farthest end before Drake turned their direction inward. When they got to the trees edging the beach, he pulled a tactical flashlight from his shoulder bag. Drake didn't need it, but he'd felt Meg's tension. He turned it on and a powerful beam of light illuminated the ground, and Meg sighed her relief.

"Thank you for bringing a flashlight. I was just about to turn around and run back to the beach."

"I would try to convince you that spiders aren't as horrible as you imagine, but it won't help. You'll always have an irrational fear of them. Don't worry, I'll shoo them all away before you see them."

"Everybody fears something," she mumbled.

"Very true."

"What are you most afraid of?"

Her question caught him off guard; he hadn't foreseen Meg asking him about his fears. Though it puzzled him, he loved these unexpected moments when he didn't already know they were going to happen. They were so rare, but he'd been experiencing more of them since befriending Meg and they were like precious gifts each time.

Drake contemplated the question and knew exactly what he feared most. "I fear being alone."

Meg swallowed back the instant lump that formed in her throat. "You're not alone right now."

"I know, and I'm very thankful to you for it." Drake frowned at his desire to say more, confused by the pleasant unawareness of his own feelings as they surfaced.

They reached a clearing at the top of a slope and Drake pointed the flashlight at a dense patch of leafy vines that appeared to be growing out of control. While maintaining the position of the flashlight's beam on the vines, he turned to her with an expectant look.

"Weeds? I just walked through a jungle in the middle of the night so you could show me a giant pile of weeds?"

He laughed. "It's more than that."

Drake led her to the front of the massive vine-covered structure and with a simple wave of his hand, a section of the vines parted to reveal a door. Meg gasped in surprise at seeing the arched doorway and her eyes explored beyond it to take in the entirety of the structure.

"It's a building," she whispered.

"Actually, it's a house. Want to go inside and have a look?"

"Obviously," she said as though he'd asked a supremely stupid question.

Meg climbed the stone steps to the door and the hinges squealed their disuse when she opened it. She stepped inside the dark house with Drake right behind her. The sound of a striking match preceded the smell of sulfur and then the room was aglow from the hurricane lantern he carried.

"I brought this here earlier so we could see."

"You were right, there are a few things I didn't know about Alaret Beach." She marveled at the interior of the house. "What is this place?"

"Besides being a house, it's a refuge of sorts. A place to go when there's very little hope left." He knew she waited for one more piece of information. "I built it a long time ago."

She nodded and turned to explore the rest of the house while he followed with the lantern. Meg eyed the barren walls in lengthy intervals, and when she continued staring at one particular spot, he reached for her hand and allowed her to see what would be there one day. She didn't question the image that burst to life in her mind, she merely studied it awhile as though it was already there.

Without a word, she moved away from it and headed toward the end of a hallway to a room made almost entirely of windows. As the house was covered in vines, the only source of light came from the lantern Drake still carried. He allowed her to see what the windows would look like once all the vegetation was removed, and with the sunlight filtering in the room from the vision, she found it warm and inviting.

"You'll create that painting I showed you a moment ago in here," he said.

Meg watched him carefully. "Is this supposed to be my house one day?"

"Yes."

She asked nothing more of him and left the windowed room. Meg paused at an empty room halfway down the hallway, but remained silent and continued on to the base of the stairs. Drake positioned himself between her and the first step, preventing her from ascending the staircase.

"No," he said. "You can see it later."

His irises portrayed a controlled swirling of color that wouldn't settle on anything final. She understood it was important to him that she not question his refusal.

"I think I've seen enough of this house for now," she said.

"I'd like to show you one more thing before we go."

Drake led her to the middle of the front room and shined the lantern on the dust-covered stone floor. Meg could just make out a distinct pattern beneath the grime—a fading rectangular border of intricately carved markings.

She kneeled to get a better look. "What is it?"

"Many things, but my favorite part is the fantastic history written into it. You'll read all about it one day, but not tonight."

They exited the house, and with another wave of his hand the vines fell back into place over the door. Once again, the house disappeared. Drake led her over to a large oak tree and turned her around to face the clearing surrounding the house. The moon cast just enough light onto the scene for Meg to see colors in various locations in what would be a yard if the house was lived in.

"Alec knows about this place," Drake said. "He'll show you soon."

Though surprised, and a little hurt that Alec hadn't told her about the house, she made no comment. Halfway back to the cart, Drake slowed their pace along Alaret Beach and pointed at the cliff wall.

"There's another place up there you don't know about," he said in a hushed whisper, as though afraid someone would hear him. "Alec doesn't know about it either, but you'll both discover it together."

"Show me now."

"I can't. Someone's up there and the last thing I want right now is for her to see me… especially with you. In fact, let's get out of here."

~

When they were a good distance away, Meg couldn't stand the nagging question anymore. "Drake?" She looked at him and frowned when he laughed. "What's so funny?"

"You, and how long you've been wanting to ask me, but not wanting to ask me. No, Meg, I don't have a crazy girlfriend hiding out at the top of the cliff."

"Oh." She felt her cheeks burning. "Do you have one hiding out anywhere else? I don't want to make anyone angry."

"Nope, no girlfriends anywhere."

"Then who were you worried about seeing you?"

"Not yet, Meg, but I promise I'll tell you soon."

Drake drove along the sole island traveling lane to the mountains and eventually turned onto a forest path. It was bigger than the other forest footpaths Meg was used to, but not paved like the traveling lanes. When they passed by a large building, Drake told her it was the mountain region's general store. He pointed out a few other buildings, explaining what each of them were and the names of the people who managed them. It was like a smaller version of the main town center and Meg was fascinated by its quaintness.

Though it was a few hours before dawn, it wouldn't be long before the first of the shopkeepers showed up to open for the day. Since it was still deserted, Drake stopped the cart and let her explore. She peeked in all the windows while he shined the flashlight inside. When she started to yawn, he coaxed her back to the cart and continued driving up the mountain.

The wide dirt path narrowed the farther they travelled higher in elevation and she wondered if he was taking her to Mors Cliff again. They were so close to it when he finally pulled the cart into a small clearing that had the worn appearance of it being his usual parking spot. She got out and looked around for a nearby house. Finding nothing, she turned to Drake to see him smiling and pointing upward—his expression akin to that of devotion. Her gaze followed the directive, and then she saw it.

There, amid the trees and perched over a moss-covered rocky crag of mountain face, was the edge of a wooden porch. Though she couldn't see it properly from the ground, Meg knew the planked deck must lead to a house. To the left, she caught sight of medium-sized boulders arranged in a staircase leading up to the side of the porch.

Her eyes returned to Drake's and an adventurous smile spread over her face. Before he could say a word, Meg took off running to climb the boulder staircase.

A sense of happiness warmed and soothed Drake, watching her make her way up to see the inside of his home. He retrieved their bags from the cart, taking his time so she could explore on her own for a while.

Meg was breathless when she reached the porch, breathless still by the sight that greeted her. The entire front of the house was open and airy by the lack of glass windows, exposing the scenery of the trees and mountains. Generous swaths of sheer white fabric—which billowed in the occasional passing breeze—covered the many openings, allowing moonlight to spill into the front room.

She knew when Drake was with her, she'd heard his footsteps and saw his silhouette go to a table against the wall. He lit several candles and the front room came alive with new light. The windowless room was for sketching and painting, several easels and canvases in various stages of completion leaned here and there against every available surface. His hand slipped into hers and he led her to the farther recesses of his home.

Drake carried one of the candles in his other hand and as they walked along, the flickering light showed more of each room, but she longed for the sun so she could see everything clearly. When they reached his bedroom, he placed the candleholder on the bedside table and she eyed the giant bed draped with delicate netting suspended from the ceiling.

He parted the netting and sat on the edge of the bed. When she came to him at his gentle tugging of her hands, he closed the netting again behind her and scooted them both up to the pillows. Then he pulled the bed sheets over their bodies and cocooned her in his embrace.

"Let's get some sleep before our next lesson," he said in a soft whisper.

~

The cheery sounds of singing birds woke her up several hours later. Meg was still in Drake's bed, but he wasn't there beside her. She sat up, parted the netting encompassing the bed, and looked up at the cathedral ceiling towering over her. It seemed impossible to have achieved and she wondered if Drake had built this house as well.

"Meg," he called from somewhere at the front of the house. "I can hear your stomach growling from here. Come have breakfast with me."

She smiled to herself and followed the smell of something wonderful. He was in the front room, sitting at a high table overlooking the porch, and spread out on the tabletop was a variety of decadent food. It was the only thing her eyes would focus on and she dashed to the chair opposite him. The mouth-watering aroma turned out to be freshly baked bread—she wasted no time, snatching off the loaf's prime heel piece and slathered on butter before devouring it. Drake watched her, smiling, and she didn't care what he thought of her ravenous appetite.

While buttering a second slice, she surveyed the rest of the options. There was a plate of beautifully arranged cheeses accompanied with fruit, both fresh and cut in artisan preparation. Drake selected what he considered to be the best of the cheeses and spread on a thin layer of fig confit, sprinkling it with walnut shavings. He held the piece up to her lips and waited for her to open up, which she did and then closed her eyes. An explosion of flavors rewarded her and she opened her eyes again at his urging.

Drake held a glass of red wine in front of her, insisting she complement the flavors with it. Meg took the offered glass and sipped it, enjoying the finishing flavors the wine had created on her palate while he nibbled on Corinth grapes from the plate of cheeses.

"I like the way you eat," she said, reaching for a different selection of cheese, topping it with a blackberry glaze.

"I thought you'd like it."

When she satisfied her hunger, Meg eyed the canvases. She could see them better now in the daylight, and she studied each and every one. One in particular grabbed her interest and she got up from the chair to examine the biggest of all the canvases in the room, also among the most completed ones.

It depicted a forest scene, but unlike any she knew of. The enormous size of the tree trunks was proof that it wasn't a Gamma forest scene. One of the trees held a nest, bigger than that of an osprey's, with multiple vines bearing gigantic leaves trailing down the sides. That alone was impressive, but it was the center of the painting that pulled her in. A tiny bird approached an enormous flower and all around the scene there seemed a busyness that escaped her full knowledge.

Meg felt Drake's presence behind her. "That's not from here, is it?"

"No. It's of where I came from. You can't see the colors properly because…" He hesitated briefly, then wrapped his arms around her. "Can you see it now?"

An incredible knowledge filled her and she saw more of the painting she hadn't noticed before. There were colors there she couldn't name and they dazzled her eyes. Not only that, but she saw the tiny bird's wings beating to stay aloft. It reminded her of the waterfall sketching lesson Drake tried so hard to make her understand—*capture the motion.*

"You see it now, don't you?" he asked.

"Yes, I can see it. I want to paint like that."

"And you will" –Drake turned her around– "in just a little bit. We should make a painting for Ila so she doesn't start doubting what we're up to."

"Think she's starting to?"

"Not yet, but she will if you don't give her something by tonight."

Drake went back to the table and gathered the rest of their breakfast. He took the bounty outside, amassing it all in a hollowed out log positioned near a small creek running alongside the length of his front yard. Meg watched him from the hammock strung on the porch until he fussed at her to follow him to the prepared scene.

He handed over her sketchpad and pencils. "I want you to sketch a drawing of the ravens eating the rest of our breakfast. Remember our first lesson of focusing on the most prominent lines, but make sure to pay attention to details so you can paint them in later."

Meg glanced at the log. "I don't see any ravens."

Drake looked up into the treetops and swept his arm in a beckoning motion. Within seconds, two healthy-sized ravens descended onto the log, cawing at each other in what appeared to be a discussion on who got first dibs on the cheese.

"You have about twenty, maybe thirty, minutes to sketch them, and don't forget to draw outlines of the trees in the background."

Drake took up residence in the vacated hammock while she frantically sketched the ravens gorging themselves on the food. Even after the cheese and bread were consumed, and while the ravens considered the feasibility of being able to eat or carry away the fruit, her pencil raced across the page. When they left, she focused on the lines of the trees behind the log.

In her peripheral vision, she saw the familiar stream of colors descend from the porch and come to a stop near her. "Well, what do you think?" she asked, holding the sketchbook up.

"You even managed to capture them arguing with each other." He took the drawing and walked back to the stone staircase. "Now, let's go make a painting out of it."

Meg followed him inside to the front room where he'd already set up an area for her painting lesson. He motioned for her to sit on the stool in front of a blank canvas. They spent hours perfecting the painting, not one second bored her and she looked forward to having her own studio one day.

There were moments when Drake enveloped her body and took her hand into his to show her how to paint a troublesome area of shadows beneath the ravens, or to teach her how to blend the oil paints directly onto the canvas. Each time he touched her, she grew more aware of their close proximity, and even more perplexing was how her body responded to it.

The painting was declared finished as early evening approached. Drake studied it and smiled his satisfaction that she had captured the essence of the scene's motion. He waved his hand across the surface and the oil paints instantly dried.

"Impressive, Meg," he said, still viewing the work. "You're very talented. Even from the very beginning..."

He turned around, noticing her silence, and found her looking out over the porch railing at the skyline. Drake had a sense he was about to experience another one of those coveted moments he hadn't foreseen.

She faced him after he'd only taken a few steps. His presence in her life had filled the hole Alec left behind when he absorbed who she really was. Meg grew stronger; Drake suspected she may even be absorbing a bit of himself. If so, he didn't care—he'd gladly give it all to her if he thought she'd have it. He stopped walking toward her and waited for her to speak.

"Our fifth day is almost over," she said.

"That's right." He hated the reminder. "I'm about to take you back to Ila so you can have dinner with her and give her the painting."

"I want to know what's really happening here."

"I know you do. I'll tell you—"

"Soon, that's what you keep saying."

Meg teetered on a thought, and then it came to him—the part Drake hadn't foreseen.

She looked up at the sky. "You know, all I have to do is think about Alec for more than a few seconds and..." She left the rest of the warning suspended and a bolt of lightning blazed across the sky above them. The sound of thunder soon followed and rain finished the procession.

"Stop it, Meg. You'll send more than just Alec after us. I swear, I'll tell you. I'll show you tomorrow. Please, don't make me tell you now."

Drake rushed the rest of the way to her in a blurry trail of light and color, encasing her in a brief eternity before returning himself to a physical form and wrapping his arms around her. Meg felt horrible again, reminiscent of when he told her his worst fear. She suspected that same fear caused his sudden anguish. Her arms went around him, hoping to calm his trembling.

"I'm sorry, I didn't mean to upset you. I trust you, Drake."

He pulled away from her and cupped her face in his hands. "Don't be sorry. I'm asking a lot of you, and I'm afraid to say there's more I'll ask. Will you be patient with me a little while longer?"

"Yes."

~

Meg sat at her dining table, informing her mother that she'd be going to bed early again. Ila finished the last of her dinner and glanced at the painting Meg had given her.

"Fine by me, especially if you keep bringing me presents."

After they cleared away the dishes, Meg showered and retired to her bedroom. She expected Drake would be there waiting for her, but the room was empty and so she went about the task of getting her bag ready. While reaching into her dresser drawer for a shirt, the thinnest trail of blue light streamed in and settled over a white one. She smiled and picked the shirt up, pulling it over her head while the animated blue light raced in and out of the shirt's sleeves, making her giggle.

"Stop, that tickles," she said, keeping her protests to a hushed whisper.

Drake materialized in front of her, fixing her collar and tucking the shirt into her shorts. "Ready?" he asked.

"Don't you need to remind my door again?"

He looked at her bedroom door and chuckled. "It still remembers."

They left out of their usual exit of Meg's bedroom window and Drake drove them to an area of vacant houses. He held her hand while they walked around all three of them. She waited for him to explain why he'd brought her here, but he remained silent.

"Why are we here?" she asked. "These are newcomer houses."

"There'll be some newcomers soon, and they'll change everything." Drake faced her. "So will you, and these newcomers will help us make that happen."

Drake led her back to the cart and drove up the mountain lane to his house. When they arrived, she waited for him instead of bounding up the stone staircase ahead of him. Once inside, Meg lit the candles herself and took his hand into hers to lead him to his bedroom.

"Can we sleep for a while?" Meg parted the netting surrounding the bed, hoping he hadn't planned on having her draw the moon. "I'm really tired."

Like before, he sat on the edge of the bed and tugged her down with him toward the pillows, encircling his arms around her as they settled among the sheets. Before she drifted off to sleep, he shared an idea with her.

"I want you to stay here for the remainder of our time together. I'll go down tomorrow evening and handle Ila myself, but you'll have to go back to her the following evening. Are you okay with this, do you want to stay with me?"

"Yes, Drake." She closed her eyes, welcoming sleep. "That's exactly what I want."

~

Meg's eyelids fluttered open, and the harshness of daylight made her squint. When her eyes adjusted to the light, she saw Drake sitting up on the bed with his sketchbook, in deep concentration on whatever it was he'd been drawing.

He glanced up and saw she'd awoken. "Good thing I'm finished with it." He turned the sketchbook around for her to see.

It was a drawing of her asleep in the very position she still reclined, its depiction was exact and flawless. Meg scanned the bed's surface and discovered several more pages of her in various sleeping positions strewn about the sheets.

She grimaced at one of them. "No way! I can't believe you drew me with my mouth open like that. It looks horrible. Please, tell me I wasn't snoring."

"You could never look horrible, Meg. Surely, you know how beautiful you are."

Meg averted her eyes at the compliment and fiddled with a crease in the bed sheet. "If I went around thinking that about myself, I'd be a vain and conceited person." Her voice was soft, but determined. "And I don't ever want to be like that."

"Vanity isn't the same thing as confidence." Drake set the sketchbook aside. He put a hand over hers, stopping her nervous fidgeting with the bed sheet. His other hand went to her chin to lift her face toward his. "Don't forget, our final lesson will be about increasing your confidence in every aspect of what makes you who you are."

She smiled. "You haven't answered me yet."

"No, Meg, you don't snore."

~

At breakfast, Drake blindfolded Meg, explaining that a good way for her to have more confidence in herself was to learn how to trust her senses. He tied a white cloth around her eyes, then returned to the seat across from her to continue the lesson.

"Open your mouth," he instructed. "I'm going to feed you and you'll have to tell me what it is."

Meg smiled first before opening her mouth. His fingers brushed past her lips as he placed something cool and soft on her tongue.

"What do you taste?"

She closed her mouth and analyzed the flavors and textures of the food on her tongue. It was a fruit for certain—the sweet was there—but it wasn't as firm and crisp as an apple. "A pear?"

"Very good. Let's try something else."

"Grape," she said quickly of the next object.

"That was an easy one."

After she correctly guessed a strawberry, an orange slice, and lemon zest, he tried a different kind of food. "Okay, what do you taste now? I'll give you a hint, it's not a fruit this time."

She squished the food around in her mouth with her tongue; its texture was noticeably different from the fruit and had a creamy quality. "Cheese."

"What kind?" he tested further.

"Well, I've already eaten it. Can I have another piece?" She opened her mouth and Drake put another cube on her tongue. "Goat?"

"Exactly. Let's try adding your sense of touch before you taste."

Something soft brushed against her lips, but its edges were course and grainy-like. It was delicate, too, as she could feel parts of it crumbling away. "I think I know this one. Can I eat it now? Bread is probably my favorite food."

Drake fed her the bread and after a few seconds of silence, Meg felt something wet pass across her lips. A droplet fell off her bottom lip and ran down her chin, falling to the table. After a second swipe of the same sensation, she asked, "Am I allowed to taste it?"

"Yes."

She licked her lips and knew instantly what it was. "Wine… red, and don't ask me the year because I don't know."

Meg heard him chuckle, and then the sound of his chair moving; she readied herself for the next object. It was soft, not wet like the wine, but not dry like the bread. Whatever it was, it gently tugged at her bottom lip. An idea presented itself in her mind, but she was afraid to voice it and tried to come up with an alternative. The object left and awaited her answer.

"Um, a flower… petals, I mean?"

"No. This is the first one you got wrong. Try again, and don't be afraid to trust what you know."

The soft objects returned to her lips, caressing, and she knew exactly what they were—she could feel his breath, and she'd memorized his scent days ago. Though still deprived of sight, she could almost see them. They felt so wonderful; she prolonged giving her answer, fearing it would end the test.

"What do you feel, Meg?" the objects whispered.

"Your lips," she whispered back.

"Yes."

His lips left hers, and then she sensed he was all around her, urging her to stand from the chair. She could barely feel the floor beneath her feet as he led her back to the bedroom. Though still blindfolded, Meg knew they stood beside the bed. Hands went to her arms, lifting them above her head, and her shirt was tugged up and then off. Her shorts were unbuttoned and pulled down, and she lifted her feet so they could be moved aside.

Delicate fingers went to her chest and unclasped the bra, slipping it away from her arms. These same hands pulled down her underwear and helped her step out of them. Meg stood there, wearing only the blindfold, feeling as though she was being studied before Drake gently guided her to lay down on the soft sheets.

He scooted himself onto the mattress, sitting beside her, and she heard the sound of charcoal scratching against paper. Meg allowed her body to relax and after a while a smile curved her lips.

"Yes, that's perfect," he said. "Keep smiling like that." The fervent race across the page resumed. When it slowed and came to a stop, she heard it being torn from the sketchbook. "Roll over and turn your head toward me."

Meg did as he asked and after another long while of him sketching her form, his hand went to the back of her head to untie the blindfold. Her gaze fell to the most recent of his drawings and a rosy color spread on her face, made redder when he showed her the first drawing.

"Too bad I'm not painting, that's a beautiful pink on your face." He flung the sketchbook aside.

Drake lay down and pulled her to him, hugging her tight. Meg couldn't begin to describe the growing sensation of heat building inside her at the feel of her nakedness against him, and was glad he still had his clothes on.

"Don't be ashamed of your body, it's wonderful. I should know, I just drew it several times," he said as though giving her perfectly sound advice.

Regardless of his assurances, Meg pulled away a little and tried to tug the bed sheet up, but he gently nudged her hand away. He propped himself up on his elbow to peruse her body from an elevated angle. She knew he'd already studied her bared physique, but it had been easier when she was blindfolded. Meg started to close her eyes, but he wouldn't allow it.

"No, keep them open. I want you to watch me looking at your body."

Meg focused on his eyes, the irises swirled intensely while they studied every inch of her, occasionally lingering in some places longer than others. Something changed in her after the initial feelings of modesty had passed—she started to feel emboldened and infinitely braver. She found the discarded blindfold and draped it over his eyes, tying it behind his head before relaxing back against the pillows.

She picked his hand up from where it rested on the bed between them and placed it palm down onto her abdomen.

"Tell me what you feel," she said.

"Downy soft skin, and delicate, like peaches. Goosebumps are rising, you're chilled."

There was some initial nervousness at having their roles reversed, but he soon regained his own confidence. Drake's fingers splayed out across her belly and he allowed his hand to explore every detail of her, as his eyes had done. At times, he felt her body quiver and he had to pause before continuing on, fearing things were going too far, too quickly.

He pulled the blindfold off, ending the exploration. "I think you mastered our confidence lesson."

Meg noted his shaky voice and his trembling hand as he tugged the sheet up. "This isn't over yet," she said, the statement laced with warning.

"I know."

She yanked the sheet away again and stood from the bed. Ignoring her clothes on the floor, she went to the closet and selected one of his white button-up oxford shirts and slipped her arms into the sleeves. When she turned around, he was already there, reaching for the buttons himself.

They went to the porch and lay in the hammock together. Meg had a new sense of ease with her body now and had no qualms about wrapping one of her legs around his. While he pulled on a rope tied to the side of the house to keep the hammock swinging, she snuggled up against his side and stared at the treetops swaying in the wind.

The hours passed by too quickly and when evening crept up on them, they got up from the hammock. Meg followed him to the kitchen and accepted the glass of wine he held out to her. After they ate, she picked up the bottle of wine and her glass and walked to the front room where all of Drake's artwork rested against the walls.

One was a composite of colors that reminded her of the flower garden he'd taken her to. Again, her eyes fell to the largest canvas in the room, the one with the small bird and gargantuan trees. She leaned over and noticed something she'd missed before. There were tiny specks all over it, forcing her to lean in even closer for a better look. The specks revealed themselves to be tiny people with wings who flew all throughout the painted scene. She stood upright again at feeling his presence.

"Do you miss being there?" She pointed at the specks. "Do you miss them?"

"Yes."

His arms went around her waist and pulled her back against him. They stared at the painting for a while, each of them longing to be there.

Finally, Meg asked, "Are you sure you don't want me to go with you to my house?"

"I'm sure. I'm going to give her last night's memory." Drake chose not to go into the details of how Ila would relive the events, even talking to Meg as though she was actually there and compliment the painting of ravens for a second time. "Wait here for me, I'll be right back."

Meg saw a flash of streaming light and color trail out of the front room and over the porch railings into the trees—he was gone. She knew he'd be back soon, but experienced a terrible loneliness at his absence. Feeling drawn there, she went back to the bedroom and gathered up all the drawings from the bed, smiling as she appraised each one.

"You're the most peculiar person I've ever known, Drake," she mumbled to herself and smiled at realizing that this was what she cherished above all about him.

She stacked the drawings on a small wooden desk near his dresser and when she turned around, her eyes widened in shock at the vision standing by the bed. The room had grown dark with the approaching night, but she could still see clear enough to know Drake was nude. It was her turn to draw him now. Only briefly did she avert her eyes out of modesty before setting about the task of lighting every candle in the room while he waited for her on the bed.

Rain began to fall again, and lightning lit up the sky as she approached him—studying the lines of his form. She climbed onto the bed, took the sketchbook into her lap and drew the lines already committed to memory. At times, the pace of her sketching slowed, coinciding with her cheeks turning crimson, and he'd smile without mentioning it.

She took her time with the shading and when there was nothing left to perfect, he held his hand out. Meg relinquished the sketchbook for his inspection, hoping he thought it as good as the ones he'd drawn of her. Drake was silent for too long, making her worry he didn't like it.

"Stop worrying, Meg, it's excellent. I was only thinking about how much you've learned in our week together. I'm proud of your accomplishments. I hope you are, too."

Meg nodded. "I am. Thank you, for everything." She took the sketchbook from him and set it aside.

"You shouldn't go thanking me for *everything* just yet, there's still more I intend to show you. Do you want me to answer some of your questions now?"

"Yes, but I get to choose what I want to know first."

Drake already knew what she wanted to learn before all else. He struggled between two parallels again. Either one led to the same result, but the essence of his turmoil was what was best for Meg. He cared for her, as was his nature, even more so for her specifically, and he wanted Meg to be at peace with her decisions. Ultimately, he decided to allow her to make her own decisions as she approached each one.

"What do you want to know?" he asked.

Meg took the blindfold that still lay on the bed and placed it over his eyes, securing it behind his head.

After a moment, her fingers delicately brushed across his chest, then down the central line of his torso and abdomen. He submitted in blind silence to her exploration of his anatomy. When it became excruciating, he reached for her hands in the effort to make her take pause.

Her hands slipped from under his, dodging his efforts. For a moment, he felt nothing at all and just when his mind formulated what was to happen, her body stretched out over his. Though she still wore his shirt, she had unbuttoned it and the feel of her skin in such an intimate way sent a glorious pulse of electrified energy shooting through his body. He knew Meg still wanted to explore, still wanted to learn—she was testing new boundaries, and he forced himself to give that to her calmly.

She branded soft kisses on his chest. Her hair fanned outward and the curls felt like needles piercing their image onto his shoulders and sides; the sensation made him shiver. The delicate kisses traveled up his chest, finding new places to discover at his neck and earlobes. Despite the intensity of it all, he did well maintaining his control. It was when her lips connected with his that the first beginnings of doubt trickled into his thoughts.

It was about curiosity and pursuing sensual knowledge for her—she grew more determined and uninhibited, and her kissing became feverish from her body's demands to discover more. His own urges became increasingly more difficult to ignore as the eager movements of her hips sought closer contact. When his hands reached for her hips, to help her find that contact, he forced himself to speak.

"Meg… please," he whispered against her lips, but it only inflamed her intense desires. If he intended to stop her, Drake knew the time to do it was presenting itself and he cared too much about her to let it slip away. *'You shouldn't be doing this with me. I know you love Alec.'*

Her body tensed at the conveyance. She wanted to ignore it, but it was like he'd thrown cold water on both of them. Meg sensed his resolve and it forced her away from him, snatching the blindfold off his face to look at him.

"Why would you say that to me?" she demanded.

Drake saw a mixture of passion and newly emerged anger staring down at him. He hated reminding her of it. "Because it's true. Are you gonna try lying to me and say you don't?"

She climbed off of him and tugged the shirt closed. "It doesn't matter. It's got nothing to do with what's happening right now."

"Yes, it does."

"No, it doesn't!" Meg's anger at having to discuss Alec became palpable. "He and I are… ridiculous, that's what we are." She refused to look at Drake anymore. "He doesn't want me, not like this."

Drake let go a heavily burdened sigh. "Actually, Meg, he does."

Meg shook her head. "You're so wrong about that." Her gaze drifted toward her clothes at the end of the bed. "He's rejected me so many times that I've given up on him."

Drake reached for her hand, but she recoiled at the touch. He refused to let her dismiss what he wanted to say. "I think your first—"

"No! I'm not having this conversation."

"It's important, Meg. We should talk about it." It became more of a struggle for Drake to continue with his noble intentions, all he wanted was to bring her back to his arms. "Alec loves you and he's finally realized it. He's so jealous you're spending time with me that I'm afraid we'll all wash out to sea if he doesn't get you back soon."

"It's not jealousy," she spat. "He's only concerned. Alec's protective over me like he's always been, but that's all there is to it."

"You're right, but he feels other things for you."

"I'm not an idiot, Drake. I know what *other* things Alec feels, but he's determined not to act on them. He's stronger than you know."

His next words tasted like venom on his tongue. "You have to show him what you want." It was a nauseating venom. "You have more confidence now."

Meg looked at Drake as though he'd attempted to rip her heart out. "When I met you at the lake by my house, I wasn't just mourning Lena's death. I'd made a decision not to suffer any more rejections from someone who didn't want me." She shook her head. "Yet, here I am… being rejected again by someone else who doesn't want me."

She'd had enough and lunged forward to get her clothes, but a stream of blue light beat her to them and flung them out of her reach. Drake was under her again and instantly returned to a physical form, sitting up and saddling her in his lap. The look on his face was agonizing.

"Please, don't go. Don't leave yet," he said, his pleading voice thick with emotions that confused her.

"Drake…"

"I wasn't rejecting you. You have no idea how hard it was for me to stop what was happening." His arms went around her waist, hugging her to him as though she meant to leave with his soul. "It's just that I don't want you to have regrets."

"You know better than I do." Her voice whispered over his bare shoulder, staring blankly at her clothes she'd so desperately wanted to retrieve. "Would I regret being with you?"

Drake pulled away from her, enough so that he could cup her face in his hands and look into her eyes. He had to answer the truth as he saw it forming. "No, not about this."

Inching forward, her lips pressed to his again. At the contact, a series of thoughts, emotions, and memories tried presenting themselves to her and she knew they came from Drake as a last offering for her to decide what was best for herself. Meg saw them and walled them off from her mind, having already made peace with what she wanted.

He felt the wall go up and ceased trying to show her more—he ceased resisting as his hands crept to her shoulders and slipped the shirt off of them. His fingers wound through her hair and reached the back of her head, turning it slightly and kissing her in the unrestrained way he'd been wanting to do since the minute his lips touched hers this morning.

His lips left hers, but only to greedily connect with her neck and chest. A yielding sigh escaped past her lips and his own returned there, wanting to taste it while it lingered. Drake leaned her back against the pillows and looked into her emerald green eyes, seeing that they accepted him more than he did himself. He gently nudged her knees apart, and she welcomed him—her whimper muffled by the sound of thunder.

They neither stopped nor slept as the night continued, it was hunger that finally forced them apart. They satiated their ravenous appetites in the kitchen, forgoing plates and discussion. Stomach hushed, Meg wedged herself between Drake and the counter. The rest of the pear fell from his hand as he hitched her legs up around his waist, using the cabinets as support while he pushed against her.

Eventually, they had no choice but to give in to their bodies' demand for sleep. Drake scooped Meg up from the kitchen floor and carried her to the bed. Still half asleep, she rolled over and he snuggled up behind her before closing his own eyes.

~

The early morning light came in through the bedroom windows and Meg opened her eyes. She knew Drake had already awoken without having to turn around to see his face, her eyelids fluttered closed again at feeling him move against her. He shuddered and whispered her name on the back of her neck.

A moment later, when his heartbeat returned to a normal rhythm, she turned to look into his eyes. His irises were swirling, but slowly with calmed passion. Meg put her hand to his face and traced the outline along his jaw and chin with her finger, trailing it up to his lips, nose, and forehead. Somewhere outside, a bird sang while she fell in love with his beautiful lines, the way he clung to her, his crazy swirling irises, and how he filled an emptiness in her life that only he could fill.

The happy song of the unseen bird brought forth the unhappy reality of what day it was. "It's our final day together, isn't it?" she asked him, hoping he'd say it was their first day of lessons.

"Yes," he said, dashing her hopes, but pulled her into an embrace that suggested there'd never be an end between them.

"Then we're going to spend the whole day right here," she said, ignoring the hideous way the future felt.

"I like that plan, but only after we get up long enough to eat."

"From what I recall, there wasn't much left in your kitchen to eat." Meg smiled at remembering their ventures in his kitchen. "Want to have breakfast at the café?"

"Yes, but certainly not the café at the main town center." Drake ran his fingers through her hair and struggled to discern his scent from her own. He enjoyed the puzzling way it made him feel. "We have a small café up here. I say we grab a bite and come back to this exact location. Good plan?"

Meg's stomach growled her answer. "Think I could get away with wearing only your shirt?"

"Hmm, sounds appealing, but I think you should put your shorts on, too."

~

Drake and Meg sat at one of the high tables by the window, having full view of the pouring rain. Meg scanned the menu and ordered the first things she knew she liked. After the waiter jotted down their order and left for the kitchen, Meg put her foot on Drake's knee under the table and inched it higher to his thigh, watching his expression. He grabbed her foot, pulling it toward where she had intended for it to end up.

The café manager, a potbellied older man with fiery red hair and a bushy mustache, frowned at them from the bar, but continued polishing the glasses. It wasn't until he saw Drake stretch his arm out under the table, toward Meg's parted legs, did he go to the kitchen to put a rush on their order.

They managed to make it back to Drake's bedroom, but their clothes trailed from the stone steps to the side of the bed.

Meg collapsed on top of him and sighed into Drake's neck a short while later; her body still tingling and his just starting to tremble beneath her while his hands clutched tight to her hips. White light escaped from him, enveloping them both. When his trembling intensified, there was more of the light, but it came from her this time. Her composition changed, shifted to a different way of being, and it amazed her. She felt so alive.

The light surrounding them dissipated when his trembling slowed and his breathing returned to normal. Though it was the middle of the day, the room became darker from the storm clouds gathering over the entire island. Sheets of rain fell, bolts of lightning burst through the air, and the sound of thunder was so loud at times, it shook the house.

Drake's eyes went to the window at one point when lightning struck particularly close by. Meg refused to let it distract him. "I don't care about the weather right now. I want to know what just happened to me."

"Did it scare you?" he asked.

"No, it was incredible."

His hands left her hips and went to her back, hugging her into his embrace. Their time together was drawing to a close and there was still so much he needed to share with her. Answering her question, though he hadn't expected it would happen, was only one of the many things he needed to explain to her. It would also be one of the more difficult subjects he'd have to reveal to Meg.

"There's a part of you that's missing. It was taken from you a long time ago. Probably because of the way we've been together, I think that part of who you really are latched on to what I am and used it to express itself."

"What do you mean by taken from me?"

Drake sighed, dreading having to show her the memory, but allowed it to flow into her thoughts. She lifted her head from his chest to look at him, her eyes wide with disbelief.

"He stole from me," she said in an eerie whisper. "He stole who I am."

"He was a child, Meg. He thought he was protecting you."

"How am I supposed to ever look at him again without demanding he give back what he took from me?"

"Don't worry about that, I'll help you deal with it." He reached up and grasped her face firmly in his hands, forcing her to look into his eyes.

The irises swirled a menacing turbulence. Meg understood more lurked there amid the colors: thoughts, memories, and emotions that he wanted to show her. The past was there, mingling with the future, slamming against one another to create this very moment—the future's past.

His fingers fanned out against the sides of her head, squeezing gently in the effort to gain her full attention. "Are you ready?"

"Show me," she said.

The images of Drake's history presented themselves first, colliding and then fusing with the history of others. Thoughts propelled through a vast expanse of time and space before moving on to a more recognizable realm—her home, but one with an accurate history. She saw her birth and ignored the shock. He showed her again what Alec took from her.

The memories careened forward and she saw herself standing with Alec in the forest through Drake's perspective. She suffered his loneliness, so sad and desolate, but it changed to hope as she examined herself through his memory, as he had done.

Everything sped up again, to their time together and to every place and thing he'd shown her, to moments that hadn't happened yet. The further through time he went, the tighter he had to hold her still, and he fought against his nature to put a stop to it to spare her. This moment of showing her was fixed now and he knew it, stopping isn't part of her future.

The memories slowed, then ceased altogether. It was all he knew to happen with certainty, but it was more than enough. He eased his grip on her, watching her carefully. Meg's eyes closed and a single silent tear fell from each one, landing on Drake's chest. She may as well have driven daggers there with both hands; he thought he may have finally found a way to die.

Yet, he continued to live and she continued her silence. He sat up a little, keeping her saddled in his lap while maintaining his hands on her cheeks. "Meg, please, say something. Talk to me. Look at me."

"What do you want me to say?" She opened her eyes. "What choice do I have?"

"You always have a choice." He was determined to make her understand this. "So much of what I showed you happens because we help make it happen, but only after you agree."

"How could I not agree?" Meg sighed with defeat. "But so much destruction, Drake. Why?"

"You saw what will happen. Either way, there'll be destruction. There's no avoiding it."

Meg knew he waited for her answer, she half-waited for it herself. There was no way to put it off, the people he showed her would be here soon, bringing with them the genesis of a war of astronomical proportions. "Lena was right, all I'll ever know is sadness and death."

"No, Meg, her words were only partly right. It was what you said to Lena that held more truth, it'll be the only way you'll ever know about happiness and living."

The reminder of her own words changed something in Meg's understanding. It was true, she couldn't have one without the other. There were others, too. Some she knew, some she hadn't even met yet, but their happiness and survival also depended on her answer.

"Yes."

"Are you sure? Do you think you can do what I showed you?"

"You showed me doing it, Drake. Obviously, I find a way. What I want to know is how I'm gonna go back to a normal life, interacting with these people who are coming here. How the hell am I supposed to pretend like I don't know these things?"

"I'll help you with that."

Her eyes narrowed at him, knowing what he meant by the statement after seeing the true nature of her birth.

"No, I won't take these memories from you. I'm not exactly pro-memory absorption. What I'll do instead is tuck them away in your own mind. They'll be suppressed for you to remember as you need to."

Meg relaxed at his reassurance, but maintained her eye contact with him. She found no deception in his eyes, but what she did see was an innocence very different from her own. It was pure and genuine, it amazed her how intact it was given what she learned of his history.

"No, Meg, don't ever think that." Drake smiled at her. "I didn't come from an oppressed race. We lived separately because it was the only way we could all be happy."

"I know, you made sure to put that sentiment in your history. It still bothers me, though." Meg brushed the conflicting feelings aside, not wanting to think about it anymore. She was stronger now, like she was meant to be before it was stolen. "Make sure you *extra*-suppress the memory of what Alec took from me. I know how I am. If I remember too soon, then our plan will fail."

"I will." Drake lay back, tugging her with him.

'You want me to name her Kai?' Meg asked him silently.

'Please?'

'I like it.'

"Maybe they'll be more like me one day," Drake said, pondering, unable to see this sort of eventuality.

"Maybe, but why does it have to be so sad?" Meg asked, more to herself.

"Are you speaking in generalities, or are you referring to the sadness of having to let someone like me go?"

"Both, I think." Meg fell silent for a while, struggling to find a better way to say what was on her mind. "I know you're all alone. Maybe we could find a way so I could stay with you."

Drake was touched, even though he heard the uncertainty in her voice. "I can already feel you wanting to leave me now that you know what I am."

"No, Drake, I'm not like that."

"Yes, you are like that, and there's nothing wrong with it. You can't share your life with someone like me. You can't be with someone who knows every thought and memory you'll ever have. No one *really* wants to know what their future holds because everyone knows not all futures are perfect and rosy."

"Well, I already know about mine. You showed me."

"You only know how much I allowed you to see. You don't know all of it," he dared to say and felt her body go rigid. He knew it would happen and as Meg's lips parted to speak, he allowed the future memory of her words to proceed her spoken ones.

"I'm strong… I… can handle…" –she frowned– "…knowing—" Meg stopped, disgusted with the way her spoken words echoed with the shared memory of them.

She fell into yet another bout of silence while hating how small and pathetic she was. Meg grimaced when she accepted there was no counter-argument to present that he wouldn't already know to be forthcoming. Even worse was the feeling of wanting to be with people like herself again—those as clueless to the future as she had been a week before.

"You understand now? Only another Lucusan could ever live peacefully alongside me," he said, hating the reality of the explanation.

"I won't lie and say that wasn't a problem for me, but I also won't lie about how I wish it wasn't like that." Meg clung to him. "I like being with you. I'm sorry for being who I am. I wish I was more like you."

"Don't be sorry for who you are, you come from a long line of superior beings," he chastised. "Without them, I wouldn't exist." Drake urged her to lift her head to look into his eyes. "Without you, Kai won't exist."

It was strange for Meg to be reminded of someone so important who'd yet to take their first breath, to think of them in a physical sense. "Will she be safe?"

"I'll make sure of it." Drake saw apprehension growing in Meg's eyes. "We don't have much more time together and I need to know now, before I take you back home, are you sure you want to do this?"

"I'm sure. I want a future." Meg placed a kiss on his chest. "Are you sure we can't spend more time together?"

Drake smiled at her question and thought about how being with Meg made him feel. It was wonderful being wanted by someone who knew exactly what he was, and still wanted him anyway. It had been a long time since he'd had any kind of a relationship. None of them had resulted in the sort of kinship he'd developed with Meg. It reminded him of the life he had before his home was destroyed, a life he had few memories of—even his true parents were long gone.

He didn't look forward to resuming a lonely existence after taking Meg back to her normal life. If he wanted a better world for her and for so many others, he had no choice. Their time together on Gamma had run out; Meg needed to return to her life and develop a relationship with Alec. Drake knew she was armed with enough knowledge and experience to make that happen. It brought a sense of jealousy to him, which he instantly recognized and it made him laugh.

"What?" she asked.

"Nothing." He shook his head. "I wish we had more time together, but you already know we don't and I want to tell you a few things before it gets much later."

"I'm listening."

"After you get to your new home, I want you to go to the library. It's enormous, not like the library here. I want you to go to the historical section and learn everything about yourself and your ancestors, where you came from, how I and people like me are created. However, and this is important" –he raised his eyebrows– "read it yourself. Don't rely on the historians to help you."

Drake showed her an image of how the historians relayed an otherwise daunting mass of material to someone without them having to actually read it all. "Because of the nature of your situation, they won't question why you'd want to read it all without their assistance."

"Okay, but why? You already showed me quite a bit."

"I care about you, Meg. I want you to know all of it. I think it'll help you find comfort in what you'll start planning after you get there."

"Yeah, I already have more questions that we don't have time for you to answer."

"I do have to take you back tonight, though." Drake half-grinned. "I laughed a moment ago because I recognized some rather petty emotions I was having."

Meg understood and it caused her to blush. "Oh."

"That same emotion will be what drives him to finally let go of all his reservations to keep you at a certain distance. You saw the memories, you'll be happy with him. You need to develop that relationship before they get here."

Meg was uncomfortable discussing this issue with Drake. She wondered why he seemed so at ease with it.

"No, it isn't easy for me," he said of her thoughts.

"Good, I'm glad I'm not the only one." Meg's brow creased at the embarrassing tension before changing the subject to one even more delicate. "That's not the only reason, though. I know who else you're worried about."

"You're right, I am worried about her," he said. "She's come down from the cave, and she's a force to reckon with. All this bad weather has finally gotten her attention. Chaza knows Alec's doing it and she wants to know what's causing his dark mood. She'll start searching for you if I don't get you home soon." His face took on a timid expression. "You should know, Chaza fears me. She knows what I am."

"I really don't care what she thinks." Meg acquiesced at Drake's frown. "She'll be fine tomorrow when she sees me again."

~

They went to the small café to have their last meal together. Though happy for each remaining second they had, there was still a somber mood that haunted their dinner. When they finished, they went back to Drake's house and he handed her an unframed painting.

"Give this to Ila in the morning. When I take you back tonight, I want you to go straight to your bedroom. I'm going to Ila first." It caused him pain knowing what he'd have to do. "I don't have a choice, I have to alter her memories. I'll have to be thorough about it, too, given what's already been done to her mind."

The idea of it hurt Meg as well, so she shifted her attention to the painting he handed her. "Really, Drake? Pegasus?"

"Too much? You're right, we shouldn't give it to her."

"Wait." Meg held the painting out of his reach. "I mean, well, it *is* kind of cruel in a way, but she'll like it for now. She won't know what it means."

~

Drake picked Ila's limp form up while Meg remained rooted to the front room floor, watching him walk down the hall and turn into her mother's bedroom doorway. She could still see the smile on Ila's face when they'd walked into the front door only moments ago; a smile that faded when Drake immobilized her. He had assured Meg this part was necessary to absorb Ila's memories thoroughly, considering the people who would try picking apart her splintered memories.

When Ila's bedroom door shut, Meg went to her own bedroom and waited.

After changing out of the clothes that had remained at the foot of Drake's bed for days, she put on a t-shirt and crawled under her own sheets. She thought they'd disappoint her after having been tangled up in Drake's, but they felt oddly comfortable and familiar. Maybe, Meg considered, this was a sign that she looked forward to starting the rest of her life, and it was better than the life she'd been living.

A stream of green and blue light slipped in under her sheets, encompassing her body in a feeling of warmth, surrounding her in everything she defined as good and beautiful in any world worth destroying or saving.

"Don't suppress them yet," she whispered to him.

Drake returned to his physical form and pulled the t-shirt off of her. He looked down into her eyes and denied himself the urge to take her away from Gamma immediately. "I wasn't planning on it."

He stood on the edge of their final moments together before delivering her over to someone else, and if insanity was possible in his breed, Drake considered he may be standing on the edge of that as well. There was no way to thank Meg for the companionship she'd given him and for the hope of a future with endless possibilities she'd chosen to help him fight for. He could take comfort in knowing her legacy would be known forever, written in historical documentation as being a monumental figure who spear-headed a movement for equality and universal peace despite all the odds against it.

"It isn't enough, but thank you," he said, rolling her onto her front and lifting her hair to kiss the back of her neck. *'I love you, Meg.'*

She closed her eyes at the beautiful sensation she'd grown to crave. Meg had wanted to say something in response to his silent declaration, but whatever it was fell to the forgotten state of waiting to say it later as he lifted her to her knees and moved her body against his.

As the night marched on, Meg finally succumbed to the drowsy pull of her eyelids while cradled in Drake's arms. Seeing her give in to the need for sleep was the moment he both dreaded and waited for—the very same reasons he'd kept her awake until the very last minute. He glanced at the window and saw the first pink tinge of the approaching dawn.

He had no choice but to leave and allow Meg to start the rest of her life. In just a few short hours, she'd emerge from her house and show those who needed the confirmation that she was fine, and they'll be too relieved to question her week-long odd behavior. Drake saw it all, the torrential weather would cease the minute Alec sees her again. Chaza would relax and return to her own lonely existence—hers of choice.

Drake looked back at Meg's peacefully sleeping face and pulled her to him. Halfway between his physical form and his expressed colors, he suppressed all the memories he'd shown her and all the intimate moments they'd shared, leaving her with only the barest memory of their art lessons for her to recall.

When it was done, he leaned over and kissed her before turning to her bedroom door. He'd already thought to keep all of her drawings, concerned they'd be reminders to tug on her suppressed memories. Drake looked at her one more time before leaving, before returning to his lonely life. His only comfort being the pact they made together to right a wrong, and to provide a home and a future for everything and everyone they cared about, and ever will.

As he drifted away from the island, Drake knew he'd come back soon. He had no choice, the future was set, and it was unbreakable. It returned to him his own confidence.

5

Infrastructure

A year had passed since Lena's death and, though it took a while, Meg had returned to her usual self. For months afterward, she tended to drift away from conversations, became lost in thoughts kept so well-guarded that even Alec couldn't get through.

Ms. Elwin's arthritis miraculously cured itself and Alec was all too thankful to see less of Drake Quinlan going into the school to substitute her classes. When he stopped seeing Drake, Alec stopped thinking about him and worrying over the time he spent with Meg.

Worse than he'd ever been, Alec kept a constant vigil over Meg; watching her closely and having no choice but to guess at where her thoughts wandered to when she seemed a million miles away.

Her twentieth birthday was fast approaching and he forced himself to part from her long enough to work on a surprise he hoped she'd like. When another idea came to mind, a frivolous gift, he refused to let it fall to the unattainable.

Alec arrived early for his next outing on the sailboat with Frank, one he hoped would finally produce a pearl of good enough quality to give Meg on her birthday. For over a week he'd been taking diving lessons from Frank, but made sure he ended each day with stopping by Meg's house to see how her day went.

He stepped out from the dunes near Gamma's boat dock, then crouched among the sea oats when he saw an unfamiliar man standing by the dock entrance. Alec spied him from his hidden vantage point and watched the man stare at the island as though he expected it to answer some question he'd asked.

The stranger turned away and left on a small speedboat. Alec went to stand, but stopped at seeing what looked like a female's figure disappear into the sea oats a few yards away. He scanned the area, but found no one. A voice from behind scared the hell out of him.

"What are you doing, Alec?" Frank asked. "You don't have a fancy for turtle eggs, do you? I'd be awfully disappointed if you did."

"No." Alec shook his head, glancing around for an excuse and found one on the sand in front of him. "I was looking at a hermit crab."

Frank smiled. "Funny little critters, aren't they? Seems like they never want to be seen."

"Yeah." Alec stood and stepped out from the sea oats. "Ready? I'm feeling lucky today."

"That's the spirit." Frank winked at Alec. "Let's get that pearl."

~

Alec and Meg left the cart by the footpath and carried their daytrip belongings the rest of the way to Alaret Beach. They dumped the lot in the sand and hot-footed it to the water to cool off.

Meg groaned. "This is the hottest summer ever."

"You said that last year," Alec said.

"And it was, until this summer."

They sat at the water's edge, letting the cool ocean waves wash over their legs. Meg scooped the water up in her hands and poured it on her shoulders and neck, but Alec lay down to get the cooling-off job done faster.

Meg laughed at him. "What are you gonna do when a wave comes and covers your face?"

"Hold my breath."

She eyed an incoming wave. "Might want to start holding it now."

As a small wave washed over them, Alec closed his eyes. Something flashed in her memory and quickly dissolved in the rippling effect of the sunlight shining on the water covering Alec. She thought the vision surreal; the white and yellow colors dancing across the water dazzled her eyes and it almost seemed like time slowed down a little to make it last longer.

"Now you have sand in your hair," she said when the wave subsided and Alec opened his eyes again.

"Guess I'll have to wash it out."

Alec stood and went farther out into the water until he was waist deep and waited for the next wave. At just the right moment, he dove headlong into it, reemerging a moment later. He turned to Meg and smiled. "You just gonna sit there all day?"

"I'm waiting for you to feed the sharks first before I go in."

"You really want a shark to eat me?"

"No." Meg sighed. "I'd probably miss you."

"Come swim with me." Alec feigned a pout. "Pretty please?"

She rolled her eyes, but got up anyway and stood next to him. "Show me how to dive into a wave."

"It's easy, it's all about timing." He looked at the next incoming wave. "Here comes a good one. Ready?"

Meg faced the wave, but kept turning her head to watch Alec, trying to duplicate his technique. When the wave got close enough, they dove into it and reemerged on the other side.

"That was fun!" she shouted over the roaring Atlantic, and they spent the next hour diving into wave after wave until they were exhausted.

Back to where they'd dumped their belongings, Meg pulled two beach towels from a bag and spread them out. Alec rummaged for food and water, oblivious to her growing irritation.

"Obviously you found the food," she grumbled at seeing he'd already demolished a good bit of the bread.

"I'm starving." He felt bad for hogging. "What are you trying to find?"

"Are we supposed to stand by the ocean and ask the fish if they have any volunteers?"

Alec scanned the items Meg had already searched through and realized his mistake. "Oh, no, I forgot to bring the fishing gear."

"Exactly." Meg scowled at him.

"I could make a spear." He shrugged, trying to ignore the bread he wanted more of.

"Yeah, right," she said, but then a thought came to mind and she laughed.

"What?"

Meg balled her hands into fists and pounded her chest. "Me Meg, you Alec. We stab fish with stick and eat."

He chuckled when she held up an imaginary spear and pretended to stab the bread with it. "I'm serious. I know how to make one, I just have to find the right kind of wood. I'm not sure how good I am at spearfishing, though."

Her playful Tarzan expression morphed into incredulous disbelief.

"Oh, come on," he said. "We'll turn it into an adventure and make it fun."

A semblance of a mischievous smile curved her lips. "Okay. What kind of wood do you need?"

"We'll have to go in there." Alec motioned toward the trees behind the dunes. "The type of wood isn't as important as the condition and length of the sapling."

She sat on the towel next to Alec. "Pass me some of that bread. I'm starving, too.

Alec handed her the rest of the loaf and a bottle of water. "Is Ila mad?"

Meg finished chewing the huge chunk of bread she'd bitten off and washed it down before answering him. "She was livid when I told her I was spending the day with you instead of her on my birthday. Don't worry, I set her straight."

"Great, more reasons for Ila to hate me."

"She doesn't hate you."

"Then why has she taken to snarling at me every time I come over to visit you?"

"Because she's Ila." Meg laughed, knowing Alec wanted to agree, but was hesitant to insult her mother. "And because she's extra-stressed out right now over the mares. Management's really hounding her this time because whoever they sold the foals to is questioning everything, especially why it's taking so long. They probably don't know the first thing about horses."

"Tell her I'm sorry," Alec said, but couldn't hide his grin. "Just so you know, I'm glad you're spending the day with me. So, how's it feel to turn twenty?"

"Not much different than turning nineteen."

"I got you a present."

"You didn't have to do that." She lost interest in the bread and eyed Alec's shoulder bag. "Where is it?"

"Close your eyes and hold out your hand."

Her eyes narrowed. "No way. You'll put something gross in it."

"No, I won't." Alec raised an eyebrow. "Do you want your present, or not?"

Meg extended her arm out and opened her hand, giving him one last dubious glance before closing her eyes. She heard him fumble around for a second, then felt his fingers brush against hers as he placed something in the palm of her hand.

"Don't open your eyes yet," he said.

There was motion in front of her and then she felt his breath on her face. The velvet touch of his lips barely brushed hers as they passed across her cheek.

"Happy birthday, Margaret Meg Arcana," he whispered in her ear. "Open your eyes now."

She did and saw a single pearl resting in her hand. The luster and inner glow of the pearl met her eyes and its simplistic beauty awed her. "Alec, it's beautiful."

"You like it?"

"I love it," she said. "I think it's the best present I've ever gotten. Thank you." Meg rolled the pearl around in her cupped hand, amazed at the size of it. "How'd you get it?"

"Frank taught me how to pearl dive."

Her mood shifted from light-hearted to ferocious in an instant. "You let Frank dive?"

"No!" Alec said. "He stayed on the sailboat and coached me from there."

"Okay." Her placid countenance returned.

"Actually, we had a lot of fun with it. He told me pearls are among the earliest gems known to man, and that according to Persian mythology they were the tears of the gods."

"That's kind of cool." Meg grinned at him. "I really do love it."

"My mom said you can take it to Chapman Peterson and he'll make it into jewelry for you."

"That's a good idea." Her gaze returned to the pearl. "I'm thinking a ring would be perfect."

~

They consumed the rest of the food, which wasn't much, and Alec got to his feet. "Want to go stick shopping with me?"

"What kind of sapling are we looking for, Tarzan?" Meg asked once they reached the wooded area.

"One that's about five feet long." Alec surveyed the puny options. "These trees are too small. Let's go farther in."

There was little foot traffic in this area, making it difficult for either of them to navigate through the brambles. Occasionally, Alec picked up a stick, or judged one still attached to a tree, but would decide against it being the right shape. They came to an area where Alec discovered more promising options and he started removing a small limb from the tree with a pocketknife.

Meg continued to wander through the trees, exploring more than helping. She noticed a familiar change on the ground in front of her and her eyes followed the narrow corridor in a winding, upward fashion.

"Alec, come here."

He went over to her with the newly severed limb.

"Look, it's a path." Meg pointed at the barely discernable sandy patch. "Where do you think it goes?"

"I don't know, this is the first time I've been to this part of the beach. Looks like an old footpath nobody uses anymore."

"Want to see where it goes?" she asked, though it sounded like she'd already made up her mind. "Please?" Meg wore a goofy smile, even batted her eyelashes a few times.

"Really, Meg? What if it goes nowhere?"

"That's not possible. All paths go somewhere." She nodded to encourage him, but had every intention of exploring, with or without him. "And we'll never know unless we check it out. I believe you mentioned something about adventure a little while ago."

"Fine." He groaned. "Let's go have a look, but let me walk in front. I can use this sapling to knock away some of the brush." He smiled and offered her the stick. "Unless you want to do it."

"No, you can go ahead of me."

They walked along the old forgotten path and a few times got confused where the forest floor had been reclaimed by natural fauna. They managed to stay on course, entering a denser stand of trees on an increasing incline.

"I have an idea where it's gonna end up," Alec said.

"Where?"

"At the top of the cliff wall. I've never been up there. I'm not sure why anyone would make a path to it."

"For the view?" she suggested.

"Maybe."

The rest of the hike continued in silence and once they reached the top, the landscape opened up to a breathtaking panorama of the ocean and Alaret Beach. They spied their towels and bags from the lofty vantage point.

"Like I said" –she nudged him– "for the view."

"Maybe," Alec repeated, frowning.

Still not satisfied the path led to only a scenic vista, Alec turned around to face the island side of the cliff and saw a cave entrance. Instant suspicion turned him back around to try distracting Meg from seeing it.

"A cave!" Meg blurted out, much to Alec's disappointment. "I didn't know there was a cave here."

"Neither did I," he muttered, his mind racing for a new plan. "We probably shouldn't go in there."

"Are you stupid? How could we *not* go in it?" Meg laughed at him. "We stumble across a cave we never knew about and you're not interested in exploring it?"

"It might not be safe, Meg."

"Oh, really? What's gonna get us? We don't have any bears on Gamma. What's the matter, are you afraid of bats?" She pushed past him, leaving him with no choice but to follow after her.

"I don't care about bears or bats." He grabbed her wrist. "It looks pretty dark, there could be a drop-off in the cave floor."

She hadn't thought of that and tried to find a way around it. "I brought a flashlight. It's in my bag."

"Of course you did," he said. "I forget fishing gear, but you remember a flashlight for a daytrip."

"I want to see the cave, Alec. Let's get the flashlight."

He chuckled—his curiosity ate away at him, too. "All right."

They raced each other back down the cliff, excitement coursing through both of them. When they reached the bottom, Meg looked over her shoulder to see how far behind Alec was and fell unceremoniously onto the sand.

"Meg!" Alec yelled and caught up to her. "Are you okay?"

"Yeah, I guess." She checked her arms and legs for scrapes. "I tripped on something."

Part of a long metal cable jutted out from the sand. Alec kneeled and swept aside more of the sand to get a better look at it. "I've seen this before, on other parts of the island. It's always around the beaches. I think it has something to do with the infrastructure, like electricity or something." He pointed at the welt forming on her knee. "Sure you're okay?"

"I'm fine." Meg stood and looked down at the cable. "Honestly, though, shouldn't that be buried deeper?"

~

Flashlight in hand, and after a last thought to move their belongings to higher ground out of the incoming tide's reach, they were off again to the cave. Back at the top, Meg stayed close behind Alec and used the flashlight's beam to inspect the safety of the floor, walls, and ceiling.

The back of the cave had a large metal door centered in the rocky wall, but had no obvious way of opening it. Where a doorknob should be, there was nothing.

"Maybe it opens from the inside," he said.

"Then there'd have to be another entrance somewhere on the island. But where?"

Alec shrugged. "I have no idea."

Further searching of the cave revealed benches along the walls, and in various places on the floor were remnants of camp fires from long ago. In one area, an old beach blanket covered in dust lay forgotten near several small bottles. Alec took the flashlight from Meg and shined it on the labels.

"Unbelievable!"

"What?"

"I recognize these labels," he said. "They were the first ones my mom made for the wine produced here."

The empty wine bottles were scattered on the cave floor, but farther away, and lined neatly against the cave wall, were at least twenty more unopened ones.

"Hmm, know what I'm thinking?" Meg asked.

"I can imagine."

"I say we open one and have a birthday toast." Meg eyed the closest bottle.

"We don't have any cups, though."

"Guess we'll have to open two then, and drink from the bottles." She gave him a wink. "I promise not to be offended."

Meg grabbed the filthy beach blanket and shook off its years of accumulated dust by the cave entrance. When she returned, Alec had already opened two bottles and after she spread the blanket out, he handed her one.

Holding his bottle up, he said, "Here's to you, Meg. Happy birthday, and may you have a hundred more. Cheers!" They clinked their bottles together, each taking a swallow, then settled down on the blanket.

"This is really good," she said, taking another sip. "Give my compliments to Kyrie."

"I'd rather not mention we were up here drinking wine she made forever ago." Alec frowned. "I wonder why they're up here. If she knew about this place, I can't believe she never told me about it."

"Who cares? I say we enjoy the spoils of our plundering." She drank several swallows while looking around the cave with the flashlight, marveling at how big it was. "Is this place cool, or what? I say we swear never to tell anyone about it, especially those brats we went to school with."

"Don't worry, I won't." Alec let out a loud sigh. "They'd get drunk and fall off the cliff. Their parents will complain and management will have the entrance boarded up."

"Wow, I've never had forever-ago cave wine before. Makes you feel kind of relaxed and giddy, huh?" Meg took another sip.

"Yeah, I'm feeling it, too. It must be stronger because it's aged. It's good, though." Alec glanced at her. "Maybe you shouldn't drink so much so quickly."

"It's okay. I like the feeling. Besides, it's my birthday. I'll have as much as I want."

He smiled. "Go ahead, enjoy it, but I'm driving home."

Several sips later Meg grew bold enough to say, "I saw you talking to Charlotte the other day. What's up with that?"

"Charlotte?" He was at a loss.

"Are you really gonna pretend you don't know who I'm talking about? She's the one with the big chest, she fawns all over you every chance she gets." Meg saw his eyebrows lift in realization. "Right, that girl."

"Nothing's up with her. She's kind of annoying, actually."

Meg snorted. "Oh, sure. I saw you looking at her chest."

"Well, Meg, she does sort of show them off. Everyone looks at them." Alec didn't know whether to be insulted or flattered. "You know she's with Bryan now, right?"

"I know, but it doesn't stop her from drooling every time she sees you. It's disgusting and I feel sorry for Bryan."

"She can look all she wants, Bryan has nothing to worry about. I'm not interested in Charlotte." Alec drank the last of his wine and picked up another bottle. As he worked on getting the cork out, he asked, "Speaking of Bryan, didn't he have a crush on you from first grade to graduation?"

"No. Well, maybe in elementary school, but I pretty much thought all boys were gross back then. When we got to high school, he developed a crush on Charlotte… right about the time she got that well-endowed chest. He used to ask me for advice all the time, wanting to know how to get her attention. I guess she gave up on you, because she finally took notice of him after graduation and they've been together ever since."

"Oh, I didn't know that. I saw him hanging around you all the time at school and just assumed he liked you."

Meg took another swallow from her bottle and held it up to the flashlight, seeing there was little left of it. After polishing it off, she put it with the other empty ones. "I'm out, open another for me."

Alec reached for another bottle and while opening it, he thought about someone else he wanted to ask her about. The trouble was sorting out how to broach the subject, mostly since it still upset him. As he handed the opened bottle to her, he wondered if she even knew how upset he'd been.

Hoping he wouldn't regret it, Alec asked, "What about Drake?"

"Who?"

"Drake?" he asked louder. "The guy you spent a whole week with… alone."

"Oh, right." Meg laughed. "What about him?"

"What were you two doing?" Alec recalled how he could never find them, no matter how long he searched, nor how far and wide. "And where?"

Meg frowned at what sounded like his anger. "I already told you, he was teaching me how to sketch, and we were all over the island."

"Is that all he taught you?" Alec muttered.

She was about to yell at him, but remembered something—though only a fragment. The harder she tried to capture the memory, the more elusive it became. Before disappearing entirely, a brief flash of Drake's face materialized, saying, *'…he's so jealous you're spending time with me… we'll all wash out to sea…'*

"Alec, what's wrong with you? You sound jealous."

"I'd hardly call it jealousy," he said, sneering, and noticing she hadn't answered his question. "Was that all you two did, draw?"

"It sounds like jealousy to me."

"Fine! You want me to admit it? I was jealous, watching you two go off together… laughing and having fun. I saw you at the café with him, and he put his hand on yours. It was all I could do not to go in there and yank him up from that table. Don't even get me started about those last few days, it was like you had vanished. It scared me, I thought he'd done something horrible to you and I… I didn't know what I'd do if I never saw you again."

Alec stopped, thinking he'd gone too far and said way more than he wanted to say. Even worse, he worried she'd be mad at some of his comments, but then her hand covered his.

"I'm sorry if I made you worry about me. If it makes you feel any better, Drake was always very nice to me. I don't remember him ever making me feel uncomfortable."

"Don't be sorry, Meg. I'm the one who should apologize." Embarrassed now, he removed his hand from under hers. "I'm probably the one making you feel uncomfortable."

For a second, an iciness coursed through her at feeling slighted by Alec's removal of his hand. She considered getting up and walking away, but then another sensation of a memory trying to elude her kept her still: '*…have confidence in yourself… go after what you want.*'

The memory of the words dissipated, but left in their wake a determination to begin the next phase of her life. She looked at Alec and somehow knew it all started with him. A new understanding evolved in her thoughts: for their relationship to develop further, she'd have to get over the urge to run away at the first hint of rejection. Resolved now, and even more determined, Meg sorted through her options of how best to approach Alec. She drank more of the wine and leaned back against the cave wall.

He followed her example and relaxed. They sat side-by-side for a while, staring at the cave wall opposite them, listening to the tunneled sounds of the ocean breezes whipping by the entrance. The silence between them had stretched on for too long and Alec knew Meg was lost somewhere in her thoughts. He tried so hard to sense them, but found an impenetrable wall, a rarity for him and he felt sure Drake was the one responsible for it.

"Tell me, Alec, what are you gonna be when you grow up?" she asked, hoping humor would set him at ease.

"Oh, I don't know, maybe I'll retire early and live out the rest of my life on an island somewhere." He laughed so hard he couldn't finish the rest of the sarcastic remark about his future job prospects.

"That was a good one," she said and pointed the flashlight at the metal door. "What do you think's on the other side of it?"

"It's probably how the maintenance workers get around without disturbing us. Or, it could be the door to the underground area we're all supposed to go to during hurricanes. Either way, it's more island infrastructure."

"I forgot about the underground tunnels. You're probably right, but it seems so mysterious. This whole cave seems mysterious to me. There's something about it…"

"What do you mean?"

"It feels" –she pointed the flashlight at the walls and ceiling– "oddly comforting."

"What?" Alec snorted.

"I don't mean comfort in the sense of creature comforts, more like in a *familiar* kind of way."

She took several long draws from the wine bottle while contemplating what she really meant to say.

"Like when you've been caught in the rain and you're soaking wet and all you want to do is get to a dry place... like home. Finally, you're home and not getting rained on anymore, even though it's still raining outside. You put on your familiar dry clothes, look out your familiar windows and see the rain is still pounding and would soak you again if you went out there, but you're warm and safe in your familiar house. It makes you feel even more warm and safe, knowing you somehow defeated a miserable existence by simply having a home to go to. Does that make any sense to you?"

Meg turned the flashlight in Alec's direction to see his response.

"I know the feeling you're trying to describe, but this cave doesn't have that same effect on me. I wonder why it makes you feel like that." He chuckled. "Maybe it's the wine."

"Oh, shut up. How many more bottles do we have?"

"More than you and I can drink, even if it is your birthday."

"This is a good birthday. I'm having fun."

Meg turned the flashlight off, but there was still light filtering in from the cave entrance, casting a soft glow inside. She scooted closer to Alec and rested her head on his shoulder. Though he tensed a little at the unexpected contact, his mind and body was languid and quickly unknotted.

A smile hinted at her lips as she finished off the last of the wine in her bottle. She set it next to the other empty ones and reached for Alec's hand, interlacing their fingers. Her other hand inched closer and she placed her fingertips on the back of his hand.

Her fingers swept delicate lines from his wrist to his elbow, and then retraced them back down again. Though he tensed, it was minimal, and he didn't stop her when she repeated the action a few more times. Then she chanced brushing her fingers up to his shoulder where her head still rested, and a shiver went through his body.

"Meg," he said, his breath uneven. "What are you" –he paused at feeling her lips on his neck– "doing to me?"

This was all the encouragement she needed. Meg released his hand to turn her body toward his and pressed her lips more firmly on his neck, trailing a line of sultry kisses to his ear. "I'm kissing you," she whispered.

Alec closed his eyes in an effort to find self-control, but her whispered breath in his ear made it impossible. She continued the delicate kisses along his jaw line until she reached his lips. Leaning against him, wrapping her arms around his neck, Meg locked her lips to his and still wanted more contact.

Her enthusiasm only added to his inability to think clearly and his hands reached for her waist to pull her closer. Alec returned her kiss, gentle with hesitation at first, then with more decisive urgency. He rotated his body to align it with hers, and leaned her back onto the blanket. As though he was starving, his lips moved to her chin and then her neck when she tilted her head.

His mouth went to her ear. "Meg, I want you."

She was consumed by the intensifying desires escalating between them. When his lips found hers again, her arms went around his waist, pulling him tighter against her. It wasn't enough, and she wrapped her legs around him and moved her hips beneath him, against him, still wanting more.

Alec opened his eyes to look at her.

Her eyes opened, too, at the sudden loss of his kissing, afraid he was going to put an end to it. His blue eyes were a smoldering black—there was no doubting it, he wanted her. "Please, don't stop," she said, her voice shaky, her body still moving against him.

"Are you sure?" he asked, surprised at how difficult it was to form the questions. "Is this what you want?"

"Yes." She nodded, still moving. "I want you. I know you want me, too… no more talking." She lifted her head up from the blanket to kiss him again, fearing he'd speak or ask what she considered to be stupid questions.

One last thought of hoping they weren't making a mistake drifted through his mind. He abandoned all thoughts of stopping and allowed his hands to explore Meg's body, impatiently pushing away clothes that would impede his progress.

~

Several hours later, they lay wrapped in each other's arms and legs, sleeping blissfully. Meg woke first and the sight of Alec's body excited her. She rubbed her hand along his chest, down toward his abdomen, going farther still until his eyes opened—awoken by his physical response to her touching him.

"No more sleeping," she said, smiling.

His scent filled her thoughts when her lips went to his neck. The taste of his sweat on her tongue caused an uprising of renewed desire for him, and she continued giving her hand the freedom to roam wherever she wanted—learning, teaching.

Alec's breathing quickened and he rolled her over, kissing her and enjoying his own exploration of her body. A gasp escaped her lips and it nearly drove him insane that he'd spent so much time pushing away the chance to hear the beautiful way it sounded.

A sudden noise that neither of them recognized came from somewhere inside the cave, putting a stop to any notion they had of going any further. "What was that?" Meg asked in a hushed voice.

"I don't know." Alec turned his gaze to the back of the cave. "It sounded like it came from that door."

They didn't hear anything else, but it had been enough for them to scramble back into their clothes. Alec picked the flashlight up to look around, but nothing had changed, the door was in the same position as before. He grabbed Meg's hand and led her out of the cave, feeling at ease only after they returned to the beach.

When Meg reached for her bag, Alec said, "Wait, I want to show you something before we leave." He smiled bashfully and shrugged. "It's another surprise I had in mind for you."

While they walked hand in hand, farther up Alaret Beach, Alec thought about what had changed between them. He was happy about the difference and wanted to kick himself for not realizing sooner that Meg meant more to him than just someone he needed to protect.

"That's new," Meg said of the recently cleared path.

"I know, I made it." A wisp of some new adventure brewed in his eyes. "Come on, let me show you where it goes."

At the top of a slope, the landscape opened to a clearing. Her gaze went to the area where a house stood covered in leafy vines, the front of which had been cut back. Meg thought she knew something of it, but the clear view of the entire front of the structure was novel to her.

"What is it?" she asked.

"It's a house. I never knew about it since we've never ventured this far up the beach before." Alec refused to admit he'd discovered it one day while scouring the island trying to find where she and Drake had gone. "Anyway, I was bored and stumbled across a house-shaped pile of vines, and I got curious. I pulled some of the leaves away and found a door."

"I wonder how long it's been here."

"I asked my mom about it. She said when management made the island a long time ago, this house was already here, created with the island. No one knows how it happened, it's a complete mystery."

"How intriguing," she said and moved in closer for a better look at the only part cleared of vegetation.

The door and its casing arched gracefully. The door itself was made of three large vertical planks of wood—decorative wrought iron hardware that had rusted from neglect adorned it.

The chimney was made of horizontally stacked stones, some were thick and rectangular, others wafer-thin, and all were varying shades of gray and pink. The exterior wall was comprised of ivory colored stucco, but the years of filth and grime had made true appreciation difficult to attain.

Another feature that caught her eye was the structure's roof; two steep A-framed borders, set at different angles gave the appearance of royal crowns. The shortest topped the door, the tallest framed the entire house, the casings matching that of the door below. Weathered, round stones of gray and white created the steps that led to the door.

"It's beautiful," Meg said.

"I was hoping you'd say that." Alec let go of her hand and walked toward the huge oak tree towering over the clearing. "When I first saw it, I thought of you and how you'd say exactly what you just said. I decided to fix it up for you, so you could have your own house. What I'm wondering now is…" He frowned, leaned against the trunk, and let out a heavy sigh. "I don't know what I'm saying."

Meg went to him. "Just say what's on your mind."

An ocean breeze played with her curls and he thought she was so beautiful standing there in front of him. "I love you, Meg. I always have."

She smiled and leaned against him. "I love you, too, Alec. And I hope you'll keep letting me, instead of pushing me away all the time."

"That's over now," he said, shaking his head, and wrapped his arms around her.

"I'd like the house more if you lived here with me," Meg said, resting her head on his chest.

She heard a chuckle in his chest before he answered.

"I was hoping you'd say that, too."

"How long will it take to fix it up?" she asked.

"I'll work on it day and night if necessary to hurry it up."

"Good. In the meantime, let's keep our plans a secret."

"Why?"

"I'm just worried about how my mom will react. She's really stressed out right now and I'd rather she be happy for me." She looked up at him. "It's kind of a big step, you know? She'll be fine once the mares foal."

Considering Ila's personality, even under the most mundane of circumstances, it made Alec cringe to think of telling her that he and Meg were going to live together. There was no way she'd love the idea of Meg not being her little girl anymore and not living under her roof. Ila was high-strung on a good day; stressed out, she was an absolute beast.

"I have to make the house livable anyway, I guess we can *try* keeping it to ourselves for now." Alec's gaze drifted to the curve of Meg's neck and had an urge to kiss it. He laughed softly and said, "I hope she's not paying attention to details, though."

"What sort of details?" Meg smiled, knowing full well what he meant.

"Like how all I want to do is undress you."

"Like how I want to let you?"

"Yeah, that sort." He leaned in and kissed the curve he'd been eyeing, and groaned at how keeping their plans a secret wouldn't last for long if he was forced to look at Meg in front of Ila. "Come on, it's getting late. I bet Ila spent all day making a birthday cake for you."

~

Chaza had been ill-prepared for the scene that greeted her when she returned to the cave. She cloaked herself and took to the darkest shadows to survey the image before her. Alec was just positioning his body closer to Meg's, and it was clear to Chaza that it wasn't their first time. Refusing to allow it to happen in front of her, she picked up a rock and hurled it at the metal door.

Remaining motionless, she averted her eyes while they dressed. After they left the cave, Chaza uncloaked herself, but continued to stand there, feeling numb as some of her worst fears came to fruition. She'd hoped Alec and Meg would remain only as friends until the day came when Alec would be taken from the island.

Sighing, weary and tired, Chaza trudged to the back of the cave and placed her hand in a cloaked hollow to the left of the metal door. She grasped the lever hidden inside and pulled; a metallic clanking sound echoed throughout the cave and the door opened.

Inside the loft, Chaza sat at her desk to think. It was her own fault; having become complacent and too dependent on Alec. It always seemed a kind of poetic justice allowing Alec to help her protect Meg, since he was one of the people she protected her from.

She was there that day in the barn when Alec and Meg were children, watching everything. When she saw Alec pick up the rock before following Meg into the barn, Chaza slipped in after him and waited, cloaked in the shadows. His thoughts were so easy to sense when he was a child and she panicked at what he planned to do. She wondered if she could kill Alec as he reached into his pocket to retrieve the rock. The thought of Sebastian's rage at hearing the news of Alec's death sent a shiver down her spine, so she waited until the last minute before taking action.

She emerged from the shadows just as the stone left his hand, and was only a foot from him when he lunged forward to catch Meg from falling. Chaza had no choice but to pause; Alec held what she tried to protect, making it difficult to use deadly force against him. Then, his thoughts shifted from that of how to incapacitate Meg to forming a sphere to make her better. It formed instantly, surprising her by its strength—disrupting it would create chaos. Chaza heard him say, *'I swear I'll always protect you, Meg.'*

With the sphere gone, Chaza realized what he'd done and almost laughed that she hadn't thought to do it herself. Absorbing Meg's abilities so that she appeared normal put many of Chaza's worries to rest. She backed away from Alec when Meg began to stir, and then she left to return to the cave.

Over the years, Chaza watched Alec and Meg become great friends. She noticed Alec's abilities strengthened at a quicker pace, too, thanks to what he'd absorbed from Meg. The guilt he developed as he grew older, fearing he'd done it out of greed, is what prompted him to erect the impenetrable wall of a protectorate guardianship with Meg.

When Chaza sensed Tavis' presence on the island, she hoped it would all be over soon. Perhaps Sebastian would finally come to retrieve Alec and slip away without ever knowing a thing about Meg. But having discovered them in a passionate embrace on the cave floor, Chaza feared that plan was probably shot to hell now. She took pen in hand and opened her journal to record the dismal turn of events as she saw them to be, forcing herself to stay within the guidelines of historical documentation—giving an emotionless, yet detailed, account of her recent discoveries.

~

"What took so long this time?"

"Did you want me to watch, or just have a peek?"

"All right, point made. How's he doing?"

"Quite well, it seems."

Sebastian eyed Tavis carefully. "Meaning?"

"Meaning things have changed between Alec and that girl he was supposed to be only friends with," Tavis said.

"Changed in what way?"

Tavis went over and sat in a chair opposite Sebastian's desk. "In the kind of way that made me feel like a pervert for watching. When I saw her sneak into his bedroom window in the middle of the night, I wanted to leave right away. Against my better judgment, since I figured you would ask me if I had, I checked it out. They were doing exactly what I thought they'd be doing. Obviously, I left and came back here."

Sebastian cleared his throat. "Are you sure about what you saw?"

"Yes."

"Maybe it was just a casual thing between them."

"I doubt it. I heard them talking about a house they plan to live in after Alec fixes it up. In my opinion, he has strong feelings for her. I suspected it the last time I went there and I told you as much."

"I know, but the last watcher said there was nothing between them." Sebastian considered the new information and shook his head in frustration. "You haven't noticed anything different about her? Nothing at all?"

"No. She appears average to me." Tavis considered Meg for a moment. "I mean, she is pretty. I can understand his attraction to her, but she hasn't exhibited any of the traits Alec has. Maybe if you allowed me to see *all* the previous watchers' notes, instead of just partials, I could study them. Maybe they missed something."

"No."

"Then watch him yourself." Tavis got up to leave.

"That's what I plan to do. In fact, I'm going there myself and I have every intention of bringing him here."

Tavis stopped in the doorway and turned around, finally noticing the suitcase by Sebastian's desk. "What?"

"I'm leaving tonight. I've been thinking about it for a while and I'm ready to get Alec off that despicable island. I hope he'll come willingly, but I'll do whatever is necessary to make it happen. While I'm there, I'll see what I can make of this girl he's so fond of. What's her name?"

"Margaret Meg Arcana, and you should know it's more than just a fondness. I'm pretty sure he has bonded to her."

"I'll see for myself. If you're right, then I'll have to decide whether or not I think she can adjust to life here."

"Sounds like you plan to stay a while," Tavis said, eyeing the suitcase again.

"If I have to. Do you want to come with me? I could probably use your help. I haven't been there in a while."

"Maybe, if you tell me why Alec is so important to you."

"...He's my son, and yes, that makes him your brother. If you go with me to Gamma, I'll tell you everything."

It was a shocking blow to Tavis. Was this why there was always a feeling of something missing? The potential for clarity proved too tempting to wait for Sebastian's return for further explanations. “Okay, but you will tell me everything as soon as we get there. I’ve had enough of all the secrets.”

“I know.” Sebastian stood. “We have to leave immediately.”

“What about council’s approval?”

“They scheduled a meeting for tomorrow morning, that’s why I want to leave tonight.”

“They won’t be happy we snuck out.”

“I really don’t care about their happiness at the moment.” Sebastian took a deep breath to steady his nerves, and to keep from shouting. “If you intend on coming with me, then pack a bag, we should go… now.”

~

Kyrie waited until Alec finished eating. “I did our laundry today. I put yours on your bed. Why don’t you go put them away?”

The unusual after-dinner request elicited a frown from Alec. “Okay, I will, after I help you clear away the plates.”

“I’ll take care of the dishes.” Kyrie didn’t move from her seat at the dining table. “Please, Alec, put your clothes where they belong.”

Halfway through the pile of neatly folded clothes, Alec groaned. “Dammit,” he muttered at seeing Meg’s laundered underwear lying atop his own. He picked them up, but there was no point in hiding them now.

“Interestingly, those aren’t mine,” Kyrie said from the doorway—he turned to look at her and tossed the underwear behind him. “I don’t suppose they were on your floor because you’ve suddenly taken to wearing women’s lingerie?”

“No.” Alec stifled his laughter.

“Would they belong to the person I saw sneaking off from the side of our house earlier this morning?”

“Yes.”

“All right then.” She nodded. “Finish up in here and meet me in the kitchen so we can talk about it.”

By the time Alec joined Kyrie in the kitchen, she was already on her second glass of wine. A smile formed on her face at seeing how uncomfortable he was, and she hid it by going to the cabinet to retrieve a second wineglass. She filled it and set it in front of Alec.

While he took a sip, Kyrie eyed the label and said, “It’s from a chardonnay grape, perfectly aged and from one of the best crops this island has ever produced. I’ve been hoarding the bottles to save for a special day.” She looked at Alec. “This was not the kind of day I had in mind.”

Alec took another sip. “It’s great.”

“I thought you and Meg were just friends,” Kyrie said, keeping her eyes locked on his.

He swirled the wine around, like he’d watched Kyrie do countless times, and then he drained the contents. When he returned the glass to the counter, he used one finger to push it toward her for a refill.

"We were. Things changed."

She refilled his glass without looking at it and pushed it back to him with one finger as he had done—the awkward conversation taking on the appearance of a chess match.

"When did things change?"

"It's been weird between us for a long time."

"I know that, Alec. That's not what I'm asking you. What I want to know is when did it go from being weird, to Meg sneaking into your bedroom at night and leaving her underwear behind?"

"Technically, it's none of your business." Alec drained his wineglass again and refilled it himself.

"I agree, but I still want to know."

"On her birthday," he said, his voice loud with frustration. "This is not a conversation I ever imagined having with you. I'm not exactly thrilled to be discussing our intimate relationship with my mother."

"Well, that answers my next question, not that I had any doubts when I found her underwear." Kyrie finally broke eye contact with him and looked into her wineglass, trying to sort out the awkward, unexpected situation. She had a lot of questions she wanted to ask him, but they were even more delicate. Instead, she chose a different angle. "What are your intentions regarding Meg?"

"My intentions?" Alec frowned, trying to sense on his own what Kyrie was thinking.

"I want to know how you feel about Meg." The conversation was as hard for her as it was for Alec. "Where do you see this going?"

He understood her concerns now. "I love her. I have for a long time and I think you know that."

His answer did bring her relief. She'd always known how important Meg was to Alec, and how protective he was over her. Truthfully, she knew he loved her, but could never be sure if it was only a brotherly affection or in some deeper way. It wasn't until Meg had spent so much time with Drake did Kyrie see the true nature of Alec's feelings, and she figured that must have been the turning point for him.

"Does she love you, too? I want you to be sure."

"Yes, she does." Alec smiled his confidence. "We've already planned out what we want to do. We're fixing up that house by Alaret Beach to live there… together."

"Has Meg talked to Ila about it?" Kyrie asked, her voice hopeful, but since her front door remained intact she highly doubted it.

"Ila doesn't know about any of this," Alec said. "Meg thinks we should wait until the mares foal. It's important to her that Ila be supportive of our relationship."

"I can certainly understand Meg's thinking." Kyrie shook her head at the hell about to unleash itself on the island when Ila learns about Meg and Alec. "Honestly, Alec, Ila won't respond well no matter when you tell her. She'll lose her mind the minute she finds out Meg's not her baby anymore."

"Maybe we should get it over with and tell her now."

"No, Meg's right. Ila was at the store today and she was a wreck. Apparently, management called her and they weren't happy that she'd been wrong about the mares' foaling date. I haven't seen her this stressed out in a long time and I have to agree with Meg, if Ila's approval is really that important to her, then just wait a little longer. Work on the house in the meantime, and try not to leave any of *your* underwear at Meg's house."

Alec grimaced. "I'm not talking to you about underwear anymore, okay?"

"Okay." Kyrie laughed, but wanted to make one more point. "Be careful around Ila, she's not stupid. I don't care how preoccupied she is with those damn horses, she'll notice if things are different with Meg."

"We'll be careful." Alec thought of something while he took his wineglass to the sink. "How do you feel about me and Meg being together?" He heard her get up from her chair and when she stood beside him, he forced himself to listen to her answer instead of traipsing through her thoughts.

"I've always known how much Meg means to you. I'll even admit that I noticed a difference in the way you were when Drake spent time with her. It did something to you, and for the first time ever I saw you were terrified of losing her. You had me a little worried, and so I was just as happy as you were when Drake drifted away." Kyrie stopped Alec from washing his wineglass a third time by taking it away from his hands. "Are you asking me if I approve of my son being with Meg?"

"I guess."

"Of course I like Meg." She laughed softly while rinsing out her own glass. "Who doesn't? All I want to know is are *you* happy with her?"

"Yes."

"Then I only have one request." Kyrie smiled at the kitchen window's reflection of Alec's face. "Give me a five-minute warning when you tell Ila."

6

Newcomers

Hiding the homing pods under the cover of darkness was simple enough, but hiking to the newcomer houses by hugging the coastline of Gamma proved an exhausting feat. From what Tavis remembered of the island's layout, they would reach them by dawn, hopefully giving them a moment to rest before trying to present themselves to the islanders as newcomers.

"Have you considered what our relationship should be?" Tavis asked.

"Exactly what it is, I'm your father."

"What about our names?"

Sebastian found the question insulting. "We are Abbotts and I will not lose my identity… nor will you. I think the truth is best, to avoid making mistakes, of course."

"You need to work on your speech, you sound too formal. I've only had a few watcher assignments here, but I learned quickly that the language is much more lax."

"I had forgotten about that." Sebastian chuckled and remembered how he liked the flow of the shortened speech the last time he'd been on Gamma. "How's this? I hope you agree that I'm improving."

"We'll learn together," Tavis said.

They reached a hilltop and stopped to survey the area. At the bottom, in a clearing surrounded by forest trees, stood three houses. They formed a sort of semi-circle, but there was plenty enough in-between space so as to not crowd each other. Each house portrayed a small, yet quaint, seaside cottage look—completing the invitation with a short wooden fence that matched the different colors of the newcomer abodes.

The scene smacked of a sickeningly sweet attempt by management to entice a newcomer into forgetting that they'd just entered an oppressive life of forever bowing to them. There were two reasons for being a newcomer: you were either invited to keep the existing population from growing overly bored, or to increase the population with your approved genetic blue-print.

"Which one?" Tavis asked when they reached the traveling lane abutting the houses.

"The left one," Sebastian said. "It's the closest to the town center and I would prefer to appear eager to join the community."

The sun had finally peeked over the horizon when they opened the front door and stepped inside to look around. It was decorated with antique furniture, some of which appeared quite valuable; a thick layer of dust covered the surface of all. They darted in opposite directions, heading for the windows. Once every window in the house was open, they sat down to rest and to discuss their first trip to the town center as newcomers.

"We should go to the general store right away," Sebastian said.

"I agree. Cleaning supplies are at the top of my list." Tavis ran a finger along the coffee table, creating a dust-free line. "Before we go, we need to decide on a place to tell people where we came from. I suggest we pick somewhere remote that no one would know anything about."

"Alaska works. I doubt management would ever bring a newcomer hailing from West America to any of their islands." Sebastian shot Tavis a look of warning. "However, if we do encounter an expert on remote Alaskan mountains, let me do the talking."

"Fine by me, you're the only one who has been there. I do have one other issue, though."

"What?"

"Cooking and cleaning," Tavis said.

"I don't suppose you have done any research on those subjects?" Sebastian asked, sounding hopeful.

"No."

"Neither have I. Oh well, we shall learn by doing. For now, we should start heading for the town center."

"Wait, I need to know something first," Tavis said when Sebastian got to the door. "I assume Kyrie is Alec's mother, is that right?"

"Yes." Sebastian closed the door again. "Do you want me to tell you everything now?"

"Not yet, I need to stay focused today. All I want to know right now is whether or not Kyrie will recognize you."

"No, I absorbed her memories." He hesitated, knowing Tavis hated memory tampering. "Kyrie thinks Alec's father is someone she was once married to. He was a horrible man and thankfully he's no longer on the island."

~

They strode toward the town center, marveling at how everything looked since they weren't cloaking themselves. The closer they got, the slower they walked. At the first sight of people, a mutual nervousness formed. This is when it would begin, with the meeting of the first islander—once introducing themselves as newcomers, there would be no going back.

"Ah, here we go. Are you ready?" Sebastian asked.

"I guess."

No one noticed either of them as they walked into the center's main square and it was an unspoken relief. They made their way to the general store, but hesitated before stepping up to the entrance.

Sebastian thought of a potential complication and groaned. "Please tell me that payment for supplies is—"

"Still the allowance system," Tavis said. "Kyrie logs everything herself and sends monthly reports to management."

It was a relief, and a curse. "We need to be sparse with our purchases. Hopefully, our names will get lost among the rest. The last thing we need is for management to come here."

Tavis stared at the doors. "When we walk in there, the questions will start."

"How about we walk around for a bit first?"

They leisured around the main square, looking in all the shop windows, taking note of any they may want to make future use of. No one paid any attention to them; there was no recognition or curiosity on the faces of the people they passed by.

"Everything is as I remember," Sebastian said, reflecting.

"Try to remember what I said about the language. We need to assimilate their speech patterns quickly."

"Relax, I have my key." Sebastian glanced at Tavis' neck, the necklace glinted in the sunlight. "As do you."

"But *they* don't, they will think us weird."

"Stop worrying, I've assimilated language before. It's easy, just listen to their words and thoughts."

As they rounded a corner, the first trial began when they ran into Frank Doscher, who took instant notice of their fretful faces.

He stopped in front of them and smiled. "Well, hello there. I'm so sorry, I almost ran you both over. Guess I should slow down and watch where I'm going." Frank's tone imbued warmth and welcome. "You're newcomers, aren't you?"

"Yes," Sebastian said.

"It's been a while since we've had a newcomer. My name's Frank Doscher. When'd you get in?"

Tavis said, "We just got here this morning. We're staying in one of the vacant houses just up the lane. This is our first trip to the town center, though, and you're the first person we've met so far. I'm Tavis Abbott and this is my father, Sebastian."

Sebastian gave Tavis a sly smile and turned to Frank. "It's a pleasure to meet you."

"You know, I was a newcomer once, but that was so long ago I don't think it counts anymore. I'm originally from Ireland. Where are you from?"

"A small town in Alaska… False Pass," Sebastian said. "Have you ever been there?"

"Nope, I'm afraid not." Frank chuckled. "Never been to Alaska for that matter. I used to want to travel there when I was a young man. I hear it's beautiful."

"It's very beautiful there, some places more than others. There's mountain after mountain, as far as the eye can see."

"Now I'm wishing I would've made time to go."

"It's never too late, my old friend. If you'd like to see Alaska, then you should go."

Frank smiled. "Leaving this island isn't as easy as you may think."

"It's easy enough, you simply choose to go."

"I'll keep that in mind." Frank winked at Sebastian. "Say, have you gotten your supplies yet?"

"Not yet. We were just about to when we ran into you."

"I'm on my way to the general store myself. Come with me and I'll introduce you to Kyrie Ellison, she runs the store."

Tavis and Sebastian exchanged an anxious glance, then followed alongside Frank, listening while he pointed out several lanes and explained where they led to on the island. When they reached the store's front entrance, Frank held the door open for them.

Kyrie was at the counter and looked up from her inventory log. "Hello, Frank, how are you today?" She glanced at the two who'd followed in with him. "And who have you brought with you?"

"I'm doing well, Kyrie. I've brought you some newcomers, Sebastian and Tavis Abbott from False Pass, Alaska. They just arrived today."

"Really? It's been a while." Kyrie watched the pair, who were content to stare at the floor. She figured they were nervous and it made her smile. "Well, don't just hang around in the doorway, come in."

Kyrie came from around the counter and stood in front of them. "It's nice to meet you." She had to lean to force eye contact. "Have you already picked a house?"

"Yes, just over the hill, the white house," Tavis said, as it seemed Sebastian had turned mute. "I'm Tavis, by the way, and this is my bashful father, Sebastian."

He wanted to scowl at Tavis, but chuckled instead and looked at Kyrie. "It's nice to meet you, too." He cringed at how timid his voice sounded.

Yet, seeing her again, an understanding came to him that he wouldn't leave her on this island again. Though Sebastian sensed a semblance of recognition pass over her face, Kyrie said nothing, and he puzzled over why he couldn't get a clearer reading of her thoughts.

"Did you open the windows?"

"Yes," Tavis answered for him, trying not to frown at his odd behavior. "Obviously, we'd like to get some cleaning supplies so we can clear out the dust."

"Right." Sebastian snapped back to the conversation.

"Okay, I'll gather the things you'll need to start settling in." Kyrie gave Sebastian and Tavis a reassuring nod. "Have a look around the store. It won't be long before you discover what else you'll need. If there's anything not already stocked, I can put in a special order for you."

When she left, Frank asked, "So, what do you think of Kyrie?"

"She's great, Mr. Doscher, thank you for introducing us," Tavis said, even though Frank had clearly addressed Sebastian.

Understanding more of the customs than Tavis did, Sebastian said to Frank, "You've been very kind to us. We appreciate it."

"You're welcome. You'll like her son, too. His name's Alec and he helps her with the store, especially with the deliveries." Frank turned to leave with his flour and baking powder, adding just before walking out, "Once you get settled in, I'll invite you over for dinner."

"How do you think it went?" Sebastian asked after Frank left.

"I think we got lucky running into Frank first. He's well-respected and he seems to like us, so we shouldn't have any problems being accepted by everyone."

Sebastian smiled and whispered, "Excellent job at assimilating the language, by the way."

"Thanks." Tavis frowned. "What's up with Frank constantly deferring to you? I'm not a child."

"Yes, we need to talk about that. I'll explain it later."

"Also, whatever sordid affair it was you had with Kyrie must still affect you." Tavis gave him a scathing look. "Your behavior was embarrassing."

While Tavis and Sebastian carried on their conversation, neither was aware they were being watched from a small window on the door to the storage area.

"Did Frank mention from where in Alaska?" Alec asked.

"False Pass," Kyrie said.

"Hope that's not an omen."

"Oh, don't you start with your ridiculous suspicions, Alec. I've already met them and they're very nice."

"Well, I haven't met them yet. What are their names?"

"Sebastian and Tavis Abbott."

"How old do you think she is?"

"She looks about your age. Why?" Kyrie nudged Alec's side. "You thinking about dumping Meg?"

"No," he said, nudging her back.

"I'm just teasing you." Kyrie glanced at Tavis' profile. "She's beautiful, though, and she has that same odd eye color you have."

"Wow, Mom, I never knew you thought my eyes were *odd*."

"I didn't say your eyes were odd, I said the color was... and I've always thought your eyes are beautiful. Since when do you have problems with self-esteem?" She elbowed him again. "All I meant was that her eyes are the same color. Actually, now that I think about it, so are his."

Alec turned his attention to Tavis, but he couldn't see her face. As luck would have it, Tavis turned toward the door he and Kyrie stood behind; their eyes met briefly through the glass pane before Alec turned away.

"Great, she just caught us staring at them."

"I'll go out there," Kyrie said. "Do me a favor, go to the store's kitchen and bag up enough food to get them through the next day or so."

Kyrie opened the door, smiling. "My son's getting a few things together for you."

"Thank you for all your help, Ms. Ellison. Tavis and I very grateful."

"My pleasure, and please, call me Kyrie." She looked at Tavis. "You, too."

Tavis offered her a friendly grin and moved to the next aisle over where she'd spotted a few items that could become a necessity depending on how long they stayed on Gamma.

Kyrie watched Sebastian pick up a box of bandages and read the instructions as though he found them amusing. His dark brown hair was a little messy, but still meticulous somehow. He was tall, and there was a confidence about him, too, with just a hint of what was probably a well-earned ego.

"You're not planning on getting injured, are you?" she asked.

Sebastian put the box back on the shelf. "I certainly hope not."

Something about his voice was familiar to her, but she couldn't place it. "Good. I hope you don't either, but we do have a physician if you need medical attention. Dr. Patrick's office is on the other side of the main square, it's the white brick building next to the school."

A hint of disgust passed over his expression. "I'll consider myself lucky if I never have to visit his office."

Sebastian looked into Kyrie's inquisitive hazel eyes; it had been a long time since he'd last seen them. No matter how hard he tried he couldn't make out her thoughts, and it puzzled him. He chuckled, as though laughing at his own joke, and put his hand on her shoulder—hoping the contact would make sensing her thoughts easier.

It was a move he instantly regretted. Though it worked, he sensed his own thoughts and memories transfer to her as well. It confused him that she could so easily absorb his knowledge and when she tried making sense of the images he had no choice but to quickly blur them.

Kyrie's eyelids fluttered closed at his attempt to alter the images and then her legs buckled, forcing Sebastian to grab her arms. The additional contact carried with it a more ancient feeling. He understood it, but couldn't fathom why he experienced it with her in such a benign touch.

"What the hell are you doing?" Alec yelled from the storage room door. "Get your hands off of my mother." He dropped the bags on the floor and barreled toward them, nearly knocking over a display rack of greeting cards, ready to push Sebastian away and escort him out of the store.

Alec's furious tone snapped Kyrie back. She blinked a few times to clear her head and looked at Sebastian.

Ignoring Alec, Sebastian asked her, "Are you all right? Think you can stand?"

Slowly, she righted herself and turned to Alec, seeing his defensive posture and how his eyes remained locked on Sebastian. Kyrie positioned herself in front of Alec to block his view and offered him a reassuring smile.

"I'm fine, Alec. I got light-headed and Sebastian was kind enough to catch me before I fell."

"You sure?"

"Of course, don't make such a fuss," she said. "Did you get what I asked?"

"Yes, it's over there." Alec gestured to where he'd dropped the bags.

"Thank you." She glared at him and mouthed, '*Be nice*', before turning back to Sebastian. "If you'll follow me to my desk, I need you to fill out a form for the store's records."

As they walked away, and while Kyrie explained what parts of the form Sebastian needed to fill out, Alec turned his attention to Tavis. Their eyes met and he knew she'd already been watching him; the study still lingered in her gaze.

He searched her eyes for many things, but particularly any duplicity about her nature. What he found was that she sized him up in the same light—boldly, too, as though she couldn't care less what he thought of a reciprocated character analysis. He hated admitting it to himself, but he liked her tenacity.

There was something else about her, Alec noted. She seemed knowledgeable in some worldly way, but naïve and inexperienced in the way the world revolved. An innocent layer of something brand new surrounded her; a thing she found cumbersome and wanted to shed.

Tavis searched and traipsed through his thoughts and memories equally. Mostly, she found him broody and arrogant, as was her opinion when she'd observed him on her first watcher assignment. She didn't like his assessments of her, but she couldn't necessarily argue against them.

Peering into his eyes, she saw how like Sebastian's they were. Tavis fiercely guarded these thoughts of comparison from Alec. It amazed her that she hadn't already questioned the similarity, even mirroring her own: the teal of an island lagoon reflecting blue skies, minute specks of green with larger flecks of violet occasioned the irises here and there.

It was hard for either of them to tell at what point the other had delved too far into something too personal. Both snapped to attention by the instinctual need to guard their thoughts, slamming shut the door for further perusal.

Alec frowned at the wall he rarely encountered in another and he broke eye contact with Tavis to turn his attention back to his mother.

~

"That went well enough, I suppose," Sebastian said during the walk back to their house.

"It went well enough if your plan was to seduce Kyrie in public and make Alec angry." Tavis waved and smiled warmly at a family of four driving by them in an island cart. Once they were out of earshot, she continued. "You should know you succeeded, I'm pretty sure Alec hates you now. He doesn't seem all that excited about me either."

"I wasn't trying to seduce Kyrie. I couldn't sense her thoughts and I figured a casual pat on her shoulder would help." Sebastian sighed. "Unfortunately, she saw a few of my thoughts instead, so I tried to lessen the damage."

"You mean you tried to absorb them. Call it what it is."

"What was I supposed to do? She saw I was there when she gave birth."

"Well, try to keep your hands to yourself from now on."

"Tavis." Sebastian's tone took on clear warning. "You're being disrespectful. I don't care how grown you think you are, I'm still your father."

"Sorry," she muttered. "I'm tired, and I'm not looking forward to cleaning that filthy house. I want one of those carts, too. I can't believe how hot it is here."

Sebastian laughed. "I agree. I'll ask Kyrie about getting one."

"Why weren't you able to read her thoughts?"

"I'm not sure exactly. Maybe Alec shielded them. He's extremely protective, I noticed, and I couldn't sense his thoughts either."

"Yeah, I tried it, too. I got that he was trying to pick my own thoughts apart." Tavis snorted. "He was surprised when he discovered I was doing the same thing, so he walled his mind from me. You're right, though, he's protective. Wait till you see him with Meg."

"He's more adept with his abilities than I expected. I'm not sure what to make of that either. For the time being, we'll exercise caution around him until I sort out what else he's capable of." Sebastian unlatched the front gate for Tavis. "Ah, here we are, home again."

"You haven't told me yet why Frank kept addressing you."

"That's because I'm not looking forward to explaining it to you." He shut the gate and ascended the porch steps. "There's a gender inequality here, one that greatly favors the males."

"Well, that explains a lot." Tavis rolled her eyes. The look of indignation gave way to fear. "Do I need to worry about my safety while we're here?"

"No, of course not. You're my daughter and no one will dare lay a finger on you." He opened the door and they looked around at the sea of dust that seemed to smirk at them. Exasperated, he said, "Let's teach ourselves how to clean."

~

The next morning, Tavis went to Sebastian's bedroom and shook him awake.

"What's wrong?" he asked, squinting at the abrupt harshness of sudden light.

"A noise woke me up. I've heard it several times now," she whispered. "Wait, it'll happen again."

Sebastian listened and when a bell-like note reverberated down the hall, he shook his head. "It's a doorbell, Tavis. Someone's at the door."

"Oh." She stood.

"Go see who it is. I'll be there in a minute." He saw her apprehension to leave. "I can't go to the door in my underwear."

"Oh," she said again and left.

When she opened the front door, Meg stood there. It was odd to Tavis, seeing her up close and allowing Meg to see her. "Hello," Tavis said.

Meg eyed Tavis' robe. "I hope it's not too early. Kyrie told me we had newcomers and asked if I'd bring you some of my hens. By the way, I'm Meg Arcana."

"I'm Tavis Abbott." She glanced at the crate sitting on the porch. "What are those?"

"They're hens. Do you want me to put them in the coop?"

"Um..."

"The coop is in the backyard, Tavis." Sebastian appeared and, to Tavis' relief, took over the conversation. "Thank you for bringing them. I'll go with you, Meg."

Tavis joined them after getting dressed and watched the hens walk around the bottom of the coop, pecking at the food Meg had also brought. She hated the latch keeping the coop door closed and wanted to open it.

"Do we really have to keep them caged like that?" Tavis asked.

"I don't like it either." Meg went to her and led her closer to the coop. "Unfortunately, it's necessary until they get used to their new home. After they get to know you, you can let them out during the day. They'll always go back to their nest boxes at night." Meg gave Tavis a wink. "You can make them like you faster by giving them treats."

Sebastian picked the crate up, carried it to Meg's cart, and set it in the back. He turned to her and took her hands into his. "Again, thank you for the hens. I promise to spoil them rotten and we'll enjoy every egg they give us."

"You're very welcome, Sebastian." Meg smiled, somewhat modestly, then remembered: "Oh yeah, my mom wanted me to ask you over for dinner. After you're settled in, of course."

"Tell her we'd love to," Sebastian said. "But only after we have dinner with Frank Doscher. We promised him first."

Meg beamed. "I'm glad you've already met Frank. He's probably my most favorite person on Gamma." She got into the cart and said to Tavis, "If you'd like, I can show you around the island. Call me when you know what night you'd like to come over for dinner."

Tavis nodded, thankful not everyone on the island felt so inclined to constantly address the male counterpart. "I will." She waited until Meg drove off and asked, "What do you think?"

"She's quite charming." Sebastian made his way back to the front porch, sorting through what he thought of Meg. He sat in one of the cushioned rattan chairs and stared off at the barren front yard. "She has an engaging personality… damn near disarming, actually."

"Is that all?" Tavis reached the top step and leaned against the porch column.

"Not exactly. Like you, and all the watchers before you, I didn't find anything out of the ordinary about her." He shook his head, dissatisfied with his own findings. "I could even detect some of her thoughts, and though they're genuine, they seem almost staged somehow. There's another thing, too. She was perfectly at ease in our presence, and I got a sense she was happy we were here."

"I noticed that, too," Tavis said. "What do you make of it?"

"I don't know yet, but I intend to find out before I make any final decisions."

~

Jack opened the front of the printer to remove a nonexistent paper jam while watching the East American military entourage file into management's boardroom. It wasn't the first time he'd seen them arrive for their private meeting, but it was ahead of schedule. Normally, they met twice a year, but it had only been three months since their last one.

At best, his job was second tier in importance. Jack could only speculate what went on behind the soundproof walls and doors of the Stone Davis Corporation boardroom. However, what he could do, and what he planned on doing, was to snoop around Eldridge Stone's office as soon as the meeting got under way.

He heard the door's lock click and wasted a few more minutes pretending to be the problem-printer savior before making a mad dash to Eldridge's office. Jack spied a stack of folders sitting on the desk and figured that was a good enough place to start. His heart already pounded at the risk he took, but he thought it would explode when he opened the top folder.

The images were disturbing enough, but as he flipped through the rest of the pages, his eyes widened in shock with every line he read. Not only did management know about the relationship with his coworker, they were planning to confront him and Michelle about her pregnancy in a meeting scheduled for the morning. Jack scanned the list of options they had in mind to present at the meeting, for both reprimand at violating company policy that prohibited interoffice relationships, and also what should be done regarding the pregnancy.

"Shit!"

He flipped back to the images of him and Michelle in compromising positions, each impossible to dismiss as anything other than exactly what they were. "No, I was just teaching her weather terminology… particularly diction," Jack mumbled.

An eerie chill ran down his spine and he closed his eyes. When he opened them again, his gaze drifted up the office wall, toward the ceiling, and he saw a camera pointed right at him. He closed the folder and left the office, checking every corridor for cameras on the way to his office.

"Meet me in your apartment in an hour," Jack said to her when he opened the door.

Michelle groaned. "Not now, Jack, I'm tracking a hurricane. All the models indicate potential landfall on Gamma. Maybe later, okay?"

"That's not why I want to meet you," he said, trying not to look at the camera. "Don't waste your time, it won't hit Gamma. They never do."

"That's what you always say. It's like a mantra with you, but I think you're wrong this time."

"Let it go, Michelle." Jack forced himself not to yell. He had no way of knowing if the camera recorded audio, so blurting out his discovery wasn't the way to get her to do what he wanted. "We both have vacation time we need to take, and I was thinking maybe it's time I meet your parents."

Michelle lost interest in the forecast models and shifted her gaze to Jack. "Why the sudden change of heart?"

Though she appeared dubious, Jack also heard a note of hopefulness in her tone and he jumped on it, taking care not to step too far out of his usual character. "I guess you wore me down, nagging tends to do that."

The flippant remark narrowed her eyes, but she tamed her anger and grabbed the stapler to attach the current naval forecast of Hurricane Anna to her report for management to look over. He already knew what they'd do with her efforts; they would thank her and wait for her to leave, and then toss the report in the paper recycling bin.

"Okay," she said. "I'll meet you in an hour."

~

When Jack opened the door to her apartment, a stapler sailed across the room. Not expecting it, and not having ducked fast enough, it made contact with his forehead and landed on the floor at his feet.

"So I'm a nag, am I?" she yelled.

Worried more office supplies were on their way, Jack stepped inside and slammed the door shut. "Stop it, Michelle," he said when she searched for something else to throw.

She looked at him and her mouth opened in surprise. "Oh my God, Jack. I'm so sorry."

"What?" An odd warmth trickled down the bridge of his nose. He touched his fingers to it and saw blood. "I'm bleeding! Are you crazy?"

"If you insult me one more time—"

"What, you gonna throw a file cabinet at me?"

"Seriously, Jack, that's enough." Michelle's expression softened. "I'm sorry I threw the stapler at you. Come with me to the bathroom so I can see how bad the cut is."

After a considerable amount of complaining about the alcohol stinging, and that she used more than was necessary out of meanness, Jack looked in the mirror, fussing at the cut just below his hairline. "It's gonna leave a scar."

"You'll survive." She applied a bandage to keep the wound closed. "Now what was it you wanted to talk to me about?"

Jack left the bathroom and looked around Michelle's apartment for cameras. Finding none, he sat down and considered how best to approach her with what he had in mind for getting them out of the research station.

"Where's your suitcase?" he asked.

"In my closet." She sat at the end of the bed. "Why? Were you serious about wanting to meet my parents?"

"Eventually, I guess." An uncomfortable expression passed over his face. "In the meantime, we need to get out of here. Pack a few things and we'll go on a little vacation together. We should probably leave… now. I'll help you if you're gonna be slow about it." Jack rolled his eyes at the way his words came out, and the reemerging irritation on her face proved he hadn't achieved the acceptance he'd hoped for. "Management knows about our relationship, they even know you're pregnant."

"How? We've been careful." The worry in her voice matched his own concerns. Michelle stood again, paced a few times, and then stopped in front of Jack. "What makes you think they know?"

"Because I found a file on Eldridge's desk, and it was full of everything about you and me." Jack shook his head. "Apparently, there's a camera in our office. There were pictures of us in the file. They're planning to call us in for a meeting in the morning to confront us."

Though her face twisted in embarrassed horror, she said, "So what? They know, big deal. They'll fire me because I'm newest, and female." She sneered at the truthful reality. "I'll go home to my parents and you can put your notice in and meet me there. Problem solved."

"No, problem not solved." Jack went to Michelle's closet to retrieve her suitcase. He put it on the bed, and continued with the rest of what he'd read while opening her dresser to pack the suitcase himself. "Let me tell you the options management has in mind for our situation. You can either have an abortion and keep your job, or give the child up for adoption to a company shareholder couple who happen to be rich, well-connected, and woefully infertile."

"They can't force me to do either one." Michelle tried yanking back the shirts Jack put in her suitcase, but he grabbed her wrist to stop her.

"Yes, they can. What are you gonna do? You're on an island surrounded by the Atlantic Ocean, and they control the transportation to the mainland."

She pulled her wrist free and asked, "How are you planning to get us out of here?"

"Steal one of the boats at the docks."

"And go where?"

"Same place I always go when I *borrow* a boat."

"Gamma? Have you lost your mind?"

"They won't think to look for us there. I'll hide the boat, and we can act like we're newcomers for a little while until I figure out a way to get you back to the mainland." He saw her doubt. "Or, you can try taking your chances with management in the morning."

"I'll pack my own suitcase," Michelle said, letting go a defeated sigh.

~

Sebastian and Tavis parked the cart Kyrie had procured for them in front of their house. After having dinner with Frank, they drove around the island for a while, but ended their exploration when it got dark. They noticed the lights on inside the farther newcomer house and saw figures moving around to open the windows.

"Who do you think they are?" Sebastian whispered.

Tavis shrugged. "*Real* newcomers, maybe."

"Let's find out, shall we?"

Sebastian got out of the cart and cloaked both of them as they neared the side of the house. They were close enough to the open kitchen window to hear a woman complaining while a man's voice grew more frustrated with his every response.

"My God! This house is filthy."

"Sorry, Michelle, they don't have janitors here."

"I hope there's nothing toxic in this dust. What if the baby comes out fluorescent?"

"It's just plain old dust, wait… you know about—"

"Yes, Jack, I know about it. You're not the only one who listens to gossip at work. Why do you think I agreed to hide here? Obviously, management wouldn't have any qualms about forcing me to do whatever they want. Just so you know, I don't want to be here for long."

"We only need to stay here long enough for them to give up trying to find us."

"What if they search here?"

"They won't. They'll think we tried heading for the mainland. Besides, a full-scale search on Gamma would freak out the residents and that's the last thing management wants."

Tavis chanced a peek through the window to visualize the faces to the voices, then tugged on Sebastian's arm. After retreating back to their house, she said, "I've seen him before, while I was watching Alec. He was always on the beach by the docks. Alec saw him once, but didn't confront him."

"Why didn't you include that in your report to me?" Sebastian asked.

"I didn't think it was important."

"Apparently, you were wrong. Those two are from the research station. Didn't you hear them?"

"Yeah, I did." Tavis frowned at him. "I don't know why you're so worried. They're hiding from management, it's not likely they'll report us."

"You have a point." Sebastian nodded. "Sounds like they ran because she's pregnant. It wouldn't surprise me if management treated their employees with the same regard they do their islanders."

"We're going to bump into them eventually. How should we handle it?"

Sebastian chuckled at the conundrum. "Fake newcomers meet fake newcomer neighbors, and neither one can out the other. I have no doubt they'll discover us in the morning and we'll all introduce ourselves as newcomers, knowing full well we're all lying. I say we just wait and see how it goes." He raised his eyebrows. "Don't forget our plan if this current situation doesn't work out in our favor."

"I won't forget, I just hope it won't come to that. I'd rather Alec come with us willingly." Tavis sighed. "I'm with Michelle, though, it better not take long."

~

The next morning, Tavis headed to the coop to check on the hens and offer them treats—last night's leftover spaghetti noodles and some lettuce. She hoped Meg's suggestion of bribery worked more sooner than later so she could allow them the space to roam at will.

Sebastian had gone to the front yard to start planting the roses Kyrie delivered. She'd sacrificed a few of her own after he expressed his disappointment at the month-long wait for new roses to arrive in the special orders shipment. Tavis had always teased him for his affection for roses, declaring they were the true love of his life, and she simply rolled her eyes when Kyrie insisted Sebastian have some of hers.

"Do we still have hens?" Sebastian asked at feeling her presence behind him.

"I didn't leave their coop door open, if that's what you're asking," Tavis grumbled. "They're still skittish when I go near them. They probably think we're the ones responsible for denying them their freedom."

"Technically, we are. They'd be happily roaming about Meg's yard if we hadn't have shown up." Sebastian finished watering the transplanted roses and turned to find Tavis glancing over at the farther newcomer house.

"Have they come out yet?" she asked.

"Not yet, but I did see his face in the front window a few times." Sebastian coiled the garden hose and put it back against the side of the house. "They're probably wondering what they should do. I have a feeling he wasn't expecting anyone else to be living in these houses."

"I'm sure he did his homework and knows there haven't been newcomers here for a long time. I really hope your mutually beneficial refugee idea works."

"Well, we're about to find out." Sebastian nodded in their direction. "Here they come."

Tavis turned and saw Jack and Michelle walking down the porch steps. Though they were both smiling at them, it seemed nervous and forced. When they made their way over, it was Jack who spoke first. "Hi, my name's Jack, and this is Michelle."

"Hello, Jack and Michelle. I'm Sebastian and this is—"

"I'm Tavis Abbott." She refused to be spoken for. Tavis held her hand out, offering it to Michelle first. "It's nice to meet you."

"It's nice to meet you, too," Michelle said—the fake smile turned genuine.

After Michelle shook her hand, Tavis then offered it to Jack. When their hands made contact, a pulse of what felt like electricity shot through Tavis' body. She looked into his eyes, assuming Jack had felt it, too, and hoped to find an explanation in his thoughts for the odd sensation. All she found was that he was just as surprised and confused by it as she was.

For a brief second, Tavis caught a whisper of a thought—or more like a memory, she considered—but it dissolved too quickly for her to fully grasp it. Yet it seemed so important, as though it involved them somehow... and time. *Time in its simplest form*, Tavis pondered and reluctantly let go of Jack's hand.

Sebastian had experienced a condensed version of what his daughter had sensed, and he stepped forward to shake Jack's hand, half-expecting a similar encounter. There was nothing at all, aside from animosity. He let go of Jack's hand and shook Michelle's, discovering a painful truth he wished his physician's knowledge wasn't able to detect.

"We just got here last night," Jack said, frowning somewhat at Tavis.

Unlike Tavis, Jack had seen more of the images—witnessing a series of expressions portrayed on her face before they dissolved. Some of them were happy and full of laughter, others hinted at passion from intimate moments. What bothered him most, before it all faded away, was a look of pain and sadness in the eyes he no longer found strange but beautiful as she looked out of a domed window—and while tears fell onto her cheeks as she realized some unknown failure. He found himself wanting to protect her from that agony, but had to shake himself loose of the painful image to focus on his current situation.

"We noticed the lights on last night when we got in from having dinner with a friend." Sebastian initiated the start of the temporary falsehood between them. "Being fellow newcomers ourselves, my daughter and I knew you'd have a lot of dusting to do… settling in and all that sort of business. We decided to let you introduce yourselves whenever you were ready."

Jack recognized the cunning attempt to establish a preplanned relationship. "Have you been here for long?" At the very least, he hoped Sebastian would squirm a little. Jack knew full well they hadn't been here more than a week.

"About a week," Sebastian answered both the question and Jack's thoughts.

"I guess that makes all four of us newcomers," was the carefully controlled reply Jack gave, keeping his eyes locked on Sebastian's.

Noting the challenge in Jack's voice, yet still needing to anchor a firm but unspoken understanding of what was to be expected, Sebastian shifted his gaze to Michelle's abdomen and said, "Indeed, all *four* of us."

Tavis put an end to the stand-off before her father's ego pushed Jack too far. "Are you planning to go to the general store?" she asked Michelle.

"Yes. I have a list a mile long." Michelle turned to Jack. "Ready?"

"Sure, let's go. It was nice meeting you both," Jack said to Sebastian and Tavis. "I'm sure we'll see each other again soon, since we're neighbors."

"Keep in mind, they'll be paperwork to fill out at the store," Sebastian said before they walked away. "They're for Kyrie's records, but special orders need management approval."

"Thanks," Jack said.

When they left, Tavis turned to Sebastian. "Well?"

"We're safe for now. Jack can't report us because he's hiding from the people he'd have to contact. He knows we're not supposed to be here, though. I dropped enough hints for Jack to know I suspect the same of them."

"Could you sense much from his thoughts?"

Sebastian chuckled. "Some, mostly that he doesn't like me very much."

"Well, that part was obvious. Even Michelle could see that." Tavis went to the porch and sat on the third step. "Could you tell how long he plans to hide out here?"

"Not really. He's too scared right now about getting caught." Sebastian stared at the newly planted rose bushes for a moment, considering a potential problem they may face. "Michelle was easier to read."

"What did you find?"

"She's been having pain, and it's getting worse. Of course, I'd need to examine her properly, but I'm pretty sure the fetus isn't viable." Sebastian glanced at Tavis, nodding at what she was already thinking. "The pain she's experiencing is consistent with the initial stages of miscarrying."

"How sad for her," Tavis said softly.

"It's sad for him, too, Tavis."

"I know." She frowned at his curious expression. "Why are you looking at me like that?"

"What happened when you shook his hand?"

"I don't know." She shrugged when he raised his eyebrows. "I really don't know. It felt like some kind of a shock, and then it seemed like a memory of his, but I couldn't make out what it was."

Sebastian relaxed. "Maybe he's hiding something else. I'll keep an eye on him and see if I can sort it out."

~

A few days later, Jack opened the front door—his nostrils flared at seeing Sebastian about to push the doorbell, yet again. "Hello, Mr. Abbott."

"Please, it's Sebastian," he said, affecting a good-natured quality to his tone.

"Okay, Mr. Sebastian, what can I do for you?"

Sebastian smiled. "Actually, I wanted to do something for you. It seems you and Michelle received a dinner invitation for tomorrow night at Ila Arcana's. Is that right?"

Jack blinked a few times. "Yeah, is there an island gossip column I don't know about?"

"Tavis and I are attending the same dinner. I just got off the phone with Ila's daughter and she asked me if I wouldn't mind offering you a ride to their house. It's quite a long walk from here."

"I was thinking about cancelling." Jack eyed Sebastian's cart parked on the lane and grimaced at the reality he couldn't order one for himself.

"That's what I thought you'd say, and I'm here to offer a solution. Frank Doscher has a spare island cart and he wanted me to tell you that he hopes you'll accept it as a gift. If you're so inclined to take the gracious offer, I'll drive you to Frank's so you can thank him and drive it back here."

The opportunity to have his own transportation was too great a convenience for Jack to reject the offer. "All right, I'll be ready in a minute."

The ride to Frank's went well enough, but just before they pulled up to his house, Sebastian said, "I don't recommend you declining the dinner invitation. It's not in your best interest to offend the residents from the start. They have very little in the form of entertainment and you wouldn't want tongues wagging about how unfriendly the newest newcomers are. They're already whispering at how unusual it is to have two sets of newcomers arrive so close together."

Jack stopped admiring the landscape long enough to acknowledge the subtle warning. "Fine, we'll go, but expect us to be fashionably late."

~

It was late that evening when Tavis insisted she take on the task of watcher again, convincing Sebastian that they needed to know whether or not Meg and Alec's relationship still continued. He'd suggested he do it, but she dismissed the notion by telling him she knew the forest footpaths better.

Sebastian relented. "Go ahead, just be careful." He picked up their plates from the table and took them to the kitchen. As she put her shoes on, he added, "Jack took that cart out for an evening drive, so make sure you cloak yourself the whole way. Okay?"

"I'm more worried about Alec. I hardly see him around anymore, it's like he's avoiding us. I knew more about what he was up to before we came here."

"I know." Sebastian drifted off into his thoughts briefly, then sighed at how disappointing it was every time Alec ignored him when they crossed paths. He looked at Tavis and considered telling her the rest of what she needed to know. He decided against it, though, and put it off for a better time. "See what you can find out."

Tavis walked along the lamp-lit lane for a while, working out the layout of the footpaths in her mind before choosing which one to take to get to Alec's house. She was close to the town center, devoid of islanders at the late-evening hour, when she sorted out the best path. It was just beyond the curve leading into the main square, and she ran to get there faster in case any shop keepers were still around.

Just as she made the turn up ahead, her eyes darted to the trees on the opposite side of the lane. With her attention diverted, distracted by a brilliant flash of trailing colors, she failed to see the cart coming around the bend. The edge of the front bumper nicked her legs as it swerved to keep from hitting her, knocking her backward onto the pavement by the entrance to the footpath she'd meant to enter.

"Are you okay?" Jack shouted, hopping out of the cart to check on whoever he hit. At seeing it was Tavis splayed out on the pavement, his eyes widened at imagining Sebastian's face looming over him, demanding an answer for why he tried to run his daughter over.

"I'm fine," she said and tried to sit up.

Jack squirreled away his panic, made easier at hearing her talk, and kneeled to help her up. He watched to make sure she could stand on her own. "Are you hurt? I'm sorry, I didn't think anyone would be out on the lane this late."

Tavis surveyed the backs of her arms to find welts forming just below her elbows. "It's nothing serious, just scrapes." She let go of his hands. "It's my fault. I should be more attentive when I go out for a run at night." It was the best excuse she could think of to explain why she'd been running in the dark.

"Let me take you back home," Jack said. "I'd rather get your father's anger over with."

She looked into his eyes at hearing the offer mixed with genuine concern over Sebastian's reaction. "Actually, I just started my run. I'm fine, you can go."

The lamplight cast a halo around her face, illuminating the blue of her eyes. He never wanted to stop looking at them. An overwhelming sense of regret came over him at the thought of letting her be on her way.

"What happened when I shook your hand?" he asked, his voice barely audible. "I saw… things."

"I don't know." Tavis shifted her eyes to his chest, then to a nearby tree to escape his study.

He stepped closer, trying to see into the eyes she meant to hide from him. "Don't do that," he coaxed. "Look at me."

"I said I was okay."

At his continued silence, Tavis met his inquisitive stare again, seeing that his expression had changed from worry to something else. Something she wasn't familiar with, but what kept her from looking away. She felt trapped, but not by him—it was by her own thoughts, and not one of them made any sense to her.

Chancing a step even closer, Tavis hoped to find an explanation for why she always wished he'd be on the beach when she came to watch Alec. At the nearness, Tavis explored the new look in his eyes. It was one she had no personal experience with, but that which she understood the ancient and primitive nature of—and it was drawing her in. She didn't resist it, she didn't want to.

Jack grew acutely aware of her proximity and read the evolution of thoughts pass over her eyes, even knowing when she'd guessed at his most basic thoughts. He watched her lips part at the realization, and then that was *all* he could see. His hands went to her cheeks, holding her head still so he could continue to look at her—afraid she'd run off and the moment would be lost forever.

Being this close to her, touching her, inhaling the scent coming from her, with each new thing he discovered, he wanted to know more. Jack's heart pounded, his body demanded he discover what hers felt like against his, and he wanted to know what her lips tasted like. Nothing else mattered more than seeking out these answers.

His hands became vice-like grips as he guided Tavis from the lane and pressed her against the nearest tree. When her back hit the trunk, she gasped at the small pain it caused and Jack's lips went to hers. The intensity scared her at first and she considered pushing him away, but the thought diminished amid stronger desires.

She responded to his kiss and her arms found their own way around his waist to pull him closer. Their kissing frenzied, became not enough, and Tavis' hands instinctively tugged at Jack's clothes. She fumbled at the buttons of his shirt until his hands connected with hers.

At the touch of his hands so close to her body, glorious heat seared through every one of Tavis' cells. She guided his hands to her abdomen, pushing them under her shirt. They inched upward; feeling, exploring—and then he stopped.

Jack's lips broke away from hers. It was going too far, she felt entirely too good to him and he feared his inability to maintain control for much longer.

"No," Jack croaked, his voice breathy and hot on her neck. "We can't do this… Michelle… your father."

Tavis tried to clear her head, but her thoughts were foggy. It wasn't until Jack put some distance between their bodies, and the chill of the night air cooled them, that she trusted her own mind again. Their eyes met, and it was Jack who turned away from her gaze this time.

"Get in the cart," Jack said, looking at the ground. "I'll take you home."

"But—"

"You need to clean those cuts on your arms." He softened his voice when hearing his barking tone. "Would you please just get in the cart? I'll be there in a minute."

She frowned at his back, experiencing a range of emotions from indignity at being ordered around, to wanting him to kiss her again. Siding with self-respect, Tavis shoved off from the tree and tugged her shirt down.

"Thank you, but I'll walk home," she said and pushed past him.

There was no point in going to Alec's anymore. Tavis knew Sebastian would worry how long she'd been gone if she tried, so she headed back home after stepping onto the lane. A moment later, she heard the cart pulling up behind her, but ignored it and continued walking.

"Come on, don't be so stubborn," he called to her. "Please?"

Tavis scowled at herself for liking the sound of his voice. After a few minutes of silent walking, with the cart rolling along behind her, she realized he wasn't going to give up. She slowed her paced and when the cart stopped, she got into the passenger side.

Oddly, he didn't speed off as she assumed he would. If anything, Jack drove the cart at a snail's pace and Tavis figured she could've gotten home faster on foot.

"Why are you driving so slowly?"

He shrugged. "I need to charge it. The battery's dying."

"That's a lie."

"How would you know if I'm lying?" He kept his eyes trained on the lane ahead, but could see she pointed to the battery-life gauge.

"It's over half charged," she said.

"Yeah, I lied."

"You think all women are stupid, don't you?"

"No. Right now, I think I'm stupid." Jack stopped the cart and looked at her. "I want to say I'm sorry for what happened back there."

"Just forget about it, Jack. I have. Okay?"

"Oh."

~

"So, how'd it go?" Sebastian asked when Tavis came in. He closed the culinary encyclopedia he'd checked out from the library and set it on the side table by the couch.

"I didn't go."

He frowned at her disheveled appearance. "Then where've you been this whole time, and what happened to you?"

"Dodging island carts." Tavis held her arms up to show him the road rash. "And not very well, I'm afraid." She'd forgotten to shield her thoughts and hoped her father hadn't seen more than she would rather he know. "Will you help me? It's starting to burn."

Sebastian gave her a warm smile and stood as she approached him. He examined the wounds and determined they weren't significant enough to worry about scarring with a simple maneuver. It was nothing for him to do it, Tavis meant more to him than she knew, and he continued smiling at her while he placed his palms flat against her damaged skin.

"No," she said, feeling horrible and guilty now.

"Hush," he whispered.

A small sphere formed around the area he concentrated on most heavily. As the burning sensation waned, Tavis saw a bit of suffering knit his brow. Though they were small wounds, there was no way for the one absorbing them to not experience some pain. A moment later, the sphere vanished and he pretended to send the memory of pain in the air as though releasing a bird, eliciting a laugh from Tavis.

"Better?"

"Yes." Tavis tilted her head to see the skin as good as new, except for the smudges of dirt. "Let me see your arms."

"Your doubt wounds me more," he said, showing her the backs of his arms.

There was the slightest tinge of red there in the same spot they'd been on hers. It never ceased to amaze her how accomplished a physician he was.

"I'm still hopeful you'll go to medical school," he said, a hint he dropped often.

"I know."

"Which island cretin tried to run over my daughter?"

"Jack," she said. "It was an accident, so don't go confronting him about it. He was worried you'd be angry."

"I won't say anything." Sebastian held her gaze. "I won't question you about the tree bark in your hair either."

7

Ripple

As they'd yet to openly explore the residential area of the island where Meg and Alec lived, Sebastian and Tavis left for the dinner engagement well ahead of time to take advantage of the opportunity.

Tavis pulled the cart off the side of the lane by one of the many forest tracts interspersed between residential houses in the lowland part of the island. "I want to show you something," she said, leading him into the adjacent forest.

Several minutes into the trek, Sebastian asked, "Are you familiar with these footpaths?"

"Yes, they're everywhere in these forests. I memorized them during my watcher assignments. I didn't have a choice because Alec and Meg use them almost exclusively, and there are no maps, and no signs."

"I was never here long enough to learn but a few of them," Sebastian said. "Sure we won't get lost?"

"What was it you said... your doubt wounds me more?" Tavis laughed at his grimace. "We won't get lost. I did some research on these footpaths from the previous watchers' notes and I think it's fascinating how every one of them were made by the islanders. I doubt management even knows about them. Even if the maintenance workers informed them, they wouldn't have the slightest clue how to navigate them."

"Are there any in the mountain region?" he asked.

Tavis' footsteps faltered, knowing he tested her, and it annoyed her. "You told me not to go there, and I didn't. Alec never went there, so there wasn't any reason for me to contemplate going against your wishes. Why is it so important to you, anyway?"

"Because we have no purpose there and I don't know much about that area. I don't want you getting into trouble, so if you'd continue to respect my wishes, I'd be a very happy and grateful father."

Grinning, she said, "Don't worry, I have no intention of making you grumpy and ungrateful."

The footpath opened up to a lake with a waterfall, and an angry-looking heron took to the sky when Sebastian ventured too close. "Exquisite," he said of the pristine landscape.

"Isn't it? I love this spot." Tavis pointed to the center of the lake. "That's where I hid the pod during my assignments. I always swam here for a while before leaving."

"You're not thinking of going for a swim now, I hope."

"No, but I will if we're here much longer."

"Enjoy it while you can," he said, chuckling to himself. "I don't plan to be here any longer than I have to. Come on, let's go be the irritating early dinner guests." Sebastian turned to head back toward the path, but stopped at catching sight of a few white flowers perched at the top of the waterfall. "Look up there, Tavis."

She followed his gaze. "Flowers?"

"Edelweiss. Did I ever tell you how hard I tried to get that flower to grow here?"

"No."

"I took more seeds than you could possibly imagine and sprinkled the entire island with them trying to get them to sprout. I even had a previous watcher do it for me." He paused at some painful memory.

Tavis knew which of the watchers he meant.

"It finally worked," he continued, "and I've always attributed the edelweiss growing here with Alec's birth."

"Why?"

"It's an Alpine flower. It only grows in mountainous regions where there's lots of snow." A bit of a smile played at Sebastian's lips. "This island shouldn't come anywhere close to the sort of climate edelweiss requires, yet here it grows. It was the first bit of proof that Alec inherited my ability to influence weather patterns."

"I'm glad *I* didn't."

Sebastian looked at her with raised eyebrows. "Oh, yes you did. You're just afraid of it."

~

"They're not here yet," Tavis said when pulling into Ila's driveway.

"If they show up at all, Jack informed me they'd be late."

They sat in the cart and took in the full view of the house and property. The enormous size of it hinted at management favoring the lucrative business of horse-breeding and wanted their equestrian breeder as comfortable as possible. The sky-blue home—built by Moretti Construction—was one of the original houses constructed on Gamma, and therefore larger and more architecturally eye pleasing than the later housing.

The small wood fences that surrounded all the houses on the island matched the color of the trim—on Ila's house, a darker shade of blue. The flower boxes hugging the entire front porch were filled with blooms of complimentary and matching colors. It was truly beautiful, and truly pretentious.

To the right of the house stood a quaint barn and the colossal-sized horse stable, a structure larger than the house and barn combined. Both the stables and the barn were painted red, with rich-brown trim that matched the fencing surrounding the expansive pastures the horses grazed in.

"Wow," Sebastian said. "Impressive, considering management's the one who approves everything."

Tavis frowned. "Is this the first time you've seen this place?"

"Yes," he said, nodding. "When I was here before, I spent most of my time at Kyrie's, or near the town center."

"Clearly," Tavis said under her breath.

A white hen followed by a black speckled rooster walked by the front of their cart and Tavis smiled at his fluffed up feathers. When the rooster ran in front of the hen and let go a raucous crow, she laughed aloud.

"And why do you find that so funny?" he asked.

"Because he looks ridiculous, and she's obviously not interested."

"She's interested enough." Sebastian watched the hen peck at the ground. "She's just being coy."

"Personally, I think she's being smart to—" The rest of Tavis' empowered opinion ended at seeing the hen crouch and the rooster taking immediate position on her back. "Never mind."

Ila came out of the stables and waved at them. After leaning the pitchfork against the stable door, she walked over to them. "You're early," she said, visually appraising their appearance, lingering longest on Sebastian.

"That would be my fault." Sebastian flashed her a winsome smile. "I was hoping to see more of this part of the island. I have to say, your place is quite beautiful."

"Thank you, I do love compliments." Ila removed her work gloves and extended her hand to each of them. "It's nice to finally meet you both. I was just about to bring the horses in for the evening. Come have a look at the stables while I'm corralling them."

Sebastian and Tavis waited by the stable doors while Ila opened the pasture gate and sounded off a whistle to call them in. All of them fell in line, appearing eager to retire for the evening.

"Your horses are beautiful, too," Sebastian said when Ila reached the stable doors.

"Yes, they are." Ila nodded, patting the stallion leading the line. "I've always enjoyed them."

He reached up to touch the stallion, but it snorted and took a few steps back, forcing a similar reaction from the other horses. Ila calmed him down with a few muzzle pats. "Horses can be leery of people they don't know, especially this guy," she explained. "I hope you're not insulted."

Sebastian and Tavis followed in after the last horse and helped Ila refill the water troughs in the stalls. Ila then showed Tavis how to slice the apples near the stable sink, confessing the horses were spoiled and the apple treats were the main reason why they were so anxious to follow her back to the stables.

"Do you need any help with dinner?" Sebastian asked Ila.

"Nope. Everything's done, just waiting for everyone else to arrive."

"Where's Meg?" Tavis asked.

"Off somewhere with Alec, as usual." Ila rolled her eyes. "She promised to be back in time for dinner."

"Oh, my God!" A female's voice shrieked from somewhere outside. "This place is gorgeous, Jack."

Ila chuckled when the horses snorted at the disturbance. "Sounds like my other dinner guests have arrived." She went to the stable doors and called out to them. "Come see my horses before I close up the stable."

During introductions, Ila appraised Jack as she'd done Sebastian. Jack seemed more interested in the stable and horses than in anyone around him. He went to the stallion's stall and lifted a hand toward his muzzle.

"Careful, that one's spirited," Ila said.

"Most Thoroughbreds are." Jack heeded her warning and moved to the next stall, where a yearling begged for his attention. "Arabians, though, they have a much better temperament."

"You know your horses," Ila said. "You're not a mole from management sent to spy on me, are you?"

Jack maintained his composure by continuing to rub his hand along the yearling's neck, even laughing softly when the other horses whinnied at him. "I grew up around horses. My parents had a passion for them. They bred them occasionally, too."

"Well, Jack, you probably shouldn't have told me that." Ila winked at him. "I'm gonna start nagging you to help me out."

"You don't have to nag, I like being around horses." Jack looked around at the rest of the stalls. "Kyrie told me you have pregnant mares."

"I do, I keep the foaling stalls in the barn," she said. "Would you like to see them? Maybe you could tell me why they're taking so long to foal."

Soon as they all reached the barn, Jack said of the two heavily pregnant mares, "It won't be long, that's for certain."

"By my calculations, they should be in labor already." Ila gave the mares at disapproving frown.

"How did you breed them?"

Ila stared at him blankly for a second. "You seem old enough to know how that works."

Jack ignored Michelle's fit of giggling. "I mean, were they inseminated, or did you allow the stallion access to the mares?"

"I was teasing, I know what you meant." Ila grinned, then let out a sigh. "Insemination equals added costs in management's opinion. Since Rex has never passed up an opportunity with a mare in estrous, I go with pasture breeding."

"Pasture breeding is perfectly fine, that's how my parents bred their horses. The drawback is that you could be off by almost a month on the mare's due date." Jack glanced at the mares munching on their oats. "And you have two due dates to consider. They could foal days, if not weeks, apart."

"But they are pregnant, right?" Ila asked, laughing again at the confused expression on Jack's face. "I'm still teasing you." She turned to lead everyone out of the barn. "Let's go in the house and have a glass of wine before dinner."

~

Meg rushed up the steps and barreled through the front door, her eyes searched for Ila's in the people gathered around in the front room. When their eyes met, Meg offered an apologetic smile and shut the door.

"Sorry I'm so late, Alec doesn't have a clock out there yet."

"Meg, these are our *new* newcomers, Jack Cavanaugh and Michelle Martin." Ila turned to them. "My daughter has been helping her friend renovate a house. Apparently, he's waiting until it's finished before he bothers to put in a phone line."

"It's nice to meet you both." Meg shook their hands and said to Ila, "I'm gonna change into something less filthy and then I'll help you set the table."

"Take your time, we're having a glass of wine before dinner."

"Hey, Sebastian," Meg said. "Hey, Tavis. Come with me to my room and talk to me while I'm getting ready?"

"I'd love to."

Meg did most of the talking while she rummaged through her closet to find something to wear. Tavis sat on the edge of the bed, listening to her excited chatter about the stone house and how great it was going to be once Alec finished with it.

Pushing past the wall of dresses, Meg reached for her jeans and tossed them over the back of a chair near the cheval mirror.

"Alec's more than just your friend, isn't he?" Tavis asked while Meg selected a shirt from her dresser.

"No," Meg said without turning around. "Why would you ask me that?"

"Your shirt's on backwards, unless you always wear pockets on your back."

Meg pulled the grimy shirt off, still not turning around. "How embarrassing, it's probably been like that all day."

"And your shorts are inside out."

Finally, Meg faced Tavis, wearing a calm but concerned expression. "Do you think my mom noticed?"

"No, she's too busy flirting with my father."

Meg put her clothes on quickly and sat next to Tavis. "Please, don't say anything to anyone. When we're done fixing it up, it's supposed to be our house."

"Why don't you want anyone to know?"

"I haven't told my mom yet." Meg picked up a brush from her bedside table and worked out the tangles that had formed throughout the day. "I'm waiting until the mares foal because I hope she'll be more supportive of our decision if she's not having to deal with two stressful things at once."

"Does Ila not approve of Alec?" Tavis took the brush from Meg and helped with the knots she missed in the back.

"She can be critical of him sometimes. To be honest, I don't think she'd ever approve of anyone. It's not so much about Alec as it has to do with me. She's stuck, I think…"

Tavis tried sensing where Meg's thoughts had gone, but met a wall she couldn't find a way around. She assumed Alec was responsible for it, leaving zero wiggle room for anyone to sort it out for themselves.

"Where's Ila stuck, Meg?"

"When and where I'm a baby."

Giving up, and even understanding to a degree, Tavis said, "She sounds like my father. She doesn't want you to grow up and make your own life, but she does love you and wants the best for you."

"Is Sebastian a tyrant father?"

"He can be." Tavis laughed softly. "Even though I haven't ever given him much reason to worry."

"No way, I can't believe you've never had a boyfriend. You're gorgeous." Meg gave Tavis a wicked smile. "In fact, the bartender at the café asked me about you. Alec has to make deliveries tomorrow, so we're not working on the house. How about you and I have lunch at the café and I can introduce you to James."

"I'd love to meet you for lunch, but I'm not interested in trying to find a boyfriend."

"Then we'll just call it me wanting to introduce you to someone… who's definitely not hard to look at, by the way." Meg put the brush back on her night stand and stood. "Let's eat, I'm starving."

They exited the bedroom and found Sebastian and Jack sitting in the front room, sharing an uncomfortable silence, while Ila and Michelle were in the kitchen making fast friends over their mutual love of fine tea.

Dinner went well, though Ila and Michelle monopolized most of the dinner conversation while everyone else listened. Every now and then, Ila directed a question to Sebastian about Alaska, particularly what sort of food he and Tavis were used to eating.

At times, she was unrelenting and it forced Sebastian to admit, "Unfortunately, I'm having to learn how to cook since coming here. I apologize if some of my answers seem ignorant."

Tavis watched every eye at the table fall to her, and this was why she didn't shoot a scathing glare at her father. "We're both learning," she said.

It occurred to Ila that she may have stumbled upon a sensitive subject regarding whatever became of Mrs. Abbott. She smiled warmly and said, "Don't worry, you wouldn't be the first newcomer who had to learn how to cook. There's a kitchen at the store and Kyrie can give you both some pointers. In the meantime, you're welcome to come here anytime for dinner."

"Thank you, Ila," Sebastian said. "We'll talk to Kyrie tomorrow."

"I have plans tomorrow," Tavis said to him. "Meg and I are meeting up for lunch at the café." Feeling a bit daring, she added, "She wants to introduce me to…" She looked at Meg. "What did you say his name was?"

"James," she said, smiling.

"So, does that mean Alec's actually going to work tomorrow instead of being a carpenter?" Ila asked Meg.

"That's not very nice," Meg said.

Ila rolled her eyes and waved her hand dismissively, explaining to her guests,

"My daughter has made it her personal duty to help her friend fix up a stone hovel he plans to live in." She glanced at Meg again. "If anyone's not being nice, it's Alec. For one thing, ingratiating his friend to help him with such a menial task. For another, slacking off when he should be helping his mother instead of reminding everyone why his father was removed from Gamma."

Tavis glanced at Sebastian and knew he was close to losing his temper. His ire always showed in his eyes first, a steely glare that holds you prisoner. That is, if you're paying attention, which Ila wasn't.

Hoping to restore her father's calm, perhaps even help Meg in the process, Tavis said, "I think Meg's smart to help him. If it turns out to be a worthy effort, especially if she decorates it, the whole island will be asking her to help them with their houses. She could be Gamma's sole interior designer."

Her assessment of Ila's personality proved precise, but only by a narrow margin.

Ila said, "It's possible, Meg is artistic. I suppose we'll wait and see. At any rate, I'm happy she's going to show you around tomorrow." She gave Tavis a sly wink. "You'll like James, he's quite the looker."

After more banal conversation over dessert, Tavis grew tired of noticing Jack avoided making eye contact with her, wearier still of how she wished he would look at her. Mix in too much Ila-flirtation with Sebastian as the evening wore on, and the clock on the wall became her focal point. She felt a nudge at her side and she turned to find Meg grinning at her.

"Of course, I'd love to get some fresh air, Tavis," Meg said, as though they'd been discussing the matter at length.

As they stood from the table and excused themselves, Jack finally cast a glance at her, noting the lack of scrapes on Tavis' arms. He struggled to remember where they'd been. After the front door shut, Jack's gaze drifted toward Sebastian and found quizzical concentration expressed in his eyes.

Jack turned his attention to Ila. "Thank you for dinner. Remember what I said earlier, if you need any help with the mares, let me know."

"I will." She smiled at Michelle. "It was a pleasure to meet you and I hope you'll come over tomorrow for tea. Supposedly, my chai tea will arrive in the morning's special orders delivery."

"I'd love to." Michelle winced a little at the pain, trying to hide it as she'd done for weeks.

Sebastian noticed it, though, and saw how pale she was.

So did Ila. "Are you okay?"

"I'm fine." Michelle looked at Jack in askance, but decided to make the announcement herself. "I'm pregnant and sometimes I get really tired. That's all."

"Oh, you poor thing." Ila stood. "Jack, take her home so she can rest. I'll take care of the dishes."

~

The next day, Ila opened the front door and had to force a smile for Michelle. "You still look tired, come inside and sit on the sofa."

"Thank you," Michelle said. When she reached the sofa, she exhaled relief at being off her feet again. She accepted the teacup, but refused the sandwich Ila offered her.

"You look pale. You were last night, too." Ila sat next to her. "Are you having any pain?"

Michelle nodded. "It's been getting worse."

"Does Jack know?"

"Not about it getting worse. I didn't want to worry him." Michelle set her teacup on the coffee table and put her arms around her abdomen when a sharp pain seized her. "I need to lie down."

Ila helped Michelle recline back onto the throw pillows and covered her with a blanket. "Try to relax," Ila said in a soothing voice. "Want me to call Jack?"

"No, I'll be fine in a little bit. Besides, he's not there. He wanted to explore the island on foot today and that was the last thing I wanted to do." Michelle gave Ila a gracious smile. "I was so glad when you invited me over. I'm sorry if I'm being a burden."

"Don't be silly." Ila patted Michelle's shoulder. "I like taking care of things. I'm gonna check on the mares, and I want you to take a nap."

Her eyelids were already closing and she mumbled something about a nap sounding perfect. Ila went to the kitchen with their plates and teacups and picked up the phone to call Dr. Patrick's office.

"Hello, Clark, how are you?"

"I'm doing very well, Ila. It's a slow medical day on Gamma, just the way I like it. What can I do for you?"

"I was wondering if you could come over." There was a lengthy silence, causing Ila to think the line went dead. "Dr. Patrick?"

"I'm still here," he said, but sounded uneasy. "Is there something wrong that you can't come to my office? Are you having headaches again?"

"I'm not calling about myself, it's about the newcomer, Michelle Martin." Ila glanced toward the front room to make sure Michelle still slept. "She's here at my house… sleeping, right now. She's pregnant and I think there may be a problem. She told me she's been having pain and it's getting worse. I'm really worried about her."

"Hold on, I have the newcomers' files right here on my desk." There was another long silent pause. Then he asked, "Is Jack Cavanaugh there, too?"

"No, Michelle said he's out exploring the island. Should I get someone to try looking for him?"

"No," he said quickly. "I'll come over and take a look at her first. No need to scare him if it isn't necessary. Let her sleep until I get there."

Dr. Patrick hung up with Ila and called management. "William, it's Clark. I just got my first update on Michelle Martin. Oddly enough, she's at Ila's house, sleeping on her couch. Ila called me because she's worried about the pain Michelle's been having. I told her I'd be right over, so you need to tell me now, what do you want me to do?"

"Is Jack there with her?" William asked.

"No. It's just Ila and Michelle."

"That's perfect," William said. "Get over there and finish it off. I'll put in a request for a coastguard ship to arrive in a few days to take Michelle to the mainland. You have the briefcase I sent you, right?"

"Yes, it's at my home. You really think she'll take it?"

William snorted. "Of course she will. Just make sure you convince Jack that Michelle will be returning. I'd rather he stay on Gamma willingly."

"Okay."

~

The sting of a needle injecting the serum into her arm that would finalize an already threatened pregnancy woke Michelle up. She looked up at the portly, grey-haired man sitting on the couch with her, at first returning his warm smile, but then becoming more apprehensive as he injected a second needle into her arm.

"Who are you? What are you doing?" she asked just before a euphoric warmth washed over her.

"I'm Dr. Patrick, Michelle. I just gave you a sedative to help you relax."

"Why?" When the sedative took full effect, she didn't care why anymore.

"What was the first injection for?" Ila asked while watching Dr. Patrick pull Michelle's shirt up to press on her abdomen.

"Just a prenatal vitamin," he said dismissively. "I'd say she's close to four months along. Michelle." Dr. Patrick tried gaining her attention through her sedated fog. "Have you had any bleeding?"

"Mm, hmm." She nodded slowly and giggled at how wonderful the simple act of moving her head felt. "You're the island doctor, aren't you? I probably shouldn't be talking to you." She pointed a finger at him, and found the extension of her arm to be amazing. "Wow, I feel so good."

Dr. Patrick felt the weight of Ila's stare. "I'm fully trained in obstetrics, you needn't worry, Michelle. You should rest now, close your eyes and relax."

"Okay," she said.

"Why'd she say that?" Ila asked him as Michelle fell into a sedated sleep.

He turned to look at Ila, putting her under a different sort of microscope, responding only when she appeared uncomfortable from his scrutiny. "Who brings the thunderbolts to Zeus?"

Ila stared at him blankly for a moment, then asked, "Can you repeat the question?"

Relieved, he said, "Try to get someone to find Jack and bring him here."

~

"Well, what do you think? He's gorgeous, right?" Meg set her fork down on the edge of her plate like Ila had taught her to do to indicate she'd finished her meal.

"Yes, he is, but hush... he's coming over," Tavis whispered.

"Meg, your mom's on the phone. She said it's important." James picked up their plates. "You can use the bar's phone."

When Meg excused herself and went to the bar, James smiled and his soft brown eyes held Tavis' gaze. "I hope you don't mind me saying this, but you're incredibly beautiful."

Tavis averted her gaze for a moment. "Thank you, James."

"Would you care to have dinner with me one evening?"

"Sure, that's sounds nice." Tavis nodded. "I'll call you."

His smile broadened. "Reach inside my apron pocket."

"What?" She glanced at the front of his bar apron.

"I'd get it myself" –James held the plates higher– "but my hands are full."

She looked around at the other tables. No one was paying attention, so she slipped her hand inside his pocket. Tavis sensed from his thoughts that she was to retrieve a piece of paper, yet it was his other thoughts that tinged her cheeks pink.

"It's my phone number," he said. "I wrote it down in case you said yes. Call me anytime, day or night."

Meg returned to the table as James left and Tavis tucked the phone number in her pocket. "Is everything okay with Ila?"

"She wants us to look for Jack and take him to my house. Apparently, Michelle's having some medical problems. Dr. Patrick's there, too, and said Jack should be there." Meg frowned. "It doesn't sound like she's doing well."

They searched the town center first, then checked by the newcomer houses, and after roaming aimlessly around the residential lanes, Meg grew more exasperated. "He could be anywhere on this island!"

Tavis had a hunch where Jack may be and as more time passed, guilt ate away at her for not suggesting it sooner. "Check the beach by the docks," she mumbled, staring at the floorboard of the cart.

"Why would he be there?"

"I've seen him there before." Tavis shrugged. "It's worth a look, right?"

"Okay."

It took almost half an hour to reach the docks. When Meg pulled the cart up by the dunes overlooking the beach, Tavis pointed at the rock wall where Jack sat at the very top staring at the ocean. "There he is."

Meg turned to Tavis at hearing a softer quality in her voice. Briefly, she saw a longing in Tavis' eyes before she shifted her gaze away from Jack. "Too bad you didn't think of it sooner, huh?" Meg asked.

Tavis heard the note of compassion in Meg's voice. "I know, I should've mentioned it earlier." She looked at Meg. "I'll wait here while you get him."

"Oh." Meg had assumed Tavis would be the one to talk to Jack. After turning the cart off, she hesitated before getting out. "Tavis, is there something going on between—"

"You should hurry, we've been gone for hours."

~

"Is she gonna be okay?" Jack asked when Dr. Patrick explained Michelle was at risk of miscarrying.

"She'll be fine, but it's too early to say about the pregnancy." Dr. Patrick handed Jack a bottle of pills. "They're sedatives, the dosage is on the label. She needs strict bed rest for now and I'd prefer not moving her for a day or so. Ila agreed to let her stay here in the meantime. You, too, of course."

"She can have my room for as long as she needs," Meg said.

"I'll swing by tomorrow to check on her," Dr. Patrick said. "Call me at my home if there're any problems tonight."

Ila escorted Dr. Patrick out while Meg finished getting the rest of what she'd need from her room. "We should let her rest," Meg said to Jack and led him to the front room. "Do you need to go to your house to get anything for her?"

"Yeah, thanks, I hadn't thought of that."

"Tavis' cart is still at the café, would you mind dropping her off on your way?"

"Okay." Jack glanced around the room. "Where is she?"

"In the barn, she wanted to see the mares." Meg stopped him before he opened the door. "Speaking of which, my mom thinks one of them is about to foal. See what you think while you're out there."

Jack went outside and saw Ila talking to Dr. Patrick by the lane. Quietly, he stepped into the barn and found Tavis giving apple treats to the mares.

She heard his approach; it puzzled her that she knew it was Jack without having to turn around to confirm it.

"I'm sorry about what's happening with Michelle," she said. "Do you trust Dr. Patrick?"

He took one of the apple slices and fed it to the mare he suspected showed signs of early labor. "I don't really have a choice anymore. He's already involved."

"Well, I hope she's gonna be okay."

"Dr. Patrick said she'll be fine, but he didn't sound so hopeful about her pregnancy."

Tavis wasn't comfortable offering false words of encouragement about a pregnancy she already knew was doomed. "All that matters is Michelle's health."

"Come on, Meg asked me if I'd take you to your cart."

~

The mare foaled during night while Jack and Ila stood vigil. By morning, Michelle had miscarried. Meg called Alec and asked if he'd help Jack transport Michelle to Dr. Patrick's office. When Alec walked in, he froze at seeing Jack's face, recognizing him as the same man he saw on the beach by the docks.

"Thank you for coming over, Alec, I really appreciate it." Jack extended his hand. "I haven't met you yet, I'm Jack Cavanaugh."

Alec shook his hand and noted Jack's haggard appearance. Sensing how worried he was about Michelle, Alec decided against confronting him, at least for now. "It's nice to meet you." He looked over at Meg and smiled. "How's the mare?"

"She and her foal are doing great." She winked at Alec. "One more to go."

Jack frowned at the exchange, noticed where their gazes fell on each other, and determined they were more than friends. Ila came into the room, and she may as well have been a knife the way Alec and Meg's intimate glances severed from one another.

"She's ready," Ila said. "Poor thing's so sad, though. She keeps asking for her mother." After walking past Alec to open the front door, she finally acknowledged his presence once she saw he'd arranged the delivery cart as she instructed. "Thank you, Alec. Just make sure you drive carefully, Michelle's in a lot of pain right now."

It was an embarrassingly cool reception, but Alec said only, "Got it."

An urge to stand up for Alec came over Jack. "Kyrie tells me Alec makes all the deliveries on the island, Ila. I'm sure he knows every pothole on every lane better than anyone. I trust him completely."

Ila gave a curt smile and followed Jack, fussing while he scooped Michelle up from the bed and carried her outside. After arguing over Michelle's comfort in the medical transport stretcher attached to the utility cart, Ila finally relented to let Alec and Jack drive away—tailgating them in her own cart.

"Kind of annoying, isn't she?" Jack asked Alec when Ila beeped her horn a third time and shouted for Alec to slow down.

"In an overly, motherly way," Alec muttered, his jaws clenched.

"You mean, bitchy?"

"That, too." Alec looked over at Jack. "Hey, that was cool of you to stand up to her on my behalf. Thanks."

"Forget about it."

Alec thought again about having seen Jack before, and though he liked him, he couldn't shake off his suspicions.

"I'm gonna come right out and say it… I've seen you before, by the docks. It wasn't that long ago either, but it was before you were supposedly a newcomer. I saw you get on a boat that management uses and leave on your own. So, tell me, who are you really and why are you pretending to be a newcomer?" He sensed Jack's panic before confirming it in his eyes.

Seeing Alec scrutinize every one of his emotions and thoughts, Jack realized he wasn't going to be able to lie his way out. Even *that* realization formed in Alec's expression and Jack knew he had to say something or else risk being turned in to management.

A heavy, defeated sigh escaped Jack. "Michelle and I are weather researchers. We work for management, but our positions with them aren't any more important than what Kyrie and Ila do for them. We're sort of in line with maintenance workers, to be honest."

"Why are you here?" Alec slowed the cart down to give Jack time to answer, and to make Ila happy since she laid on her horn again.

"Relationships among colleagues are strictly prohibited at the research station and all employees sign contracts agreeing to that. Michelle and I obviously broke that agreement, and not only that, she got pregnant. I discovered management found out about it and were planning to confront us, so I decided to run and hide before they got the chance."

"Why here?"

"Because it was the only island, the closest island, I knew anything about. If you paid any attention to that boat, then you know why I couldn't use it to take Michelle all the way to the mainland." The guilt Jack felt sat on both he and Alec. "That's where she'd rather be, and that's why she keeps asking for her mother. I'm the one who insisted on coming here. I've always been fascinated with this island, and for the life of me, I don't know why."

"What are you gonna do now?"

"I don't know, Alec." Jack shook his head. "I'll have to prepare myself for whatever management has in store for me after you tell Dr. Patrick who we really are. I guess my idea to hide under their sniveling noses was poor judgment and I'll suffer the consequences of dragging Michelle down with me."

The hatred Jack had for his employers was loud and clear, but what had caused it was heavily guarded by what came across as fear. For once, it didn't matter to Alec not knowing the full story; the fact that Jack hated them so much created a camaraderie that he rarely ever experienced with others.

More so, it was the tremendous weight of Jack's oppressive guilt that stirred Alec's compassion. "I won't say anything to Dr. Patrick. I've never trusted that man, and you shouldn't either."

Relief flooded Jack's bloodstream. "Thank you."

"We're almost there and I want you to tell me what you know about the other *newcomers*."

Jack closed his eyes for a moment, considering the unspoken arrangement he'd formed when he met Sebastian and Tavis. However, he knew his own status hung precariously in the balance—all seemed to hover over Alec.

"I know they aren't from the research station." Jack decided to stick to the absolute truth as he knew it to be. "I'd never seen them before until I came here. Technically, they could be newcomers, only management has access to island census records."

"I don't think they're newcomers, and I don't trust Sebastian."

"Well, he's a different sort of nut, but I think they're harmless." The memory of a passionate embrace flashed through Jack's thoughts. "Tavis seems like a nice person."

Alec glanced at him and frowned. "What would happen if they were reported to management?"

"Management would come here to investigate, at the very least."

"I don't want that." Alec pulled up to the front of Dr. Patrick's office. "I'm not telling anyone what I know. Keep an eye on Sebastian for me. If you see anything unusual, let me know. Okay?"

"You want me to spy for you?" Jack asked in a hushed whisper at seeing Ila already checking on Michelle.

"Yeah." Alec's eyes narrowed at Jack. "You don't have a problem with that, do you?"

"I guess not."

~

"How are you feeling this morning, Michelle?" Dr. Patrick asked when her eyes opened.

"I'm still tired all the time." Michelle sat up. "Where's Jack?"

"I sent him home to get some much needed rest."

"Is Ila gonna come sit with me?"

"You've grown fond of Ila, I've noticed." Dr. Patrick smiled. "She's quite fond of you, too. She wanted me to tell you she'll bring some tea for you later. In the meantime, I want to talk to you while we have a moment alone."

There was something false in his smile that made her nervous. "About what?"

"A coastguard ship will arrive this evening to take you to the mainland for further medical treatment. It happens from time to time, certain procedures require a full surgical room and this clinic isn't set up for that."

"I need to have surgery?"

"Some miscarriages have complications that require surgery." Dr. Patrick retrieved a briefcase from the floor and placed it on the roll away table by her bed. "Your miscarriage wasn't complicated at all, but that's not what you're going to tell Jack."

"I don't understand."

"Then I'll make it simple for you." He sat on the edge of the bed. "You're leaving Gamma permanently, Jack is staying. The reason he'll stay is because you and I are going to convince him that you'll be back as soon as you've been medically released from the mainland hospital."

"Why would I do that?"

"Because you're not supposed to be here, Michelle. Management wants you gone, immediately." Dr. Patrick wheeled the table closer, positioning it in front of her. "By the way, they wanted me to tell you that you're fired."

"What about Jack?"

"He's not your concern anymore."

"Then why should I help you convince him to do anything?"

He opened the briefcase. "Here are half a million reasons to persuade you. The other half will be wired to your personal account once you return to East America, provided you successfully convince Jack to wait here for your return. Since Ila likes you so much, convince her, too."

The bundled stacks of money had a profoundly numbing effect on Michelle. Unlike the sedatives Dr. Patrick had been giving her, the money seemed to dull her ethics instead. She looked at him and asked, "What if he refuses to let me go to the mainland hospital without him?"

"He won't." Dr. Patrick chuckled at the insulted look on her face. "Be smart, girl, take the money and buy yourself a new Jack."

"Fine, I'll do it." Michelle closed the briefcase. "I'll try anyway. Jack can be unpredictable sometimes."

"You minored in theatre, I'm sure you'll do just fine." He stood and walked to the door, adding before he left, "Think of it as a million-dollar performance."

Convincing Jack turned out to be more like an elementary school puppet performance, in Michelle's opinion. Her theatrics made him all too ready to enjoy a break from her, so she focused her efforts on Ila instead. She implored Ila's help to watch over Jack until her return, and Ila adored the attention—swearing her oath to keep Jack from growing overly bored while Michelle was away.

~

Meg sat on a blanket under the sprawling oak tree in front of the stone house, wondering where Alec had gone. Then she remembered, he went to get her some water after she refused to eat her sandwich since it tasted funny. He had told her the water still ran black from the faucets and he'd have to go hunting for bottled water with his spear. She turned her head to look at the house she and Alec had spent weeks working on and smiled at how beautiful it looked.

Earlier in the morning, once Alec had put the last segment of fencing around the house, he stood guard over her while she planted the first of her flowers. When she protested, he told her it was necessary to protect her from evil. It occurred to her that he forgot to leave a guard while he was out hunting for water.

The clop of horse's hooves galloping up the newly finished lane leading to the stone house startled Meg and she feared what evil came for her. She sighed with relief at seeing it was only Sisco Horton dismounting from the horse, using his walking stick to make his way over to her.

"Hello, Margaret," Mr. Horton said. "Love what you've done with the place."

"I thought you were blind," she said, scooting over so he could sit with her on the blanket.

"I am, but I can feel this house," he told her. "Where's Alec?"

"He's out hunting bears… or was it water?" Meg frowned, trying to recall what Alec said. "I can't remember."

"It doesn't matter, Alec's a good lad." Sisco let go a hearty laugh. "Tragic fellow, but he loves you. I see he put down the foundation for the barn."

Meg looked at where Sisco pointed his cane. "He insisted I have one for my flock."

"And the first of your flock will announce their arrival in that barn."

"I'm sure I don't know what you mean," she said, keeping a respectfulness in her tone.

"Oh, yes, you do." Sisco picked up Meg's uneaten sandwich and ate it in front of her. "Doesn't taste funny at all."

"I wish you'd stop, Sisco," Meg said. "I'm not supposed to know until it's time."

"It's time for some of it." His voice had softened.

The horse snorted and raised its head, ears pricked forward, sensing a change in the wind. Clouds formed overhead and lightning struck over the ocean. The sound of whispers came from the trees behind the stone house, growing louder and louder over the wind. Meg struggled to hear the words, but couldn't make out anything that made any logical sense.

"Who is that?" Meg shouted.

"The dead."

His answer reminded her of a truth that struck instant fear in her mind. "I thought you were dead, Mr. Horton." For just a second, he didn't look like Sisco Horton, but someone else Meg desperately wanted to remember better.

"I am." The blind Sisco she remembered from her childhood turned to her. "And you will be, too, if you don't get a move on. I don't want you to join these voices." The wind stopped and the clouds rolled away faster than they should. "Heads up, child, it's about to start."

Both Sisco Horton and his horse exploded in a beautiful array of colors, forcing Meg to wake up. "Oh, my God!" she said, panting. "It was just a dream."

As the details of the dream faded, Meg saw her bedroom door was open and that a figure stood there. "Mom?"

"I'm glad you're awake, sweetie," Ila said. "I want you to do something for me."

"Did the other mare foal?" Meg got out of bed and turned her bedside lamp on.

"Not yet." Ila stepped into the bedroom and held out her hand, waiting patiently for Meg to come to her. "I want to show you something."

Together, they walked down the hallway. Once they arrived at the bathroom's threshold, Ila turned Meg around, guiding her backward a few steps until they stood next to the sink counter. Though Ila smiled, Meg thought it eerily strained with forced control.

"What's wrong?" she asked.

"I want you to pee on that stick for me." Ila pointed at the edge of the sink's marble counter.

Meg looked at where Ila pointed and struggled to control her own temper. "You went through my bag?"

"Pee on that stick," Ila repeated, glaring at Meg. She slammed the door shut and leaned against it, crossing her arms as though she'd stand there for hours waiting for Meg to relieve her full bladder.

"No." Meg crossed her arms as well.

"All right." Ila clutched the doorknob. "I'll call Dr. Patrick then."

Snippets of the dream replayed themselves in her thoughts: *...it's time for some of it... heads up, child, it's about to start.* Meg glared back at Ila while she picked up the pregnancy test, ignoring the shameful way it felt when urinating on it—glaring still while they waited silently for the results.

When the positive sign smirked, Meg asked, "Feel better now?"

"Should I bother asking whose it is?"

"No."

"Where'd you get the pregnancy test?"

"Kyrie."

"So, she knows?"

"Yep."

"I'll deal with her later. For now, you're going to end things with Alec and I'm going to call Dr. Patrick and" –Ila glanced at Meg's abdomen, thankful she wasn't showing yet– "beg him to fix this problem."

"I'm not a little girl anymore, Mom. You can't force me to do anything I don't want to do. Now, please, get out of my way."

Ila opened the door, but refused to let the matter drop. "You deserve better than Alec, I don't want to see him drag you down. You may not be a little girl, but while you still live under my roof, you'll do as I say."

While trying not to let Ila's angry words upset her, Meg continued to get dressed. She eyed the clock on her nightstand. "He'll be here any minute and it would mean a lot to me if you'd stop insulting him. I love Alec, and you're just gonna have to find a way to accept that."

A knock at the front door sent Ila rushing down the hallway with Meg following close behind. Ila got there first and snatched it open, not bothering to hide her disgust at seeing Alec standing there.

"Get off of my porch, you filthy piece of shit." Ila's voice, though clipped, imbibed pure venom.

She tried to slam the door shut, but Alec prevented it by pushing past her. He went immediately to Meg. "Are you okay?"

"Yes." Meg nodded, but her quivering chin was heartbreaking. "She knows about us."

"I sorted that out."

"Get out!" She snarled when Alec took Meg's hand into his and led her out to the porch. "I don't think so, you're not going anywhere with my daughter."

"Yes, I am," Alec said. "That house we've been working on is *our* house. I love Meg and if you think I'd leave her here with you as angry as you are, then you're crazy."

Ila stood in the doorway and watched them drive away. A fresh surge of anger trickled through her at recalling that Kyrie knew all along about Meg and Alec. She shut the door and drove off in the direction of the general store.

Before entering, Ila paused to calm herself—preferring to go in quietly and let the element of surprise guide her. She stepped into the store and scanned the floor, finally spotting Kyrie at the counter. After closing the distance, Ila waited for Kyrie to look up and then slapped her when she did.

Kyrie stumbled backward, but caught herself from falling. Stunned, she held a hand to her burning cheek and the other went up defensively in case another slap was on the way.

"I guess you know now," Kyrie said.

"You knew about it, you bitch! You should've kept your dog of a son on a shorter leash instead of letting him come sniffing around my daughter." Ila leaned forward and added in a hateful tone, "Looks like he's turning out to be just like his father."

"Ila, they love each other," Kyrie reasoned, keeping her voice calm.

"Oh, is that what you call it? I was thinking of a different word."

"Alec would never treat Meg badly."

"No, he just gets her pregnant." Ila's voice trembled. "And they're not even married. They haven't even been living together... but, I guess that's all gonna change now."

"That's what this is really about, isn't it? You're terrified of losing Meg."

"Yes." Ila was stunned by her own admission. Her shoulders slumped forward in telling defeat. "I don't know what to do without her."

Kyrie came from around the counter and hugged Ila. "You're gonna be fine. Meg and Alec are in love, they're not leaving us. You've been in love before. Don't you remember what that feels like?"

"I remember, it's wonderful." Ila closed her eyes for a moment and inhaled, trying not to scream, or worse, cry. "I'm sorry I slapped you, but don't be surprised if I hold a grudge for a while for keeping their relationship from me."

"Of course, I'd be shocked if you didn't." Kyrie hoped Ila felt a little better, but she was concerned about Meg and Alec. "Where are they?"

Ila pulled away from Kyrie and leaned against the counter. "I don't know. I screamed at Alec and told him to get out of my house, but he wouldn't leave without Meg. Maybe I should go find them and try—"

"No, no," Kyrie said quickly. "Cooler heads prevail. Give it time first. You should know that they wanted to wait until the mares foaled. It was important to Meg to have your support and approval. She hoped that if you weren't under so much stress, you might be happy for her."

"Are you trying to make me feel like a monster?" Ila's voice went up an octave.

"No, I just wanted you to know how much you mean to Meg. You're her mother, she loved you first."

A movement by the entrance caught Ila's attention. "Tavis," Ila said at seeing her standing there looking worried.

Kyrie spun around and gave Tavis a warm smile while walking over to her. "Hello, Tavis, I'm sorry I didn't see you. Have you been waiting long?"

Tavis figured Kyrie was more curious about how much had been overheard. "Not very long. I came to get milk, my father's trying to teach me some of the cooking lessons you gave him."

"How's that going?"

"He seems to have picked up on it." Tavis sighed. "Me, not so much." The tension in the room made her nervous, but there was no way she'd leave without knowing. "Are Meg and Alec okay?"

"They're fine, sweetie. I'm sure they're at the stone house. Ila was just about to tell me how the new foal is doing."

Ila came over to them. "The foal's perfect, and I need to be getting back because the second mare's showing signs of going into labor. Tavis, if you'd like, come over later and have a look. Okay?"

"I'd like that, thank you."

"Can I see, too?" Kyrie asked Ila.

"Sure." Ila rolled her eyes.

"Tavis, I'll swing by your place after I close the store and we'll ride over together."

"How much do you think she heard?" Ila asked after Tavis left.

"All of it," Kyrie said. "Who cares? The whole island will know soon enough."

~

When Ila left, upset by the prospect of island gossip, Kyrie rushed around the store to gather basic supplies for Alec and Meg. She filled the push cart with everything she thought they'd need right away. In the end, she shoved three push-carts full of stuffed boxes out the store and piled them into the utility cart. As she drove off, Kyrie glanced at Chapman Peterson's shop and an idea came to her that she thought would help smooth things over between Alec and Ila.

Kyrie was relieved when she saw Alec's cart parked in front of the stone house. A smile curved her lips when she knocked on the door, her son's front door. Alec was living separately from her now, and with someone he loved—it made her happy.

Alec opened the door. "Hey, Mom."

"Hey, son. Will you help me unload the cart? I brought some supplies I figured you and Meg might need."

"Sure." Alec stepped outside. "Ila knows."

"I'm aware of that. She told me at the store, quite passionately in my opinion." Kyrie raised her eyebrows. "What happened to giving me a warning?"

"I didn't have one either." Alec shrugged. "I showed up in the middle of it. Did Ila make a scene?"

"Nothing I couldn't handle, but she was angry."

Alec snorted. "Yeah, I know."

"How's Meg?"

"She's inside, resting. I haven't been able to get much out of her about what happened, she's really upset. She just now stopped crying, but only because she's exhausted."

Kyrie frowned. "Meg hasn't told you?"

"Told me what?"

The front door opened again and Meg looked at Kyrie. "Don't," she said.

"I want to tell him. It's just that everything happened so fast and not the way I had planned."

Alec was close to losing his temper at not knowing what they were going on about. He resisted the instinctive urge to pry the thoughts from them. "What do you want to tell me, Meg?"

"I'm pregnant." Her chin quivered. "Are you mad?"

"Meg, don't cry again. You're killing me." Alec wrapped his arms around her. "No, I'm not mad, you silly goose. I love you."

Kyrie had to fight back her own tears, watching them interact together for the first time in the open. "Congratulations to both of you, or all three I should say."

Meg leaned back from Alec. "Thank you, Kyrie, for everything."

"Don't worry, I'm working on Ila. She's already calmer and I have an idea that'll make her more receptive to you and Alec being together now."

"What?" Alec asked.

"It's a surprise. I want you both to come to the store in the morning, Meg needs to start ordering furniture for this house and I need you to run an errand for me." Kyrie walked down the stone steps. "For now, I need help unloading this cart so I can get back to the store."

8

Altered

Tavis tried to make it seem like a casual thing when she told Sebastian of her plans to see the new foal with Kyrie.

"Will Meg be there?" he asked, finding it odd that Tavis and Kyrie were chummy all the sudden.

"I doubt it."

Sebastian closed the Gamma civics book he'd been reading and stared at Tavis until she fidgeted at his attempt to sense her thoughts. "What's going on?" he asked.

"I walked in on Ila confronting Kyrie about Meg and Alec. She was mad that Kyrie knew about them."

A bit of a smile adorned Sebastian's face. "I've been able to sort out more of Kyrie's thoughts lately. I guess Alec's been busy. She did know about them and helped them keep it a secret. It made me curious why Ila's so against it."

"What about you, have you made any decisions about Meg?"

"No." Sebastian shook his head. "Alec won't let me anywhere near her. I'm no closer to a decision about her than I was before I came here."

"I like her," she said. "I think she'll fit in fine—"

"It's not a popularity contest, Tavis. I know nothing about her."

"Then I suggest you start learning soon because she and Alec are living together now. I think it's safe to say that Alec won't part from her willingly."

"I know that already!" Sebastian felt horrible at seeing fear in Tavis' eyes. "I'm sorry, I shouldn't have yelled at you."

"It's okay." Tavis went to him and took his hands into hers. "I know how much Alec means to you. He's important to me, too, now that I know he's my brother. I want him to be happy… even though he can be a sourpuss sometimes." She hoped the playful jibe would lighten her father's mood.

"He's only like that because he doesn't trust me."

"From what I can tell he doesn't trust most people." Tavis frowned at his continued sullenness. "Something else is bothering you. What is it?"

Sebastian gave Tavis' hands a gentle squeeze before letting them go. "I can't quite figure it out, but there's more going on here than I'm aware of." It still worried him that he'd yet to talk to her about the nature of his involvement with Kyrie.

"What do you mean?" she asked, following him to the front room window.

"I rode out to the stone house one evening after you went to bed. I was just curious to see what Alec was doing with the place."

"And?"

"I sensed Chaza's presence there." Sebastian stared at the flourishing roses, adding in a whisper, "I'd know her scent anywhere."

"My mother?" Tavis tugged at his arm to make him look at her. "She's alive, she's here?"

"I don't know, I didn't see her. I only sensed that she was there, or had been. Tavis, I need to tell you—"

"Kyrie's here," Tavis said at seeing the cart pull up in front of their house.

Sebastian was thankful for the reprieve. "Go, we'll talk about this later. While you're at Ila's, see if you can explore what's going on in that woman's head. Just be careful around Kyrie, she's observant."

He stood in the doorway after Tavis walked out, and waved to Kyrie. She grinned and asked, "Would you care to come with us?"

"No, thank you." The smile on his face broadened. "I was in the middle of reading a… satire. Maybe next time."

"Okay," Kyrie said, thinking to herself that no man should be so easy to look at. "I'll have Tavis back later tonight."

Unusually quiet, Kyrie drove at a fast clip toward the town center. It wasn't until they were past all the shops, heading for the old village, did she slow down—yet still maintaining her silent reserve. Tavis attempted sensing where her thoughts were, but stopped when Kyrie suddenly glared at her.

"What are you doing, Tavis?"

"Nothing."

The cart slowed to a stop and Kyrie turned to study Tavis' face. When Tavis squirmed in the seat, Kyrie finally spoke, "Your eyes are truly remarkable, a beautiful color."

"Thank you," Tavis said, but knew Kyrie didn't stop the cart simply to pay her a compliment.

"Until you and your father came here, I'd only seen that same color in one other person." Kyrie's voice took on a steely edge as she leaned in closer to Tavis. "Can you guess who?"

"No," Tavis lied.

"My son." There was no mistaking the accusatory undercurrent lacing the answer.

"Oh, I hadn't noticed." Tavis was surprised by how submissive she felt and sounded. "I'm sorry."

A fretful crease knitted Kyrie's brow at realizing she was scaring Tavis. "I shouldn't have spoken to you that way."

"It's all right. I know you're worried about Ila."

"I'm very worried about her, but that doesn't give me the right to make you feel like you need to apologize for the color of your eyes." Kyrie tilted her head and gave

Tavis a doleful pout. "Give me a smile so I know you don't think I'm as crazy as Ila? Please?"

Not only did Tavis smile, she couldn't help but chuckle at this. "She won't hit you again, will she?"

"So, you did hear all of it?"

"I was right behind her when she went into the store," Tavis admitted. "I assumed she hadn't seen me since she didn't hold the door open for me. I saw her slap you through the store's window and I went inside thinking I'd try to stop her if she did it again. I still can't believe she hit you."

"Management has always catered to her, and I'm afraid to say that it's made her rather spoiled. She could place a special order for a diamond tiara today, and though they'd gripe about the cost, I bet you anything it would arrive in next week's shipment."

"I already knew about Meg and Alec. Meg told me when I asked her about it."

"Soon, that won't be an exclusive club anymore."

"Why doesn't Ila like Alec?"

"What was the reason Meg gave you?"

"That Ila's stuck and refuses to view her as an adult."

"Meg's right. It's not just Alec, no one will ever be good enough for who Ila considers to be her baby. She's known to be like that with the yearling horses, too." Kyrie sighed. "I'm going over there because I don't want her spending too much time on her own. She'll dwell on it and get angrier with every passing second that Meg's not there, and living with Alec instead. I have a plan that I think might help Ila focus on something else, something new and, hopefully, exciting for her."

Intrigued, Tavis asked, "What?"

"I don't want to jinx it. Just try not to mention their names and follow my lead. Do I have your support?"

Tavis looked at Kyrie's patiently waiting face. She wanted to try gaining entry to her thoughts and plans, but somehow knew better than to attempt it again. While studying her face, Tavis noted how beautiful Kyrie was. Her exotic appearance, coupled with soft hazel-green eyes, forced anyone present to become lost in the allure. And her company and personality was a pleasure to be around.

Tavis thought she understood why her father acted the way he did around Kyrie, as she felt her own head nodding to agree. "I'll do whatever I can to help you with Ila."

~

Sebastian was in the front room, lost in his thoughts while the book he'd been reading lay open in his lap, waiting for him to pick up where he'd left off. He was glad for the time alone, as he needed the calm to squash the instinct to turn the island upside down to flush Chaza out.

His intellectual, more prudent, instincts begged he bide his time and not ruin the pristine opportunity to bring Alec home by chasing down what may only be speculation. Yet, he was certain he'd felt Chaza's presence. It was unshakable, growing stronger with each passing day, even while sitting here contemplating it—

She maintained her position, hiding in the shadows of the hallway, watching him weigh his options... or lack of them. Chaza knew when Sebastian was deep in thought, but she also knew it wouldn't be long before he realized just how near she was to him. Weighing her own options, Chaza considered the idea of putting an end to it all.

Chaza had long since given up on ever returning home, so killing Sebastian would come at no great cost to her. Though a tempting solution, there was no way she could go through with it, Tavis would be lost without her father. The concept of *home* meant nothing to Chaza anymore, but the principles of nonviolence were what truly kept her from carrying out the act of ending Sebastian's heartbeat.

The only other option was to deliver herself to him, a thought that almost made her reconsider the previous option. She knew he was thinking about her, and probably had been since the night she'd barely made it out of the stone house unseen when he showed up to snoop around. Chaza shook her head at thinking how alike they were.

"Ah." Sebastian's sudden voice yanked Chaza from her reminiscing. "Our mutual love of flowers gives you away, dear wife."

Chaza uncloaked herself, stepping out of the shadows simultaneously, and marched over to the chair he continued to sit in like it was a throne. "Why are you here?" she demanded.

"You know perfectly well why I'm here."

"Let me be clear, why are you *still* here? And why did you bring Tavis with you?"

"Tavis was the last watcher."

"I know, I watched her watching."

Sebastian set the book aside and stood, towering over Chaza. "You look well, for someone I thought was dead. Where've you been?"

"I've been right here on Gamma. I never left." Chaza squared her shoulders, lifting her chin defiantly. "I stopped believing in what you believe in."

"That's not a good enough reason for you to let everyone think you'd been killed. Your parents are still insisting—"

"I didn't come here to talk about the past. I want you to get what you came for and go home."

"It's not that simple. It seems Alec was aware of being watched and became quite adept at escaping observation. I decided to stay awhile first to watch him myself before taking him home."

She stiffened. "Have you learned anything new?"

There was a nervous edge in her tone that he easily sensed, and his eyes narrowed. "What are you hiding?"

"I'm not hiding anything."

The infuriating obstacle of not being able to probe each other's minds stood in the way, preventing either of them from seeing what the other thought, remembered, planned, and more importantly, what lay hidden. Sebastian often wondered if this was the true demise of their marriage. Emotions were a different matter however, particularly fear. If there was one thing Sebastian could be certain of, she was hiding something—something she was deeply afraid of.

"You know how determined I can be, Chaza." His tone was foreboding. "If there's something going on here that I'm unaware of, I'll find out what it is. By the way, I told Tavis my suspicions about you being here. She was shocked. You should know that even though she was only a baby when you left, Tavis grew up feeling your absence, and she still does."

Chaza suffered the heavy burden of guilt that Sebastian intended for her. "Leaving her wasn't an easy decision for me to make."

"Easy or not, you left. You let everyone think you were dead. How could you do that to the people who care about you?" Sebastian tried, but he couldn't hide his pain. "How could you do that to me?"

She stepped closer. "That wasn't an easy decision for me either."

Something in her eyes begged forgiveness for something more than simply having left him over a difference in ideals. Slowly, not sure how she would react, Sebastian lifted his hand to touch her face. Relief swept over him when she didn't recoil.

He wanted to forgive her for leaving him and Tavis so long ago without so much as an explanation, but it wasn't easy to forgive something he'd yet to fully understand. Watching her eyes close at their nearness, he sensed her torture from some guarded secret she had no intention of revealing to him. It angered him, yet it also stirred his compassion—knowing that whatever it was, he was equally responsible for its creation.

"I still care for you, Chaza," he said in a bare whisper. "Won't you tell me what's troubling you?"

"You meant everything to me, and you know how badly I wanted a family with you." She paused to regain control of the emotions that threatened to bring her to a wretched pile of tearful groveling. "But I'm not going to tell you, and I hope that you'll have enough respect for me to let it go."

It pained him further to say, "So now I know, you are hiding something."

Chaza laughed at realizing her mistake. "You're a smart man, Sebastian, and that's why I married you... and why I left you." She reached up and cupped his face in her hands. "I have to go, but before I leave I want to tell you to keep an eye on Tavis. She's not a baby anymore, she's bloomed into the exquisite rose you imagined. Expect company in your garden."

"I've already seen one or two lurking nearby, nothing I can't handle."

"How long do you plan to be here?"

"For as long as it takes." Sebastian watched her walk away. "Where are you staying?"

Pausing at the hallway entrance, Chaza turned to him and said, "I don't accept visitors." Seeing his puzzled expression, she added, "I have no identity on this island. If you asked anyone about me, they wouldn't know who you were talking about and you'll only raise suspicion among an already skittish population."

~

When Tavis returned later in the evening, she sat next to Sebastian on the porch.

"How's Ila doing?" he asked.

"Better than she was this morning. Kyrie's idea is for Ila to busy herself planning Meg and Alec's wedding."

Sebastian nearly spit his tea back into the cup. "I didn't know they were considering marriage."

"I don't think they are," Tavis said. "On the way back, Kyrie told me she plans to talk to Alec in the morning."

"What if he refuses?"

"He won't. I think he'll agree with Kyrie." Tavis poured a fresh cup of tea for both of them. "I want to show you the memory of what Kyrie said to me on the way to Ila's."

"Are you sure?" He chuckled when she rolled her eyes. "I know how protective you are of your thoughts."

"Stop teasing me. Do you want to see the memory or not?"

A beautiful warmth washed over Sebastian at the allowance into Tavis' mind.

It takes a lot of trust to show someone a memory, a trust which could be lost forever if taken for granted. Any little stray thought could allow the viewer to see more than what had been intended.

She showed him from when Kyrie noticed her thoughts were being sensed to where Tavis agreed to help her with Ila.

"I believe I mentioned to be careful with Kyrie before you left," he said.

"Sorry, I didn't think she'd be *that* sensitive."

"I'm sure she's had lots of experience dealing with Alec."

Sebastian looked at her and considered the wisdom of changing everything Tavis knew about her life. If he continued to put it off, he'd risk damaging the close relationship they shared. This thought alone was enough to put an end to his silence.

"I need to tell you something. Actually, I want to tell you a few things. Turns out I was right, Chaza's here. After you left with Kyrie, she came to me."

"She waited for me to leave?"

"Don't be upset," he said, feeling the crushing blow of Tavis thinking her mother didn't want to see her. "Chaza wanted to show herself to me first because she didn't want to hurt you."

"It's too late for that." Tavis' emotions went from disappointment to anger. "She let me think my mother was dead. Has she been here the whole time?"

"Yes."

Tavis shook her head, trying to get her thoughts together without being disrespectful to her father. "Whatever happened between you and Kyrie had nothing to do with me. I can't believe my own mother would treat me like this."

Sebastian closed his eyes and said in a soft whisper, "Chaza's not your mother." He opened them again at her silence, seeing an eerily placid waiting expression on her face. "She raised you for a little while before she disappeared from our lives, but you're not her biological daughter."

Breaking eye contact with him, Tavis turned her head to look at anything but him. Her gaze fell to the roses just beginning to bloom near the porch railing. A sardonic laugh escaped her. "I guess it would be stupid of me to ask who my mother really is. Does Kyrie even know she has a daughter?"

"No. She thinks she gave birth to only one child."

"Alec and I are twins?"

"Yes."

"Why didn't you take us both home?"

"I wanted to." Sebastian set the teacup on the table between them and leaned forward. "But when a baby mysteriously disappears, it draws a lot of attention."

"Oh, no one knew she was pregnant with twins." Tavis nodded, clarity crystallizing now. "You could take one of the babies without anyone noticing."

"Dr. Patrick suspected it, but I altered his memories the night I helped Kyrie give birth to you and Alec."

"Is that why Chaza left you? Because you cheated on her and wanted her to raise another woman's child?" Tavis looked at her father as though he was immeasurably cruel.

Sebastian scoffed at the accusation. "It was all done medically, I didn't betray my wife." He frowned, unconvinced by his own explanation. "However, I think part of the reason she left was because she had trouble accepting the fact that I fathered two children with someone else. Chaza and I couldn't have children. We tried, but she miscarried every time."

"Why did you pick me over Alec to take home?"

"There were so many reasons, Tavis, I don't remember anymore which one was more important to me at the time. Chaza always wanted a daughter, and I wanted to give her one. I thought it would make her happy again."

"Obviously, you were wrong."

He heard a note of sadness in Tavis' voice. "Actually, she was happy for a while and she loved you very much, but she kept an eye to her work here on Gamma. I think she may have become obsessed with the fact that Alec still remained here. Chaza grew more and more withdrawn from me, it seemed I'd lost her already before she vanished altogether."

It didn't take special abilities to feel the sorrow and loss resurfacing in Sebastian's emotions. Compassion stirred Tavis and she got up from her chair to sit on the porch by his feet, resting her head on his knee as she did as a small child. "I'm glad you picked me. I can't imagine my life having grown up without you."

"I can't imagine my life without all the joy I got being your father, ever since the day I first held you in my arms."

"Even when you had to chase off boys interested in me?" Tavis ribbed. "Ila reminds me of you a little bit."

"Not funny, but I'm glad you brought that up. You've read enough of the files and documents about Gamma, so you know what management's objective is. There was no way I was going to allow my daughter to be subjected to their plans and influences." Sebastian hooked a finger under Tavis' chin, tilting her head up to look into her eyes. "You'll make your own choices, especially when it comes to who you decide to be with. As long as I approve of him, of course."

Tavis narrowed her eyes, but there was a playful glint to them. "I'll pretend you didn't say that." She rested her head back on his knee and tried to sort through the mass of information she'd learned this evening. "What did Chaza say to you?"

"That she wants me to take Alec and leave as soon as possible."

"Why?"

"I'm not sure exactly, but I know she's hiding something from me. I told her I'd figure it out and she didn't seem thrilled about it."

"Anything else?"

"She said she left me because she stopped believing in what my goals were. Chaza knew, as we all do, that we're a dying race and she was never all that excited about my ideas. She wasn't the only one, there were others who were against my plans." Sebastian chuckled. "Particularly, every member of our council."

"But why leave you and come here? It doesn't make sense."

"I agree, and I think it has everything to do with whatever it is she wants to keep secret."

"Think it has something to do with Alec?"

"Maybe."

"I wouldn't mind knowing how he's able to use his abilities so well without proper training. If we're twins, why is he so much more skilled?" Tavis asked. After several seconds of silence, she looked up at him and saw the reality etched in his frown. "You don't know, do you?"

"I have no explanation for it. Alec was twice as strong as he should've been from an early age. I'm hoping to sort it out before we take him home because right now, he's behaving like a young tyrant in the making and that won't be well received."

"Yeah, no kidding." She grimaced at another reality. "We're already in trouble for sneaking off without council approval."

"It's getting late, we should go to bed soon," Sebastian said, dismissing the subject of Chaza and Alec. "Was there anything else you wanted to tell me about Ila?"

Tavis stood and glanced over at the far newcomer house. "She asked me about Jack. All I could tell her was that he keeps to himself. When was the last time he came out?"

"I don't know." Sebastian looked over at the house and saw only one room lit in lamplight. "I tried knocking on the door earlier, but he wouldn't answer it. I rang the doorbell several times, but he just shouted for me to go away. I'll try again tomorrow."

"Are you worried about him?"

"I'm more worried about you. Will you be okay around Kyrie now that you know she's your mother? I don't want her to know just yet, for obvious reasons."

"I'll be fine." Tavis inhaled a deep breath of calm. "But she's coming home with us. We're not leaving her here."

Sebastian pulled Tavis into a hug. "I have every intention to bring her home. I hate that I didn't do it sooner."

~

The first light of day illuminated the bedroom in the stone house, waking Alec. Meg still lay next to him, sleeping, and he nudged her awake. Her eyes opened, then squinted immediately at the harsh light.

"We're getting curtains right away," she said, stretching.

"I'm all about curtains." He tickled her until she laughed. "Let's get dressed so we can pick some out."

Meg got up and went to the closet where the boxes were. She rummaged through all of them, looking for the clothes Kyrie mentioned she'd thought to add to the supplies. It became clear to Meg that her options were limited.

"It seems I have only sundresses to pick from," Meg said.

Alec turned to find Meg waving a pink dress at him and he laughed at the sight of her grumpy face.

"You think it's funny, do you? Well, there's plenty of them, how about you wear one, too?"

"I'm sorry. My mom raised a boy, she doesn't know how to pick out clothes for a girl."

"*Girl* being the appropriate word. I'm gonna look like I'm five years old." Meg went back to the box and stared inside it. "And, of course, there's no underwear."

"I promise you, if you wear that dress with me knowing you're not wearing anything under it, I won't be thinking five-year-old thoughts," he said, hoping to smooth things over. "In fact, if you want, I'll help you get dressed."

A suggestive smile curved her lips. "No, but you can take it off me later."

When they arrived at the store, Alec parked in his usual spot and went inside hand-in-hand with Meg. Kyrie smiled at seeing how happy and comfortable they were to announce their status to the whole island.

"Good morning," she said. "Aw, Meg, you look so pretty. Did I get the right size?"

Though Meg found the poker face a little painful, she said, "It fits perfectly. Thank you."

"Excellent." Kyrie came from around the counter and led Meg to her desk. "Look over this catalog and start picking out the furniture you want to order. All the forms are right here. I'll help you with them after I talk to Alec about an errand I want him to take care of."

Kyrie met Alec outside.

"What do you need me to do?" He looked around for the typically laden utility cart, but found it nowhere. "Are there deliveries?"

"No deliveries," she said. "I want you to pick something up."

It wasn't unusual. Alec often had to retrieve items in addition to delivering them, especially for the older residents. "Who from?"

"Chapman Peterson's shop."

Alec looked over at Chapman's store and frowned. "Is that all?"

"That's all."

Confused, he asked, "Is it heavy?"

"Not at all." Kyrie gave him a sly wink. "It should fit right in your pocket."

"All right, Mom, what's going on?"

"Chapman told me the other day that Meg's pearl ring was ready for pickup. I thought it would be a lovely idea if you got it and gave it to her as an engagement ring when you ask her to marry you."

"What?"

Her eyes fixed on his, the perky expression shifted to a pinching severity. "Do you have some sort of a problem with marrying Meg?"

"No, of course not. You just surprised me."

Her expression softened again.

"Good. You need to do what's right for Meg, and by extension, Ila." Kyrie sighed and patted Alec's shoulder. "If there's one sure fire way to win Ila over, it's giving her something else to think about. Planning her daughter's wedding" –she raised her eyebrows– "*before* Meg starts showing, would probably put an end to Ila's perceived notions of shame and dishonor."

"You really think it'll help?"

"What do you think, Alec? Would it be in Meg's best interest if her mother was happy for her? You're gonna be a father, you have to think about these things."

Alec stood there like a stone statue while the weight of impending fatherhood finally sank in. Though a little frightening, it also made him happy and he smiled. "You and Meg will be working on furniture orders for a while, right?" he asked.

"Probably."

"I have an idea, but I might be gone for at least an hour. Okay?"

"Your idea doesn't involve skipping town, I hope?"

"No." He laughed and jumped into his cart, driving away in the direction of Ila's house.

As he stood at her front door, he was suddenly nervous about knocking on it. Several minutes passed while he judged the wisdom of his idea. At one point, Alec started to leave, thinking he'd changed his mind, but stopped before reaching the porch steps.

He looked back at the door and grimaced at imagining what insults Ila would hurl at him, if only he could pluck up the nerve to carry out his plan. Alec understood what Kyrie hoped to accomplish; she knew Ila wouldn't be able to resist getting excited about a wedding. She would want to be involved in every step, plan every detail, and it would heal the rift between all of them.

Determined to make it right, Alec returned to the door and lifted his hand, letting it hover in the air an inch away so he could ready himself. Without warning, the door was yanked open, surprising him.

"I can't take it anymore!" Ila glared at him. "You've been standing on my porch, staring at my door for over ten minutes. What the hell do you want, thief?"

"I wanted to ask if you'd help me with something."

"You want *me* to help *you*? Oh boy, I can't wait to hear this," she said, perturbed by his audacity.

"Chapman said Meg's pearl ring is ready to be picked up."

She waited for him to continue, but he only looked at her. "I know you did not just come to my house and ask me to run an errand for you. Have you lost your mind?"

"No! I'm just nervous right now." Alec inhaled deeply to steady his nerves. "I want to give the ring to Meg when I ask her to marry me. I was hoping you'd come with me to help pick out wedding bands you think she'll like because, well, I don't know much about jewelry."

Ila crossed her arms and raised an eyebrow at Alec. "I'm surprised you didn't ask Kyrie to help you out with that."

"She doesn't have much experience, my father didn't even give her an engagement ring."

Some of Ila's icy reserve melted. "I know."

Alec thought he may actually stand a chance of getting her to come around. Risking a light chuckle first, he said, "And if the clothes she picked out for her to wear are an indication, she wouldn't be very helpful at selecting wedding bands that Meg would like."

Miffed at hearing Kyrie provided clothes for Meg, but still curious, Ila asked, "What kind of clothes did she give Meg?"

"Sundresses. Pink ones, yellow ones. One of them had purple flowers and ruffles."

Ila snorted, imagining the expression on Meg's face when she discovered the dresses. Meg hadn't worn frilly dresses since she was a child. "Hold on while I get my shoes."

Alec waited on the porch for Ila to get ready, relieved his plan seemed to be working out. On the way back to the town center, they sat in the cart quietly while he drove. The silence became maddening and he wondered if he should try pushing his luck.

Bringing the cart to a stop, he turned to Ila and looked at her with the most pleading set of blue eyes she'd ever seen in her life. It was all she could do to keep from laughing.

"I can't tell you enough how sorry I am for upsetting you. However, I'm not sorry for loving Meg. I want to spend the rest of my life keeping her safe and making her happy, but right now she's not as happy as she could be because Meg needs you in her life."

"I need her in my life, too," Ila said and stared off at nothing.

She appeared somewhere far away. Alec tried sensing where her thoughts had drifted to, but all he found were vague images of Meg's infancy and a confusing menagerie of unfamiliar memory fragments.

"Please, Ila, be happy for Meg… for her sake. You have no idea how much it hurts her thinking she disappointed you."

"Yes, Alec, I'll be happy for Meg." She gave him a reassuring nod. "As long as you continue to protect her and make her happy every day of her life, I'll be happy for both of you."

~

At Chapman's shop, Ila helped Alec pick out the bands she knew Meg would love—white gold engraved with Trinity knots. She went with him to the general store after he insisted she be there when he proposed to Meg. Before Alec opened the door, Ila stopped him.

"You only need to present her with the engagement ring for this part. I'll hold on to the wedding bands for you. When do you think the wedding will be?"

He shrugged. "This weekend, maybe?"

"Absolutely not." Ila waved a dismissive hand. "I can't possibly get out all the wedding invitations by this weekend."

"Well, I'll leave it to you and Meg to decide when." He hoped this was the right answer.

"Very good, Alec, that's much better." A satisfied smile settled on Ila's face. "All you have to do now is propose and hope she says yes."

The thought of Meg rejecting his proposal hadn't occurred to him and a frown formed on his forehead.

Ila guessed at what troubled him. "Don't worry, she'll say yes."

Alec opened the door and found Meg still seated at the desk while his mother finished a phone call, with an elderly resident based on how loudly she spoke. Kyrie's voice faltered when she saw Ila follow in after Alec, but smiled after he winked at her. Ila rolled her eyes at both of them.

Meg looked up from the order forms and saw Alec walking over, and her mother standing next to Kyrie at the counter. She wanted to ask him if their mothers were all right, but then he knelt on the floor by her chair. He held a small box up to her and opened it, showing her the pearl ring nestled inside the blue velvet base.

"Margaret Arcana, will you marry me?"

Her lips parted in surprise and she looked from the ring to Alec. "Yes, Alec Ellison, I'll marry you."

He pulled the ring out and slipped it on her finger. They gazed at it for a moment and then smiled at each other.

"I love you."

"I love you, too, Alec."

Meg slipped her arms around him, drawing him closer for a kiss, not caring that their mothers were watching. Alec wound his arms around her waist and stood, lifting Meg up from the chair. He spun her around a few times before placing her feet back onto the floor. She swayed a little from dizziness.

"Better not spend too long planning their wedding," Kyrie said to Ila. "Here, I picked out the finest we have."

Ila glanced at the box of silver-embossed wedding invitations, then eyed Kyrie again. "Not bad," she said. "Think the newsletter office can print them in a hurry?"

"I already talked to them, Henry said he'd be delighted to print as many as you need." Kyrie grimaced apologetically. "Provided he gets an invitation, too, and that you dance with him at the reception. I told him you'd love to."

"Thanks." Ila scowled. "You didn't promise anything else, did you?"

"I said you'd sleep with him." Kyrie laughed at the horror on Ila's face. "I'm just kidding."

Sebastian and Tavis came in and joined Ila at the counter. "Who's the lucky man, Ila?" he asked at seeing the wedding invitations.

Smiling demurely, Ila said, "Did I forget to tell you, darling? I decided to have a spring wedding, so we should get our invitations out right away."

"But I was looking forward to eloping, sweetheart," Sebastian said.

"Actually, the *extremely* lucky man is sitting right over there with my daughter." Ila gestured toward Meg and Alec, who were perusing a bedroom furniture catalog. Meg giggled and blushed when Alec pointed at something in the catalog and leaned over to whisper in her ear.

Despite his misgivings, Sebastian smiled. "Ah, new love… so sweet."

Alec looked up and saw Sebastian watching them. He tensed, but refused to allow his mistrust of the man to spoil his day. When Frank Doscher entered the store, Alec took hold of Meg's hand and they went over to the crowded counter.

"We just heard." Tavis grinned at Meg. "Congratulations."

"Thank you, Tavis." Meg held her hand up to show off the ring. "What do you think?"

"It's beautiful." Tavis admired the pearl and stepped back for everyone else to see.

"'Bout time." Frank clapped Alec's shoulder. "Let me know when you're ready to get that barn built, Alec."

"I'd love to see the house my daughter *will* be living in," Ila said. Batting her eyelashes at Alec, she asked, "You don't mind giving us all a tour, do you?"

Both Alec and Meg understood Ila's meaning—they wouldn't be living together until after the wedding. More importantly, this was to be the understanding among all the island residents, starting first with Frank.

Meg gave Alec a slight nudge, hoping he would understand her next words. "That's a great idea. It's been weeks since I was last there and I'd like to see it again so I can work out what furniture I should order."

Alec sensed how elated she was to be in cahoots with Ila again. He pulled her close, mostly to vex Ila, but also to enjoy the nearness again before having to hand her back over to her mother until the wedding. "Okay, let's show everyone where I plan to spend my honeymoon."

"Well, look who decided to join the living," Ila said and went over to the newest arrival.

Everyone turned to see Jack contemplate leaving again. "I just came in to get some razors," he said to Kyrie over Ila's shoulder.

"Looks like you should've gotten some days ago." Ila appraised Jack's unkempt appearance. "Not that you care, but the second mare finally foaled."

"I'm sorry, Ila, I've had other things on my mind. How'd it go?"

"It went well," she said, her voice softened. "Have you heard any news about Michelle?"

"Yeah, I just talked to Dr. Patrick before I came in here. He said she's having to stay at the hospital longer than they'd expected because she had an allergic reaction to the antibiotics."

"I'm sure they're taking good care of her. She'll be back before you know it." Ila hooked her arm under his to keep him from leaving. "You look like you could use a change of scenery. We were all about to go see the stone house Meg and Alec are going to live in after the wedding. Why don't you come with us?"

"Wedding?" Jack looked over at Alec and Meg and saw they stood as a couple. He gave Alec a knowing grin and nodded his head in approval. Suddenly, he recognized the term Ila used. "Wait, what stone house?"

"It's old, weird, and mysterious. Want to see it?"

Having heard many times about the unexplained stone structures that seemed to build themselves with the formation of each island the Stone Davis Corporation created, Jack was very interested in seeing it with his own eyes. "Yeah, I do."

~

"Wow, this place is beautiful," Jack said, following everyone inside the house. "A lot nicer than the newcomer houses. Too bad it's so far out from everything."

"That's my favorite part," Alec said.

"It's a fine house," Sebastian said. "Looks like you've put a lot of hard work into it, Alec."

"Yep," Alec said.

"What's back there?" Ila peered down the hallway.

"It's a sunroom. Come on, I'll show you." Alec led Ila around the staircase, and Frank, Tavis, and Sebastian fell in line behind them.

Jack's attention was focused on the strange faded carvings on the front room floor. Meg went to him, frowning, thinking he might know what they were and why they were there—hoping he'd have an explanation for why they seemed so familiar to her. When their eyes met, she knew he had no more understanding of them than she had, but it was obvious they had the same effect on him.

He scanned the rectangular border once more and shrugged. "You should put a rug there," he muttered and left to join the others.

Alec and Meg showed everyone the entire first floor, all that was left to show was the upstairs bedroom. Neither one of them were keen to extend the tour to that area, knowing the state they'd left it in earlier.

"What's upstairs?" Ila asked.

"Another room," Alec said. There was an awkward moment of silence that filled the space where Alec should be offering to show them the room. When it stretched on forever, he asked, "Would you like to see it?"

"Sure." Ila moved past Alec and Meg to ascend the staircase.

When Ila reached the top, she saw the air mattress, sheets, and clothes—particularly Meg's underwear—strewn about the floor, and panicked at the thought of Frank seeing the tattling mess.

Turning around, Ila said, "Oh, it's not ready to show off yet. It's completely filthy. Dust everywhere. We'll all have to wait until Alec gets it cleaned up." She gave them both a scornful look as she passed them, shooting one to Jack as well at hearing him snicker.

~

Ila, Kyrie, and Meg decided the wedding would take place in three weeks, just enough time for Ila to pull it all together seamlessly if she worked day and night. "But no longer than three weeks, you don't want to be showing at your wedding," Ila had said. When Meg appeared insulted, Ila added, "Like you're not concerned about it, too."

The wedding was to take place at Ila's house, as there was more outdoor space, and since she insisted on it. Meg wanted a small attendance at the ceremony, but as she and Ila sat down with the list of people to invite, the number of attendees grew larger and larger. It wasn't long before half the island population received an invitation.

During a session of counting the RSVPs, Alec noticed one in particular that made him angry. He looked closer at it, making sure he'd read it correctly, and tossed it over to Meg.

"Why'd you invite *him*?"

"Who?" she asked, picking up the RSVP.

"Drake." He sneered. "Why would you invite him to our wedding?"

Meg scanned the invitation and saw that Drake had accepted and would be attending. She looked back at Alec. "I didn't, I guess my mom sent him one. Why do you have a problem with it?"

"Why do you think, Meg?"

"You're being ridiculous!" Seeing the shock on his face at her outburst, Meg lowered her voice. "It's you I'm marrying… I love *you*."

Her words had a soothing effect on him. "You're right. It just surprised me."

Both Meg and Alec flat out refused to wear anything formal at their wedding, but Ila did get them to compromise. Meg agreed to wear one of the white sundresses Kyrie had given her and allowed Ila to have her fun selecting a maid-of-honor dress for Tavis. Alec agreed to wear dress slacks and an oxford shirt with a tie, scoffing at Ila's suggestion of a bowtie.

Some of the older ladies got together and made a bridal veil, using pieces from their own wedding gowns to assemble it. When they presented it to Meg, they said it was her *something old*.

With Meg back at Ila's, Alec spent most of his time at the stone house, putting furniture together that started arriving almost daily. Though he was busy, the house felt lonely without Meg.

Frank Doscher got a group together to help Alec with the task of building the barn, and with their hard work, it was built in five days. With the barn complete, and the furniture deliveries slowing to a trickle, Alec began spending more time at Kyrie's. It was Meg he wanted to see, but Ila kept running him off after only an hour long visit, and she never let them be alone. When he told Kyrie about it, she fell into a fit of laughter, making him prefer the solace of his old bedroom.

Chapman Peterson was to officiate the wedding. Before he came to the island, he'd been an ordained minister and as such, performed all the weddings on Gamma. Meg asked Frank to walk her down the aisle, a request he proudly accepted.

Ila had decorated a restored antique horse buggy in the wedding colors, to which she'd rig to one of the horses after the reception for Meg and Alec to ride off in. She'd gotten up before dawn the morning of the wedding to diamond braid the horse's mane, interlacing it with blue silk ribbons.

After finishing the braid, Ila went inside the house to wake Meg up. "Time to get out of bed, it's your wedding day. Would you like some breakfast?"

She'd come to dread discussing the subject of food. Some days, Meg wouldn't eat anything other than bread. Then, for a few days, she'd eat like she always had—with one exception, she hated the smell of food cooking no matter what kind of day she was having, save for the aroma of baking bread. Ila knew exactly what to give Meg for her *something borrowed*, the bread maker.

"Yes, I would. I want scrambled eggs, and buttered toast with strawberry jam, and orange juice sounds good." Meg sat up, wide-eyed with excitement. "Oh, and pears! Do we have any goat cheese?"

Ila grimaced. "Meg, are you sure you want to eat all of that? I don't know if I can handle hearing you retch another day. To be honest with you, I'm almost glad it's Alec's turn to listen to it for a while."

Meg smiled and said, "I feel fantastic, and I'm starving."

~

Kyrie came over after Ila and Meg had finished their breakfast, bringing with her Meg's *something new*. It was a crate housing a Dominique hen sitting on seven eggs, Meg's favorite breed.

"I put them in the stable away from the other hens to keep her calm," Kyrie said to Meg. "I'll put the crate on the back of the buggy before you and Alec leave from the reception."

"Thank you, Kyrie," Meg said, giving her a hug.

When Meg left to shower, Kyrie asked Ila, "How's she been feeling?"

"Don't get me started." Ila groaned. "Thankfully, it seems like she's having a good day. We'll know in a minute if it's not by the sounds of her breakfast being heaved into the toilet."

A few silent minutes later, all they heard was Meg singing in the shower. "I guess it's a good day," Kyrie said. "Where's Tavis? Shouldn't she be here by now?"

"She'll be here around noon. I didn't want her to come over too early in case Meg vomited all morning. Tavis is helping James with the food and drinks at the reception, so I didn't want to risk disgusting her."

For the next few hours, Kyrie and Ila readied the front lawn for the wedding ceremony. While they were setting up the table for the reception, Sebastian pulled into the driveway to drop Tavis off. She went to Ila. "My father wanted me to tell you not to worry about Jack, he'll help taxi the elders and usher at the wedding."

"Good." Ila sighed her relief. She eyed the small white box wrapped in metallic blue paper that Tavis carried. "What's that?"

Tavis glanced at Kyrie, then said, "It's Meg's *something blue*."

"Oh, Meg's in her bedroom. Go inside and give it to her," Ila said. "See if you can do something with her hair while you're in there."

Meg opened the box while Tavis brushed her hair. "Oh, Tavis!" Their eyes met in the cheval mirror. "I didn't know you had it in you." She lifted the blue garter belt and skimpy slip of a silk nightgown from the box. "It's beautiful, I'm sure Alec will love it."

Tavis shook off the unexpected awkwardness at imagining her brother enjoying the gift. "Well, Kyrie helped me."

"She's great, isn't she?"

"Yeah." Preferring to change the subject, Tavis asked, "I'm curious, have you seen the dress your mother picked out for me to wear?"

"Nope. She's hiding it from me, too. So, I want to apologize now if it turns out to be hideous."

A breeze blew through Meg's open window, billowing the curtains and knocking over the bridal bouquet of roses interspersed with edelweiss from the dresser.

"Want me to close the window?" Tavis asked.

"No." Meg took the brush from Tavis' hand. "You should go see if Ila's ready for you to get dressed now."

Assuming Meg wanted to be alone for a while, Tavis left, even though it was too early to get dressed. Later, when the afternoon began to bow to the approaching evening, Ila opened the bedroom door and smiled at Meg, who still sat in the chair in front of the cheval mirror where Tavis had left her.

"Tavis did a wonderful job on your hair," Ila said, shutting the door behind her. "I fixed hers in a French knot after she got dressed. She looks stunning, by the way. Are you okay? You look a million miles away. You're not feeling sick, are you?"

"I'm fine." Meg looked over at her window. "Can you shut the window?" Her eyes drifted over every aspect of what defined her bedroom. "It's time to close it now."

Ila helped Meg get the dress and veil on, then wasted time smoothing out perceived imperfections. "Well, this is it. All of the guests are here, even the old biddies that Frank, Jack, and Sebastian chauffeured in. Are you ready? You can always change your mind, you know."

"Mom."

"I just want you to be happy."

"Alec makes me happy."

"He better." Ila hugged Meg. "Frank will come for you when the ceremony starts."

Just as Ila reached the bedroom door, Meg said, "I love you, Mom."

"I love you, too, Meg."

Ila returned to the front room to find Sebastian hovering over Tavis, trying to cover her back with the cardigan sweater he'd plucked off of Kyrie's shoulders. Tavis appeared mortified by his behavior, looking around to see who all bore witness to it.

It was all Ila could do to contain her anger, and failed to keep it out of her voice. "What the hell is wrong with you?" she shouted at Sebastian and marched over to Tavis, snatching the sweater off her back.

She wedged herself between them and appraised the dress she'd personally selected for Tavis to wear. Ila was pleased with the results, finding the blue satin evening dress complemented her form beautifully. She turned Tavis around and discovered what was undoubtedly causing Sebastian so much stress.

The back of the dress was devoid of fabric, except for two wispy thin straps crisscrossing Tavis' upper back. Her entire back was exposed, all the way down to the lowest point of her waistline, and the dress was loose enough to provide a peek-a-boo showing of the sides of her waist. The bottom half of the dress billowed midway down the front of her thighs, with a longer train gracefully falling down the backs of her long legs. With her hair up off her slender neck, Tavis looked regal and statuesque.

"Is that what's bothering you? A back?" Ila blasted at Sebastian, hoping to shame him.

He was almost scared to answer her. "Well, there *is* a lot of it showing."

"Really? And everyone thinks I'm bad about Meg." Ila narrowed her eyes, daring him to argue with her. "In case you haven't noticed, Tavis is a woman, not a little girl. Now, if you'd tell Frank to get the ceremony started, I'd be very grateful." With that, she dismissed him.

Sebastian looked at Tavis' exposed back one more time before giving up and going outside to find Frank. When he was gone, Ila turned to Tavis. "Are you okay with the dress? You look gorgeous, but if you're not comfortable, Kyrie and I will help you find something else."

"Ila's right, you do look amazing." Kyrie came over to Tavis and put an arm around her shoulder. "Do you like it? I'll rummage through every closet in this house if you don't."

Tavis smiled and whispered, "Actually, I love it."

"Perfect." Ila felt victorious that the unforeseen dress issue was resolved. "Let's get this wedding started, shall we?"

~

With the wedding music playing in the background, Frank escorted Meg down the aisle to Alec. He was so happy to see her again, as Ila had refused to let him visit Meg for over three days, insisting it would make the moment of their nuptials more special—especially for the photographs.

When the ceremony ended, the reception went into full swing. Glasses of wine and champagne were poured and passed around. Ila planned the music for the evening. Most of it was lively for energetic dancing, but every so often some classical or haunting melody played, giving couples an excuse to dance closer together.

"You've been very busy lately," Sebastian said to Ila an hour into the reception.

"Yes, I have, but it has been kind of fun." She grinned at him. "Do you forgive me for the dress?"

Sebastian chuckled. "Yes, and I'm sorry for making a scene on your daughter's wedding day. Are you happy for Meg?"

"As long as Meg's happy, then I'm happy," she said after a thoughtful moment.

"Well-spoken," he said, amused. "May I congratulate the mother of the bride?" Sebastian set his wine glass down and held his arms wide for a hug.

Ila laughed and allowed him to fold his arms around her. Within seconds, Sebastian's body tensed and she backed away. "Is something wrong?"

"No. It's just that you smell quite wonderful. Are you wearing perfume?" It was the first idea that came to mind for him.

"I am, you like it?"

"You should wear it always, it suits you. I should probably congratulate the mother of the groom. Make sure you save a dance for me," he said and hurried away.

He went to the back of the crowd and leaned against a tree, watching everyone enjoy themselves. A glance at Tavis dancing with yet another fellow he couldn't put a name to, forced a reluctant acceptance on him he'd rather not have to think about at the moment. Instead, Sebastian considered what he'd just discovered in Ila's mind while hugging her.

What he found was a wall he was all too familiar with. There were vague and blurry images of Meg as a baby, leading into clearer images of Meg growing up. The most pristine of Ila's memories were the recent ones of her anger, then her resolution to be happy for Meg and Alec. Yet, so many of her memories were broken fragments, riddled with numerous gaping holes as if much of her history had been rewritten—possibly altered.

It was the messiest accumulation of memories, and lack of, he'd ever encountered. There was no denying it; someone, or maybe more than just one person, had altered Ila's memories in great detail. It seemed to him that most of it happened long ago, as he would've known any recent absorption of thoughts and memories. More troubling was the signature of embedded false memories, which could only create a time-line that didn't truly exist.

But why, and for what purpose? Sebastian wondered, he couldn't fathom why someone would do that to Ila.

"You look deep in thought," Kyrie said.

He snapped out of his reverie and focused on Kyrie. The outdoor torches cast a glow around her and he found her captivating—native and alluring in the sense that the island was made with her in mind. Part of him wanted to drag her away and see what became of his increasing desires for her.

He brushed the notion aside. "You caught me. I was just thinking about how I'll feel when Tavis weds. I worry I won't handle it well."

"You'll do fine, and so will she… as long as you're not the one picking out her clothes." Though teasing, Kyrie's eyes were on him, watching him, studying him acutely.

He found it rather curious.

"I've forgotten my manners. I haven't congratulated the mother of the groom yet," Sebastian said, holding wide his arms as he'd done with Ila.

"Thank you, I'm very happy for my son," Kyrie said, avoiding his attempt at physical contact by stepping to his side to watch the crowd. "Lovely evening, isn't it?"

"Indeed, it is." Sebastian smiled and brought his empty arms back to his sides. "You look beautiful tonight, but then again, you always do."

"You don't look so bad yourself, Sebastian." Kyrie looked up at him. "But, then again, you probably already know that." Her gaze drifted back to the crowd and she pointed. "I'm glad you convinced Jack to get out of that house."

He searched the sea of faces and found Jack sitting alone at a table, watching Tavis. She was dancing with James now, the only man whose name Sebastian knew as James called often to invite Tavis to some gathering or another. The expression on Jack's face was pure and simple jealousy, an easy and ancient emotion to detect. His angry scowl was directed at James, who'd put his arms around Tavis' waist to pull her closer. Sebastian found it both odd and entertaining.

~

The music stopped and Tavis reminded James of their hosting duties. "There's a line of people waiting for you to get their drinks." She nodded toward the bar table.

James glanced at the swaying line of people waiting for the bartender to return. "Looks like most of them need coffee." He shook his head and went back to his post.

Tavis surveyed the refreshments table, finding the plate of finger sandwiches depleted, save one that had a bite missing from it. Once inside the kitchen, Tavis took her time searching for a clean platter, enjoying the quiet stillness. She opened the refrigerator and found the container of pre-made sandwiches—nearly jumping out of her skin when she shut the door and there stood a man just on the other side.

"You're almost out of punch, too," he said, smiling at her.

She looked at the near empty punch bowl he carried. "I should wash it first."

"I'll help you."

While he stood at the counter, arranging sandwiches on the plate, Tavis studied the man she was sure she hadn't seen all evening.

"I'm a friend of the bride," he said aloud, as though aware of her thoughts. "My name's Drake, I live in the mountain region."

Her eyes evaluated him with more savvy intent when he turned to look at her. His expression was friendly, and somewhat studious. If ever a man could be called beautiful, Drake's face would certainly claim that title. The shape of his eyebrows gave him an almost elfin appearance, his nose was thin and narrow, ending in a button tip. Below it, were a set of plump cupid lips placed elegantly over a whisper of a cleft chin.

His entire face was framed in chestnut curly hair that looked so soft, Tavis had to fight the urge to reach out her hand to touch it. She became more aware of his height and realized he was somehow closer than when she'd first begun her appraisal of him.

He lifted his hand and traced a gentle line along her jaw with his forefinger. "And you're Tavis," he said softly. "An Abbott through and through… classic Abbott lines."

A crease formed on her forehead.

"Hmm, even your frown forms perfect lines," he said. "I've noticed how jealous your dancing with James is making someone else."

"Who?"

"Jack Cavanaugh." Drake tugged a wisp of Tavis' hair to settle it against the jaw he had traced. "In fact, he's sitting at a table right now, staring at the kitchen window and hating how I'm standing so close to you."

"He's with Michelle."

"Michelle's not coming back, she chose money over love, not that she ever really loved him."

"How do you know that?"

"Have Sebastian introduce himself to Dr. Patrick." Drake shrugged. "A simple handshake ought to help your father discover the lie."

Tavis looked into Drake's eyes with more purpose, leaning closer to see a myriad of colors swirling gently. Her eyes widened at the discovery. "I know who you are," she said, her voice almost a gasp. "Why are you here?"

"Yes, Tavis, you know who I am." Drake gave a light tap of his finger to her temple. "And, now I'm gonna have to take that part away, but I insist you keep the rest."

Her eyelids fluttered closed and when they reopened, she found James asking her if she needed help carrying the punch bowl. "What?" she asked, shaking her head to clear her thoughts.

James grinned. "Have you been sipping on that punch?"

She laughed. "No, but I feel like I need to."

"Come on, everyone has fresh drinks and I want to dance with you again."

~

After several more rounds of dancing with James, Tavis declared she was done for the night as the shoes Ila picked out to go with the dress were killing her. James led her back to the table and sat in front of her. He leaned over and removed her shoes, putting her bare feet in his lap.

"Better?" he asked.

"Much better." Tavis sighed, thinking weddings here were far too exhausting.

"So, I hear Ila has new horses. Have you seen them?"

"Yes, and they're so adorable. She keeps them in the barn away from the rest of the horses. Would you like to see them?"

A wicked smile formed on James' face. "Why do you think I asked about them?"

They walked slowly to the barn, since Tavis refused to put the wretched heels back on. Inside the barn, Tavis turned on only one of the lamps so as not to disturb the roosting hens and led James to the back where the two foals were.

She leaned over the enclosure and pointed to the grey dappled foal. "That one's my favorite."

"Yeah, I like her, too."

Tavis turned to him when his fingers brushed against her bare shoulder and traced a delicate line down her arm. When his hand went to her bare waist, he pivoted his body and took a step closer to her. James stared into her eyes for a moment; then, so fast it almost made her dizzy, encapsulated her in his embrace in one sweeping motion.

His lips were on hers in a flash. At first, Tavis' instinct was to struggle, as she wasn't in the habit of letting just anyone handle her in such a way. Yet, something else prevented it, a longing to learn more stopped her. Even when his hands flattened against her back to pull her closer to his body, and though the intoxicating experience lacked something more perfect, Tavis felt powerless to stop him.

Just when Tavis thought she'd give him anything he wanted of her, a voice boomed from somewhere near the barn door, forcing them apart. "What's going on in here?"

They turned and found Jack looming in the doorway, a recognizable rage flashing in his eyes. He advanced toward James and for a second, Tavis thought Jack meant to hit him. Instead, he positioned himself between them and stared hard at James.

"Guests are thirsty. Ila's been looking for you," Jack said, his tone menacing. "You know how testy she can be. Shall I go out there and tell her I found you, or do you want to go back to doing your job like a good little boy?"

James backed away from Jack, but looked around him to speak to Tavis. "I'll see you out there?"

"I'll be out soon," she said.

Jack faced Tavis once James was gone. "What the hell was that about?"

"What?" she shouted, annoyed by his ill-placed anger.

"Forgot already? I'm sure he'd be disappointed. You should join the rest, Alec and Meg are about to leave. Or did you forget why you're here as well? Nothing better than a good romp in a barn, huh?"

Tavis frowned at his harshness and turned to leave, wanting to escape his unchecked temper. She'd only taken two steps when he grabbed her wrist and spun her around. He cupped her face in his hands and kissed her before she could say a word. Different than James' kiss, her body responded instantly, as it had done the first time Jack kissed her.

His hands left her face and groped at her dress, searching for the hemline. At the contact of his hands brushing against her thighs, she moaned, further driving his passion. He hitched her leg up, wrapping it around him so he could feel her body even closer. Tavis' fingers found Jack's belt and unbuckled it while his hands made contact with her hips. It was the sound of his zipper and a voice from nearby that froze Jack. He pulled away from Tavis, trying not to look at her, fearing the sight of her would make him ignore Ila's call for everyone's attention.

As he headed to the barn door, he straightened his clothes. Before walking out, with his back still to her, he said, "I'm sorry, Tavis. I want you so much, it's killing me."

When he left, Tavis inhaled deeply, taking a moment to gather her wits and conceal her thoughts before rejoining the reception. She smoothed out her dress from all the groping she'd been subjected to, deciding to do her best to prevent it from happening again. Lifting her chin, Tavis marched out of the barn, allowing herself to dump the memories on the barn floor behind her as she left.

Still, there was one memory she clung to and Tavis made it her mission to introduce her father to Dr. Patrick. Just as they shook hands, she brought up the subject of Michelle. "Will she be back soon?"

"I'm sure it won't be long, my dear," Dr. Patrick lied.

Tavis watched her father's handshake linger a moment longer, then saw his face contort from a false tolerance of the man to one of deep loathing.

"We should see the bride and groom off," Sebastian said, leading Tavis away from Dr. Patrick.

Everyone gathered near the horse and buggy where Meg and Alec stood, forming a line to congratulate and wish them well. When it was Sebastian's turn, he took one of Meg's hands and brought it to his lips. "Congratulations on your marriage. Alec's a fine young man," he said with a smile and bowed.

"Thank you, Sebastian."

He leaned closer to kiss her cheek while Alec glared at him. Just when Sebastian's face made contact with Meg's, he caught a familiar fragrance coming from her, not unlike flowers and it reminded him of Chaza. He looked down at the bouquet in her hand and smiled at seeing the edelweiss and roses.

"My favorites," he said to her and as he went to pluck a petal from one of the roses, his hand brushed against her abdomen. He detected a truth he knew well. *She's pregnant*, he thought to himself. There was more he wanted to learn, but he sensed Alec's growing impatience, so he passed Meg off to the next in line of well-wishers.

Sebastian shook Alec's hand; both of them reluctant to do it, but each for different reasons. There was a small current that passed between them at the contact. Unlike Alec, Sebastian understood the nature of it. Rather than sort it out, Alec chose not to think about it, or Sebastian for that matter—all he wanted was to take Meg home.

"Make every second with Meg a cherished one, Alec," Sebastian said after releasing his hand. "Make those seconds last a lifetime."

Alec hadn't expected the sentiment from Sebastian. "Thank you," was all he could say.

Tavis motioned for Sebastian to join her near the front of the buggy and as he came over, he saw a familiar figure standing among the trees on the other side of the lane abutting Ila's property. Chaza smiled at him before cloaking herself and disappearing into the forest. He found it puzzling that she'd be here, but then he remembered having first detected her presence at the stone house. It made him wonder if Tavis had been right to question whether Chaza's hiding on Gamma had something to do with Alec.

"Pay attention." Tavis interrupted his thoughts. "They're about to do that weird ritual I was telling you about."

Sebastian looked in time to see Meg toss her bouquet up and over her shoulder. It soared through the air over the crowd, heading directly toward them and Tavis reached up to grab it just before it smacked Sebastian's face.

Alec pushed the bottom of Meg's dress up to her thighs and pulled the blue garter belt down to her ankle, sliding it off her foot while she giggled. He postured as if it were a bow and arrow and sent it sailing through the air. The crowd laughed and cheered when it landed on top of Jack's head. Even Jack chuckled as he pulled it off and tucked it in his pocket. Instead of rice, everyone threw rose petals at the couple while they climbed up into the buggy.

"She's pregnant," Sebastian whispered to Tavis as Meg and Alec drove away. She looked at him as though worried, but not surprised. "You knew?"

"Yes, I did. That was another part of the confrontation between Ila and Kyrie I overheard that morning. I didn't tell you because I was afraid you might... I don't know..." Tavis' words faltered along with her meaning, but he knew full well what she meant to say.

"Tavis!" Sebastian chastised, disbelieving she'd think him capable. "I would never do such a thing."

"But you keep wavering on how you feel about Meg, and you've seen for yourself how important she is to Alec. They chose each other and that's a lifelong bond. Have you considered what will happen if you try to tear them apart?"

"I've thought of little else lately, and now I have something new to consider, something I had least expected when we came here." His whispered voice became agitated. "On top of all that, I find Chaza, too. Not only hiding on this island, but lurking over in the trees just now."

Her eyes darted to every tree in the vicinity, searching for Chaza, but found no trace of the woman she'd spent her whole life thinking of as her mother. "Why would she want to see Alec and Meg's wedding?"

"I don't know, but I intend to find out."

9

Ante Finem

Alec and Meg pulled the horse and buggy up in front of their home, but weren't in any great hurry to get out. The night sky was cloudless and the stars shone bright and wondrous. A soft breeze blew in over the incoming waves of the vast Atlantic Ocean, bringing with it the delicate sounds of whispering that Meg occasionally heard.

It was an odd thing with the whispers: Sometimes they came from the island; other times from off the ocean… and could be from anywhere on Earth.

"Do you ever hear them?" she asked.

Not sure she meant what he thought, Alec looked at her, but her gaze remained on the stars above. "Hear what?" he asked.

"The voices in the wind."

"Yeah. I didn't know you could hear them, too, though." Alec took her hand and interlaced their fingers. "What do you hear?"

"I dreamt once that they were the voices of the dead."

"That's kinda morbid."

"What do you hear?" she asked.

"I've always liked to think of them as the voices of the living." Alec thought about his answer for a moment, then amended it. "More like those not living yet."

"I like that idea better than mine."

Meg turned her attention to the stone house. Not having seen it in three weeks, she smiled at the changes that had taken place in her absence. The house was lit up with warm lamplight and she could just make out some of the furniture through the front room's windows. Meg had no doubt Kyrie and Ila were responsible for the arrangement.

Directly in front of them stood the most noticeable difference. The barn seemed to beckon her to corral the horse and hen inside so she could start her new life. "Come on, let's get this horse and bird in the barn. I want to see our house."

Alec got out of the buggy and released it from the horse while Meg picked up the crate housing the hen, following behind him through the barn door. She was thrilled to find a proper coop and though it took several minutes of wrestling with the hen, Meg finally convinced her to resume sitting on the eggs in one of the nest boxes.

"That's a good girl, *Antony*," Alec said, petting the horse's muzzle after filling the water trough.

"Oh, shut up. I was five when I named her."

They left the barn and when Alec opened the front door, he turned around to block Meg from entering.

She looked at him, confused. "What are you doing?"

"No arguments, I'm gonna carry you over the threshold."

"Forget about it."

She tried to duck under his arms, but he swooped her up before she could get past him.

"I said no arguments," he said when setting her back down in the front room.

"Show me around."

Alec went to the windows to draw the drapes, explaining that their moms took over the task of installing them. "I couldn't figure them out and I was about to nail them to the wall."

He led her from room to room on the first floor, showing her all the furniture that had arrived by special order and which ones were given as gifts from the islanders. The front room and kitchen were completely furnished, but the two spare bedrooms only had rugs.

The walls were covered in framed paintings, some of which were quite good, causing Meg to study them. She knew which ones Kyrie had selected over the ones her mother had, but one was especially difficult to figure out. It was a swirling mass of flowers in an open field, surrounded by distant trees of enormous size, bigger than any tree on Gamma. Yet, it was the flowers that captivated her—every color imaginable with a hint of some that eluded her.

"Tavis and Sebastian ordered that for you," Alec said.

"I like it."

"Want to see upstairs?"

"Not if you're planning to carry me up there."

"I promise, I won't carry you," he said. "Besides, that's a lot of stairs."

"Hey!" Meg pushed him away.

"I'm teasing you." He caught her before she walked away. "You know very well I'd carry you up those stairs. I'm considering dragging you up there if you keep staring at the paintings for much longer."

They ascended the stairs and Meg was amazed at the transformation. The huge canopied bed took up a third of the room, ivory crocheted netting graced the arches above it. Against one wall stood an armoire that matched the wood of the bed and a dresser flanked the opposite wall.

"This room is mostly finished," Alec said. "There're a few more pieces on the way, the cheval mirror, nightstands, and Ila insisted you have a vanity. So, what do you think?"

"It's wonderful, I love it."

Again Meg was swooped up into Alec's arms. "I said I wouldn't carry you up the stairs, but I am carrying you to that bed. You have no idea how much I've missed you."

Alec laid her on the bed and loosened his tie, flinging it across the room. He slipped Meg's shoes off her feet and kicked his own off before lying down beside her, happy she was back in their home again.

"I think I have a pretty good idea." Meg giggled. "My mom's not here to chase you away, either."

"I'll chuck her out the window if she dares."

He was content for a while just looking at her. A question plagued his thoughts, but he didn't want her to get angry at him for bringing it up. He toyed with the top button of her dress while he contemplated whether or not he should ask.

Seeing his distraction, she put her hand over his to stop his fidgeting. "What are you thinking about?"

"I saw him whisper something to you during the reception," Alec said, shrugging, embarrassed for asking. "What did he say to you?"

"Who are you talking about?"

Alec sighed. "Drake."

"Oh." Meg recalled Drake leaning in closer and whispering something to her. The words were muffled among the din of people talking and the music playing. She concentrated to hear the whisper again, '*...she forgives when she asks to be forgiven.*' But that didn't make any sense, so she said, "He couldn't stay for the rest of the reception, that's why he left early. It was hard to hear him over the music, but I think he was wishing us well since he wouldn't be there to see us off at the end with everyone else. Please tell me you're not still worried about Drake."

"No, of course not," he mumbled and saw her frowning doubt at him. "I'm sorry, Meg. I don't know what it is about him that makes me act like a jealous idiot."

"Because he's good-looking and mysterious?" She risked at joking and laughed when he scowled. "What are you worried about? You're not exactly a dog, you know."

He shied a little. "You really think I'm handsome?"

"Well, Alec, I haven't been chasing after you all my life because of your charming personality. And your dimples are ridiculously distracting."

"I'll take the compliment and ignore the insult." He smiled, flashing said dimples, and tickled her until she pushed his hands away. "Speaking of jealousy, did you notice how grumpy Jack was all night?"

"I sure did. I was beginning to worry about James' safety." She raised an eyebrow. "I think Jack's hot for Tavis. And if I'm right about my suspicions, I think Tavis feels the same way about him."

"Then I feel sorry for Michelle if she ever comes back."

"You don't think she's coming back?"

"Nah, she acted like she hated it here. I say good riddance, I didn't really like her either."

Meg snorted. "You don't like anyone."

"Hush." Alec leaned in for a kiss. "Let's not talk about them anymore."

"I agree, but I want to ask you something else."

She sounded somewhat sad, and it was all he could do not to invade her thoughts to find its source. It had been bothering him more and more, bypassing her willingness and knowledge to see her thoughts—it felt awkward and there were times it seemed she was aware of it.

"What's wrong?" he asked instead.

"I know you were kind of… *encouraged* to get married. You were always so protective of me, and I came to think that you'd never want me as anything more than a friend. I guess what I'm trying to ask you is, do you regret marrying me?"

"I don't know yet, we haven't been married very long."

"I'm being serious, Alec. Do you think you'll ever regret it?"

"No, Meg, I don't regret a single thing. You know how protective I am and that's never gonna change, *I'm* never gonna change. It's who I am and I feel like you accept that part of me. I'll never regret marrying you, no matter what."

"Okay." A relieved smile formed on her face. "I trust you, I always have."

"Can we do the wedding night thing now?" he asked, tickling her again until she giggled.

His hand returned to the buttons, unfastening them while holding her gaze. When he reached the last one, he pushed the dress aside and looked down at the blue lingerie.

"It was my something-blue gift," Meg explained.

"It's nice, but I think it'll look better on the floor."

While he took his time undressing her, Meg studied his expression and determined he really was happy. "I love you, husband," she said softly.

"I love you, too, wife."

~

Alec was off for a week from the general store following the wedding. He and Meg spent most of their honeymoon upstairs, leaving the bedroom long enough to eat and take an occasional walk along Alaret Beach.

Ila gave up on them bringing the horse back to her, so she went to their house to retrieve Antony herself on the third day. Making as much noise as she could without being too obvious about it, Ila squashed the idea that either of them were going to come out to greet her. She quietly retrieved the horse and buggy, blocking out the images of what could be keeping Meg from at least saying hello.

On Alec's first day back to work, Meg looked around at the clutter that had accumulated from a week's worth of caring for nothing else but wrapping her legs around Alec. She spent the first half of the day tidying up the house and devoted the afternoon to where she really preferred to be—outside, creating color with flowers. Meg wanted a great big garden and decided to try duplicating the colors in the painting Sebastian and Tavis had given her.

As Meg fussed and fawned over which flowers to plant next, Chaza watched her from the forest that edged the stone house. She laughed at times, seeing Meg change her mind about a particular arrangement, starting all over again before committing to planting them in the flower beds.

Chaza made the impulsive decision to uncloak herself, and waited to see what would happen should Meg look in her direction. Having watched Meg and Alec work tirelessly to turn a dilapidated hovel into a home, Chaza grew fond of hearing them quarrel over differing opinions of what should go where, what color to paint the front room, or how big the barn should be. Chaza came to accept that Meg was no longer a baby, no longer a little girl, or an adolescent teenager, but a beautiful woman who wanted to make her own life.

Meg stood, assessing the look of the flowers to see how their colors blended with the rest. She was about to kneel again to pluck away a stray weed when she caught sight of a woman standing near the trees. For a moment, Meg thought her familiar, but was sure she'd never seen her before. After removing the garden gloves, she went over to the woman.

Until now, Meg thought Kyrie was the most beautiful woman on Gamma. But the stranger standing before her was undeniably exquisite in her own way—a foreign and timeless elegance. She looked more like a painting, perhaps even a sculpture, than a real woman to Meg. Her hair was an iridescent black, much like the feathers on the migrating ravens who visited the island. Sunlight showed the barest hint of reds one moment, then blues the next, among her long flowing tresses.

The complexion of her skin was so flawless, so like ivory, that Meg almost wanted to touch it to see if the woman was real. The emerald green of the woman's eyes was mesmerizing, pulling you into a place worth getting lost in.

Sudden awareness that she was gawking dawned on Meg. She recalled her manners and extended her hand to greet the woman.

"Hello. I don't believe I know you. I'm Meg."

Chaza shook Meg's hand. "It's nice to meet you, Meg. I'm Chaza." The emotions of having her first conversation with her daughter formed a painful lump in her throat. "I was just out for a walk and saw you working on your garden. Looks like it's coming together quite well."

"Thank you." Meg smiled. "Would you like to come inside, maybe have some tea? I was just about to take a break anyway."

It was still early afternoon and Chaza figured it would be a few more hours before Alec returned. "I'd love to."

After a small tour of the first floor, Meg led Chaza to the kitchen, inviting her to sit at the table while she prepared the tea. "Are you a newcomer? I don't recall ever seeing you before."

"I've been here for a long time. I live in a remote part of the island," Chaza said.

Meg assumed she meant the mountain region and didn't question her further. She set the teapot on the table and asked, "Do you need milk and sugar?"

"Yes, please."

Upon opening the refrigerator, the smell of leftovers greeted Meg and her stomach lurched. She grabbed the milk and slammed the door shut, snagging the sugar bowl off the counter on her way back to the table.

"You look pale. Are you all right?" Chaza asked.

"I'm fine, just tired," Meg's nostrils flared and she held her breath in the attempt to quell the surging bout of nausea.

"This is a lovely home you have."

"My husband and I fixed it up together. We just got married a week ago."

"No wonder you're tired." Chaza saw Meg blushing, so she clarified: "I meant fixing the house up yourself would make you tired, but I suppose being a newlywed could make anyone tired as well."

Meg laughed at the misunderstanding. "My husband's name is Alec. He went back to work today. He works at the general store with his mother."

"I'm familiar with the store, and Kyrie." Chaza set the teaspoon down and took a sip. "So, this is your first day alone in your new house. How do you like it?"

"It was weird at first, but then I liked how quiet it was. That lasted an hour before the messiness in here started getting loud, so I shut it up by cleaning it up." Meg grinned. "I probably wouldn't have invited you in if I'd seen you earlier this morning, that's how horrible the house looked. After that, I went outside to work on my flower garden. To answer your question, it was nice having the house to myself, even though I'll be glad when Alec gets back."

"Well, Meg, you've got it all figured out and you're wise beyond your years. You sound happy."

"I am happy. How about you, are you married?"

"Yes, but we're separated. Sometimes it's not so figured out." Preferring to change the subject, Chaza returned the conversation back to the garden. "I noticed you didn't have anything blue in your flower beds."

"You're right," Meg said, recalling the layout of her flowers. "I don't, do I? I'll have to order some."

"If you'll allow me, I'd like to bring you some. I know where some are growing wild and neglected. They're not meant to grow that way, they need attention and care."

"You're sure you don't mind?"

"Consider it my housewarming gift to you and your husband."

"I'll look forward to them, thank you."

"I should be going before it gets much later." Chaza took her teacup to the sink. "Thank you for your hospitality."

"I enjoyed the company. Come by anytime." Meg stood to walk Chaza to the front room, but had to grab the table to steady the dizziness and fight back the nausea.

Worry forced Chaza to her. "What's wrong? You don't look well at all."

"I stood up too fast." Meg tried to smile. "I'm so sorry... I'm gonna be sick."

Aside from the initial handshake, Chaza had meant to avoid touching Meg, but it became unavoidable as she rushed her to the downstairs bathroom. Meg heaved into the toilet while Chaza held back the mass of curls, rubbing and patting Meg's back occasionally until it was over.

Chaza flushed the toilet discreetly and handed Meg a glass of water, which Meg refused at first.

"You don't drink it, just rinse and spit."

Meg did as she was told, then looked at Chaza with an apologetic expression. "I need to lie down."

"I agree. Come on, that big fluffy sofa in the front room looked perfect for messing up again."

"I'm so embarrassed," Meg said once Chaza helped her to the couch. "I bet I'll never see you again this side of Alaret Beach."

"I doubt that," she said in a soft voice, holding Meg's wrist until she was fully sedated.

Chaza continued to kneel by the couch, even after Meg slept peacefully, smiling at the childlike quality of her slumber. "I think you're the only thing I've ever gotten right," Chaza said as she reached over to grab the blanket, draping it over Meg and tucking it under her chin. The stolen moment of being able to take care of her was wonderful.

Though she already suspected what caused Meg to fall ill, Chaza couldn't resist the temptation to find out for sure. "Meg?" she tested.

At no response, Chaza slipped her hand under the blanket and flattened her palm against Meg's abdomen. As if the small rounding wasn't proof enough, she continued and was amazed by the sound of a second heartbeat. It was strong, close to surpassing Meg's.

What if she isn't strong enough? Chaza wondered, but dismissed the thought, reminding herself that Meg's strength could be restored. She closed her eyes and concentrated, unable to let go of one question. After a few minutes, Chaza's smile broadened.

"Ah, you'll feel his kicking soon enough. Get your rest, sweetheart, you'll need it with this one." Chaza removed her hand and leaned over to place a kiss on Meg's forehead. "I love you," she said and saw herself out.

~

"Want any more bread?" Alec called from the kitchen later that evening.

"No," Meg answered from the couch.

Alec came into the front room to join her, exhausted by delivering a week's worth of orders in one day. "Did you miss me today?"

"Not a bit."

"Not even a smidge?" Alec mock-pouted until she giggled at him.

"Okay, maybe a smidge. I did meet someone today, though. A woman I've never met before, she said her name was Chaza."

"You've never seen her before?"

"No, she said she lived in a remote area. I assume she meant the mountains."

Though suspicious, Alec conceded it was possible for a person not to have met everyone on the island. There were many people in the mountains and some of them kept to themselves—it was a big island. What bothered him was the coincidence that someone new came along the first time Meg was alone all day.

"Chaza," Alec said, testing the name. "That's kind of unusual."

Meg knew the look on Alec's face all too well. "Don't you start that."

"What?"

"Your suspicions. Chaza was a very nice woman. I was working on my garden when I saw her, she even pointed out that I hadn't anything blue planted yet and offered to bring me some as a gift to us. I graciously accepted, because *I* have manners." Meg glared at him. "Oh, and by the way, I invited her in to have tea with me and guess what? Nothing horrible happened. I like her very much and I'm looking forward to her visiting again."

"Did she mention when she'd bring the flowers?"

"No, Alec. I'm sure she doesn't plan to bring them tonight if that's what you're worried about."

"I'm not worried, I'd just prefer to be here. You know I'd feel better about it if I met her for myself."

"I know," she said, sounding grumpy. "I have no idea when she plans to bring them. If she shows up while you're out, I'm not gonna be rude and decline her gift, but I'll mention I'd like for her to meet you. Okay?"

"Okay." Though still unsure of the situation, he dropped the matter since Meg seemed so irritated.

Alec looked at her to see if she had anything more to say on the subject before he moved on from it entirely. Her eyes widened and she pushed the blanket away from her lap, covering her mouth before sprinting down the hallway.

"Meg? What's wrong?" Alec followed after her.

"Go away," she muttered through her fingers, her voice low and sickly awful.

"No, I won't!"

Arguing with him was impossible, making it to the bathroom in time held more importance. While she emptied the contents of her stomach into the toilet, Alec stood sentinel behind her and held her hair back. After flushing the toilet, Meg sat on the side of the tub. Alec sat beside her and waited for her to be able to talk again.

"I feel better now," she said, but felt like she needed to rinse her mouth.

Sensing it, Alec got up and poured her a cup of water from the sink. She took it, swished several mouthfuls and spit into the toilet, sending the lot with a final flush.

"You were sick the other day, too," Alec said. "Do you think there's something wrong?"

"Yeah, Alec, it's called *pregnant*."

"Oh." He felt woefully inadequate on the subject. "Guess that's normal, huh?"

"For some women." She sighed. "Apparently, I'm one of those women. So, unless you like the sounds and smell, I suggest you go away the next time I give you warning."

"Nope." Alec shook his head, grinning. "I'm half responsible, the least I can do is hold your hair back and pretend not to be grossed out."

Embarrassed all over again, Meg frowned. "I got sick earlier while Chaza was here. She held my hair back, too, and even helped me to the couch. She had to see herself out because I fell asleep. I wouldn't blame her if she never sets foot on Alaret Beach again."

"Don't worry about it. If she did all that for you, then maybe she is a nice person." He took Meg's hand and led her out of the bathroom. "My mom wants you to come with me to the store in the morning so you can start ordering furniture for the nursery. While you're working on that, I'm gonna get a haircut since she insulted me all day."

Meg tugged at his arm when they got to the front room. "Let's go outside and sit under our tree, I need some fresh air."

While they sat under the massive oak tree limbs, looking out at the ocean waves crashing onto Alaret Beach, Meg thought of an idea she'd contemplated several times in her life. "Have you ever thought about getting on one of the sailboats and just keep going?"

"What do you mean?" he asked.

"I mean, just get on a boat." Meg nodded toward the ocean. "Leave this island and never look back."

Again, Alec was surprised by the things he didn't know Meg thought of. "All the time, all my life."

"We could keep sailing until we reach East America," she pondered aloud. "Make a new life and live like the people management sells the horses to."

Alec risked sensing her thoughts and saw the life she imagined. "It's tempting, Meg, but you know what always stopped me from doing it?"

"What?"

"Everyone I care about. My mother… you. We couldn't leave everyone behind and there's no sailboat big enough to take them all with us."

"I know, but it would've been great for a while."

"We'll make it great here, Meg."

~

The next day, Meg selected everything she wanted for the nursery and left it to Kyrie to place the orders in the intervals she thought was best so as not to cause complaints from management.

"What's all this?" Kyrie asked, finding Meg in the art supply aisle with a cart full of paints and brushes.

"I have a project planned for the nursery walls."

"All four walls?"

"Yeah, I know." Meg laughed at Kyrie's doubt. "I need to get started. I want to paint my and Alec's favorite places on the island."

"Then you're gonna be very busy."

While recording the supplies in the inventory log, Kyrie said, "Speaking of busy, your mother has decided to make it her personal duty to drag Jack out of his house and turn him into a stable boy."

"For once, I hope her meddling works." Meg piled the supplies in a box. "Alec mentioned people are starting to gossip about his reclusive behavior."

When Alec and Meg returned home, they noticed a glaring difference. "Chaza brought us our blue flowers. Look at them, Alec!"

"I see them." He hid his frown.

"She was right, it ties everything together, it's perfect. And it's your favorite color… I can't believe I hadn't already thought of it."

In various locations throughout their yard, blue hydrangea bushes were planted. The color lit the flower beds up in a glowing coolness and Meg understood why Chaza suggested the blue to compliment the other flowers.

"She left a note," Alec said, grabbing the slip of paper tucked under the ornate doorknocker. He read it while Meg admired the transformation of her flower beds.

Dear Meg and Alec,

I took the liberty of planting the blue hydrangea bushes in your yard. I hope you don't mind. They're one of my favorite flowers and they bring me renewed hope of a happy future every time they bloom. May their beauty bring as much joy to you as they do for me.

Sincerely,

Chaza

"That was nice of her to do that. I hope I get to meet her soon," Alec said.

The coincidental timing still bothered him. He brought the letter closer and inhaled, but all he could smell was Meg and that also bothered him. He looked around their yard, into the trees surrounding their home, turning around to scan Alaret Beach, searching for an explanation or some reassurance that he worried unnecessarily.

Only the familiar sight of the trees, the ocean, and Meg enjoying the gift from Chaza greeted his eyes. It dawned on him at this very moment that the ever-present and ceaseless need to protect Meg had extended two-fold. He looked back at the letter and read it again. Maybe it was something in the wording, but he had a strange sensation that there was nothing to fear from the writer.

~

"James called again," Sebastian said, startling Tavis.

"What'd you tell him?" she asked when he shut the door.

He sat next to her. "I told him you were busy sitting on the porch staring at Jack's house."

Tavis frowned at him. "I wasn't staring at his house."

"Yes you were, just like you've been doing more often than not lately."

"Did you really say that to James?"

"No, I said you'd already gone to bed." Sebastian peered into her eyes until she turned away to avoid the scrutiny.

"I feel sorry for him, more so after you told me Dr. Patrick was lying to him about Michelle." Tavis glanced over at the house again. "What if he's just sitting in there, waiting and waiting for nothing?"

Sebastian found her curiosity intriguing. He wanted to question it, but thought better of it, feeling he may already know the cause of it. "Though I don't like the way it was handled, I think it's the best thing for Jack that Michelle isn't returning."

"Why?"

"Because he didn't love her. Apparently, she didn't love him either."

"Maybe we should tell him what we know," Tavis said. "Maybe he'll feel better if he knows Michelle's not coming back."

"You know we can't do that. Technically, we shouldn't know it, and it's also none of our business." Sebastian saw her fidgeting, appearing as though she was about to stand. He stopped her with one question: "Am I right about that, Tavis? Is there some reason you would make it your business that I'm unaware of?"

Tavis met his eyes with reticent caution. She detected a similar reserve in his expression and knew it was born of him controlling the instinct to invade her truest thoughts. Not quite sure, certainly not willing to trust her own feelings, she decided to lie. Though she suspected he'd sense the incomplete truth, it was better than trying to explain what she didn't understand herself.

"You're right, it's none of our business." She settled back down in the chair. "Besides, he might report us if he has no reason to stay here anymore."

He experienced an odd disappointment that Tavis didn't try making more of a stand, and it occurred to him the cause was probably his own doing. "Don't worry," he said. "Ila called me earlier and said she's coming over in the morning to put an end to Jack's seclusion. Maybe you should try to help her, befriend him and see what his intentions are when he realizes Michelle's not coming back."

"I'll try, but Jack's thoughts aren't easy to sense." Tavis shrugged. "Most of the time, anyway."

Sebastian felt horrible for tricking Tavis into the admission of having intimate knowledge of Jack's mind. "You'll do fine."

~

Tavis woke up hearing Ila and Sebastian's muffled conversation. She left her bedroom and found them sitting at the dining table, sipping on the tea Ila had brought.

"Good morning, Tavis," Ila greeted at seeing Tavis make her way to the refrigerator.

"Hi, Ila. How are you?"

"I'm doing well, thank you." Ila waited until Tavis finished pouring a glass of orange juice and had brought it to the table to sit with them before continuing. "Your father just informed me that you've never been horseback riding."

Tavis eyed Sebastian. "No, I haven't."

"Well, we're gonna put an end to that travesty today."

"How so?" Tavis asked, still eyeing her father, who was suddenly interested in reading the steeping instructions on the back of the over-priced tea container.

"I have the unfortunate task of gelding an unapproved quarter-horse who's showing signs of..." Ila paused and glanced at Sebastian. "Um, let's just say he's reaching a certain age where he could pose a potential breeding issue that management has decided is unacceptable. Dr. Patrick's meeting me this morning at Mrs. Hamilton's barn to show me how to do it so I can perform the procedure on my own in the future."

The few images Tavis was able to sense of Ila's thoughts were not only disturbing, but had nothing whatsoever to do with riding a horse. "Did you want me to come with you?" she asked, desperately hoping that wasn't what Ila wanted.

Laughing, Ila set Tavis' mind at ease. "No. With everything that's been going on lately, I haven't been able to exercise the mare that recently foaled, and the stallion's getting restless, too. After you get dressed, I want you to come with me to Jack's so I can call in the favor he offered a while back. He can start by working the horses and teaching you how to ride."

"I don't mind trying, but shouldn't you be there if he agrees?"

"Jack knows his way around a stable, I'm not worried." Ila batted her eyelashes primly. "What do you say, won't you help me coax that mule-headed man out of his house?"

She relented. "Okay, I'll go get ready. Just don't get your hopes up, it's not likely he'll answer the door."

"I'll handle it. Just hurry up, sweetie, I really do have to get going."

Tavis got up from the table, looking back over her shoulder at Sebastian as she walked away, but he seemed more interested in talking to Ila than giving her a reassuring thought of approval. It was a different matter altogether when she exited, ready to go, and bumped into him in the hallway. He wanted to say something to her, but kept it to himself as Ila stood impatiently nearby.

"Are you ready?" Ila asked.

Giving her father a curious glance, Tavis stepped around him to join Ila. Sebastian fell in line behind them and stopped her midway to Jack's house. "Tavis, I want to tell you something before you go." Aware that Ila listened, he left it with: "Promise me you'll be careful if Jack agrees to take you horseback riding."

"I will."

"Give your father a hug," he said, opening his arms wide to receive her.

Frowning, Tavis gave up trying to understand what he was up to and went to his open arms. A gentle, euphoric warmth greeted her, a feeling not unlike standing in the sun, allowing its light to warm you on a chilly day.

Sebastian released Tavis and looked into her eyes, satisfied by their sublime appearance. "You better come back in one piece," he warned, but chuckled.

"Is something wrong?" she whispered to him. "You're acting weird."

Before he could answer, Ila interrupted him. "For goodness sake, Sebastian! Tavis isn't a fragile piece of crystal. My horses aren't going to smash her to smithereens."

"Thank you," Tavis said to Ila as they approached Jack's house.

"Quite a protective father you have there."

Ila walked up the steps and knocked on the door. When no response came, she rang the doorbell, yelling, "Jack, I know you're in there. Open the damn door now."

They heard a stomping advance toward the door and when it opened, a disheveled, irritated-looking Jack leaned against the door casing. "I'm not up for visitors, Ila."

"That's a good thing, because I don't have time to visit with you this morning." Ila pushed the door open wider and sauntered in, sneering at the untidy mess strewn about the house. "I've come to call in that favor you offered."

"What favor?" he asked, but was suddenly aware of Tavis' presence as she came in to join Ila. When she passed him, a sweet fragrance left a trail behind her. He followed her, hoping she'd turn around so he could see her face again.

When she did, Tavis was surprised to find him hovering over her. She looked up into his eyes, thinking he may intend to escort them out of his house, but saw a recent memory lurking in his thoughts. He was remembering the way her lips felt and how soft her hips and thighs were. She also sensed Jack's overwhelming desire to recreate that memory, causing her to turn away to hide the blush forming on her cheeks.

Ila concluded her judgment of the filthy kitchen and returned her attention to Jack. "Meg's unable to help work the horses right now. I'm doing the best I can, but I'm only one person. If you're not too busy *not* shaving or cleaning anything, would you mind exercising the stallion and mare for me today? Oh, and take Tavis with you, she's never been horseback riding."

Jack blinked a few times, sure he had to be dreaming, or perhaps he'd misunderstood Ila. "You want me to give horseback riding lessons? To Tavis?"

Her eyes narrowed. "I'm sorry, is that beneath you?"

"No," Jack scrambled, "I was just trying to be clear about what you wanted."

Ila glanced at the wall clock and groaned. "I have to meet Dr. Patrick for a gelding lesson. If you'd prefer, I could go with Tavis while you take my place and learn how to castrate a horse."

"Nah." Jack looked at Tavis again and thought himself the luckiest fool on the island. An image of Sebastian popped into his head. "Is Sebastian okay with you getting on a horse?"

"Yes, Sebastian's perfectly fine with it," Ila answered over her. "We'll wait outside while you change into something more appropriate. My saddles aren't robe friendly."

~

Jack drove to Ila's with Tavis in the passenger seat and neither one of them spoke during the lengthy trip. The entire drive consisted of Jack inhaling the sweet scent he first noticed at his house; he spent half the time enjoying it and the other half being annoyed for liking it. When he brought the cart to a stop in front of Ila's house, he continued to sit while staring at the stables.

"If you've changed your mind, you can go back home. It's okay," Tavis said.

"I haven't changed my mind. I like riding, and I could use some fresh air." He looked at her for a moment, considered asking her why they never talked about their previous encounters, but shrugged it off. "Come on, let's go."

After leading the two horses out of the stall, Jack focused his energy into explaining everything he did as he saddled them. He told her it was important she pay attention to the saddling process if she ever wanted to ride on her own.

They led the horses outside and Jack helped Tavis mount hers, nervous about standing so close to her. When she was securely seated in the saddle, he suppressed the urge to pull her back down and drag her to one of the empty stalls. Once Jack mounted his own horse, they went off at a slow pace at first so he could teach her how to direct a horse. Tavis got the hang of it quickly and he allowed the horses to go at a faster trot.

"Have you explored the forest footpaths yet?" Tavis asked.

"No. There aren't any trail markers, I'm afraid I'd get lost. Have you?"

"Yep, and I've memorized most of them. They're so peaceful and the scenery is beautiful. Want me to show you one of them?"

Intrigued by the notion of exploring something new about the island, he said, "How could I refuse peace and beauty?"

Tavis told him where to lead their horses to, choosing a nearby path that went from Ila's house to the town center. A narrow creek meandered alongside the length of the path and large moss-covered boulders dominated in various locations where a bird would land on occasion to watch horse and rider go by. Jack looked down into the stream, seeing schools of small fish dart in and out of the shadows their horses cast on the surface.

"Are there paths in all the forests?" he asked after Tavis explained the reason for them.

"Pretty much, and there are no maps, you just have to learn them."

When the path ended at the town center, they turned the horses around and headed back into the trees. "Where does that one go?" Jack pointed to a well-worn path that intersected the one they were on.

"To a lake."

"Is it a path you've memorized?"

"Yes." She rolled her eyes at his doubtful tone. "I know that one particularly well. The only paths I haven't memorized are the ones in the mountain area. Do you want to see the lake?" She slowed her horse. "It's one of my favorite places here. There's a huge waterfall and hardly anyone goes there. I usually have the whole lake to myself when I go there to swim."

"Yeah, let's take a look." He turned his horse around and followed the path.

Tavis stayed behind him, watching how he commanded the horse to stop when they reached the lake. Jack dismounted from his with ease and she was about to duplicate his method, but he stopped her.

"Dismounting a horse can be tricky, let me help you for now." Jack held his hands up to her and waited.

Not sure what she was supposed to do, Tavis put her hands into his. He frowned at her. "What are you doing?"

"I don't know what you want me to do," she said, embarrassed.

Jack laughed heartily. "Swing your other leg around to this side of the horse. You'll hold on to the saddle while I grab your waist and help you down."

"Oh." She removed her hands from his and clutched the saddle horn.

"You have to let go of the saddle," Jack added when he was unable to plant her feet on the ground.

Tavis let go and slid off the horse while Jack guided her down. Their bodies were so close that Jack caught that scent again. He closed his eyes and held his breath, hoping to block it out.

"Thank you," she said when his body swayed toward hers.

His eyes opened again and he forced himself away, shuffling over to the edge of the lake to look out over the rippling water. On the other side of the lake, where the water was calmer, the occasional fish or turtle broke the surface, causing a circular ripple. He thought Tavis' assessment of the lake's peaceful beauty was absolutely correct.

He glanced over at the waterfall and saw Tavis climbing to the top of a boulder positioned next to it, and then she descended to the other side. A surge of excitement pulsed through his veins at wanting to check out the waterfall himself.

After tying the horses to some nearby trees, he headed in the direction he assumed Tavis had gone before he lost sight of her. Climbing over the same boulder, he got a better look at the cove the wall of water fell into. The waterfall's immense power was breathtaking and he knew by the shape of it that it held a secret most people were clueless to. He looked around, but didn't see Tavis anywhere.

"Tavis?" No answer came and he worried. "Tavis?" he called louder, looking in every direction.

"I'm in here," Tavis called back.

He spun in the direction of her voice and found her in the water. "Oh. I didn't know you were thinking of going for a swim."

"I already told you, I swim here all the time. I like it better here than swimming in the ocean."

The only visible part of Tavis was her head and neck; he wondered if she jumped in with her clothes on. He looked around again, searching for signs that she had disrobed and hated himself for hoping she had. On a smaller boulder, at the back of the one he'd climbed, he saw her shoes. Next to them were the shorts and t-shirt she'd been wearing.

He turned to her; she was still in the same position—he half-hoped she still wore her undergarments. Tavis swam closer to the water's edge and he caught sight of white straps on her shoulders, eliciting a sigh of relief from him.

"The water temperature is perfect, you should come in." She misinterpreted the apprehension on his face. "I'm sorry, I didn't think to ask… do you know how to swim?"

"Of course I know how to swim," he said as though his swimming ability had been challenged.

"Well, I wasn't implying you didn't. I was just being polite."

Jack felt bad for barking at her. "Sorry, I have an ego problem sometimes."

Tavis started to emerge from the water and at seeing more of her bra, Jack held his hands up. He looked at the waterfall to block the image of Tavis clad in only her underwear, knowing he wouldn't be able to stop himself from ogling her if she meant to walk past him like that.

"I was thinking I might enjoy a few laps myself," he said.

She bit her lip to keep from laughing at what looked like Jack talking to a waterfall. Stopping her advance from exiting the water, she asked. "Are you sure? We can head back to the path if you want."

"I like swimming." He shook his head at hearing his own stupid-sounding response.

He turned around from Tavis while she waited in the water, watching him fidget with his clothes. After unbuttoning his shirt, he slipped it off and put it on the rock next to Tavis' clothes. His hands went to his pants button and he froze, remembering that he'd forgone underwear when he got dressed as there were none clean. He glanced over his shoulder and saw Tavis abruptly stifle a giggle.

Annoyed with himself for behaving like a shy prepubescent boy, Jack turned to face her fully and locked his eyes onto hers. Taking his leisure about it, Jack unzipped his pants, and pulled them off his legs while still holding her gaze. Not once did she flinch or avert her eyes when he walked toward the water.

"Can you dive?" she asked before he entered.

"Yes." He tried to keep the arrogance out of his reply.

"Climb the boulder and dive in. The water's deep in the cove, it's safe. I do it all the time."

Jack ambled up the large boulder; it seemed a high perch to him and he did wonder about the water's depth. He decided to take a leap of faith in the name of adventure and dove in head-long. When he resurfaced, he felt free and liberated from everything that had been dragging him down.

"That was amazing!" he shouted, slinging the water off his face and hair.

He went to dive again and Tavis smiled at the transformation of his mood. She watched Jack climb the boulder, taking advantage of his preoccupation with diving to examine his body. His wet brown hair glinted in sunlit highlights and his eyes were the color of blue-grey slate. The stubbly beginnings of a beard framed his animated smile. Her eyes traveled down to his shoulders; they were broad, and his arms were tightly muscled, but not the bulging kind.

He was a little taller than her; his legs especially longer. His skin tone was that of an olive complexion, one the sunlight loved appreciating. Her gaze trailed up his legs and she blushed at his emboldened decision to remove all his clothes.

The dive off the boulder ended her visual appraisal of his physique. When he resurfaced near her, he said, "I see why you like this lake so much."

"It's the best place, in my opinion," Tavis said, musing. "I've yet to encounter another person here since I discovered it."

Jack found this hard to believe and only smiled at her. He was about to leave to dive again, but stopped when she submerged under the water. Staying put, he waited to see where she'd resurface. He spun around at hearing her laughter behind him and was met with a wall of water she splashed in his face.

"Oh, yeah?" He laughed, slanting his hand through the water to send an even higher wall arcing toward her.

The water cascaded over her head and face, trickling down in molasses-motion off of her and back into the lake. Jack took notice of her eyes again. The daylight made their color more intense—the blue was indescribable. His gaze followed the curve of her face, down to her neck. Her facial lines traced a chiseled appearance meant for a purpose he suddenly wanted to be a part of. A deep and primitive longing heated him from the inside.

Tavis saw the subtle shift in the way Jack looked at her and it forced an equal shift in her own thoughts. She chanced a step closer and waited to see his reaction. He matched her step and took several more, stopping short of their chests making contact.

She wanted to touch him, hungry and thirsty for things that weren't food or water. The inch of space separating them became unbearable. An ancient urge encouraged her and she placed a hand on his chest while instinct brought her lips to his neck; the contact made him shiver, coaxing her to explore.

Jack hitched her legs around his torso, and he wrapped his arms around her waist. The buoyancy of the water and his hands coming to rest at the small of her back kept her firmly latched to him while he walked them toward the waterfall. He knew there was an alcove on the other side, but they'd have to pass under a torrent of water to get there. If they made it, he was certain a paradise waited for them.

As they passed through, the water beat down on their bodies—neither one noticed, nor cared. Having made it to the alcove, Jack surrendered to everything his body wanted, pressing Tavis against the closest wall and kissing her in a slow and experienced manner.

All of it was new to Tavis, and the unfamiliar emotions intensified exponentially. As wonderful as his kisses were, her body wanted more. The few remaining clothes she wore became an obstacle to be rid of and her hands tugged impatiently at them.

Her wanting drove him to near madness. Experience had prompted him to go slower, but her urgency called out a more primitive edge to his desire for her; eventually winning the battle. Jack reached for the underwear she tugged at and had them off within seconds.

He guided her to a flattened area of the undercut gorge and laid her down to look at her form. She was beyond beautiful, her body beckoned him to end the torturous longing he'd harbored for her since the day they met. Jack moved his face level with hers, positioning his body over her. Tavis' eyes were closed and she arched her body receptively. There was one last moment of apprehension that tried to pull him away from the moment—until she opened her eyes.

That unworldly blue color, accentuated by passion, met his earthy gray ones and any thought he may have had of turning away vanished like it never existed. Jack ended their torture. Instantly, one torture replaced another and a cry of pain escaped her lips. He recognized the situation for what it was and it both surprised and scared him.

"Did I hurt you?" he whispered at her ear.

"Yes, but..." Her voice was husky and heavy with passion. "Jack, please, don't stop."

Tavis locked her ankles together around his backside, urging him to keep going. As he pushed against her, his mouth covered her, kissing her slowly—never releasing, not even when she whimpered at his lips. He paced his movements in rhythm with hers, wanting Tavis to view the experience as pleasurable. It became difficult, though, for him to steady his tempo. Again, she flashed her eyes at him, and there was a smoldering dark tint to the blue.

"Now, Jack," she said, begging him, her body trembling beneath him.

There came and went another question in his mind, its time for asking was so past and forgotten now. A guttural sound was born in his chest and escaped as a roar as his own body shook with tremors.

They fell into a blissful silence afterward, wrapped around each other and watching the back of the waterfall. Eventually, Tavis sat up and reached for her undergarments.

She caressed his cheek and said, "I'm gonna swim back now." Then she stood and dove through the waterfall.

"Wait," Jack called, but doubted she heard him through the wall of water. He dove in and found her halfway back to the lake's edge. When he reached her, he pulled their bodies together. "Why'd you leave?"

"We've been gone awhile and we shouldn't leave the horses tied up so long."

"Don't you want to talk about what just happened?" It confused him when she shook her head. "Tavis, I think it's important—"

"Shh." Tavis put a finger to his lips to quiet him. "I know what you're worried about and I want you to stop, everything's fine. What happened will stay just between us. Okay?"

An odd mixture of relief and disappointment came over him, he resented even the concept of Michelle. "Okay, we don't have to talk about that right now."

"Good." Tavis stared into his eyes for a moment. She wanted to tell him Michelle wasn't coming back, but there was no way to do it without divulging how she came to have that knowledge. "Ready to go?"

"In a minute." He smiled. "I want to look at these pretty eyes of yours a little longer. What color would you say they are?"

"Blue, like yours, but less gray."

He laughed. "They're blue all right, but nothing like mine." Jack cupped her face to study them. "My parents took lots of vacations and they hauled me around all over the world with them. We went to the Maldives once and even though I was a little kid then, I can still remember the blue of the water there. It's a close match… almost."

Jack took her hand and they left the water. He leaned against the large boulder, watching as she put her clothes on.

When dressed, she looked at him. "You're not riding back to the stable like that, are you?"

The smoldering look in his eyes suggested he wished she'd take her clothes back off. Tavis retrieved his shirt and handed it to him, then leaned against the boulder to watch as he had done to her. He held her gaze while he buttoned it.

"Your hair's turning lighter," he said.

"I mentioned I come here a lot."

His expression turned serious. "With no one else, I noticed. Tavis, why didn't you tell me? I didn't know I'd be your first—"

Again she shushed him with her forefinger. "You were, and I'm not sorry about it."

He took her wrist and pinned it to the rock above her head, leaning in to kiss her. Tavis' body relaxed and molded to his, causing him to sway against her—pressing more urgently as their kissing continued. Recognizing the quickening of his pulse, Jack stopped while he still could.

"Let's go," he said, pulling away from her. He slipped his pants on and zipped them up with great difficulty.

After helping Tavis onto her horse, they rode off in the direction of the path. Jack thought about what had changed since they were last on it. He imagined he should feel guilty, but he just couldn't, and regret was certainly out of the question. When he looked back at Tavis following him, the only thing he felt was jealousy of the horse she rode.

He continued peeking over his shoulder at her, fearing he'd look and she wouldn't be there, and that he'd only been dreaming. At one point, he caught a look of pain on her face.

"Are you hurting?" he asked, bringing the horses to a stop.

"A little," she admitted, wincing.

Jack unbuttoned his shirt and removed it again, folding it up to make a cushion on his saddle in front of him. He brought his horse next to hers and grabbed Tavis' reins, helping her onto his saddle to sit on the make-shift pillow.

"Better?" he asked once they started moving along.

"Much better, thank you." Tavis looked over Jack's shoulder. "What about my horse?"

"Don't worry about him, it's in his nature to follow this one." Jack patted the mare. "He'd follow her round and round this island till he dropped from exhaustion."

She let her head rest back on his chest as his body cradled hers. Jack directed the horses at a snail's pace, prolonging his time with Tavis for as long as possible. Something was different, something he'd never experienced before. Not sure what to call the feeling, he decided it was right despite everything else that was wrong.

Thankfully, Ila was still out and therefore missed seeing Tavis and a shirtless Jack return to the stables. She also missed seeing him chase Tavis around the stalls after they secured the horses, and how when he caught her, he carried her to the hay bales.

"Stop," Tavis protested. "What if she comes home and catches us?"

"All I'm doing is lusting after you with my eyes."

Jack placed the tip of his finger on her forehead and traced a line down to the tip of her nose, then down over her lips and chin. He continued down her neck, through the center of her chest, and at reaching her belly button he paused and looked at her questioningly. A slight smile curved her lips, so he flattened his hand and continued downward, nudging her leg over a little to explore.

"Jack," Tavis said in a breathy whisper.

"Want me to stop?" he asked, watching her eyes close.

"No."

~

There was a lot Ila missed this day, but her horses saw it all. Sebastian, too, had a pretty good understanding when Tavis returned home. The new rosiness in her cheeks was telling enough on its own. When she walked to the kitchen to investigate the wonderful smell of the quiche baking in the oven, the hay sticking out the back pockets of her shorts, along with the pieces clinging to her messy hair, affirmed the obvious.

There were so many questions he wanted to ask her, but they were all inherently personal and to broach the delicate subject too soon would damage their trust. Sebastian had no choice but to wait until a more appropriate time.

"You don't appear to have any broken bones," he said when she joined him in the front room. "I take it the horseback riding lesson went well."

"Yes." Tavis guarded her thoughts, thinking only of the horses. "It's kind of tricky getting on and off the horse."

"I'm glad you had a good time." Sebastian did want to know one thing, though. "Were you able to find out his plans once he learns Michelle's not returning?"

"Not really, he wasn't thinking about her much." Changing the subject, Tavis asked, "Do I have time to take a shower before dinner? The quiche smells amazing, by the way, and I'm starving."

Sebastian chuckled. "Yes, it still has to finish baking and then we can find out if it's edible."

10

Multiply

There were more excursions to the waterfall lake in the weeks following Tavis' initial horseback riding lesson. Her new ritual of daily swimming came with, *'I'll be back later this afternoon'*, to her father before driving away in the cart. Within minutes, Jack would speed off in the same direction as Tavis—with a joyful smile plastered on his face.

It was during the third week when Sebastian finally had enough of their secrecy. He paid a visit to Dr. Patrick and *encouraged* the man to make the announcement of Michelle's decision not to return to Gamma.

The next day, Dr. Patrick and Ila stood at Jack's front door. Dr. Patrick leaned in toward Ila and said before knocking, "Thank you for meeting me, I'm afraid I wouldn't know how to handle it if he gets emotional. I've never really been all that great with comforting my male patients."

The door opened while Dr. Patrick still knocked on it, surprising all three of them. "Well, that was fast," Ila said.

"What are you doing here?" Jack asked Dr. Patrick.

"I'm afraid I have some bad news, Jack. It's about Michelle. May we come in?"

Jack saw Tavis had just stepped out of her house, but had gone no farther than the front porch upon seeing Ila and Dr. Patrick at his door. "Sure, come in," he told them. When they passed by him, Jack shook his head at Tavis, hoping she understood he wouldn't be able to meet her at the lake.

He shut the door, but could still see Tavis' concerned expression in his mind. He went over to the dining table where Dr. Patrick and Ila had taken their seats. At spotting the sympathy expressed in Ila's eyes, Jack grew uneasy.

"Has something happened to Michelle?" Jack asked and sat opposite Ila.

"She's fine, Jack," Dr. Patrick said. "However, Michelle has decided not to come back here. She left an apology letter for you in her hospital room."

"What did it say?"

"She wanted you to know she was sorry and hoped you'd understand. There was also mention that she'd be at her parents and if you weren't too angry with her, you could pack the rest of her belongings and have them shipped there." Dr. Patrick leaned over and patted Jack's shoulder. "Don't worry, Ila will help you gather her things and I'll make sure they're sent to the address she listed in the note."

"That won't be necessary," Jack muttered to Ila.

"I don't mind at all, that's why I'm here," she said.

Jack was about to argue, but Dr. Patrick put a stop to it. "It's customary for someone to volunteer to help with these sorts of things. Normally, it's when someone has passed away. For all practical purposes, it's been decided to treat this matter in the same way. They'll be a condolence dinner for your loss at the café tonight before the fishing tournament. You don't have to attend the fishing trip, but you'll be expected at the dinner, of course. Do you understand?"

The command in Dr. Patrick's voice left zero wiggle room for Jack to protest. "Okay," Jack said, feeling like a scolded child.

"Very good," Dr. Patrick said. "Also, you'll be moving into the vacant newcomer house. There'll be no arguments on that front either." Dr. Patrick gave Jack a stern look. "Some of the older ladies think you need a fresh start so that you won't dwell on reminders of Michelle in this house. A group of volunteers will ready the house today and you'll be expected to return there after the dinner. Any questions?"

"May I be excused from the table, sir?"

Dr. Patrick mistook Jack's sarcasm as him needing to leave to deal with his emotions. "I understand," he said, nodding. "I have patient appointments I need to get to. Ila will stay to help you and offer support. I'll see you this evening at the café."

~

Two hours into listening to Ila's supportive encouragement while they gathered both his and Michelle's belongings—pointless crap, in his opinion—and he thought he'd lose his mind. At the very least, he feared he'd speak his inglorious gratitude if he heard one more: *'Give it time, you'll be able to move on'*; or, *'One day, this will all make sense'*; even worse was, *'Do you need a hug?'*

"Ila." Jack focused on keeping the impatience out of his voice. "I need to go outside for a little bit." He saw her apprehension. "I just need a moment to myself… you know, to be emotional and stuff. Okay?"

"Go ahead, but don't be gone too long." Ila smiled sweetly at him while folding one of his shirts. "Dr. Patrick's trusting me to keep an eye on you today."

"And I'm so grateful," Jack said, it almost hurt keeping his lip from curling in disgust.

As he walked out the back of the house, he glanced at the group of people who had descended on the vacant newcomer house. He noticed Sebastian talking to Frank Doscher, but didn't see Tavis anywhere. Assuming she was inside her house, he darted to the trees and nearly ran her over.

"What are you doing out here?" he asked, grasping her shoulders and peering over her head to make sure no one saw them.

"I've been watching your house, hoping you'd come out."

He chuckled, still spying the fray unfolding by the vacant newcomer house. "It's a good thing I like you so much because that's kind of weird, Tavis." Satisfied they hadn't been spotted, Jack led her farther into the trees.

"I was worried about you," she said.

Her face had taken on a sad expression and for the first time, Jack sensed an innocence about her. It comingled with the hurt he caused, and dangled on the hope that he didn't think ill of her.

"I shouldn't have said that, I'm glad you were out here. I was trying to sneak over to your house to talk to you." Seeing she wasn't convinced, he asked, "Remember when I told you I have an ego problem sometimes?"

"Yeah."

"Well, sometimes I say stupid things, too."

Tavis grinned and averted her eyes to his chest. "I know."

This was the moment when—watching her look away bashfully, no doubt recalling some of his passionate utterances—Jack realized what it was he felt for her.

And he wasn't about to let it slip through his fingers.

"Hey," he said, tilting her chin up. "Michelle's not coming back and I want to talk to you about it."

"I'm listening."

Jack shook his head. "Not now, my babysitter put an expiration stamp on how long I can stay outside. Is Sebastian going on that fishing trip tonight?"

She nodded. "Are you?"

"Hell no." Jack contemplated an idea. "He'll be out for a while. Does he check on you after you've gone to bed?"

Tavis snorted at the notion. "Not since I was a child."

"Apparently they do creepy things to people in mourning here. I have to go to a commiseration dinner at the café tonight." Jack nodded toward the middle vacant house. "I'll be living there starting after the pity party. Will you meet me there tonight? I really need to talk to you about… well, stuff."

"I think Ila's looking for you." Tavis pointed toward Jack's back porch.

"Shit! I have to go." Jack leaned over while keeping his eye on Ila, accidentally kissing Tavis' nose. "Promise you'll meet me tonight?"

"I'll be there." Tavis cradled his face in her hands to get his attention. "I promise."

Tavis waited for him to leave before she made her way back to her house. Sebastian came in soon after and explained some of what had happened. "The matriarchs decided to turn the vacant newcomer house into Jack's bachelor pad. Some of them were even going on about setting him up with this or that lady… after a respectful waiting period, of course." He chortled. "Funny, huh?"

"What's funny is that thing on your head. What is it?"

"It's a lucky fishing hat, Frank just gave it to me. You like it?"

She looked at all the various lures and hooks adorning the crown and brim. "You're sure you want to go?"

"Yes, I'm sure. Alec's going, too, and we know how much he enjoys my company." Sebastian smirked. "I'm hoping to learn more about how he and Meg are doing."

"Fine, just please be careful. Fishing is different here from the way we do it at home."

"I'd invite you along" –he winked– "but it's for men only."

"Oh, what a big surprise." She rolled her eyes. "I wouldn't go anyway. From what I've seen of it, I prefer our way."

"Me, too." Sebastian took the hat off and set it on the table. "We're expected to go to that dinner at the café, are you okay with that?"

"Why wouldn't I be?"

"It was just a question, Tavis. No need to be so defensive."

"Sorry." She turned away from his quizzical staring. "I'm just tired, I'll probably turn in early tonight."

"Well, I'm told these fishing tournaments can last well past midnight, so I'll make sure I'm extra quiet when I get back."

~

It was a strange dinner. Half in attendance—mostly the elderly women—insisted it be a solemn occasion. The other half expressed a range of emotions. The men discussing the fishing tournament were entirely too excited to be somber, and the boastful talk of their fishing prowess grew louder with each beer consumed. Those not going on the excursion didn't seem to care one way or the other.

Jack spent a good bit of his time gazing at Tavis, who sat several chairs away on the opposite side of the long table that had been set up for the dinner. He smiled when she laughed at someone's joke, he wanted to fuss at the waiter when her water glass needed refilling, and he wanted to trade seats with Sebastian so he could sit by her instead. Most of all, Jack wanted to take her home and see how she looked on his new bed sheets.

When James started lingering too long near Tavis' chair, stealing opportune peeks down her blouse, Jack thought he handled the situation well by not clobbering him where he stood. He waited for a better moment to present itself so that he could set James straight, and it came right after Tavis left with the rest of those having no desire to stay any longer than was absolutely necessary.

He strode over to the bar, sat on one of the stools, and waited for James' return to pour another round of one-more beers for the men at the table. When he did, Jack was satisfied to see the nervous apprehension in James' expression—who was probably recalling their last run-in at Meg and Alec's wedding.

"Can I get you anything?" James asked, setting the tray of empty mugs in the bar well.

"Yeah, I'll have another beer," Jack said.

James grabbed a mug from the cooler, asking while he poured, "You going on the tournament?"

"Nope. Are you?"

"No, I'll be here late cleaning up." James set the beer in front of Jack. "Sorry to hear about Martha."

It took him a moment, but then he realized who James meant. "Actually, her name's Michelle and to be honest, her leaving me isn't exactly what I'd call a loss. Certainly nothing like yours."

"Oh, really?" James grinned the typical bartender's smile when addressing someone he figured had drank too much and made no sense. "What have I lost, Jeff?"

"So we're getting names wrong, are we?" Jack downed half his beer. "Okay, asshole… that's your new name, by the way." He let go a loud belch. "Your loss is Tavis. She's not available and if I ever catch you looking down her shirt again, I'll tie you to a chair and make you stare at my balls until you can't remember what breasts look like anymore. You get the point, don't you?"

"Yeah, I got it," James said.

"Well, I think I'll be heading home now. I have an important meeting with a certain blouse I plan to unbutton." Jack finished off the rest of his beer and belched again before standing. "Excellent beer, asshole."

~

Jack followed the sound of the shower running and the glowing sight of candles flickering in the master bedroom, discovering Tavis had already made herself at home. He disrobed quietly and walked into the bathroom, pausing to admire her silhouette through the clear shower curtain.

"I thought you'd never get here," he heard her say.

"I was tying up some loose ends." Jack moved the curtain aside and looked at her for a moment, forcing himself to think of something else to keep from reacting immediately. He stepped in and slid the curtain back into place. "Where'd all the candles come from?"

"It seemed the women wanted you to have plenty for when you're ready to start romancing again."

He took the bar of soap in his hand. "You missed a spot," he whispered into her ear, sending a shiver down her back. After lathering the soap over her body, he handed it to her. "My turn."

Tavis made him turn around and she ran the soap along his backside first, then took her time with his front—exploring every inch of him. She trailed her soapy hands up his arms, moving to his chest to form lathered circles that inched farther down his abdomen. Her exploration continued along the front and insides of his thighs, finally ending in the center. She delighted in the instant response it created and heard a low rumbling sound rise from Jack's chest, escaping past his lips as a groan.

"You see what you do to me," Jack said.

He was determined to keep control for a while longer and pulled her closer to the stream of water to rinse the soap from their bodies. Then he pulled the shower curtain back and took his time drying off Tavis' body before toweling his own. Lacing his fingers into hers, Jack led her out of the bathroom, to the bedroom, and to the still untouched bed sheets.

She lay down and he stood above her, taking in the way she looked reclined on a bed he had every intention of making theirs. The entire drive back from the café, he thought about their relationship. Though it wasn't a long one yet, there was no doubt in his mind he wanted one with her.

She was fond of him, and he knew this. However, he'd begun to suspect that he may only be an exciting diversion for her. She wouldn't be the first who viewed him in this way, but she was the first he wanted more from than just mind-blowing sex.

His experience and intellect—and even something more in the form of elusive memories Jack couldn't quite recall with sensible clarity—hinted that he'd have to approach her just right if he wanted to truly win her.

The time he spent contemplating his plan reflected back at him as emerging impatience forming in her eyes. It occurred to him what the precise way was to make her finally agree to talk. Jack smiled to reassure her that nothing was wrong and joined her on the bed, scooting them up to the pillows. He caressed her face with his fingers and gave her a somewhat chaste kiss before leaning back again to look into her eyes.

What he saw there was a thing he wanted to always see, Tavis looking at him expectantly in a bed he hoped she wanted to share with him exclusively. Jack was done with the secrecy, done with the stolen moments; he wanted the whole island to know so they could be liberated to do as they pleased. His only concern was not knowing how Tavis felt about him.

Jack banked on the one thing he knew for certain that she was feeling right now. He slipped his hand inside the towel he'd wrapped around her and positioned his thumb in just the right spot while staring into her eyes. He coaxed and teased until he saw the beginnings of Tavis' eyelids flutter and heard her breath catch at the tingling sensation.

Just when the first of her breathy whimpers began, Jack slowed, stopped, and then removed his hand. Her eyes refocused on his, expressing a confused and frustrated look.

"Can we talk now?" he asked, his voice soft, but full of intent.

The stronger, well-established side of Tavis wanted to yell at him for the trickery. Yet, the burgeoning side of the woman who wanted him for herself was the one who gave Jack what he'd already decided would be their future.

"Yes, but after, okay?" Tavis said, hoping he'd give her release first—feeling perfectly fine for wanting it, and would take it gladly if he granted it.

The intense moment allowed Jack his first glimpse into Tavis' thoughts, and he considered himself lucky she allowed his egocentric plan to work. His lips returned to hers, his hand returned to where it had been and before he could do it himself, Tavis plucked their towels away. She pushed his hand aside and climbed atop him, as though to take what she wanted and show him he didn't control all. He understood it and remained pliant and patient until her body trembled. Only then did he grasp her hips and move them methodically against his until his mind swam in a sea of ecstasy.

"I love you, Tavis," he said, sighing into her neck and hair when she collapsed onto his chest.

"I love you, too, Jack," she whispered in his ear.

They rolled to their sides and snuggled close to each other. "Are you mad at me?" he asked.

Tavis swept her lips across his chest. "No, but I will be if you ever do that again. Don't ever use this part of our relationship as a strategic tool to get what you want."

"I agree." He smiled a little. "Actually, I don't see that ever being a problem. Certainly not from me anyway."

"I have to admit, it surprised me."

"I really am sorry, Tavis. It's just that every time I've wanted to talk to you about us over the last few weeks you always hush me."

"I know." She frowned. "It was wrong of me and if I'm being honest with myself, I used our intimacy to hush you."

"Well, I wasn't gonna mention it, but that was how I got the idea—"

"Jack." Her voice held warning. "I believe you wanted to talk to me about something."

"Right." For all his blustering, he was suddenly nervous. "I don't want to hide us anymore. I've decided I want you with me all the time, any time of day or night I want. Anywhere and everywhere I want. In any way I want, and in front of any—"

"Is that all?" she asked when he paused.

"I said all that and forgot to ask what you wanted first. Do you want to be with me?" Jack lay flat on his back and stared at the ceiling. "Or did I just embarrass myself?"

Tavis propped herself up on her elbow and looked at him. "You really need for me to say it?"

His hand went to her cheek. "I'd feel better if you did."

"I want to be with you all the time, too."

A smile of relief and happiness graced his face for a moment, and then a look of concentration formed. "Okay, now that that's settled, we should talk about whether or not you'll like being with a corpse. Will Sebastian try to kill me?"

"I can't tell you how my father will react because I truly don't know. All I can say is that it doesn't matter what he thinks, I'm an adult and I can make my own decisions."

"Yeah, well… I was hoping you'd say something like he's been wanting to kick you out for years and that I'm exactly the man he'd always wanted for you." When she made no comment, he decided not to think about Sebastian anymore. A different sort of question nagged him and he wondered if it was in his best interest to mention it.

He fidgeted and no matter how hard she tried, there was no getting past the guarded wall surrounding his thoughts. "What's going on in that head of yours now?"

"Something I *should* tell you, but I don't want to tell you." Jack pulled Tavis closer and rested her head on his chest. "You haven't had much experience with anyone else, and, um, I can't say the same. Obviously, you know about Michelle and for a while before her I wasn't with anyone, well, except myself." Jack shook his head and groaned. "Okay, so college was like an endless sea of opportunity for experience. Before that was high school, less like an endless sea, but still a decent-sized swimming pool. I won't disgust you by bringing up my middle school experience. So, there it is. Does it bother you that I've been around the block, the neighborhood, numerous cities, and everywhere else that put out a welcome mat?"

Tavis laughed. "Not at all. In fact, I like the way you already know what to do and when to do it. Does it bother you that I'm not so experienced?"

"Hell no!" Jack snorted. "I'm loving this teaching job way too much."

"Now you're just being bad." She nudged his ribs.

"When should we talk to Sebastian?" Jack asked. "And should I wear a suit of armor when we do?"

"I'd rather talk to him alone. To tell you the truth, I don't think he'll be as difficult as the rest of the people on the island. Have you thought about how everyone else is going to react when they learn how quickly you moved on from Michelle?"

Jack thought about it for a minute, considering whether or not he'd risk losing one more day with Tavis just to adhere to some archaic notion of waiting an appropriate amount of time before moving on with his life.

"Okay, I just thought about it. I don't care what other people think."

"All right, I'll talk to him tomorrow. You hide in the waterfall cave until I give you the all-clear." Tavis laughed when Jack's body tensed. "I was only joking. My father's a peaceful man. I assure you, you'll probably get a cooler reception from the likes of Ila and a few of the older islanders."

"We'll find out soon enough. Let's get some sleep before I wake you up for one of those *anytime-I-want* moments."

~

Despite everything she told Jack, Tavis was skittish around her father the next morning. She attempted to make breakfast, but only succeeded in waking him by the horrendous smell of having failed. While Sebastian tried to salvage anything edible from the mess, Tavis put off talking to him about Jack, thinking a full stomach of better food would be more to her benefit.

Well into the afternoon, after bypassing several opportunities, she laughed at herself for being scared to talk to the one person in her life who knew her better than she knew herself.

Tavis left her bedroom and found her father sitting on the front porch having a cup of tea. She sat in the chair next to him and poured herself a cup, sipping while plucking up her courage. When she emptied her cup, Tavis wasted more time by reaching for the teapot to refill it, but stopped at finding Sebastian staring at her.

"Will you ever get around to telling me whatever it is you want to talk to me about?" Sebastian took the teapot himself and refilled both their cups. "You've become very skilled at shielding your thoughts. The only thing I can sort out is that you're a bundle of nerves and that I'm the reason for it. You'll either have to tell me verbally what's troubling you, or let me in."

Looking into her teacup, Tavis realized her folly—she could block her thoughts, but not the intensity of her emotions. Sensing emotion was easy, not being a thought or a memory, but a state of being that affects everyone around you. Clearly though, she wasn't about to *let him in*, as he would see far more than either one of them wanted.

"I'm waiting, Tavis."

"I know."

"Just say it." He tried to encourage her with an empathetic expression, but her apprehension continued. "Would it help if I guessed the subject?"

This got her attention. "Maybe," she said, curious.

"Does it have anything to do with where you've been spending all of your time lately?" Sebastian chose his words wisely. He needed Tavis to tell him about Jack herself.

"Yes."

"Then I wish you'd tell me. It's causing me pain to see you so tormented."

"Okay, I will." Tavis took a deep breath to steady herself. "Jack and I have become closer. A lot closer, actually. I know you didn't plan on this kind of thing happening when we came here, but it did."

Tavis got up from her chair to face him. She wished he'd look at her, but he seemed determined to stare off into the distance. She put her teacup down and sat on the floor by his feet, resting her chin on his knee. "Won't you even look at me?"

He did, and asked, "When you say *closer*, do you mean as more than just friendship?"

"Yes," she said, nodding. "We want to be together. *I* want this. He told me he loves me."

"And how do you feel?"

"I feel the same way." Tavis saw the dissatisfaction of her answer in his eyes. "I love him, and he knows it."

Sebastian fell silent. He did it for effect as he'd already made up his mind on the matter. He suspected from the beginning that there was something between them and had even helped make it happen. Yet, looking into her hopeful eyes, he could never tell her that.

Her resolve to shield her thoughts and memories weakened briefly and he saw glimpses of passion he would've preferred not to have seen of his daughter. However, it did offer proof of her declaration. Sebastian sensed their love; it was new and growing stronger. He knew that if he scrutinized Tavis further, he would find still more proof of another bond between them.

"Is Jack home?" he asked and set his teacup down.

"Yeah…"

"Go inside and wait for me. I'll be back in a little bit."

She stood, and when he reached the porch steps, she asked, "Wait, what are you gonna do?"

"I plan to have a talk with Jack."

"Wait," she repeated. "Will you allow it?"

He couldn't help but smile. "Stay here. Inside, please. Do you understand me?"

"Yes," she said, encouraged by the smile he meant to hide.

He stood at the bottom step until Tavis went inside, then headed over to the center newcomer house. As he ascended the front porch steps, he caught sight of the dining room window blinds snapping shut. Holding back a chuckle, he marched up to the door and knocked loudly for good measure. When Jack opened it, Sebastian found a respectable amount of fear in his eyes and it took a great deal of effort not to laugh.

"Jack," Sebastian said.

"Sebastian," Jack greeted back.

"My daughter just gave me some interesting news. Would you say what she told me is true and factual?"

Jack looked at Sebastian's hands for potential weapons. "I'd say she made true and factual statements."

"And what exactly are your intentions for my daughter?"

Jack came out onto the porch, shutting the door behind him. If Sebastian wanted to know, then he had no problem telling him. Yet, standing in front of the man, Jack wished himself a little taller as Sebastian suddenly seemed a looming giant who stood at the gate of what he most wanted.

"I want to spend every day and" –Jack cleared his throat–"night with Tavis for the rest of my life."

"And?" Sebastian held the gate-keeper's vigil.

"I want to make her happy, and be happy with her." Jack supposed this was the appropriate answer.

"Obviously, I didn't imagine you wanted a life of misery with Tavis."

Averting his eyes to the porch railing, feeling like he was on the verge of failing an important test, it occurred to him what Sebastian waited for. "I love her, and I want to be just as important to her as you are. I don't want to know what a day is without her."

Sebastian approved. "Shall we get going then?"

"Where to?" Jack frowned.

"To my house, to help Tavis gather her things." Sebastian rubbed his chin thoughtfully. "That is the plan, I assume. You want my only daughter, my pride and joy, to move in here with you and live a carefree life of no real commitment, right?"

Jack was confused, he thought he'd been doing well. "So, you don't approve?"

"Approve of what?" Sebastian asked.

"Of me. You probably don't even like me."

"I like you well enough." Sebastian shrugged. "My daughter says she loves you, so there must be something worthy about you."

"But, you act like you don't want her moving in here with me." Jack watched Sebastian's eyebrows raise. "Oh."

"Right." Sebastian shook his head. "I was beginning to think your worthy quality must be something other than intelligence."

"Hey!"

Sebastian chuckled. "Come on, I want to see you propose to my daughter. I'll try not to laugh if she declines."

"Wait a minute."

"Why? You don't want to marry Tavis?"

"I'd love to, I just hadn't thought of it." Jack was overcome with nervous energy. "I've never done this before. Isn't there supposed to be a ring… and surprises, and knee-bending?"

"Don't worry, she'll definitely be surprised. If she says yes, you can get a ring later." Sebastian smiled, somewhat mischievously. "Personally, I can't wait to see you bend the knee to Tavis."

~

Jack led Tavis to a wing-back chair in the front room, and then kneeled down in front of her.

"What are you doing, Jack?"

He took her hands into his and looked up at her, wearing his best smile and most hopeful eyes. "Tavis Abbott, will you marry me?"

She glanced at her father, who stood by the kitchen entrance watching the scene, trying not to seem too amused. "My father put you up to this, didn't he?"

"He only reminded me of something I already want. I'd be the happiest man alive being your husband." Jack brought Tavis' hands to his lips and kissed each one. "What do you want?"

"I want us to talk about this privately. Later, at your house." She witnessed the hopeful look in Jack's eyes vanish, quickly replaced by dejection, even shame. Tavis refused to let him feel this way and brought his hands to her lips, kissing them as he had done hers. "That wasn't a no, okay?"

Optimism animated his eyes again, highlighted by a broad smile. "Can I take that as a *maybe* that I can turn into a yes if I woo and charm you long enough?"

"You mean nag and drive me crazy?"

"Probably."

"Yes, Jack Cavanaugh, maybe I'll marry you."

He hugged her to him and whispered in her ear, "He said he wants me to help you pack. Was he being serious?"

Tavis leaned back and glanced at Sebastian again, saying loudly for him to hear, "No, I think my father likes having fun with you. Why pack? Your house is next door." She focused her attention back to Jack. "I'll meet you over there in a bit, I want to talk to my father."

When Jack left, Sebastian initiated the conversation with Tavis. "He does love you."

"Did you influence him to want to marry me?" she demanded.

"No, Tavis, I didn't lay a hand on him. I skirted around the topic verbally and the notion came to him by way of his own thoughts."

"Sounds like a loophole to me."

"And, to me, it sounds like you're dodging," Sebastian said, raising his voice a little. "Is it possible you don't love him?"

"No."

"Did you sense how happy he was at the idea of making such a commitment to you?"

"Yes." Tavis crossed her arms and shouted, "And before you ask, yes, I sensed how hurt he was when I didn't accept his proposal. It hurt me, too."

"Then what's the problem?"

"I saw how Alec and Meg's wedding went." Tavis' face expressed a pouting that Sebastian hadn't seen in years. "That's not how we do it back home, and I'd rather it be real."

"Ah, I see now."

Sebastian sat on the coffee table in front of Tavis and waited for her to meet his gaze. When she did, he continued.

"Marriage is a symbolic way of expressing love and commitment between two people who want the whole world to know how happy they are. It's a ceremonial declaration of love. It's the only kind Jack's familiar with, and he wants that with you. There're only two places that it truly matters." Sebastian tapped his finger to her forehead. "Here." He lowered his hand and gave another gentle tap to her chest. "And here. If it's real in these two places, it's real anywhere."

"Thank you," she said. "You're a wonderful father and I don't know what I'd do without you."

~

Three days later, Jack had asked Tavis to marry him several times over. He decided to switch tactics when she walked out, saying she wanted to visit her father for a while. When she returned, the house was decked in flowers of every variety known to the island.

It was the roses on the dining table that widened her eyes and made her gasp. "Oh, no, Jack." She snatched the curtains back from the front room window to confirm what she already suspected. She saw two things: her father's plucked rosebushes, and him marching up the porch steps.

Though he knocked as customary, Sebastian opened the door himself—his eyes zeroed in on the neatly arranged roses sitting on the table. He glanced from Jack to Tavis and said, "Marry that man or I'll do a bit of clipping myself." And then he slammed the door shut.

"He loves his roses," Tavis explained. "You shouldn't have done that. It's sweet, but—"

"I'll fix it," Jack blurted out. "I have an idea, come with me to the store and I'll put in an order for the very best roses. I'll even plant them myself and then Sebastian will be all happy again."

"Okay." Tavis frowned at Jack's eagerness.

Approaching the town center, it occurred to Tavis that it was the first time she and Jack would be arriving there together for no other purpose than to go shopping. Technically, no one other than her father knew about them yet, but there were a few faces that appeared wise—particularly those who worked at the café.

Jack parked in the middle of the square, even though there were several spaces available closer to the general store. "Let's walk around first," he said.

"Why?" she asked, eyeing him.

"Because it's a beautiful day." He saw she wasn't convinced. "I haven't seen all the different shops yet."

She got out of the cart and rushed to keep up with Jack as he made his way over to Chapman Peterson's shop.

"Can we look at this one first?" he asked when they got to the entrance.

Tavis peered into the windows, seeing several wedding portraits lining the walls of the shop. She sighed. "Jack—"

"Tavis, I love you. I want to marry you, I want you to marry me. I can't even think about anything else."

"Why do you want to marry me?" Tavis stepped closer, standing between him and the door. "And don't say it's because you love me. I want to know why it's so important to you."

"I can see the rest of my life with you." Jack pulled on memories he had no explanation for. "I can see that the beginning, middle, and end should be with you. That looks like forever to me and I want forever to start today."

She blinked a few times to rid the stinging in her eyes. "That was beautiful, Jack." Tavis nodded and took his hand. "Will you marry me?"

Several quips came to mind, but he pushed them aside. "Yes, Tavis, I'll marry you."

~

Chapman Peterson joined them in matrimony after Jack selected the *'doorknob'* of a diamond he insisted Tavis have for her engagement ring, and after she decided on a more conservative set of wedding bands.

Over the course of the following weeks, the middle newcomer house became their home. Word of their nuptials spread quickly among the islanders, bringing with it scandalous rumors and hushed whispers of why Michelle really chose not to return.

Though he didn't acknowledge it, Tavis knew it upset Jack that not everyone was as happy as he was about their marriage. Ila was disgusted with him, but treated Tavis the same as she always had. She went so far as to start another rumor that Jack had seduced Tavis, taking advantage of her innocent nature to trick her into marrying him.

Kyrie didn't appear to have any reaction, other than being surprised at first, then helpful to them anytime they visited the store. Meg and Alec weren't shocked at all, and Meg was quick to chastise anyone who dared speak ill of them in her presence. Frank seemed disapproving, but didn't treat Jack any differently and he refused to ever think of Tavis in any kind of bad light.

Eventually, Jack grew more hurt by the treatment he received whenever he and Tavis went out. He was finally happy in his life and instead of being joyful with him, everyone treated him like an undesirable tramp in their otherwise perfect society. Tavis told him to give them time, and that it wouldn't be long before they found something new to gossip about.

Still, it chafed him, so he took to not-so-subtle ways of appeasing his resentment. Any time they were seen in public, and when given a cold reception, Jack pulled Tavis close and kissed her shamelessly just to spite them. Sometimes, he even laughed maniacally when he heard their gasps—intent to shock them further. It made him feel better, but only fueled their fervent whispering.

After a while, most of the islanders got used to seeing them together. Jack was tentatively forgiven and received back into the island fold. It was the pretentious sorts, such as Ila, that lingered unforgiving in the wake of Michelle's past.

One night after they'd gone to bed, Jack cuddled Tavis close to him, her back against his chest. It was especially comforting this evening, as it helped soothe his bad mood. Earlier in the day, after he stepped out of the barber's shop, he saw Ila talking to another woman who had her teenage daughter with her. He was curious if Ila was still sore at him.

Jack started walking over to them and was about to say hello when they saw him approaching. Ila bristled and when the other woman saw the reaction, she ushered her daughter away as though afraid Jack would pounce on her if he got close enough. Ila turned her back to him and strolled into the general store. Not only had it been humiliating, it also made him angry.

He dismissed the ugly memory. "Can I ask you something?" Jack stroked Tavis' hair.

"Of course." Tavis considered reading his thoughts, but set the urge aside.

"I've been curious about something for a long time. You and Sebastian weren't really newcomers, were you?"

It was a subject she knew would come up sooner or later, but knowing it didn't help her much. "No, not in the sense you mean. We weren't invited to come here."

"You're not from Alaska, are you?"

"No."

"Where did you and Sebastian come from?"

"I can't say."

"Why not?" A twinge of irritation laced Jack's tone.

"I won't betray my father's trust."

"Well, what about me?" He raised his voice. "You don't care whether or not I trust you?"

"Jack—"

"Dammit, Tavis!" He sat up. "You're my wife and I have every right to know where you came from. Why won't you tell me? Is Sebastian a criminal? Is that why there's no talk about your mother… did he kill her?" Jack grew angrier with each of his mean-spirited questions. "Maybe you're both just side-show freaks looking for a better life."

Tavis sat up and looked at him. "You're being cruel."

She reached for her pillow and turned to leave. Just before she stood from the bed, Jack's hand clamped down around her wrist.

"Where do you think you're going?"

Tavis turned her head to look at him again, and then her eyes went to her wrist. His gaze followed hers and the sight of his hand squeezing her wrist horrified him. "What the hell am I doing?" He released her immediately and pulled her to him. "I'm so sorry, Tavis. Tell me I'm not a monster."

Tavis felt the anguish radiating from his emotions as he hugged her close to his chest. "You're not a monster, Jack. I wouldn't love you if you were. But just so we're clear, don't ever touch me like that again."

"I'd rather die first. I shouldn't have said those nasty things to you either. I was in a bad mood because of what happened with Ila earlier and I took my anger out on you. It was childish, inexcusable behavior and I'll regret it for the rest of my life."

"The way Ila's been treating you is wrong. To be honest, it's starting to make me angry, too. We're just gonna have to ignore her."

"I know, you're right. I'll stop trying to make peace with her." Jack leaned back a little to look into Tavis' eyes. "You're right about something else, too. You should never betray your father's trust, not even for me. I don't care where you're from, I'm just glad you're here."

~

After their impromptu nuptials, they rarely left their house and when they did, they developed a reputation for being perpetual newlyweds who seemed to think they were honeymooning on a deserted island. On many occasions they were found in passionate embraces, anywhere from the beaches, to the waterfall lake, and even in the forests. Once, Alec had to turn his cart around on the way home and take a different route at finding them stopped in the middle of the lane, completely oblivious to their surroundings.

Chaza had also stumbled upon them, several times. Though it was a shock finding Tavis in these intimate moments, Chaza was happy for her. She laughed at imagining how Sebastian was handling the newest island scandal.

One Sunday afternoon, Sebastian went over to their house and knocked on the door. Jack opened it, wearing only a towel, causing Sebastian to grimace at the sight.

"If you can endure the separation, I'd like to talk to my daughter for a minute."

"Sure, come in." Jack opened the door wider.

Tavis walked into the front room and Sebastian raised an eyebrow at the small scrap of red silk she wore. He shot Jack a disapproving glance, assuming he was responsible for Tavis' attire.

"Hey." She slipped on a robe and smiled at him. When she saw the stand-off between her father and Jack, she asked, "Did you come to see me, or fuss?"

"I wanted to make sure you weren't being held prisoner to start with," Sebastian said, staring at Jack a moment longer before turning to Tavis. "Also, I'm here to invite you both to dinner tonight at Ila's house. Do you think you can leave this house for a few hours to eat in a civilized manner?"

"What's that supposed to mean?" Tavis demanded.

"It means you two should pay more attention when you *do* manage to go out. You're not the only two people on this island," Sebastian said to both of them. "People are making jokes about where you'll be found next."

Tavis' face flushed red and she mumbled, "Okay, I get it." She peeked at Jack and saw a worried frown on his face. "Wait… did you say dinner at Ila's? Are you sure she meant to invite us?"

"Yes, she specifically wanted you both there, along with Kyrie, myself, Alec, and Meg."

"All right, we'll go," Tavis said.

"Good, I'll let her know you'll be there." Sebastian approached Tavis and held his arms wide. "Give me a hug, I haven't seen you in forever."

She gave him a chastising look, but hugged him anyway. Though he did miss their time together, Sebastian was more interested in discovery. He inhaled a deep breath, listened intently, used every technique both old and new known to him, and confirmed what he already suspected. He kissed her cheek and said, "I'll see you later. Dinner starts at six o'clock, don't be late."

When he left, Jack pouted. "I don't want to go," he said. "I'm not looking forward to more dirty looks from that… from Ila."

Tavis shrugged. "Maybe ignoring her worked and she wants to make things right."

~

Surprisingly, dinner went well. Every now and again, Tavis had difficulty looking at Alec and Kyrie, knowing who they were to her. The discomfort had been growing stronger; they were her family and she wanted to be as such. Her gaze would then drift to Sebastian, only to find him already watching her. There was a silent understanding between them as he gave her a reassuring smile.

Ila appeared cordial to Jack. It was still a chilly reception, but at least she wasn't snarling as much. Alec watched the interaction between Jack and Ila and laughed to himself from time to time. At one point, Jack noticed the amused expression and he frowned at Alec—who'd been seated beside him. They both realized it wasn't a coincidence that Ila had put the two of them together at the table.

"I'm just glad it's *you* and not me now," Alec whispered to Jack, trying hard not to laugh when Ila glared at them.

Tavis was happy to see Meg again, whose previous little belly wasn't so little anymore. Tavis thought Meg looked radiant and happy, almost aglow in warmth and color—even more than she was used to seeing from her.

"Tavis, would you like a second helping?" Ila asked.

Everyone at the table stopped talking and looked at Tavis, who'd started nibbling at the food on Jack's plate.

The fork Tavis was about to put in her mouth, laden with rosemary roasted potatoes, hovered in the air briefly before she set it back down. She was embarrassed now and wished everyone would stop staring at her.

"She can eat whatever she wants," Jack said, meeting every curious eye at the table with anger.

"I'm fine," Tavis answered Ila.

Alec experienced an odd twinge of outrage at seeing her avert her eyes to the table, and was about to speak up on Tavis' behalf when Ila spoke again.

"Perhaps Jack's not feeding you enough." Ila's intent was to be funny, but everyone looked at her as though she'd tricked them all there to further shame Jack and Tavis.

Every eye was set in judgment, except for Tavis', who'd fixed her gaze on the floral centerpiece adorning the table.

"Oh, come on," Ila said, exasperated. "I had a good reason for asking Tavis that. I made a dessert, especially for her... and Jack, too, I guess. I spent all day working on it. I just didn't want her to get full from dinner. I *was* going to wait a little longer, but I'll bring it out now."

Sebastian was ready to get up from his chair and take Tavis home himself after trying to sense Ila's thoughts, only to find the frustrating and chaotic maze of memories he normally encountered. What kept Sebastian seated was detecting Ila's genuine emotion of having wanted to do something nice for Tavis.

"Kyrie, can you help me bring my surprise out?" Ila asked.

"I'd love to." Kyrie set her linen on the table by her plate and followed after Ila. "I can't wait to see the dessert that can change a lovely dinner into a potential lynching."

A few minutes later, Kyrie returned to gather the plates from the still somber table. "We're all gonna feel exceptionally bad in a minute," was all the hint she gave before scooting off.

"Tavis, you haven't been over to see me in a while." Meg attempted to lighten the atmosphere. "Would you like to come over soon and see the baby's room? I'm almost finished with it."

She appreciated Meg's effort to restore normal conversation. "I'd like that, thank you."

Kyrie returned and winked at everyone before she shut the overhead light off to give the dining room a softer glow. Right behind her came Ila, carrying a huge cake of pink and white icing with red marzipan roses circling each of the four tiers. At the very top of the cake stood a bride and groom figurine—it was truly beautiful.

As Ila approached the table, she said, "Even though Tavis and Jack eloped, there's no reason why they shouldn't have a wedding cake. I hope you like it." Ila smiled at both of them as she set the cake down.

Tavis' eyes stung, but she refused to allow the tears to fall. She stood and went over to hug Ila, whispering, "Thank you, Ila. Jack and I are so happy."

Everyone enjoyed watching Tavis and Jack cut into their cake and feed each other a slice. Sebastian was particularly pleased, as he found these little rituals fascinating; marveling at how they united people, even if only for the moment.

Jack and Tavis took the rest of their cake home and stuffed themselves so full they fell asleep with the plates still resting at the end of their bed. It was Jack who woke first, when the first few rays of daylight dawned over Gamma and peeked around their window blinds.

He removed the forgotten plates to the kitchen and returned to watch Tavis sleeping. As always, he found her peaceful repose to be one of the most beautiful sights his eyes would ever witness. She had kicked the covers off and his eyes drifted down her torso, stopping at her abdomen. Gently, he flattened his palm there.

Tavis' eyes opened at the contact and found Jack smiling at her.

"Good morning, sleepyhead," he said.

"Good morning."

"Tell me, how've you been feeling?"

"Fine. Why?"

Jack patted her belly. Though small, there was a noticeable roundness to it. "What's this?"

"My abdomen."

Ignoring her sarcasm, Jack asked, "Do you think it's possible you're pregnant?"

"Well, Jack, considering what our favorite activity is, I'm sure it's a possibility."

"When did you last have your period?" Jack couldn't recall her ever having one.

"Not since before you and I were together."

"That was quite a while back, Tavis. Shouldn't we find out for sure if you're pregnant?"

"It'll become obvious all on its own if I am."

"Yeah, but I'm all curious now." He stuck out his bottom lip.

Tavis sighed. "I suppose we could go to the store and get a pregnancy test. It's still early, no one will be in there yet. But if I am pregnant, I'd rather keep it private for a little while longer."

"Kyrie might guess it's possible," he said.

"She won't say anything to anyone."

Excitement lit Jack's face. "You really mean it? We can get one? Come on, let's go."

"We have to put clothes on first."

He jumped out of bed and nearly tripped on the rug. After a mad dash to the closet, he snatched the first dress he saw off its hanger and brought it to her. "Is this good?" he asked, holding it up for her approval.

"Good enough," she said, laughing at him.

Jack pulled on the pants he'd worn to dinner at Ila's since they were at the top of the clothes hamper. One leg went in easily, but he started hopping to keep from falling as the other pant leg had twisted up, refusing to allow entry. He groaned, sat on the bed to unwind it, and shoved his leg in. With a quick flap to air it out, Jack pulled the shirt he'd worn to dinner over his head—wrinkles and all.

"Ready?" he asked.

"Your shirt's inside out," Tavis said as she got up from the bed. "And please brush your teeth."

Once she was ready, Jack raced them to the store. When they went inside, Jack pretended to be interested in light bulbs until he heard a tapping sound. He turned to the source and found Tavis glaring at him with her arms crossed and foot tapping on the floor.

"Are you really gonna let me stand there alone in front of Kyrie and ask her to put this on our account?" She uncrossed her arms and waved the pregnancy test in front of him.

"No." Jack slipped Tavis' hand into his and they walked to the counter together.

"Good morning, you two. You're up early today," Kyrie said and then caught sight of their sole purchase. She picked it up and tucked it inside a brown paper bag. "Did you need anything else?"

Tavis looked at her, wondering what life would've been like if Kyrie had raised her. It was becoming almost like torture to be around her, to not tell Kyrie that she had a daughter, to not tell her the true significance of what she had just handed Tavis in a brown paper bag.

"That's it. Thank you, Kyrie," Tavis said.

~

When they got back home, they returned to their bedroom. Tavis ripped the package open and put the test piece on the bed in front of them; they looked at it as if they expected it to do something magical. She picked up the paper provided in the box and unfolded it. After reading the instructions front to back, she set the paper down by the crumpled box.

"Well, should I pee on it?" Tavis asked, looking at the test.

"What?" Jack frowned at her.

"That's how these tests work," Tavis explained. "It detects certain hormones in urine that are only present during pregnancy. My question is, do we really want to know right now?"

"Yes, we really want to know… right now."

"We could wait, like I said before. Let it be obvious on its own."

"Why are you changing your mind again?"

She bristled. "I have my reasons."

Jack hid his frustration when she didn't elaborate. "Are they private reasons?"

"No, but" –Tavis looked sideways at Jack– "they're embarrassing ones."

He smiled at her unusual behavior. "You shouldn't feel embarrassed to tell me anything."

She was still reluctant.

"I would never laugh at anything important to you."

"I'm afraid you'll treat me differently if it turns out I'm pregnant."

"Treat you differently how?"

"You might not want to…"

"Want to what?" he prodded.

"You know, *be* with me."

It was a puzzling admission, but after a moment it dawned on him what she alluded to. "You're afraid I won't want to have sex with you if you're pregnant?" he asked for confirmation.

"Right," she said with a quick nod.

"Tavis, you can't possibly be worried about that! Have we met?"

"But I *am* worried about it."

"As a fully functioning member of the male gender, I can assure you that won't be a problem."

"You can't know that for sure."

"Oh yeah? Since I already think you are pregnant, I'll prove to you how much it doesn't matter. Allow me to refresh your memory, madam."

Jack grabbed hold of her and pinned her to the mattress, kissing her neck and growling playfully. His hand started pulling her dress up to her thighs while she laughed and tried pushing him away. He continued his pursuit by nudging her legs apart with his knees. Still, she struggled and laughed at his effort to prove himself right.

In the worst ever French accent, Jack stopped long enough to say, "Theese wooman, she prrotests my lahve. Eet cannot be, I shall weether away weeth deesire fer her."

"No!" She giggled when Jack's lips returned to her neck. "I have to pee, I've been holding it for the test. But yes, that's what I was worried about."

"You don't have to worry about it, I'll still want you with shameless abandon even when you're nine months pregnant."

"Okay, I'll do it." Tavis snatched the pregnancy test off the bed and headed to the bathroom. She turned to shut the door and found that Jack had followed her. With her hand still on the doorknob, she said, "I don't need an audience while I pee on a stick."

"I won't look."

Jack wouldn't budge from the doorway; she knew he intended to stay and would even argue if she refused him.

She relented and handed him the instructions. "Fine, turn around."

Even though she'd already memorized them, Tavis let Jack read the instructions aloud. He wanted to be involved and she wouldn't deny him that. When she said she was finished, he turned around wearing an expectant look.

"It's gonna take a few minutes, at least," she said. "Didn't you read that far?"

He looked at the paper in his hands, scanning the parts he hadn't bothered reading. "Oh." He put the instructions on the sink counter. "Want to go back to bed while we wait?" he asked and winked.

Tavis was the one who resisted Jack's attempts to be intimate after returning to their bedroom. "I'm too jittery, I can't."

"Who's rejecting who, hmm?" he asked, chuckling.

"I can't take it, it's been long enough." Tavis pointed at the bathroom. "Go get that stick."

"Did you just tell me to fetch?" Jack got up from the bed. "Great, now I'm a dog." He retrieved the test, smiling from ear to ear as he handed it to her. When her eyes met his, he said, "You're officially my pregnant wife."

11

Discover Me

They'd only been realized parents for an hour when Tavis asked, "How do you feel about it? Is it too soon?"

It wasn't so much the question as it was her doubting tone that got Jack's attention. He suspected what she really wanted to know. "Too soon for us, or too soon after losing one with Michelle?"

"Both."

"I love you, Tavis. If you'd be willing, I'd have a hundred babies with you. Starting now is perfectly fine with me." He sighed before going on to the more delicate issue. "What happened with Michelle was a mistake. We always took precautions, but she got pregnant anyway. I didn't love her, and I know she didn't love me. Hell, half the time she acted like she didn't even like me."

"I saw how upset you were when she miscarried."

"Yeah, it stung. It was my baby." This was a loss that Jack had quietly suffered from and he hated thinking about it—and for a multitude of reasons. "When it happened I felt relieved, too, and that made me feel worse."

"I want to ask you something else." Tavis closed her eyes for a second to rally her nerve. "Remember when you asked about whether or not my father and I were invited to come here?"

"I remember," Jack muttered, still ashamed.

"Were you and Michelle really newcomers?"

The question hit Jack hard, he had assumed it didn't matter to her. "I think we all knew that none of us were really newcomers."

"Would you be betraying anyone if you told me why you came here?"

Jack shook his head. "No." He swallowed a nervous lump and plunged headlong into the truthful abyss, hoping it would change nothing between them. "Michelle and I were weather researchers working for the corporation who founded, developed, and most importantly, maintain this island."

He paused to see if Tavis was shocked, but she wore only a patient expression. Not being a true islander, hearing that he worked for management wouldn't horrify her like it would everyone else, so he continued.

"Employee relations are strictly forbidden. Management discovered we were involved and were planning to confront us. I got scared and convinced her to come here and hide. I should've already told you all of this before you married me. Now that I have, I suppose you'll be wanting a divorce."

Tavis squeezed his hands to keep him from moping. "Don't be silly. Why would I want that?"

"You haven't lived here very long. If you had, then you'd know how everyone feels about outsiders, especially management and their scientists." Jack looked at her with sheepish eyes. "They even view the maintenance workers suspiciously. If the islanders knew I worked at the research station, they'd hate me and have me removed."

"Well, then" –she smiled at him– "let's not tell anyone."

"Someone already knows."

"Who?"

Before he answered, she remembered.

"Alec," Jack said. "The research station isn't very far away from Gamma. Before everything happened with Michelle, I used to sneak over here whenever I thought I could get away with it. I was always careful to not be seen, but I guess I wasn't careful enough. Alec confronted me and said he'd seen me once, walking near the docks. After he grilled me, I told him what I just told you and he said he'd keep my secret. So far, he has."

Having been there herself that day, Tavis knew Alec had seen Jack by the docks, but didn't know for sure if Alec had ever confronted him about it. "Why do you think he decided to keep quiet?"

"Um…" Jack squirmed. "Well, he wanted me to spy on you and Sebastian. He doesn't seem to like Sebastian very much. I didn't want to do it, but I sorta let him think I would. I avoided it by barricading myself inside and letting everyone think I was hopeless without Michelle."

"Has he mentioned it since then?"

"Nope." Jack grinned. "I did spy a little, but not on Sebastian."

She hugged him tight. "None of what you've told me changes how I feel. I don't care who you worked for, or who you were involved with before me."

"I'm so relieved to hear you say that," he said. "I'm glad you know now. In fact, you know what?" He leaned back. "I want to take you somewhere on this island that few people have seen. I've only seen it once."

"Where?"

"Have you heard anyone talk about the underground bunkers since you've been here?"

Tavis wished she could deny knowing about them, but she'd have to lie to do it. She'd been noticing a peculiar thing with Jack: lying to him was becoming increasingly more difficult, as the evidence of a lie reflected back at her in his frowning expression. She found it odd and decided to talk to her father about it later. In the meantime, the absolute truth would have to suffice.

"No, I haven't heard anyone mention them."

"There are tunnels under Gamma. They were built for weather emergencies, but most islanders have never seen them. I was taken on a tour of them after they hired me." His excitement kept building on itself. "They're really interesting, and a little spooky. You want to see them?"

"Interesting *and* spooky?" she said. "Who could refuse that?"

"We'll go in the morning. I'll ask Frank if I can borrow his rowboat. There're only two entrances, the one I went through is only accessible by water."

She knew about the bunkers, but not how to get to them. The entrance Jack meant was by way of the ocean and she wasn't all that thrilled with the idea. "Where's the other entrance?"

"I have no idea, maybe we'll find it tomorrow." Jack saw her apprehension. "Don't worry, I know how to row and the ocean entrance isn't far from the docks."

"Okay, we'll go. You've got me all curious now."

"You'll like it." Jack gave her a quick peck on the lips. "I'm gonna have a shower and get ready. I'll need to ask Frank about the rowboat today and check the tides for tomorrow. Want to come with me?"

"No, you go ahead. I'd like to visit with my father," she said. "Unless you wanted me to go."

"You should visit Sebastian, I think he misses you." Jack rolled out of bed and winked at her. "Besides, I was talking about joining me in the shower."

"You're impossible," she said, rolling her eyes.

He stopped in the bathroom doorway. "Who's treating who differently? You used to always want to take a shower with me."

Jack ducked when Tavis threw the pregnancy test at his head, laughing while he turned the shower on.

He started humming a tune and goosebumps formed on Tavis' body. She knew the melody well, but Jack couldn't have ever heard it before. Though it wasn't exact, most of what he hummed was close enough to be undeniable.

Tavis got out of bed and walked toward the bathroom, barely breathing. There was no mistaking it, Jack was humming a lullaby sang to children by her people. She crept through the doorway, peering past the clear shower curtain. Seeing the water cascade down Jack's sun-darkened backside caused an instant reaction in her body.

"There you are, I was wondering when you'd get in here," he said, his back still facing her.

"How did you know I was standing here?" she asked, knowing she'd made no sound that would've given her presence away.

"I don't know, I smelled your perfume or something." He turned around, wearing a wolfish smile.

Watching the water roll down his chest increased her longing, but she suppressed it. "I'm not wearing perfume."

"What difference does it make? Get in here, I'm lonely." Jack pulled the curtain back, inviting her in. "Please." Jack looked at her with begging puppy eyes, making her smile. She stepped into the shower, happily giving in to her desires.

~

"I'll probably be gone for a few hours," Jack said and kissed Tavis before he got in the cart. "Enjoy your visit with Sebastian. Tell him I send my love."

Tavis laughed. "Sure I will, he'll think you've lost your mind. Tell Frank I said hello."

"I will. Kiss me again, your father's watching." She kissed him and gave him a good pinch, too.

When he drove away, Tavis went over to where Sebastian waited on his porch. "How much time do I have with my daughter before Jack returns to continue seducing you?"

"Stop," she said and sat in the rattan chair, relaxing back against the cushion.

"So Jack sends me his love, does he?"

"You're an eavesdropper now, huh?"

"It's in my nature." Sebastian chuckled. "Where's he off to?"

"If you were listening, you'd already know where he's going."

"I do, but why's he going to Frank's?"

"Jack wants to borrow his rowboat so he can take me to the underground bunkers tomorrow morning."

Sebastian raised an eyebrow at Tavis. "He confessed?"

"Yes. He said Alec knows, too, but that he'd keep quiet if Jack spied on us for him." Tavis eyed the serving tray on the table. "Is that fresh tea?"

"Of course." He pointed at a linen-covered basket. "And I mastered the art of baking fine pastries. They're all for you and Jack. You can take them home later, or eat them all now if you want."

"I would've never guessed it, but Jack can cook." She lifted the linen and went for a croissant. "I love these things."

"I'm glad Jack can cook, I don't have to worry about my daughter starving."

Sebastian waited, hoping Tavis would tell him herself, but she seemed more interested in pulling apart the buttery layers of the croissant and then eating the flaky strands.

"I learn new things about him all the time. Unfortunately, I can't find an explanation for some of it and I wanted to talk to you about it while he's gone."

"What sort of things?"

"Hold on." Tavis finished off the croissant and resisted the urge to get another. "Not that I want to, but I can't seem to lie to Jack. I have to either keep my mouth shut, or answer in absolute truths. Even then, sometimes I get this feeling like he might sense more than I think he can."

Sebastian smiled; he knew what was happening with Jack. It did seem to be advancing at a faster-than-average pace, but it pleased him. "I'm surprised you don't already know, Tavis. You and Jack chose each other, it's a bond. He's assimilating."

"Oh." Tavis smiled. "Is it supposed to happen so quickly?"

"I admit, I've never seen it happen this fast before."

Her prideful smile morphed into a mystified frown. "What do you mean, *before*?"

"A long time ago, our own scientists did some experiments. It's a touchy subject, and it was one of the things that Chaza and so many others came to oppose." Sebastian wavered, as he hadn't planned on discussing this horror with Tavis, but he continued—at least with some of it. "We took some people from this island and brought them to our home, let them mingle with our own, and waited to see what bonds would form, if any at all."

"Were there any?"

"Only a few," he said. "Those that failed to create a bond with anyone were returned here with their memories absorbed. I'm afraid to say it, but the ones we brought back here didn't do so well afterward and that's why the experiments were stopped."

Tavis was intrigued and had a million questions. "What about the ones that stayed at our home?"

"They're still there, doing quite well. They assimilated beautifully, inherited some of our unique abilities, and their lives are better than what they had here."

"Did any of them assimilate as quickly as Jack is?"

Sebastian chuckled. "Well, Tavis, you only gave me one example. Being able to pick up on the subtleties of lying is meant to strengthen the bond between two people. There are very few ways of getting around it, and you've already discovered keeping silent—" He considered Chaza, and the similarities astounded him. "...and distancing yourself. A person doesn't have to worry about lying or hiding a truth from their mate if they're not around them."

"I'll give you another example," Tavis said, interrupting his bewildered thoughts. "I heard him humming one of our lullabies in the shower earlier."

"Which one? Hum it to me."

Tavis duplicated the correct version and said, "He didn't have it exactly right, but it was close enough."

"Ah, yes. The lullaby we sing to infants." He couldn't resist it any longer. "It seems Jack's already bonding with the baby."

She was floored. "You know?"

"Of course I know."

Tavis wanted to protest, wanted to be mad at him for invading her privacy, but blaming him was pointless. Of course he would know she was pregnant. She was, however, curious about one thing. "How long have you known?"

"Why do you want to know that?"

"Just curious."

"I'm reluctant to answer."

"I can tell."

"I confirmed it when I invited you to dinner at Ila's, but I'd already suspected it long before then."

"How long have you known about Jack and me?"

"From the very beginning."

"Why didn't you say anything?"

"Contrary to what you may think of me, I was respecting your privacy… as much as I could anyway." Sebastian gave her a reassuring smile. "I'm glad I did. I can see how happy you are with Jack."

"I am." She nodded, grinning.

"Do I need to act like I don't know about the baby when I'm around Jack?"

"No, I'll tell him you know later, but I want to keep it private for a while. The only other person who might suspect it is Kyrie. We got a pregnancy test from the store this morning."

"You're secret's safe with her."

It took her a moment, afraid it would worry her father, but eventually said, "It's getting harder to look at her and ignore the fact she's my mother."

"I'm sorry, Tavis, but there's nothing I can do to fix that right now."

"I know." Tavis refilled their teacups while she thought of Alec. "I imagine it would be just as hard to look at my brother, but he's practically walled himself and Meg away from everyone. I hardly ever see him, except in passing. Dinner at Ila's was the longest visit yet, and more like a shock really. I was surprised he even came."

"You know how he is with Meg." Sebastian shrugged. "And it's normal for him to be even more protective while she's carrying their child. Don't be surprised when Jack starts behaving that way."

"Think Meg's assimilating?"

"I don't know, Alec doesn't come to me with questions like you do." Though he grinned at his quip, a groan of failure soon erased it. "Short of kidnapping her, I'm not sure how I'll ever find out more about her. I will say this, though, she's an odd enigma and I hope that's not a bad thing. I just can't shake the feeling that I'm missing something important that would explain not just Meg, but Alec, too."

"She invited me to come have a look at the baby's room." Tavis winked at him. "Maybe you should come with me when I go."

"Well, I'd be delighted, Tavis."

They had a good laugh and then Sebastian broached a subject he'd been meaning to discuss with Tavis. "There's still time, but you need to start thinking about the conversation you'll have with Jack."

"I already have been. To be honest with you, I'm not as worried about Jack as I am Alec." Tavis cautioned, "You're gonna have a lot of trouble with him. He's not gonna want to leave here."

"I know, and I don't look forward to forcing him if it comes to that." Sebastian waved his hand dismissively. "Enough of this oppressive subject. How about you let me see if you're having a girl or a boy."

"No," she said. "I want to find out for myself. Besides, I was thinking we could go see Meg now."

"What about Alec? Is he working today?"

"Yeah, I saw him loading the utility cart this morning at the store, and it was stuffed. He'll be gone all day."

"Let's go pay a visit, shall we?"

~

Meg was sitting outside in the shade of the oak tree, reading a book on roses, when they pulled up in front of the house.

"Pretty little thing, isn't she?" Sebastian whispered to Tavis.

"She is, and she looks adorable with that belly."

"Won't be long before you're *adorable*."

Tavis shot him a warning look. "Hush, she's coming over."

"Hello, you two. I'm so glad you came to see me."

"You've been busy planting." Tavis looked around at all the flowers exploding in color. "You have three more flower beds since the last time I was here. It looks amazing."

"Thank you." Meg turned to see what all Tavis viewed. "I've been having a lot of fun with it. I was thinking about making a rose garden on the other side of the house. I've always wanted one, but my mother says they're too fussy."

"Only for those who don't know how to treat them," Sebastian said. "Personally, I think you should put them on the other side of that oak tree. There's more sunlight there and roses love the sun. Also, when they're blooming you'll enjoy the scent in the ocean breezes while you sit under your tree."

"That's a good idea." She cast a curious look at him. "Are you a gardener, too?"

"I've always had a fondness for flowers."

"Especially roses," Tavis said.

"Come inside and have tea with me. I can't wait to show you the baby's room." Meg was already leading them to the front door. "I finished the last bit this morning."

Tavis and Sebastian were stunned when they walked into the room. Hand-painted on one wall, where the canopied mahogany crib stood, was a scene of Alaret Beach. Part of the ocean and beach were included with the sea oats in a frozen state of blowing in the wind.

The cliff wall was positioned in the left most corner, continuing on to the adjacent wall. You could just make out a dark hollow at the top of the cliff, and dotted along the edges were small white edelweiss blooms.

The rich green forests of Gamma decorated another wall. Stepping closer, you could see paths that wound through the trees and had, in places, been taken over by vines and roots. The last wall showed a scene of the stone house, complete with the garden and Meg's favorite oak tree.

The door to the room was painted ivory and centered in the room was an intricately carved wooden rocking chair; a cushioned footstool sat in front and a small table with similar carvings stood nearby.

"Meg!" Tavis leaned in to get a better look at the individual oak leaves and clusters of acorns. "It's beautiful. Who painted all these murals?"

"I did," she said, blushing, but proud of her work.

Sebastian was just as awed by them as Tavis. "*You* painted these?"

"Yes." Meg said, sounding somewhat insulted.

His atonement was quick in coming. "No, Meg, I wasn't doubting you. It's just that I didn't know you were capable of such artistry. It's truly magnificent."

"Thank you." Her smile returned. "This is what I've been working on. Once I got started, I couldn't stop painting. Sometimes I was in here all day and halfway through the night."

Sebastian moved closer to study the mural of Alaret Beach and the cliff wall. Meg had paid close attention to detail while painting the scene and he wondered if she had to use a photograph or if she painted it directly from memory.

The illusion of movement and sound was unmistakable, further confusing him as to how she possessed such a trait. His gaze drifted up the cliff wall and came to a stop at the dark hollow perched near the ceiling. Though he wanted to, he thought better of asking Meg for a ladder.

"What's that?" he asked her instead, pointing at the hollow.

Meg glanced up at it. "Oh, that's just an old cave at the top of the cliff."

"There's a cave up there?"

She grinned at the fond memories she and Alec shared there. "Yes," she answered, but said no more.

He sensed her unwillingness to divulge more about the cave, so he let it rest, deciding he'd explore it himself later. "Well, I'm very impressed by your painting abilities. You've captured these island scenes with absolute perfection," he said, still admiring the murals.

"He's right, Meg," Tavis said. "You should keep painting, your work is amazing."

The piercing sound of the whistling teakettle commanded their attention. Tavis peeked at Sebastian before turning away to follow Meg out of the room. She knew what he was thinking, and it confused her as well.

When they reached the kitchen, Meg insisted Sebastian and Tavis sit and relax at the table while she prepared the tea. As she set the serving tray down, she steadied herself on the edge of the table with one hand and her other went to her abdomen.

Sebastian got to his feet. "Are you okay?"

"I'm fine," Meg said to reassure him. "The baby's kicking… quite hard, too."

"May I?" Sebastian asked, holding his hand near her belly.

"Sure." Meg grabbed his hand and placed it on the spot where she'd felt the most movement. "He's jumping around right now."

He took full advantage of the unexpected opportunity to gather anything he could about the health of the baby. He closed his eyes to concentrate on the things he most wanted to know and opened them again at the sudden kick that greeted his palm.

Meg's eyes widened at him. "Did you feel that?"

He nodded to acknowledge her question, but something familiar in her wide, vibrant eyes tugged at his attention. He snapped out of the reverie at feeling yet another kick to his flattened palm.

Sebastian detected an increase in Meg's heart rate. "Did you eat something sugary recently?"

"Cookies," she said, sighing. "It seems I want them all the time now."

He laughed and continued with his exploration. There were several more thumps to his hand and he concluded the baby was healthy and strong. Interestingly, he also confirmed what Meg had mentioned before.

"You said *he* was kicking. So, you think you're to have a boy?" He'd already discovered the fact.

"I just have a feeling it's a boy."

After having their tea, they moved to the front room. Sebastian sat on the bench by the huge bay window so Tavis and Meg could sit together to chat.

"Jack must be good for you," Meg said to Tavis. "I've always thought you were so pretty, but now you look absolutely beautiful, and happy, and radiant." She gave her a sly smile.

Tavis' cheeks reddened at the compliment, and at the rest of what Meg meant. Her eyes darted to Sebastian's briefly before returning to Meg's. "Jack and I are doing very well."

Unable to contribute much to the conversation, Sebastian shifted his gaze to the window. It had a direct view of the enormous oak tree and beach beyond it. The leftmost window panes gave a partial view of the forest edging the back of the property. A movement by the tree line caught his eye; he saw Chaza standing there, staring right at him.

He glanced over at Tavis and made a quick decision. Even though he may suffer her ire later, he gave them something more to talk about. "I think I'll have a look at that barn that was built in record time. Tavis, you should tell Meg, I'm sure she'd love the company in her journey to motherhood."

"Tavis!" Meg was an instant bundle of joyful excitement. "Are you really pregnant?"

"Um, yes… I *had* wanted to keep it private for a while, but it seems my father has other plans." Tavis smiled at Meg, then turned her eyes to her father in disgust.

With an apologetic shrug, Sebastian stood and walked to the door, seeing himself out while Meg promised Tavis that she wouldn't tell a soul.

Nearing Chaza, watching her as she waited for him to approach, he suffered a painful guilt for everything wrong between them. Sebastian felt to blame for her being on Gamma—a hellish place she didn't belong in. He wanted her to go home.

He was just about to tell her this when she demanded, "What are you doing here?"

"Tavis wanted to see Meg," he said, scowling at her abrupt nature.

"I'm sure you wanted to see her, too."

Sebastian hadn't wanted to engage in a verbal battle with her, but she seemed intent on it. All he really wanted at this point were answers. "What are you hiding from me?"

Chaza was surprised by his equal abruptness, but maintained the conservative calm she reserved especially for him. "We've already had this conversation."

"I could always start guessing."

"And I could always refuse to answer."

"That itself would be an answer."

"Maybe, but you'd never know for sure." Chaza sighed, as if already bored with the discussion. "I could always just walk away from you right now."

"I could follow you."

She laughed. "You could, but you won't. You came here with Tavis, she'd worry why you left."

"You know me well, Chaza, *I* would never do that to Tavis," Sebastian said with a single purpose in mind. He saw the sting of his harsh words pass over her face. "Speaking of Tavis, she's pregnant."

"I imagine she is. I've seen them together, sometimes they make me blush," she said, satisfied he experienced a bit of her own sting.

"I've spoken to her and Jack about that," Sebastian mumbled.

"Ah, but it's new love, dearest. Don't you remember how that is?"

"I remember quite well."

"Are you happy with their union?"

Sebastian wondered if Chaza truly cared about Tavis' happiness, or if she was only trying to distract him. "They chose each other, and Jack's beginning to show signs of assimilating."

She nodded, even smiled a little. "That's good. They must be well-suited and very happy together for him to be assimilating so quickly."

Sneaking in the forewarned guessing, he said, "I'm curious if the same is true of Meg and Alec. Unfortunately, he keeps her thoughts so well-shielded I can't discover for myself if she's a good match for him. I can only assume that since they've chosen each other, and that's she's still pregnant, she must be."

"I've seen them together, they're very happy." Chaza took a risk, offended that Meg's worthiness was being questioned. "I've befriended Meg and I can assure you they chose each other a long time ago."

"Alec trusts you?" Sebastian could hardly believe it possible. He also found her sudden defense of Meg and Alec out of character.

"He tolerates me because Meg's fond of me." Chaza smiled. "I tread lightly to appease him. He seems to be getting used to me."

Sebastian leaned against a nearby tree and crossed his arms. "How does he accept the fact that he can't sense your thoughts?"

"Really?" She snorted, amused. "It never occurred to you? I give him false ones to sense."

"Huh." He was impressed. "Very smart. However, that's rather devious for our kind."

"I've been living on this island for a long time, Sebastian. Deviant behavior, even for our kind, is unavoidable. Assimilation works both ways."

He hadn't thought of this before and it worried him briefly, but he shut it down and dismissed it as an eventuality he had no intension of ever experiencing.

"It's too late for me to try that on Alec, he's already decided he doesn't trust me.

I wasn't expecting him to be so advanced and I still don't understand how he came to be as strong as he is at his age. Tavis is only just now starting to come into her own."

"You shouldn't take it personally," Chaza said. "Alec's like that with most people."

"You know an awful lot about Alec, and this is the second time I've caught you lurking around this house. You were at their wedding, too. Why are you so interested in them?"

Chaza's body stiffened and the air around them became thick with tension.

"You know something about them, I can almost see the proof of it in your eyes. Tell me what it is."

"You need to be getting back," she said. "They'll be wondering why you've been gone so long."

A half-smile formed on Sebastian's face. "Is this you *walking away* from me now?"

Chaza turned and stepped into the forest. Sebastian watched her go until he could no longer see her before he went back to the stone house. He found Tavis and Meg still sitting on the couch, laughing at something he hadn't been present to hear.

"Still mad at me?" Sebastian asked Tavis.

"No," she said. "Just don't do that again, okay?"

"I won't tell anyone else from here on out."

Tavis' eyes narrowed slightly, knowing there was hidden meaning in his promise. "We should go now. I wanted to get stuff done before Jack gets back from visiting Frank."

Meg winked at Tavis. "I know what you mean. It's impossible to get anything done when they're around. Come see me again soon."

"I will," Tavis said.

"It was good to see you, too, Sebastian." Meg walked them to the door. "You can help with the roses, if you want."

"Anything for you and the little one," he said. "I'll root some of mine and bring them to you."

~

Sebastian veered from the path that would've led them back to their homes. Though she already knew the answer, she asked anyway, "Where are we going?"

"To that cave, obviously."

Tavis sensed his edginess. Her own curiosity nagged her about the cave and why Meg included it in the mural, but that wasn't all that begged an answer. "What do you think about Meg's paintings?"

Sebastian looked over at Tavis as though she'd asked the most stupid of all questions. "I think they're impossible, if she's just ordinary," he said, hinting at Tavis' previous attempts to observe Meg. "You know perfectly well what kind of ability it takes to create that kind of art."

"I never saw her doing anything that remotely suggested she was capable of it. You only allowed me a few assignments, how was I supposed to—"

"Tavis, I'm not blaming you. I don't understand it either and it infuriates me to no end. I feel like the answer is staring me right in the face, but I just can't seem to figure it out."

"I know you weren't looking at the barn." Tavis shifted her gaze to her lap. "After you left, I looked out the window and saw you talking to Chaza."

"Did Meg see?"

"No, she'd gone to the bathroom and I got up to see if you were coming back inside." Tavis frowned, recalling how Chaza looked among the trees while talking to Sebastian. The only memories she had of Chaza as her mother came from photographs. "She still looks like the pictures we have of her."

Sebastian slowed the cart to a stop. "I'm sorry, I just realized it's the first time you've seen Chaza since..." Sebastian grimaced. "Are you all right?"

"I'm fine, it was just weird seeing her." Tavis shook her head, dismissing the feelings of abandonment. "What were you two talking about?"

"I told her I could start guessing at what she's hiding, but like I told you earlier, she could simply refuse to answer. When I told her that would be the same as an answer, she said if my questions worried her she'd just walk away."

"Did you try anyway?"

"Not really." Sebastian rubbed his chin, recalling bits of their conversation. "Guessing would sound more like wild speculation. Interestingly, Chaza has befriended Meg, and Alec tolerates their friendship."

"Why does she want to be friends with Meg and Alec?"

"Why, indeed. I asked her why she was so interested in them and that was the question that bothered her. Of course, that was when she refused to answer and walked away."

"Well, it's pretty clear then. Whatever secret Chaza's keeping from you must involve Meg, or Alec, or both of them." Tavis shrugged. "I can't imagine what, though."

"Neither can I and it's so damn infuriating!"

Sebastian slammed his hands against the steering wheel. It scared Tavis seeing him react this way to stress. For the first time since their arrival, she wondered if his being here for so long had become *too* long.

Concerned, she put a hand on his shoulder. "Please don't get upset. I don't like seeing you this way."

He regretted his outburst. "I didn't mean to worry you. I'll be fine once I sort it all out."

"If I have to, I'll seek her out myself and demand an explanation."

"I don't want you to do that," he said, then sighed. "I should tell you, I told her you were pregnant."

"I figured you had." Tavis didn't want to care what Chaza thought, but the reality was that she did. "What'd she say?"

"That she's seen you and Jack together and that you both look very happy." He left out the jibe Chaza made about *how* she discovered their happiness.

"She watches me?"

"Yes, she watches you. That doesn't surprise me at all and it shouldn't surprise you either. Chaza does love you, Tavis, and she cares about your happiness. Don't ever forget that."

~

Sebastian drove farther down Alaret Beach and parked among the sea oats at the cliff wall's base. They searched through the brambles for a way to the top. "Over here," Tavis called. "This looks like an old path."

He joined her by the overgrown footpath and they cast a weary glance at each other. *'Don't even look at it,'* he warned.

Tavis heard the thought as though he'd yelled it aloud. They turned to the path and began the climb to the cliff top. Once they reached it, and looked out over the beach and ocean, he asked, "Amazing view, isn't it?"

"Breathtaking," Tavis said, the high wind carried her answer away as soon as it escaped her lips.

"There's another cliff on the island. It's at the very tip of the mountains and easily twice the height of this one." Sebastian looked down the cliff wall to where their cart was parked. "There's no beach at the bottom, it leads straight into the ocean. It has a rather tragic history, people have leapt to their death from it."

"That's horrible." Tavis felt sick to her stomach by the grisly image that had formed in her mind. "I don't remember reading about that in the watchers' documents."

"It's not exactly a heart-warming story, so I omitted it from the files I gave to you." He grinned at her. "It's in the medical journals, though. I'm surprised you didn't read about it there. Oh, silly me, I forgot, you've yet to study medicine. Still, I'm hopeful you will one day."

"Hush, you know I will when I'm ready," she said, amused by his constant hinting that she follow in his footsteps.

She returned her attention to the scene before them. Looking down at the cliff's base, she doubted anyone could ever survive a fall from even this height. It made her wonder what would drive a person to intentionally do such a thing.

"Why would anyone ever jump to their death?"

"Because they chose to," he muttered.

Sebastian glanced at the cave entrance. The wind picked up, lashing their hair into their eyes. He looked back at Tavis and found she hadn't moved to follow him and it made him nervous seeing her there. "Come away from the cliff, Tavis. Let's have a look at this cave."

She turned her head to him. Their eyes met and it amazed Sebastian how similar Tavis and Alec looked. The both of them were an equal blend of himself and their mother. He wondered if Kyrie saw it.

He snapped out of his thoughts when Tavis faced the ocean again, still perched at the edge. Sebastian took a few steps closer to her and saw images of the thoughts she'd forgotten to keep private. She, too, was thinking of Kyrie and he sensed her sadness; born from wanting a closer relationship with Kyrie. Tavis wanted her mother.

The crushing pain and guilt for what he'd done overwhelmed him. Sebastian struggled with the urge to comfort his daughter and the desires to respect her privacy. He fought harder still to keep the tears from his eyes—she'd know what put them there if she saw them. After forcing the pain away, he set his focus on getting her away from the cliff.

"Now, Tavis!"

A shiver ran through her body. She shook off her burdensome thoughts and shuffled over to Sebastian, tucking her arm under his. "The wind has a chill in it."

Before her thoughts had turned to Kyrie, she'd been thinking of what Sebastian said. It was unimaginable to her that someone would choose death. She'd felt something unfamiliar on the cliff; what it must feel like to be truly mortal and to choose death—it felt hopeless.

They walked into the cave and stood in the center, observing and memorizing every detail. Sebastian went over to the discarded old blanket and bent down to examine it when noticing the wine bottles lined up against the cave wall. He observed that a good many of them were empty and the unopened ones were thickly layered with dust.

Returning his attention back to the blanket, he brought it closer to his face, trying to discern a scent and any memory associated with it. Frowning, Sebastian studied the scene as a whole and remembered the look of fondness in Meg's expression when she told him about the cave.

He smiled and said, "I think we may have stumbled across a private place of Meg and Alec's."

Tavis turned to assess the items Sebastian had discovered. "I'd say you're right." She pointed at the back of the cave. "Where do you think that door leads to?"

"It's probably an entrance to the underground bunkers." Sebastian dropped the blanket and stood. "When Jack takes you there tomorrow, see if they lead here."

Neither of them could find an obvious way of opening the door. Sebastian detected a scent, though, one he was all too familiar with and he closed his eyes to concentrate on what memories could be had. His eyes opened again at the clarity; the scent was too recent, too reminiscent of a conversation he'd just had. Most telling was Chaza's entry shortly before he and Tavis had made the trek up the footpath to the top of the cliff.

"Look over here," Tavis said.

Tavis found a small alcove that had been cloaked in the cave wall, adjacent to the steel door. She reached her hand through the small sphere and felt a handle at the top of the stone cubbyhole. Thinking it would open the door, she was just about to pull it down when Sebastian put his hand on her arm to stop her.

"Don't open it. I just discovered where Chaza's been hiding," he said, his voice imbued compassion. "This must be where she lives."

"Oh." Tavis removed her hand and stared at the steel door.

"Keep that in mind when you're with Jack tomorrow. Make sure he doesn't see her."

"I will."

"Thank you." Sebastian gave her a severe look of warning. "One more thing, please be careful and don't be gone for very long. I'd hate to have to rip this island in half looking for you."

"Okay," she said. "Stop worrying so much."

"We should go." He kept his voice low. "Chaza warned me she didn't accept visitors."

12

The World Beneath the Island

"I want you to wear this," Jack said to Tavis, holding up a bright orange lifejacket with numerous pockets, each of which contained several items.

They stood on the dock at the northern end of Gamma, near a piling he'd tied the rowboat to. Tavis took the jacket from Jack and put it on.

"What's this for?" she asked, finding the lifejacket uncomfortable.

"For your safety."

Jack fastened the buckles and safety straps on the vest, testing them repeatedly for their tautness. Several times, he stuck his hand inside to make sure it was tight against her torso. Giving the straps one last tug, he stood back and waited for her approval.

"I can't breathe. It's too tight."

"It's supposed to be tight. You can take it off when we get to the entrance." He frowned when she didn't express her gratitude at his thoughtfulness. He'd spent a considerable amount of time preparing for their outing, especially on the precautionary aspects.

"If I don't suffocate before we get there," Tavis mumbled.

"I heard that. Don't be so difficult. I want to tell you what's in the pockets in case you need them… but you better not need them." Jack offered a broad smile, hoping it improved her mood.

"I'm serious, I really can't breathe. Can't you loosen this thing a little bit?"

Though he grimaced his displeasure, Jack loosened the straps enough for Tavis to breathe freely again. When she accepted the adjustment, he pointed to one of the front vest pockets and waited for her to look at it before explaining its contents.

"In this pocket are several flares." He delved right in to his preplanned discussion of the emergency gear. "If the boat were to capsize, you'll need these for me to find you. All you have to do is point it at the sky and pull the tag on the bottom."

"But it's daylight."

"In these other pockets," he continued, "you'll find water packets. They're to prevent dehydration if rescue is taking too long. Just rip the tab off the top and drink. Make sure you ration them."

"Jack—"

"This side pocket contains a waterproof stun gun, should you encounter any sharks in the water. You simply touch it to the shark's nose and push the red button. Do you want me to show you how to use it?"

Pausing to see if she had any questions, or if she wanted him to demonstrate any of the survival tools—having brought extras in case she did—he waited patiently for her command.

Tavis had no intention of going through a survival class before getting into a rowboat and heading out over an ocean she didn't trust. Especially not after glimpsing the image in Jack's thoughts of the creature the stun gun was meant for. Instead, she turned around and started walking up the dock.

"Hey! Where are you going?"

"I'm going home," she said, keeping her eyes trained on the beach ahead.

Jack trotted after her and blocked her view of dry land. Not to be thwarted, Tavis fumbled with the lifejacket buckles to pry the offensive thing off, but he took her hands into his.

"What's wrong?"

"Sharks? Really, Jack? Flares? Just how far out into the ocean were you planning to row us?" Tavis tried getting around him.

He encased her into his arms, which wasn't easy with the stuffed lifejacket she'd failed to dislodge from. "I'm just trying to keep you safe, Tavis. We're not going out into the ocean, we'll only be hugging the coastline. Okay? I didn't want to take any chances, just in case. Do you really want to go back home?"

She sighed at his dejected tone. "Fine, I'll go. But if I have to wear this jacket, then you have to wear one, too."

"Mine's in the boat." His goofy grin returned. "I'll put it on, I promise."

~

Halfway to their destination, Tavis counted the notches on the rowboat and wondered where the other two oars were. She saw beads of sweat forming on Jack's forehead as he struggled to row while wearing the cumbersome lifejacket.

"You should let me help row."

"No," was all he said.

"Your chivalry is touching, but I think I can row a boat."

"There are only two oars," he said, recognizing the obvious trap.

"And yet, there are four notches on this boat. Where are the other two oars?"

"You're awfully ornery today. I took the other oars out because I don't want you rowing. It's too hot and you're pregnant." Jack realized he sounded rather gruff, so he added, "Besides, I wanted the workout."

Hearing the edginess in his tone, Tavis tried sensing what caused it. All she found was that Jack had become more adept at guarding his thoughts. She chose to let the matter drop and spend the rest of their lives reminding him that she'd *let* him win this battle.

Not long after the missing-oar debacle, they arrived at a rocky overhang that the rowboat could easily pass under since it was low tide. Once they passed underneath, it opened up to reveal a huge cave—appearing as though nature had created it, but that which management had tweaked to their own purposes.

Jack continued rowing until they reached the back of the cave where wooden eyelets were secured to the wall. Near the eyelets, steps had been carved into the stone, creating a staircase to a landing. At the farthest end of the landing was an archway leading to a corridor that had all the appearance of manmade construction.

After tying the rowboat to one of the eyelets, Jack helped Tavis to the first step and followed behind her. At the top, he told Tavis about the length of time they'd have to stay in the bunkers. "We won't be able to leave until it's low tide again, about twelve hours from now."

"What?" she yelled, and her *what* echoed throughout the cave. "Twelve hours? Why didn't you tell me that before?" She thought of her father's warning, but couldn't exactly tell Jack he'd tear Gamma to pieces to find her. "I didn't bring any food."

"We just had a huge breakfast. You can't possibly be hungry again."

"That wasn't very nice." Tavis tapped her foot, refusing to move. The more she thought about it, the more she *was* concerned about being stuck without food and water.

"I was only teasing you," he said. "It's a survival bunker, there's lots of food stored here for us to plunder. Besides, we don't have to wait for the tide to go out completely. It just needs to be low enough to clear the cave opening."

"There's water? And proper bathrooms? I'm not squatting anywhere, Jack." Tavis cast a longing glance at the cave exit.

He laughed and slipped her hand into his. "Yes, there's water and plumbing."

At the end of the corridor was a large steel door, identical to the one at Alaret Beach. To the left of it was a similar cubbyhole and Tavis watched Jack reach inside to pull the handle down, opening the door. She hoped he'd forgotten about wanting to find the second entrance to the bunkers.

Jack went through the opening and fumbled around in the dark passageway, searching for the main breaker box. When he found it, he opened the metal cover to reveal a panel board. A series of sharp clicks reverberated off the walls and the entire corridor in front of them lit up. Able to see better now, Jack flipped several more switches and the area beyond the hallway flooded with light, offering a glimpse of what promised to be a huge expanse of space at the end.

Satisfied he'd lit up enough of Gamma's underworld, Jack turned to her with an adventurous look. "Hello and good morning, ma'am. My name's Jack Cavanaugh and I'll be your tour guide today. Be sure to wear your name tag in a visible location, and please stay with your group."

"You're so silly." Tavis grabbed two fistfuls of his t-shirt and pulled him closer to give him a quick kiss. "That's half your tip, I'll give you the rest if I like the tour."

"Then let's get started, shall we?"

They headed down the long corridor and entered an enormous dining room. Oak tables were set in long rows, with all the chairs neatly tucked under them. Along the tabletops, in front of each chair, stark white placemats had been set in an orderly fashion. Hanging from the ceiling, in alternating lengths, were hundreds of lanterns shaped like upside-down umbrellas—each a soft-brown that cast a beautiful glow around the room.

Three of the walls surrounding the tables were faux windows, complete with drapes that had been tied back to form diamond shapes. Florescent lighting constructed behind them gave the appearance of daylight coming through the windows.

To the right, was an industrial kitchen equipped with everything imaginable to run a Michelin three-star restaurant. It was in pristine condition, as it was rarely, if ever, used. The copious amounts of unused stainless steel gleamed under the fluorescent ceiling lights. The floors and walls were of black and white tile, further enhancing the kitchen's look of cleanliness.

Leading from the dining area were numerous passageways. Tavis followed Jack through the first one, nearest the kitchen. On either side of the hallway were doors that opened up to individual living quarters, each with their own private bathroom.

When they reached the end of the first corridor, Tavis noted it ended with a tall stone archway that had been bricked in. They turned around and went back to the main dining area to explore the next hallway. Each corridor was more of the same, individual living areas, each ending in the same bricked archway. At the farthest end of the dining area was another large archway. They passed through it to find the longest of all the corridors and the rooms here were mostly management related, but a few were community related.

The first room on the left was a physician's area with several trauma stations. On the right was a smaller version of the general store, fully stocked. Spanning the rest of the corridor, was a recreational area. It had everything from games, to exercise equipment, and even a small library tucked away in the back with lots of cushy couches and chairs with coffee tables placed nearby.

The left side of the corridor had another room to explore, but Jack wanted to see the rest of the medical office. At the back of the examination rooms was a large apartment for the resident physician to use as a living space during natural disasters.

"Nice spread, huh?" Jack snorted.

"Did you really think Dr. Patrick would stay in the dormitories with the rest of the islanders?"

"No, of course not," he said, his voice full of scorn as he surveyed the glaring overclass.

The biggest room in the apartment was the bedroom, decorated in a masculinity that Jack found strangely insulting. He was certain there'd never been a female physician assigned to Gamma, or any other island for that matter.

By far, the largest object in the room was the grand king-sized bed that five people could easily sleep on. Its massive mahogany bedposts and canopy, carved in European classical style, almost reached the ceiling. The drapery adorning the four corners of the bed was made of the finest silk available and undoubtedly cost a small fortune. The mattress itself, puffed up like a giant marshmallow, lay undisturbed until Jack flopped face-down on it and mumbled something Tavis didn't catch.

"What?" she asked.

"Goose down," he repeated after rolling over. "It's a goose down mattress."

Jack looked up at the canopy, then at the headboard, finding more carvings. Wrought iron had been worked into the mahogany headboard in intricate scrolls that smacked of professional artistry. His gaze traveled over to the wall constructed in the same manner as the dining room. A total of seven faux windows were dressed in wispy sheer curtains that accentuated the false daylight coming in.

Like those in the dining room, they were synced to reflect real time. After explaining it to Tavis, Jack got up from the bed and went over to a control panel tucked away behind an oak armoire. Adjusting the timer, he told Tavis to watch the light.

What had been midmorning *sunlight* began to intensify to reflect high noon, and then mid-afternoon. The light faded to an early evening glow as Jack continued to fast-forward the clock. Once most of the light waned, she saw an image of the moon begin to take shape in the upper left corner and stars twinkled along the faux night sky.

"Wow!" Tavis stared wide-eyed at the moon. "It looks so real."

"It's also linked to a weather satellite." He turned the timer back to its original position. "If the programmed perfection gets too boring, you can mix it up with reality... rain, meteor showers, eclipses, whatever's out there."

Off to the right of the bedroom was an expansive office and library with bookshelves lining all four walls. The books consisted of everything from medical texts and journals, to classic literature and modern poetry. Soft lamplight was the sole source of lighting, giving it an old university library feel.

The bathroom was bigger than the front room and dining room of their newcomer house combined, and just as decadent as the rest of the apartment. Not only was there a domed standing shower, but also a recessed tub with a saltwater fish tank surrounding two sides. The tropical fish, and even a small octopus, swam around in their artificial environment—oblivious to Jack and Tavis' presence.

"How is their upkeep maintained?" she asked. "What about their food?"

"It's a self-sustaining tank and the food is programmed to dole itself by a timer." He tapped a finger against the glass and the only creature to take notice was the octopus, who appeared to make direct eye contact with Jack. "Maintenance workers come here periodically to replenish the food supply."

The only room left to explore was the kitchen, turning out to be just as typical as the rest of the rooms. The giant island in the middle consisted of a second washbasin surrounded by butcher-block wood, shiny copper pans hung from the suspended rack above it. Tavis opened the cabinets to find them well-stocked with nonperishable foods.

There was only one thing out of place and Tavis noticed it first; a teacup with the remnants of liquid that hadn't quite dried out rested in the base of the double sink. On the counter was a small plate with fresh crumbs on it.

"Come on, let's go to the next room," she said, afraid he'd discover the teacup and plate.

Tavis went to the doorway and held her hand out to Jack. Anxious to leave the pompous display of elitist lifestyle, he took her hand and led her out of the apartment.

Unlike the rest, the door to the next room was a large heavy steel one, reminiscent of the two entry doors to the bunkers. Though it was pulled to, it wasn't completely shut and Jack pushed it open to reveal a large office-type room. There were desks with chairs, and all along the walls and tabletops were monitors, all of which were off, with a thick coating of dust on each of them.

Jack let go of Tavis' hand and went to the first monitor to try turning it on. After testing them all, only one lit up; a view of the ocean-side cave they'd entered through. They saw the rowboat was higher up the piling from the incoming tide.

At the back of the surveillance room loomed another steel door, but not only was it closed, it was locked. Jack peered through the keyhole, but with no light on inside there was nothing to see. He ransacked all the desk drawers searching for keys, but none that he found allowed him entry. Not one to give up so easily, he found paperclips and unbent them to try picking the lock open—still it wouldn't budge.

"Humph… pick proof," Jack muttered. Tossing the paperclips aside, he looked at the door again, checked the walls beside it for a cubbyhole, and finally decided it was impassable. "I wonder what's in there," he pondered aloud, frowning at the door.

When Jack began his mission to open the door, Tavis slipped out of the room to investigate the rest of the corridor. At the end was another stone archway, but not bricked in like the others. Once she passed through it, she had the option to go left or right, but the right side ended with the typical brick wall. To the left was a narrow stone staircase and Tavis had a feeling she knew where it would lead to.

She ascended the stairs, assuming Jack was still preoccupied with the locked steel door. Halfway up, she heard him call out from the corridor, "Tavis? Where are you?"

A movement at the top of the stairs stopped her from going to him. It was Chaza. She looked down at Tavis with a fearful expression, and equal fear showed on Tavis' face.

'Jack's with me. Cloak the end of the stairs to look like a brick wall,' Tavis told Chaza silently before rushing back down to the archway.

"Tavis, where are—" Jack bellowed again, but stopped when he saw her emerge from the archway.

"I'm right here," she said, smiling.

"Find anything interesting in there?" He headed toward where she still stood in the archway.

Glancing at the base of the stairs, Tavis was relieved to find it cloaked—appearing as a continuation of the bricked back wall. She could just make out the iridescent quality of Chaza's cloaking. "Looks like more walls."

Jack looked at each end of the short hallways, seeing only brick walls on each and along the back. A frown formed on his face and he motioned to the left wall. "That's weird," he said.

Her eyes widened. "What's weird?"

Motioning to the right side as well, he said, "What's with all the brick walls?"

"Future expansion, maybe?"

"Probably." He shrugged. "I was hoping one would lead to the second entrance to the bunkers. I know there's supposed to be one around here somewhere."

"Did you get that door open?" she asked to distract him.

"No. That's probably where it's at."

"Want to go back to that kitchen and dirty a few dishes?" Tavis batted her eyelashes, Ila-style.

"Sure, let's go see what kind of food they stock in here."

He looked back at the locked steel door in the surveillance room again when they passed by, as if he expected a way in would suddenly make itself known. "I should've tried going in there when I was here before," he mumbled.

While they continued on to the kitchen area, Tavis tried to sense why Jack was so obsessed with the door. Unfortunately, his thoughts had become jumbled and none of the few things she could discern made any sense.

"Jack?" Tavis stopped walking when they reached the dining room. "What's wrong? You seem… I don't know, distracted."

As he'd continued walking when Tavis stopped, Jack was several feet in front of her with his back to her. It took him a moment before attempting an answer—he struggled with how much he should tell her.

"I was hoping to get into that room because I think it may have particular importance besides just being a second entrance to the bunkers. I wanted to see it, I wanted to study it more. It could have a lot of information that may be relevant to us."

Tavis still looked at his back since he'd yet to turn around. The situation seemed pressing and she wanted Jack to answer her more directly. She went over and stood in front of him.

"What kind of information do you think's in there?" she asked.

"I heard some things." Jack looked into her eyes. "Things that bothered me at the time, but they worry me even more now."

"Heard things from who?"

"From other researchers, and maintenance workers."

"Are you gonna tell me about it?" Tavis didn't like how Jack's growing concern made her feel.

"I don't want to."

"Will you tell me anyway?" She took his hands into hers.

Jack knew she waited for an answer, but there was an innocence poised behind the beautiful blue irises, defining her, and he dreaded destroying it. "I'll tell you what I heard, but I don't know if it's absolutely true. It's one of the things I'd hoped to find out for sure by coming here."

He let go of her hands and put his arm around her shoulder, continuing their way to the kitchen, remaining silent until they got there. As a distraction, he rummaged through the cabinets while talking.

"Like I said, I'd heard things… long before I came to work for management, so I asked a coworker about it after I'd been there awhile and he confirmed it. Management has a plan in place, they call it the End Plan." Jack fell silent again and started looking for pans, even though he hadn't decided on what to cook yet.

"What's the End Plan?" she asked, her voice more grave than he'd ever heard from her.

Jack slammed a pan down on the stove with too much force, startling her. She stood from the chair and turned to leave the kitchen. He bolted over to her, encasing her into his arms, molding her back against his chest—his hands moved to her abdomen and found peace there.

"I don't want to scare you," he whispered.

Tavis stared at the dining room wall's faux windows. They were brighter than they were before and she thought they, too, must be set to reflect real time. Her senses were more heightened than usual now and she could hear her own heartbeat as well as their baby's.

"I don't care if it scares me or not, I want you to tell me what you're worried about."

"It was planned from the very beginning, that should anything happen here that couldn't be fixed..." Jack didn't want to say the rest, but he blurted it out anyway: "This island is geared with nuclear devices for the purpose of total destruction."

A chill crept down her spine. She was shocked at first, but remembered everything she'd been taught about how people were here—how they relied on extreme violence to solve what they considered to be an inconvenient problem. Tavis realized what Jack had said was probably the truth and she wondered if her father knew about it.

Jack waited for her to respond. Minutes passed and still she didn't say anything. "Do you understand what I just told you?"

"That's why you wanted to unlock that door. You wanted to find proof?"

"Yes," he said.

"Do you have any idea what would have to go so horribly wrong here to qualify as not fixable?"

"No, I don't. I was hoping to find some clues in that room, but now that I think about it, management wouldn't keep that kind of information here."

This supposition was for her sake, as she'd sensed the lie. Or perhaps, Tavis considered, she wasn't the only one who relied on telling absolute truths.

Jack turned her around to face him, cupping her face in his hands. "Was I wrong to tell you?"

The sadness in his voice caused her physical pain. She wanted to reassure him they'd be okay, no matter what may happen to Gamma. "You were right to tell me, and I respect you all the more for it. I don't know what management has in store for this island, but you and I are gonna have a very long life together. You'll just have to trust that I know this. Can you do that for me?" Her eyes wore a pleading expression. "Can you trust that we'll be okay?"

A strange new feeling came over him; a growing trust that made him understand and accept that Tavis' confidence was enough—that perhaps she may know more than he did. He chose to believe her, and experienced more warmth from it than he figured he was entitled to.

"I can do that," he said, pulling her head to his chest.

"This island's going nowhere for now," she said. "Everyone here is safe. I want to be happy here with you awhile longer."

"You're right." He nodded over her head. "Gamma's been set up this way from the beginning. If nothing's happened yet, nothing probably will for a long time," he said, trying to convince them both.

Tavis stared straight ahead, still transfixed by the glowing faux window walls. She made no reply, not answering Jack—avoiding a lie.

"Babe?"

"What?"

"Let's not talk about this to anyone," he said.

"I agree." Tavis stood on her tiptoes and kissed him. "I'm getting hungry now. Feed me."

~

When they finished eating, they cleaned their dishes and put them away, making sure to leave everything exactly as they'd found it.

"Have you ever played billiards?" Jack asked while he wiped the counters.

"No. Is that in the recreation room?"

"Yeah." He frowned. "It was the big green table with pockets on the sides sitting in the middle of the room."

She ignored his teasing. "Nope, I've never played. Is it fun?"

Jack nodded. "Want me to teach you?"

"Do you think I'd like it?"

"I think so."

"Okay, let's play." Tavis gave him a playful scowl. "Or should I say, game on?"

"Ha, ha, woman!" Jack bellowed and stood tall to emphasize his declaration, walking with an exaggerated gait through the dining room. "Prepare yourself for defeat, for I am the lord and master of billiards."

After racking the billiard balls on the fine worsted wool surface, he explained the basics of the game and helped her pick out a cue stick. Once he scattered them with the break shot, he sank the solid three-ball and the game was officially started.

"I thought you said you'd never played before." Jack grimaced as he watched Tavis sink the eight-ball and win the game.

"I haven't." Tavis shrugged and put the cue stick away.

"But you just beat me."

"Beginner's luck, I'm sure. What, are you a sore loser?"

"Of course not." He sounded insulted and it made her laugh.

"I'm a quick learner. Besides, there's some skill involved, but mostly this game seems to be about prediction and luck."

Jack raised an eyebrow at her, looking at Tavis in a new light. "So, you're either a very lucky psychic, or I have an exceptionally intelligent wife." Smiling wolfishly, he added, "Sexy, too. Want to play something else on the table?"

"Stop it." She ducked from his nearing mock-predator embrace and looked around the room at the other games.

Feeling competitive and curious, he put his cue stick away and went over to the dartboard. "Let's see how well you do with darts," he said, a note of challenge in his voice. "Ever played?"

"No." She giggled when he shot her a suspicious look.

She paid close attention while he explained the rules of the game and they spent ten minutes practice throwing before beginning a game of Cricket. This time Jack won, but only in the final throw.

"Yes!" Jack clapped his hands while jumping up and down. "I won!" He punched the air victoriously and gave a bow to his imaginary fans.

"Jack, you're being silly."

"I know, I don't care… let me have this," he said, still elated by his win. When he calmed down, he looked at her. "Okay, I'm good now. Tell me, what do you think about darts?"

"Obviously, it requires skill in hand-eye coordination to a high degree of accuracy. I'd say a great deal of luck is involved as well. Trying to calculate potential outcomes doesn't seem to be much help though." Tavis eyed the dartboard. "Basically, you either hit your intended target, or miss."

He frowned at Tavis as though she'd just answered him in fluent Pig Latin, then he smiled. "Damn, you're a smart cookie, aren't you? Gettin' sexier with every word, baby."

Jack pulled Tavis into his arms, pressing his body against hers. He took the three darts out of her hand and threw them all at once at the dartboard. He breathed softly on her neck and swept his lips past her earlobe, saying, "You smell delicious."

She didn't want things to escalate here, not with Chaza just at the end of the hall and aware of their presence. "What's that table for?" she asked, hoping to divert his attention.

He turned to see what she pointed at and said with a gleam in his eye, "That's an air hockey table. I can take you down in air hockey."

"Show me how to play?"

Proceeding in much the same fashion as she did with billiards, Tavis excelled. When she won, she imitated Jack's earlier response when he won the Cricket match.

"I won, I won," she said while clapping.

"Okay, I get the point. You sure do know how to bruise a man's ego," Jack said. "Go ahead, give me your thoughts on air hockey."

"Well, there's some skill involved with hand-eye coordination, but being able to predict your opponent's next move is the best way to win this game."

He blinked a few times. "Are you saying I'm predictable?"

She laughed at his pouting face. "Only at billiards and air hockey, and maybe a few other things."

"We should look at the camera to see how the tide's coming along." Jack turned the air hockey table off. "Unless you want to check out the bunk beds in the dormitory, in a *predictable* way." Jack smiled, hinting at fun.

Tavis knew he was teasing, but he wasn't against it if she wanted to take him up on the offer. "No." She shook her head. "Not here."

~

Back in the surveillance room, Tavis peered over Jack's shoulder at the screen when he sat in the chair. The water level in the cave had fallen considerably and the rocky overhang appeared high enough to allow passage beneath it.

"We can leave whenever you want." He swiveled the chair around and pulled Tavis down into his lap. "Keep in mind, though, if you plan to try beating me at any more games we'll have to stay overnight."

"No way. Everyone would think we drowned at sea." Tavis looked at all the dusty screens. She ran a finger across the one nearest them, creating a dust-free line. Frowning, she asked, "What are the rest of these for?"

"Same as this one, for observation," he said. "I don't know where the other locations are because I can't get them to turn on. When we went back to the kitchen earlier I looked for cameras, but I didn't see any, so they're not for monitoring the bunkers. Wherever the cameras are, they must be out of commission."

"When you were in here before—"

"They weren't working then either. I was so thrilled just to be touring the place, I didn't want to ask too many questions."

"If the cameras aren't in here, then they must be above, on the island."

"Maybe at some point in the past, but these monitors haven't been turned on in ages." He pointed to the clean line she'd created in the dust. "They were probably meant to be used as a way to let people know when hurricanes had passed over the island."

"Maybe." She tilted her head. "It just seems like one or two cameras would be enough to show it was safe to come out after a hurricane."

"What a suspicious mind you have," he said, chuckling. "But I agree, it does seem a bit overkill. Not to mention it's never mattered."

"What's never mattered?"

"These bunkers have never been used for their intended purpose. No hurricane has directly hit Gamma in over twenty years."

Tavis knew this already, but she liked hearing him talk about it. She also knew Jack struggled with understanding why certain things happened and didn't happen on Gamma. "Why do you think that is?"

"I honestly don't know." Jack sighed. "It used to drive me crazy. There's no scientific reason for why hurricanes seem to always repel away from Gamma. I finally gave up trying to figure it out, maybe that's why I started getting bored with my work."

"I'm glad you got bored." She gave him a quick kiss. "Let's go home."

Jack turned the monitor off and helped Tavis to her feet. Just before turning the lights off, he glanced at the steel door, dismissing it when Tavis tugged at his arm. As they exited the surveillance room, he turned toward the archway instead of going back to the center of the bunker to leave.

"Where are you going?" Tavis asked.

"Hold on, I just want to see something before we go," he said and kept walking.

Tavis panicked as Jack approached and then turned left at the archway. She ran to catch up to him, fearing the worst—that the stairway may not be cloaked anymore and that he'd find Chaza. When she reached him, she sighed a quiet relief to see the stairs still cloaked, still appearing as a brick wall.

"Tavis, what do you see there?" He nodded toward the cloaked stairs.

"I want to go home."

He was too curious. If she lied, she worried he'd sense it. Tavis hadn't expected Jack to question the existence of what should look like a wall to him. Somehow or another, he detected the shimmering iridescence of Chaza's cloaking. Jack continued standing there, ignoring her request to leave. When he lifted his hand, she knew he meant to test what he saw.

"Fine! I'll leave without you." Tavis stomped off in the opposite direction in a last ditch effort to force his attention.

It worked. Jack turned to find Tavis halfway to the dining room archway. He glanced one more time at the strange opaque brick wall before trotting off after her.

"What's the matter?"

"I'm just ready to go home," she answered truthfully, but was growing weary of relying on this technique.

Jack checked the kitchen again to make sure they'd put everything away while Tavis waited by the hallway leading to the entrance. He turned off all the lights in the bunker and when they got back to the cave, he stuffed her back into the lifejacket while she scowled at him. At seeing her face, he loosened the straps so she could breathe.

"What did you think of it?" Jack asked while he rowed them back to the dock.

"It's an interesting place, thank you for showing me." Tavis smiled at him. "I know where we can go if I ever feel the need to bruise your ego."

~

The next day, when Jack left to take the rowboat back to Frank, Tavis went to Sebastian. If he did know about the potential destruction of the island, she wanted to know why he kept it from her. She'd gotten little sleep thinking about it and she was angry that it was Jack who told her instead of her own father.

She walked in without bothering to knock. "Did you know this island was rigged for complete destruction?" Tavis demanded.

"Hello to you, too," Sebastian said, turning a page of the book he was reading on the rise and fall of ancient civilizations.

Several long seconds passed while he continued to read; the silence became almost more than Tavis could stand.

Finally, he looked up from the book to address her question. He worried his answer would only make her angrier.

"Yes, I know." He closed the book and set it aside. "I take it Jack knows as well?"

"He told me about it yesterday while we were in the bunkers."

"I'm surprised management would discuss such matters with a weather researcher," Sebastian said, but it sounded more like a question.

"He said he'd heard rumors before he even worked for them and that a maintenance worker confirmed it."

"It's top secret information, Tavis. I seriously doubt rumors fly beyond the scope of management—"

"I don't care how he came to hear about it," Tavis shouted. "All I care about right now is you telling me why you chose not to let me know about something so important."

"Why would I tell you something so terrible?"

"Because I have a right to know!"

"Your right to know didn't influence my decision. It was my compassion as a parent that stopped me. What would you have done?"

The question gave Tavis pause. Of course it was a horrible thing; she knew why he didn't tell her. "Do you think they'd ever do that?" she asked, a desperation in her tone now.

"They have no need or reason to use their End Plan at the moment."

Tavis was shocked he knew the name for it.

Sebastian saw the fear forming in her eyes and decided to smooth over some of the damage of her newly found knowledge, without disclosing too much information.

"If the conditions were right, I believe they would destroy Gamma, and every living thing on it. They wouldn't even tremble with regret afterward. At the moment, there's nothing happening here that would cause them to make such a hasty decision. You have nothing to worry about, for now. Don't forget our own plans should they become necessary."

She thought about their recovery plan and it brought her comfort until she realized some things had changed since they'd arrived. "But—"

"I know what you're thinking and I want you to stop worrying about it. I have a plan," he said, hoping this would be enough to reassure her.

"Our recovery plan didn't include—"

"Enough!" he roared, cutting off her arguing. "I know very well what our recovery plan allowed for. I told you, I have another plan and it will work. Don't question me again, do you understand?"

"I understand," she said, nodding humbly.

"I don't mean to scare you." He softened his voice. "All I want you to know is that I have another plan in place that solves everything you're worried about. Too much stress right now isn't healthy for you or the baby." Sebastian smiled, flashing his dimples at her. "Will you trust me, daughter?"

Tavis joined him on the couch and he put his hand on hers, patting it reassuringly. She relaxed at the gesture and smiled back. "I trust you. I always have and I always will."

"Very good." Sebastian hid the totality of his relief well. "Now, tell me, were there any problems in the bunkers I should be aware of?"

"You mean with Chaza?"

"Of course."

"I found the end of a hallway that led to the second entrance where she's living before Jack did. I guess Chaza heard our voices because I found her at the top of the stairs."

"Did you talk to her?"

"Only silently, and only to tell her Jack was with me and to cloak the end of the stairs."

"So, he didn't see her?"

"No, but the ocean entrance has the same kind of metal door with a cubbyhole handle like the cliff cave does. If Jack were to ever discover it, he'd know how to open it." Tavis shook her head and sighed. "Chaza's cloaking on the cubbyhole won't matter."

"What do you mean?"

"Right before we were about to leave the bunkers, Jack wanted to see the end of the corridor again. He noticed something was different about it, like he could see the cloaking. I had to threaten to leave without him to keep him from trying to touch it."

"I wouldn't have expected that yet." An amused expression formed on Sebastian's face. "Seems like I keep saying that about Jack. I have no idea how he's able to assimilate so quickly. Apparently, you've chosen an exceptional mate to share your life with. I'm happy for you and your future with him." He gave Tavis a wink and added, "Don't tell Jack I said that."

Tavis laughed and thought of Meg and Alec again. "What about Meg? Do you think she's an exceptional mate for Alec?"

Sebastian groaned. "I don't know, Tavis. When we were visiting the other day, I was able to tell more about the baby she's carrying than I could about Meg. If it's not a basic emotion that *anybody* could sense, then I'm not privy. Alec wasn't even there and still I couldn't break through the shield protecting her thoughts and memories."

"You don't think it's possible, do you?"

"I know it's not possible," he said. "If Alec has that kind of ability, he'd almost match my own… maybe even surpass it, to be honest."

"Have you thought any more about why Chaza's so interested in them?" Tavis asked, almost hinting Alec had help.

He knew what she alluded to. "I've considered that, too, but there are several flaws in that theory. Alec would never form a coalition with someone like Chaza. Not to mention, she told me the only reason why Alec tolerates her friendship with Meg is because she fronts false thoughts and memories for him to sense."

"Wow, that's pure genius," Tavis said. "Too bad we didn't think of that."

"Yeah, I know. I hate admitting it, but it's a great strategy." Sebastian stared off for a moment. "I'm beginning to think Chaza's interest has more to do with Meg than it does Alec."

"Why?"

"She said she befriended Meg, not Meg and Alec." Sebastian raised his eyebrows. "She was a little too quick to defend Meg when I questioned her worthiness for Alec. And then there's the wedding, Chaza was there, but hiding in the trees. I can only assume it was because she hadn't *befriended* either one of them yet. If I'm right about this, then what I need to be asking myself is, why is Chaza so interested in Meg."

"Have you tried getting any more information from Ila?"

Sebastian snorted. "That woman's mind is pure chaos. I'd need a map, and still I don't think I could find my way around her thoughts and memories. I can't even recognize her memory structure because they're so fragmented and confusing."

"I wonder what happened to her."

"So do I." He remembered his encounter with Ila. "The last time I tried sensing information from her was at Meg and Alec's wedding. Part of what I found was that her memories have been heavily altered, and for a long time. Some had elements of our own memory modification, particularly absorbing and implanting false ones, but the vast majority didn't and seemed a rudimentary attempt."

"Do you think Alec did it?"

"No." Sebastian dismissed the suggestion immediately. "I don't care how advanced Alec is, memory tampering requires at least some medical knowledge. That only leaves the scientists and Chaza as options. I'm sure the scientists haven't reached our level yet, and if they did try experiments on Ila, that would explain the crude quality I discovered."

"You really think Chaza's responsible for some of it?"

"I think she's responsible for the parts that were clean," he said. "The parts that only one of our physicians could accomplish, which leaves Chaza as the only possibility. Unfortunately, she's also the only one with the real memories, and she's not talking."

Tavis frowned, still at odds with how much she hated messing with someone's memories. "Why would Chaza do that to Ila?"

"There'd have to be a good reason, wouldn't it?"

She considered it for a moment, thinking of memories taken versus reality, and tried to come up with something helpful. An idea, though maybe a stretch, came to her. "What about Kyrie?"

"What about her?"

"You can take memories and implant false ones, but you can't change history, right? Based on the watchers' files I read" –she narrowed her eyes– "the notes not removed anyway, Kyrie and Ila grew up together. If you think you can behave yourself, maybe you should try finding out more of Ila's history through Kyrie."

"Behave myself? What's that supposed to mean?" he asked and when Tavis smirked at him, he dropped the matter. "As we've both discovered, Kyrie knows when her thoughts are being sensed. I haven't bothered trying in a while."

"You could always try just striking up a conversation." Tavis let out a derisive snort. "You do still remember how to get information from someone verbally, I hope. When I say *verbally*, I mean spoken words, not sensing… and no touching either, please."

"Oh, stop it, Tavis. I think I know how to handle myself around Kyrie."

She laughed. "Yeah, right. I've seen how you are around her. It's the silliest thing I've ever seen."

"I'm not silly."

"Whatever you say." Tavis rolled her eyes. "By the way, I've seen the way she looks at you, too. Especially when you're not paying attention. I assure you, her thoughts are—"

"All right, that's enough."

"Fine. I do want to ask you something else, though." She held her hands up when he shot her a warning look. "Not about Kyrie."

"Go ahead."

"There was a room in the bunkers with a bunch of monitors. The only one that worked showed the ocean side cave entrance. So, I was wondering, are there cameras on this island?"

"There used to be," he said. "They were scattered all around the island, most of them placed discreetly on the trees. All the ones I know of don't appear to be functioning anymore. However, I don't like taking risks and I'm glad you're aware of them now."

"Me, too. I'm happy they're not working. It's so creepy thinking someone's sitting in a room somewhere, constantly staring at you through a camera."

They heard Jack's cart pull up outside. "Ah, Jack's back. I think I'll go visit Kyrie at the store. Maybe I'll ask her to have dinner with me." Sebastian stood. "Do you need anything while I'm there?"

Tavis thought he sounded way too eager to start trying to get information from Kyrie about Ila. Resisting the urge to tease him, she smiled and answered, "No."

After they walked outside, Sebastian went to his cart, "Jack," he greeted as he passed by him.

"Sebastian," Jack greeted back.

13

A Different Perspective

"How are you today?" Sebastian asked Kyrie when he entered the store.

"Fantastic." She closed the inventory log and smiled. "How are you?"

"Fine, thank you." He smiled back and almost asked her right then, but chickened out and feigned interest in whatever was on the shelf in front of him.

After a moment of seeing him stare mindlessly at the boxes, Kyrie got up from her desk and went over to him. "Did you have any questions about the feminine products?" she asked in a mock-professional tone.

Confused at first, Sebastian focused on the items he stood in front of. Then he realized why Tavis said he behaved silly around Kyrie. "No," he said. "Actually, I was curious if you had plans this evening?"

"Yeah, I've got a hot date tonight."

"You do?" Sebastian was not only surprised, but also disappointed at the idea that Kyrie was dating someone.

"No." She laughed. "Why do you ask?"

He inwardly chastised himself for being jealous. "Would you like to have dinner with me? There's this recipe I want to try out, but I'd like it if I had someone to join me. Naturally, I thought of you."

Compassion swept over Kyrie. With Tavis being married, and with a baby on the way, she thought Sebastian was undoubtedly at a loss—not knowing what to do with all his newly found free time.

"That's sweet you thought of me. I'd love to. What recipe did you have in mind?"

"Brown butter risotto with lobster."

"Oh! Feeling ambitious are you?"

"Well, I had an excellent teacher," he said and pointed at her. "We could think of it as my final exam."

Briefly, Kyrie wondered who had been cooking for him before he came to Gamma. It certainly wasn't Tavis since she didn't even know how to boil an egg.

"That does sound like a good recipe," she said. "Do you want to use my kitchen? At my house, I mean?" Kyrie hoped the question didn't sound too eager.

"If you don't mind. My kitchen's nowhere near as stocked as yours and we'll need a pot to cook the lobsters in. I don't have one big enough." He shrugged. "I also wouldn't mind having a dinner you helped me with somewhere else other than in this store."

"Wait, you have *live* lobsters?"

"Yeah." He sighed, thinking of their current living arrangements. "Frank showed me how to catch them using a trap. I checked it yesterday and there were two lobsters in it, big ones, too. They're in my refrigerator now. I'm either gonna try this new recipe with you, or take them back to the ocean."

"Forget about it, those lobsters are as good as cooked and I can hardly wait for dinner." Kyrie thought of everything she'd need to do to get ready. "Okay, I'll close the store early. You get the lobsters and meet me at my house in a few hours."

"I'll see you soon," he said.

~

Sebastian went back to his house and scanned the titles of cookbooks he'd accumulated, trying to remember which one contained the recipe. "There you are," he said, snatching up, *The Chef's Guide to Atlantic Crustaceans.*

He reread the recipe, memorizing every ingredient and detail before setting it by the door—the bag of lobsters soon joined it. A glance at the clock suggested he had plenty of time for a quick shower.

Afterward, once he'd settled on wearing slacks instead of shorts and was about to pull on a white polo shirt, he caught sight of his reflection in the mirror. He'd been noticing it with Tavis, but was shocked at seeing how island life had bronzed his own skin tone. His brown hair, though still wet, was reflecting a similar fate. The blue eyes stood out and he found this odd because he'd never thought of himself as different until now.

The resemblance between him and Alec were becoming uncanny. He frowned at this as he pulled the shirt on and convinced himself not to fret over it while straightening the collar. Back in the front room, Sebastian scowled at the clock and tried wasting more time by picking up where he'd left off in the book he'd been reading. It was useless, unable to focus, he tossed it aside.

"What am I doing?" he muttered to himself as he clipped some of his roses to take to Kyrie.

When he came back inside, a rustling noise got his attention and his gaze went to the bag the lobsters were in. "Oh, yeah? Ready to go to Kyrie's? Me, too." He shook his head and stomped off toward the kitchen to rinse the roses, mumbling, "Great, I'm talking to lobsters now."

Finally, the clock hands pointed at an acceptable enough hour and he grabbed up the cookbook, lobster bag, and bundled roses—remembering to turn the front porch light on as he left the house.

~

He pulled up in front of Kyrie's and saw her through the kitchen window putting a large stockpot on the stove. She'd changed clothes and wore the ubiquitous island spaghetti strap sundress. One of the straps had slipped off her shoulder and hung loosely by her arm, perfect and apropos. Sebastian considered the wisdom of being alone with her.

Kyrie went to the sink and while filling a container with water, spotted Sebastian sitting in the cart; she smiled and waved. He pushed his sense of foreboding aside and smiled back. When Kyrie met him at the door, she held a glass of chardonnay in each of her hands; he noticed she'd righted the wayward strap.

"Are those for me?" she asked, nodding at the roses.

"Of course." He traded the roses for a wineglass. "And these are the lobsters." He held the bag up.

"I want to see them."

"Let's get them to the kitchen first."

Sebastian followed Kyrie to the kitchen and set everything on the counter. He finished filling the stockpot with water and when he turned toward her, said, "Don't open that yet."

Kyrie yanked her hands away from the lobster bag and held them at her sides. She looked at him, her eye-blinking expression that of a naughty child who'd just got caught sneaking a cookie before dinner.

"Oh, don't you give me that look." He chuckled. "Their claws aren't secured. You wouldn't want to get pinched. When the water's boiling, I'll take them out and show them to you."

"Yes, sir." She grinned and went to the sink to fill a vase with water. "Thank you for the roses. I haven't received flowers from anyone since Alec was little. He used to pick every dandelion he could find and bring me an entire bouquet. It wasn't until he got older that he realized he'd been doing me a favor by weeding the yard."

"You're very welcome. Although, I did feel a little guilty since technically they're your rose bushes."

She corrected him. "*Used* to be mine. I gave them to you, so they're yours now and you've been the one taking care of them."

"We both have." He took the vase from her and centered it on the dining table. "Let's get the ingredients ready."

He joined Kyrie by the counter and opened the cookbook to the recipe, each scanning the ingredients list. "You smell great." She leaned in closer to him. "What is that?"

"Must be the soap I get from you," he said, shrugging.

Sebastian was a little surprised that Kyrie could discern his scent, he hadn't expected it. Though they shared two children together, she'd never chosen him; he wondered if that really mattered in their case. *Ah, but I chose her*, he thought to himself.

"Maybe," she said. "I might start using that soap myself. I didn't know it smelled so good."

They both took a generous sip of their wine in unison.

"Have you ever cooked risotto before?" Kyrie asked, changing the subject after an image of Sebastian naked in the shower popped into her head.

Sebastian's eyes widened slightly as he'd caught the image. It was evident to him that Kyrie's thoughts weren't as shielded as they had been. He cleared his throat and took another sip of wine. "Nope, have you?"

"Yes, there's lots of stirring involved."

Kyrie went to the cabinets for the ingredients they'd need while Sebastian opened the refrigerator to get the butter, stock, and onions. Once the water boiled, he pulled the first lobster out of the bag; it wasted no time trying to get hold of its captor.

"Here's the first, ready for battle," Sebastian said.

"Wow!" She watched Sebastian pull the second angry lobster out and join it with the other in the pot. "I'm glad you caught me trying to open the bag."

For the fifteen minutes they needed to cook, Sebastian and Kyrie busied themselves with readying the ingredients. Then, while the lobsters cooled on the counter, they sat on the porch to enjoy more of the wine and watch the sun disappear behind the forest on the other side of the lane.

"Tavis and I went to visit Meg the other day," Sebastian said. "Won't be much longer before she and Alec are parents."

"I know, and Meg's so excited. She has everything ready and now it's just a waiting game."

"She showed us the baby's room, it's truly remarkable. I didn't know she was so talented. Did she inherit her artistic abilities from Ila?"

"No way!" Kyrie snorted at the notion. "Ila isn't creative that way. She's good with horses, pretentious home décor, and entertaining. Oh yeah, she can cook, too."

"What about Meg's father?"

"Joseph? I knew him well, I never saw him paint, though." Kyrie sighed. "He died in a boating accident just before he and Ila were to be married. It devastated her."

"It's a shame he never got to meet his daughter."

"He never even knew about her," Kyrie said, refilling their wineglasses.

"I imagine Ila was heartbroken, knowing she'd have to raise her baby alone."

"Actually, no one knew she was pregnant, not even Ila. Not until she came home with a baby one night after she'd been out riding her horse on the beach."

"What? How's that even possible?"

"Ila was so depressed after Joseph died, and she didn't want to be around people. I convinced everyone to leave her alone and give her the time she needed to grieve. She spent most of her time alone, or with her horses."

"She would've had to have been in complete isolation. How could everyone not notice she was getting bigger?" He doubted the entirety of the story. "How could she not know it herself?"

"The doctor said it's very possible for a woman to carry a baby to term and not know she was ever pregnant until she went into labor."

"Dr. Patrick?" He could barely keep the disgust out of his voice.

"Yeah, he's been Gamma's physician since before I came here."

As a precaution, Sebastian shielded his thoughts at the mention of her arrival on Gamma. Still fascinated by the new information, he continued pressing Kyrie for more. "So, Ila had a baby… all alone… on a beach?"

"Apparently." Kyrie laughed. "I'm sure Ila didn't find Meg under a seashell."

"It's an astonishing story, though."

"I agree, but Ila turned out to be a good mother. She guarded Meg fiercely while she was a baby. The first friend Meg ever had was Alec." Kyrie looked over at Sebastian. "Think those lobsters are cool enough yet?"

"Yeah, let's crack 'em open."

~

While cracking open the hard shell of the lobsters, Kyrie cut her finger. She went to the sink to wash out the debris—blood flowed profusely down the drain.

"Dammit!"

"Let me see it." Sebastian held his hand out.

She put her wounded hand in his and he examined the gash to determine its severity. It wasn't very deep and he told her a bandage would suffice.

"You don't think it needs stitches?"

"Needs what?"

"Stitches," she repeated and blank-stared at him.

"Right, stitches." Sebastian recovered, remembering how wounds were healed here. "No, it's not that bad."

He wished he had access to his own medical supplies; a cut this size could be healed in a matter of minutes. Absorbing the wound was also an option, but she'd notice and demand an explanation. *Archaic remedies it is,* he thought to himself.

"Where do you keep the bandages?"

"In the bathroom."

Sebastian found the bandages in the bathroom's closet and scanned the instructions before leaving so he wouldn't look like an idiot not knowing how they worked. As he headed back to the kitchen, he thought of a way to absorb a little of the wound.

"Thank you," she said and went to take the bandage from him.

"I'll do it."

He wrapped her finger in a tissue to dry it before putting the bandage on. Part of him wanted to heal the cut while it was still exposed, but she watched him intently. After securing the bandage to her finger, he gave it a gentle rub, as though smoothing flat the adhesive, absorbing some of the wound so it would heal faster. Sebastian looked up at her and found her staring in awe at him.

"Thank you, again," she said in a soft whisper.

"You're very welcome." He smiled and winked at her. "If you don't mind, I'll finish opening up the lobsters. You can get the risotto started."

~

"You weren't kidding, this risotto does require a lot of stirring," Sebastian said, having constantly moved the contents of the pan around for over twenty minutes.

"That's right, so keep stirring," she said from her seat at the kitchen island.

Sebastian had taken over, insisting she relax and allow him to do the cooking.

Kyrie wondered, though, if he'd only said that because they kept bumping in to each other.

"I just added the last of the stock, it shouldn't be too much longer before it's ready to serve."

"Good! I'm starving, and since you banished me to this chair I can't even sneak a bite."

A few minutes later, while reaching into the cabinet for plates, Sebastian continued his quizzing. "Does Meg look like her father? I noticed she doesn't look much like Ila."

"Meg looks nothing like Ila, but she does resemble Joseph. Same curly blonde hair, same face shape." Kyrie recalled Joseph's angelic face. "He had green eyes, too, but Meg's are more intense. She even has his same personality."

"Sounds like you miss him."

"He was a great friend to me, to everyone. I don't think there was anyone who didn't like him. It was a sad day when he died."

When the risotto was declared done, they finished the final preparations of the dish and took their plates to the dining table.

"This is fantastic, Sebastian," Kyrie said of the first taste. After several more, she added, "I completely approve and give you an A plus for your final grade."

"You know, I never thought I'd enjoy cooking so much."

While they continued their meal, Sebastian fell into his thoughts. The story of Meg's birth was incredible, unbelievable really. He thought about how Ila's memories were either altered or implanted, or most likely both. Though still uncertain, Sebastian entertained the possibility that the two were connected.

Sebastian insisted he be the one to wash the dishes, saying she shouldn't get her bandage wet. His real worry was that if she changed it too soon, she'd see it was almost healed.

"I'm stuffed," Sebastian said, patting his full belly. "Care to go for a stroll?"

"I'd love to."

Kyrie put her shoes on and pulled a sweater over her shoulders. While walking down the lane, chatting about everyday occurrences, Sebastian decided to broach another subject—one more potentially sensitive to Kyrie. He already knew the background, but he found himself wanting to hear it from her perspective.

"You never speak of Alec's father. Is it too personal for you to talk about?"

When she bristled somewhat at the question, he regretted his insensitivity. He remembered how humiliated Kyrie was during her brief marriage to William Davis. As it did then, it brought him a feeling of wanting to protect her from the pain she suffered at William's callousness.

"I shouldn't have asked, I'm sorry."

"William Davis, that was his name," she said, regaining her composure. "He was the only person forced to leave Gamma for debauchery. We were married, but not even marriage could keep that man from chasing skirts. He caused quite a few problems, even broke up a couple of marriages in addition to our own."

"Was he really that bad?"

Nodding, she said, "He was really that bad. Eventually, enough of the husbands complained and William was removed from the island."

"That must have been difficult for you."

"When he cheated the first time, it was hard for me. After several more of his affairs, I stopped caring. I was glad when management came to remove him, but I was so embarrassed… everyone looked at me with pity. Management took care of the divorce quickly. About a month later, I found out I was pregnant."

They'd already started walking back to Kyrie's house and when reaching the front steps, they sat down to continue the conversation.

"Did it ever bother you having to raise Alec on your own?"

"Are you kidding me?" Kyrie's eyes widened with disgust at the idea of having co-parented with William. "I preferred it. I can't imagine how Alec would've turned out if William had had an influence on him." She smiled and admitted: "Besides, oddly enough, I've always felt lucky to have Alec all to myself."

Kyrie picked up their empty wineglasses and went inside to refill them. Sebastian followed her in, feeling better at hearing her peacefulness with being a single mother.

While she was in the kitchen, he walked over to the fireplace mantel and looked at the framed portraits. The most recent picture was of Meg and Alec on their wedding day. After studying Alec's face, Sebastian's gaze drifted to Meg's. He stared at her green eyes and remembered Kyrie's comment about them being the same color as Joseph's… '*but Meg's are more intense.*' There was a familiarity there he couldn't quite name.

"Mrs. Abbott?" Kyrie interrupted his thoughts.

"What?"

"You know so much about me and Ila now. I was curious to know a little more about you. If it's not too private, was there a Mrs. Abbott?"

Amused by her candor, Sebastian took the wineglass Kyrie held out to him. Hearing the term, he realized why Meg's eyes seemed so familiar—the emerald color reminded him of Chaza's.

"Yes, but she left me. I had to raise Tavis alone, too." Sebastian brought the wineglass to his lips and glanced back at the photograph. He drained half the glass while considering the coincidence of the similarity.

"I'm sorry to hear that. How long ago did it happen?"

Sebastian turned his back to the mantle. "When Tavis was still very young."

"Here's to single parents." She raised her wineglass.

They clinked their glasses and each took a sip.

Kyrie set her wineglass on the coffee table and stood in front of Sebastian—close, but maintaining a touchless space between them. She stepped to his side and then behind him, admiring what she considered an exquisite physique.

For the longest time, he felt the heat radiating from her body against his back, but nothing more. Sebastian almost wished she would finally make contact to end the unexpected torture; and then she did. She took the wineglass from his hand and placed it next to hers. Her hands pressed softly against his back and caressed upward to his shoulders.

Her fingertips trailed down the length of his arms, continuing the study of the lines she found there. When she reached his wrists, her body moved closer and pressed against his back. As her arms wrapped around his waist, she slid around to face him again, leaning into him, allowing him to feel the curves of her body. Her hands were on his chest, inching higher to his neck until they reached the back of his head and she ran her fingers through his hair.

Sebastian's body responded to hers and it scared him for a multitude of reasons. He wanted to stop what was happening, especially when the face of a dear friend popped into his thoughts, reminding him of who Kyrie really was. The face vanished when Kyrie tilted her head and pulled his to her neck. Her longing woke a passion in him that had been sleeping for a long time, urging him to abandon all reason.

There was one last weak idea to stop, but his body refused to allow the thought to win. He groaned in defeat, lifted Kyrie off the floor, and wrapped her legs around his waist. Sebastian carried her to the bedroom, unzipping the back of the dress along the way while showering her neck with kisses.

He stood her by the bed and the dress slid down her body to the floor—she wore nothing beneath it. She lay on the bed, waiting, watching as he removed his clothes. Then he stood there to admire her: studying every inch of her, memorizing her every curve, and when their gazes met, he joined her on the silky sheets.

"You are divinity, Kyrie," he whispered against her lips. Soon as her arms were around him, their bond was sealed for life.

It was power and beauty, and it was well past midnight when Sebastian woke to find Kyrie curled up next to him. He grappled with his thoughts when he sensed the newly strengthened bond between them; worried about how difficult it would be to hide it. A look at her sleeping face made him smile; he was drawn to her. He pushed the nagging thoughts aside and woke her, pulling her close—wanting her to make them go away forever.

When Sebastian stirred again, just before dawn, he had Kyrie cocooned in his arms. With the start of a new day not far over the horizon, his thoughts were clearer. Part of him wanted to wake her again, but he resisted the urge to consider what the rest of the day would bring; it made him uneasy.

This was a mistake, it shouldn't have happened, he thought to himself.

He felt Kyrie's body tense in what seemed a reaction to his thoughts and he realized she hadn't been asleep. Kyrie lifted her head and peered into his eyes; she looked crushed—she'd sensed his thoughts of regret. He remembered telling Tavis about the reason why Jack had begun to sense some of her thoughts.

Sebastian had chosen Kyrie for a mate and he'd been foolish to think of it in a clinical sense. This was why Chaza was so opposed to it, and so hurt by it. She had worried about the inevitable connection that would be created between them, and she'd been right.

Looking into Kyrie's eyes, Sebastian saw he'd hurt yet another who meant so much to him. For some reason, one that terrified Sebastian to acknowledge, Kyrie's pain hurt him more. He decided to try absorbing her memories of their night together.

He hugged her to him and closed his eyes while running his fingers through her hair.

"Wait," she said.

Her voice broke his concentration. He frowned, confused by her command and its meaning.

Kyrie added quickly, "I want to talk to you about something. Not here, somewhere else… a place I know."

She knew he wasn't convinced and was about to tell her no. "Management knows more than you think they do." She hoped this would have an effect—and it did.

Sebastian nodded, though still frowning.

"I'll call Alec and tell him to open the store because I have a headache," she said. "Get dressed, we should go while it's still dark outside."

~

She drove them to Mors Cliff. Between the high winds and the roar of the waves crashing against the rocks below, it was difficult for them to hear each other. "Do you know the name of this place?" she asked him.

"Mors Cliff."

"I assume you know its history as well?"

"Yes." He was jittery being near where there'd been so much death. "Do we have to stand so close to the edge?"

Ignoring the question, she said, "I know you were about to change my memory of last night."

"I don't understand what you mean."

"Yes you do. I want you to remove the memory, not just alter it. Can you do that? I know some people can."

He'd hoped she didn't remember much about her life and family before she came to Gamma. It appeared that hope was lost now. "That's not an easy thing to do."

"Management's more aware of what happens here than you realize, Sebastian. They know you're here, they track the store's paperwork and Dr. Patrick reports everything to them." Kyrie's eyes expressed a desperate sort of pleading. "I have a feeling they're waiting for something, and I think it has everything to do with you."

Sebastian closed his eyes for a moment to think. He worried that the complex circumstances of their relationship would prevent him from doing what she wanted. Taking her hands into his, he tried hard to absorb her memories of their night together, particularly to keep them from Alec. It was a miserable failure.

"I can't do it." He shook his head, defeated. "I can't, because I…"

"Because you what?"

"We have a bond, Kyrie. I chose you a long time ago and I chose you again last night. Short of bringing you to the brink of death, that bond prevents me from taking certain memories from you."

Kyrie appeared confused and he wanted so badly to tell her everything. Even though it would hurt her to know what he'd done, Sebastian wanted to share it with her. He wanted her to know they shared two children together, he was finished with her thinking William Davis was Alec's father. More than ever, he wanted her to know Tavis was her daughter.

"Close your eyes and see what I want you to see," he said.

She did, and images began pouring into her head. The night she got sloppy drunk when William was removed from Gamma, she saw herself about to fall asleep in her bedroom. Sebastian was there, and with someone else, a much older female who was also wearing a white physician's lab coat.

The next images were of the day she gave birth and again Sebastian was there, but alone this time. She watched his memory of him helping her deliver Alec while Dr. Patrick lay in a heap on the floor, and then there was a second baby, a girl.

Though she was still in his memories, half of them were hers before they were taken, and she remembered what had belonged to her. Kyrie had known she carried two babies, but dismissed it over the years as having been her imagination.

She watched the memory of Sebastian smile at the female infant and say her name would be Tavis, then he named Alec. He placed the babies side by side in the infant warmer and returned his attention back to Kyrie. His purpose and sole desire was to heal her body, not wanting her to suffer a lengthy recovery from giving birth to their children.

Seeing it all through Sebastian's perspective, Kyrie also experienced his emotions and she sensed he struggled, feeling guilty for the bond he knew had been created between them. She went through the anxiety he had for not discussing his plans with people who meant a great deal to him. Above all, Kyrie felt that he loved her.

Kyrie watched Sebastian pick her head up and lean her against his chest, swaying and humming to her while she still lay on the delivery table—he was altering her memories. The act had been easy then, Kyrie still weak and exhausted, the bond still new. When he was done, Sebastian laid her head back down again and kissed her forehead first, then moved to place another on her lips.

She saw him pick Tavis up and felt the pain it caused him having to leave both herself and Alec there when all he wanted was to take them all home. He looked one more time at her sleeping form and left. This was where the memory ended and he started to speak again, bringing Kyrie back to where they stood on Mors Cliff.

"So, now you know, you and I have a bond. I chose you a long time ago and last night, *we* chose each other." Sebastian looked at her timidly. "Truthfully, we've been skirting around choosing each other since I came back here."

Her eyes left his and stared unfocused at his chest. "Is that why you can't absorb my memories now?"

"I can't do things like that to you now," he said. "Memories can't be erased, they can only be absorbed, altered in varying degrees, or false ones can be implanted. No matter what, though, the memories aren't gone. The real history is always somewhere. Short of overpowering you physically, and I'd never do that, our bond protects us."

Tears formed and rolled down her cheeks. Kyrie wiped them away, though plenty threatened to replace them. "Tavis is my daughter, and you took her away from me."

Though it was a statement, it sounded like a question. "I did." Sebastian braced himself to feel the anguish of her anger.

"You should've taken Alec, too, and never have come back here," she said, surprising him. "I know you're gonna leave, I can sense it. Make sure you take Alec with you this time."

Kyrie turned around and looked out over the ocean. She closed her eyes to clear her mind of all thoughts so he couldn't see them. It wasn't easy thinking of nothing, so she focused her attention on a singular theme.

The swirling images of the general store's inventory that she allowed him to see confused him. Her arms had been resting by her sides and Sebastian watched them rise slowly. She fanned her fingers apart, as though to feel the breeze flow between them. Gusts of wind whipped her hair and dress toward the sea. The images he'd sensed from her came to a stop and were replaced by a feeling of regret.

'I'm sorry,' she said silently.

Leaning forward, Kyrie willed the wind to take her to the rocks and sea below, hoping there wouldn't be pain. The sphere around her was instant, freezing her in time. The wind stopped blowing and the waves stopped crashing against the rocks.

His voice thundered: "I don't care if you choose it or not, I won't allow it."

He grabbed one of her wrists and snatched her off the cliff; out of the sphere. It dissolved as quickly as it had formed. Relief swept over him as he realized he'd just saved Kyrie from certain death, his promise to watch over her still intact.

"It's the only way." She struggled to free herself from his arms. "Get Alec and Tavis away from this horrible place."

"I will," he said, trying to calm her.

"Alec won't make it easy for you." Kyrie shook her head. "He doesn't like you, he's suspicious of you. I don't know what he'll do if he finds out about all of this."

Sebastian sighed. "I know he doesn't care for me very much. He has warmed up to Tavis, though. I'm thankful for that because it might be the only thing that prevents him from contacting management himself." He scowled at her, at what she'd meant to do. "Don't you ever try that again. Do you understand me? Never. Nothing is ever so bad as that."

"He's gonna know, Sebastian. I can't hide this from Alec."

He knew she was right. The minute Alec sees her again, he'll know something's different and won't stop until he sorts it out. It occurred to Sebastian just how alike he and Alec were in that respect. Kyrie was nowhere near as adept as Chaza at secreting her thoughts and memories—she was simply too inexperienced.

"There's another way." It tormented him to even consider it. "*I* can't change your memories, but I can take you to someone who can."

"Who? Tavis?" Kyrie leaned back to look into his eyes, but he wouldn't let her leave his arms.

"No, Tavis isn't capable of that yet. Nor would she be willing to try." Sebastian cupped Kyrie's face. "Even if she could, I wouldn't allow it. Tavis means everything to me and the last thing I want to do is bring any stress into her life right now."

"Then who?" Kyrie frowned at him.

It was a miserable feeling to say it. "My wife. I won't lie to you, Kyrie, it'll hurt me to ask for her help. It won't be easy for her either.

"Wife? She's *here?*"

"Yes." He nodded. "This is where she's been since she left me. I didn't know until after I came here."

"If it's gonna hurt her, then we shouldn't ask her to do it."

"I'm afraid I have to insist." There was compassion in his expression, but also clear warning that he'd take her there kicking and screaming if need be. "I'd prefer it if you went willingly."

"I'll go," Kyrie said.

~

Not taking any chances, Sebastian gripped her hand while they walked away from the cliff's edge. As they walked the long stretch of the cliff top in silence, Sebastian looked around at the landscape and thought of the people who had come here to die. All of them had walked up the cliff, as he and Kyrie had done; however, none of them walked back down again.

When they reached the cart he got in on the passenger side, but moved to the driver's seat, refusing to let go of her hand. Once she was seated, he fastened her seatbelt.

"I'm not going to jump out," she said.

"For the most part, I believe you, and I trust you." Sebastian leaned forward to meet her eyes. He wanted her to see how it would've affected him had she been successful. "But choosing to end your life is insurmountable and I'd never forgive myself if anything happened to you. A very good friend of mine wouldn't forgive me either. So, if you don't mind, I'd rather not suffer my own self-loathing and his wrath. Okay?"

Sebastian watched closely for her response, searching for any indication that she knew who he referred to. Kyrie stared back at him, and either due to Alec's protective shielding or because of her own abilities, Sebastian met an all too familiar wall. Instead, he relied on finding the answer in her eyes and there was an unmistakable knowing shining back at him.

"You know who I'm talking about, don't you?" He needed to know, once and for all, how much she remembered of her family before coming to Gamma.

Without hesitation, she said, "Yes, I do."

He smiled at her answer and laughed inwardly at his foolishness. Sebastian thought he may kick himself for the rest of his life for thinking she didn't know her own ancestry, that she couldn't feel it.

Though it was a long drive from Mors Cliff to Alaret Beach, he took advantage of the early morning hour and drove as fast as the cart would allow. He parked amid the sea oats and unbuckled her seatbelt. For added measure, he cloaked the cart.

Kyrie watched as it disappeared, and continued to stare as though noticing the opaque haze surrounding it.

Sebastian followed her gaze. "You can see the strange blur around the cart, can't you?"

"Yes."

"Okay, come on." He wondered if he was about to waste his time, and Chaza's.

Sebastian walked away from the beach and toward the old footpath leading to the cave. Kyrie recognized it immediately. "Where are we going?"

"To the cave."

"She's in that cave?" Kyrie was shocked at first, but remembered the steel door. "In the bunkers?"

"Yes," he said. "That's where she's been living."

"What's her name?"

"Chaza."

The name held no familiarity, but Kyrie thought it sounded pretty. "That's a nice name." She grew more nervous with each step closer they got to the cliff top. "Does it mean anything?"

"It means oyster."

Sebastian considered the answer and came to an abrupt halt. Certain pieces of a complex puzzle seemed to fit together, but he couldn't force them into logic.

"What's wrong? Why did you stop?"

He cleared his mind again, deciding to think about it later. There was a more pressing issue at hand and he couldn't risk Kyrie sensing his thoughts and suspicions just before meeting Chaza.

"Nothing's wrong."

Before entering the cave, Sebastian picked up a large piece of driftwood. He tested its durability by hitting it against the side of a large boulder just outside the opening. The brittle end shattered and fell to the ground. He looked around for another and found an even bigger, sturdier one that held together after he put it through the same test.

"Why do you need that?" Kyrie asked, eyeing the large stick in his hand and hoping it wasn't for defensive purposes.

"I don't know how thick that steel door is. I'm sure a simple knock won't be sufficient." He knew how to open the door, but didn't want to do that out of respect for Chaza's wishes.

They went into the cave and Kyrie marveled at the sight of a place she hadn't seen in so long. Her eyes drifted over to where the wine bottles rested against the cave wall and saw the old beach blanket she and Joseph had used to drag them back there with.

"Sit here on the bench while I try to get her to see us," Sebastian said.

She ceased her reminiscing about the ways in which the islanders had resisted prohibition before management gave up on the futile attempt to keep them all sober. And though not as lucrative as the horse business, wine production turned out to be a pretty-penny endeavor.

Sebastian waited for her to settle down on the bench before going over to the door. He knocked the wood to it in three light taps and stood back to see if the door would open.

It didn't budge. He wondered if she was even in there, but given the early hour she had to be. The second knock came with more force, sending an echo reverberating throughout the cave. Still the door remained shut and after a few minutes, he tossed the stick aside and tried verbalizing his request.

"Chaza, I need to talk to you," he said and waited.

Still nothing. "Chaza, please come out here. It's important."

Nothing.

Tired and weary, Sebastian rested his forehead on the steel door, trying to keep his growing frustration at bay. "Chaza, please. I know how to open the door. I don't want to do that, but I will if I have to."

He waited a few more minutes, then went over to the cloaked cubbyhole in the cave wall. With a sigh, he reached his hand inside to find the handle. Just before he was about to pull the lever down, the steel door opened. Chaza stood in the doorway and watched Sebastian withdraw his hand.

"How did you find out about the cave?" she asked, not bothering to hide the magnitude of her irritation.

"Meg's painting."

"Of course."

Chaza stepped out from the doorway and into the cave, ready to go into verbal battle with him. She didn't appreciate being woken up so early and she was even angrier that he had discovered where she'd been living. Though she had hoped it wouldn't come to it, she planned to set him straight about how unwelcome a visit of any kind from him was.

She took a few decisive steps toward him, the assault just at her lips when she stopped—feeling the presence of another with them. Chaza looked past Sebastian and saw Kyrie sitting on one of the benches, watching them with keen interest. More importantly, and most telling, was the well-informed expression in Kyrie's eyes.

"What's she doing here?" Chaza asked, astonished that he would dare such cruelty.

Sebastian remained silent, so Chaza risked her own perceived dare by attempting to make her way over to Kyrie. There was a fleeting sense of dread as she passed by Sebastian, but as he allowed it, she kept going. Chaza extended her hand and said, "Hello, Kyrie."

Kyrie gulped back the nervous lump that had formed in her throat and put her hand in Chaza's without saying a word. It was the longest handshake she'd ever shared with anyone in her life, either by factuality or by way of the uncomfortable tension. Whichever, it felt like an eternity to Kyrie.

Chaza let go of Kyrie's hand and looked at Sebastian as if she expected him to deny what she'd just learned. He averted his eyes to the cave floor at her feet; confirmation enough. She fought her own internal battle with guilt. How could she fault him when she'd done the same, several times, and once in the very spot he averted his eyes to?

"Just so I'm clear, you *both* want me to alter her memory of last night and everything you showed her today?" Chaza asked.

"Yes," Sebastian answered for all three of them, still finding it difficult to make eye contact with either woman.

"I can't absorb the memories from her. At best, what I *can* do will only be a temporary fix. What happened between you will happen again." Chaza struggled to maintain her dignity. "This is exactly why I opposed your plan in the first place."

"What would you have had me do, Chaza?" Sebastian roared, startling all. "Let us die out?"

"No, Sebastian, I wouldn't have that." Chaza paused in the effort to gain control over her emotions. "I just wish there could've been another way."

"But there wasn't… there isn't," he said, lowering his voice.

"There's hope now, though. So it would seem, anyway," Chaza said with the barest glimpse over her shoulder to where Kyrie sat, enrapt and quiet.

"Maybe *all* of us will live on in future generations." Sebastian finally made direct eye contact with her, waving his arms to indicate each of them. He added, in what sounded like an accusatory tone, "Could it be possible?"

Silence filled the cave as Chaza studied Sebastian's words and the impenetrable hint they provided. He was challenging her, but made it impossible for her to sense even the smallest fragment of his emotions. She could only speculate at his meaning and it brought her a panic that she had to squelch before he found it.

She attempted to be the voice of reason. "Considering who she is, it may not work."

"Try anyway," he said.

"There's also the issue of management most likely being aware of your presence. Have you considered that?"

"I've considered it, and so has Kyrie. If you help with her memories, maybe it'll buy us more time."

"I can't change how you both will react when you see each other again," Chaza said with warning. "And you still need to understand, Sebastian, it might not work on her."

"I'm aware of that." The mental anguish threatened to undo his resolve. "I plan to avoid her afterward to prevent her from remembering. Just… suppress the memories." He shook his head emphatically. "But please, don't take them away from her. Do whatever you can, Chaza, I'm begging you."

She sensed a glimmer of what he was going through, his torture, and only because he allowed it. Encouraged by the unexpected openness, she closed the distance between them and reached for his hand.

Sebastian wanted more time to develop a better relationship with Alec and he feared what happened with Kyrie may have destroyed that hope. He was still, as he always had been, tormented over the promise he made to keep Kyrie safe and had every intention of keeping that oath. Moreover, Chaza understood, even felt it herself, why he prolonged leaving Gamma—he feared the stress alone would have an irreversible effect on Tavis and he wasn't all that certain about the safety of her traveling either.

She also detected his guilt. It hurt Chaza to know he still had a sense of obligation to her. "I'm to blame for what's failed between us, too, Sebastian." She squeezed his hand to reassure him. "I'm so very sorry that I hurt you."

"Will you do it now?" He'd let her get a sense of what he felt to make her understand how important it was that they come together, even if it only amounted to a temporary solution, to deal with a situation that could potentially ruin everything.

Her shoulders slumped forward and she removed her hand from his at feeling the sudden wall he had erected. Chaza turned, went back to Kyrie, and sat beside her on the bench. She had serious doubts her efforts would achieve what they wanted, but decided to try doing what she could to help them.

"How do you want the memory arranged?" Chaza asked whichever one would answer.

Kyrie spoke up, looking at Sebastian as though to seek his opinion. "Probably having you leave right after dinner. I'll notice differences in my kitchen, so we should leave that part."

He nodded.

"I'll have to implant a memory of her waking up with a headache and calling Alec to open the store for her," Chaza said, seeming to seek approval for the additional false memory of her own creation.

It took a great deal of bravery and effort, but Kyrie took control and even chanced looking directly into Chaza's eyes. Something of an ancient and mutual design passed between them—a kinship that Sebastian wasn't privy to—and they both nodded simultaneously at what they knew would be their only hope to buy more time.

Speaking to Kyrie, Chaza said, "When I do this, you'll fall asleep. You'll wake up like normal, but with a different recollection of last night and this morning. I'm going to put my arms around you and all you need to do is relax and let me in. Okay?"

"Go ahead, I'm ready," Kyrie said and closed her eyes. She relaxed her muscles and felt Chaza's arms wrap around her shoulders. Just as she thought how awkward it was, she fell into a dreamless sleep.

Chaza swayed slightly while she concentrated on what she meant to do. It was hard for her, seeing the images of Sebastian and Kyrie together, but there was no way around them—only through. Absorbing the memories hit an immediate wall of resistance, one she expected. Instead, she focused all of her energy into suppressing them.

Confident as Chaza was of her abilities, she frowned her uncertainty. Rather than dwell on whether or not she'd successfully suppressed the memories, she worked next on implanting a false memory of Kyrie waking up with a headache and calling Alec. Most of that memory was already there, she needed only to eliminate the sense of falseness and diminish Sebastian's presence.

The last thing Chaza did before releasing Kyrie was to examine other aspects of her body for any forgotten details that may be discovered later. She tensed at what she found and eased Kyrie down onto the bench before standing up to face Sebastian.

"Make sure she stays asleep until you get her back. Check for anything that may confuse her when she wakes up."

He nodded once and walked over to the bench to scoop up Kyrie's sleeping form.

Just before he left the cave, Chaza called out to him, "Sebastian." She hesitated for a moment. "You may want to examine her before you leave her house."

~

Sebastian parked the cart behind Kyrie's house, preferring not to take any chances that someone would pass by and see him carrying her inside. After he put her on the bed, he looked around the bedroom and removed all traces of their night together.

Satisfied with the appearance of the house, he sat on the bed beside her and listened to the sound of her breathing. Reluctantly, he placed his hands on her body; his own responded right away at the contact, but he ignored it. A quick search revealed no sign of a medical problem and he wondered what Chaza had found.

He thought of the things that made Chaza an excellent physician, particularly what field she was most skilled in. Almost scared to do it, Sebastian slid his hands down Kyrie's torso, relying on the quiet stillness of the room to calm him. He focused his concentration on the pathways Chaza must have singled out.

Then he saw it; Kyrie had ovulated, the egg fertilized now. Sebastian opened his eyes and looked at Kyrie's sleeping face, wondering what he should do. There was always a chance it wouldn't implant, and it would be easy for him to make sure of it. Yet, he couldn't bring himself to do it; it would go against everything he fought for. He removed his hands from her abdomen, feeling sick and ashamed for having considered it.

Sebastian stood; he wanted only to be alone with his thoughts and he desperately needed sleep. He passed no one along the way to his house. When he entered through the front door, he headed straight for his bedroom and collapsed onto the bed without removing his clothes or shoes.

~

The next few days were hard for Sebastian to get through. He avoided Kyrie at all costs, even leaving his house before dawn, fearing she may come over to thank him for dinner. Occasionally, his telephone rang in the evening and he refused to answer it. Simply hearing her voice could be problematic and he didn't want to test it.

A month passed and the phone finally stopped ringing. Sebastian would've allowed himself a sense of calm if it weren't for one prevailing thought. He fought against it, but nevertheless found himself standing over Kyrie's bed in the middle of the night, cloaked in case she woke up.

Looking at her produced feelings he knew would surface the minute he saw her. He closed his eyes to steady himself and to remember his purpose for being here. *I have to know*, he thought.

He placed the tip of his forefinger against her wrist to find her pulse. When he felt it, he forced it to slow down, just a bit, below its rate of resting. Then he influenced her into a peaceful dreamlessness so she wouldn't wake up when he placed his flattened hand on her abdomen.

Ignoring the warmth and softness of her skin, Sebastian focused on what he came here to find. He moved his hand slowly across her belly, concentrating to detect the sound of a growing new life. For a moment, he thought he would find nothing and, as he'd predicted, it made him sad. Then he caught the barest hint of a second beating heart tapping out in rhythm with Kyrie's. He listened carefully to confirm it and tried to stop himself from going any further, but it was a weak attempt—a lingering moment longer would satisfy his curiosity.

A son, he discovered and allowed himself to smile.

He knew he'd have to release Kyrie immediately, or risk not being able to. After removing his hand from her abdomen, he paused a moment to return her pulse to normal. Though it took a great deal of effort, he turned his back to her and walked away; leaving quietly out the back door he'd entered through.

14

Luke

Meg had worked out the design for her rose garden and, though the ones she ordered hadn't arrived yet, it could be made official by planting the rooted ones Sebastian had given her.

Alec had been working the whole day getting the soil ready to transplant the roses to. Occasionally, Meg got up from her chair by the oak tree to help Alec, but he would lead her back and suggest she help him by letting him know if he strayed too far from her intended borders.

"Being pregnant doesn't make a woman fragile," she said, fussing at him as he led her back to the chair a third time. "I'm still capable of doing my own garden work."

"You're almost nine months pregnant. I'm not letting you dig." Seeing the mutinous look on her face, Alec said, "You can't bend over anymore. I had to help you shave your legs last night." The reminder only made her pout. "Oh, come on, Meg—"

"But I'm so bored just sitting here. In fact, I'm tired of just sitting all the time, and I'm tired of feeling like a giant balloon."

Alec tried not to laugh, but Meg looked and saw his amused expression and she scowled at him.

"You certainly don't look like a giant balloon. I think you get more beautiful every day."

"You're only saying that so I'll stay in this chair."

"I am not." He leaned over and asked, "Would you like for me to take you inside and show you just how beautiful I think you are?"

"What if I said yes?"

Alec smiled and moved to lift her from the chair. She laughed and pushed his hands away, but they returned to tickle her.

"Stop!" she squealed. "You're gonna make me pee on myself."

"Are you sure you don't want to go inside?" he asked, still hovering over her. Alec was glad to hear her laughter; for days she'd been cranky.

"Yes, I'm sure. Besides, you'd probably hurt your back lugging me up the steps."

"Here's good." He winked.

"Not happening." Meg rolled her eyes and stood. "I *am* gonna walk around for a little bit, though. I was serious when I said I'm tired of sitting, my butt's numb. I promise not to lift anything too heavy. Okay?"

"All right, but don't walk too far away. I'll end up following you and then you'll be mad at me because the roses still aren't planted."

He gave her a kiss and returned to his work. Meg stretched her back, amazed at how much it had been hurting over the last several days. She meandered over to the other flower beds and found them boringly perfect, not even a stray weed to pull. Making her way to the barn, she stopped before going in to see if Alec was watching her—he was.

"I'm just gonna feed the hens and check for eggs. Eggs aren't too *heavy*, are they?"

"Go ahead," he said, laughing to himself.

Meg went inside, calling to the hens to let them know she was there. They gathered around her feet and clucked softly amongst themselves while she scooped up several helpings of their feed, sprinkling it onto the barn floor. Watching them quarrel and carry on conversations about who got the prime bits was entertaining for a while and then she went to the nest boxes to retrieve what eggs there were.

After gathering seven of them, she stopped abruptly at the last box she meant to check when seeing a burnt-orange colored hen sitting there. "Oh." Meg frowned and looked over her shoulder at the hens still pecking at the feed. A quick count confirmed she suddenly had an eighth hen.

"And who might you be?" Meg asked the unfamiliar hen. "Mind if I slip my hand under and see what you've got?"

Carefully, not knowing the hen's temperament, Meg slipped her hand under her and felt three very warm eggs. She was impressed the hen allowed it without so much as a cluck and she promptly removed her empty hand. "Well, you sure did come to the right place. I can't wait to see your chicks," Meg said to her and stepped away.

Moving past the hen gallery, Meg put the gathered eggs in one of the baskets by the barn door and looked around for something else to do. The water containers were almost empty and needed a good scrubbing in her opinion, so she collected the pails and took them to the sink at the back of the barn.

When they were squeaky clean again, she set the empty pails back in their places near the coop and looked around for the bucket Alec used to fill them. Finding it under the sink, Meg filled it with water and lifted it. She was halfway there when she heard the sound of water splashing onto the concrete slab at her feet. Thinking she'd spilled some from the bucket, Meg frowned at seeing it still full.

She set the bucket down and turned to make sure she hadn't left the tap on. There was no water coming from the faucet, nor were there leaks in the pipes beneath the sink. "Weird," she said and reached to pick the bucket back up.

An intense pain sliced through her abdomen. Her hands let go of the bucket handle and went to her belly. Stunned by the severity of the pain, Meg leaned over and went to her knees. Finally seeing the bottom half of her dress completely saturated, it dawned on her where the water came from.

"ALEC!"

The hens scattered in every direction at the unexpected yelling. She was about to bellow again when she felt Alec's hands reaching for her.

"Meg? What's wrong?"

"Um," was all she said.

Alec surveyed the scene around her. He saw the full bucket of water and wondered why the barn floor was wet. "Where'd all this water come from? And why were you lifting that heavy bucket?"

"My water broke. I'm going into labor."

Was he scared? Yes. His first thought was to find someone else, someone better able to help Meg. Would he do that to her, let her know how terrified he was? No. He scooped her up from the floor and hurried out of the barn, scattering more hens as he left. Alec hurtled all the way to the front door, trying not to jostle her too much, then struggled with the doorknob. Once inside, he started to put her on the couch.

"No, not here," she said.

"Then where?"

"Upstairs, to our bed."

"But Meg, if you're in labor we should probably go to Dr. Patrick."

"No, Alec," she said, frowning. "I want to have our baby in our home. I thought you understood that."

"Yeah, but I was thinking you might change your mind when we got to this point. Are you absolutely sure?"

"I'm very sure." Meg gave him a tentative look. "I don't trust Dr. Patrick. I don't even like him all that much."

"I don't either." He shook his head. "Just keep in mind that he's the only doctor we have, okay?"

"Okay."

He carried her upstairs, slowly, hoping she thought he was only trying to be careful. When he got to the second floor landing, somewhat winded, she was eyeing him, appearing affronted. "Well, technically, I'm carrying two people."

When he tried to put her on the bed, she stopped him again. "Wait!"

Alec froze with Meg in his arms, hovering over their bed while his back protested. "What now?"

"I want to change out of this dress, it's all wet."

"Do you think you can stand?"

"I think so."

He stood her up on the floor, and they waited to see if she could handle it.

"I feel fine right now," she said, shrugging. "Go get another dress for me."

Alec went to their closet and rummaged through the maternity dresses that Meg called *tents* on her crankier days. Since she put him in charge of the task, he picked his favorite color—a blue one. He turned around to take it to her and found her nude. With the protruding belly, Alec thought she never looked more beautiful and he stumbled a little on the rug on the way to her.

"Do you need underwear?"

Meg chuckled. "I think they'd get in the baby's way."

"Right." He smiled. Instead of handing her the dress, he slipped it over her head and smoothed it out. He rubbed his hands across her belly.

"Are you ready?" she whispered, feeling nervous and happy all at once.

"I'm ready." He gave her cheek a kiss. "How're you doing? Are you in pain?"

"No, but I was. I think I had a contraction after my water broke."

"Let's sit on the bed for now and see how things go."

~

An hour later, Meg put down the book she'd been reading when a small pain formed in her abdomen. Though not excruciating at first, it was increasing in severity. She shook Alec awake.

"What?" He sat up. "Do you feel something?"

"I'm having a contraction, it's starting to hurt." Meg put her hands on her abdomen and leaned as far forward as she could in an effort to lessen the pain, but it didn't make a difference.

"Want me to do anything?" he asked, hating his uselessness, how it equated to his inability to keep her from hurting.

"Get our stuff… track the timing," she said a little too loud, lifting a hand from her belly long enough to motion toward his bedside table.

"Right." Alec reached over and opened the top drawer to retrieve the notepad, pencil, and the watch Meg had placed there a month previously. He wrote down the time and waited for her to tell him when the contraction passed.

She started nodding and inhaled deeply, exhaling the breath in a relieved sigh. Then she relaxed back against the pillows. "That was definitely a contraction. It's over now, write the time down again."

"What kind of a pattern are we looking for?" he asked while scribbling down the time.

"When the contractions are five minutes apart, and each one is lasting about a minute, that means it's getting close." Meg picked the book up and scanned a few lines. "I'm supposed to start pushing once they're about a minute apart."

It took ten minutes for the next contraction to hit her, and it was more painful. Alec wrote the time down and held her hand until it was over.

"That one really hurt," she said.

"Do you want me to get you something to drink?"

"Just some water."

When Alec returned with the water, he saw a look of anguish on Meg's face. "You're having another one?"

Alec rushed to the notepad and jotted the time down. It had only been five minutes since the last one. He waited for her face to relax and her breathing to return to normal before handing her the glass. She drank half of it and gave it back to him.

"The last two were only five minutes apart," he told her.

Meg glanced at the dark windows. "What time is it?"

"Eight thirty. Are you getting hungry?"

"No, just thirsty."

He gave her back the glass and she drained the rest of it. Alec ran back downstairs to the kitchen, devouring what he could of the dinner leftovers while filling a pitcher full of water. A third of it spilled on the staircase on the race back upstairs.

"Maybe you should wait a little while before you have more water. It's just gonna make you have to go to the bathroom more often," he said at seeing her gulp down another glass.

"I already have to go. Help me up."

He waited outside the bathroom door until she was finished.

"Another's coming," she said when she opened the door.

Alec guided her back to the bed and watched the pain contort her face. He wrote the time down and waited for her to indicate that the contraction had passed.

"Five minutes again, and it lasted for longer than a minute," he said.

She didn't answer him right away, focusing instead on steadying her breathing. After a moment, Meg turned to him and admitted: "They're getting a lot more painful."

~

Beads of sweat began to form on her forehead. Alec went to the bathroom closet to get a hand towel, patting away the sweat as it formed. He'd recorded seven more contractions, each lasting about a minute long over the last hour. Sometimes they were five minutes apart, sometimes longer. Meg grew more tired with each contraction, and more silent between them. She didn't seem to want water anymore.

"Meg, are you sure you don't want me to take you to Dr. Patrick?" he asked, growing more worried at her lethargy.

"I'm sure. I shouldn't be traveling anywhere right now anyway." Her voice sounded exhausted and weak.

She'd taken to falling asleep between contractions, but when one did start, her eyelids popped open and she started panting right away. Alec diligently wrote down the start and end times on the notepad.

At times, he would put his hands on her abdomen during her contractions and could feel it tighten and become hard to the touch. He spent most of his time drying the sweat off her forehead and lifting her head up to give her small sips of water.

Meg got to a point where she no longer wanted to talk, or hear updates about the timing of the contractions. Eventually, she stopped waking up on her own when another one started. Alec relied on watching her abdomen go taut again as a sign and would wake her up.

After a while, that procedure started to annoy her and she grew more irritated with him for disturbing her sleep.

"Alec, I'm tired. I just want to sleep." She pushed his hands away when he tried shaking her awake at the start of another contraction. "Leave me alone."

"You're having another one," he told her, but her eyes closed again.

He looked at the times on the notepad and noticed a pattern emerging—her contractions were growing farther apart. She hadn't mentioned anything about this scenario, or what it meant. Alec yanked up the book she'd been reading and flipped through the pages. Everywhere he searched for a match to what was happening, it ended with the same sentiment: *Call your physician immediately.*

Gently touching her shoulder, he tried waking her up, but she wouldn't open her eyes. He started to panic and tossed the book aside to try shaking Meg awake. Still no response, so he shook her vigorously and shouted her name.

All she did was mumble that she was still sleeping and didn't want to get up yet and asked if he would put the teakettle on the stove. Alec reached for the phone and dialed Dr. Patrick's home number, as it was close to midnight now. The phone rang and rang, but no one answered. He was nervous and edgy, but tried maintaining a semblance of calm.

Just in case he dialed the wrong number, he redialed, and still it rang. He slammed the phone down and tried rousing her again. "Meg, wake up!"

Nothing. She didn't even mumble this time and the sweat formed and rolled down her face. He wiped it away, only to watch it return. He felt her abdomen, the contraction had stopped.

Alec got up and paced the floor, continuing to stare at her abdomen for any sign of another contraction, but there was no tightening. None of it felt right to him and he decided to go against her wishes. There was no way he'd risk losing her, not even if she stayed mad at him forever. He ran downstairs, grabbed the keys to the house, and locked the door behind him.

It went against everything that defined Alec's nature to leave Meg alone and so vulnerable, but he had to get Dr. Patrick here to help her. He jumped into the cart and sped off in the direction of the lane that would take him to Dr. Patrick's house. Well on his way, feeling a bit better for making the decision to involve Dr. Patrick if it meant helping Meg, the cart slowed and came to a stop right in front of the forest footpath he'd wanted to take.

"Dammit!" Alec yelled. He hadn't charged the battery yet, as he usually did this at night, so he left the cart on the lane and took off into the woods on foot.

He ran at a fast clip and was halfway to the group of houses where Dr. Patrick lived when he saw a figure up ahead in the middle of the path. For a moment, Alec thought he was about to be met with the strange occurrence of swirling light he'd not seen since childhood. A closer look revealed the figure as being typical of any islander, and feminine in stature.

His brow creased, not expecting he'd encounter anyone out so late. As he trotted closer, he saw it was Chaza; the surprise brought him to an abrupt halt.

"Where are you going?" she asked, taking a few steps toward him.

"Chaza, I don't have time to talk right now. I need to get Dr. Patrick to my house. Meg's in labor and it's not going very well." Alec moved around her.

"I'm afraid I can't let you do that," she said.

Alec gave a brief glance at her over his shoulder, but kept walking.

"Don't walk away from me," Chaza said, her tone resonated with sinister warning.

Alec wondered if she was crazy and he regretted mentioning anything at all about Meg being in labor. Though he continued walking down the path, his scattered thoughts distracted him, causing him to move at a slower pace.

"I won't warn you a third time, Alec."

The mood of the entire forest shifted. Every night creature suddenly fell quiet. The wind ceased blowing in off the ocean, making the trees appear to have frozen in time. Without the wind, the whispered voices were somehow louder.

If time in forward motion had a scent, perhaps it could be considered as fresh, like clean laundry. But when it isn't moving, it's stale, like ancient dust.

Still, Alec kept walking, ignoring her and the strange silence. Up ahead of him, he saw something shimmering, appearing as a pearlescent glow that looked vaguely familiar—growing higher and wider. Alec's footsteps faltered as his eyes followed the intensifying light move upward, then arc over the trees above him.

The wall of light formed a sphere around him and he recognized it. He'd made the same kind of sphere himself many times before, but he wasn't creating this one and he'd never created one so large. Alec turned to face Chaza, the only other possible source of the anomaly and found her standing directly in front of him—her eyes were wild with rage.

Chaza's hands shot to Alec's neck and she forced him backward, pinning him to the nearest tree. Alec wanted to pry her hands from his throat, but he couldn't induce his arms to move from his sides. He felt his entire body become lifeless, paralyzed, and all he could do was stare into Chaza's eyes.

"Don't bother fighting it," Chaza said, her voice controlled, but fierce. "As long as I want you to remain motionless, you'll remain so. I told you I wouldn't warn you a third time. Keep that in mind in the future."

"Who are you?" Alec was stunned at how different she seemed—the extreme opposite of the nice, mild-mannered woman who visited Meg and brought her flowers.

Ignoring the question, Chaza asked, "What did you mean by Meg's labor isn't going very well?"

"I thought you liked Meg, I thought you were her friend," he said, hoping the words would have an effect on her.

They had an immediate effect. The green of her eyes grew more illuminated as her face took on a conflicted expression. He became more aware of a similarity he hadn't noticed before. It was as if he was staring into Meg's eyes. Never being one to put much stock in coincidences, Alec felt there had to be a reason for it.

"Putting things together, are you?" she asked, seeing his thoughts with unapologetic ease.

"Right now, Meg's in our bed at home, in labor, and I can't wake her up. There's no one there with her. I'm not a doctor, but I'm sure she should be trying to push by now." Alec's voice had taken on a discernable note of pleading. "I have to get Dr. Patrick to her."

"She won't wake?"

"No. Please, Chaza, let me go."

"I won't allow you to bring that foul man to Meg. I'll help her."

"But we need a doctor."

"Where I come from" –Chaza's eyes narrowed into slits– "I am a doctor. You can't trust Dr. Patrick, he works for management… and he's a very loyal dog."

She waited for the words to sink into Alec's head. When they did, the sphere around them vanished. Her hands left his neck and she grabbed his wrist. The velocity at which she raced through the forest with him in tow seemed impossible. Though Alec couldn't, nor had he ever thought he was capable of doing it, he suspected that Chaza shifted time at a faster rate now to get to Meg as quickly as possible.

When they arrived at the stone house, Chaza released Alec and waited for him to unlock the door. She bounded upstairs to Meg, who still lay sleeping on the bed. There was intense worry on Chaza's face as she looked at Meg.

Chaza put her hands on Meg's abdomen and closed her eyes. Alec stood at the end of the bed and watched her concentrate. When she opened her eyes, she turned to Alec—the worried expression had been usurped by fear. Her eyes flitted to his wrist before she spoke.

"She's very weak, Alec. Neither she nor the baby are doing well. Meg needs to wake up and she needs to be stronger to start pushing." She paused, shook her head, and then nodded in what seemed a final battle with some decision. "You're gonna have to help her become stronger again."

"How?" His voice choked. He couldn't lose Meg; he didn't know if he could, or even wanted to, live without her.

"You need to give back what you took from her. All of it," Chaza said, refusing to feel bad for interrupting his musings of contemplating a life without Meg.

The fierceness had inched back into her voice and Alec had an uncanny feeling that she was about to force something out of him if he refused her. He thought of only one thing that could justify her words. Shocked, he stared disbelieving at her.

"How do you know about that?" Alec's voice fell to a whisper as he glanced at Meg.

"Because I was there," she said in an equally controlled whisper. "I've always been there, watching over *my* daughter since the day I gave birth to her."

Alec wanted to challenge the revelation, but the power Chaza emanated subjugated him. He looked at Meg and realized what he had to do. Not bothering to verbalize acknowledgement of Chaza's declaration that she was Meg's mother, he lay on the bed. Alec pulled her limp form to him, cradling her in his arms, and formed the sphere around them.

He kissed her sweat-drenched forehead, kissed her closed eyelids, her cheeks, finally placing a gentle kiss on her lips and closed his eyes to focus on what he meant to do. He began to allow the part of Meg he took so long ago to leave him, and soon it found its own way back to her—settling back seamlessly to the rightful owner. There was more pain involved this time and the aching surrender showed on his face.

At last, it was done, and he said to her, "I swore to you that I'd always protect you. I'm trying to save your life now. Please come back to me, Margaret Arcana."

The sphere faded, and he could feel the part he had absorbed from Meg was gone from him. Though there was a hollowness inside him that hadn't been there before, it refilled when he looked at her face and he was more at ease for having returned her strength.

Chaza went to the side of the bed again and tried to convince Alec to leave the room so she could help Meg give birth.

"I won't leave," he told her with finality. Alec stood, ready to throw her out of the house however way he could and take his chances with Dr. Patrick. "I mean it, Chaza. Don't fight me on this."

Not exactly thrilled with his belligerence, she understood why he had no intention of going anywhere. Chaza figured she may need more of his help before the end of it and so she offered him a warm smile.

"Help her push when I need her to. At the moment, she's still weak and it might not be easy for her to sit up and do it on her own at first. Stay beside her and lean her forward when I tell her to push." Chaza glanced at Meg's still-sleeping face. "Encourage her, give her some of your strength if she needs it. For now, I need you to make her wake up. I'm worried we're running out of time."

He nodded and sat back down on the bed. "Meg," he said softly.

Chaza busied herself with pulling the bed sheets up to Meg's knees and examining how far along she was. "Wake her up, Alec."

"Meg," he called louder, shaking her shoulders.

"Leave me alone, Alec, I'm tired," she mumbled and swiped his hands away.

"Wake her up!" Chaza sounded more urgent, almost scared again. "She needs to start pushing. Now, preferably!"

"You can go back to sleep later, Meg. There's something important you have to do right now," he said in a gentle tone. He hated yelling at her and hoped reasoning with her would help. Still, she slept.

"Alec." Chaza calmed her voice, though she wanted to kick him. Since it was reasoning he considered, she had no problem giving him a proper lesson on how to use it. "If she doesn't start pushing immediately, your son will die. Meg will survive, but she'll die emotionally and you'll have lost her just the same. Stop being gentle with her and wake her the hell up."

He needed no more convincing than that. Alec got to his feet again and leaned over Meg. Given what he intended to do, he looked apprehensively at Chaza. She didn't like it, but nodded her head.

Turning back to Meg, muttering a plea for forgiveness, Alec lifted his arm. With an open hand, he slapped her face as hard as he could. It was like a piece of himself died with the act and he grimaced at the physical pain it cost him. Meg's reaction was instant. Her eyelids flew open and after an initial look of confusion, the emerald green of her eyes appeared to flash red with undeniable rage.

"YOU HIT ME?" Meg screamed her furious disbelief at him.

For a second, he thought she was about to leap from the bed to strike him back, but then her face contorted in agony as a contraction ripped through her body.

"You need to push," Alec told her. He sat next to her, gripped her shoulders, and leaned her forward. "Come on, push now."

"Alec's right, it's time for you to push. Now, Meg," Chaza said.

It hurt too much for Meg to question why Chaza was there. She leaned forward more with Alec's help and started pushing as hard as she could. A guttural scream escaped her as she exhaled and sat back against the pillows, panting. Fresh beads of sweat formed on her forehead, which she wiped away before Alec could.

"That was good, Meg. I can see the baby's head now. Another contraction should be coming soon and you'll have to push again," Chaza said.

Meg was already exhausted. "It's too hard."

"I know it is, but Alec will help. You have to do it, though. The baby needs to get out."

"Okay." Meg nodded. "When the next contraction—" Again, she was seized with searing pain.

Alec leaned her forward and wedged himself behind her to keep her in this position. "Come on, baby, let's do this," he said to her.

"Push, Meg. Keep pushing… that's right… very good." Chaza began to feel more confident with the progress. "The baby's head is out. You're doing a great job, sweetie. When the next contraction comes, I want you to push this baby all the way out. One big final push. I know you can do it."

Meg's breathing was still labored as she rested back against Alec. Her head rolled side-to-side on his chest and he thought her eyes seemed out of focus. He swept away the sweat-saturated curls from her face and smiled when she looked up at him, her eyes focused once more.

"I love you, Alec."

"I love you, too, Meg."

Lines formed on her brow and she turned to Chaza. "I'm about to have another contraction. Can I push now?"

"No, wait until you feel it."

Meg started panting heavily, saying between breaths, "Oh God, I have to, I gotta push… now."

She lifted herself forward and strained to push. Her scream started out low, increasing to a loud pitch, and still it grew louder.

"Scream as loud as you want, Meg. JUST PUSH!" Chaza's bellowing rivaled that of Meg's screaming. "He's almost out. Keep pushing."

Meg's body quaked and trembled, her face turned a fiery red from the exertion. The very tresses Alec had swept back came forward again and plastered themselves against her forehead and cheeks. He concentrated all of his thoughts on helping her, willing some of his own strength outward to her. Beads of sweat formed on Alec's face and a newly formed sphere surrounded them.

Chaza heard them both screaming with the birth of their son.

"You did it, Meg," Chaza said.

Exhaling her biggest breath of air yet, Meg collapsed back onto Alec's chest, her own chest heaving while she tried to steady her breathing and heartbeat. Chaza held the baby up for Meg and Alec to see him and when he started crying, so did Meg.

"Your son," Chaza said and placed him in Meg's arms.

Alec and Meg looked at their son's face, each of them feeling an existential sense of joy and pride. When Alec ran his thumb along the baby's forehead, Meg looked up into his eyes and kissed his cheek.

"I'm so happy right now," she said.

"Me, too." Alec hugged her tight. "You had me so worried. Please, don't ever scare me like that again."

"Alec, would you take the baby and clean him with fresh cloths?" Chaza interrupted them. "I need to finish up with Meg. It shouldn't take but a moment and you can bring him right back so she can nurse him. Don't forget to wrap him securely in a receiving blanket."

He glanced at her, still uneasy about leaving. "It's fine, Alec," Meg told him.

"Okay." He slipped out from behind Meg and took the baby into his arms. He kissed the top of her head, left the room, and headed downstairs with his newborn son.

"All right, little guy, this is your room." Alec flipped the light switch on in the nursery with his elbow. "Your mom spent a lot of time getting it ready for you, so make sure you thank her later."

Carefully, he placed the baby on the changing table by the crib and kept one hand on him while rummaging through the drawers for hand cloths and towels. After a good wipe down, Alec smiled and said, "You look so much better. How about a diaper?"

From the same drawer, he grabbed a diaper and put it on the infant easily enough, once he sorted out which side was front-facing. A few drawers down, he pulled out a blue one-piece newborn outfit. With a bit of wrangling, mostly due to the baby wiggling, Alec maneuvered the onesie over his head and put the arms through.

"Can't forget the booties," Alec said to him and slipped them on the tiny feet. "I wish Meg would settle on a name for you soon. In the meantime, I'm gonna call you my favorite of the ones we picked out."

A blue knit cap finished off the dressing of the newborn. Being his first time, Alec thought he'd done an excellent job. That was, until he got to the blanket part. He struggled with how to swaddle him and tried several times before giving up.

"We'll go with the taco look. That okay with you, Luke?"

Alec scooped Luke up, and the corner of the blanket that trailed down was gathered and piled on top. "Good enough. I bet you're hungry, right? You'll have to see your mom about that one. Let's go see if she's ready for us."

After turning the light off, he climbed the stairs and knocked on the door. Chaza opened it and smiled at the sight of Alec holding the baby. "We're done, and Meg's very anxious to have him back."

He stepped in to find Meg sitting up and looking much more refreshed. Chaza had helped Meg out of the sweat-drenched dress and into a fresh nightgown. Her hair was neatly brushed and almost dry again. Somehow, Chaza managed to change the linens on the bed and re-fluffed the pillows for Meg to rest against.

Meg smiled and held her arms up. "Gimme."

"How're you feeling?" Alec asked and put the baby in her arms once she'd unbuttoned the front of the gown.

"Still tired, but otherwise I feel great." Meg looked at the infant. "How's our baby? I see you dressed him all in blue."

"Of course." Alec chuckled. "I think he's hungry."

Meg pulled an extra blanket over the upper half of her chest and began nursing with instant success. "I'd say you're right."

"Have you decided on a name yet?" Chaza asked.

"Luke. That's what Alec's already decided," Meg said without taking her eyes off Luke.

Alec eyed Meg, puzzled. She'd known Luke was his favorite name of the list they had put together, but she couldn't have known he'd already started calling him that. Meg had her true self back. He would have to get used to the idea that she'd be different. She would be more like him, he considered.

"Luke's a great name. I like it," Chaza said.

"Well, that's four votes. Luke Arcana Ellison it is."

"*Four*?" Alec questioned Meg.

"Yes, four. Luke likes it, too," she said, looking up at Alec and Chaza with an untroubled smile.

"Do you want me to get you anything?" he asked.

"I'd love some tea."

Chaza gathered the pile of bed linens and started to follow Alec out of the room, but Meg called out to her. "Chaza, thank you for helping us."

"My pleasure, Meg. Don't forget to thank Alec later for letting me." Chaza smiled at Meg and winked at Alec. "It took a lot of convincing to get him to accept my help."

~

When they arrived downstairs, Chaza dropped the bundled linens by the door before meeting Alec in the kitchen. She stood near the table, waiting patiently while he readied a tray. Much as Meg had gone through giving birth to their son, she knew Alec had undergone many new changes of his own and she wanted to talk to him about it before leaving.

"You can never lose abilities, or unlearn them either," she said. "You haven't lost anything by returning Meg's identity. It's not possible for you to become weaker, only stronger as you age. You'll have to get used to her being different now, more like you."

Alec put the teakettle on the stove and turned to face Chaza. "I considered the idea of absorbing it again," he said, curious to see Chaza's reaction to the admission.

"Are you going to try hitting her on the head with a rock again? You wouldn't be able to do that now, it would bring you too much pain. And she won't part so easily from her true self now that she's older."

Again he was astonished at how much Chaza knew. However, he didn't argue with her, as he understood what she meant. He would never be able to hurt Meg and he seriously doubted she would be as pliant either.

"You're right," he said. "I'm not gonna try absorbing her abilities again."

"You'll have to help her, and teach her, when she begins to notice differences about herself." Chaza shrugged, knowing the next question Alec wanted to ask. She wasn't sure herself. "It probably won't happen right away since she'll be preoccupied with Luke. I'm guessing you'll notice more than she will at first. At some point, she'll have questions and you'll be the one she turns to for answers."

He listened to everything Chaza had to say, but struggled with his usual mistrust and wondered if he should trust her.

She sensed his thoughts, but as he remained silent, she continued: "Dr. Patrick will be disappointed he didn't deliver Luke. When the news gets out, I'm certain he'll come here to examine Meg, but especially Luke. Don't let him be alone with the baby. He'll be wanting to get blood samples for management."

Alec had every intention of doing exactly as Chaza instructed, but he wanted to know the reason. He wanted answers to questions he'd had all his life. "Why?"

Not keen about the disrespect in his voice, Chaza gave him a look as though he'd insulted her.

He found her glare uncomfortable. "I'll do what you say, but I just want some explanations." It felt odd to him to be so supplicant.

She softened at his words. "I know you do. You want answers to a lot of things. If you allow Dr. Patrick to examine Luke, it's very possible management will take him away. If their scientists like what they see in his blood work, I'd say it's most probable that you and Meg will never see Luke again."

Her warnings were eerily similar to the very same his mother had when he was a child. Kyrie had been terrified someone would take him away from her if he flaunted his abilities. As he grew older, he understood it wasn't some phantom monster out to get him, but the very people who lorded over the island. For what purposes and designs, Alec still didn't fully comprehend.

"No matter what Dr. Patrick says, don't trust him," Chaza said. "His allegiance falls with management and their scientists. You need to know something else. Those people whose thoughts you can't read, or are barely able to, are either us, them, or somewhere in between. Don't forget that… ever."

"Don't worry, I can handle Dr. Patrick," Alec said. Lowering his voice, he asked, "Are you really Meg's mother?"

"Yes. Obviously, Meg doesn't know that and neither does Ila. I'm trusting you not to say anything right now. Trust isn't so easy for me either, Alec." Chaza sighed at her inability to explain more to him. "As for the rest of your questions, you'll need to ask someone else. It's not my place to tell you."

"Who?"

Excitement lit up his face at the prospect of finally getting answers to everything he wanted to know.

"Sebastian."

"Sebastian?" The excitement turned to utter disappointment. "Why him?" he asked, sounding somewhat disgusted.

"Because he's like us… you, me, Meg. Luke will be like us, too, when he's older." A frown formed on Chaza's face, worried she'd already said too much. She accepted that there was no going back, Alec knew enough to know there was more to discover.

"Is there something else you want to say?" he asked.

"Not really, but I'm going to anyway. Sebastian's my husband, but we've been separated for a long time. I was unfaithful to him with Joseph. The result of my infidelity is Meg. Sebastian doesn't know that Meg's my daughter, no one does. He's the one you need to take your questions to. But prepare yourself, Alec, you may not like the answers."

"Fine, I'll have a chat with him," Alec grumbled, deciding that if Sebastian had the answers, then he had no problem demanding he share them. "If I need you for anything, where can I find you?"

"I'm never very far away. You're not the only one who watches over Meg. If I'm needed, I'd probably know it already. All you really need to do is want me to hear your thoughts and I will, if I'm listening." She smiled. "Make sure Meg gets some rest, she needs it."

"I will."

She turned to leave and Alec walked her to the door. As she bent down to retrieve the bundled-up bed sheets, Alec said, "You don't have to do our laundry. I'll take care of it."

Chaza exploded in laughter. "You're so funny, Alec. I am no one's maid. I have no intention of washing your bed linens. I'm going to burn them."

"What? Those are Meg's favorites."

"There's a lot of *blood work* in these sheets. Management would have no problem ordering Dr. Patrick to get what they want, one way or the other. Tell Meg you ruined them trying to be helpful and order a replacement set. Problem solved."

Alec waited in the doorway, watching Chaza disappear into the night toward Alaret Beach. He thought she was an interesting woman and was glad to have made an alliance with her. If the teakettle wasn't screaming for his attention, Alec imagined he would see a fire on the beach within a matter of minutes.

15

Lani

Jack woke up to a pleasant tickling sensation on his hip. He'd been dreaming he was in a forest surrounded by monolithic trees, even bigger than the giant redwoods of West America. In the dream, he knew someone was there with him, but couldn't see their face. There was a haunting melody playing from somewhere in the tree he stood in front of.

His gaze drifted up along a flowering vine that clung to the massive tree trunk, and paused when he noticed something different about the colors of the flowers. They were unlike any he'd ever seen before and he struggled to find the exact word for it. Something enormous flew over his head and distracted him from the flowers. Whatever it was, it temporarily blocked the sunlight filtering through the tree canopy.

He'd just caught a glimpse of vines sporting impossibly sized green leaves moving overhead when he felt a tickle at his hip. The dream dissipated when he looked down to see who it was. His eyelids fluttered open and he saw Tavis was lying beside him, looking down at his torso.

Still early morning, the first light from the sun came in through the window drapes and cast a soft glow in their bedroom. The tickling sensation that woke him was Tavis tracing circles around the small tattoo on his hip. She'd pushed the bed sheet down to his thighs and was studying the lines of the tattoo. Jack watched her for a moment, noting she appeared deep in thought.

"I want to wake up just like this for the rest of my life," he said to her.

Tavis looked up at him and smiled. "I seriously doubt you'd want to wake up next to a great big watermelon for the rest of your life."

"Oh yeah? I think you're the prettiest watermelon I've ever laid eyes on. Besides, as long as you're willing, we can have a watermelon farm."

"You plan to keep me always pregnant?"

"Well..." Jack contemplated the idea. "As long as there's plenty of in-between times."

"I wouldn't mind some of that in-between time now. I'm ready for our baby to be born," Tavis said and returned her attention back to the tattoo.

"Why haven't you ever asked me about that?"

"I assumed it was personal and if you wanted to talk about it, you'd tell me." She traced another delicate circle around it. "Is it personal?"

"No." Jack was amazed by her patience. "I got it when I was a freshman in college. Me and some of my friends got tattoos one night after we had way too much to drink." He laughed. "*Naturally*, I got a hummingbird tattoo because I'm extra macho when I'm drunk."

"What possessed you to get a hummingbird?"

"I don't know." Jack snorted. "Too many beers and idiot friends possessed me? My parents were so mad when they found out about it."

Tavis studied it again and frowned. "How did they find out? It's not exactly in a visible location."

"I was stupid and charged it on my debit card. Since they paid the bill, they saw the tattoo parlor's fee. When I refused to show it to my mother, my father said he would send me to work at the local grocery store as a bagger before sending me back to college if I didn't let her see it."

"So, you had to show it to her?" She chuckled at imagining Jack having to drop his pants in front of his mother. "What did she think of it?"

"She laughed at first, but then said how happy she was it was hidden. She also said if I did anything that stupid again, they'd take away my debit card, hence why I don't have any more tattoos. Even drunk, I could remember the threat of poverty."

"That's a funny story," she said. "I'm glad you told me."

Tavis sighed, reclined back on the bed next to him, and stared at the ceiling. He rolled to his side and rubbed her belly, occasionally tracing a few of his own circles around her belly button, the bottom of which was at the surface now.

"Anything wrong?" he asked.

"No, I'm just restless. I feel cooped up in here."

"How about we take a shower and then have breakfast?"

"I don't know if you've noticed, but it's getting a little cramped in the shower lately."

Jack nuzzled her neck. "Please?"

"How can I resist a beggar?"

~

During breakfast, Tavis asked Jack what he wanted for lunch.

"I don't know, I'm still eating breakfast," he said, laughing.

"I want to know what to pack."

"Are we going somewhere today?"

"We're going swimming at the lake."

"What? Are you crazy? Look at you," Jack blurted, nearly dropping his fork. One glance at her and he immediately regretted his words.

"Are *you* crazy?"

"I think so." Jack stared at his plate to avoid her glare.

Rather than throw the rest of her uneaten eggs at his face, Tavis picked up her plate and went to the kitchen. When she leaned over the top of the picnic basket to put napkins in, a twinge of pain nipped at her abdomen. She grabbed the edge of the counter and waited for it to pass.

"Should you be swimming as far along as you are?"

"Swimming is a perfectly good form of exercise." The last of the pain subsided. "And it doesn't matter how far along I am. Water's buoyant, I'm not going to sink like a stone."

"Well, if you're sure it's safe, that does sound like a good idea." He risked a stern look at her. "But no diving off that boulder."

She smiled at the protective warning. "Okay. No jumping or diving, just swimming for me."

"Sandwiches are fine." Jack finished the last of his toast and took his plate to the kitchen. He kissed Tavis' cheek then bent over to kiss her belly. "How's our baby doing this morning?"

"She's fine."

"You really think we're having a girl?"

"I really think so."

"Have you thought of any names yet?"

Tavis rolled her eyes. "Not since the last time you asked."

"I guess we could just call her *Baby* until you decide on a name. Or, how about Agnes, Phoebe, or Gertrude?"

"Nope."

"Frances… Bernice?"

"Jack!"

~

Tavis hid a few items in the duffel bag Jack had packed and went outside to join him in their garden. He had become obsessed with trying to grow everything imaginable. Though they never admitted it, Sebastian and Jack were competing with one another's gardening skills. The differences between the two were visually obvious. Jack had taken a more practical approach with clean lines and in choosing plants with multiple uses: vegetables, fruits, and a bounty of herbs.

Sebastian, on the other hand, had planted a garden of whimsy. Color was his muse in the garden rather than orderliness—all things fanciful, as opposed to useful.

Jack's garden had grown from a simple small one to stretching all the way back to the edge of the forest and his herb garden flanked the entire right side of the house. He'd taken his time with the area, plotting out the height and width of individual spices to complement each other.

In the center of the herb garden, Jack had built a koi pond made from rocks he found on the island. When it took too long to transport the rocks on his own, he enlisted the help of Alec, Frank, and Sebastian. After that, it became a group effort to get the koi pond built along with plenty of male bonding. Though it wasn't perfect, Alec seemed a little more tolerant of Sebastian by the end of the project.

When it was halfway built, they erected a temporary wall blocking the view since Jack had decided to add a surprise for Tavis. On the day of the unveiling, she was delighted to find that Jack had included a waterfall to the pond to remind her of their favorite place.

Jack had to argue with Kyrie about ordering koi fish. She was concerned it wouldn't be allowed since nonnative animals were forbidden on Gamma. She explained that, aside from the horses and chickens, even domesticated animals were strictly forbidden by management. Jack countered that koi would be considered garden decorations and would be exempt from the rule.

After an hour of arguing with Jack, Kyrie gave up as it was clear he wasn't about to. She placed the order and to her surprise, and Jack's, *'Told ya'*, the koi arrived in the end-of-the-week's shipment of special orders.

With the koi in the pond, flourishing and hatching baby koi, many islanders came by to see and oh and ah at it. Some of them were the very ones who'd shunned Jack after the Michelle fiasco.

However, there was one morning that threatened to tarnish his reputation anew. Tavis had been jolted awake by yelling and clanking coming from somewhere outside, and Jack wasn't in bed with her. She scrambled off the bed and put on a robe, finding him out by the koi pond with a pot in one hand and a wooden spoon in the other. Jack was wearing one of her robes, and he hadn't bothered tying the belt.

"What are you doing?" Tavis yelled.

Startled by the unexpected voice, Jack spun around and saw disapproval and shock on her face. "There was a heron hunting in our pond."

He looked like a child who feared the consequences for having done something naughty. She couldn't help but smile. "Jack, fish have been dealing with this sort of thing since fish evolved. That heron can't possibly catch and eat every one of them. Even if it ate a lot of them, there are hatchlings in there that will repopulate the pond."

"You're right," he said. "I'm sorry I woke you up."

"Let's go back inside." She held her hands out to receive the pot and spoon. "And please tie that robe before someone sees you."

Jack looked down at the satin pink robe to find the entire length of his naked front half exposed for all the world to see. He snatched the robe together and looked around, making sure he hadn't flashed anyone more than they wanted to see of him.

"Maybe that's why that heron flew off so quickly," he said, chuckling.

Tavis laughed at the memory before sneaking up behind Jack. In a mock-dignified tone, she asked, "Excuse me, sir, have you seen a big grey heron around here?"

"Ha, ha, very funny."

"Everything's ready whenever you are. We just need to load it into the cart."

While waiting by the cart for Jack to retrieve the basket and duffel bag, Tavis saw Sebastian come out of his house. "Wait," she called to him before he reached his cart.

Sebastian smiled at how she ambled toward him and thought she seemed more heavily burdened by her pregnancy than usual. Guilt twisted his gut for having spent so much time away from her since falling into habits that prevented him from bumping into Kyrie.

"Where've you been going every day?" she asked.

"Visiting with Frank. We've been going out sailing around the island."

Tavis noticed his haggard appearance, atypical for him. Sebastian always took great care of himself and was meticulous about his grooming. She dismissed it as his usual worrying and hoped that what she had in mind would bring him around.

"I miss you." She held her arms out. "Can I have a hug?"

"Of course." Sebastian wrapped his arms around her as best he could. Within seconds, he pulled away and looked at her belly. "Daughter," was all he could say and Tavis wasn't sure if he meant her or the baby.

"Hush, don't say anything. I have it all planned out and I want to surprise him."

Jack came out of the house carrying the duffel bag and basket.

"Where are you going?" Sebastian asked quickly, as Jack was heading over to them now.

"To the lake, for a *swim*," she whispered.

"Ah, tradition," Sebastian whispered back. "Ancient, but still, it is the best. I'm so proud of you. I can't wait to meet her."

"Your daughter seems to think it's okay for her to be swimming. What do you think?" Jack asked.

Sebastian grinned at Tavis. "She'll be fine. Just make sure she doesn't dive off anything."

~

At the lake, Tavis insisted they set up a spot for them to have lunch later. He helped her spread the blanket out on a nearby grassy area and stared at her funny when she kept repositioning the duffel bag and basket around the blanket corners.

"Are you worried about the wind moving the blanket?"

"Yeah." She looked up at him. "I don't want it to get dirty. Is there something in the cart we can use to hold the other corners down with?"

"Just use the towels." Jack went for the duffel bag.

"No!" she shouted, but forced a laugh when he frowned at her. "Our clothes will work."

Jack tried convincing her to leave her underwear on while they swam, but she refused and said he could wear them if he wanted. She swam out to the middle of the lake and he stayed close to her, amazed at how late pregnancy hadn't slowed her down.

"That's enough swimming for now," he told her. "Let's float on our backs and stare at the sky for a while."

They floated in this manner for a long time while Tavis gazed up at the cloudless sky. Occasionally, she would have a contraction—inching up on the pain scale, but so far they weren't what she'd consider agony. Her belly protruded above the water and she noticed how it hardened when she felt the pain. Having paid attention to the timing, Tavis figured she'd have to tell Jack soon.

"Do you think I'll be a good father?"

"Yes."

It was what he wanted to hear, but it felt too simplistic. "I mean it, Tavis. I want to be a great dad. You know, like how your father is... don't tell him I said that."

She laughed, thinking she'd have to start a list of what not to say the other admitted to. "I have no doubts in my mind that you'll be a fantastic father. You might even rival that of my own."

He smiled at her confidence. "Think our baby will have blue eyes?"

"Now *that* I can't be sure of. We'll just have to wait and see." Tavis watched a small flock of migrating arctic terns fly overhead. A name for their daughter finally came to mind. "Lani."

"Nah, I'm pretty sure those were arctic terns," Jack said.

"No, silly. Lani Abbott Cavanaugh, that's our daughter's name. I hope you like it because I'm not budging."

"Lani." He tested the sound. "It's pretty." Jack reached over and patted Tavis' belly. "I like it."

Another pain sliced through Tavis, and more pronounced. There was no putting it off—their child was ready to be born. Knowing Jack would follow her, she swam closer to the lake's edge, nearer to the waterfall until her feet could touch bottom again.

"Nope, forget about it. I'm not letting you go under that waterfall." Jack was ready for battle if necessary.

"I wasn't planning to. I just wanted to be near it."

Tavis took Jack's hands and flattened them on her belly. He waited to feel the familiar kicks he thought she wanted him to feel. Instead, he noticed her abdomen was unusually hard and he looked into her eyes, waiting for her to explain it. There was something different in her expression; pain.

"Are you ready?" she asked.

"No, Tavis. Not here."

Jack wrapped his fingers around her wrist and tugged to leave the water. Tavis dug her feet into the sandy bottom of the lake, refusing to move. Defiance knitted a crease on her forehead, so he decided to hear her out.

"This is where I want to have our baby, and I want you to be here to help me."

"I'm worried something could go wrong."

"Nothing will go wrong, I promise. Can you trust that?"

"I want to," he said, but was still afraid.

"My water already broke. The contractions are getting more painful now and I can feel the baby's in position. All I need to do is push a few times and she's born. If we left, you'd end up having to pull the cart over and then our daughter will be born on the side of the lane. Is that what you want?"

"No, I don't want that." Jack groaned. "Shouldn't we get out of the water at least?"

"I want to have her here. She won't breathe air until she's exposed to it."

"Tavis, I really do want to trust you, but I'm scared. What if there are complications? What do I do? Take you to Dr. Patrick? Bring him—"

"No!" Her eyes bored into his. "I don't want that man anywhere near me or our baby. If there are any complications, which there won't be, you're to take me to my father."

"Sebastian?" Jack snorted. "What can he do?"

"More than you realize."

The defensive expression on Tavis' face told Jack he'd better respect her wishes and that the subject wasn't open for further discussion. He relented with a sigh, gave her a kiss, and hoped nothing would go wrong.

"All right, preggers, I sincerely hope you know what I'm doing."

Tavis smiled. "When the next contraction comes, I have to start pushing." She was all business after winning him over and led him to the boulder. "Lean back against this rock and give me your hands. Bend your knees so I can put my feet on them."

Jack understood exactly how Tavis intended to push, so he positioned himself against the boulder and dug his heels into the lake bottom. He took her hands and waited for her to get a proper footing on his knees. When the next contraction came, Tavis pushed. Other than her face turning a little red and a bit of trembling, you wouldn't know she was trying to give birth—her calm awed him. She finally exhaled and relaxed her grip on his hands.

"I thought there'd be screaming," he said.

"Some women do. Who knows? I'm not finished, I could scream yet."

"Is it very painful?"

"Yes, Jack, it's painful."

"How much progress did you make?"

"Her head's crowning."

"That's good, right?"

"That's very good." Tavis nodded and tried to relax before the next contraction came. "It also means my labor is progressing quickly. Between each time I push, I need to relax, like I'm doing now." Her abdomen tightened. "I have to start pushing again."

She braced her feet against his knees and readied herself to push. Using her hands, he balanced himself between her and the boulder for better leverage. As she took a deep breath and pushed harder still, the rough edges of the boulder threatened to cut into his skin. When she exhaled and allowed her legs to relax, she focused on steadying her breathing and trying to rest for the next contraction.

"How was that one?" he asked once her face looked peaceful again.

"Her head's fully crowned now. The next push will have her head free."

"Really?"

"Yes, but there'll be more pushes after that, and it's gonna take longer for me to relax enough to be able to talk. So, listen to me." When he nodded, she continued. "Once I push her all the way out, you'll need to let one of my hands go to bring her to the surface."

"How will I know she's out?"

"You'll know." She saw he wasn't convinced. "I'll kick you if you don't. Okay?"

He laughed. "Okay. Don't worry, I'll get her when she's out."

Tavis wasn't worried; she knew Jack had long since bonded with their daughter. He'd sense what his baby needed at the precise time she needed it. "I meant what I said earlier, you're gonna be a wonderful father. Our daughter will love you unconditionally."

"I hope so. I can't wait to meet her."

"It won't be long." A sudden frown appeared on her face and a look of pain chased away the peaceful countenance. "This one's gonna hurt."

The contraction sliced through her abdomen like a knife hell-bent on causing as much pain as possible. Instead of screaming, the first and only sound she gave was a heart-breaking whimper. Jack would've preferred her to scream.

Tavis took a deep breath and pushed hard against his knees—her fingernails cut into his hands while she pulled at his arms. Jack watched the veins bulge out on her forehead and neck; he wished there was a way to do the work for her. It seemed too long, and he worried she held her breath longer than she should. Finally, Tavis exhaled; for once looking beaten by sheer exhaustion.

"Her… head… is… out," Tavis said through frenzied breaths.

"Shh, shh, shh," Jack cooed softly to sooth her. "Focus on breathing. I can't imagine it's easy, but try to find a way to relax for the next one."

Jack matched her breathing by exaggerating his own, then slowly brought it down to encourage her to steady her pace. After a minute or so, Tavis breathed normally again. Her lips pursed, as though wanting to say something.

"You're gonna try pushing her all the way out on the next one. Is that right?"

She nodded, thankful to not have to waste her concentration on speech.

Her face became his study for signs that she was about to start pushing. Tavis seemed almost completely relaxed again when her eyes widened, and he waited for her to pull at his hands and push on his knees. When she did, it seemed the most enormous effort yet. She took a deep breath, and pushed so hard that the boulder finally won the battle on Jack's skin.

What felt like an eternity passed and Jack didn't like how long Tavis had gone without exhaling. He was about to dismiss the look of concentration on her face, the warning it gave him, to tell her to stop pushing. But then he began to feel something else, something tugging at his protective awareness that had solely belonged to Tavis. It was more than something, it was *someone*. Tavis' grip on his hands loosened and her blue eyes disappeared behind her eyelids.

Jack let go of her left hand and reached down into the water. He felt something soft and silky and he latched on to it as though all of life depended on it and brought Lani to the surface. He looked down into his daughter's face and tears sprang to his eyes at the overwhelming feeling of infinite joy. He pulled Tavis' exhausted body to his chest, cradling both mother and child.

"Oh, Tavis. Look at her, she's beautiful."

The baby started to make audible sounds and Jack remembered what Tavis said about her beginning to breathe once exposed to air. Never in his life had he been so happy to see another person do something so simple as take a breath.

"She's breathing, Tavis. Oh, my God… that's beautiful, too."

"Let me see her," Tavis said, her voice weak and spent.

Jack leaned Lani forward so Tavis could see her.

"She's perfect," she said. "Give her to me. There's a sterile set of scissors and a clamp in the basket. You need to cut the umbilical cord."

Carefully, Jack leaned mother and child against the boulder before sprinting to the basket. He found the items at the bottom, underneath everything edible she'd packed that morning, and he trotted back to the boulder. At brandishing the scissors, part of him wanted to repair the cut and Tavis sensed the thought.

"Nothing will ever truly separate us in the way that matters most," she told him.

"I know, I think I just fell in love with you having our child inside you. I'll have to work on making that happen again."

"Not too soon, I hope."

"Oh, of course. I can wait until we get the baby asleep tonight. Come on, it's time to get my ladies out of this lake."

~

Jack made a fluffy cushion of the towels for Tavis to sit on and packed everything else in the back of the cart. When he returned to the blanket, Tavis was already asleep. Nudging her awake, he told her to hold Lani while he carried them both in the blanket to the passenger side of the cart.

He eased her down onto the seat and ran around the cart to the driver's side. At hitting a few bumps on the footpath and seeing Tavis wince, Jack had no choice but to drive at a snail's pace until reaching the smoother travelling lane.

When they got home, he scooped them both up again and carried them inside to their bedroom. Jack laid them on the bed and stood back to admire how beautiful they looked.

"Do you need anything?" he asked.

"Just water."

After he got back with a pitcher of water and a glass, he found Tavis fast asleep. He set the water on the bedside table and pulled the blanket at the end of the bed over her and Lani. Too happy and excited to sleep, Jack forced himself to leave the bedroom so they could rest.

He busied himself with unpacking the cart and putting away the uneaten food from the basket. Later, after washing all the towels and clothes, he gave the house a thorough cleaning. Since it was late afternoon, he thought Tavis might be hungry when she woke and he prepped the ingredients for all her favorite foods. Whether or not they paired well in one meal was irrelevant, in his opinion.

He picked the best of his romaine lettuce leaves and set them in ice-water. Between the dashes outside for ingredients and getting them cleaned and chopped in the kitchen, Jack peeked into the bedroom to check on them. Each time, he found them still sleeping.

Just when the brie soup tested done and was set to the back of the stove to rest,

Jack heard an unfamiliar noise resonating throughout the house. He followed the sound to the bedroom and opened the door, finding Lani crying and Tavis just waking up.

"She's probably hungry. How long were we asleep?"

"About five hours," he said.

Tavis pulled Lani closer. "Yep, hunger woke this baby."

The overwhelming feeling of pride flooded Jack again, yet he was also a little jealous. Not so much for Tavis' attention, but for feeling left out of being able to feed his own daughter.

Tavis sensed the emotion, not that it took any special ability; the pitiful look on his face was obvious. She'd already planned in advance for this very situation.

"I ordered a nursing pump and some bottles last week. You'll be able to feed Lani, too."

Jack sat on the side of the bed and looked into Tavis' eyes. His heart fluttered at the compassion he found there. "Thank you for thinking of that."

"I want you to participate in every way," she said. "It's important for the bonding between you and Lani."

He leaned over and kissed Tavis, then kissed the top of Lani's head.

"I hope you're hungry," he said while helping Tavis take a few sips of water. "I'm cooking all your favorites. The brie soup's done. I have everything ready to make Caesar salad and chipotle shrimp. You can decide whichever one you want."

"Wow. You're just a bundle of energy, aren't you? That's a good thing, because you're gonna need it." She smiled. "They all sound great. I'm pretty hungry, I might eat all of it. Thank you for making dinner."

"Leave it to me, sweetie-pie," Jack said in a mock-salesman's voice, making her giggle.

"You're so silly," she said. "And stop making me laugh."

"Okay, I'll put on my serious hat now. I just want you to focus on yourself and getting as much rest as you can."

"After I'm done feeding her, I want to take a bath. Will you take care of Lani while I have some time to myself?"

"Are you kidding me?" Jack's eyebrows raised. "I'll go prepare a bath for you right now. I can't wait to spend time with her."

Jack made another mad dash to the garden with the idea of making the bath more special for Tavis. He plucked several stems of lavender, sage, rosemary, and chamomile, then eyed Sebastian's garden. He peeked at the front of the house and saw that Sebastian was still out, so he snagged a couple of his prized roses.

Back in the kitchen, he dumped the bounty in the sink to rinse them off and freshen the blooms. Once the tub had filled with warm water, Jack floated a few of the selected herbs in the water along with some yellow rose petals and put the rest in a basket by the side of the tub for Tavis to add as she wanted. He drizzled mineral oil in the water, lit the aromatic candles, and went back to the bedroom.

"Everything's ready and waiting for you," he told her and picked Lani up from Tavis' arms. "Is she fat and happy now?"

She couldn't help but laugh, even though it caused her pain. "Yes, dutiful daddy, she should be fat and happy for at least an hour. You might want to change her diaper though."

He recognized the jab for what it was and refused to be bothered by it. "I look forward to changing her diaper," he said, holding his chin up in a dignified manner. "Even if it is disgusting." Jack walked out of the bedroom with Lani and marched off in the direction of the nursery.

Tavis eased to the edge of the bed, finding every inch of her body was sore and tender. She slowly made her way to the bathroom and a smile spread over her face at the sight of the bath with the herbs and rose petals floating on the surface. After disrobing, she lowered herself into the water and enjoyed instant relief. She had no idea how Jack knew which herbs to put in her bath water, nor did she care.

It was glorious, and she soaked in the bath until the water chilled. She briefly considered refilling it with warm water, but forced herself to get out and dry off. Slipping on her robe, Tavis opened the bathroom door to a silent house and figured Jack must've taken Lani outside. She went to the bedroom closet and put on a sundress, looking forward to the day she could wear shorts again.

Tavis found Jack on the front porch talking to Kyrie, who was looking at Lani in the carrier sling that Jack had strapped against his body. He was just finishing up the story of how he helped Tavis give birth.

"Congratulations, Tavis," Kyrie said, smiling. "Lani's perfect and beautiful. How're you feeling?"

"Like I need to sit down." Tavis sat in one of the cushioned rattan chairs. She saw Sebastian hadn't returned yet and that Kyrie had to leave his order on the porch.

Kyrie sat in the chair beside Tavis and held her arms out to Jack for him to hand over Lani. Disappointment showed on Jack's face as he relinquished Lani from the sling to Kyrie's waiting arms.

"Proud and protective much?" Kyrie whispered to Tavis.

"Yeah." Tavis chuckled.

"You did a great job, Tavis," Kyrie said, looking at Lani's tiny face. She glanced at Tavis and saw her blinking back tears. "What's wrong?"

"Nothing." She waved her hand in the air to dismiss the flood of emotions at seeing her mother hold her daughter. "Stupid hormones. And I want my father to meet Lani, but he's still out."

"The hormones will straighten themselves out over the next few days." Kyrie's voice had a comforting effect. "Sebastian will be home soon enough. Frank's really taken to his company and I think it's nice that your father has been giving him something else to do besides sit around the house and miss Lena all day."

"I know." Tavis nodded and smiled. "I'll be fine in a few days."

Lani stirred and started nuzzling at Kyrie's chest. "I think Lani wants her mother."

She stood and placed Lani in Tavis' arms. At the contact, Tavis sensed a difference in Kyrie, a difference she was still very much accustomed to. It was a shock and she wondered how it could be possible.

Tavis felt a pull from Jack and when she looked at him, found him frowning at her. He'd sensed her troubled thoughts and was worried about her. She still found the changes in Jack an obstacle at times and she cleared her mind of what she'd been thinking about Kyrie.

"I should be going now," Kyrie said, interrupting the staring between Tavis and Jack. "I still have a few more deliveries to make today."

"Where's Alec?" Tavis asked.

"I've been making him take more time off to spend with Luke and Meg."

When Kyrie drove off, Jack took the seat next to Tavis. "How was your bath?"

"Absolutely wonderful. Thank you so much." She grinned. "I'll be wanting one a day for a while."

Sebastian's cart pulled up at full speed and he practically launched himself out of the driver's seat. He rushed up the porch stairs and said, "Let me see her."

Tavis lifted Lani up to him, happy he was back now. He looked down into Lani's face while she still remained in Tavis' arms. After a moment, he took Lani into his own arms and turned his back to Tavis and Jack, walking out into the sun to see her clearly.

He studied and examined every inch of Lani, deciding she was entirely perfect and as strong as he'd been hoping for. Gratitude and completion swept over him. Closing his eyes, he brought her closer to his face and fixed her scent to memory so that he would recognize her anywhere and anytime.

If only he could get close enough to Luke to do the same, but Alec had become more protective than ever. Sebastian had no choice but to assume Alec protected something as equally perfect as what he held in his arms.

Sebastian placed a delicate kiss on Lani's forehead and sang to her, swaying with the gentle breeze. The soft sound of the melody was calming and peaceful. It held a long history that both Tavis and Sebastian understood, but one that Jack had yet to be told of. Still, it brought a sense of order that he'd already begun to familiarize with. When Sebastian's song ended, he turned to face them again.

"Both of you have made me more proud then you'll ever know. Lani is superior in every way," Sebastian said as he walked back up the steps.

To Jack's surprise, Sebastian placed Lani in his arms instead of Tavis'.

Having easily picked up on it, Sebastian said to him, "The bond between a father and his daughter is unbreakable and more everlasting than time itself."

With a knowing smile and a simple nod to Jack, Sebastian turned his attention to Tavis and took her hands into his. He peered into her eyes, searching for any signs of physical distress. "You're well, it seems."

"I'm fine, just tired."

"You're growing stronger by the minute. It won't take long." He kissed the backs of her hands and put them in her lap. "I'm tired myself," Sebastian said and retreated back down the steps. "Feed my daughter, Jack, I heard her stomach growling. For goodness sake, she just gave you a child."

Tavis put her hand on Jack's arm to stop him from saying anything. "He's only having a little fun. Don't be mad."

"*Is* your stomach growling?" he asked.

Tavis nodded and took Lani from him when he stood.

"Let's go inside and put some food in that belly."

~

In the middle of the night, Tavis woke to the sound of Lani crying—the sound much louder than it should've been. She and Jack had put Lani in her crib in the nursery before going to sleep, yet somehow Lani seemed to have made her way to their bed.

Jack also woke at Lani's crying and found Tavis' expression set in blaring reproach.

"What?" He attempted innocence. "I knew she'd wake up to nurse soon and I didn't want you having to get her."

"Thank you for thinking about *my* comfort."

"I'm sorry, Tavis." Jack gave up on the not-guilty plea. "She's just so little and I couldn't stand seeing her sleeping all alone in such a big crib."

The next morning, Tavis called Kyrie to inquire about ordering a bassinet for their bedroom. Kyrie chuckled into the phone when Tavis told her about Jack sneaking Lani into their bed.

"There's no need to order one, I still have Alec's. Meg wanted to use her own bassinet that Ila had saved when she and Alec had a similar problem with Luke. I'll bring it to you after I close the store."

Later that afternoon, after Kyrie reassembled the bassinet in their bedroom, Tavis gave her a big hug to thank her. Though truly thankful she could sleep again without worrying about Lani, Tavis was interested in confirming what she'd sensed before. Not only did she confirm it upon embracing Kyrie, Tavis found a stronger shielding of her thoughts—as though Kyrie were the one in full control rather than Alec's usual doing.

~

Over the next few weeks, Tavis increasingly found herself chasing Jack down to retrieve their daughter. Just as often, he chased after her as well—with the pump. When he bottle-fed Lani for the first time, there was no denying him what he felt was his right to participate in feeding her and Tavis began to feel like a dairy cow.

Early one morning, Tavis stared into the refrigerator and counted five bottles of her recently pumped milk sitting on the top shelf. Jack had diligently written the date and time on each one.

"Jack?" Tavis called out, still eyeing the bottles.

"Yeah?" he answered back from the nursery. He'd washed and dried all of Lani's blankets and was folding them before putting them in the dresser.

"There are five bottles in the refrigerator. I'm gonna visit with my father for a little while. Do you mind feeding Lani while I'm out?" Tavis asked, shutting the refrigerator. Her eyes fell to Jack's other obsession, Lani's feeding chart affixed to the front of the refrigerator door.

"Are you well enough?" Jack came into the kitchen, still folding a baby blanket while his eyes scanned the feeding chart.

"Yes. I just need to get out of the house for a little bit. Are you sure you're okay with feeding Lani?"

"Not a problem." He opened the refrigerator and counted the bottles. "Looks good. Enjoy your visit with Sebastian."

She was mildly insulted that he was so willing to let her go, even though she'd go anyway if he tried to stop her. Stepping out into the early morning air was sublime, a feeling to savor, and she took her time walking over to Sebastian's. When she got to his front door, she let herself in as she always did, and found him in the kitchen scrambling eggs.

"To what do I owe the pleasure?" he asked with a glance over his shoulder.

"I needed a change of scenery. Hope you don't mind."

"I would never pass on a visit from you," Sebastian said. "Jack's testing your limits, I presume?"

"Yes." Tavis sighed and sat at the dining table.

"He's behaving normally, I hope you know that."

"I know, but it's still… maddening." She shrugged. "Sometimes I get so irritated with him. Like just now, before I left to come over here, he was more interested in counting milk bottles. I'd already told him there were five, but he counted them anyway."

"Give him time, it'll balance out." He brought the plate to the table and offered some to her.

"No thanks, I already had breakfast. How much time?"

With his fork full of eggs, Sebastian paused and looked at her. He realized Tavis truly didn't know the answer and he set the fork down. "Well, how are you feeling, physically?"

"Fine. Better every day. I thought it would take longer to heal from giving birth."

"It does for the women here, but you're different, stronger in that respect. It won't be much longer before you have Jack's full attention again." Sebastian picked his fork back up and began eating his breakfast, watching the blush stain his daughter's cheeks.

"Okay," she muttered. "I understand, we don't need to discuss it further."

"Lani's absolutely perfect and new. Jack wants to protect her and care for her like he does for you. I can't tell you enough how happy this makes me. I'd be willing to bet that if you were to become overly distressed right now, he'd sense it and break the door down to get to you."

"You think so?"

"Do you want to test it?"

"No!" Tavis glared at him, then thought of something and rolled her eyes. "Besides, right now he'd only be worried about the potential loss of the milk source and then he'd probably chase Meg around with the pump."

Sebastian nearly choked on his toast; he hadn't had a good laugh in a while.

When he finished his breakfast, Tavis picked up his plate and carried it to the kitchen. She wanted to broach the subject of Kyrie with him, but it would be awkward if her suspicions proved to be correct.

"I want to talk to you about something," she started while putting his plate in the dishwasher.

"I already know what's on your mind and we'll not be discussing it."

"So, I'm right?"

"I'm not going to answer you."

"It's yours, isn't it? Kyrie's not seeing anyone that I know of. Does she even know she's pregnant?"

"No more questions, Tavis."

"Why?" she pleaded for any answer at all.

He got up from the table and headed toward the front door to leave. Tavis reached it first and positioned herself to block his passage.

"Why?" she repeated.

"Because of the inescapable bond I made with her a long time ago, the one that gave me you and Alec. I need to leave now. I have to avoid seeing her and the answer is no, she has no idea she's pregnant. She can't know right now." He sounded like he had doubts, but shook his head. "Please, Tavis, move out of my way."

She hated seeing him so distraught and stepped aside to let him leave. It hurt still more watching him get into the cart. It dawned on her how little time they had left on Gamma.

"Wait!" Tavis cried out to him.

Sebastian turned the cart off to address her unspoken question. "No, we don't have much time left. Come here."

Tavis went to the cart and sat in the passenger seat.

"We'll be fine, stop worrying. Go for a nice walk to clear your head and to strengthen your body, then go back home to Jack and Lani." He took Tavis' hand and brought it to his lips. "Everything will work out just fine. It's all planned out." Sebastian smiled at her and willed her to accept his reassurances.

"Okay," she said, returning his smile.

Tavis trusted him because he wanted her to. She trusted him because *she* wanted to. She trusted him because she had to.

16

Father and Son

"I think he wants you." Alec hovered Luke in the air above Meg.

"Oh? Did he tell you that?" Meg looked up from her book and set it aside.

"No, but he keeps trying to find a place to nurse on my chest." He handed Luke to Meg and sat on the couch beside her.

"Is it still just you and Sebastian fishing tonight?" she asked, settling Luke to her.

"Yeah."

"Did you try calling Jack?"

Alec snorted. "He can't part from Lani long enough to bother with fishing."

"Hush, I think it's sweet."

"He acts like you do with Luke."

Meg grimaced at him. "What's that supposed to mean?"

"What? You said it was sweet." Alec chortled. "I like the way you are with Luke. You're both so calm and happy when you're together."

"He's happy with you, too."

"I know he is. When he's not hungry we get along great." Alec brushed his fingers along Luke's cheek. "That's my boy, I'm proud to be his father." He'd much rather stay home with them instead of dealing with Sebastian. "I'm thinking about cancelling the fishing trip."

"No, don't do that," she said. "It's too late to cancel, and besides, that would be rude. Sebastian's probably got everything ready to go by now."

Alec was silent for a moment. His hand found hers and he brought it to his lips, letting it linger there while he thought things through. "You're right." He put her hand by Luke's side and stood. "I'm gonna get the fishing gear ready. I'll be right back."

He went out to the barn and stood in the doorway, listening to the soft clucking of the hens roosting in their nest boxes. Most of the daylight was gone and he'd have to leave to meet Sebastian before long. After retrieving the fishing poles from the back corner and leaning them against the barn door near the tackle box, Alec thought again about whether or not he wanted to confront Sebastian—everything about it made him nervous.

His eyes scanned the darkened trees edging the back of their house and he recalled the conversation he and Chaza had the night Luke was born. Oddly enough, he was less nervous asking for Chaza's help than meeting Sebastian.

He headed over to the forest. "Chaza? Are you there?"

A few minutes passed of no response, so he turned to go tell Meg he was leaving and nearly bulldozed Chaza.

"What do you need from me, Alec?"

"Right now? A drink sounds good. You scared the hell out of me." Alec frowned at her. "It's unnerving how you do that."

"Do what?"

"Just… appear like that. So quietly."

"Years of practice," she said, half-smiling. "How are Meg and Luke?"

"They're doing well."

A strained silence passed between them and when his eyes averted to the ground, Chaza said, "All right, out with it. Obviously, you want to say something."

"Actually, I wanted to ask you a couple of questions. I want to have my facts straight."

"Do you doubt what I told you before?" Chaza lifted her chin.

"No, I know Meg's your daughter." Alec gazed into Chaza's eyes. "You said you'd cheated on Sebastian with Joseph… I mean, well…" He wasn't so sure how to word his question. "Wasn't Joseph Ila's fiancé?"

Chaza had a hunch where his questions were heading. "Joseph and Ila were having some problems when I got involved with him. I'd already left Sebastian, he just didn't know it yet because I was too big of a coward to tell him. When I said that I was unfaithful it was because we were, and still are, technically married."

"Why did you leave him?" Alec half-expected she'd yell at him for asking personal questions.

"Sebastian and I disagreed on an issue and there didn't seem to be a resolution to it."

"Does he know you're here?"

"Yes."

"Are you sure he doesn't know Meg's your daughter?"

"Only you and I know." Chaza sighed in defeat. "However, Sebastian's a smart man and he knows I've been hiding something from him. He'll figure it out, unless someone tells him first. Is that right? Is that what this is about… why you want to have your facts straight?"

Alec nodded. "Are you sure Ila doesn't know Meg's not her daughter?"

"She has no idea." Chaza was curious what Alec would think at learning how Ila came to be clueless. "I altered her memories and created false ones for her to believe and remember." He was unfazed. "Have you ever done anything like that, Alec?"

"Once, when I was a kid. I tried it on my mother so she wouldn't worry about me being different. I don't think it worked, though." Alec shook his head. "I don't know, she's never said anything about it."

Chaza cleared her throat. "Yeah, that can happen with some people." The last thing she wanted was to address questions about Kyrie. "Is that all you needed?"

"No." Alec grew concerned about how late it was getting. "There's no record of your name anywhere, so I assume management doesn't know about you. To be honest, I don't think the islanders know about you. You mentioned you've been here for a long time. Why were you here to begin with?"

It was the start of the more important questions Alec wanted to ask and Chaza knew she'd have to be careful with her answers. "I came here as a watcher. Not for management, obviously, but for someone else."

"Does management know someone else is observing their island?"

"I don't believe so." Chaza knew what his next question would be, could almost see it forming in his eyes.

"Who were you watching for?" Alec waited, but realized she wasn't going to answer. "I've decided to get my answers, like you suggested."

Chaza remained silent.

"It's him, isn't it?"

"I can't answer any more of your questions, it's not my place. You'll have to ask Sebastian."

"That's what I intend to do tonight. Will you stay with Meg for a while? She's been talking about you more lately, she really wants to see you."

"I'd love to." Chaza smiled, but then gave Alec a weary glance. "Are you going to tell Sebastian that Meg's my daughter?"

"Yes." He frowned, unsure of how she'd react.

"It's okay. I knew you would when I told you." A sardonic laugh escaped her when she thought of her weaknesses. "Maybe that's *why* I told you. Perhaps I'm too chicken to do it myself. I only asked so I'll know to expect an ugly confrontation."

"Will he hurt you?" Alec hadn't considered this and it worried him to think his actions would bring her harm.

"No, not in the way you're thinking. We're not capable of bringing that sort of physical harm to anyone."

"I'm not so sure about that."

She was impressed by his doubt of the concept. "You're thinking about when you slapped Meg to get her to wake up." Chaza knew the true source of Alec's burden. "You're remembering the time you hit her on the head with a rock so you could take everything that defined her."

He suppressed his budding anger. "You're the only one I know who's this good at sensing my thoughts. Stop it."

Resisting the urge to laugh again, Chaza continued. "Think about it, Alec. Each of those times, and any emotional pain you caused as well, didn't come without a price. It caused you equal pain, sometimes more."

"Yeah, it did. Not that I make a habit of it with Meg, but it's happened. It hurt enough to know that I never want to do it again. Ever."

Ah, but the trouble with 'ever' and 'never' is that these words don't care what we want. And neither does the Trinity of the Cosmos: the accurate history of all our yesterdays; our day-to-day entropic realities; and fate's arrow of time—which points at our mortal finalities.

"Then you know how I'm gonna feel when Sebastian hears what I did. Our marriage may be over, but we did love each other once. I never told him that I was leaving him, I just left and he thought I was dead. Instead, I was here, in the arms of another man, and having that man's baby. I'd say, at the very least, Sebastian will be hurt and might have a question or two for me."

It was a thorny subject and Alec had to admit to himself that Chaza did owe an explanation to Sebastian. Something else came to mind. "Are you Tavis' mother? Is she Meg's sister?"

"No, I'm not Tavis' mother. Someone else is." Chaza tread dangerously close to revealing too much. She waited to see if her answer caused more questions. If they did, Alec chose not to voice them.

He changed the subject instead. "You were right about Dr. Patrick, he came over wanting to examine Luke. I didn't have to do anything, Meg wouldn't let him near Luke."

"That's excellent," Chaza said, sounding relieved. "Just keep an eye on that, Dr. Patrick won't give up so easily. Come on, I want to see Meg and Luke."

~

"Look who I found," Alec said to Meg.

"Chaza!" Meg's eyes lit up. "You haven't come to see me in a while. Have you been well?" Alec picked Luke up from Meg's arms so she could button her shirt.

"I'm fine. I was letting the new parents have their time for bonding. How's Luke?" Chaza's eyes went to the bundle in Alec's arms.

Alec brought Luke to Chaza, offering him for her to hold. She looked into Alec's eyes to make sure he meant to let her before taking him into her arms. A genuine smile graced Chaza's face when she looked at Luke; no pretext, no pretense, no fear—just pure love.

She studied Luke's face and supposed his eyes, and those twin dimples, would be like Alec's—like all those of his ancestors. The rest of him was all Meg, in her opinion, especially that crazy, curly hair.

"He's such a good baby," Meg said. "He rarely cries, except when he's hungry. I should warn you, he's particularly hungry today."

"That's because he's a healthy growing baby boy," Chaza said, addressing Luke more so than Meg.

Chaza positioned Luke against her chest, resting his face against her shoulder. Though he wasn't a newborn anymore, he still had that distinctive baby scent. To Chaza, it was the most wonderful scent in the universe.

"He seems to like you," Meg noted.

Luke let out a loud burp. After a good laugh, Alec said, "I should get going. I'm already late."

Meg turned to Chaza. "Alec's having dinner at the café before surf fishing later. Would you like to have dinner with me and Luke?"

"It just so happens, I'm hungry, too," Chaza said.

Alec pulled Meg close and gave her a kiss before leaving. It wasn't as chaste as he had intended and Chaza averted her eyes for a moment.

"Enjoy your dinner, ladies." Alec patted Luke's head. "And young man."

Chaza watched him leave, sensing his resolve to finally get the answers that had always plagued him. Whether or not Sebastian was ready to give them was unpredictable, but Alec was armed with enough information to tip the balance in his favor—leaving Sebastian with no choice but to talk to him.

~

Alec put the fishing gear in the back of the cart and drove off toward the town center. The whole way there, he thought about how he would approach Sebastian with his questions. No matter what scenario came to mind, the result was the same: getting the answers out of him wouldn't be easy.

Chaza's warning that he may not like the answers kept coming to mind and by the time he pulled up in front of the café, he'd convinced himself that it didn't matter. Even if he ended up hating the answers, it was still better than never knowing.

He saw Sebastian through the café windows, sitting at the bar talking to James. Inhaling deeply to steady himself, Alec turned the cart off and entered through the glass entrance doors to the bar, and took a seat next to Sebastian.

"Alec," Sebastian greeted. "I just got here myself. James was telling me about the new seasonal beer and convinced me to give it a try."

"I'll have one, too," Alec said to James and picked the menu up to peruse the dinner specials.

Sebastian also studied the menu and, once James was out of earshot, said, "The café asked Jack about using some of his herbs in their menu items."

This bit of news surprised Alec. "Really?"

It was a prestigious honor to be asked for any of your produce by the café. The chef was notorious for being picky about the ingredients in his dishes and always preferred island grown ingredients to ordered foodstuffs from the mainland. If Jack accepted, and rejection was unheard of, his name would appear on the dining room billboard as a contributor to the evening's meal.

"Yes, and he's quite puffed up about it," Sebastian said.

James returned with Alec's beer. "What'll it be, gentlemen?"

"I'll have the grilled trigger fish." Sebastian handed the menu back.

"Winter squash ravioli with a Caesar salad."

When James left to put their order in, Alec picked up his beer mug and brought it to his lips, draining a third of it in one hearty gulp. Sebastian watched and followed Alec's example, finding the experience rather indulgent, but palatable. The flavor was excellent and reminiscent of the last time he'd had it; bringing back memories of his previous time on Gamma.

"How're Jack and Tavis doing with Lani?" Alec asked, interrupting Sebastian's thoughts of whether he should have beer made when he returned home.

"They're enjoying parenthood very much. Jack's quite smitten with Lani, as am I."

Alec and Sebastian drained the rest of their beer and stared at their reflections in the mirror behind the bar. Alec noticed they were the same height and build, and that their hair parted in the same direction.

"Another round?" James asked, taking their empty mugs.

"Yes," they answered in unison.

They continued with the small talk until their food arrived. By the time they finished eating, they'd consumed two more beers and ordered some growlers to take with them. Driving in separate carts, Sebastian followed behind Alec to the beach near the docks.

Once they unloaded the fishing gear and were settled in their beach chairs, Alec reached for the beer and poured them each a mug.

Sebastian held his mug up. "Here's to catching lots of fish."

After a clink of their mugs and a gulp from each, Alec's fishing rod arced with the first catch of the evening, revealing a sea bass. Sebastian reeled in two more and Alec released a juvenile nurse shark before they were half an hour into the fishing excursion.

Things quieted down after the initial catches and the reeling-in slowed to a more predictable pace. When they weren't busy re-baiting, they engaged in idle chitchat at times, and just as often, silence fell between them.

Knowing Alec was sensitive to the invasion, Sebastian had long since refrained from aggressively probing his thoughts. However, it was clear to him the minute Alec sat down next to him at the café that something was on his mind. Yet, nothing had been mentioned outside of the usual island happenings.

They'd consumed over half the beer and caught several more fish that were acceptable for keeping when the awkward silence came—different in nature, and stretching on longer than the previous moments of silence had. Their fishing rods hadn't bent in the obvious sign that something nibbled at the bait in over twenty minutes.

Alec poured them another beer and looked up at the starry sky. It was a clear night, spectacular, not one cloud to prevent a single star from shining. But he suddenly felt very small, like he was merely a speck of dust. The beer had loosened him up and he failed to guard his thoughts as he was so apt to do.

Sebastian followed Alec's upward gaze at sensing the pensive thought. He took a risk and hoped he wouldn't regret it. "There's no such thing as a life so small that it has no importance. However, it's true that some lives are more important than others, it's all a matter of perspective. Is there something on your mind, Alec?"

Time to ask, or leave it alone? The decision was an easy one for Alec to make. *"A life so small,"* Alec quoted and contemplated the words. "But what about a life so different? Is that life important, too?"

"Again, Alec, it's all a matter of perspective."

"What about the person who *is* different? What if that person starts to question their difference from that of all the people around him?"

Sebastian became acutely aware of the change in Alec. Though he knew he'd have to answer Alec's questions one day, he didn't know his son had already made the choice for him and had decided to confront him tonight.

"Then that person would need to start asking his questions aloud, rather than brood over them silently," Sebastian said.

"I agree, maybe it is time to start asking questions. I met someone not so long ago who suggested I should start by asking you."

"Is that so?" Sebastian looked over at Alec, who continued to stare at the stars instead of facing him. "And who might that be?"

"My wife's mother."

"Ila?"

"Nope, it wasn't Ila. It was someone else, someone I think you're familiar with. Her name's Chaza… I believe she's your wife."

Sebastian's demeanor froze over at once. He'd already experienced a whisper of suspicion concerning that riddle, but had dismissed it as impossible. To hear the words spoken was quite a blow. "Did she tell you that?"

"Yep."

"Chaza and I weren't able to have children. I know Meg's not my daughter, I'd feel it if she were. Who's her father?"

"Still the same father, Joseph, just a different mother. Apparently, your wife was unfaithful."

Alec took sick pleasure in relaying the information, even though he couldn't understand why he felt this way. Yet, there was something else—a shameful feeling crept over him. He turned to look at Sebastian, who'd found a sudden interest in watching the sand beneath his feet.

An overwhelming sense of sadness exuded from Sebastian and spread outward in all directions. The first pangs of remorse hit Alec, until he saw Sebastian reel in his line from the ocean and stand from his chair. After he folded it, he gathered the rest of his belongings.

"Hey, where are you going?" Alec asked.

"I'm going home."

"Oh, no you're not! I have questions I want some answers to." He stood and threw his fishing rod down.

"Not now, Alec. I'll talk to you later." Sebastian started walking toward his cart.

Alec was furious and went after him, refusing to let him get away without at least hearing his questions. "I know you've been watching this island, just like management does. I know Chaza used to work for you, but she won't tell me why, she said I had to ask you. Tell me, Sebastian, why are you so interested in Gamma?"

Sebastian stopped and faced him. "I'm not so interested in watching this island as I am in watching you… since you were born."

"*Me*? Why?"

Shaking his head, Sebastian turned around again and continued on.

Disgusted, Alec spat out, "You're nothing but a coward."

The retreat away from Alec came to an abrupt halt. Sebastian had wanted to be alone, but his son's hateful words cut through him.

Alec watched Sebastian slowly turn to face him again, and for the first time in his life, he felt submissive. The look on Sebastian's face expressed not only disapproval of the insult and complete lack of respect, but an unmistakable intent to let him know it was unacceptable and would never be tolerated again.

"THAT IS ENOUGH!"

Alec stumbled back from Sebastian, who loomed over him with leviathan reverence.

"I can be accused of many things, most of which are probably true." Sebastian's eyes bored into Alec's. "And I can be called a lot of things, but I am no coward. You will never address me with that word again."

Sabastian saw a respectful amount of fear form in Alec's eyes and he relaxed a little. The fact remained, though, that the insult came from Alec's quest for answers.

"I'm curious, Alec, did Chaza tell you why you had to ask me? Why didn't she just answer your questions herself?"

"She said it wasn't her place."

"Did she say anything else?" Sebastian asked, but Alec remained silent. "What else did she say, Alec?"

"That I may not like the answers," he blurted out.

Sebastian chortled. "She's right, you probably won't like them."

"I don't care. All my life I've wanted to know why I'm so different from everyone else. You and Chaza seem to know, so why don't you tell me?"

"I'm different from everyone else on this island, too. So is Chaza, so is Tavis. After what you've told me of Meg's true parentage, I assume she is as well."

Alec averted his eyes. "She was, until I took it away from her."

"Ah, of course." Enlightened, Sebastian let go a hearty laugh. "So, you absorbed that part of her energy. You must have done it when she was quite young, you wouldn't have gotten away with that if she were older."

"We were children when I did it."

"That solves the mystery of why you were so strong at such a young age." Sebastian raised his eyebrows. "And why Meg never seemed anything but ordinary."

"Who the hell are you?" Alec's voice was filled with awe, but there was also a pleading.

Sebastian sighed and put his fishing gear back down. There was no way he'd answer all of Alec's questions, but he would answer a few. The problem was settling on which ones to address. He sat next to the gear and motioned for Alec to do the same.

They stared out at the ocean while Sebastian gathered his thoughts. The water looked so different at night. It was as dark as the sky, but lacked the beauty of the light from the moon and stars.

"I can't possibly answer all of your questions in one night, but I'll do what I can. First, I need to know how you'll handle yourself if anything I say upsets you."

Alec frowned. "I'm not sure what you mean."

"If I told you something that turned everything you thought you knew into something else, how will you behave around the other people in your life and on this island? Will you act in haste, or do anything that disrupts the current flow of life here?"

"Do you mean, will I run around like I've lost my mind and tell everyone what you told me?"

"Right, that."

"Do you plan to harm anyone here?"

"Absolutely not." Sebastian scoffed at the notion. "We're not capable of harming anyone and don't plan to start doing so."

"Chaza said the same thing."

"While I admire your protective nature, I'm still waiting for your answer."

Alec nudged a few divots from the sand with his shoes while he considered the question. "As long as you don't plan to hurt anybody, then I don't plan to lose my mind," he said. When Sebastian continued to wait, Alec added, "And no, I won't tell anyone."

"You're a man now, and as such, there's honor among men. I trust you to keep your word and to use your best judgment. What you tell Meg is up to you."

"I gave back what I took from her the night Luke was born. She had difficulty with the birth. Chaza helped deliver Luke, but Meg was weak and Chaza told me to give it back or they could die."

"How's Meg dealing with it?"

"She hasn't asked any questions yet." Alec shrugged. "I'm not even sure she's noticed a difference yet. Luke keeps her busy."

"She *will* have questions, Alec, and soon I suspect. It'll be your responsibility to help her. Don't be surprised if you find *yourself* having to face a few angry questions from Meg."

"I'm still waiting for your answer," Alec said, mimicking Sebastian's earlier words. The last thing he wanted was to think about Meg's potential anger at learning what he'd done to her.

"You want to know why you're different." Sebastian chose his next words with purpose. "It's because of your lineage."

"I never got to know my father, he was sent away before I was born." Alec considered his mother and shook his head. "My mother's not different, not like me."

"Maybe not like you, but she is in other ways. William Davis wasn't special in any way and what made him different is what got him booted off Gamma."

"Then why did you say it's because of my parentage?"

"Alec…" –Sebastian braced himself before continuing– "William Davis isn't your father."

Alec said nothing. It was a shock, but he knew in his gut that it was probably the least shocking thing he was to hear. He felt he almost knew what was coming next. Hadn't he wondered why Tavis compared the color similarity of their eyes the day he met her? She'd walled her thoughts off so quickly, that walling off his curiosity came with ease—and with too much relief in the rearview mirror of hindsight.

"You're different because I'm different."

"Just say it." Alec's hands started to tremble.

"You're *my* son." He decided to tell him about Tavis as well. "And Tavis is your twin, that's why you two look so similar."

Still, it stunned Alec. As though the revelation wasn't enough of a bombshell, to say that Tavis was his twin sister mystified him. He wanted to deny it, accuse him of lying, but there was no point. It was the truth, and Alec knew it. No matter what he thought of Sebastian, he was not the sort to make up such outlandish lies, and he would never involve Tavis in them.

More than anything else, what prowled among his thoughts was his mother. Alec was positive she couldn't have known about any of it. He would've sensed it long ago had she been aware William wasn't his father and that she had a missing daughter.

"Did you take advantage of my mother?"

Alec kept his voice calm, but Sebastian detected the underlying turbulence.

Knowing what Alec meant, and trying not to think about a recent memory, Sebastian said, "I'm a physician. When you and Tavis were conceived, it was done in a clinical way. I altered her memories afterward and that's why she thinks William's your father. She has no memory of giving birth to twins, or that I was there to deliver them."

"Why did you take Tavis away from her?"

"No one knew she was carrying twins. It was easy for me to take one of you with me without creating complete chaos on the island."

"But why Tavis?" Alec was surprised by his need to know the answer.

"There was absolutely no way I was going to leave my daughter in this... petri dish," Sebastian spat, disgusted at the thought.

"Does Tavis know all of this?"

"Yes, but not until recently. I told her after we came here and it was a shock for her, too. Tavis spent her life thinking Chaza was her mother."

Alec thought of what he wanted to ask next. There were many questions and he couldn't be sure which ones Sebastian would answer. "I'm different because you're different. So, why are you different? And don't say it's because of *your* father."

Sebastian smiled. "Where I come from, and it's your home as well, we're all the same. We're not stuck on one island feeling different from everyone else and worrying about what that means."

"Are you from the mainland?" Alec asked, it was all he knew of besides the island he'd lived on all of his life.

"No, we're from much farther away than the mainland."

"You're planning for me to go there, aren't you?"

"Yes," Sebastian said flatly.

"What if I refuse?"

"You won't."

"You don't know that, you don't even know me."

"You'll go because you have to, our people need for you to come home."

"People need me here, too," Alec said.

"Meg and Luke will come with you."

"What about my mother?"

"I've already told you, Kyrie's different, but in different ways." Sebastian stared at the individual grains of sand in front of him. "She'll be going, too. You can't tell her, Alec, about anything I've told you."

"Why not?"

"Well, for one thing, she'll think you're crazy. There are other reasons, none of which I prefer to discuss with you tonight."

"Why do people need me somewhere else?"

"Our people are suffering and barely able to exist for much longer." Sebastian teetered on the brink of becoming an emotional mess trying to convey what he wanted Alec to understand. "We're good people who made mistakes in the past, but we've learned from them."

"I still don't know how you think I can help."

"By coming home. You can help by keeping our people from going extinct."

A low rumble formed in Alec's chest and escaped as disgusted laughter. "So, what you need is breeding stock? Are you nuts?"

Desperately trying to maintain his placid reserve, Sebastian said, "Don't ever say that again, here, or at our home. We, you, *all* of us aren't as base and depraved as Ila's horses. We are a noble race of people and you should consider yourself proud to be a part of us."

It was all Alec could do not to laugh again. "You went and impregnated my mother without her knowledge or consent, how noble can you be?"

Though he wanted to, Sebastian knew reminding Alec of his disrespectful tone wasn't the way to win him over. Good old-fashioned knowledge was the only logical way of getting through to Alec, and Sebastian was all too ready to hand it over.

"Why do you think this island exists? We only took advantage of what management and their scientists had already started. They're trying to do what our people did a millennia before, but it's doomed to failure and we learned that the hard way. What's even worse is that they're doing it for all the wrong reasons, and in all the wrong ways. To them, you are, at best, a few notches up from Ila's stallion."

"Let me see if I have this right," Alec said. "All of *their* reasons are wrong, but all of *yours* are right. Oh, and noble, of course. Does that about sum it up correctly?"

Still controlling his temper, Sebastian answered, "Yes. I'd say that's it exactly."

"Assuming I'd be willing to go, when were you planning to leave?"

"The sooner, the better. I've been recently made aware that management knows I'm here and that they're watching more closely than they ever have. I imagine leaving will be trickier now."

"I'm glad you brought that up." Alec folded his arms over his chest. "Exactly how did you plan to leave? No one leaves Gamma without management approval."

"That won't be a problem for me." Sebastian realized he was succumbing to the back and forth banter, yet he couldn't resist it. "Supposedly, no one gets *in* without management approval either, yet here I am… again."

Humbled a little, but still wanting to know how determined Sebastian was to make him leave, Alec asked, "How much of a choice do I have?"

"I'm afraid I can't give you much of a choice."

"It seems to me I always have a choice."

"In an ideal world that's true, but this" –Sebastian swept his arms in an arc to indicate everything around them– "is not such a world. You don't belong here and nothing good will come of you trying to stay."

"I'll be the one who makes that decision. Meg and I will decide together where we belong."

For more times this evening than he cared to count, Sebastian tried to maintain an even temper when what he'd rather do is incapacitate Alec and send him off. Normally, he'd be proud of Alec's determination to make his own choices in life, but not here, not on Gamma.

"I encourage you to talk to Meg, but I'll warn you to tell her how important it is to keep it between only yourselves. Trust no one here."

"Wouldn't that include you, too?"

"You're my son. I only want for you and your family to have a future, one that's happy and peaceful. I want you to have everything you're entitled to have, everything that belongs to you by your true birthright. You've only known life on this island, don't let that cloud your judgment."

Alec said nothing in response, so Sebastian added, "I'm begging you, please trust me, so much depends on it."

"Part of me wants to trust you."

"That's the part of you who's a father, who knows what it means to want the best for your child." Sebastian hated to, but he offered the uglier side of his insight. "The part that doesn't is the result of having grown up here. The side of you that's influenced by how life works in this world and especially on Gamma. Management is monitoring your mother now and as long as she's here, they'll continue to extract information through her."

"Then why aren't you trying to protect her?"

"I am."

"How? It seems to me you've been avoiding her."

"That's how I'm protecting her, by avoiding her."

"What? That doesn't make any sense."

"It would if you knew more."

"Then tell me more!" Alec demanded.

"I don't think it would be a good idea right now."

"If it involves my mother, then I highly suggest you tell me. If you don't, I'll find out for myself."

It was a threat that Sebastian knew Alec meant to follow through with. There would be no rest until Alec figured it out and it wouldn't be difficult to do at Kyrie's stage of pregnancy.

"Kyrie's pregnant with your brother, but she's not aware of it yet. If she were to discover it, then management would find out and everything would change in the blink of an eye. They would come here."

Alec jumped to his feet and paced back and forth in front of Sebastian.

Occasionally, he stopped to glare at him. At last, he asked, "Did she become pregnant in a *clinical* way?"

"No."

"How could you?"

What Sebastian felt was akin to shame. He recognized the base emotion for what it was and refused to be defined by it. He looked up into Alec's accusing eyes and tried to find a way to explain it to him.

"She and I have a bond that began many years ago. It really is all about the choices we make. I chose her, there's a pull between us that's inescapable." None of what he wanted to say came out right. "It's not unlike the bond you have with Meg. Alec, it's complicated."

"Un-complicate it."

"I love her," Sebastian said softly, admitting it to both Alec and himself. "I love the child she's carrying. She wanted me to alter her memories so you wouldn't find out, but I couldn't do it, so Chaza helped. It's a delicate situation and I'm afraid she'll remember if I spend too much time around her, and that's why I've been avoiding her."

No matter how hard he tried, Alec couldn't find an ounce of deception in Sebastian's eyes. Still, he was skeptical. "What about Chaza? Didn't you *choose* her when you married her? Did you not have a bond with her?"

Sebastian grimaced. "That's a harder one to un-complicate."

"Forget it, she already told me anyway." Alec sighed. "Conveniently, she left out the parts involving my mother." He turned away from Sebastian and faced the ocean, watching the waves break against the beach. "I still have a lot of questions, but it's getting late. I need to get back to Meg and Luke."

"I want to tell you a few more things before you go." Sebastian stood and joined Alec's side. "Come closer to the water with me."

Alec looked at him, confused. "Why?"

"Come with me and I'll tell you why."

They went to the water's edge. The waves and wind drowned out most of what Sebastian said. Alec had to step closer to hear and began picking up on the thoughts Sebastian allowed him to see.

"Years ago, management placed cameras at strategic locations all over Gamma. I think they're all out of commission, but it's best to err on the side of caution."

"I've seen those cameras, they don't work." Alec snorted. "I'm the one responsible for wrecking most of them."

"Never assume you're not being watched."

"I never have."

"There's something you need to be aware of. Management has what they refer to as an End Plan. Do you know what that means?"

"No."

"They devised a way of destroying Gamma in the event that if ever things got out of hand... uncontrollable, so to speak, they'll detonate a series of nuclear explosions for the purpose of erasing the whole of the island."

Stunned, Alec asked, "What about the people who live here?"

Sebastian frowned at Alec, wondering if he should show him rather than answer the question verbally. Deciding that a picture was worth more than a thousand words, he inundated Alec with images of total and complete destruction of life and land.

The emotional agony overwhelmed Alec and he fell to his knees. He couldn't stop the bout of nausea and got sick on the sand until there was nothing left, but still his body convulsed and heaved. Though the waves washed away the sick, they left behind the vivid memories of what Alec saw.

"That's what they'll do if they feel they've lost control of their island." Sebastian grabbed the back of Alec's shirt and pulled him back up to a standing position with a strength that surprised Alec. "Never kneel down on this island again."

"They wouldn't do that," Alec said, refusing to think it possible.

"Oh, yes, they would, and they have. Where do you think those images I showed you came from?" Sebastian let go of Alec's shirt, confident he wouldn't fall again. "They'd do it without flinching and start all over again somewhere else. They'd start a new island, or focus their energy and resources on one of their other ones."

"Why?"

"To bring about what they think is a better and stronger race of people."

"Like us?" Alec wiped his mouth on his sleeve.

"In how they *define* us, but it's a distorted image of who we are and what we stand for. What they're trying to do is wrong, and how they go about it is even worse."

"What would make them feel they've lost control?"

Sebastian didn't want to answer this. What constituted management's decision for destroying an island had evolved over time. Things were different on Gamma, and Sebastian feared he knew exactly what it would take for them to view the island as a waste of space.

"In the past, it was rebellion," was Sebastian's controlled answer.

Alec stared at him, somewhat disappointed. "There're two things wrong with that answer. I wasn't asking about the past, and your thoughts are still showing. You think management will destroy Gamma if their brightest and best get away."

"Yes." Sebastian nodded.

"If you succeed in getting us away, then they failed. Management destroys Gamma and everyone left on it."

"Yes."

"But if you fail, they won't—"

"You can't stay here, Alec. I won't allow it."

"You may be my father, but you don't own me, or control me either. I make my own decisions. I choose my own life."

"The other side of that argument is if you stay, management owns you, management controls you, and management makes your decisions, which means you'll never *really* make your own choices. You accept what they give, you accept what they take away. And I assure you, Alec, it's not balanced. Management takes way more than they give."

Alec recalled what Chaza said about the possibility of Luke being taken away and how it would destroy Meg. "Chaza said Dr. Patrick's really a member of management. Is that true?"

"He is."

"Are there others?" A list of names and faces presented themselves as likely candidates in Alec's mind. It was a long list.

"I believe there are others living on Gamma, posing as any other normal inhabitant, but who are really aligned with management. However, they're exceptionally adept at escaping our attention." Sebastian shrugged. "That's probably why they were put here."

It bothered Alec to bring it up, but he had to for Tavis' sake. "Do you know about Jack?"

"Yes, but he's different. He and Tavis have chosen each other." It was encouraging to Sebastian that Alec felt obligated to speak up for Tavis' wellbeing. "He'll become more like us, it's already happening."

"I've had enough for tonight, but we're not finished and I haven't made any decisions. I won't until I discuss it with Meg." Alec stood his ground. "Can you accept that?"

"Yes, but don't put it off. We're running out of time."

~

Alec pulled the cart to a stop in front of the stone house. It was late and most of the lights inside were off, save the one outside Meg had left on for him. He assumed Chaza had left due to the late hour, but he was wrong.

"How'd it go?" A voice jolted him.

"Chaza, I'm beginning to think you enjoy scaring the hell out of me."

"Well, you do look funny when you're startled."

"Thank you for staying," he said. "Sorry I'm so late getting back."

Chaza nodded and waited.

"He knows now, and you were right, it upset him." A pained expression framed his face. "He's my father?"

"Yes."

"And Tavis is my sister, my twin." Alec ran his fingers through his hair, feeling exhausted and frustrated. "I don't know how I missed it."

"Because you weren't looking for it," Chaza said. "Stop beating yourself up. You're lucky to have them."

"I'm tired, Chaza. I'd rather just let you see the rest, if you want."

Chaza thought about it. She could decline, but figured she'd regret it later. When she nodded, Alec let her see the memory of his conversation with Sebastian.

"He's worried they'll use the End Plan here," she said in a whisper, more to herself.

"You think they will?"

"You've been told a lot tonight. You should get some rest." Chaza put her hand on Alec's shoulder. "Everything he said was the truth. I know that doesn't make things easier for you, but Sebastian decided it was important for you to know how far management will go. He really does want you to have a better life and that's why he wants you off this island."

17

Mea Culpa Genus

When Sebastian reached the cave, he hesitated and thought about what his presence would do to Chaza. He didn't want to create any more problems for her than he already had, but the need to see her surpassed the want to respect her wishes.

With tamed determination, he pulled the lever that would open the steel door. Once inside the loft, he closed the door behind him and went in search of Chaza.

He found her asleep in the room she'd been living in for all the years they'd been separated—the years he thought her dead. Seeing the peaceful serenity expressed on her sleeping face made him want the same for himself. He sat on the settee flanking the end of the bed with the intention of waiting for her to wake so they could talk, but fell asleep as soon as his head found a comfortable position.

A gentle nudge woke him several hours later. He looked up and saw Chaza standing over him. Worry marred her otherwise flawless face.

"Do you hate me?"

"I could never hate you." Sebastian swung his legs around and sat up on the settee, noticing that a blanket had somehow made its way to him during his sleep. "You're a huge part of my life, Chaza, part of me will always love you."

She sat next to him. "I should've been the one to tell you. It was wrong of me to let Alec do it."

"Actually, I'm glad he did. I finally told him what he needed to know."

"Yeah, he told me about it when he got back. Or rather, he showed me."

Sebastian stopped staring at the carpet and looked at Chaza, wearing a puzzled expression. "Odd how chummy he is with you."

"Jealous?"

"Don't be ridiculous, I'm not jealous." His gaze returned to the carpet. "Well, maybe a little." A chuckle escaped him. "I'm very jealous."

"Truthfully, it's a weird sort of friendship. I'd call it more of an alliance." A nervous apprehension kept Chaza rooted for a moment. However, knowing that if it stretched on for too long, she'd get up and start pacing. It would eventually make her angry enough that she'd demand he leave at once. "How long?"

Too late, anger had crept into her tone.

"Still the same fretful beast, aren't you? Maybe Alec recognizes like minds." He thought she'd enjoy the jibe, but she only glared at him. "Not long, Chaza."

The answer calmed her, yet brought new worries. "What's your plan?"

"There's transportation, safely hidden."

"How many?" Her eyes narrowed when he seemed to hesitate. "Don't you dare lie to me. I know your weaknesses, I'll go straight to Tavis and ask her if you told me the truth."

"Three."

She went through a mental list of those who would need to leave. "Is it possible to request more?"

"No." Sebastian knew she'd sorted out the predicament. "Everything will work out. I don't want you to worry about it."

Chaza shot him an incredulous look of disbelief—angry that he thought blanket reassurances would placate her as though she was a child. She took pause, though, seeing how tormented he was at knowing that everything wasn't going to work out.

Instead of yelling, Chaza calmly said, "I can count, I know there's one too many that need to go. Someone needs to stay and it should be me. I already know how to live in the shadows of this island. When you get everyone home, send someone to come for me. See? Problem solved."

Before he could point out a flaw in her solution, a clanking sound reverberated off the walls from somewhere in the underground bunkers. They remained quiet, waiting to hear if there would be any more noises. Footsteps joined the clanking, then a series of doors opened and shut. Occasionally, they heard muffled voices followed by brief moments of silence.

"There're people down there," Sebastian said, staring at the door that he figured would lead to the narrow staircase Tavis told him about. "Does that happen often?"

"Not really. About twice a year maintenance workers show up, but they never stay long."

"Will they come up here?"

"They never have before."

Sebastian started to get up, but she tugged at his arm. "Don't," she whispered.

"We should be prepared to leave if they decide to come up here."

"It would be the first time if they did."

"You could be wrong about them being maintenance workers."

He didn't like the coincidental timing. Kyrie had told him she believed his and Tavis' presence on Gamma had been discovered. Shaking his arm free of Chaza's hold, he approached the door and listened.

"Is the end of the staircase cloaked?"

"Yes, ever since Jack and Tavis were here." Chaza saw him pull down on the door handle. "What are you doing?"

"I have to know who it is and what they're doing down there."

She rolled her eyes and got up. If he was determined to go into the bunkers, then she'd have to go with him. Of the two of them, she was the only one who knew how to navigate the bunkers and it terrified her thinking he'd get caught.

After easing the door open, he waited for any sound at all to present itself now before moving on. Hearing nothing, save the clanging, they cloaked themselves and descended the staircase.

Though they couldn't be seen, they couldn't conceal any abrupt sounds, so they crept down the stairs until reaching the bottom. Standing under the archway, both of them growing exponentially more anxious, they watched for signs of movement. Nothing happened for a while and then they heard two distinctly different voices talking to one another.

"Go check on the wiring," a man's voice grumbled.

They saw a man in a white uniform walk out of the surveillance room and continue on toward the center of the complex. *'That was a maintenance worker,'* Chaza said to Sebastian silently.

"Yeah, I need to talk to Eldridge," the man still in the surveillance room said.

Sebastian urged Chaza forward into the corridor, pausing long enough to make sure the maintenance worker wasn't returning. Satisfied the errand would take a while, he led Chaza to the doorway of the surveillance room.

The man they'd heard sat in a desk chair with his back to them, holding a phone to his ear. Atop the desk, and along the wall above it, were monitors. Some of them had been turned on, while others remained black. The ones displaying images were of various locations on the island.

The closest screen to Sebastian and Chaza displayed several angles of the town center in real time. People were walking in and out of shops and Sebastian recognized Alec leaving the general store in the delivery cart, full of packages to be delivered for the day. Only then did he realize how long he'd slept on the settee.

Other monitors revealed images of beaches, some were of traveling lanes abutting nearby houses, one dedicated solely to Kyrie's. Sebastian wondered what the still black screens were supposed to be monitoring.

The desk chair swiveled around, giving them a profile of the man's face. He used his shoulder to prop the phone to his ear and typed in a command on a keyboard. Still, the monitor remained black.

"Yeah, I'm still here," he said into the phone and gave up on the monitor. He swiveled the desk chair toward the open doorway. "No," he continued, "tell him it's William calling and that I need to talk to him now."

William was put on hold a second time and he leaned back in the chair, staring blankly at the doorway where Sebastian and Chaza stood invisible to him. Sebastian was shocked and confused, hearing his name and seeing his face. It had been a long time since he last saw Kyrie's ex-husband, but he and the man sitting in front of him were one and the same.

"Eldridge, awfully nice of you to take my call," William said. "I'm at the surveillance room. Do we want *all* the cameras functioning again?"

He fell silent for a moment. "I had Ron work on the wiring during the night, but only half of them are working so far. You want me to have him check the End Plan infrastructure wiring while he's fixing the rest of the cameras?"

After another pause, William said, "Okay. Have you notified the scientists of the meeting yet?" Silence again and then he said, "Whatever, they'll get over it. Ron probably won't finish up for several more hours. I'll let you know when everything's up and running. Oh, do me a favor, find the blueprints to these bunkers and put them on my desk. This place is huge, I can't find the loft."

William placed the phone back on its receiver and leaned in closer to the screen showing Kyrie's house. She had just gotten out of her cart and as she bent over to retrieve a bag from the back seat, William zoomed the image to her backside.

"Damn, Kyrie, looks just like I remember," he mused aloud. "Sweetest ass on Gamma."

Chaza felt Sebastian's body stiffen at William's rakish comments and she tugged at his arm to get him to follow her. Sebastian obliged and they went back to the hidden stairwell. Once safely back in the loft, they allowed the sphere around them to dissolve.

"You remember who that was, right?" Sebastian asked.

"I remember him. What do you make of it?"

"He was talking to Eldridge. Obviously, he's a member of management."

"Why do you think they want the cameras working again?"

"Why do you think, Chaza? They know we're here, they probably know we intend to leave. You know what they'll do if they fail to keep us here."

Sebastian sat in a chair next to the table Chaza used as a desk. He saw several piles of neatly stacked journals and knew right away what they were. His fingers twitched from an ancient instinct to read the historical documentation. Knowing Chaza wouldn't allow the intrusion, he forced his eyes from them.

Though the journals would one day become part of a vast catalog of historical documents, as they sat on that desk, they represented her still ongoing life—one still fundamentally private.

"You can't stay here anymore, it's not safe." There was finality in his tone, as though he expected a fight and was determined to win it. "Pack up whatever you want to take. I'll help you."

"I hardly think that's necessary—"

"No!" Sebastian stood. "You heard William, he'll be coming back with blueprints. Cloaked or not, he will find this loft and you know I'm right." He saw the fiery, independent spirit take root in her expression. "There's a vacant newcomer house, you can hide there."

Chaza sighed and began gathering what items she wanted to take with her. Of all the things she'd collected over the years in the loft apartment, it was the journals she went to first—protecting them and packing them away with attentive care into her shoulder bag. Clothes was her second priority and he helped her pack them into duffel bags.

She looked at the stairwell door when they were ready to leave. "Should I uncloak it now?"

"No, I'd rather not risk it. He might find it right away and we need the time to get far away from here."

Glancing one more time at the loft she'd lived in for so long, Chaza realized that as soon as she left, it would become part of her past. It was strange to walk away from it. But she did, and went through the steel door leading to the cave to yet another set of memories she would leave behind. She waited until Sebastian shut the door before dropping her bags and facing him.

"What are you doing? We need to get out of here," he said as she stepped closer to him.

"I want to show you something first," she said and placed her hands flat on his chest.

Bewildered at first by her behavior, it occurred to him what she wanted when the peaceful tranquility took hold of him at being allowed access to her memories.

There could only be one thing she wanted him to see. "You don't have to do this," he said.

"I want you to know."

When he nodded his consent, Chaza showed him her memories, starting first with when she met Joseph. Sebastian watched her give birth to Meg, alone in the very room they'd just left and how she chose Ila to be the one who would raise her child. She showed him Ila accepting, and the process of altering her memories. Then, experiencing part of it himself, he felt her intense pain as she ran off from the cave.

She took her hands away from his chest. "I wanted you to see it because you deserve an explanation for why I let you think I was dead."

"Chaza…" He hadn't been prepared to see the memories and therefore didn't know exactly what he should say.

"Let's go," she said and picked her bags up.

~

Once they reached Sebastian's cart, hidden in the sea oats at the base of the cliff, he chucked the bags in the back. His gaze swept over their surroundings, scanning every surface, contemplating a memorized map of every tree from Alaret Beach to the newcomer houses.

Chaza watched the familiar cerebral countenance fondly—at least up until the point in which he glanced skyward and then closed his eyes.

"Hey," she called to him, but he ignored her.

Clouds formed, slow to build at first, but then foreboding of an incoming tropical storm. Lightning streaked across the sky over the ocean.

"Why are you doing this?"

Still he ignored her, maintaining a direct connection with his intended purpose.

More clouds rolled in, turning the entire skyline over the island a menacing shade of dark grey. The wind picked up and grew fiercer by the minute, bending the reeds, sea oats, and trees in all directions. Sebastian opened his eyes and bolted to the cart.

He said while driving away, "I'm trumping Alec's ability to control the weather. I'd prefer to drive you to the newcomer houses without William seeing us. If we're lucky, the storm will reduce the visibility of the cameras, maybe even knock a few down."

Chaza looked over her shoulder at a set of ominous-looking black clouds rolling in from the ocean. "You need to go faster!"

The cart sped off toward the traveling lane. "I'd hoped to keep it simple, but it's been a while since I've messed around with the weather. I bet Alec's surprised."

There was a touch of playful excitement in Sebastian's voice that Chaza hadn't heard in a long time, even before she left their home.

"You almost sound like you're having fun," she said and grabbed hold of the cart's side rail.

"Why not?" He veered around a sharp turn and left the traveling lane for the seclusion of the forests. "It felt good to do that again and thwarting that detestable man felt even better."

"Have you learned these footpaths yet?"

"Not all of them, but I've memorized this one in particular. I suppose you know them all?"

"How do you think I get around on this island? I've even created a few of them myself." Chaza thought about the paths in and around her garden and hoped Sebastian's destructive weather wouldn't do any damage there.

The storm made it to land and was gaining speed. Rain started as a trickle, but increased to pounding the roof of the cart. Wind whipped the rain in from the sides, drenching their clothes. Some of the smaller trees in the forest bent at awkward angles and slapped against the edges of the cart.

Sebastian drove as fast as the cart would allow and finally made it to the end of the path. It was a mixed celebration, the trees were no longer a threat, but the rain had become torrential. Though he could barely see the lane in front of him through the wall of rain, it was what he wanted since neither could William if he still sat in front of the monitors.

Thankfully, there were no foolhardy islanders left in the town center as Sebastian barreled through and relied on memory to reach the lane leading to the newcomer houses. He passed his house first, then squeaked past Jack and Tavis', and only relaxed again after pulling up to the back of the vacant house.

They grabbed up her bags and ran to the back door. Soon as they entered the house, thunder shook the windows and scared them into dropping everything on the floor to huddle together—watching the ceiling as though they expected it to burst into pieces.

They broke apart from the childlike stance at realizing the house still stood intact. Chaza glowered at him.

"Sorry," he said, shrugging, "Guess I made it a little too strong."

"I'd say you achieved zero visibility. I'm certain no one saw us."

He picked up her bags and motioned for her to follow him on a quick tour of the house. The kitchen cabinets had been stocked with the typical canned food, but the refrigerator was empty.

"You should get dry and settled in," he said, wanting to go back to his own house and do the same. "Have a look around, see what you need. I'll bring you a decent dinner later tonight, and whatever else I can think of you may need. Think you'll be okay for now?"

"Thank you, Sebastian. I'll be fine." Chaza nodded, but frowned.

"What's wrong?"

Her gaze fell to his sodden shoes. "Do you forgive me?"

Sebastian stepped back from the doorway he'd been about to leave through and shut the door. "Come here," he said.

When she did, he brushed aside the wet strands of her hair before tilting her face up so he could look into her eyes. It seemed her spirit had broken from all the turmoil of not only the past few hours, but all the years she'd spent from home. Sebastian sensed her need for him to acknowledge her question and all the memories she'd shown him.

He wrapped his arms around her wet shoulders. "It's not about forgiveness anymore. If it was, then I'd have to beg for it myself. But I won't, because three people were created over what you and I are asking forgiveness for. I don't regret any one of them being alive, and I'm sure you don't either. It's up to us to forgive ourselves, not each other."

She considered his words, and knew she wouldn't trade Meg for anything, not even for absolution in a moment of weakness. Chaza pulled away from him. "I hate it when you're right. Go away, I'd like to change out of these wet clothes you caused."

He laughed at her unspoken epiphany; that which had erased all her doubts and had returned the confidence Sebastian was used to dealing with from her. Just before he left, he said, "This storm will probably last a few more hours. Make sure you pull the window blinds down and close the curtains."

~

The rain had chilled his body and the warm shower was both invigorating and relaxing. Afterward, clean and dry again, Sebastian went to the kitchen to gather food and beverages to give Chaza later.

He was trying to figure out a way to talk to Tavis alone about everything that had happened, when his front door opened. Tavis leaned her umbrella against the porch railing and stepped inside. To his immense relief, she was alone.

"What's with this freak storm?" she asked, finding him in the kitchen. Her eyes darted to the large basket filled with food resting on the counter.

It hadn't occurred to him that Tavis would be curious about the rare storm and would seek him out for answers. "I'm responsible for it."

"*You* did it?" Her gaze returned to him. "Why?"

"So I could get back here without being seen."

She seriously doubted he'd go to such extremes just to prevent Kyrie from seeing him. "Seen by who?"

"They're using the cameras again. I convinced Chaza to leave the bunkers and since I didn't want her being seen with me, I figured the heavy rain would obscure the camera views."

"Where is she now?" Tavis looked into the front room as though she expected Chaza to be sitting on the sofa.

"In the vacant house."

Tavis sat at the dining table and waited for him to join her. "What makes you think they're using the cameras again?"

"I went to see Chaza last night, after Alec and I were done fishing. While we were talking, we heard noises coming from the bunkers. Chaza said they were probably maintenance workers, but you know how I am. We found a member of management and a maintenance worker trying to fix the cameras."

"Management was there?"

"Yes, William Davis."

"What?" Tavis was floored by the name. "Was he always with management?"

"Apparently." Sebastian frowned; he had a million questions himself, none of which Tavis could answer. "We listened to him talking to Eldridge on the phone."

"What was he saying?" The goose bumps forming on her arms had nothing to do with the chill of the storm.

"William was updating Eldridge about getting the cameras working again, and asking about checking the wiring of the End Plan infrastructure. They were discussing a planned meeting with their scientists, too, and he wanted Eldridge to find the blueprints to the bunkers because he couldn't find the loft."

"Anything else?" she asked, exasperated.

His lip curled in disgust. "He was leering at Kyrie through one of the cameras."

"They already had some of them working?"

"Yes."

Her shoulders slumped forward. "They're gonna try to stop us from leaving, aren't they?" Tavis spoke as though she was solving a riddle. "They know we're here and they want to watch us constantly. But, the End Plan…" Her gaze met his. "Oh. If they fail to stop our escape, they destroy Gamma."

"I believe that's an accurate assessment."

"That's not gonna help you with Alec. He'll blame you for it."

"I know."

"How long do we have before we leave?"

"Not long," he said. "And I'm afraid it'll be trickier when we do."

He wondered if Tavis would question the transportation again. If so, he was fully prepared to lie as he'd done before. Her thoughts were somewhere else, though.

"I'll have to talk to Jack sooner than we planned, won't I?" She worried, thinking it was too soon.

Sebastian put his hands on the table, palms up, waiting for Tavis to place hers in his. She did as he wanted, seeking any solace and wisdom he could give her.

"Yes, daughter, you'll need to have a difficult conversation with Jack. I'll help you if you need me to." He smiled. "I don't think you have anything to worry about. Jack would follow you to the ends of the universe, maybe even to the beginning."

A stubborn lump formed in her throat. She tried hard to control it, but tears formed in her eyes—welling, then spilling down her cheeks and coming to a rest on the table cloth.

"Let's have none of that." Sebastian pained at her tears. "Don't you know a star dies when someone cries?"

Tavis laughed softly at his words and removed one of her hands from his to wipe away the streaks left behind by the tears. She gave him a smile and put her hand back in his.

"That's a myth and a story for children," she said, her mood lightened somewhat and it made Sebastian feel better.

"Oh, but is it?" He winked.

"Stop it."

"I'd like to tell you something else, if you're up for it."

"Is it more bad news?" Her eyes narrowed at him.

"I wouldn't call it *bad*, it's more like mystery-solved news. But it will surprise you."

"Go ahead," she muttered.

"I know what Chaza's been hiding now."

"She told you?"

"No, Alec did. Chaza told him first and then he took great pleasure in telling me."

She frowned. "Alec?"

"Chaza had an affair with an islander. That was part of what she wanted to hide from me."

Tavis' mouth opened in surprise and creases formed tight lines on her forehead. She tried to stand, but Sebastian's hands went from cradling hers to securing her wrists, refusing to let her.

"Let me go!"

"I will not," he said sternly. "I'd never allow you to go to her with such anger."

A fierceness of the darkest kind clouded her blue eyes, turning them a nasty shade of black. Though he feared the primitive response may surface, it was still a shock to see it from Tavis.

"I've been the one who's had to watch you suffer from the pain of thinking she was dead all these years. She owes me an explanation at the very least!" Tavis struggled against his hold on her.

"Stop it right now!"

"No!" she dared, the fire and determination in her eyes turned almost sinister, a thing Sebastian never wanted to see from her.

"I'll immobilize you if I have to." His warning was omnipotent. "And I will absorb the memory of what I just told you."

Tavis stopped struggling at the threat and looked into his eyes; she saw he meant it. Her gaze drifted to their hands and realized that he was not only prepared to follow through, he was about to do it.

"Don't!" She flinched as though it was already too late. Tavis couldn't bear the thought of her father absorbing *any* memory from her.

"Will you be calm?"

"Yes."

Sebastian released his daughter's wrists, hoping it would relieve his agony for bringing fear to her. They looked at each other, stand-off style, waiting for the other to sit back down. Tavis decided to be the first and he followed after.

"Chaza had already left me when she got involved with someone else," Sebastian said in Chaza's defense.

"You know what? I might be able to accept that, if only she would've mentioned to you that she was leaving you. But, no, she decided to let you mourn her *death*." Tavis inhaled deeply to steady herself at feeling her temper flare again. "Please tell me she's still involved with whoever it was she left you for. At least I could pretend it was for love."

"You're being disrespectful, Tavis."

"Oh, I'm sorry."

He chose to ignore her sarcasm. "Actually, it was a brief affair and the man she was involved with died later in an accident. Chaza had other reasons for why she didn't come back."

Oddly enough, Sebastian was nervous to tell Tavis the rest. He stood and went over to the window, seeing that the rain still poured in buckets. He thought about how out of practice he was at influencing weather patterns and laughed inwardly at his rustiness.

Tavis got up and joined him by the window. "What were the other reasons?" Her voice had softened.

"Chaza didn't come back because she had become pregnant, and carried the child to term. She gave birth on this island, but gave the newborn to another woman here to raise as her own. Chaza altered the woman's memories so she'd believe the baby was hers. But then, I think, Chaza couldn't bear to leave and she stayed to make sure the child was being cared for properly."

The hairs on the back of Tavis' neck stood on end. Her mind raced through the possibilities and came to a stop on one single face. "Margaret Arcana," Tavis whispered while staring at a puddle in the front yard. "Of course."

"Yes," Sebastian said, watching the same puddle.

"Well, I feel stupid." She remembered something he'd said about Chaza's lover. "She had an affair with Joseph?"

"Yes."

Tavis' body stiffened again in anger and he turned his head to look at her face, watching for any sign that she wanted to rush out to confront Chaza.

She noticed the renewed attention. "It makes me angry, but I won't go against your wishes."

"I'm going to tell you what I had to say to Chaza when she asked for my forgiveness. Had she not left me and had an affair, there'd be no Meg. She's been a powerful motivation in your brother's life and we can never know how Alec would've turned out if Meg was never a part of his life. There'd also never be Luke."

Sebastian focused all his energy and levity onto Tavis. He wanted her to fully understand the weight of his next words. "And if there was no Meg to confound all my watchers, myself included, you and I may not have stayed here as long as we did. I may not have even needed you to come along."

She contemplated his meaning. It was true, one of the driving forces that brought Sebastian back to Gamma was to sort out what creature had so claimed Alec's attention and yet not come up as anything particularly different or special. Above all, Tavis would've never developed a relationship with Jack—there would never be Lani. The thought forced a shiver down her spine. What world was worth living in, worth saving, without all of them?

"I agree completely," she said and her entire body relaxed. Tavis turned from the window and took a few steps toward the kitchen. She eyed the basket sitting on the counter and made an obvious assumption. "Is that for Chaza?"

"I'll take it to her tonight. I told her to keep the windows covered, so you shouldn't have any trouble with Jack noticing someone's in the house."

After investigating the basket's contents, Tavis said, "Tell her I'll leave a basket for her as well. I'll put it on the back porch."

"You don't have to do that."

"Yes, I do." Tavis smiled at him. "Women have need of things other than food."

"Okay." Sebastian nodded. "I'll tell her."

Tavis thought of something, and though it didn't matter to her anymore, her curiosity forced the question out. "Since Meg's Chaza's daughter, why weren't we able to detect any special abilities from her until recently?"

"Because Alec absorbed that part of her when they were children, and that's why he was always stronger than he should've been for his age."

"How is that possible?" She was somewhat horrified. "I didn't know we could absorb abilities."

"I assure you, I've never done it. In my medical opinion, it could only be done to a child." Sebastian shook his head at the ethical implications of ever performing such a procedure. "Alec had to give it back to Meg the night Luke was born. There were complications and Chaza convinced him to restore her abilities."

"Does Meg know about any of this?"

"No." Sebastian sighed. "I need to tell you something else."

"Oh, fantastic. What now?"

"Alec knows I'm his father, that you're his twin sister, and that Kyrie's pregnant. He also knows I want him to leave Gamma, and I told him about the End Plan."

"That was quite a fishing trip you had." Tavis maintained her composure, but dreaded the inevitable awkward moment when she'd see Alec again. "How'd he take it?"

"Well enough, I suppose. He said he wouldn't make any decisions until he talked to Meg." He looked at Tavis keenly. "Nothing's changed, Alec will leave this island whether he agrees to it or not. If he puts it off for too long, I'll talk to Meg myself."

"How'd he handle Kyrie being pregnant?"

Sebastian looked away, but said, "Sort of like you did, only worse."

~

After leaving her father's house, Tavis paused on her front porch before going inside. The worst of the storm had passed over Gamma and the rain had begun to slow to a drizzle. She closed the umbrella and set it by the door while looking over at the house Chaza was in. It would be so easy to walk over there and ask her the questions that remained unanswered, but keeping her word to Sebastian meant more to Tavis.

She shook the temptation off her shoulders and went inside, finding it mostly quiet except for the sound of Jack's singing. He was in the shower, belting out some hideous rendition of a sailor's ballad in a mock-drunken fashion.

Lani slept in her crib, in her own room, which was a rare occurrence. The savory aroma of something delicious cooking lured Tavis to the kitchen and she found a manicotti baking in the oven. She spied an open bottle of wine and two wineglasses sitting on the counter, one of which had already been used. Maybe it wasn't *mock-drunken* singing, she thought to herself and laughed softly.

She poured a glass for herself, refilled Jack's, and headed down the hallway.

"Hi, honey, I'm home," she bellowed over his singing once she reached the bathroom doorway.

The song stopped mid-verse and Jack turned the water off. He pulled the shower curtain back and reached for a towel, draping it around his waist without drying off first. "Are one of those for me?" Jack pointed to the wineglasses Tavis held.

"Yeah." She handed him one, watching the water droplets roll down his chest and had to force herself from reaching out to touch them.

"Is Lani still sleeping?"

"Yes, I just checked on her." Tavis took an appreciable gulp of her wine. "The manicotti smells wonderful. I checked on that, too."

"I wanted to cook dinner for you." He smiled at her.

Jack took a sip from his glass and wrapped his arm around Tavis' waist. The heat of his body warmed her and all she wanted was to forget dinner and lead Jack to their bed.

"How was your visit with Sebastian?"

"Fine." Tavis remembered to guard her thoughts. "He was surprised by the storm, too. It's almost over, just raining now."

When he released her to walk out of the bathroom, Tavis followed him to their bedroom and watched him remove the towel to dry himself off. After draining the rest of her wine in one swallow, Tavis headed back to the kitchen with the intention to refill it.

A quick check on the manicotti hinted that it would be a while before it was done, so she grabbed the wine bottle to take back to their bedroom. She found Jack reclined back on the bed, propped up on their pillows, and reading a book. The thin bed sheet covered his naked torso and he had one foot resting on top of the sheet, showcasing the state of his undressed silhouette.

Tavis was already refilling her wineglass when he looked up and saw her standing in the doorway. "I need a refill, too," Jack said and picked up his empty wineglass.

She came over and poured him another before setting the wine bottle on the bedside table and joining him on the bed. Instead of looking at the *elephant* in the room, Tavis turned her attention to the book he still read.

"What are you reading?" she asked, sighing.

Jack raised his arm for Tavis to curl up next to him. She happily scooted her body as close as she could get next to his and rested her head on his chest.

"A medical book," he said.

Her head turned toward the open book. The chapter he read was on women giving birth and the page he was on provided an in-depth overview of what to expect after childbirth.

"Why are you reading this?" Tavis glanced up at him.

"I just wanted to educate myself on your health."

Looking back at the page, Tavis saw a few paragraphs describing the duration of healing time. She smiled and said, "You could've just asked me."

"I was going to, but I wanted to read about it first so you wouldn't think I was an idiot." He didn't say anything for a moment, pretending to still read the text. "Well," he continued, "since we're on the subject, how are you feeling? Has everything healed properly?"

Something close to relief and wanting to cry for joy was how Tavis felt. "I feel great, other than the fact that I've been feeling great for so long now that I'm about ready to start begging you."

He slammed the book shut, sent it flying to the floor and rolled over, pinning Tavis to the bed and playfully growling like a wild animal. "I can't tell you enough how happy I am to hear this," he whispered in her ear.

"I'd rather you show me," Tavis said, grabbing his face and pulling it to hers to kiss him. She stopped long enough to tell him to undress her, but changed her mind and did it herself when he tried to be romantic about it.

They had two joyful hours before Lani woke up and they took care of her needs quickly, watching and waiting for her to fall asleep again. When she did, they ate the burnt manicotti in bed, enjoying every crispy bite between trysts the rest of the blissful night.

~

Tavis woke just before the first rays of light brought night to a close. She slipped out from under the sheets and grabbed her clothes before easing the bedroom door shut to keep from waking Jack. After readying a basket for Chaza, she secured Lani in the sling and left out the back door.

Meaning to leave the basket on the porch, Tavis had a brief thought of apprehension about not having checked on Jack one last time before leaving, and that was exactly when Chaza opened the back door.

"Tavis." Chaza smiled at her. "If you can, would you come in for a moment?" She held the door open wider.

Her uncertainty had been correct. Jack stood in front of their bedroom window and watched Tavis walk over to the house he once shared with Michelle. Tavis had been about to turn around after setting a basket on the porch when the door opened by a woman he'd never seen before. Though Tavis seemed familiar enough with the woman to have entered the house with their child, he was not at all happy about seeing the door shut his family from his view.

Jack snatched open the dresser and put on the first pair of shorts that presented themselves, donning a t-shirt while he walked down the hallway to the back door. Hastily, he shoved his feet into the flip-flops, groaning when he realized he'd been trying to put Tavis' on.

On his way over to the house, he considered what he'd seen. Clearly, Tavis knew the woman and had to have known she was there. It bothered him that she hadn't mentioned it to him.

Refusing to consider the possibility that Tavis didn't trust him, Jack continued on until he stood at the back door, stopping to listen for sounds coming from inside. Hearing nothing, he raised his hand and it shook a little as he reached for the doorknob. He opened the door softly and heard their voices coming from the direction of the front room. Jack crept down the hallway and gradually picked up on some of their conversation.

"So, you're happy?" Jack heard the woman ask.

"Yes," Tavis answered her. "I don't think it's possible to be happier."

"That's all that ever really matters. You've done well, Lani's healthy and strong. She's alert, too. I think she'd make an excellent observer, but I hope that one day that won't be necessary."

Jack chanced a peek around the corner he hid behind and saw the woman holding his daughter. She seemed friendly enough; however, seeing his child with a stranger didn't sit well with him. All he could see of Tavis was her back, but she appeared at ease.

The woman looked up from admiring Lani's face and gave Tavis a concerned look. Jack experienced a small start of panic, worried he'd been seen.

"Our conversation is no longer private," the woman said to Tavis.

He flattened his body against the wall in a pathetic attempt to keep hiding. Embarrassed now for eavesdropping on their conversation, he considered trying to slip out of the house, but it was too late for that. Taking a deep breath, Jack moved away from the wall and stood in full view of them. Tavis had already turned her head toward the hallway and wore a tense expression. She stood and went to him.

"Jack," was all she said.

"What are you doing here? And who is she?"

Tavis turned to Chaza as if she expected an answer to appear on her face that she could give Jack, but Chaza said nothing—leaving it up to Tavis to sort out.

She turned back and said, "Her name's Chaza Abbott. She's Sebastian's wife and she raised me as her daughter for a while when I was a baby. I came here to bring her some things I thought she might need."

Taken aback at hearing the woman was married to Sebastian, Jack looked at her more closely, examining what kind of a woman would love Sebastian enough to be his wife. He thought her beauty was classic and timeless. Similar to Sebastian's persona, there seemed a wisdom in her eyes that commanded reverence and respect from all who was in her presence. If he was correct in his initial assessment of her, Jack imagined their personalities clashed like dueling Titans more often than not. Out of nowhere, he sensed Chaza dissecting him as well.

He shifted his gaze to Tavis. "Why isn't she staying with Sebastian?"

"Because they've been separated for a long time. He suggested she stay here."

Giving a slight nod, Jack went over to the sofa Chaza hadn't moved from. "It's nice to meet you, Chaza." He extended his arm.

She smiled and shook his hand. "It's nice to meet you, too, Jack. I've been getting to know your daughter and I think she's a delightful little sweetheart." Chaza looked at Lani again. "And such a beautiful baby girl, aren't you?"

A smile spread over Jack's face. "That's Tavis' doing." He sat next to Chaza and slipped his pinky into Lani's tiny hand.

"Oh, I don't know about that," Chaza said. "I see a good bit of you in there."

"Really?"

"Of course, can't you see it?" Chaza rotated Lani toward Jack. "She has your nose, and the shape of her eyes are just like yours."

Jack studied Lani's face in a new way. "Yeah, she does."

Tavis watched the conversation flow between them and it amazed her how easily Chaza won Jack over. It was like Chaza knew the precise buttons to push to get the job done quickly.

"I agree," Tavis said, taking her seat again. "I see a lot of Jack in Lani."

Though he didn't want to, Jack removed his finger from Lani's hand and stood from the couch. "I should let you two finish with your visit. I'm sure I'll see you again soon, Chaza. Please, don't hesitate to ask if you need anything."

"Thank you, Jack," she said.

"I'll be home soon, it's getting time to feed Lani again and she still needs her bath. We'll see you in a little bit," Tavis said and stood to give him a kiss.

He welcomed her lips and flashes of last night replayed in his memory. Tavis saw them, as did Chaza and so she refocused her attention to Lani out of respect for their privacy.

"Invite her over for dinner," Jack said to Tavis.

"I will."

When he left, Tavis sat next to Chaza, waiting for her to say something.

"I like him," she said. "He has a rare strength and power about him, not like the typical kind I'm used to seeing here. Also, he's unusually guarded with his thoughts... mostly."

"I know," Tavis said, blushing. "Even I have trouble reading his thoughts sometimes, except for when... well, you know."

"Yes, I noticed."

"I'm glad you got to meet him." Tavis grimaced. "I don't think you living here without his notice would've lasted long."

"He heard my comment about observers. Do you think he'll ask you about it?"

"Probably."

"You're going to have to talk to him soon, Tavis."

"I realize that. My father and I have already discussed it, and he even offered to be there if I couldn't do it on my own."

"How do you feel about that idea?"

Tavis snorted at the notion. "It's a terrible idea. It would be better if I talked to him alone."

"I'm glad to hear you say that. It proves to me how brave you are, a thing I've always known since the day Sebastian put you in my arms."

"Why did you become so opposed to my father's mission?"

Chaza was somewhat shocked by the question and realized just how close Tavis and Sebastian were. Apparently, he must share a lot of information with Tavis, Chaza surmised. However, she doubted he shared every gory detail.

"I was all for it in the beginning," Chaza said. "I became disillusioned when I learned the fate of the ones who weren't chosen by our people after they were returned here. Did Sebastian tell you what happened to them?"

"Only that things didn't go very well for them, and that had he known he would've let them stay."

"Did he tell you *how* things didn't go very well for them?"

"No, Chaza, he didn't go into details," she said, her tone testy now. "Why don't you go ahead and tell me all about it."

"They threw themselves off of a cliff."

It was a shock and Tavis stared off at nothing. "Mors Cliff," she said softly.

"I thought you said he didn't tell you."

"He didn't tell me those were the ones who jumped."

"Well, it was because of what happened to them that council put an end to bringing anyone else to our home. Not one to give up, Sebastian came up with the plan you're more familiar with. I was opposed to that as well."

Tavis' eyes darted back to Chaza's, remembering what Sebastian had told her about the difficulty she had accepting Kyrie being able to provide him with children when she never could. "Why weren't you able to carry a child to term with my father?"

"Our DNA wasn't compatible, too many differences." Chaza sighed, it was still painful to talk about. "I could get pregnant, but it was always the same, the fetus wasn't viable. I couldn't take it anymore, I stopped trying. I thought I could handle Kyrie's involvement, but I was wrong."

"It's okay, Chaza." Tavis stopped her from going on. "So much has changed for me since I've been here, I don't think I could handle something like that either." Tavis smiled and patted Chaza's shoulder. "I'm glad you had Meg, I like her."

"So, am I dining with you tonight?" Chaza asked, steering the subject to neutral ground.

"I think so, unless something changes. I'll let you know before this evening."

"You'll do fine answering Jack's questions. You have a very level head, always calm and collected no matter the situation." Chaza laughed. "You must have gotten that from Kyrie."

"Remember what you said to Jack?" Tavis joined Chaza's laughter. "I promise you, there are times when some of my father's personality's in here, too."

Chaza helped put Lani back in the infant sling Tavis still wore. Since it didn't matter anymore, she left out the front door. When she returned home, she found Jack had gone back to bed and had drifted off to sleep waiting for them. With Lani still in the sling, Tavis lay down on their bed and gave in to her own need for sleep.

~

Tavis woke up later, swiping at her face. Jack had woken and held a strand of her hair, using it to tickle her nose. "Stop it," she said, giggling when he went to tickle her ear.

"Time to wake up, lazybones."

"What time is it?"

"Noon."

"Really? I can't believe I slept that long."

"We both did. I'm lazy, too. I just woke up a few minutes ago." Jack laid his head back down on his pillow. "How was the rest of your visit?"

Tavis readied herself mentally to answer his questions. "Good."

"She seems like a nice person." Jack continued to fiddle with Tavis' hair.

"Chaza's a great person, and she's exceptionally intelligent."

"But she's not your real mother," Jack said, yet there was a question lurking behind his words.

"No, she's not, but she did raise me for a while before she and my father separated."

"Why'd they separate?"

"There were several reasons. One was they were on opposite sides of an issue that was equally important to both of them. That was the start of it and other issues developed because of it. Chaza chose to leave."

"She left you, too."

"I was Sebastian's child, not hers. She couldn't take me away from him, even if she wanted to."

"Was this morning the first time you've seen her since she left?"

"Yes."

"Where's she been all this time?"

A small part of Tavis wanted to lie. However, not only did she not have a choice, but a bigger part of her knew it was time for truthful answers. Lying would only damage their trust, and she understood how much she would need it when it came time to talk to Jack about leaving Gamma.

"She's been living here since the day she left him."

"Here?" Jack was astounded, but kept his voice calm. "On Gamma?"

"Yes."

"Did Sebastian know she was living here?"

"No, not until after we got here."

"That's quite a coincidence."

"It's true though, and we were shocked when we found out."

"I believe you. I'm not trying to upset you." Jack brought one of her hands up to his lips and kissed it. He looked into her eyes, hoping to convey to her that he trusted her. "What about your real mother, where's she?" He felt her hand, arm, and whole body go rigid. A frown etched his forehead at her reaction.

"I'm not ready to talk about her yet."

"Will you ever be ready?"

"Yes." She saw an inkling of disappointment in his eyes. "Soon, I promise. I'll be ready to tell you so many things. Will you be patient with me for just a little while longer?"

Jack hadn't the foggiest clue why it was so important for her to put it off, but he knew that she needed his patience. The pleading look in her eyes was unnecessary in his opinion. If he had a million years in his pocket, he'd reach right in and hand them over.

"I trust you as much as I love you, Tavis, and that's a lot by the way," he murmured to her. "I don't want you to feel pressured to talk about it. And, yes, this is what I should've said to you that night I was so awful and tried to bully you. You can tell me whenever you're ready. You could say your mother's the queen of Atlantis, and though I'd think you're a little nutty, it wouldn't change how I feel about you."

"Thank you, Jack. I love you, and I trust you, too. When I'm ready to talk about it, I know you'll be understanding and accepting."

The statement was more reminiscent of a question in Jack's opinion, and the waiting expression in her hopeful eyes validated it. It proved to him there was still so much to learn and explore about her—he decided to welcome it as an adventurous challenge, whenever she felt ready.

"Then you know me well," he said.

He saw the relief chase away her worry and doubt. Though it puzzled him, Tavis and Lani meant too much to him to question why she'd been so afraid. Pulling them closer, wrapping his arms around them, it felt like embracing everything that defined his already settled-upon future.

There was still one thought that nagged him. "Can I ask you one more question?"

"Yes." She already knew what it was.

"What did Chaza mean when she said Lani would make an excellent observer?"

Tavis pondered what it took to be considered a skilled watcher. It meant your observational skills were beyond that of someone simply paying attention—it required the patience that even saints would fail at and that was usually what most would-be observers lacked. Little to no details escaped a watcher's attention, no matter how small or seemingly insignificant. Above all, paying attention meant always watching, never forgetting what you saw, unrelenting comparisons of what you have seen against what you will see, and forever learning from all of it.

"Everyone's good at something. My father told me Chaza used to say I was an exceptionally alert baby. She values observational skills, and I guess Lani reminded her of me when I was an infant."

"Then why did she say she hoped it wouldn't be necessary?"

"Not everyone uses such traits for good purposes. You know very well how observation can be used against people and with potentially destructive consequences. Chaza hopes for a day when none of that will be necessary, especially here."

"She knows about management and the scientists?"

"Who doesn't on this island?" Tavis frowned. "Even if no one talks about it?"

"You're right," he said. "So, is she thinking about reconciling with Sebastian? Is that why she moved closer?"

"You said *one* more question."

"I know, but I thought that one would be okay."

"I'm only speculating, but in my opinion, I don't think reconciliation is possible for them. They've been apart for too long and there's been betrayal on both their parts. My father brought her here because he was worried about her safety, he does still care about her."

"Her safety?"

"While he was visiting her, they discovered a member of management and a maintenance worker in the bunkers. They were working on getting the cameras to work again."

Jack sat up, his mind racing, trying to come up with the potential scenarios that would bring a member of management to Gamma. "Are they sure about what they saw?"

"Yes. They overheard them talking."

Confused, Jack asked, "What were they doing in the bunkers? Did you tell Sebastian how to get in there?"

"Chaza knows how to get in the bunkers by the second entrance."

"Where is it?"

"In a cave by Alaret Beach."

"I want to see it." He was almost frantic. "Where's the cave?" Not bothering to wait for her answer, Jack rolled out of bed and searched for his shoes.

"No."

"*No?*" Jack turned to her, surprised by the refusal.

"That's right, I said no. I didn't tell you so you'd run off to the bunkers and risk getting caught. They could still be in there." Tavis sat up and patted Lani's back. "Don't you think it's possible they'd recognize you if they saw you?"

He'd been so anxious to investigate the new development that he hadn't thought about being recognized if caught. Jack sat back down. "Yeah, they'd recognize me. Did Sebastian happen to mention any names?"

"They heard William Davis on the phone with someone named Eldridge. Do you know them?" Tavis was sure he did, but was particularly interested in what he knew of William.

The snarl on his face was instant. "Yeah, I know who they are. Eldridge is CEO of management and William's right under him. Technically, they're equal partners, but Eldridge takes on more of the leadership role. I don't know much about Eldridge's history, and I only know a little about William's. Both of them made me nervous, but William especially irked me. It seemed like he paid way too much attention to me than what was necessary." Jack glanced at her, wearing a curious expression. "Have you heard his name mentioned since you've been here?"

"I know Kyrie was once married to him."

"Yep, that's right, and they don't talk about it either. I heard about it through the rumor mill. He's a jerk and does whatever he wants to do. He came here pretending to be a newcomer until Eldridge forced him to leave or risk losing his stake in the company. He married Kyrie to fit in with everyone, but he has a reputation for being a womanizer and he cheated on her all the time. Unfortunately, he's Alec's father."

"There's probably good reason why no one talks about it, I certainly don't want to." Tavis cleared her thoughts. "All I want is for you to promise me you'll stay away from the bunkers."

"Don't worry about it anymore, okay? I have no intention of bumping into William Davis." Jack kissed Tavis' forehead and peeked at Lani. "In fact, I think I'll go to the store in a bit and get a few hats and some sunglasses so he won't recognize me through the cameras."

"Are we still having Chaza over for dinner?" she asked.

"Yeah, I told you I liked her."

"Can you control your curiosity?"

"Yes," he grumbled, then thought of something. "Maybe we should invite Sebastian."

"I'll walk over later and ask if he'd like to join us."

~

Later in the afternoon, Tavis went to her father's house with Lani in tow, finding him pruning his roses in the back yard. She sat in one of the rocking chairs on the back porch and waited for him to finish.

With one last clip of a long-stemmed burgundy rose, Sebastian handed it to Tavis before going inside. She followed him, waiting while he washed his hands, and promptly handed over Lani afterward so he could fawn over her.

"You're growing more beautiful every day, Lani," Sebastian said, cooing to her. "And as happy as I am that your mother brought you to see me, I know that's not the only reason she's here. Maybe she'd like to say what's on her mind?"

"You're impossible," Tavis said.

"I've been told that before."

"Fine, here ya' go then." Tavis smiled and began: "Jack knows Chaza's staying in the vacant house. He saw me going over there earlier this morning when I thought he was still sleeping and he followed after me and Lani. He and Chaza met, and they like each other."

Tavis paused to see if he was upset about Jack discovering Chaza, but he only waited for her to continue.

"He knows you two are married, but separated, and that we didn't know she was living on Gamma until after we came here. He knows Chaza's not my real mother and was okay with me saying I wasn't ready to talk about my real mother yet. I told him about the cameras and management being here, and he already knew about William Davis."

She stopped to think about anything she may have left out. "Oh, yeah, we invited Chaza over for dinner and I'm here to invite you, too."

"Now that was quite a report! What do you think, Lani?"

Crossing her arms, Tavis waited for her father to take her seriously. "Well?"

"Is that all, or is there more?" Sebastian asked, finally looking up at Tavis.

"Not really, he knows the second entrance to the bunkers is in the cave now. He was all about wanting to check it out until I reminded him that William Davis would recognize him. He promised to stay away and said he'd wear hats and sunglasses if necessary to avoid being recognized in the cameras. That's all I can think of that you need to be aware of."

"I only have one question."

"What?"

"Which one of you is cooking dinner?"

Tavis rolled her eyes, marched over to where he stood in the kitchen, and held her arms out. Sebastian kissed Lani's forehead and handed her back to Tavis.

As she opened the front door, Tavis said, "Jack's cooking shrimp Au Poivre."

"I'll be there," Sebastian said and she slammed the door.

~

Dinner went well. There was no discussion of anything sensitive—talk centered mostly on life and events on Gamma. The conversation flowed easily and everyone was grateful for it. At the end of the evening, Jack took possession of Lani, securing her in the infant sling and announced he'd walk Chaza home.

Tavis knew he did it to avoid being alone with her father. Sebastian knew it, too, but found humor in it. When they got to the front of his house, they looked up at the sky, longing for something they both decided should remain unspoken.

"I'm glad that went well," Tavis said.

"I knew it would. I noticed Chaza and Jack seem to have a mutual respect for each other. It reaffirms to me just how unique Jack is and it makes me wonder where he came from… originally, I mean. Have you asked him about his family?"

"No, he barely mentions his parents. Sometimes he'll talk about certain memories from his childhood. I asked him once where he grew up and he said he was from a state called South Carolina, somewhere on the coast of East America. He said his childhood home was in an area called Charleston and that it was rich with history, both good and bad."

"Sounds like most of the places on this planet." Sebastian snorted. "But he doesn't mention his parents?"

"No, not really, only as necessary characters in one of his rare childhood stories. He's never even mentioned their names. It's also one of the subjects he'll guard his thoughts on." Tavis shrugged. "I can't read a thing, he has it completely closed off."

"Maybe I'll ask Chaza if she's able to sort anything out."

"Don't bother. She already noticed how guarded Jack was with his thoughts."

Sebastian sighed and changed the subject. "You have a birthday coming up. Saturday, I believe?"

"Yes, November fifteenth is Saturday." She eyed him. "Why are you bringing it up?"

"Well, since it's Alec's birthday, too, I think you two should celebrate it together. You, Jack, Alec, and Meg could go to the café for a nice dinner, and afterward go to the beach with a few bottles of wine." Sebastian gave her an encouraging smile. "And I do mean without the babies, just the four of you."

"Why?" Tavis suspected an ulterior motive.

"I think it would be good for all of you to spend time together."

"Why else?"

"Because I said so!" he all but bellowed.

Tavis was surprised by his gruffness and it showed in her widened eyes. Sebastian immediately regretted letting his impatience get the better of him. He looked back up at the sky and tried to find an inkling of calm. He ran his fingers through his hair, messing it up so that it stuck out in all directions—he had the look of an overworked genius.

"It's time for you and Alec to form a sibling bond. You both know you're brother and sister now. More than that, you're twins and you need to connect. It's long overdue, Tavis."

She remained silent, listening, knowing there was more he needed to say to her.

"He's going to need you, it's as simple as that," Sebastian said, finally acknowledging and admitting to the harsh reality. "He's going to need convincing and I think you'll have better luck with him than I will."

"Convince him to do what?"

"To go home."

18

Birthday

"Since my birthday's the same day as Alec's, my father suggested we go out and have dinner with them, just the four of us. What do you think?" Tavis asked when Jack was almost finished bathing Lani.

"You and Alec have the same birthday, *and* you're both the same age? How weird is that?"

Ignoring the comment, she asked again, "What do you think of the idea?"

"It's your birthday, is that what you want to do?"

Jack took the baby towel Tavis held out for him. She held her breath while he lifted Lani out of the infant tub and wrapped the towel around her—relaxing only after he'd placed Lani against his chest.

"Yeah, I'd like to. We don't have to cook or clean, just relax and have fun." Tavis used a small hand cloth to dry Lani's hair. "Do you mind my father watching Lani for us?"

"Maybe Chaza could help him?"

"What? You think he'd do a bad job?" Her eyes narrowed at him. "He did raise me, remember?"

"Not while you were an infant."

"Good point." She frowned, then sighed. "Fine, I'll ask Chaza to help him."

"Have you talked to Meg and Alec yet?"

"I'm gonna visit Meg in the morning, I'll ask her then."

~

"Jack!" Tavis had grown weary of him checking and rechecking the infant carrier's straps. "It's a cart. Is reckless driving even possible?"

He looked at Tavis, wearing a pouting expression.

"Sure you don't want to come with us?" she asked him.

"I'm sure. I have to clean the koi pond, the algae's taking over." Jack leaned in and kissed Tavis, taking his time about it. He whispered, as though afraid Lani would overhear, "I could let the algae win and you could call Meg instead."

"It's a tempting offer, but I'm still going to Meg's." Tavis swept her fingers along his neck. "You can tell me all about your algae battles tonight."

He shivered. "You might want to go. I'm not opposed to dragging you back inside."

She laughed and drove off after he checked the straps one last time. When she arrived at the stone house, Meg was outside pushing Luke in the baby swing that Alec had hung on the oak tree.

"I was just thinking about you," Meg said when Tavis and Lani joined them by the tree.

"Good thoughts?" Tavis asked, teasing. She stood in front of Meg, looking at her and analyzing her in a new light.

"Always. I'm so glad you brought Lani, I've been wanting to see her. Let me hold her." Meg held her arms out.

Tavis placed Lani in Meg's waiting arms, then went over to Luke. She asked, "Can I hold him?"

"I'd be insulted if you didn't," Meg said, not taking her eyes off of Lani.

Luke smiled at Tavis as she lifted him from the swing; she smiled back and memorized every detail of his face. Most of Luke resembled Meg, but those eyes and that winsome smile was all Abbott. He was heavier than Lani, so she went over to one of the chairs nearby to sit with him on her lap. She continued studying his every feature while he sat perfectly at ease, seeming to take in a few of her features as well.

She bonded with her nephew, right there on Gamma, beneath the massive limbs of the oak tree before she'd even bonded with her own twin. It didn't matter to her, deciding to work on Alec later and enjoy the moment with Luke and his irresistible smile. His hands reached out for her hair and she leaned forward so he could grasp it.

"Be careful," Meg said as she sat down with Lani in the chair next to them. "He's pulling hair now, and I don't mean gently."

"With a face and smile like his" –Tavis cuddled Luke closer– "he can have whatever his heart desires."

While Luke tugged at her hair, Tavis watched Meg study Lani's features. She seemed enrapt in the process, more so than just typical observation. She thought Meg appeared casually lost in memories and considered perusing her thoughts to see them for herself. The only thing that stopped Tavis was the potential that Meg may sense the invasion. With Alec not around, it would be obvious where it came from.

"I have an idea I wanted to run by you," Tavis said.

"What is it?"

"How about the four of us, just you, Alec, me, and Jack go out for dinner on Saturday?"

"I'd love to, but it's Alec's birthday on Saturday."

"I know, it's my birthday, too. I thought we could all go out together for a birthday dinner." Tavis waited for the inevitable response.

"Your birthday's the same day as Alec's?"

"Yep. So, what do you think? My father agreed to watch Lani. Do you think Kyrie or Ila would watch Luke?"

"Are you kidding me? They'd fight over who got to." Meg laughed, but saw Tavis still waited for an answer. "Well, I need to ask Alec about it first, but I already like the idea."

"I hope he agrees because I'm already looking forward to it. I don't know about you, but I'd love a few hours of conversation with people my own age. We can talk about anything but diapers and spit up and how beautiful our babies are."

"Actually, that does sound wonderful." Meg thought of a few additional things to add to the don't-mention list. "I'd like to ban mention of who gets up more during the night, who our babies like best, or who can carry a better lullaby tune."

"Agreed."

"So, what do you want for your birthday?" Meg asked.

"Nothing but an enjoyable evening with friends."

Meg rolled her eyes. "Don't hand me that, you have to want something."

Tavis considered what she most wanted. It was the same as what had been plaguing her more and more—to see her home again, to be there again. Too much time had passed since leaving it and she desperately longed for it. She wanted to see the familiar buildings, she missed the turquoise oceans and rivers she'd spent every free moment of her life enjoying. Like Meg had done, Tavis wanted the experience of decorating her first-born child's bedroom in her own home.

Her eyes met Meg's again and realized she'd been scrutinizing her thoughts. It worried Tavis for a moment until seeing a deep compassion, and what almost seemed a requited longing in Meg's eyes. Curious as to how developed Meg's thought sensory was, Tavis tested it.

"Nothing comes to mind."

"You want a place of your own, don't you?" Meg asked.

"We like our house." Tavis maintained eye contact. It was clear to her; Meg was quite adept at picking up on thoughts, at the very least.

"I mean something like what Alec and I have, you want something farther away."

Not only thoughts, but memories, Tavis deduced. "All in good time."

Meg accepted the diffused reply and settled back in the chair to dote on Lani again. After a moment, she said, "I've been working on something for you and it's almost finished. I hope you like it because it just turned into your birthday present."

"I wonder if I could guess what it is," Tavis said, still testing.

"Forget it." Meg looked at her, all thoughts well-shielded now. "No guessing and no peeking, it's a surprise."

Tavis smiled, simply to keep the frown off her face. "I love surprises," she lied. "Whatever it is, I'm sure I'll love it. Speaking of presents, do you have any idea what Jack and I could get for Alec?"

"Not a clue, he's impossible for gift giving."

Still probing, Tavis said, "I just thought of the perfect gift to give him."

"Really? What?"

For the first time since having met Meg, Tavis had to aggressively wall off her thoughts. "You'll have to wait till Saturday."

"Fine, it's only a few days away," Meg said, winking. "I'll have to finish up your present tonight."

They spent several hours visiting before Tavis announced it was time to head back home. "Call me later and let me know if we're on for Saturday night," she said while getting into the driver's seat.

"I will."

~

As Tavis approached the curve in the lane just past Alaret Beach, she saw an unfamiliar man walking alongside the forest. He was rather well-dressed for an islander; he was looking at her and waved when she noticed him.

She thought about slowing down to talk to him, but decided against it. Instead, she smiled, waved back, and continued driving on. As she rounded the curve, Tavis chanced a look back and found him standing in the middle of the lane watching her with a strange expression on his face—his lips curved into a half-smile.

The way he looked at her made Tavis uncomfortable, bringing a fear to the surface she wasn't familiar with. The last image she saw before losing sight of him was him talking into a communications radio.

Finally past the curve, Tavis relaxed a little, but knew she'd feel a lot better once she put more distance between them. Nearing the town center, she saw Sebastian driving in her direction. They slowed their carts down as they neared each other.

"Visiting Meg?" he asked.

"Yeah. I asked her about the birthday dinner and she's all for it. After she talks to Alec about it, she'll call me."

Sebastian frowned at Tavis. "Why's your adrenaline so high?" He reached for her wrist and didn't like the accelerated pulse rate. "What's going on? What scared you?"

"There was a man I'd never seen before on the lane just past Alaret Beach. Something about him made me nervous."

"Show me." He saw her reluctance to allow access to her thoughts and memories. "Then describe him to me."

"No, that's silly."

Tavis remembered the event and concentrated on the man's face. Still holding her wrist, Sebastian saw the memory with pristine clarity and experienced how Tavis had felt. But he knew more of the leer on William's face, and it sickened him.

When there was nothing more to show, Tavis asked, "Who was he?"

"That was William Davis. I suppose he's decided to spend more of his time on Gamma."

"Do you think he's monitoring the cameras himself?"

"I'm certain of it, but that doesn't surprise me. What *is* surprising is that he's out in the open and taking a risk at being seen. It shows his arrogance, and possibly his intentions."

"Do you think he knows who I was?"

"He definitely knows who you are, and I don't like the way he looked at you. I don't want you to go out alone again. You'll either have Jack or myself with you at all times."

Tavis scowled at the restrictions he tried saddling her with. "That seems a bit extreme."

"Well, Tavis, you have two choices... you can either heed my warning, or force me to send you and Lani home right now."

Though his tone was firm, he still maintained an elegant calm. However, Tavis sensed the struggle and knew better than to coax the calmness into becoming a full-fledged tempest. "Will you at least tell me why?"

"It wasn't a ruse that management created in their reasoning for removing William from Gamma. He really was all that his reputation portrayed him to be, fully and rightfully earning his title as a philandering womanizer. William looked at you as though you were a potential conquest, a prize of sorts."

She recalled the remembered face of William Davis and what Tavis found was what her father had. Not only did it disgust her, but the fear she had experienced returned—only it had more knowledge behind it now. Tavis dismissed the memory of his face and gave her father a baleful look.

"I won't go out alone again." A thought occurred to her and she tugged at his hand. "I'm worried about Meg now. He was close to the stone house and she's alone when Alec's working."

"I was thinking about that, too. I'd hoped it wouldn't be necessary, but I don't have a choice anymore, I have to tell Alec about management's presence here. I'm just afraid he won't handle it very well."

"What do you mean?"

"Alec's headstrong, he's more likely to confront William than avoid him." A defeated sigh escaped Sebastian. "I worry William's arrogance pitted against Alec's protective nature could create a chaos that won't bode well for us. I have no idea how much they're aware of, but there's a good chance William knows Alec isn't his biological child. If management and their scientists know *everything* about us..."

"What?" Tavis urged.

"I think they'll go beyond just keeping a watchful eye, and move toward captivity if they suspect we're about to leave. What I fear most is that it wouldn't take much for them to not wait and try detaining us anyway to minimize the risk."

"Then we'll just have to be extra careful until we do leave. Explain it to Alec just like you did to me, I know he'll listen. He doesn't want anything bad to happen to Meg or Luke."

"I hope you're right. I should find him. You go straight home and don't forget what I said about being out alone."

~

Sebastian watched Tavis drive off into the heart of the town center before figuring out a way to track down Alec. To his delight, it wasn't necessary, as Alec entered the lane ahead of him. To Sebastian's dismay, it appeared as though Alec was none too thrilled at being caught in a situation of having to acknowledge him.

Brushing the disappointment aside, Sebastian said when Alec drove within earshot, "I'm glad I ran into you, I need to talk to you."

"Can it wait? I'm kind of busy right now."

A glance at the back of the empty utility cart exposed Alec's lie and Sebastian met his eyes with disapproving disdain. Alec tried to ignore the annoying sense of shame, and even though he despised it, he found himself waiting for Sebastian's response rather than driving off immediately.

"It's important, Alec, I don't think you'd appreciate it if I let you carry on with your… hectic work schedule."

"All right, follow me."

Alec U-turned the cart and sped off in the direction of a wooded area, hoping the ridiculous shame would leave him alone. They parked alongside each other on a footpath in the forest and he waited for Sebastian to speak.

"I assume you know about the bunkers?" Sebastian asked.

"Yep."

"That's where Chaza's been living. After our fishing trip the other night, I went to see her and she and I discovered something you need to be aware of. A member of management was there with a maintenance worker to fix all the cameras so they can resume monitoring the island."

"Why? Because you're here?" Alec didn't bother disguising the accusation in his tone.

"Probably, and I want you to know *who* in management is monitoring. It's William Davis, he was never just an ordinary islander. He's always been a member of management."

Though surprised, Alec decided on the spot not to care about William Davis, or about any of his attempts to spy on Sebastian. "So what? Let them stare all they want. Maybe they'll get bored and leave."

"I'm afraid it's not that simple," he said, ignoring Alec's bravado. "He's also coming out of the bunkers. Tavis saw him today and she showed me the memory of her encounter with him. I didn't like the expression on his face. I'm sure you've heard stories of William's notoriety."

"Yeah, Sebastian, I heard." Alec stared off at the trees. "The kids I went to school with constantly reminded me of his self-indulgent behavior." He left the painful memories and looked back at Sebastian. "If you're worried about Tavis, tell her to steer clear of him."

"I've already told her not to go out alone again." Sebastian paused before continuing. It seemed a constant theme with Alec—it never took much for Sebastian to suffer agonizing guilt for having left him on Gamma. "Tavis saw William walking near Alaret Beach, right after she left from visiting Meg."

Sebastian watched the light of his unspoken warning fully dawn on Alec, and as worry and fear replaced the flippant attitude.

"I have to go." Alec started his cart and put it in drive. "Thanks for letting me know."

"Alec?"

"What?"

"You'll need to warn Meg however way you think's best, and don't tell Kyrie about William Davis' real identity."

"Why not?" Alec thought his mother had a right to know.

"William's philandering hurt her more than you know. I can't think of any good reason to tell her that those were the least of his lies. I'm hoping he plans to avoid her seeing him."

"Fine. I won't say anything, but I need to go now, Sebastian."

"One more thing, let me show you the memory Tavis shared with me. I want you to know what William looks like."

Alec's eyes narrowed; he hadn't the benefit of several beers loosening his usual reserve. Sebastian sensed, understood, and even knew exactly how to deal with Alec's concerns—Tavis had already broken him in and wore him down.

"Alec, it's a simple thing for you to see from me. If anything, it would be riskier on my part. Do you want to see him, or regret having not?"

"Go ahead."

As before, when Sebastian showed him the horrible images of people suffering and dying, Tavis' memory presented itself instantly and with even more definition. He recognized everything surrounding William as he'd seen it just this morning when he left for work. Through the memory, Alec saw the man he'd known to be his father leering at Tavis as she accelerated away from him. He felt how scared she was and it bothered him more than he thought it would.

When the memory ended, he looked at Sebastian. "Not a nice guy. I'm glad you showed me, but if you don't mind, I'd like to go check on my family."

"If you see William, don't confront him. Ignore him, Alec."

"As long as he doesn't bother me or anyone I care about, then he doesn't exist to me," Alec said and drove away.

~

Driving as fast as he safely could to the stone house, Alec's eyes darted to the sides of the lane looking for William in case he was still around. When he pulled up in front of the house, Meg wasn't outside as she sometimes was. He ran to the steps and leaped to the top.

"Meg?" he called after opening the door.

"I'm in the back room."

Alec sighed his relief at hearing her voice and calmly shut the door. Still, he hurried down the hallway to the room she used for painting. Peacefulness returned to him at seeing her seated in front of the canvas she'd been working on for weeks.

"Finished?"

"Almost." Without turning around, she asked, "Where's my kiss?"

He came up behind her, wrapped his arms around her waist, and kissed the top of her head.

"You can do better than that," she said.

Meg swiveled her chair around to face Alec. He leaned in and kissed her as she roped her arms around his neck, pulling him closer.

"How was your day?" Alec asked.

"Good. Tavis and Lani came over to visit for a bit."

"Yeah, I heard." He nodded to keep from frowning. "I ran into Sebastian on my way home and he told me."

"What's wrong?" Meg eyed him keenly. "You're really tense."

Lying to her was pointless, Meg grew stronger and more aware every day. He wondered sometimes why she hadn't asked him about it. "He said Tavis had a little situation after she left here."

Dread contorted Meg's face. "Has something happened to Tavis and Lani?" she asked, half-hoping he'd lie if it had.

"No, they're fine," Alec said quickly. "There was some man she'd never seen before on the lane near Alaret Beach. He was leering at her and it scared her a bit. Since it happened close to our home, I was worried about you and Luke."

"What do you mean, *leering* at her?"

"I mean exactly what you think I mean."

The crease that formed on Meg's brow told Alec she had the same concerns he did.

"Do you think it's anything to worry about?"

"Men leering at women they don't know isn't exactly a common occurrence here. So, yeah, I'm worried about it. Until it's resolved, I'd prefer it if you went to Ila's while I'm working." Alec readied himself for Meg's resistance to the idea. "I don't want you being here alone."

"I'm not gonna argue with you. I have no desire to be home alone with Luke if there's a creep hanging around out here. Besides, I've been slacking off on my daughterly duties. Visiting Ila while you're at work is fine by me."

"I don't have to work the rest of the week, so there's no need to worry about it till Monday."

"I'm glad you brought that up." Meg gave him a bright smile. "I want us to go out to dinner for your birthday, with Tavis and Jack. Did you know Tavis' birthday is on Saturday, too?"

Clearing his throat, Alec said, "Sebastian mentioned it." He saw how hopeful Meg looked. "So you want to do the dinner thing, huh?"

"Yes, I do. Please?"

"Okay." Alec chuckled. "Did you really think I'd say no to you?"

"Nah."

Alec looked at the painting Meg had been working on, studying it in its entirety. Her talent at painting had become nothing short of amazing to him; on a level of genius, he thought. The waterfall was so realistic, it sometimes seemed to be moving—he could almost hear the roar of the water.

"Is it to be Tavis' birthday present now?" he asked, still looking at the painting, thinking he might spot a bird fly through the trees surrounding the lake if he stared at it long enough.

"Yep, all I need to do is sign it and let it dry. It'll be ready by Saturday night. Think she'll like it?"

"She'll love it, so will Jack. I'm almost jealous you're giving it away."

The smile on Meg's face was full of pride, yet something else lurked behind it, a mischievous knowing that Alec picked up on immediately. He tried in vain to get a sense of what went through her mind, but she had become too adept at preventing him from doing so.

"What?" he asked.

"Nothing," she said. "You'll have to wait till your birthday."

"Oh, sure, I'll wait. I won't even try getting up in the middle of the night to have a peek."

"You better not!" Meg nudged his ribs. "I'm gonna call Tavis to let her know we're on."

~

"So how's Luke getting to our moms?" Alec asked Meg when the night of the dinner had arrived.

She sat at the vanity table in their bedroom, putting on her make-up; their eyes met in the mirror. Alec stood in the doorway holding a sleeping Luke against his chest. The vision of them made her heart flutter and her lips spread into a smile.

Meg knew what worried Alec; if he took Luke to Ila's, then Meg would be alone at their house. If she took him, then she'd be traveling alone and neither one of those scenarios pleased Alec.

"Both of them are coming over here to pick him up. I used the excuse that I wanted to show them the presents I have for you and Tavis so they wouldn't question it."

"Good idea. When will they be here?"

"Won't be long. I told Jack and Tavis to come over early so we could all go to the café together after I give Tavis her gift."

With a spritz of perfume, Meg turned away from the mirror and stood. She went over to where the dress she'd picked out for the evening lay on the bed. After untying her green silk robe, she let it fall to the floor in a puddle at her feet and glanced at Alec. She wore nothing beneath it except for the pearl ring she sometimes wore as a necklace. His gaze lingered where it rested on her chest and he thought it looked more perfect there than it ever did in the oyster he plucked it from.

"I really don't know how it's possible, but you get more beautiful every day. How do you contain all that beauty?" Alec asked, refusing to take his eyes away from her body.

Meg smiled at the compliment and retrieved the dress, picking it up by its spaghetti straps. She stepped into it and slowing inched it up her torso while her gaze remained locked on his. She saw the disappointment in his eyes at being robbed of the vision once the dress was in place. Languidly making her way over to him, Meg presented her unzipped back to him.

With his free hand, Alec pulled the zipper up and snaked his arm around her waist, pulling her closer. He inhaled the scent of her perfume mixed with her own personal scent and a rush of longing raced through his veins.

Meg sensed his desire for her as she allowed her body to lean back against his.

"How long do we have before they get here?" Alec whispered thickly against her neck.

"Long enough," she whispered back.

Alec eased Luke into the basinet, so as not to wake him. Returning to Meg, he slipped his hand behind her and unzipped the dress he'd just fastened. With the speed of a fleeting thought, he had the dress off her again and the both of them on their bed.

Half an hour later, Alec opened the front door for Kyrie and Ila. They looked at his disheveled appearance and surmised why it took so long for him to answer the door.

"Hey, come in," Alec said, his cheeks still red. "Meg's getting ready, she'll be down in a minute."

Ila and Kyrie shared a knowing glance before walking inside. Kyrie kissed Alec's cheek and smacked his butt. "Enjoying your birthday, are you?"

Meg bounded downstairs carrying Luke in her arms. When she reached the bottom, Alec took Luke so Meg could give Ila a hug. "Luke and I are gonna get his bag ready," he said and left them to fuss over the present he'd yet to be given.

"All right, show us," Ila said when Alec was out of earshot.

She led them down the hallway to her studio. Once inside, Meg shut the door to keep Alec from peeking.

The waterfall painting sat in the center of the room, still resting on the easel, and a bright red bow christened the top. "It's beautiful, Meg!" Ila stepped closer to inspect it. "Tavis is going to love it."

Meg went around the back of the easel and faced them both. An element of mystery and anticipation floated around her. "Ready to see Alec's present?"

"Yes," they answered in unison.

Meg came out from behind the easel carrying an already framed painting. Kyrie recognized the frame as the one she ordered several months back and how Meg refused to say what it was for. Seeing it, Kyrie was so astounded by it that tears sprang to her eyes.

"I'm speechless, Meg." Kyrie sat down to compose herself.

"Does that mean you like it?" Meg brought Kyrie a box of tissues.

Kyrie dried her eyes and looked at Meg. "I love it, I wish it was mine. You captured a very precious moment in time in such a beautiful way." Her gaze drifted over to the painting and she smiled. "Alec's gonna love it, too. You'll probably want to keep this tissue box handy."

~

When Kyrie and Ila left with Luke, Meg and Alec sat on the front steps of the stone house, feeling out of place without a baby to tend to. They looked at each other and laughed.

Alec took Meg's hand and led her inside to the kitchen to open a bottle of wine. She pulled four glasses from the cabinet, pouring wine into two of them so they could officially begin the start of their carefree evening.

When Jack and Tavis arrived, Alec and Meg were sitting under the oak tree, already on their second glass. "You have some catching up to do," Alec said, holding up his near empty glass.

"Well, I'm glad I thought to bring a few bottles with me." Jack held up two bottles of chardonnay. "Happy Birthday, old man!"

"Thank you." Alec laughed and got up with Meg to greet them.

"Happy Birthday, Tavis," Meg said.

"Yes, Happy Birthday," Alec added, giving her a hint of a smile.

"You, too, Alec." She reciprocated a tiny smile of her own.

Since they had an hour before their reservation at the café, they chatted in the front room for a while. As it got closer to the time for them to leave, Meg announced she wanted to present their gifts.

She unveiled Tavis' first and pulled the sheet away from the painting, letting it fall behind the easel to cover Alec's. A breath of air escaped from Tavis when her eyes fell to the painting. The quality of Meg's work on canvas surpassed even that of the wall murals. It was a cherished talent in Tavis' home and she could only imagine how delighted some would be to have Meg there.

"That's the best damn painting I've ever seen, Meg," Jack said.

Meg nodded at him, but watched Tavis, who'd yet to say anything. She went over and kneeled down in front of the chair. "Please tell me you like it," she said. "Maybe I shouldn't have painted such a personal place of yours and Jack's."

Tavis shook her head and took Meg's hands. "I love it, and I'll cherish it always. Thank you."

She wished she could tell Meg more about the painting, how there were others from her home who could create such beauty in artistic ways. Tavis hated being the only one among them who understood the true nature of Meg's talent.

Seeing the glassy look of potential tears in Tavis' eyes, Meg discreetly set the tissue box in the chair by her side. "You're very welcome, Tavis. I enjoyed painting it for you."

Glancing at Alec, Meg wondered if she could take his tears if his gift had the same effect. She considered waiting until they were alone, but he looked at her expectantly. After going back over to the easel and picking up the still-covered framed painting, she pulled the sheet off while keeping her eyes locked on his face.

Alec stared at the painting for several seconds before bringing his gaze back to Meg's eyes. She knew how much he wanted to stop it, but his eyes glistened anyway. For a brief moment, she thought his tears would kill her. Thankfully, a smile spread across his face.

"When did you start that?" he asked her.

"Right after Luke was born. I woke up from a nap and found you two sleeping that way on the sofa," she said. "The sunlight coming in through the bay window cast a glow on you and Luke, and it was too perfect to let it slip away. I had to paint it. I was so afraid one of you would wake up while I sketched it out, but you both slept for over an hour. That was all I needed."

Meg had painted a moment in time and captured the very essence of it. A father who had fallen asleep with his newborn son resting peacefully on his chest. Alec's hand lay atop Luke's back and both their sleeping faces were facing toward the painter. The entire scene had a dreamlike quality to it, amplified by the rays of golden sunlight coming in through the bay window.

"You amaze me every day," Alec said and at last the tears rolled down his cheeks.

Meg had never seen Alec so moved to tears and she closed the distance between them. He engulfed her into his arms and if he could, he would've absorbed her completely just to make them closer. "I love you, Meg," he whispered against her ear.

'I love you, too, Alec,' she said.

Though he recognized it instantly, he doubted she was aware that she hadn't said it aloud.

The tissue box had found its way into his chair and he took one when Tavis started to speak. "We have a gift for you, Alec, but I want to wait until after dinner to give it you. Maybe we could all go for a walk on the beach tonight."

"Sure, that sounds great," he said.

~

Jack drove to the café, as his cart was the biggest and most accommodating. When they arrived, the hostess led them to the table Meg had requested when she made the reservation—in the middle of the main dining area and in the thick of other diners. Being a Saturday night, during the dinner rush, the restaurant was packed. Even Frank was there having dinner with Effie Henderson, who was also widowed. They came over before leaving to wish Alec and Tavis a happy birthday.

The evening flew by as they laughed and enjoyed themselves, particularly Jack having way too much fun with James by giving him a wink every time he delivered their drink orders.

"Thank you… I'm sorry, what was your name again?" Jack asked after a wine bottle opening.

James couldn't resist the open invitation to speak. Standing just behind Tavis, making sure Jack saw him have a glance down her generously plunging neckline, James leaned in closer to whisper over his shoulder, "My name's asshole."

With a fresh new bottle of wine and a slice of birthday cake for each of them—complete with embarrassing candles and song—the couples resumed the idle chatter of nothing in particular until Meg asked, "So, Jack, where are you from originally?"

Both Tavis and Alec stiffened at the question, each of them knowing Meg was unaware that Jack had worked as a researcher for management. Jack, on the other hand, didn't seem to care at all about it. Though normally a private person, perhaps the wine had loosened him since he answered her question without the slightest apprehension.

"I was born and raised in Charleston," he said. "It was a coastal city in South Carolina." Briefly, Jack wondered how much geography they taught on Gamma. "It's in East America."

"*Was* a city?" she asked.

"Well, obviously, Charleston's still there, but it's nothing like it was. It used to be a great city, but it's…" Jack's voice trailed off for a moment, as though following along with his troubled thoughts. "It's very different now, unrecognizable to the city I grew up in."

"Do you miss it?"

"I miss the city I knew, not what it became. It's a military base now."

"I'm sorry."

"Charleston's not unique, many great cities aren't what they used to be."

Jack had reached the extent of Meg and Alec's history lessons on East America—that which was taught in a biased cooperative school. At a loss, Meg shifted the subject to what she thought would be a happier one.

"What about your parents, do they still live there?"

Though her intentions were benign, Jack still bristled at the question. Meg sensed the wall of privacy erect itself around Jack's thoughts and her curiosity dueled with her compassion over what must be a sensitive subject for him.

At the awkward silence, Meg's compassion won the duel: "I'm sorry if I asked something personal."

"Oh, no, Meg, it's okay." Jack felt terrible at seeing her discomfort, and he only made it worse by saying, "My parents died."

"Forgive me, Jack, I didn't know," Meg said, scrambling. "I shouldn't have brought it up."

"Don't worry about it. That was a long time ago."

All eyes were on Jack, but it was Tavis who watched him as though looking at a specimen on a microscope stage. She fought against the urge to yank him up from the table and demand he tell her more about his parents' deaths. Instead, she set it aside, knowing he had nowhere else to go but home with her and Tavis had every intention of quizzing him later.

Granting a reprieve to all of them, Tavis changed the subject to one truly neutral. "I don't know about the rest of you, but I sure could use that walk on the beach." She turned to Alec. "And I still need to give you your birthday present."

~

Jack drove off toward Alaret Beach, but kept going to the stone house when Alec mentioned going to the barn to get a few torches for staking into the sand. While Alec was in the barn, Meg ran inside to grab a beach blanket, another bottle of wine, and four glasses.

"I want to talk to you later," Tavis said to Jack.

"I know."

"You do?"

"Yeah, you want to know more about my parents." Jack chuckled. "I could almost hear your unspoken questions at the table. I promise, I'll talk to you about it later. Let's enjoy tonight, okay?"

"Okay."

Meg came back out of the house with a giant basket in one hand and the waterfall canvas in the other. "Talk to Kyrie about ordering a frame," she said, putting everything in the back of the cart.

Alec returned with the torches and slipped them in the back. They drove along the beach until settling on an area to spread the blanket—near the sea oats at the base of the cliff. Once Alec drove the torches in the sand and lit them, a steady flickering glow illuminated their immediate surroundings; the full moon lit up the rest of the beach.

The couples sat down on the blanket, opened the bottle of wine, and toasted to birthdays and friendship. Soon, Tavis pulled out a small box wrapped in blue birthday paper and handed it over to Alec, who sat next to her.

"Yeah, me, too," Jack said to Meg at seeing her excitement for Alec to hurry up and open it. "Tavis refused to tell me what we got him."

Thinking he'd have a bit of fun, Alec tore the paper slowly, acting as though he meant to save it. He chanced a peek and found Meg glaring at him.

"Need any help?" she asked.

Chuckling, Alec ripped the paper off the box and lifted the lid. He pushed the tissue paper aside and pulled out a small, but surprisingly heavy, pyramidal object made of some silver-like metal. Its sides were intricately carved in what appeared to be ancient Egyptian hieroglyphics, except for the bottom—where it was flat and smooth, save a small circular indention in the center and a slight furrow running alongside the edges. Alec returned his attention to the etchings and discovered they weren't *exactly* Egyptian hieroglyphics, none that he'd ever studied.

In one respect, they looked like Chinese symbols; in another, they seemed Hebrew. It was more like they were neither, yet all of them combined. There was a large stone on each of the four triangular sides; a most brilliant blue. The light from the torches made the gems glint and stand out to be the most notable features on the pyramid.

"They're sapphires," Tavis said in response to Alec's inspection of the rare form of the gem. "Second only to diamonds in durability."

"These symbols, are they some kind of a language?"

"Yes, but it's..." Tavis paused to choose her words wisely due to their audience. "Ancient. Not one they teach in schools."

He wanted to ask Tavis silently if she understood the language, but Jack and Meg were so enthralled by the vision of the pyramid that he dared not risk it. "What are the sapphires for?" Alec flipped it back and forth in his hands to look at and compare the four gems.

"It's best to inspect them under certain light," she said, her voice filled with the whispering undercurrent of a hint. "At the moment, a full moon's good enough."

Alec held the pyramid closer to his face, but still only saw the gems' obvious beauty.

"No, look inside… like you're trying to look *through* them," she said.

Though he brought it nearer to his eyes, he could've pulled it still closer. Alec felt Tavis' hand touch his wrist, gently guiding his hand until two opposite gems lined up, and then a little farther until aligning all with the moon.

Rays of light burst to life throughout the pyramid, casting a wondrous glow on the image held within. Alec felt Tavis' hand leave his wrist when he spotted what was inside the pyramid and no longer needed her guidance. The vision Alec saw defied explanation, but he knew what it was. He had an overwhelming urge to somehow climb inside it, to be closer to what he looked at—to *be* there and not just looking at its representation.

It startled him to feel so drawn to it; he lowered the pyramid and looked at Tavis. He had to know, and no longer cared that Meg and Jack were watching them. Their blue eyes met, so similar in nature to the sapphires, and Tavis tried desperately to let the answer show in her eyes for Alec to see. She sighed with relief when he did. They both realized too long of a silence had passed and they turned their attention to Jack and Meg.

Jack and Meg were shocked by what they saw when Alec and Tavis looked at them. The side of the pyramid that faced them was still aglow in Alec's hands and illuminated the blue of his and Tavis' eyes so that they appeared a perfect match. For a fleeting moment, it was impossible to tell them apart.

"What is that thing?" Meg asked, glancing at the pyramid.

"A paperweight." Alec recovered quickly and set it down on the wrapping paper.

"Nice." Jack snorted. "Beats all the rocks I ever used."

Alec used the distraction of Jack's quip to put the pyramid back into the box and Tavis picked up the wine bottle to refill everyone's glasses. Afterward, Alec turned to her and said, "Thank you, and you, too, Jack. I'll think of you both every time I weigh my papers down."

The couples polished off the bottle of wine and as it was still early they decided to have one more before calling the evening officially over. Meg suggested getting another bottle from their house, but Alec had a better idea.

"Let's have a bottle of that *cave* wine." Alec winked at Meg.

"Oh, yeah, I forgot about those." She turned to Tavis and Jack. "You're gonna love it." When Alec stood, Meg added, "Jack, you should go with Alec and look at the cave, it's just up there." She pointed to the top of the cliff.

Jack's gaze drifted up the cliff wall. It was hard to make out much detail from where they sat, but the light of the full moon lit it up enough to make the trek feasible. To make it more so, Alec grabbed one of the torches to bring along.

Jack turned to Tavis, knowing her worries and remembering his promise to stay away from the underground bunkers. He leaned in as though to give her a kiss, but whispered, "Don't worry, I'll keep my promise. We'll be right back."

~

When they reached the top of the cliff and entered the cave, Alec went over to the unopened wine bottles while Jack's eyes darted to the steel door at the back of the cave. His gaze traveled to the left of the door and saw the cubbyhole in the cave wall.

The fingers on his right hand twitched at the recognition of how to get inside. So strong was this side of his answer-seeking nature that he had to turn away from the door to avoid the risk of breaking his promise to Tavis. Though it worked, it made him angry.

"Okay, I decided to get two bottles," Alec said as he passed by Jack. "You never know, we may keep going for that never ending *one more glass*." When he got to the cave opening, he turned around to find that Jack hadn't moved. "You ready?"

"Sure."

They were just about to retrace their steps back down the old path when Jack put his hand on Alec's arm to stop him. "What was that down there?"

"What do you mean?"

Jack's eyes narrowed. "Your paperweight… what did you see inside of it?"

Alec handed one of the bottles to Jack while grasping for seconds to come up with an acceptable answer. "It's hard to describe, it was an illusion created by light," he settled on.

"Okay, moving on from your generic answer." Mid-stride on testing boundaries with Alec, Jack asked, "You never told Meg about me being a researcher, did you?"

"Nope." Alec stood his ground, knowing his testimony was up for examination now, and he feared only one question.

"I saw something down there on the beach," Jack said. "Something I guess I've seen hundreds of times before, but for some reason I've only just now really noticed it. I'm pretty sure Meg picked up on it, too."

"And what was that?"

"Just how much you and Tavis look alike. So much so, that it can't possibly be by chance. Your birthdays are on the same day, and you're the same age. Seriously? I want to know right now, what connects you and Tavis."

This was it, the question Alec feared. No skirting around the issue, no easing in to it, not even a bit of foreplay leading up to it—just good old-fashioned laying it out and Alec half-hated, half-admired that about him.

After a glance over the cliff to make sure Meg and Tavis were still as they left them, Alec returned his attention back to Jack. "Tavis and I are twins."

If Jack was stunned by the information, he didn't show it other than allowing several seconds to pass before carefully asking his next question.

"Kyrie and—"

"Right."

"Well, I have a bunch more questions now, but I need to know one thing first." Jack frowned at what the answer would mean. "Who all doesn't know about it?"

Alec found the question odd and he searched in vain to find the reason for it, both within himself and in Jack, but came up with nothing. "Meg, my mother, Ila…" He grew agitated. "Why do you ask?"

"Obviously, there's a lot of secrets being kept around here and I need to know who to keep my mouth shut around." Jack started walking away from Alec.

"Jack, it's more complicated than you know. Tavis and I have only just been told ourselves, please don't be mad at her for something neither one of us has yet to process."

"I'm not mad at Tavis." Jack spun around to face him again. "It's not her fault."

"Are you trying to find someone to blame?"

"There's always someone to blame."

"As much as I hate to admit it, there's no point in trying to find fault with Sebastian. Clearly, you've sorted out that William Davis isn't my father."

"How much do you know, Alec?"

"More than *you*," Alec dared to say, but regretted it at seeing Jack try to walk away again. "Hey, wait. You have to keep this a secret."

Jack glanced over his shoulder and looked at Alec as though he was a stupid child who'd been given way more information than he should be entrusted with. It shamed, embarrassed, and more than anything, angered Alec to be the brunt of this demeaning assumption.

"Up until this very second, I've liked you," Alec said through clenched teeth. "And that's saying a lot coming from me. But if you think for one minute that I'm gonna let you cause trouble, especially with William Davis showing back up, then you can think a little harder. I'll walk right back in that cave and open that door… and yes, I know how to open it. I'll find him and tell him you're hiding right under his nose. You don't want to hurt Tavis, do you?"

His retreat from Alec faltered and came to a stop. "If you did that, *you'd* be the one hurting Tavis. You'd be hurting Lani, too."

"If you start attracting attention to us, then you'll leave me with no choice but to expose you. If it comes down to my family or yours, mine wins," Alec said with finality. "I'll stop you any way I can."

Taking a moment to consider the eventualities of what would happen should Alec follow through with the threat, Jack assumed he'd be removed from Gamma before the night was over.

"And they'd probably take Lani right after you," Alec said, no longer caring about secreting his ability to sense Jack's thoughts, who was doing a poor job of maintaining his precious guard of them anyway.

Frowning quizzically, Jack asked, "How do you know what I'm thinking?"

Ego surpassing compassion, Alec answered, "You're an open book right now and, well, I did mention I know more than you do."

The defeated look on Jack's face devoured whole all of Alec's egotistic feelings of victory. His words drove the final death blow.

"Fine, I don't care what you know," Jack said, thinking he'd get on his knees and beg if necessary. "I'll do whatever you want, or *not* want me to do. If William finds out I'm here, it's over. He'll have me removed and I don't want to lose Tavis and Lani."

"Look, I shouldn't have threatened you." Alec shrugged. "I just wanted you to understand how important it is that we don't draw attention to ourselves."

"And I agree with you."

"Be careful around my mom. She doesn't know about any of this and I'd rather keep it that way for now."

"I'm not gonna say anything, Alec." Jack tried not to think of the growing list of secrets. "We should get back down there before they come looking for us."

When they returned to the beach, it was Meg's eyes that Jack's met before he turned to Tavis. He sat on the blanket next to Tavis and pulled her into his arms, hugging her as though he was afraid she would disappear if he didn't hold her close.

The interaction didn't go unnoticed, and Alec hated himself for being the one who caused Jack to feel he had something to lose. His only solace was Meg, who'd already picked up on Alec's shifting emotions.

She cuddled up to him and laced her fingers into his. "You okay?"

"I'm fine." Alec kissed the top of her head and looked up at the night sky.

A peaceful silence fell over all of them for a little while. The sound of something musical filled the air around them and all eyes fell to the gift box.

"Wow, and it plays music, too," Alec said, chuckling.

19

The Cavanaughs

Jack and Tavis returned Meg and Alec to the stone house, traversed the island to scoop Lani up from the bassinette at Sebastian's, and took her home.

As they lay in their bed, Jack held Tavis close, clutching her to his chest, and still suffering from the fear of losing her. He knew she waited. Though he wanted to tell her about his parents, it was difficult for him as it was always painful when he thought of them.

"I know you're waiting," he said.

"I don't want to push you." Tavis waited briefly, then said, "You never told me your parents had died, so it was a bit of a shock when you told Meg. Also, it seemed like you weren't being completely honest about it."

"Well, I wasn't being *dis*honest, I just chose not to go into details."

"Are your parents dead?"

"Yes. As their only child, I was the one who had to identify their bodies and make the arrangements for their burial."

Tavis caught a glimpse of Jack's memory of his parents lying side-by-side on slabs in a morgue. She forced the image from her mind, but not before it left her feeling cold.

"I was still in college, between semesters when things got really bad back home."

"How'd they die?"

"They were killed." Jack's voice remained evenly controlled, but there was a hard edge to it. "They were executed, shot in the back of the head by people working for the government at the time. They killed a lot of people besides my parents."

"Why?"

"Same reason as always, you oppose what the government's doing and you paint a target on your back. In my parents' case, they joined an organization trying to raise awareness about these islands. They wanted to put a stop to what goes on here, but the government wanted this." He waved his arm around in the air above them. "This damned island. Oh, wait, let me be clear… not just this one, but the rest of them, too."

"How many others are there?"

"Besides Gamma, there're two more." Jack hesitated, wondering if it would scare her to mention the first two islands. It felt wrong not to. "There were others."

"*Were* others?"

"Remember what I told you in the bunkers, about the potential for Gamma to be destroyed?"

"Yeah."

"The first two islands were destroyed. Management had names for them, too. The first one was Alpha and it was destroyed in a particularly horrific way. The second island—"

"Wait, what do you mean by *particularly* horrific?" Tavis sensed his reluctance and put an end to it. "Jack, I want to know."

"It was the first attempt at destroying an island, so they had no idea what kind of explosives to use or how much was needed to do it quickly. Apparently, it was miserable and there was a lot of suffering. Alpha proved to be the learning curve in what explosive isn't efficient and how using too little will cause some islanders to die a slow, torturous death."

Steadying herself, so as not to make Jack regret having told her, Tavis took a deep breath. He had shed a spotlight on a wretched piece of history, yet another her father had decided was inappropriate for her to know about.

"What of Beta?" she asked.

"Beta was destroyed as well, the difference was that they had learned from Alpha. That was when they started rigging nuclear explosives in the islands' infrastructure. Doing it that way makes for a complete and quick annihilation of a land mass and all of its inhabitants."

"We're on Gamma." Tavis recalled his mention of other islands. "There's a Delta?"

"Delta still exists with people living on it, just like here. A new land mass was created a while back, Epsilon, but there's no population on it yet. It's nearing the end of the vegetation stage and soon there'll be building construction going on for its future population. Management's also mapping out a new area for Zeta. Don't forget, there's another island, the research station. That's where management is. Can you guess the name of it?"

"Tyrant Island?"

"Digamma," he said. "It literally means double gamma and it's not only twice the size of this island, it's also the closest to Gamma."

"How much do you know about Delta?"

"Not much. Each island is assigned its own team of employees. Of course, management and the scientists rule over all. My work focused on the weather patterns affecting Gamma."

"Why'd they destroy Alpha and Beta?"

"Resistance, rebellion, anarchy. The screening process for who they bring to the islands is carried out by the scientific team now. They clearly do a better job than management did at selecting candidates."

"Your parents were opposed to the creation of the islands?" Tavis asked, but he remained silent. "Jack?"

"They weren't opposed at first, they were originally one of the investors." Jack sighed. "They voiced their misgivings about the way Alpha was destroyed. When Beta was destroyed, they threatened to rescind their endorsements. Management promised them it wouldn't happen again, but then they found out about the partnership with the East American military. That's when they pulled out and began advocating for an end to the experiments. At least that's what they told me before they died."

"Why did you start working for management if you knew your parents were against it?"

"I wanted to know why they had to die." Jack reflected on everything he'd learned since taking the research job. "I think they were right to campaign against the Stone Davis Corporation. It's all about greed and they're hurting people to achieve status and wealth."

"Have you ever worried they might know who you are? That they could connect your last name to your parents?"

"Cavanaugh? When I first applied for the job I worried about it, but they never brought it up during the interview and nobody questioned it in all the time I worked there."

"What if they do know and decided not to question you?"

"Why? What would be their reason?"

"I don't know." Tavis' mind raced for potential scenarios that would make management want to keep their knowledge of who Jack really was to themselves. "My guess is that they'd prefer to keep you close, to keep an eye on you."

"That doesn't make any sense, Tavis. I'm pretty sure they hated my parents."

"Exactly! Maybe they were worried you'd follow in their footsteps and were trying to gain inside information."

"That seems a bit of a reach."

"Oh, really? Isn't that precisely what you were doing?"

"Okay, I concede, it's possible." He grimaced at the prospect. "I hope that's not the case, though. If you're right, then that means they probably know where I've been this whole time, and that kind of freaks me out thinking about it."

"Why?"

"Because I haven't been carted off yet. Why would they let me stay if they knew I was here?

"Why do they want any people here?"

Jack snorted. "Because they're performing experiments on people, on carefully screened—" He sat up, trying to make sense of the thoughts beginning to form in his mind.

Tavis sat up, too, looking at his face in the moonlight coming in through the window—there was a bit of a wild look in his eyes. "Could it be that you're now part of their experiments?" she asked and wondered if it were true of herself.

"It sort of looks that way, doesn't it?" he whispered. "God, I hope not."

"Even if it's true, don't worry about it. We'll be fine."

"There are plenty of reasons to worry, Tavis. If at any moment they wanted to, they could take Lani away from us for testing, regardless of how we felt about it. We'd be sitting around, hoping they'd decide to give her back. It's happened before, lots of times. There've been times parents never saw their child again… ever."

"They'll never take Lani from us, and I'm certain of that."

"No one can be certain of that."

Tavis put her hand over his to calm him. "*I* can be sure. We'd escape this island before they had the chance."

Contemplating her mention of escape, Jack thought of the boat he hid in the forest when he came to Gamma with Michelle. "You're right, we will get off this island. I'll never let them get their filthy hands on Lani."

She caught the image of the boat he recalled and had no intention of leaving Gamma by such a crude means of transportation. "Jack—"

"I hid the boat I used when I came here with Michelle," he said, meaning to give Tavis hope. "We can use that."

"That's fine, Jack, but I don't want to worry so much about that right now. There's still time."

"Yeah, I know, babe. We don't have to talk about it anymore tonight." He wanted to set her mind at ease, but he didn't want her to become too complacent. "However, with William Davis hanging around, you need to understand we might not have as much time as you think. Speaking of which, I don't want you going off any more on your own, with or without Lani."

"I'm not planning on it."

He relaxed at her reassurance and rested back against the pillows, bringing her with him and wrapping her into his embrace. "I'm gonna check on the boat tomorrow to make sure it's still usable. Stay close to Sebastian while I'm gone."

Tavis struggled with the realization that her talk with Jack about their future would have to happen sooner than she had anticipated. "Jack?"

"Yeah?"

"I want to talk to you about something that's important to me, and to you as well. You asked me once where I came from and I wouldn't tell you then, but I think it's time you knew."

"You don't have to tell me." Jack still hated being reminded of that night, and to make matters worse was knowing what Alec had revealed to him. "You love me, that's all I need to know."

"But I want you to know. I talked it over with my father and he agreed I should talk to you about it."

"All right, I'm listening."

"Not yet, later."

He groaned. "Why wait?"

"Because I'm tired and I want to get some sleep before Lani wakes up."

"Oh." Jack chuckled, gave her a kiss, and closed his eyes.

~

Soon after Jack left the next day, Tavis and Lani went to Sebastian's house.

"How was the birthday dinner?" Sebastian asked, setting aside the book he'd been reading.

Tavis sat on the couch beside him and handed Lani to him before he had a chance to demand her. She eyed the book's title, *The History of Native American People*, and thought the text seemed rather thin.

"It was nice, we had a lot of fun. Meg gave me a painting of the waterfall lake. You should come over later and take a look at it, it's just like her wall murals, but even better."

"Did Alec like his present?"

"He was fascinated with the amulet, and that was just the outside of it. I had to prod him to look inside. You were right, the moonlight worked. He was able to see the image you left and he knew what it was."

"I knew he would," Sebastian said, satisfied and proud.

"I found out more about Jack's parents. It seems they were killed by the East American government for their efforts to raise awareness about these islands. Interestingly, they came to oppose the Stone Davis Corporation" –Tavis raised her eyebrows– "after first being investors."

"That *is* interesting."

"Know what else is interesting?" she asked.

"What?"

"That you didn't tell me about Alpha and Beta being destroyed."

"Sorry, Tavis, but I left that part out of the lullabies I sang to you."

"I'm not a child anymore."

"If I had told you before we came here, would you have come along?"

"No, I wouldn't have! And I probably would've tried to do everything I could to prevent you from coming here."

"Exactly."

Tavis got up from the couch and paced a few times in front of him, thinking about everything Jack had said. "There's no point in being mad at you and since I *am* here now, I'd like to know more about what happened to the first two islands. Can you do that? Can you stop protecting me long enough to tell me, Alec… oops, I meant, Father."

"Don't be impertinent." Sebastian tread carefully, knowing Tavis struggled to keep from losing her patience with him. "Okay, I'll tell you what I know. What did Jack say about it?"

"That they destroyed them after the inhabitants rebelled."

"And that's exactly what happened. What more did you want to know?"

"He said there was a lot of suffering on Alpha. Is that true?"

"Yes. Before there was a scientific team, management selected people to come to the islands. They didn't do a very good job and found themselves saddled with a quarrelsome lot that refused to live quietly and obediently, especially when they found out they weren't allowed to leave the island."

"Were they trying to leave?" Tavis asked.

Lani fell asleep and Sebastian put her in the bassinet still sitting in the front room, then motioned for Tavis to follow him to the dining table.

Sebastian said, "It became a never ending battle to pluck would-be refugees from crudely built rafts out of the ocean. When it appeared as though the whole of Alpha was in rebellion, management decided it was a failure and destroyed it. It was horrible, people suffered for days, some of them took weeks to die from their injuries."

Though not as much as he inundated onto Alec, he showed her a few of the memories that he'd been given.

"How could anyone ever do that?" she asked, her voice a bare whisper.

"You said you wanted to know, Tavis."

"I do want to know." Tavis rotated in her seat to look out the window, fixing her gaze on what she could see of the sky. She longed to be rid of Gamma. "What was their problem with Beta?"

"The same thing, an uprising against restrictions," he said. "Management had already aligned themselves with the East American government by that point, so they had access to nuclear explosives."

"Was there suffering on Beta?"

"No. It went from a bustling island to nothing but silence in the blink of an eye. Gamma was more of a success thanks to the new government appointed scientists. They rooted out undesirable traits and screened people for their more desirable ones in the effort to create a better being."

"Do you know about Delta?" Tavis turned away from the window. "Do you know there's another island that's fully populated?"

"I know about Delta, but I've only concerned myself with Gamma."

"Why is the East American government involved?"

"I don't know for sure," he said. "But I imagine it's to have exclusive rights to the scientific team's discoveries. I'm quite certain they don't have noble purposes in mind."

"Are we gonna be able to leave?" Her voice trembled with vulnerability and fear. "Will we ever see our home again?"

"Don't be afraid, you'll be home again. You'll have Jack and Lani with you and all this will seem like a bad dream not worth remembering. Their technology is nothing compared to ours. You know that already."

She nodded and let go a relieved sigh. Tavis remembered where Jack was and it made her laugh. When Sebastian frowned at her, she said, "Jack's checking on the boat he hid when he and Michelle came here. His plan is to use it as our escape."

Sebastian burst out in laughter.

"Oh, that was so funny. I needed a good laugh," Sebastian said. "But seriously, Tavis, you need to talk to him soon."

"I know." Tavis leaned back in the chair. "I mentioned it last night."

"Stop putting it off, just tell him."

"I'm nervous about it. What if he doesn't believe me?"

"Then you'll have to prove it to him."

"How?"

"Be creative, use some of your abilities. Jack's intelligent, he'll know you're telling the truth."

"He's really worried about William Davis being back here." Tavis gave Sebastian a tiny half-smile. "I'm to stay here with you until he gets back, so I hope you didn't have any plans."

"Nope, no plans today. Would you like to go visit with Chaza? I bet she'd like some company."

~

A few hours went by and Tavis took to looking out the window every few minutes, concerned that Jack was gone an awful long time just to check on the boat. She was relieved when she saw his cart pull up outside.

"I'll be right back," Tavis said to Sebastian and Chaza before walking outside.

"Visiting Chaza?" Jack asked.

"Yeah, Lani and my father are there, too. What took you so long?"

"I decided to put the boat in the water to check the engine. It runs great." Jack smiled at her as if he expected her to shout with joy. "We can leave whenever we're ready."

It was all Tavis could do not to scream how ridiculous and utterly preposterous this idea was. An image of a tiny lifejacket for Lani popped into her head and she realized it came from Jack.

"Oh, that's it!" Her eyes narrowed with her new found resolve and determination to tell Jack everything. "You and I are going somewhere. Wait here while I tell Chaza and my father to watch Lani for a little while."

When she returned, she got into the passenger seat and waited for Jack to drive off. After a few seconds, she frowned at him since he hadn't turned the cart back on.

"You haven't told me where we're going."

"Oh." Tavis considered where she should talk to Jack. Preferably, she wanted somewhere private, and away from cameras. "To the lake."

Jack drove off and once they got there, he followed Tavis to the large boulder near the waterfall and sat beside her. Tavis slipped her hand into Jack's and worked up the courage to tell him all the things he needed to know.

After several sighs from her, but nothing more, Jack asked, "What's wrong?"

"Nothing's wrong." She hoped this was true as she leaned against his shoulder. "I'm ready to talk to you about… stuff."

"Okay." He gave her hand a reassuring squeeze. "I'm listening."

"First, I want to tell you why William Davis is here and why he's trying to get the cameras working again. Management wants to prevent certain people from leaving because these people have every intention of doing just that."

"They'd want to prevent *anyone* from trying to leave."

"I know that, but they especially don't want certain people escaping."

"Are you talking about us?" he asked. "Are you worried about my plan?"

"They particularly don't want me and Sebastian to leave."

Jack frowned. "Why just you two?"

"How much do you know of what the scientists are working on?"

"Only a little. I know they're experimenting with genetics, trying to isolate certain traits and DNA. I think they're trying to create some kind of superhuman. That's what these islands are for, to have a controlled environment for the experiments."

"Sounds like you know more than just a little."

"My parents told me bits of it, but I always knew they weren't telling me everything. I think they were scared for me to know too much."

"Well, your parents were right. That's exactly what the scientists are doing and they know they've achieved many of their goals on Gamma."

Jack pulled back from Tavis to look at her. "How would you know about that?"

Tavis ignored the question and continued: "Some people possess more of the traits the scientists are looking for. I don't know about Delta, but on this island, there are plenty of them and the scientists have undoubtedly discovered it. The scientists report their findings and management takes care of the rest."

"How do you know all this, Tavis?" Jack released her hand and ran his fingers through his hair, trying to make sense of what she was telling him.

"I'm one of these people, so is my father, and there are others."

"How long have you known about what goes on here?" Jack looked back at her.

"For a very long time."

"Did someone help you and Sebastian get here?"

"No, we came to Gamma on our own." Tavis shrugged. "I guess you could say we snuck in."

"How?" Jack was dumbfounded. Though he and Michelle had also snuck in, they didn't have far to travel as Digamma was close by.

"We came in our own transportation."

"That's not possible." He shook his head emphatically, thinking of management's safeguards and protocols. "Nope, not possible."

"Their current technology can't detect our machines."

"Is that right?" Jack worked to maintain his composure. "I think you need to tell me where you and Sebastian came from."

"You sound upset, maybe we should talk about something else—"

"No, Tavis!" he shouted, startling a few birds from a nearby tree. "Just tell me now."

"We're not from here, or any other island for that matter. We didn't come from the mainland either. We came from an altogether different world." There, she said it—she finally told him, and for a moment she enjoyed how great it felt.

"Why are you saying this?" Jack's tone was beaten and his shoulders slumped forward as though they were suddenly too heavy with undue burden.

He didn't believe her.

"It's true, I can prove it." Tavis' mind raced for an idea. "Okay, in a minute I want you to think of something. It can be anything, but I want you to focus really hard first on keeping that thought private."

Jack turned away from her and looked out over the lake. She knew by his now easily read thoughts that he wasn't complying. Even worse, he wondered if there was something wrong with Tavis.

"There's absolutely nothing wrong with me," Tavis spat. "I'm your wife, and you'd rather think I'm crazy than give me a chance to prove I'm telling the truth."

He was stunned by her commanding and somewhat disgusted tone. As her eyes bored into his, shame crept up on him. When she started to get up, he stopped her by taking her hand.

"I have a thought," he said. "Actually, it's more of a memory."

Hard as she tried, Tavis couldn't break through Jack's wall of guarded privacy. She leaned in closer to him and whispered into his ear, "Relax now, don't keep it private anymore."

The sensation of her breath sent a shiver down his back.

Knowing it was the fastest way to chip away at his resolve to guard his thoughts, Tavis brushed her lips against his neck and trailed her fingertips up his back to the nape of his neck where they traced a few delicate circles.

Images began presenting themselves to her and she closed her eyes to concentrate on them. She saw herself being helped from the horse she'd been riding to Jack's horse and experienced what her own body felt like resting against his and how much he liked the feel of it.

"You remembered our ride back on the horses." She opened her eyes. "Why that memory?"

"I was amazed at how much I didn't want to let you go when we got back," he said. "I also thought of how my life would never be the same and that I didn't want it to be the same either. How were you able to see that? Do you know everything I'm thinking?"

"No, not everything, and not all the time. Compared to other people, you're unusually guarded with your thoughts."

"But you know what other people are thinking who aren't so guarded?"

"Yes." She nodded. "Where I come from, we can all do that, but it's different there. Everyone knows not to pry, and how to keep their thoughts private when they want them to remain so. But when you're not being so guarded, well, it's kind of like what happened when I told you to relax. You've been starting to sense my thoughts, haven't you noticed that?"

"I'm sure that's normal for married people."

"That's not the only reason. I'm thinking of something right now and I want you to see what it is." Tavis focused all her attention on one single memory and pushed it outward to him.

Jack studied her eyes and saw what she thought of. His gaze went to the pool of water at the base of the boulder. "Lani."

"Yes, I remembered you helping me give birth to Lani."

"I don't know, Tavis, this is hard for me to accept."

"Fine." She stood and loomed over him. "Let's up the ante, shall we?"

"Please don't be upset with me, I'm trying to understand."

"Look at me, Jack."

His eyes drifted away from the base of the boulder to her. Imperceptibly, Tavis disappeared right in front of him. He didn't trust what he saw so he looked around the boulder trying to find her, but she was nowhere to be found. Panic settled in and he jumped to his feet.

"Tavis! Where are you?"

"Right here," she said, uncloaking herself.

"How the hell…" He stared at her, disbelief and awe framed his expression.

"It's called cloaking, and probably one of the most coveted traits the scientists are trying to isolate. I can cloak other things besides just myself."

"You can?" Jack's mind raced to catch up, but still he thought there had to be a plausible explanation.

"Yeah, watch your reflection in the water." She leaned over to stare down into the lake.

Jack leaned with her and looked at their mirror images. When his reflection nodded, Tavis cloaked them both. The images disappeared as though they weren't still standing there. Jack gave a quick wave, nothing. A spit, which Tavis scowled at, produced nothing—save a ripple in the water that moved in slow-motion.

"My, God, how are you doing this?" Jack murmured.

"It's just messing around with time. Some people are really good at it where I come from."

"If someone came along, would they see us?"

"No, unless it was someone experienced with the ability. Even then, they couldn't see us, they'd only recognize a sphere of disruption." When Jack frowned at her, she added, "They'd know someone or something was being cloaked because of the odd appearance surrounding the person or object. It's mostly visual though, sound is harder to cloak. If someone came along that we didn't want seeing us, we'd have to be quiet or else risk them hearing our presence."

"This is amazing," he said. "If this is real, then I know why the government's interested."

"*If* this is real." Tavis resisted the urge to push him into the lake. "What else do I have to do to prove this is real?"

"I'm sorry, you have to know how hard this is to accept." Jack sighed. "You know how much I trust you, and I want to believe you." He smiled a little. "If it makes you feel any better, I'm more convinced than I was a few minutes ago."

Tavis considered dragging Jack back home and letting Sebastian show him a few things that would be more convincing. She dismissed the notion—the last thing she wanted was for her father to scare the hell out of him, and she was determined to convince Jack on her own.

"We can modify memories," she muttered like it left a bad taste in her mouth to say it.

"What?" He sounded horrified. "You can mess around with my memories?"

Tavis could empathize; it wasn't so long ago that her father had threatened her with memory modification. When someone stronger than you threatens you with the possibility, it makes you feel weak and oppressed. Memories are easily taken for granted until you're forced to lose them or have them changed into false ones. Of all her people's abilities, this was the one she liked the least and felt controls should be in place to prevent its abuse.

"Yes, I can do that, but I don't like using this ability. I can alter one, or more, of your memories. I can change them slightly so that you remember something else instead of actual events, or I can absorb them altogether so you have no memory at all of any given event. It's also possible to implant false memories."

"I don't like the sound of that."

"The usefulness of this ability can't be denied, but it's not to be taken lightly. In my opinion, changing someone's memories is like taking away their basic right to have them in the first place."

"Ya' think?" Jack scoffed.

"I can show it to you in a small way," Tavis said while contemplating an idea. "If you're willing, anyway."

"I don't know, Tavis."

"Let me explain my idea first."

"Go ahead."

"First, go get me a rock and a flower."

He blinked at her a few times. "You want a flower?"

"And a small rock."

Jack climbed down the boulder and looked around for rocks. After she dismissed several, he finally found one that met with her approval. He picked the first flower he saw, headed back up the boulder, and sat next to her.

"Did you need any toadstool?"

She had no idea what he meant, nor did she care; Tavis only wanted to get the deed over with. With the flower tucked behind her ear, she said, "Put the rock in your pocket."

He leaned over to shove the rock in his pocket. "Done," he said. "Tell me what you have in mind before you do anything, please."

"I'm gonna absorb this whole memory," she explained, "and the last thing you'll remember is telling me you don't like the idea. Then I'll tell you to check your pocket and you'll be confused to find a rock in it, you'll also be confused about the sudden appearance of a flower in my hair. I'll tell you that I already absorbed a memory from you and I'll offer to restore it. If I know you as well as I think I do, you'll probably demand I give it back immediately."

"Do it," he said.

"Are you sure?"

"Do it now, before I have a chance to think about it and change my mind."

Tavis took his warning to heart and snaked her arms around him. The memory was new and fresh in his mind, and Tavis had no problem finding the exact point in time she wanted to absorb his memories to. When she released him, his eyes went to the flower in her hair, confused by its presence.

It took a moment, but he remembered what he'd been about to say. "I don't know, Tavis," he said for the second time.

"Check your pocket," she said.

"What?"

"I want the rock you put in your left pocket."

Jack reached into his pocket and was surprised to find a rock; he was sure he hadn't put it there. Looking back at Tavis, he sensed what she was about to say.

"I absorbed a memory from you after you gave me permission to do it. I want you to let me give it back now," she said in a cautious manner.

"Yeah, I think you'd better do that," he said, just as cautiously.

Once again, Tavis grabbed hold of him. Since it was a small memory, and still recent, it took only seconds to restore it. When she released him, his eyes went back to the flower and then to the rock in his hand.

"The flower was in case I thought you had slipped the rock into my pocket earlier without my noticing." He looked at her. "Is that right?"

"Right."

"Thank you for finding a simple way of showing me. I agree, though, this ability is arguably more dangerous than the cloaking."

"I don't know about that." Tavis eyed their surroundings and considered the wisdom of showing him one more thing. "I can show you another one that you may be particularly interested in."

He thought of telling her he was done for the day, but curiosity laughed at him. "What is it?"

"The weather. We can influence it, but it isn't an easy thing to do and it's by no means a common ability. I'm not very good at it because I'm scared of it." She sighed and hoped he wouldn't want her to test it. "Some of us are more gifted than others with this kind of ability and experience seems to help keep it controlled. Also, individual use is highly restricted back home."

Jack's attention was catapulted to Tavis. In all the years he worked as a researcher, there was one thing that drove him almost insane at times trying to come up with an explanation for—the undeniable and inexplicable weather anomalies governing Gamma.

"Wait a minute. You can influence weather?"

"Some of us can, but like I said, I'm not very experienced with it."

"That freak storm we had recently, did you do that?"

"No."

"That storm was almost tropical in nature, and Gamma hasn't had a tropical system in over twenty years." Jack raised his eyebrows at her. "Who did it?"

"My father, he wanted to get Chaza back without being seen in the cameras."

"Impressive… don't tell him I said that." Jack thought of something. "You and Sebastian only just got here recently, who was influencing the weather before?"

Suddenly, Tavis was a clam. She didn't know she needed to be prepared to tell Jack about Alec as well. The intensity of Jack's interrogator's stare caused her to back up from him. He leaned in closer as she tried leaning farther away until he had to grasp her shoulders to prevent her retreat.

He peered into her eyes, insisting on knowing the answer. When they grew wide, he saw it reflecting back at him from the simplicity of blue irises—the same that belonged to only two other people on the island. Jack knew exactly who had been responsible for the beautiful-all-the-time weather.

"Of course." He loosened his grip on Tavis' arms. "Your twin brother, Alec."

He laughed at his discovery; finding it electrifying. After he'd given up trying to figure out the impossible weather patterns of the island, he finally found an explanation and under even more mystifying circumstances.

Tavis was shocked. "How did you know he's my brother?"

"He told me last night. By the way, your brother's a gnarly piece of work. I asked him what the connection was between you two when we went to the cave. The only thing that surprised me was finding out your mother is Kyrie."

"She doesn't know she's my mother, or that Sebastian's our father."

"I know." Jack snorted. "Alec made sure I understood that. Don't worry, I'm not gonna say anything to her, but I'm getting a little weary of all the secrets."

They sat on the boulder in silence for a while, looking out over the lake while Jack tried to sort through all he'd learned and seen.

Tavis leaned against his shoulder and was happy he allowed it, as she'd been terrified he would treat her differently.

"You can influence the weather, huh?"

"Um—"

"We'll keep it simple," he said. "Try making the wind blow a little harder."

Tavis looked at the sky, but stopped at worrying she may produce rain clouds. Instead, she looked at the trees and tried to imagine how they would look if they were bending in a slight breeze. Almost as soon as the thought formed, the wind picked up and after a moment, blew with an audible howl.

Concerned the trees were bending far more than what she pictured in her mind, Tavis glanced at the sky again and saw it darkening. She shut her influence down by closing her eyes and thinking of any and every thing that made her happy. When she opened them again, the trees were back to swaying in the typical island breeze and the newly formed clouds moved offshore.

"That was incredible," Jack said. "What do you think, did you like influencing the weather?"

"No, I didn't. I did it for you. I found it hard to control and it scared me." Tavis shuddered at the thought of uncontrollable weather and buried her face into his chest, trying to block the thought out.

A familiar protectiveness washed over Jack at seeing her reaction and he wrapped his arms around her, hoping to shield her from her own thoughts. "I'm sorry, I'll never ask you to do that again. We'll let Alec be in charge of the weather." He kissed the top of her head. "Come on, let's get back to our daughter."

~

They'd just made it back to the traveling lane when Jack asked, "Is there anything else you wanted to talk to me about?"

"A lot." Tavis grimaced at how much more they needed to talk about. "How about you ask me what you want to know?"

"Who else on Gamma is like you?"

"You already know about Alec and my father. Chaza. Meg is, too."

"Meg?"

"Chaza is Meg's real mother. She gave her to Ila to raise and altered her memories so Ila remembered giving birth to Meg."

"Who's Meg's father?"

"Joseph, Ila's fiancé."

"Oh!" Jack assumed that must be one of the betrayals Tavis had mentioned being part of the reason Chaza and Sebastian were separated. "Let me guess, neither Meg nor Ila know about it, right?"

"Right."

"Damn, I'm gonna need to hire a secretary to keep track of all the secrets for me."

"I've found it's best just to stay quiet in general," Tavis said.

"Well, that makes five of you. Anyone else?"

"Luke and Lani," she said. "That's all as far as I know."

"Lani will have the same abilities you have?"

"All of our children will. You, too, eventually." She chanced a quick peek at him to see what he thought of this.

"What?" He turned to her for an explanation.

"Watch where you're going!"

Jack narrowly missed hitting a tree before correcting his steering back onto the lane. Keeping his eyes focused in front of him, he considered what Tavis had said about him being like her *eventually*.

"How's that possible? With me, I mean."

"Our physicians call it assimilating, and it has a lot to do with bonds that form between people. It's more likely to happen than not."

"It's happened before?"

"Some people were taken from here a long time ago and brought to our home to see if they would form a bond with any of our people. The ones that did, assimilated over time."

"And the ones who didn't?"

"They were sent back here with their memories absorbed." Tavis had to close her eyes before she could say it. "They're not alive anymore, they all took their own lives."

"I've heard stories about the people who committed suicide on Gamma, it confused the scientists because it wasn't happening on Delta. Apparently, they freaked out trying to find a reason for it, but then it stopped happening."

"It stopped happening when the last one jumped off Mors Cliff. They did it because they couldn't escape the feeling that they'd missed out on a better life and that life here was meaningless compared to what they could've had, even if they couldn't remember it."

"That's a terrible story, Tavis."

"It's one our elders aren't proud of."

"*Elders?*" Jack found the reference archaic.

"Yeah, the younger ones like my father and Chaza, and the really old ones like everyone on our council."

Jack snorted. "Frank Doscher's an elder. Your father can't be more than…" Jack stopped the cart abruptly, sending Tavis forward. He put his arm out in front of her to keep her from hitting the windshield. "Exactly how old are Chaza and Sebastian?"

"Hmm, he gets all squirmy when I ask him that question." Tavis thought about it and shook her head. "There's the time difference, too, and the cloaking… especially the cloaking." She was muttering to herself now. "I don't even know how old I am here… I could be a hundred. Or ten. Ha! So weird."

"Tavis," he called her attention back.

"Oh, I don't know for sure. A few hundred years, maybe. But like I said, he won't give me a straight answer."

"Well, I'll be damned!"

"Jack."

"Sorry."

He drove the cart again, musing to himself over the new information and hoped it wouldn't make him view Sebastian differently. Jack rather liked their relationship and thought it would be a shame if things like manners and respect got in the way of him giving Sebastian a hard time once in a while.

They rode in silence for a few minutes while Jack contemplated what he wanted to ask next. "What was inside that pyramid you gave Alec?"

"Alec saw a three dimensional replica of our home. It's called an amulet and technically it's my father's, but he wanted Alec to have it. It does a lot of other stuff, too, as long as you have the key to it. For the time being, my father decided to hold on to it."

"It must have been beautiful, based on Alec's reaction," Jack said, fishing for more information.

Tavis smiled at his curiosity. "Think of everything you ever thought was beautiful and add them all together, it's even more beautiful than that."

"Sounds like you miss it."

"I do, very much. I'm looking forward to going back."

"That's the plan? To go back to your home?"

"Yes, Jack, that's always been the plan, ever since my father and I first arrived. The only thing that's different now is that I'll be taking something back with me, my family, you and Lani."

"Have you considered I may not *want* to go?"

"No, I haven't. Should I?"

They were in an uninhabited part of the island, the traveling lane surrounded by forests, when Jack stopped the cart a second time. Tavis had been waiting for his answer and saw fear form in his eyes; she followed the direction of his gaze. A maintenance worker was on a ladder leaned against one of the trees set back a ways in the forest, working on the wiring of a camera affixed to the trunk.

William Davis stood at the bottom of the ladder, dressed in more typical island attire. He was turning his head in the direction of what he thought was the sound of an approaching vehicle when Tavis cloaked the entire cart.

'Please, be very quiet. We're cloaked, but he can still hear us,' Tavis said silently.

Tavis needn't worry, Jack was frozen in his seat, watching William's perplexed expression as he looked up and down the lane for a cart. He walked out into the middle of the lane, and at one point was only a few feet from them. A menacing smile formed on his face and he gave up on his search.

"Okay, Ron, we're done here... for now," William said to the maintenance worker, but Jack knew it was an all-inclusive message.

After they left the area, Jack started the cart again and turned to Tavis. "I'd say that's a very useful ability."

"Yep."

When Jack pulled up in front of their house, he asked, "They're gonna know you told me, aren't they?"

"Yes, I told them I was before we left."

"Do you mind if I don't go in with you to get Lani?"

"No, I'll get her and meet you inside."

Tavis went over to Chaza's to retrieve Lani and related to them that she had told Jack. Before leaving, she said to Sebastian, "We're still talking it out, so I'll see you tomorrow and tell you how it all went."

~

Later, after they'd had dinner and put Lani in her crib, Tavis rested her head on Jack's chest as they lay in their bed. The evening had been quiet and lacked any real conversation between them. She feared Jack was having trouble accepting everything now that he'd had time to think about it.

"You never answered my question," she said.

"What you're wanting me to do is leave the only home I've ever known to follow you to a place I know absolutely nothing about. What if I were to ask you to stay here instead? We could have our family here."

"On Gamma?"

"Here, the mainland, wherever, just not your home."

Tavis' spirit deflated at his response. Tears threatened her, stinging her eyes, but she refused to give in to them—understanding that she'd have to pull herself and her demeanor together in a presentable fashion for him.

"Sure, Jack, if that's what you really want," was her only reply before she shut down the access to her true thoughts. She closed the bridge to his thoughts as well, deciding to let ignorance be bliss. For once in her life, she preferred the unawareness rather than trying to find out what made someone think what they did.

When Jack fell asleep, Tavis extricated herself from his arms and slipped away from their bed—she wanted nothing more than to hold Lani in her arms.

Jack found them in the early morning light, sleeping on the couch in the front room. It puzzled him that he'd slept the whole night through not noticing Tavis' absence.

Jack tried to lift Lani from Tavis' arms, thinking she may be hungry. Lani cried the second her contact with Tavis had broken and it confused him as this had never happened before. Tavis' eyes opened at the sound of Lani's distress and her arms shot up to seize her daughter from Jack.

"I just thought she might be hungry," he said.

Relaxing her face so she wouldn't cause him to think anything was wrong, she said, "There aren't any bottles in the refrigerator. I'll have to feed her myself."

A little while later, Jack tried to hold Lani again, but got the same response. She cried until Tavis took her into her arms again. The rest of the day brought similar results, it seemed his own daughter wanted nothing to do with him and he thought Tavis was unusually silent.

"What's going on?" Jack asked at dinner.

"We're having dinner."

"That's not what I mean." Jack had grown accustomed to being able to sense whatever Tavis was feeling and didn't realize how much he relied on it until now—when he was no longer able to.

"Then what do you mean?"

"I feel like something's wrong, so would you please just tell me what it is?" Jack shouted and slammed his fists against the table.

Tavis calmly put her fork down on her plate and stood from the chair. She said nothing as she walked away from the table and he watched her go down the hall and turn in to Lani's room. He assumed she was just checking on their daughter and would be right back, but then he saw the back door open on its own.

Jack got to his feet. The vision of the self-opening door confused him at first, then he realized Tavis had cloaked herself so she could leave unseen.

"Where the hell do you think you're going?" he yelled as the back door closed. He was already walking toward the hallway to follow her when the sound of the opening front door grabbed his attention.

"Sit down, Jack," Sebastian boomed and slammed the door closed. "I think it's time for us to have a talk."

"Now's not a good time, Sebastian."

"Oh, now's a perfect time. Don't worry about Tavis and Lani, they're going to visit with Chaza for a bit." Sebastian took a few steps closer to Jack. "You have two choices. You can sit down on your own, or I can force you. But either way, we will have that talk."

Jack felt miniscule in the looming shadow of Sebastian, and he had an eerie feeling the threat of being forcefully sat was on the cusp of happening. Wisely, Jack sat back down at the table to listen to what he had to say. Sebastian took the seat Tavis had vacated and pushed the plate aside.

"Thank you for not making me force you, Jack."

"What do you want to talk about?"

"It seems my daughter is distraught about something."

"And how would you know that?" He knew they could read thoughts, but from a different house?

"I've already told you once about the bond between a father and his daughter. Of course I'd know if my daughter was in pain."

"Pain?" Jack scoffed.

"That's what I said. Tavis has resolved herself to abandonment. Do you mind telling me why she feels this way?" Sebastian eyed Jack carefully and with purpose.

"I don't know why she feels that way, she's the one who left."

"Did you not ask her to stay here with you instead of returning to her home?"

"Did you get that from your bond, too?"

"No. I got that just now, from your own head."

"What's so wrong with her deciding to stay here?"

"Tavis would never agree to stay here because this island is doomed. Management will likely order Gamma's destruction the second they realize we've escaped. She'd never agree to stay anywhere else on this planet because death and destruction is the common denominator everywhere, not just on these pathetic islands."

"But—"

"Nope, I'm not finished yet." Sebastian stared Jack into obedient silence. "The pain she's experiencing comes from thinking she'll have to leave you behind. Tavis knows she could never be happy if she stayed here, even with you by her side. However, she formed a bond with you and whenever it feels like that bond is broken there will always be sadness. It won't be long before we have to leave Gamma. Like you, we also hid our transportation when we arrived. Great minds think alike, don't we, Jack?"

"Yeah, I guess we do," Jack muttered.

Sebastian got up from the chair and went around the table to stand next to Jack. His hand flattened on Jack's shoulder. What seemed like an eternity to Jack passed before Sebastian spoke again.

"Tell me, Jack, is Tavis to go home without you? Is Lani to go home without her father?"

"No, of course not, and you know that. You know better than anyone what will happen to me if I let her go," Jack said, staring at the plate in front of him.

"Do you love Tavis and Lani?"

"More than I've ever loved anything."

"Then you're right, what you're thinking is exactly your fate if you try to live a life without her." Sebastian removed his hand from Jack's shoulder and walked to the door.

"Wait," Jack called. "If I'd have given you a different answer, you were gonna absorb my memories, weren't you?"

"Great minds, Jack," Sebastian repeated. He opened the door, adding before he left, "Try not to upset my daughter again, I might not be as friendly the next time."

20

Margaret Arcana

"So, what was it you saw in here?" Meg held the pyramid up to her eye and squinted through one of the sapphires.

Alec was almost asleep on the couch in their front room when she spoke. He opened his eyes and saw her standing by the fireplace mantel where he'd put the amulet. Though he was still tired from the late night out, and somewhat hung over, Meg was wide awake.

"Pretty stuff," Alec said, yawning. "You can only see it in certain light. I'll show you tonight, the moon will still be bright enough. Come here and let's be lazy spoons on a couch."

Meg set the amulet back on the mantel and made her way over to the couch. Alec scooted over so she could lay down beside him.

"Do you like the painting there?" Meg pointed to the wall opposite them where she'd hung it earlier. "Or would you rather I hang it somewhere else, like in one of the bedrooms?"

"I think it's perfect where it is. Don't you?"

"Yeah," she said. "I just wanted to hear you say it."

"Oh, you did, did you?" Alec tickled Meg's sides, making her laugh and squirm.

"No!" she squealed through her laughter.

He stopped and settled her back down in his arms. "Where's Luke?"

"Taking a nap."

"I'm jealous."

"Shut up." Meg elbowed his side. "Did you enjoy your birthday?"

"It was very nice, thank you for making it so special." Alec kissed her cheek and buried his face in her soft hair.

"You're welcome. It was Tavis' idea, though."

"When you see her again, tell her I said thank you." He closed his eyes and snuggled Meg closer to him.

"Alec?"

"Hmm?"

"I was wondering about something. Do you think it's possible you and Tavis are related somehow?"

His eyelids popped open. Though his body had been relaxed, he tensed at her question. Meg rolled over and looked into his eyes. Her questioning expression, with just a hint of suspicion, told him he wasn't going to be able to put it off any longer.

Maybe it's time, he thought to himself.

"Time for what?" she asked.

Shocked, Alec's eyes widened. At least about some things, it was definitely time to have a talk with Meg.

"Did it occur to you that you just asked me a question about something I was only thinking about?"

"I guess." She shrugged. "It's happened before, but I don't really think about it as much as I used to."

"You've thought about it before? Why haven't you asked me about it?"

Meg heard the frustration in his voice and it worried her. "Because that's how it's always been, ever since we were kids. I never question you about these kinds of things. I thought you knew that, I thought that was what you wanted."

"I do know that, but that was when it was about me. I'm talking about *you* now. This is something you're doing, not me."

"Alec, I'm sorry if I upset you. Forget I said anything."

She tried to snuggle up to him, but he put his hand on her shoulder to prevent it. Their eyes locked and he saw her worry turn to fear. He focused on calming his voice and said, "We can't forget it. I'm not upset with you, I want to help you."

"Help me do what?"

"I want to help you understand. I've been waiting for you to ask me questions and I want to answer them, but you have to ask first."

"I don't know what questions I'm supposed to ask," she said, flustered.

"What's the first question that comes to mind?"

"How about the first one I asked?" Meg rolled her eyes. "The one about you and Tavis."

He grimaced at the idea of explaining his connection to Tavis right away. "Okay, maybe not that one. I'd rather not get into that just yet. Ask me something about yourself, something you might be curious about."

"All right, why did I hear your thought? Why do I hear a lot of your thoughts? Are you making it happen? And what exactly did you mean by *maybe it's time*?"

"There ya' go, those are the questions I've been hoping you'd ask." Alec smiled at her. He wanted her to feel comfortable, and more importantly, accepting. "You've always known I'm different from everyone else, right?"

"Yes."

"Well, you're different, too. You're like me." Alec waited to see how she would react to this; she said nothing, so he continued. "I've always been able to sense your thoughts and pretty much everybody else's. You're able to do that, too, and you've probably already noticed it lately. And no, I'm not making it happen."

"Why am I just now noticing it?"

"Because your abilities, the things that make you so different, were only just recently given back to you… the night Luke was born."

She thought back to that night. Most of it was a blur, but she remembered wanting to give up. She remembered Chaza and Alec being there and with their help, she'd been able to continue.

It occurred to her that ever since then, she'd been noticing things about herself and everyone around her that she'd never paid attention to before. Unable to come up with an explanation for it, she just assumed it was Alec's doing.

"To say that it was given back to me would imply that I'd lost it at some point. I don't recall ever being like you, or different in any way."

"You didn't lose it," Alec said. "It was taken from you. All of the things that made you different were absorbed from you when you were a child."

"Who took it from me?" she asked in a whisper, feeling she already knew the answer, but that it lurked in a memory just out of reach.

"I could show you, if you want. I could show you the memory of how it happened."

"Yes, I want to see it." Meg put away her fears, wanting to learn more about the things unknown to her—she had a hunch it was long overdue.

Alec pulled her tight against him. Although it wasn't necessary, he formed a sphere around them before showing her the memory. It had happened so long ago and he wanted her to see every detail of that day. He paused to enjoy her wide-eyed awe at seeing the shimmering sphere.

Because he didn't look forward to what may come next, he stared deep into her eyes and said, "Please try to understand that all I've ever wanted is for you to be safe. I'm asking for your forgiveness now if you see something that upsets you."

"Show me," was her only reply.

He recalled the memory of that entire day when he had absorbed her abilities. Beginning when he and Kyrie had arrived for Meg's birthday party and ending it after Ila scooped Meg up from the barn floor.

When the memory was over, Alec allowed the sphere to dissolve and he waited for Meg's response—hoping she wouldn't be disgusted with him for what he'd done. Instead, her expression was blank, as though still processing what she'd seen. Trying to sort through her thoughts came to nothing. Her continued silence scared him and he feared the worst.

"Meg, please, tell me you don't hate me."

Finally, he saw a flicker of emotion in her eyes. Though it wasn't pure hatred, whatever else it may be was carefully controlled.

"That entire memory was from your perspective," she said. "Did you know that? Did you know that I'd be able to sense the thoughts and emotions you'd had as well?"

He hadn't thought of that, but she was right and it left him with no choice but to tell her everything. "I do now," he mumbled.

"It scared you to find out I was like you, and you didn't want whoever was watching to find out about me, too. That was your main purpose for taking away who I was, right?"

"Yes, you got that part right."

"You swore you'd always protect me," she said, recalling from his memory. "And you have." Meg's eyes narrowed. "*Maybe it's time* for you to relax a little on that promise. At least long enough to tell me why you were so afraid to let me be different. Who were you scared of? Who was watching you, Alec?"

"You already know about management," he said, it was a weak and watered-down offer. "Everyone knows about them, even if we don't talk about them."

"They were the ones you thought were watching you? Management?"

"They weren't the only ones watching."

"Who else?" Meg demanded.

"People who weren't approved to be here." Alec frowned, not knowing how to explain it to her without revealing who Sebastian and Chaza really were. "They were watching over certain people that were important to them, like me, and you, and…"

"And?"

"Well, and Luke, too… now. He's only a baby, but he'll be different."

"Are we the only ones?" She saw his hesitation. "Don't you dare lie to me. Considering what you did to me, you owe me, and I want the truth, Alec."

"There are a few others who are different, like us."

"So, that brings us back to my original question." Meg's voice took on a steely edge. "Is it possible that you and Tavis are related?"

"Yes, Meg, Tavis and I are related." Alec let out a defeated sigh at realizing he couldn't share only selected parts of what he wanted to share with her—it was all too interconnected. "She's my sister."

"I knew it!" She sounded like she'd won a victory, the menacing edge in her voice more pronounced. "How long have you known? How long have you been keeping this a secret?" Her confidence and courage grew exponentially, but it was apparent she lacked the experience to control it.

"Meg," he murmured, hoping to calm her down, "I haven't known for very long, neither has Tavis."

Her eye's widened. "Tavis knows, too?"

"Yes."

"Exactly how are you two related?" The question seemed more directed to herself. Meg was putting the obvious genetic pieces together and when she paired the right ones, she scrambled off the couch. Looming over him, she stared at him in wonderment and said, "Oh, my God! Sebastian's your father. I'm an idiot, how could I have missed it? Look at you." She waved her arms at him. "You look just like him."

Her eyes had a wild appearance, almost like an untamed animal trying to free itself from captivity. Alec got to his feet and reached for her, but she pushed him away.

"Meg! Stop it." He tried reaching for her again, but she dodged him.

"Absolutely not, I'm just getting started," she spat. "Why are we different, or should I ask, *how* are we different?"

"I think that's enough for now. We can talk more about it later, after you've had a chance to absorb what I've already told you."

"*Absorb*? Really, Alec?" Meg scoffed at his poor choice of words. "How about I *absorb* some more answers out of you. Let's see how you like it."

Two things happened when she advanced on Alec: the sound of Luke's cries penetrated the room, seeming to reverberate off of every wall in the house; the other was the sudden and urgent banging on the front door. Meg appeared torn between her focus on Alec, Luke's crying, and the unceasing clamoring on the door.

Alec wondered who would be so adamant to have their knocking acknowledged and went to take a step toward the door, but Meg blocked him.

"Fine," he said. "Then you get the door. I'm gonna check on Luke."

He was halfway down the hall when Meg came at him. The sphere she had created was mere inches from him when the front door was thrown open, flooding the room with daylight. Both Alec and Meg turned to face the intruder, and he glimpsed the fading sphere she'd meant for him before it dissolved.

Chaza stood in the doorway, wearing a stern business-like expression. She strode into the front room, her eyes sparking fierceness as she glared back and forth between them.

"Alec," Chaza said, but kept her eyes locked on her daughter now. "Go see about Luke while Meg and I have a nice visit. A walk sounds like a good idea."

He backed up slowly, reluctant to turn his back. Meg glanced at him before turning to deal with their uninvited visitor. Soon as he saw Meg approaching Chaza, he swiftly made his way into Luke's room, leaving the two of them alone.

"Chaza, as always, I'm so happy to see you," Meg said pleasantly enough, but it was forced. "Unfortunately, I'm a little busy at the moment."

"Alec can handle taking care of Luke."

"I'm not feeling very well," Meg lied.

"Then some fresh air will do you good."

"I really don't want to." Meg did a lousy job of keeping the irritation out of her voice, the false civility gone and forgotten.

"And I really don't care, put your shoes on. Now!"

Meg was shocked by the unexpected command at first, but quickly recovered. "I think it's time for you to leave, please see yourself out," she dismissed and turned to go down the hall, ready to pick up where she left off with Alec.

"You can put your shoes on, or go barefoot," Chaza said. "Whatever works for you, but we are going for a walk."

The retreat down the hall came to a halt, and after a few seconds, Meg turned around. Through narrowed eyes, she looked at Chaza in a different way, and then a crooked smile spread across her face. Meg sauntered back into the front room and stood in front of Chaza, staring into her eyes, but her anger wouldn't allow her to see more than what she wanted to see.

"Oh, I get it now."

"Really? What do you get?" Chaza asked.

"You're different, too. I suppose Alec already knows that, right?"

"He does."

"Seems like my husband keeps a lot of secrets."

"Only to protect you."

"You know what? I'm about done with everyone being under the assumption that I need protecting. I can't tell you enough how sick I am of hearing it."

Ignoring her daughter's sinister mood, Chaza inhaled a steadying breath. "It's time for you to learn everything you have a right to know, but you don't have the right to extract that information from Alec the way you were about to before I showed up. You would've caused yourself a great deal of pain by hurting him that way. Your son sensed it, that's why he started crying, he was trying to stop you."

The hardened expression on Meg's face melted, usurped by a frown when she comprehended Chaza's words. It was true, Luke had only just gone to sleep and it wasn't like him to wake up so soon. A horrible pain sliced through Meg's chest as she caught on to the fact that she'd caused Luke's distress. Though her tears were instant, they fell silently down her cheeks.

Chaza worked through her own pain, brought on by Meg's tears. She guided Meg to a chair to help her into some shoes. Meg sat pliant, still coming to terms with her guilt, still crying—chin quivering. When Chaza finished tying the laces, she wiped Meg's cheeks dry.

"Let's go for that walk now," Chaza said. "Alec and Luke will be fine."

~

Chaza led Meg to the edge of the forest. "I want to take you somewhere, but it's located in the densest part of the forest. To get there faster, I'm going to hold your hand while we walk and I want to warn you that it won't feel like normal walking. Okay?"

"Okay."

After taking her hand, Chaza formed a sphere around them. It was similar to the one Alec had made, but Meg noticed a slight difference in color. Whereas Alec's was more opaque, Chaza's had an iridescent quality. She barely had a chance to study the colors before they began to move and it was unlike any kind of moving Meg had ever experienced.

Through the sphere, she saw the trees weren't swaying in the wind and on one limb she saw a bird perched, unnaturally motionless. Chaza veered to the left to avoid hitting a butterfly that appeared frozen in mid-air. Yet, everything stuck in stillness moved by so quickly, Meg had no time to try making sense of the odd visions.

They came to a sudden stop and the sphere dissolved simultaneously. The breeze began blowing through the trees again and motion took on its normal speed once more.

"Here it is, my most favorite place on this entire island," Chaza said proudly.

Beyond the trees up ahead, Meg saw an explosion of colors. They seemed to be beckoning her to come closer so they could spend time together again. She stepped forward, past the trees, and stood at the edge of an immense and beautiful flower garden—she closed her eyes to feel the warmth and strange familiarity.

Opening her eyes again, she walked to the middle of the garden, turning around in all directions to take in the wonderful colors so vividly displayed—the very same colors she tried to achieve in her paintings.

"You're appreciating the colors, aren't you?" Chaza asked.

"More than you know," she whispered, more to herself. Her eyes fell to the blue hydrangeas in front of her. "Is this where you got the hydrangeas you gave me?"

Chaza smiled. "Yes."

"You said they were growing wild." Meg turned to her. "Doesn't look that way to me."

"It's a different kind of wildness than what you thought I meant."

"What other kind is there?"

"The kind that comes from the gardener."

"Is this your garden? Did you plant all these flowers here?"

"I did, a long time ago."

"Are you saying you have a wildness about you?" Meg watched her carefully.

"Sort of." Chaza grinned at the scrutiny. "It's the kind of wildness that comes from desperately wanting to do something with yourself besides thinking about the sadness in your life."

Meg continued along the garden path until she reached the source of the sound she'd been hearing since first arriving. It was a fountain, similar to the one Jack had made for Tavis, but there were several differences. Chaza's was smaller and absent a waterfall, yet it had something even more spectacular than mere falling water.

There was a pool of water at the base and several streams shot upward from the crystal blue pool, ignoring the laws of gravity. Stones had been piled up to form a wall at the back that curved just enough at the top to create an overhang for streams of water to cascade down. From the two sides of the structure, individual streams shot out horizontally.

The streams of water, each shooting out from all four directions, formed a woven pattern in mid-air without creating a disturbance in any single rivulet. The flow of the water was flawless, exquisite, and impossible in Meg's opinion.

"You made all of this to keep from thinking about something that made you sad?"

"I had a baby once, but I had to give her away. I felt it was the best thing to do for her and myself, even though it was hard for me to give her away to another woman to raise as her own. That was when I started working on this garden."

"You have a daughter?" Meg frowned at the surprising revelation. "Where?"

"She's here, on this island."

"You had to watch another woman raise your child?" There was disgust in Meg's tone and it caused Chaza to turn away from her. "I'm sorry, I didn't mean to be insensitive. I was just imagining what it would feel like watching someone else raise Luke."

"Don't apologize," Chaza said, staring at the trees.

"We don't have to talk about it anymore."

"Yes we do," Chaza whispered, but it was loud enough that Meg heard.

The hairs on the back of Meg's neck stood on end. There was something in the whisper that hinted at a bigger event on the horizon of their conversation. Meg walked away from her, and from the nagging thoughts that emerged in her mind. She sat on a stone bench near the fountain, knowing Chaza would join her soon.

"There's something you want me to know," Meg said when Chaza came to sit by her.

"That's why I brought you here, but I'd rather show you than tell you. I know Alec showed you his memory of when he absorbed your abilities, I can sense it in your own memories now. I want to show you something else, in the same way."

"That didn't turn out so well," Meg said, her face burning with shame. "As you clearly saw."

"You were being overwhelmed with information. It's too much, too quickly, but I'm afraid it's also necessary now. Things are about to change on Gamma, and not in a good way. What I want to show you may cause you to have similar feelings to what you had with Alec earlier, but I'll help you through it. Are you ready?"

"No," Meg answered honestly.

"This can't go on any longer, Margaret Meg."

Meg wondered how Chaza knew what her birth name was. "Go ahead, show me." She closed her eyes and waited for the onslaught of memories.

The first she saw were of Chaza, looking the same way she did before Meg closed her eyes, but she was smiling and laughing with someone. Then she saw a man; he laughed, too, at something Chaza had said. They were in the cave at the top of the cliff and they were both drinking from the bottles of wine. Meg recognized the man right away as her father, Joseph, from the photographs Ila had given her.

"You knew my father?" Meg asked, breaking the sphere Chaza had created.

"Yes, I knew Joseph, but please don't interrupt me again," Chaza said, the warning was gentle.

"I'm sorry, I won't do it again."

The next memory Meg saw confused her. It was still of Chaza and Joseph laughing together in the cave, but there was a new intensity that strained their conversation. The smiles vanished and were replaced with strong desire. A scene flashed where the two of them were embraced and kissing, pushing and tugging at each other's clothes. Just as Joseph guided Chaza to the cave floor, there was a blinding light and then the memory shifted to another scene.

The memory was of Chaza, lying alone on a bed, panting as she gathered her strength to push through the pain one more time. At last, she pulled the crying newborn up to her chest and rested back against the pillows.

Tears of happiness ran down Chaza's cheeks as she looked into the face of her baby. Meg watched her wipe the baby clean and nurse her for the first time. She was amazed at how quickly Chaza seemed to recover from giving birth when she cleaned herself and changed clothes.

Meg heard Chaza hum to her baby and it was a melody she'd heard Alec hum to her and Luke—the same as what came from the amulet on the beach. Chaza's tears of happiness became tears of sadness while she continued to hum and stare into the face of her baby.

A pain born of sympathy weighed heavily on Meg's chest as she watched the scene unfold between mother and child. The memory faded into a different one and Chaza was in the cave again, talking to a woman—Ila. Meg listened intently to this conversation.

"Would you like to hold her?"

"Yes, I would."

Meg watched Chaza hand her baby to Ila. The emotions Meg began experiencing were almost more than she could stand. She wanted to dissolve the sphere again and run away, run all the way home and beg Alec to forgive her for acting so horribly toward him, but she had told Chaza she wouldn't interrupt the memory again.

She listened to the rest of their conversation and heard Ila agree to take the baby and raise her as her own. Ila had even agreed to have her memories absorbed and allowed Chaza to give her false ones.

The last memory Chaza showed her was of how difficult it was for her to change Ila's memories; to relinquish her right as Meg's mother and hand it over to someone else—then finally running out of the cave as though so much depended on it.

The memory dissolved into blackness and the sphere dissolved after it. Meg still wanted to run away and she couldn't bring herself to look into Chaza's eyes.

"All that I know is a lie," Meg said and buried her face into her hands.

Chaza wrapped her arms around Meg's shoulders and pulled her close. "Not everything. All that really matters is that you and Alec love each other. You chose each other and Luke is proof of that. That much is true and nothing will ever change it."

Meg took her hands away from her face and rested them in her lap. "You're my mother, not Ila?"

"Yes, Meg, I'm your mother."

"Why did you give me away?"

"I did what I thought was best for you, and you have no idea how hard it was for me. What you felt through my memories doesn't begin to do it justice. It wasn't easy for me to let you go, so I left the only home I've ever known just to be here, to watch you and protect you."

"To protect me? You sound like Alec." Meg moved away from Chaza.

"It's true, though. I've been hiding on this island since you were born, watching to make sure you were safe from everything and anyone that could or would hurt you. I watched your relationship with Alec from the beginning and I should tell you, he almost suffered my wrath when he threw that rock at your head."

"You were there?"

"Of course I was there. Alec didn't show that to you because he wasn't aware of my presence in the barn. Alec was young, he had no hope of detecting my presence back then. In fact, he still can't, but that isn't unusual. I'm particularly gifted at being able to avoid detection."

"Were you angry that Alec absorbed who I am?"

"Only for a second," Chaza admitted. "His thinking was for you to appear ordinary in management's opinion. There's very real potential for children with unique gifts to be taken away, forever."

"I understand, but I still feel like it was wrong for him to do that."

Chaza raised her eyebrows. "I can tell." When Meg frowned, Chaza added, "Sometimes people make decisions that seem reasonable at the time and only later can we see that there were other options."

"So, all my life, you've been watching me?"

"Yes," she said. "Well, that is until your relationship with Alec progressed into something more. That was difficult for me to accept."

Meg tried to hide her embarrassment, but the red on her cheeks gave her thoughts away. She changed the subject. "In the memory of the conversation you had with Ila, you mentioned your husband. Was that… is…" She was unsure, but suspicious enough of the possibility. "Sebastian?"

"Yes."

"That's kind of hard to imagine."

Chaza laughed softly. "We've been separated for a long time."

"Do you still love him?"

"Part of me will always care for him."

"Did you leave him because of me?"

"I had already left him before I became pregnant with you."

"But I'm sure getting pregnant with another man's child took reconciliation off the table."

"Reconciliation was never a possibility," Chaza said. "I left him because we had a lot of problems in our marriage."

"Did those problems have anything to do with Kyrie?"

"In some ways, but our relationship was already strained when Kyrie became pregnant with Alec and Tavis."

"They're twins." Meg shook her head in disbelief. "I feel like I should've known."

"I'll tell you what I told Alec, you weren't looking for it." Chaza sighed. "You need to know that Kyrie has no idea that Tavis is her daughter, nor that Sebastian's their father. She still thinks William Davis is Alec's father and she needs to keep thinking that until—"

Chaza worried that she may be telling Meg more than what Alec intended for her to know. Unfortunately, so many of the details were linked and it wasn't easy leaving out some parts while telling Meg others. Also, she was still concerned about Alec's position on leaving, knowing he was in turmoil over it.

Meg's eyes narrowed at the abrupt stop. "Until what?"

"Until it's time to go." Chaza decided that Meg had a right to know and that it would be irresponsible to keep hiding information this important from her, no matter what Alec may think of it.

"To go where?" Meg scoffed. "No one leaves Gamma. Not without approval and that's very rare, I assure you."

"We can. We have the means and the know-how to leave this island and go home."

"But this is my home."

"I meant *my* home, where I came from. As my daughter, it's your home, too."

"But—"

Meg had trouble imagining living her life anywhere but on Gamma. She thought of Alaret Beach and how much she would miss it; she thought of the stone house she and Alec had worked on to make a home. Then there were the people she'd never get to see again.

Chaza sensed every one of the thoughts as they formed in Meg's mind.

"Leaving anything, leaving anyone, or any place, whether you love it or hate it, is never easy. It can be the most difficult thing to do in life, but there are no choices this time, you'll have to leave Gamma. It's not safe here anymore."

"Why not?"

"William Davis is a member of management, he was only pretending to be an inhabitant when he was married to Kyrie. He's been seen back here and he's fixing all the surveillance cameras so they'll function again. Sebastian thinks our presence here has been discovered and that they'll try to prevent us from leaving."

"Then maybe we should stay," Meg said. "Maybe they'll leave us alone after they see that we're not going anywhere."

"It's beyond that kind of simplicity, they'll never leave you at peace now. They know we're different and they want to exploit it. If you can imagine what that means and what it entails, then you'd be wrong. It would be much worse than that." This time her warning wasn't as gentle, but not exactly threatening.

"But what about my mo—" Meg caught herself. It dawned on her for the first time that Ila wasn't her mother.

"I'm sorry for what this is doing to you."

Meg's shoulders slackened with the heavy burden of the new knowledge she now carried. "I want to go back to Alec, please."

Chaza concentrated all of her attention onto Meg, wanting to make sure she'd calmed down enough before taking her back home. It appeared that Meg was only weary from all she'd been told and that all she wanted was to be comforted by Alec.

"I can tell what you're doing," Meg said. "You don't have to worry, I'll never try to do that to Alec again. I only hope I can convince him of that."

"If you mean it, he'll know." Chaza patted Meg's hand. "Before I take you back, is there anything you want to know?"

There was one nagging question still lingering, begging to be asked. "If we leave, what will happen to this island and the people on it?" Meg stared hard into Chaza's eyes, waiting for a truthful answer whether she gave it or not.

"Why do you ask that question?"

"I've been seeing strange images, I think I'm seeing them from Alec. They're horrible scenes of people screaming in agony because they're all dying. I haven't asked him about it yet, but I'm going to unless you tell me first."

"Gamma's not the only island. There's another just like this one, with people living on it. There were two others initially, but management destroyed them because they weren't happy with the results. Sebastian showed Alec the chaos of the first island's destruction so he'd understand the reality that this island faces. If Alec's still thinking about it enough for you to see the images, it must be bothering him a great deal."

"Is it a reality for this island if we leave?"

"Most likely." Chaza frowned. "No matter what we do, even if we stay put, there's always the potential for management to destroy Gamma."

"Have you seen those images?"

"Yes, but don't ask me to show you, because I'll refuse."

"I wasn't planning on it," Meg said, dismissing the notion of seeing more. "Besides, I saw enough through Alec's dreams."

"You mean through his *thoughts*, not dreams." Chaza shook her head. "Even we aren't capable of seeing someone's dreams."

"Right." Meg felt it better to let the matter drop.

"How about we walk back normally?" Chaza asked, smiling.

Meg stood from the bench and took a few steps, but stopped in front of a rosebush in full bloom. She stared at the deep-red color of the petals and leaned closer, looking for something that tried to escape her memory—but even if it did, it wouldn't stop her from tearing the bush apart if she had to. Her hands reached out to grab the stems and then she saw it; the dried end of a stem where a rose had been carelessly plucked away. She remembered being here with Drake.

Chaza watched her curiously, wondering why Meg was so enthralled with the rosebush. She tried sensing her thoughts, but a sudden wall erected itself and refused entry. Chaza frowned at this new oddity and asked, "Meg, have you been here before?"

Smiling, she plucked one of the roses and turned to Chaza. "No."

She was happy to have remembered a little. Usually, every memory of Drake escaped full realization and somehow she knew to keep even the fragments a secret from everyone. Meg was thankful for the knowledge of who she truly was and happier still about having her abilities restored—none more so than the ability to keep her thoughts private. She brought the rose close to her face and inhaled its fragrance. A beautiful warmth filled her and she closed her eyes to savor it, to feel the light burst forth from her every cell.

"No, Meg!"

Meg opened her eyes and her light vanished as she stared at Chaza, noting the usual reserve and formidable countenance was now tangled with fear.

She stepped closer to Meg and gripped her shoulders. "Don't ever do that again. Not here, not while you're still on this island. Do you understand me?"

"Okay," Meg said.

Chaza let go of Meg and relaxed, but was still somewhat nervous. "Have you ever done that before?"

Meg shielded the lie before saying, "No."

"We should go, it's a long walk."

~

They were almost back to the stone house when Chaza saw Meg twirling the pearl ring between her fingers. She remembered watching over Alec while he dove day after day searching for the perfect pearl to give Meg on her birthday. It wasn't until after Chaza flagged an oyster containing a pearl that would meet with his approval did he stop his diving.

"I gave you your name," Chaza said. "I suppose you already know it means pearl."

"Why did you pick Margaret?"

"Because of my name and what it means, but I also happen to like the name Margaret, don't you?"

"Yes, I like my name. What's yours mean?"

"Chaza means oyster." She and Meg laughed.

When they got to the stone house, Chaza was comfortable leaving Meg at the front door, knowing she'd never attempt to force her will on Alec again—an act considered unforgivable between a husband and wife in Chaza's home.

After opening the door, Meg spotted Alec sitting on the couch waiting for her to return; worry framed his face. When he saw her in the doorway, relief melted away the frown. Though she didn't know what to expect from him, she was glad to know he was relieved to see her. She shut the door quietly and went to him.

Alec saw a look of anguish in her eyes, and then she fell to the floor at his feet. Meg wrapped her arms around his legs and started sobbing—the behavior shocked Alec.

"Alec, please forgive me," she sputtered out between sobs, burying her face against his knees.

Her misery was causing his own hell. "Meg, stop it." Alec tried encouraging her to get up, but she continued crying and slumped lower still. "I SAID, STOP!"

Meg sat back, startled by his outburst. He stood, yanking her up with him, and grabbed her shoulders. Hoping to get her attention, he gave them a slight shake.

"Don't you ever bow down to anyone."

"But you know what I tried to do to you," she said, her eyes still wet with tears.

"And what? Is that worse than what I did to you?"

Her gaze fell to his chest as she took in his words, and while other words echoed in her thoughts, *'He stole from me…'*

She found strength in the rose still clutched in her hand. "You were just a kid trying to protect me then. Today, I was only trying to protect myself," she said, almost trance-like.

"You never would've felt that way if I hadn't taken away your true identity."

"Then we're equal in our mistakes and intentions, maybe we should work on never making the same mistakes again."

"I like that plan." Alec released his hold on her shoulders. "How much do you know now?"

"A lot more than I did," she said. "Where's Luke?"

"I got him back to sleep after you left with Chaza."

"He was trying to protect you from me."

"I'll thank him later," Alec said and chuckled softly.

Meg smiled and put her arms around him. He smelled a sweet scent of flowers and wondered where she had gone to with Chaza.

"I'll take you there soon," she said.

Alec sighed inwardly—she was still not aware of when he actually spoke or when he was only having a thought. "How was your talk with Chaza?"

"She told me a lot of things, Alec." Her voice sounded weary again.

"You could just show me, if you want to."

She nodded and allowed the memory of her conversation with Chaza to flow from her mind to his. Afterward, she noticed a great deal of the burden had lifted from her.

"I imagine you want to know what Sebastian and I talked about, right?"

"You could just show me, if you want to." Meg glanced up at him.

Laughing, Alec said, "Yeah, I could do that."

He not only showed her the conversation he had with Sebastian, but all of his memories he thought she should know about. Save one, and she noticed.

"Why did you leave out what you saw in the pyramid?"

"Because I want you to see it for yourself."

~

Later in the evening, when the moon was at its highest point in the sky, Alec and Meg took the amulet outside. They stood under the oak tree and he handed it to her.

"Walk farther out, away from the tree and look through the sapphires," he said.

He watched with curious patience as she walked with the amulet to the very edge of their yard. She held it up above her head, letting the light from the moon shine down on it, causing the sapphires to illuminate.

Meg brought the amulet closer to her face to peer inside of it. Alec couldn't see her face and hoped she would allow him to sense her thoughts. She did. He saw her looking at what he had witnessed and he sensed her desire to know more.

"Oh, Alec! Is that where we come from?"

Alec went over to Meg and stood behind her. "That's where Sebastian, Tavis, and Chaza come from," he corrected.

She lowered the amulet and turned around to look at him. "You're not ready to call it your home yet, are you?"

"No."

"Are you thinking we should stay?"

"No."

"Then what *are* you thinking?"

"I don't know yet, Meg. Maybe we should just go somewhere else, try to get to the mainland somehow."

"We don't have to make any decisions tonight." She handed the amulet back to him. "Though I have to say, what I just saw was pretty amazing."

"Is it more amazing than all of the people here?" he asked. "Is it worth all their lives?"

21

The Meeting

William Davis sat at the desk in the surveillance room watching the camera monitors. He'd seen Meg reemerge from the forest with the unknown female islander. More than ever, he wished they could equip audio with the cameras, but the wind coming off the ocean made it impossible.

He looked at the clock and groaned as he pushed the chair away from the desk—he had less than an hour to get back to Digamma. After grabbing his briefcase, he ran the entire length of the bunkers to the main entrance. While descending the staircase to his boat, he took note of the water level in the cave and figured he had plenty of time to get back once the meeting was over.

With the boat in full throttle, William sped off out of the cave, as this was one meeting he didn't want to miss. The scientists had finally agreed to sit down to a meeting with management and they were notorious for trying to avoid any and all of them. The truth was that neither of the groups liked each other and viewed one another as a necessary evil. Only the threat of acting without their input made the scientists agree to attend.

William looked back at the island when he'd gained a considerable amount of distance from it, trying to imagine it not there, but he couldn't because he was especially fond of Gamma. Thinking of its destruction disturbed him more than it should, and more than he cared to admit.

Delta was fine enough, but William thought of Gamma as his personal project—his baby. He considered the layout of the island to be the most spectacular and beautiful of the original four. The mystery surrounding it after its creation added all the more intrigue for him.

Gamma was the third island created that brought with it a strange anomaly, an unexplainable stone structure. Somehow or another, they came with the creation of the islands. Neither the scientists nor management were ever able to find a geological explanation for their existence.

And without a doubt, Gamma's was the quaintest of them all.

After they ran tests on the structures, that produced nothing conclusive, they considered destroying them. It was William who talked Eldridge out of it by arguing they could run tests in the future if more information became available. In the interest of science, of course, they agreed to leave the structures standing.

It was the first of many victories concerning the decisions made about the islands, Gamma in particular. Unfortunately, he lost a few along the way. The one that bothered him most was when he was forced to leave Gamma after he'd been living there as one of the inhabitants.

He pulled his boat into one of the slips at the Digamma docks and secured it to a piling. Snatching up the briefcase, he ran up the dock, and then all the way to the meeting hall of the main headquarters building. Just as he reached the already shut meeting room door, he glanced at the wall clock.

"Dammit," he grumbled and opened the door.

"So glad you could join us, William," Eldridge Stone said when William rushed in.

"Sorry I'm late." Contempt laced William's voice. "I was busy doing what you asked me to do."

"Then our next meeting will be to hand out awards to those who do their jobs."

His eyes narrowed at Eldridge as he took the empty seat next to him. The room remained quiet while everyone waited for him to prepare for the meeting. The scientists were seated along the length of the table opposite the members of management. They, too, seemed prepared, judging by the amount of paperwork placed in front of each of them.

Eldridge informed everyone: "I have requested this meeting so we can discuss the current situation on Gamma and to reach an agreement on the best course of action regarding its future. Is anyone present not clear about the purpose of this meeting?"

No one spoke, but William noticed a few of the scientists wore disapproving expressions. They didn't bother hiding their dislike of Eldridge, as most of the management team was accustomed to doing. Eldridge spotted it as well, but chose to ignore them.

Turning to William, Eldridge asked, "Is the equipment functional now?"

"Yes. All the cameras are working again and the End Plan infrastructure is still in pristine condition."

There was an instant stir among the scientists at the mention of the End Plan and several of them turned to each other to whisper. Dr. Han, head of the scientific team, stood to address both Eldridge and William.

"I speak on behalf of my entire team by saying we're vehemently opposed to the End Plan being implemented on Gamma."

"Please, sit back down," Eldridge said to him with pseudo kindness. "No one has any intention of taking such drastic measures tonight. We're all here to discuss the recent developments occurring on Gamma."

Dr. Han looked at all the faces around the table before taking his seat again and whispered something to his colleague next to him, who nodded agreeably to the comment. Eldridge liked being in control and watching the private exchange didn't bode well with him.

"However, Dr. Han, you need to understand that it will happen if our plans fall apart." There was a sickening smile on Eldridge's face as he took delight in reminding Dr. Han of this.

William wanted to steer the discussion away from talks of the End Plan. He knew how the scientists felt and it would lead to arguments if Eldridge were to continue to push the issue.

"Dr. Han," William said, "I was looking over these copies of the test results you forwarded to me last week. Did you bring them with you today?"

Dr. Han rifled through the pile of folders set in front of him, found the ones William referred to, and placed them on top of the rest. "I have them."

"I see here that you have confirmation on some of our main subject matters. The results indicate that the DNA has greater proportions of our target anomalies. Is that correct?"

"That's correct."

"How were you able to collect the samples?" William asked.

"The female subject had taken a pregnancy test and it was retrieved from the garbage collection site." Dr. Han opened a second folder. "The other came from a saliva sample taken from a glass at the café."

"So the female, Profile A, is the daughter of Profile B? Am I reading this right?"

"You are. From the DNA profiles, it has been determined that the male is the biological father of the female."

"Have you compared these profiles with the one we have on Alec Ellison?"

"We have, and the comparisons found that Profile B is the biological father to Alec, and Profile A is his sibling." Dr. Han's tone became delicate.

William had known since Alec was a baby that he wasn't Alec's biological father; he personally demanded the tests be done. Still, it wasn't easy for him to not only hear it again, but to finally have confirmation of who Alec's father really was. It didn't help matters that everyone present in the meeting knew about the history involving William and Kyrie.

"Have you made any progress with Margaret Arcana?" William asked a little too hastily.

"No. We know she's the daughter of Joseph Arcana Sterling, but as you're already aware, she's not Ila Smith Arcana's daughter, not biologically speaking. We've yet to find a match linking her to anyone."

"What about her child?" Eldridge injected himself into the conversation. "What is it? Luke, I believe his name is? Have you run any tests on him?"

"Dr. Patrick wasn't able to get a blood sample at birth because of the child being born at home," Dr. Han said. "He hasn't been able to examine the child due to Margaret's refusal. Since he's not yet a year old, we can't use the required inoculations excuse to force her."

"I suppose we don't have any information on the child of Profile A and Jack Cavanaugh either?" Eldridge checked his notes and found nothing.

Dr. Han shook his head. "Getting a sample from that child is even harder than the other due to the nature of the situation."

"I may have a way of getting those samples," William said to both Eldridge and Dr. Han. "I'll get our informant to do it."

"Do you think she can?" Eldridge frowned. "More importantly, can she do it without getting caught?"

"They trust her, so naturally she won't get caught. It'll be easier for her to get a sample from Luke, though. The other one might be a little trickier."

"It's worth a try," Eldridge said. "As long as she doesn't get caught by the mothers. There'll be instant chaos if they realize what she's up to."

"Before we leave here today, give me the equipment she'll need to collect the samples," William told Dr. Han.

"Have you already brought her back as an informant?" Eldridge questioned William, not liking the idea of him making the decision without discussing it with him first.

"Of course not, Eldridge. I know how involved you like to be." William kept his tone evenly flat. "She still thinks she's one of them. All I need is for Dr. Patrick to help me bring her back as our informant and she'll do whatever I tell her to do."

"I'm not so sure about this idea. As I recall, the last time we used her there was some sort of an issue with her memories."

"Dr. Patrick thought it was because we were switching her back and forth too often. We haven't touched her in years, I think she'll be fine."

"Are you going back to Gamma after the meeting?"

"Yes."

"Go to Dr. Patrick and have him reevaluate her file. If he thinks it'll work, then go ahead. We could certainly use her help getting the information, but I'm warning you, there better not be any repercussions."

Confident with his plan, William said, "There won't be."

"On to other matters," Eldridge said. "As everyone is well aware, there are three people on Gamma that we didn't formally approve of, or invite there. We believe there may be a fourth, but we're having trouble confirming that. If it turns out to be true, then it's possible this person has been living on Gamma for a very long time without our knowledge."

"If you'll turn your attention to the screen." William brought up the image of Chaza standing next to Meg. "This is the woman in question."

Everyone at the table turned their attention to the large screen on the wall to see a woman walking out of the forest alongside Margaret Arcana. It appeared as though they were comfortable enough with each other to be smiling.

"We have no information on this woman, we don't even know her name," William said. "I suspect she was living in the loft area of the underground bunkers, but abandoned it when I showed up."

There was a murmur along each side of the table. The scientists and management members talked amongst themselves as they were all equally surprised by the news. Dr. Han asked, "Are you sure? Have you checked the island census to compare the numbers?"

"I've checked and double-checked," William said. "Including the new arrivals, approved departures, births, and deaths, there's still plus one."

"Could she have come in with Profile A and B?" Dr. Han suggested.

"I don't believe so, because someone had been living in the loft for quite some time. I think it's this woman," William said. "Also, can we refer to Profile A and B by their names? Profile A is Tavis Abbott and Profile B is Sebastian Abbott. I'd appreciate it if everyone updated their notes."

The sound of papers shuffling, along with the scribbling of pens filled the room. When they were finished, their eyes fell to Eldridge and William, waiting for whichever one to continue.

Instead, Natasha Hammond, third in command with management spoke next. "Have we found where they're keeping their transportation?"

"Unfortunately, no," William answered her. "They've hidden it well. The only transportation we've found is the boat Jack Cavanaugh and Michelle Martin used to get to Gamma."

"How are we supposed to stop them from leaving if we don't even know where they've hidden their transportation?" Natasha asked in a clipped voice.

"Believe me, I understand your frustration. Everyone in this room knows that's one of our biggest problems. The best chance we have at the moment is trying to predict when we think they'll attempt leaving. If we're successful with that, then we simply detain them before they go."

"Why don't we just take them now?"

"Well, we need to be sure we're detaining the right people for one thing," William said, his tone somewhat annoyed. "Now that we have a pretty good idea, and considering what we know about them, we have to make sure we're doing it properly."

"William's right," Eldridge said. "It's extremely important we don't act too quickly. I don't want to lose this opportunity, we're so close now. There's also the matter of how we'll explain their absence to the rest of the islanders."

"Speaking of detaining them," Dr. Han interrupted, "if and when we decide to take them, is the holding cell ready?"

"It's ready and waiting for occupants," William said.

"How do we know it can hold them?" Eldridge asked them both.

"We don't know that," Dr. Han said. "But given what we know of their abilities, we've done the best we can to build a relevant vault. If it fails, it'll most likely happen because of any abilities we don't know about, or because of our own blunders while we have them in custody."

"I've thought about that myself," William said. "My plan is to have only two people watching them, working in shifts. I'll be one of the two."

"Who's the other?" Eldridge asked.

"Would you like to volunteer?"

"Not particularly."

"Then perhaps you could offer a suggestion. Someone you trust?" It took more patience than William felt he had not to choke the life out of Eldridge when he looked at Dr. Han as though he expected him to volunteer.

"I'm sorry, Eldridge, with all the work I have to do there's not enough time for me to be a watchman as well," Dr. Han took great delight in saying.

Eldridge's eyes swept over the rest of the faces along the meeting table. Occasionally, he'd pause to consider some unlucky scientist or member of management.

Each one would squirm under his scrutiny and secretly hope he wouldn't ask them to take on the task of trying to restrain what they considered to be unrestrainable.

At last, his gaze fell to William again. "I guess it's you and me then," he said, sounding dismally defeated.

"Don't worry Eldridge, you have time." William sniggered. "They haven't been detained yet."

"How do we predict when they'll attempt to leave?" Natasha's gaze went from Eldridge, to William, and finally rested on Dr. Han. In her opinion, neither one of them held the answer in their expressions. She began to feel the first pangs of disappointment when William finally braved a response.

"The biggest concern on everyone's mind in this meeting room is failure. But we won't fail, because we can't. We're so close to achieving all of our goals. Failure isn't an option, we *will* succeed."

Almost everyone at the table was electrified by William's words and it brought them a sense of confidence and empowerment, but it was Natasha and Dr. Han who still maintained skepticism as they viewed the situation in a logistical way. They both understood the potential for failure and refused to allow overconfidence to cloud their judgment and rational thinking.

"Oh, thank you, Coach Davis." Natasha gave him the fakest smile she could muster. "I hope we are successful, but since you didn't really answer my question, I assume you don't know how to predict when they're about to leave. So let me ask you this, what are our plans if they do escape?"

"I'd like to know that answer myself," Dr. Han said.

Eldridge interrupted the tension-laden triangle. "I'll remind everyone again, the purpose of this meeting is to discuss the recent developments on Gamma."

For all his blustering and occasional goading, Eldridge knew far better than William how opposed the scientists were to the End Plan being executed on Gamma. Though initially selected and teamed by the East American government, the scientists had become excited by their discoveries and wanted to continue with the progress they'd made on Gamma and Delta. So much so, that there were moments when Eldridge doubted their loyalty to their original employers.

The last thing they wanted was Gamma's destruction, regardless of who may or may not escape. Eldridge also knew how important it was to mollify the scientific team. Without them, there was nothing. William understood their importance, but not their necessity and how integral their role was in the overall plan.

However, Eldridge was a businessman. In his experienced opinion, if the people they wanted to keep did manage to escape, then there would no longer be a reason to maintain the expense of Gamma. He would make a business decision: remove valuable resources, allow the island's destruction, and focus their attention on Delta, which was already showing great promise. When it came down to it, it was the investors and the East American government who kept their project alive and Eldridge had to answer to them.

Dr. Han said, "My question has everything to do with the developments occurring on Gamma. Would you please answer it."

"You know perfectly well what the answer is, Dr. Han, but I'm on your side," Eldridge lied diplomatically. "I don't want that fate for Gamma either. So like William said, that's why we can't fail. They won't escape, I'm sure of it."

Eldridge watched Dr. Han's expression soften at his words of fake, but convincing, camaraderie. He'd done it countless times before in his business career—convince all your naysayers and upstarts that you're on their side for as long as it takes to achieve your own goals. Eldridge Stone was as ruthless as they came in the business world.

"Back to this unidentified woman." Natasha redirected their attention to the image of Chaza. "Do we know where she's staying now?"

"I'm not a hundred percent sure yet, but I think she might be living in one of the newcomer houses," William said. "I sorted out that she left with Sebastian the day of that recent storm. Unfortunately, the weather obstructed what few cameras were working by then so I wasn't able to find out where they ended up. I'm keeping a close watch on those houses and I've been seeing a lot of traffic going in and out of what should be a vacant house."

"Well, see if you can get a clear image of her coming in or out of it," Natasha said. "And I want a testable sample from her if we can get one. Have someone monitor the garbage coming out of that area."

"I'm already on it, but it appears she either doesn't produce very much garbage, or she's extremely smart. I'm thinking if she leaves the house long enough I can try sneaking in to find something we can test."

Dr. Han said, "Hairs from a brush would be good enough."

"Excellent," William said. "All I need to do is confirm she's staying there and come up with a reason to get her out long enough so I can get the sample without being seen."

Eldridge pointed at the image still on the screen. "Maybe she'll visit Margaret again, it seems like they're friendly with each other."

"Yeah, I'm already working that angle."

"What about Jack Cavanaugh?" Natasha asked.

"Jack's a done deal." William laughed. "He's completely forgotten about Michelle Martin and seems very happily married to Tavis Abbott. They certainly had a kid quick enough."

"That's not what I meant," Natasha said. "Does he, or anyone else, know where he really comes from?"

"No, he doesn't." William was getting irritated with her constant needling. "Jack has no idea who his real parents are or that he was born on Delta. Only the people in this room know that. Oh, and Dr. Patrick."

"But *how* can we be sure of that?" Natasha's eyes narrowed. "We're not privy to their conversations, he could know more about his past than we're aware of."

"William's right," Eldridge said. "The only thing Jack knows is that Anthony and Rebecca Cavanaugh had been investors originally, but left because they developed ethical issues with our protocols."

"Don't you find it odd that he applied for a job with us?" Natasha was frustrated by their lack of suspicion. "I think it's very possible he knows more than he lets on."

"We know it because Anthony and Rebecca admitted what they told Jack before they were killed by the East American military." William grinned and winked. "And more importantly, what they didn't tell him."

At seeing Natasha's nostrils flare with dissatisfaction, Eldridge detailed the facts that William had scrimped on.

"During their interrogation, they said they'd only told Jack about the history of our mission, their initial investment, and after changing their minds, they joined a resistance campaign. They never bothered telling their son the biggest reason they invested in the first place was to finally have a baby they couldn't make on their own. They disgusted me then, and talking about them disgusts me now." Eldridge slammed his fists on the table. "They certainly had no ethical problems with taking a newborn infant away from his birth parents."

Natasha still wasn't satisfied, but prodded in a more respectful tone now. "Why do you think he wanted a job with us if he knew his parents were campaigning against us?"

"Curiosity? Closure? I'm sure it had something to do with one of those base ideologies." Eldridge waved a hand in the air dismissively. "It doesn't matter, we got lucky when he came to us. We were already planning out his retrieval, he saved us a lot of effort and money."

"Why did you give him a job instead of putting him on one of the islands?"

Eldridge looked at Natasha as though he couldn't believe she would ask such a stupid question. William decided to intervene, worried Eldridge would start yelling again.

"It was my decision," William said, glancing at Eldridge. "We couldn't just dump Jack on Gamma or Delta because he didn't grow up on either island, so I'm pretty sure he would've protested. And no way would he have accepted an invitation. Brainwashing takes time and it's sometimes flawed. Hypnosis doesn't work on everyone, especially someone like Jack. I figured I'd give him the job to keep him close while I worked out some other way of getting him back on one of the islands."

"Michelle Martin was your plan?" Natasha snorted. "I mean no disrespect, William, because it worked, but how could you plan on Jack becoming sexually involved with Michelle?"

Every man in the room shifted in their seat. Some of them used the excuse of reviewing their notes to avoid making eye contact with anyone, and William blank-stared at Natasha.

At looking around the table and noticing the evident change among her male colleagues, she sighed.

"Another stupid question, I suppose," she said, disgusted with all of them.

"I hired Michelle because of… if you'll forgive me, her physical attributes. I was hoping Jack was getting—" William paused at the sound of more uncomfortable seat shifting and paper shuffling. "I went on a hunch, thinking Jack might be getting *lonely* since he hadn't taken any of his allotted vacation time. His bloodwork concluded he was heterosexual" –he glanced at Dr. Han, who gave an emphatic head nod– "and all of his coworkers were men. So, I created a new position and purposely hired a female to fill it."

"Fine, I get it," Natasha grumbled. "But you couldn't have predicted she'd get pregnant, or that Jack would get the idea to hide her on Gamma."

"Actually, I did plan her pregnancy," he said. "She asked Dr. Han for birth control pills and I told him to give her placeboes. I knew he'd run to Gamma because he was obsessed with it, he snuck off over there every chance he got. Besides, where else was he gonna take her?"

"Sounds like you got lucky to me." She rolled her eyes. "Especially when she miscarried and Jack moved on to Tavis Abbott."

"It wasn't luck," William said flippantly. "Dr. Han and Dr. Patrick helped me out with the miscarriage, too."

Natasha had finally had enough and started gathering her folders. Not only was it horrifying to her that William would exert his power to control a woman's right to birth control, but to make a woman miscarry was more than she could stand.

Dr. Han knew right away that William had disclosed more information to Natasha than was prudent. He decided it was time for him and his team to leave the meeting.

"If that will be all, we have a lot of work to do," Dr. Han said when he stood from his chair. "William, I'll have my assistant bring the test kits you'll need to collect the samples."

"Thank you, Dr. Han," William said as the scientific team began filing out of the room.

Natasha stood from her chair as the last few scientists headed for the door and she silently stuffed the notes and folders into her briefcase. Though the scientists were leaving, the meeting for management was still technically in progress. No one said a word to her as she shot William a warning glare before walking away—slamming the meeting room door shut behind her.

"Was that really necessary?" Eldridge asked William.

"She asked, did she not?" William shrugged. "Maybe I should've told her how quickly Michelle sold out and how filthy rich she is now." He saw Eldridge was not at all impressed with his callous candor. "She'll be fine after she cools off."

Natasha Hammond was a smart, tough businesswoman in her own right, but she didn't come by it easily. She had been born into poverty and grew up in a house where her mother never spoke up for herself, which did nothing to help prevent the occasional beatings from her husband. Natasha learned to keep her own mouth shut so she wouldn't suffer the same fate and waited until she was old enough to leave. When that day came, she never looked back and swore to herself to never endure a life of being controlled by anyone—especially a man.

"She better be," Eldridge said. "Natasha's damn good at her work. If she leaves because of your insensitive remarks, I'll fire you and offer her your job."

"You're getting rather deluded in your old age," William said, his tone amused. "You know you can't fire me."

"Enough of this useless prattle," Eldridge barked. "Now that our squeamish scientific team is gone, we need to discuss the topic they can't seem to stomach."

"They can't stomach it because they don't want to see all of their hard work obliterated."

"Careful, William, your weakness is showing," Eldridge coldly noted before addressing the rest of the management staff. "Do any of you have any questions or comments regarding the End Plan infrastructure on Gamma?"

Gustav Anderson was the only one brave or stupid enough to speak up. "I think we'd all like to know what criteria will have to be met to warrant Gamma's destruction."

Eldridge couldn't believe he was hearing this infernal question again. It seemed the lot of them had lost sight of the ultimate goal of the whole operation. Though he would prefer to shake them all awake from their fantasy world where everything worked out exactly as they wanted, he instead chose to remain calm and collected.

"Some of you are new, and some of you have been here since the inception of our endeavor." Eldridge's eyes focused on each of the original members. "The first two islands were a joke, and not even a good one. Finally, things started looking up for us with Gamma, and we've achieved a rather nice degree of success."

He flipped through his notes at random to illustrate his point. "The success I speak of is pretty much our main purpose, our sole reason for maintaining these isolated islands with scientifically controlled populations. We have a handful of the kind of people we're looking for, right there on Gamma. They've found partners of equal value and unique abilities, and these unions have already produced offspring. This is exactly what we want."

After setting the notes back down, Eldridge turned his attention to the image of Chaza still on the screen. He scrolled through the other images until he found a zoomed-in photo of Sebastian's face.

Sighing with an air of drama, Eldridge continued: "But these very same people have no intention of staying on Gamma. I believe they want a similar thing that we want, but they want to take it back to where they came from and we can't let that happen. Oh, and let's not forget our deal with the East American government and what they want. If we fail, then Gamma is worthless."

"I hope it doesn't happen," Gustav said when it seemed Eldridge waited for a response to his speech. "However, in the event that they do escape, we could always start over. The money and time we've invested in Gamma ought to persuade you to think about it at the very least."

"And what do we do with the rest of Gamma's inhabitants?" Eldridge asked. "Are you suggesting we leave them as they have been?"

"Why not?" Gustav frowned at Eldridge's eerily calm demeanor.

"How will we explain the sudden disappearance of these people… infants, too? They'll certainly demand answers. What will we tell them, Gustav? What excuse could we possibly come up with that will ensure they won't panic?"

Gustav began to realize the dilemma of what would happen, and there was no counterargument. The inhabitants would panic, throw the whole island into chaos, eventually the society would degrade—leading to the End Plan being implemented anyway.

William saw the disappointed look on Gustav's face and said, "The last thing I want is to see such waste. That's why we have to keep them all on Gamma. I won't allow them to escape."

"How's Epsilon coming along?" Eldridge asked Gustav to shift the focus of the discussions. "Have you finished the survey? Any news on the stone structure?"

"Yes, the mapping is complete now. As for the structure, it's made of the same kind of stone, and slightly larger than the one on Delta."

"Have those expensive geologists come up with an explanation yet?"

"No. Or, only what we already know… that with each island we create, there's always a stone structure and it's always just slightly larger in square footage."

"Fire the geologists and destroy the damn building."

"I don't think that's a good idea," William said. "By all means, get rid of the geologists, but leave the structure. We don't know how or why these buildings exist, I'd rather not risk there being a problem if we destroy them."

"Fine, leave it alone then," Eldridge grumbled. "Plant the usual vegetation around it to cover it up." He'd grown weary of the meeting and so had everyone else left in the room, based on the apathetic looks on their faces. "Unless there are any more questions or comments, then this meeting is officially over."

Everyone at the meeting table gave a quick glance around and immediately began gathering their notes, stuffing them in their briefcases without conversation and then left like a migrating herd of buffalo—all except William and Eldridge, as was customary.

When they were gone, William waited for Eldridge to say whatever was on his mind without the rest of management hearing.

"They're right, we have so much invested in Gamma," Eldridge said, sounding somewhat defeated now since he didn't have to keep up the pretense. "I really don't want to see it come to nothing."

"I'm feeling confident," William said to reassure him. "We know what we're up against, all we have to do is watch closely and pay attention. If it looks like they're about to leave, we detain them. My plan is to go for Sebastian first, I feel like his daughter won't leave without him. Once we switch our informant back to our spy, we'll get more information and start formulating a long-term plan."

"This better work, William. If they find a way to escape, we both know what will happen." Eldridge shook his head. "I've got General Legare calling me every other day for updates. And when he isn't, Lieutenant General Raynor's calling me with threats to storm Gamma himself to secure their transportation." Snarling, he added, "I can't tell you enough how much I hate Arden Raynor. I swear, that man's up to no good. He scares the hell out of me."

"Don't worry, I'll make this happen." William hoped his reassurances would pacify Eldridge enough so he could leave.

A sharp knock on the door interrupted Eldridge's reply. After retrieving the test sample kits from Dr. Han's assistant, William put them in his briefcase and asked, "Is there anything else? I should leave before it gets dark."

"No, that's all for now," Eldridge said and walked with William to the door. "Let me know what Dr. Patrick says about your idea."

~

The sun was setting as William drove the boat back to Gamma. One of his favorite things was to watch the island from a distance and see it grow larger with his approach; the sunset made it all the more spectacular. Things were about to get heated up there and the intoxicating thrill of the adventure awaiting him flooded his bloodstream, making him push the boat harder to get there faster.

William was more than ready to begin the start of his intrepid plans; knowing it was his purpose in life. It seemed to him that he was born for such bold ventures, and it was what he was willing to die for to make a reality.

As he neared the northernmost tip of the island, where the yawning cave entrance waited to receive him, William slowed the boat down for safe passage under the rocky overhang and secured it to the cave wall. When he got to the steel door, he punched in the code on the new digital lock he had Ron install. After rereading Jack's employment records, William discovered he'd been taken on a tour of the bunker. The new locking mechanisms were precautions placed at both entrances to keep Jack, and anyone else for that matter, out.

Back in the surveillance room, William set his briefcase down and scanned the camera monitors before walking back out. He took the stairs, two at a time, to the loft he'd been staying in to change into more island appropriate attire. It occurred to him that Eldridge would want the loft for himself when it came time for him to help guard the prisoners.

The thought of sharing the loft with Eldridge disgusted him, so he packed up his clothes and moved the rest of his belongings to the physician's living quarters. It took three back-and-forth trips to move his accumulated things and on the fourth, he gave the loft a once over to make sure it was void of all things related to him that Eldridge would object to. Once he was satisfied, he exited through the steel door and entered the dark cave.

Since it was night, he could drive to Dr. Patrick's home under the cover of darkness. At the bottom of the cliff, William turned into the forest where he'd been hiding his cart from view, mostly from Alec and Meg as they were the only ones who lived this far out.

William drove by Ila's house on the way to Dr. Patrick's to see if she was there and to make sure she didn't have company. Through her front room window, he saw she was seated at her desk scribbling away, probably filling out the necessary paperwork involved with shipping horses to the mainland.

When he arrived at Dr. Patrick's house, he tapped lightly on the door so the neighbors wouldn't hear. All of Dr. Patrick's neighbors were the island's elderly and they had a knack for noticing anything that goes on amongst themselves. William glanced around at the other houses, half-expecting to see curtains moving aside with a face peering out at the sound of a late-night visitor. He sighed with relief when the door opened.

"William," Dr. Patrick said, surprised. His eyes also darted to the houses around his before opening the door wider and ushering William in. "What are you doing here?"

Going straight to the spacious and well-decorated front room, William sat on the large brown suede couch and his gaze went to the coffee table. He leaned over and picked up one of the medical journals that were fanned out, then flipped through the pages without bothering to look at or read any of the pages.

"I need for you to get Ila's private medical files, the classified ones," William said, tossing the journal back on the table.

"Why?" Dr. Patrick eyed him keenly.

"Because I'm in need of her services again, and I'm not referring to her horse-breeding skills." William mused, amazed at how much people would pay for a horse. "Although, that has turned out to be a lucrative business."

"I told you a long time ago we were going too far in messing around with that woman's head. If you'll remember, that's why I put a stop to it." Dr. Patrick sounded as if this was to be the final word on the matter.

William groaned inwardly. It was like the meeting of placating opposing minds was still in session.

"I remember very well, Clark, but as you said, that was a long time ago. Do you have her file?"

Dr. Patrick hesitated, wanting to say more, but thought better of it. Instead, he left the room to retrieve Ila's file from his basement, where he kept all the classified files on the islanders. When he returned, he dropped the thick folder on the coffee table, sat in the chair opposite the sofa, and gave William a stern look.

"Have you reread her file lately?" William asked.

"I don't need to, I remember her case quite well."

"Eldridge requested we go over her file together."

"What is it that you need her to do exactly? Maybe I can get it done myself and leave her out of it."

"I wish you could, but you haven't been able to do it so far. What we need are testable samples for the scientists on both of those babies. Since their mothers won't let you anywhere near them, it's time for an inside job. Ila's perfect, as Meg's mother, she's completely trusted."

"You know very well Ila isn't Meg's mother."

"Well, *I* do, but they don't." William grinned and pointed at the folder. "We've left her alone long enough, I think she can handle it. I don't plan to switch her back and forth this time, just the once is good enough for what I need."

Dr. Patrick appeared to be already concentrating when he picked Ila's file up. He settled into the chair and began going over the notes; some pages he lingered on longer than others, especially toward the end of the file. William sat patiently, watching him and hoping Clark would agree to it on his own as he wasn't looking forward to telling him he had no choice in the matter.

He closed the file and looked at William. "Assuming that time has helped bring equilibrium back to her mind, and assuming you're telling the truth about not constantly switching her, then my professional opinion is that it shouldn't be a problem. How do you plan to avoid detection?"

"This time I'm relying solely on her training to avoid having her thoughts and emotions being sensed by others." William shrugged. "I wish I would've given her more of a chance to practice before. It's more important than ever considering who we're dealing with. It doesn't matter anyway, I don't think it'll be much longer before there's an attempted escape. When they try to leave, we'll detain them."

"Oh, yeah?" Dr. Patrick snorted. "How?"

"The old-fashioned way, irresistible bait."

"Nothing like old-school, huh?" Dr. Patrick chuckled.

William stood. "Shall we get going?"

"You mean to do it tonight?"

"Yes, we're running out of time. Let's go."

~

They drove in separate carts to Ila's house, as William intended to stay with her a little while after she was switched to give her the instructions. He stood back in the shadows of the porch while Dr. Patrick knocked on Ila's door.

"Dr. Patrick," Ila said when she opened the door. "What brings you here at this hour?"

"I hope I didn't disturb you, dear," Dr. Patrick said. "I was wanting to get your opinion on a problem I'm having with one of my horses."

"Oh, absolutely. Come in." Ila held the door open for him. "Forgive my pajamas, I wasn't expecting company."

"I'm your doctor, Ila, I've seen you in less."

Ila laughed as she shut the door. When they moved from the foyer, William let himself inside, then crept to the kitchen where he could still hear them in the front room. He listened with perked ears to their conversation, waiting for Dr. Patrick's initiation of the switch.

"So, what kind of problem are you having with the horse?" Ila asked.

"Who brings the thunderbolts to Zeus?" Dr. Patrick asked, leaning in closer to Ila and maintaining strict eye contact with her. After her initial look of confusion, her eyes glassed over and she stared straight through him as though he wasn't there.

"Can you repeat the question?" Ila's voice was monotone, almost lifeless.

"Who brings the thunderbolts to Zeus?"

Reborn clarity replaced the blank look in Ila's eyes and they refocused on the individual seated in front of her. A winsome smile spread across her face.

"Clark! Why, Pegasus, of course," she said. "You look" –she didn't want to say *old*, even though that was what she thought– "different. How long have I been down?"

"Quite a while."

"Oh, God, really?" Ila stood and looked around the room for the mirror she remembered hanging on the wall. When she located it, she ran to it to examine herself. "Thank you, thank you," she said to the mirror.

Dr. Patrick chuckled at Ila's vanity. She'd feared having aged like he had, but Ila carried the gene for slowed aging and therefore had nothing to worry about. Unfortunately, he considered, this was the only thing unique about her."

"How're you feeling, Ila?"

Ila backed up from the mirror to get a fuller view of herself; she grimaced at the drab pajamas. "I feel fine. I look a little frumpy, but I can fix that." She turned to him and her eyes narrowed. "Where is he?"

"I'm right here, my pet."

William came out from the kitchen with his arms outstretched. When Ila saw him, she ran over and jumped into his arms, wrapping her arms and legs around him and giggling. He hugged her tight and laughed with her.

"I sure have missed you," he told her, rocking from side-to-side until she dislodged herself from him. He took the clip out of her hair to allow her tresses to fall down around her shoulders. "There, that's better."

"I should be mad at you." Ila pouted, turning her back to him. "How dare you keep me down for so long?"

"We're good here," William said to Dr. Patrick, dismissing him. "Thank you."

"Don't forget what we discussed," he reminded and stood to leave.

After seeing him out, William locked the door and went around the house to close the blinds and curtains. As a precaution, he turned off most of the lights, leaving only a few lamps on. Finally satisfied with their privacy, he retrieved his briefcase from the kitchen and placed it on the coffee table.

"Apparently, there's a lot you need to tell me," Ila said.

William looked up and saw her studying the photographs on the fireplace mantel. "Yeah, we should probably talk about that first."

Her gaze went from a photo of Meg and Alec at their reception to one of herself with a small child cradled in her arms. "Do I have another kid?" She sounded none too thrilled with the prospect.

"No." William laughed. "That's Luke, Meg's child with Alec. They're married now."

"Kyrie's son?" Ila blurted. "I'm gonna need a drink. How about you?"

Ila trotted off to the kitchen and returned with a bottle of wine and two glasses. She poured one for herself, downed it while staring at William, then poured herself another before finally filling his glass.

"Thank you, nice of you to share."

"Don't get snippy with me. I'm the one who's been kept in the dark." She sneered at him. "Go ahead, tell me everything I've missed."

It took no less than two hours for William to tell Ila all the things she needed to know and to answer all her questions. He told her everything he knew about Sebastian and Tavis: when they arrived, how they disguised themselves as newcomers, and especially their abilities. Though he explained the true parentage of Alec and Tavis, he dodged the subject of Meg's. As always, more so than ever, William needed Ila to continue thinking Meg was her daughter.

"What is it you need for me to do?" Ila asked when it seemed William had finished with the gossip column updates.

"Before I answer that, I want to ask if you still remember your training about avoiding detection. Particularly, avoiding thought sensory abilities."

"I remember everything I was trained for. Why do you doubt me?"

"Because it's more important than ever, especially when you encounter..." William had been about to list off the names, but settled on the overwhelming reality. "Pretty much everyone I told you about. I can't risk switching you back and forth, it wasn't going so well the last time." He took her hands. "Dr. Patrick decided you needed a break, that's why you've been down for so long."

"Fine, not a problem. I feel rested now." She raised an eyebrow at him and smiled. "You still need to tell me what you want me to do."

"The usual, I only warned you because it might not be as easy as you're used to. I'm gonna leave you with two test kits. I need for you to collect a sample from Luke and Lani. Everyone trusts you, so you shouldn't have any problems finding a way to be alone with the babies." William sighed. "Don't worry if you can only get one from Luke for now, but if you can get both at the same time it would be fantastic."

"Sounds like a challenge," she said. "And you know how much I love a good challenge."

"I should go now, it's getting late," William said, unconvincingly.

"So soon? I was hoping you'd help me out of these ugly pajamas before you left."

"I thought you'd never ask," he said and leaned her back onto the couch.

22

Ersatz

Ila was flipping through the paperwork on the horses, sipping coffee while still in her robe, when the front door opened without so much as a knock.

"Meg! What are you doing here?"

"What do you mean, what am I doing here?" Meg set Luke's diaper bag on the dining table. "I told you on the phone yesterday that Luke and I were gonna spend the day with you."

Alec came in carrying Luke. "Anything wrong?"

"Apparently my mother forgot I was coming over today," she said loud enough for Ila to hear.

"Oh, stop it. I only forgot because I've been busy filling out all these forms." Ila shuffled the top few layers of the paperwork. "How are you, Alec?"

"Good, how are you?"

"Better, now that Meg and Luke are here. I could use a break. Are you off to work?" Ila pushed her coffee mug toward the back of the desk so Meg wouldn't notice it.

"Yeah, a ton of special orders came in over the weekend and I told my mom I'd help her sort through it."

Alec seemed preoccupied about leaving so Ila wasn't too worried about him. Meg, on the other hand, looked at her wearing an odd expression. As a precaution, she mentally focused on the lines of the paperwork that still needed filling in.

"Well, you better get going or everyone will start calling the store asking why they haven't received their orders yet," Ila said.

He gave Meg a kiss and handed Luke to her. "I'll pick you up this afternoon."

When Alec left, Meg went to her old bedroom to retrieve the playpen. Once Luke was happily gnawing away on a teething cookie, she turned her attention back to Ila, who'd resumed going over the shipping forms. Meg frowned at Ila's lack of interest in either herself, or Luke.

She considered everything she knew now. The woman sitting at the desk, filling out forms, as Meg had watched Ila do all of her life, wasn't her real mother. But it didn't matter to Meg. It was Ila who raised her, who cared for her when she was sick, and who put the bandages on all her cuts and scrapes.

Meg went over to the desk and caught a whiff of the pungent aroma right away. "Why are you drinking coffee? Are you out of tea?"

"It sounded good at the time."

Ila stood from her desk, grabbed the coffee mug, and went to the kitchen to pour it down the sink. It frustrated her to do it as she really had been enjoying the coffee, but it wasn't worth risking Meg's suspicion.

On her way back to the front room, Ila stopped at the playpen to look at Luke. There were several similarities that made Ila think of Alec; those eyes foremost, but she was most proud of the mass of blond curls that only Meg and Joseph could lay claim to.

"And how's Luke this morning?" Ila asked him and he smiled up at her. "Hmm, Alec's dimples."

"I know." Meg laughed. "But he's got my hair."

Ila hadn't figured she'd need to rely on her training with Meg. It may be nothing, but she didn't like the coincidental timing of Meg's guesswork.

"What's wrong?" Meg asked.

That's it! Ila decided—she had to rely on her training, even with Meg. She focused all her thoughts on imagining herself taking a shower, and as it being the most important task that needed immediate attention.

"Nothing's wrong, sweetheart," Ila said in a cajoling voice. "I'm just starting to feel silly about being the only one not dressed for the day. Let me go have a quick shower and put some clothes on. You should take Luke to the stables to see the horses while I'm getting ready."

Meg leaned over the playpen to retrieve Luke and after they walked out the front door, Ila rushed to the window. She waited until Meg was inside the stables before darting to her bedroom to call William.

On the fourth ring, he finally answered. "Hello."

"It's me," she said. "I guess you didn't know Meg and Luke were supposed to be spending the day here with me? Alec just dropped them off before going to work."

"Sorry, I had no idea that was their plan. Were you able to recover the situation?"

"Of course."

"This could work out to our advantage. Meg's good friends with Tavis, see if you can get Meg to invite her over with Lani. If she does, find a way to be alone with the babies."

"I'll make it happen," she said. "There's something I should probably mention."

"First of all, where's Meg? Can she hear you?"

"No. I'm not stupid, William. I sent her to the stables with Luke while I'm *supposed* to be having a shower. Something's different about Meg, I swear it seems like she's reading my thoughts. It worried me enough that I had to rely on my training."

William hadn't considered this, and it further emphasized how much they still needed to know about Meg's true parentage. His mind kept going back to that image of the unknown woman walking out of the forest with Meg. "It has to be her," he muttered to himself.

"What?" Ila asked, annoyed. "Are you even listening to me?"

"Yeah, sorry. That's interesting, I'm not sure what to make of it right now.

Sounds like you're handling it well. Just keep your wits about you, especially if Tavis does come over. Let me know if you get those samples."

"I'll get them, stop doubting me," she said. "I have to go. I'll call you later."

William placed the phone back on its receiver and drummed his fingers on the desk. What he needed was to get the hair sample from that woman, the sooner the better, but he had no idea how to get her out of that house. Based solely on a hunch, he formulated a plan and picked the phone up again.

"Dr. Han, it's William. Good news, we may have those samples sooner than we expected. I'll deliver them as soon as I have them in hand. In the meantime, I need for you to get a flu virus ready and have someone get them over to me immediately. Something substantial, but not life threatening, and two infant vaccines against it as well. I have an idea that might flush out our unidentified islander."

~

After showering, Ila went to the bedroom and rolled her eyes at everything hanging in the closet. "Why would anyone ever dress like this?" she mumbled, amazed at how opposite her taste in clothing was from her islander alternative.

She went to the dresser, hoping for a better selection, and settled on shorts and a tank top. With a scowl, she pulled on a pretentious ivory sweater to cover her shoulders.

"I should've brought the camera with me," Ila said when she walked into the stables, seeing Meg hold Luke up to one of the yearlings so he could pet its muzzle.

"Don't you have a million pictures already?" Meg glanced at Ila's shorts. "Need to do laundry?"

"Stop picking on me so much," Ila said while thinking about the yearlings in front of them. An idea came to her as she watched them munch on their oats alongside the mare. "They need a good workout."

"Haven't you been riding them?"

"Yes, but only one at a time, obviously." Ila sighed. "And the poor mare, she hasn't been taken out in a while."

It occurred to Meg that with her no longer living here, Ila didn't have the help she used to have. "I'm sorry." Meg put her hand on Ila's shoulder.

"You have nothing to be sorry about. Besides, I have an idea."

"What?"

"You should invite Tavis and Jack over if they don't already have plans for the day. The three of you could give the horses a workout, and it would help me out so much. What do you think?"

"I'll go inside and call her right now," Meg said and smiled. She was glad for the opportunity to help her in any way that she could and pulled her into a hug with Luke between them.

The sudden gesture surprised Ila, but she welcomed the hug from her daughter. "Feeling sorry for me, are you?" Ila chuckled—she truly loved Meg, no matter which Ila was at the surface.

"I just want to help you, that's all."

"Then give Luke to me and call Tavis." Ila beamed at her. "And don't take no for an answer."

Meg handed Luke to Ila and bounded out of the stables. Ila made her way over to the stable doors with Luke on her hip. The daylight lit up his blue eyes.

"You're a handsome devil, Luke." Ila went to the front porch and took a seat to wait for Meg. The front door opened and she closed her eyes briefly in anticipation of good news.

"You're in luck, they said they'd be over after they get ready." Meg sat in the chair next to Ila. "I told them you'd watch Lani. You don't mind, do you?"

"I'd love to watch her," Ila said. "I'm looking forward to it."

"Tavis liked her birthday present, so did Jack. They love that waterfall."

Ila knew it had been Alec and Tavis' birthday, since William explained to her they were twins. Unfortunately, small details like gifts hadn't been included in the need-to-know updates.

Before the silence stretched on for too long, Ila went with a generic response. "You weren't *really* worried she wouldn't like it, were you?"

"No, not really." Meg's admission came with a sly grin. "Alec loved his, too. Maybe I'll paint one for you next. Any ideas on what I should paint?"

Yet another detail William didn't mention. Or didn't know, Ila surmised. She assumed Meg made reference to artwork, but went with yet another generic answer. "You know me well enough, what do you think I'd like?"

"Horses, and a great big painting, too. One you can hang on the front room wall." She considered what Ila would like most. "How about a painting of the horses on Alaret Beach?"

"I already love it."

"Maybe we'll ride the horses out there today so I can draw a quick sketch and get started on it tonight."

Ila knew the trip to Alaret Beach would take some time and everything seemed to be working out perfectly, so far anyway. All she needed was for Tavis and Jack to show up and leave Lani with her. She forced herself to stop thinking about it since she needed to focus on utilizing her training. Though Meg had stopped badgering her, she'd yet to deal with Tavis.

~

"They're here," Meg said, looking out of the kitchen window.

Meg opened the door and the first to enter was Tavis; it shocked Ila how much she looked like Alec. Jack followed in behind her and Ila stood to get a better view of him. He was tall, standing several inches above each of them. Jack put his arm around Tavis' waist and his fingers subtly caressed her hip while they maintained their conversation with Meg. Viewing Jack and Tavis as a couple, Ila appraised their symbiotic appearance; deeming they were made for each other—they were simply beautiful together. The intimacy between them was almost tangible and Ila quickly squashed the feelings of jealousy when they turned to her.

"Tavis." Ila greeted them with a smile. "Jack. How are you and little Lani doing?"

"We're doing well, how are you?" Jack smiled back at her. "Meg mentioned you were knee-deep in paperwork."

"It's ridiculous how many forms have to be filled out just to ship one horse, and I have two." Ila shook her head. "It's nice to have a break, thank you so much for coming over today to work the horses. One of the mares desperately needs the exercise and the yearlings need more saddle training."

"Well, that's easy enough to do. My parents used to rely on me to train any difficult horses they bought." Jack chuckled. "They said I had more patience with them."

Current task, envision Jack's skills in equine training; repeat gratitude. "I'm so relieved to hear that," Ila said, eyes wide with appreciation. "I can't tell you enough how much this helps me."

It worked; an expression of pride came over Jack's face. Tavis looked at him and grinned in a knowing way, as if she'd sensed a thought she found amusing. With a glance at Meg, Ila saw the same knowing look on her face as well. William had been right, but more than he knew—she'd have to be more careful than ever.

When Ila sat on the sofa, Tavis joined her and extracted Lani from the infant sling. Ila approved of what she considered to be the most beautiful baby girl she'd ever seen—save Meg.

Current task, make Tavis comfortable with leaving Lani with you. "Would you like to trade?" Ila chuckled, holding Luke closer to Tavis.

"Of course I would."

Ila took Lani into her arms. "Oh, Tavis, Lani's so pretty. You're gonna have to chase away a lot of boys when she gets older."

"I'll be in charge of that." Jack winked at Tavis and picked Luke up. "Look at you, rascal, you're getting so big. Maybe we can talk Ila into breeding some ponies for you to ride."

"Absolutely not!" Ila blurted. "I have my hands full enough with the horses."

"Oh, well. Sorry, Luke, guess you're just gonna have to keep eating whatever your mommy's feeding you so you can ride the big horses soon." He handed Luke back to Tavis. "I'm going out to the stables to saddle the horses."

"It's going to be a beautiful day for riding and Meg just finished making a lunch to take with you," Ila said to Tavis when Jack left. "She wants to sketch the horses while they're on the beach. I think she's worried I'm jealous over your birthday present. You know what? I am."

"Mom, I haven't had a chance to talk to them about that," Meg said as she set the tote bag of sandwiches by the front door.

"Are we riding all the way out to Alaret Beach?" Tavis asked Meg.

"It won't take me long to draw a quick sketch, but I understand if you don't want to ride out that far. I could always take one of the horses out there myself tomorrow."

That was the last thing Tavis wanted; Meg riding through the footpaths alone. She looked from Meg to Ila and then her eyes fell to Lani, still cradled in Ila's arms. It worried her how long Ila would have to watch Lani. A crease formed on her forehead and Ila guessed at Tavis' concerns.

"Tavis, I have handled a baby before." Ila gestured toward Meg. "She's standing right here in front of us. I hope that counts for something as to my ability to take care of Lani for an hour or so."

Tavis blinked a few times and shook her head. "I wasn't doubting you. I'm just being a new mother, I guess. Riding out to the beach sounds fun. If Lani gives you any trouble, just call my father, he's very good with her. I already told him Lani would be here while we took the horses out."

"Lani won't be any trouble at all, but I promise to call Sebastian if I have any questions."

When Jack came back in from saddling the horses, Meg and Tavis explained the new plans to him. He was fine with the idea and it helped reassure Tavis further that she needn't worry.

Ila waited in the doorway until they exited the stables and made their way down the lane. When she could no longer see them, she still waited, just in case they came back for some forgotten item. Once twenty minutes passed, she deemed it safe to think clearly again.

Still holding Lani, she went to Meg's old bedroom and laid her on the bed, placing two pillows on either side of her in case she got any ideas about rolling over. Ila went to the closet to get the shoebox she'd hidden the test kits in earlier, thankfully before Meg and Alec had arrived.

She took the kits out, placed them on the bed, and opened one of them. After slipping on the sterile gloves, Ila collected the cheek cells on three separate swabs. On the third swab, Lani tried suckling on it and Ila chuckled at her. "Not yet, I'll feed you after I get Luke's samples."

With Lani's samples secured, Ila returned her to the playpen and lifted Luke. "Your turn," she said to him, bringing him to the bedroom where his kit was already set up.

When she finished with Luke, she propped him on her hip and headed for the front room—leaving the completed test kits on the bed.

Just as she walked out of the bedroom, a trail of brilliant colors streamed in through the open window, covering the entire surface of the bed.

Mission accomplished, Ila went to the refrigerator for a bottle. While it warmed, she called William.

"Hello?" he answered on the first ring.

"I have both your samples. Meg, Tavis, and Jack are riding the horses to Alaret Beach, so you have plenty of time to come get them."

"I'll be right over."

~

Ila was still feeding Lani when the back door opened and closed. "So you can fly now? How'd you get here so fast?"

"I'm starting to learn the shortcuts through the forests," he said. "Where are the samples?"

"On the bed in Meg's old bedroom."

While squirrelling them into his briefcase, he couldn't believe how fortunate they were to have both samples so quickly. "Thank you, you never cease to amaze me." He grasped the sides of her face and kissed her.

"I'm just shocked by how easy it was," Ila said after he released her. "But you were right, I did have to rely on my training. They trust me, though, so it went smoothly enough."

"Excellent!" William looked down at the child still in Ila's arms. "So, this is Lani."

William went to transfer Lani into his own arms, but Ila tensed. "What?" He frowned. "I *can* hold an infant."

She put Lani in William's arms while he took the bottle, continuing to feed her. He walked to the front room and sat in one of the wing-back chairs. Ila watched William study Lani, wondering what he was thinking.

"She's a cute baby," he said.

"Have you seen her parents? They look like Grecian Gods!"

"Yes, they are quite handsome." William laughed at her description. His gaze drifted over to the playpen where Luke had fallen asleep. When Lani finished her bottle, he propped her up on his shoulder and while patting her back he went over to have a closer look at Luke. "What color are his eyes?"

"Blue, like Alec's," she said; and his jaw clenched. "It still bothers you that Alec's not your son, doesn't it?"

William's gaze shifted to Ila; her expression was that of mere curiosity. "A little." He sighed. "But it seems that everything has worked out the way it should, for the better."

Lani had fallen asleep, so William leaned over the playpen and settled her down next to Luke. He took a blanket draped on the side of the playpen and covered the sleeping babies. Their comfort was important to him, they meant everything to William. His entire life's work lay in that playpen, and he had to fight the urge to take them away immediately.

Instead, he turned away from them to clear his head. He picked up the empty bottle and took it to the kitchen. "Would you mind getting my briefcase for me?"

He sat at the dining table and thought of how best to convince Ila to do what he had in mind for her next task. It wasn't going to be easy, considering how much she truly cared about Meg, but he needed to get the hair sample from the unknown female.

Ila returned with his briefcase and he motioned for her to sit next to him. Opening it, he pulled out three vials, two of which were filled with a pink liquid and the third, clear. He laid them out in front of them and turned to her.

"I need you to do something for me and you're not gonna like it. However, I can't express to you enough how important this task is."

His tone and words produced an instant glare from her. "What is it?" Ila pointed at the vials. "I assume it has something to do with those."

William picked up the one filled with a clear liquid. "This vial is a genetically altered form of a flu virus. It'll seem like a dreadful illness for about a day, but then the virus dies spontaneously. In other words, it's a very safe version of the twenty-four hour flu. The other two vials are inoculations to give to the babies as a safety precaution."

"Who are you wanting me to give this to?" Ila took the clear vial from him.

"Meg."

"Why?" she asked without looking at him.

"Because we need to get a testable sample from that woman I told you about. She seems to have formed a friendship with Alec and Meg. Short of setting the house she's hiding in on fire, this is the only idea I can come up with to get her out long enough so I can sneak in and collect a hair sample. I'm hoping she'll want to check on them if it appears they're suffering horribly."

"What you're asking me to do is purposely make my daughter sick."

"I know." William forced a tenderness into his tone. "Our own scientists provided us with this vial. If I had even the slightest doubt of their competence, I wouldn't have agreed to it, nor would I ask this of you. I thought you trusted me."

"I do trust you, William, so stop patronizing me. I didn't say I wouldn't do it, I only wanted you to know how difficult it's going to be for me. How the hell am I gonna get Meg to drink from this vial anyway?" Ila was frustrated, and if it weren't for sleeping babies in her house, she would've screamed at William.

"When they get back, serve tea to everyone. Just make sure Meg's getting the right cup." William offered a sympathetic smile. "She and Alec will start showing symptoms tonight. Tomorrow will be the worst day for them, and by tomorrow night they'll start feeling better."

"What if their illness comes and goes without this woman ever knowing Meg and Alec were sick?"

"I've thought about that, too. Find some reason to call Meg in the morning. If Alec can even answer the phone at that point, he'll tell you how sick they are. Make up an excuse that prevents you from going over there yourself to check on them. That's when you'll call Tavis and tell her what's going on… you get the idea."

"Yeah, William, I think I can handle lying to everyone." Ila rolled her eyes.

"I've seen Tavis going into that house numerous times. I'm hoping she'll go over there and tell the woman how sick Meg and Alec are. I'll be watching from the monitors and if she leaves, I'm going over there myself to get the sample."

"How are we gonna keep everyone else from getting sick?"

"If you're careful with Meg's cup, then no one else should get sick." William grimaced and added, "You might want to avoid giving her a goodbye kiss when she leaves."

Ila was silent for a moment, contemplating everything he'd told her—ideas were already formulating in her mind for how to carry out the plan. She picked up the two pink vials and stared at them while rotating them between her thumbs and forefingers. Finally, she stood and looked down at William.

"Help me vaccinate these babies." She leaned in close. "But I'm warning you, William, if anything happens to them or Meg, I'll personally make it my mission to kill you myself."

William was stunned at her words, and yet he knew by her demeanor that she was entirely serious with the threat. He hoped his trust in the scientific team's assurances didn't turn out to be naïve.

"Don't worry, Ila, I don't want anything happening to them either."

When they were done, William retrieved his briefcase and walked to the back of the house with Ila. Instead of opening the door, he pressed her against it. "Want me to come over tonight?" he whispered in her ear.

"Not tonight, maybe tomorrow night." She swayed against him. "I want to make sure everything turns out as well as you say they will first."

He groaned. "Fine. I'll see you tomorrow night then, when everything works out to our advantage. One word of caution before I go, it has to do with Sebastian. You had it easy today because Tavis trusts you, and she's still young and inexperienced. Sebastian, on the other hand, is a clever man and I'd prefer it if you avoided him at all costs. Should you find yourself having to deal with him face to face, you will *not* have it so easy. Okay?" William raised his eyebrows.

She nodded. "I'll be careful."

~

When he left, Ila went to the kitchen to get the serving tray ready for tea. The best way for her to ensure that Meg got the tainted cup was to use a mismatched tea-set and she opted to give Meg the one decorated with green accents. After assembling the serving tray, Ila slipped the vial in her pocket.

Luke was the next one hungry; she gave him one of his bottles and let him nibble on one of the teething cookies Meg had left in his bag. Then Lani decided it was time for her to have another bottle, but she also needed a diaper change, and definitely first in Ila's opinion.

"I'm so happy I didn't have twins," she murmured to Lani while feeding her. "You two are worse than the horses." As Lani finished off the last of her bottle, Ila worked out the details of her plans.

Ultimately, she decided to leave her engagement ring in Luke's diaper bag. In the morning, she'd call Meg and ask her to check the bag for the ring. At that point, she'd hear of their illness, setting the rest of what she had planned in motion.

Lani drifted off to sleep and Ila set her back next to Luke and glanced at the clock on the front room wall. There was still enough time left to prepare the poultices she'd normally use on a horse with a punctured sole. She felt it better to at least have it on hand should anyone come by the next day.

Using only cold ingredients, as the smell would reek should they come to room temperature, she mixed it quickly and hid the container at the bottom of the refrigerator.

It was none too soon; when Ila got back to the front room to check on the babies, she heard the trio returning.

She went into task mode and returned to the kitchen to put the teakettle on the stove and dropped a teabag into each of the cups. "Did you have fun?" Ila greeted them at the door. "Are the horses all worn out now? They didn't give you any trouble, I hope."

"Not a bit," Jack said. "They're fine horses. Whoever's getting them is very lucky."

"I'll take that as a compliment."

Meg and Tavis made their way over to the playpen and peeked at the sleeping babies. "How'd it go looking after two babies on your own?" Meg asked.

"Surprisingly easy. They're perfect little angels," Ila said, thinking about having just finished feeding Lani. She turned toward the kitchen. "How about some tea? I just put the kettle on and I hope you'll join me before you rush off."

The three of them sat at the table and waited for Ila to join them. She slipped the engagement ring off her finger and tucked it into her pocket, trading it with the vial. After pouring the contents into the green-trimmed cup, Ila watched the teabag absorb the liquid.

Ila inhaled deeply to relax her nerves and poured the hot water from the teakettle into each of the cups. Focusing on the day's events with the babies wasn't working anymore, so she switched to thinking about the mound of paperwork she still needed to finish in order to get through the agonizing moment of sickening her own child.

"Thank you," Tavis said when Ila placed a teacup in front of her.

"You're welcome." Ila moved on until she'd given everyone their teacups.

Ila refused to look when Meg sipped from the tainted cup, knowing all would be lost if she did. However, after a moment, she chanced a peek and found Meg looking at her—holding the teacup to her lips. Meg winked and sipped her tea before returning her attention back to Tavis and Jack.

When they finished, Meg cleared the serving tray to the kitchen while Ila gathered up the diaper bags. After dropping her ring in the bottom of Luke's, she set it aside to say goodbye to Tavis and Jack. Alec showed up before long to take Meg and Luke home.

With everyone gone, Ila went into action. She brought the stallion in from the pasture and led him to the largest stall, then put the poultice container and all the equipment necessary for a punctured sole on a table nearby him.

"Don't worry," she said, petting his muzzle to calm him when he caught the scent of the poultice. "I'm not gonna use it on you."

Ila called William when she got back inside. "It's done and I want you to know how much I hated doing it."

"Thank you," he said softly for her benefit. "I'm sorry I had to ask you to do that."

"I dropped my ring in Luke's bag, that'll be my reason for calling Meg in the morning. I've staged it so the stallion appears to have an injury that needs round the clock treatment, which will be why I call Tavis and tell her about Meg and Alec." She sighed into the phone. "You better hope this works, I don't want to have made my daughter sick for nothing."

"I'll be waiting by the monitors. Just make sure you tell Tavis how gravely ill Meg and Alec are."

~

The next morning, Ila picked up the phone. On the fourth ring, Alec finally answered. "Hello?"

"Alec, it's Ila. Can I talk to Meg, please? I think I may have lost my ring in Luke's bag."

"No, Ila, Meg's not feeling well."

"What do you mean? What's wrong with her? She was fine when she left here yesterday."

"Hold on," he said.

Ila heard what sounded like Alec retching, but it was muffled as though he'd set the phone down to spare her. After a minute or so, he continued to speak and he sounded awful.

"Neither one of us are feeling well. I can't talk right now. I need to check on Meg and Luke. I'll try to call you later."

He hung up then, and Ila dialed Tavis' number.

She picked up right away, "Hello?"

"Hey, Tavis, it's Ila. Are you feeling okay?"

"Yes, why?"

"Apparently, Meg and Alec are very sick. I just got off the phone with him and he could barely talk, and he said Meg was too sick to come to the phone. I'm worried about them, and Luke, too. I want to check on them, but my stallion has a medical emergency and has to be dosed every thirty minutes. Maybe I should call Dr. Patrick to go—"

"No. I'll send Jack over to check on them first."

Ila hadn't thought of this scenario and had to come up with a quick solution. "Do you think he should? What if it's contagious?"

"Oh." Tavis conceded Ila may have a point. "It could be, I'll ask my father to go instead. I'll tell him to call you after he checks on them."

It was the best Ila could do. "Thank you, Tavis."

After Tavis hung up with Ila, she explained to Jack what the call was about while putting her shoes on. She'd already knocked on Sebastian's door when it occurred to her that Chaza should know as well. As she headed back down the steps, the door opened.

"What's wrong?" Sebastian called out to her. "Where are you going?"

"I need to talk to you, come with me to Chaza's," she said and continued on her way.

Sebastian shut the door and caught up to her. Once they were inside, Tavis told them what Ila said on the phone. They, too, were concerned about Luke if Meg and Alec were so sick they couldn't talk on the phone. Sebastian and Chaza agreed to go over there together and Tavis suggested that Chaza cloak herself instead of relying on a storm.

~

William watched on the monitor as Tavis and Sebastian walked out of the house the woman was staying in. Though he didn't see the woman, he guessed by their movements that she must be with them. Still, he worried he could be wrong. Sebastian drove away, and William watched him traverse to the side of the island where the stone house was; not too far from where he sat, tracking their every move.

He waited for confirmation that the woman was with Sebastian. Finally, he got it when Sebastian came around to the passenger side of the cart and waited for what could only be someone to join him before going to the front door. William jumped to his feet.

Avoiding the traveling lanes, William took the forest footpaths to the newcomer houses and parked the cart deep in the woods. He eased around the back of the house and spied on Jack and Tavis' to make sure they weren't outside. Seeing no one, he crept up the back stairs, opened the door quickly, but shut it slowly once inside. Before releasing the doorknob, William held his breath to listen for any sound that he wasn't alone.

The house was silent, yet he still worried someone would come in and catch him. He forced himself to let go of the doorknob and went straight to the nearest bathroom. The beautiful sight of a hairbrush on the sink counter made him almost want to cry joyful tears. If he weren't so nervous, he figured he probably would.

He managed to get the sterile gloves on despite his shaking hands and started pulling hairs from the brush, stuffing them into the collection bag as fast as he could. Satisfied he'd collected enough, he sealed the bag and shoved it into his pocket.

William didn't concern himself with removing the gloves, he only wanted out of the house. It wasn't until he was back in his cart and driving away did he feel secure enough to trust that he'd actually gotten away with it.

Back in the surveillance room, William poured himself a glass of scotch. After draining it, he poured another full glass—not caring at all that it wasn't noon yet. He glanced at the monitor showing the stone house and saw Sebastian's cart still there.

The scotch finally did its magic and relaxed him. He called Dr. Han to give him the good news and said he'd bring the sample to Digamma right away. Before he left, he called Ila to tell her they'd been successful and that he would see her later.

Feeling confident and powerful, from both his luck and the expensive scotch, William stared at the stone house on the screen. "Enjoy the last of your freedom, Sebastian," he said and walked out of the room.

~

Inside the stone house, Sebastian and Chaza forced Alec into bed with Meg by reassuring him they'd stay however long it took until they were well enough to take care of Luke on their own. Alec didn't have the strength to resist; he fell into a feverish sleep alongside Meg.

Chaza placed empty trash bins on each side of their bed in case either of them woke up sick. From what she had seen of the place, she'd prefer they didn't try making it to the bathroom since a good half of their previous attempts hadn't been successful.

"What do you think's wrong with them?" Chaza asked later in the kitchen, stirring a bland vegetable broth while Sebastian fed Luke a bottle at the table.

"I'm not sure exactly." Sebastian considered their symptoms. "It seems like they've contracted some sort of a viral illness, but what confuses me is that Luke isn't showing any symptoms."

"Maybe it was something they ate."

"Can you tell what they had for dinner last night?"

"It doesn't look like they had anything." Chaza turned the stove off when the broth came to a boil and put a lid on the pot to keep it warm. "The only dishes I've found are all Luke's."

"Tavis said Alec was at work all day yesterday while she, Jack, and Meg were at Ila's. The little bit Alec could answer was that Meg got sick first and then shortly after, so did he." Sebastian frowned. "Maybe they picked up something from Ila's, after Tavis and Jack left." He handed Luke to Chaza. "I should call Ila and find out if she's been feeling okay."

Sebastian dialed Ila's number. On the seventh ring, he hung up. "No answer, maybe she's out in the stables. Tavis mentioned something was wrong with the stallion."

"I hope that's where she is. What if she's sick, too, and can't get to the phone?"

"I'll ride over there and check on her," Sebastian said. "If there's anything wrong, I'll call you from there."

~

He knocked several times on Ila's front door to no avail. Sebastian thought about letting himself in, but decided to check the stables first. As he stood in the stable doorway, he heard Ila consoling the stallion.

"That's a good boy." She petted his muzzle. "It's okay, I'm not gonna put that smelly stuff on you."

Ila seemed to be feeling well, certainly not suffering like Meg and Alec. He stepped into the stable and the scratchy-crunching sound of his shoes on the gravel got her attention. She swung around at the unexpected noise and her eyes widened when he approached.

There was no recognition in her eyes, only bewilderment. The reaction confused Sebastian and he stopped his advance to study the situation.

"Hi," she said.

"Hello, Ila. I just came from Meg and Alec's. I tried calling you, but didn't get an answer… guess you were out here."

So, this is Sebastian, she thought. Her eyes raked across his form appreciatively.

Though Kyrie was a beautiful woman, it was obvious to Ila where Tavis and Alec got their extraordinary appearance from—the man standing in front of her was a paragon. She took a few mindless steps toward him, but stopped when her eyes met his again and realized she was doing a lousy job at guarding her thoughts.

"I'm sorry, Sebastian. Please, tell me how they're doing? Are they gonna be okay?" Ila imbued grave concern in her voice. Worried about the look on his face, how he seemed to bore into her every cell, she plunged into a world of meaningless images.

"They're resting for now," he said. "I was wondering how you were feeling."

"I'm fine, so far." She concentrated on the blank lines of the shipping forms. "Are you thinking they may have caught something?"

"Possibly, but it could also be they ingested something." Sebastian saw the same blank lines Ila thought about and it made no sense to him. He wondered why she'd concern herself with paperwork while Meg lay sick in bed.

"Are they gonna be okay?" she asked again.

It seemed Ila was distraught when she asked the question, but it was over-inflated and she continued thinking of random things—Sebastian was forced to read a list of poultice ingredients repeatedly.

He frowned at what appeared to be a mantra she silently chanted over and over again, making her seem addle-minded. It occurred to him that she hadn't asked who was staying with Alec and Meg while he was here checking on her. Sebastian moved closer to her, hoping to find an explanation for her odd behavior. She avoided him by side-stepping at the last moment and she thought about a moment when she'd been feeding Lani.

Sebastian felt it better to answer her question first. "They'll be fine, once whatever's wrong with them runs its course. I'm just glad you're not sick, I was worried when no one answered the phone."

He was being cautious with her and she knew it.

"I'm so relieved," she said with a hand over her chest. "Thank you so much for going over there to check on them." Ila remembered waving goodbye to all of them as they left her house.

It was clear to him now that Ila deliberately thought of things to shield something else, or to hide some memory. Frankly, it surprised him that she was capable of doing it. What bothered him was that Ila thought only of recent events.

He quizzed her. "You're very welcome, it was no problem at all. You know I like helping others." Sebastian shrugged, grinning, as though recalling to mind some previous folly. "Like that time when Tavis and I first met you. Meg was helping you bring the horses in from the pasture" –he pointed at the stallion– "but this one walked away from the others. Of course, I thought I'd be helpful and get him back for you, but you said I'd be lucky if all he did was run off since he didn't know me yet."

"And he would've, too, he's very spirited." Ila turned and smiled at the stallion.

"Thankfully, he and I are great friends now," Sebastian lied again—he'd not set foot in Ila's stables since that very day.

"Yes, I'm sure he'd come to you now."

"Let's not test him." Sebastian shook his head. "I imagine he's not in the mood. I should be getting back, I promised Alec I'd stay and help with Luke."

"You will? Oh, thank you again. That makes me feel so much better."

Some of the tension left Ila and it was the first real emotion Sebastian had detected from her yet. Though truly relieved and thankful, it was born of guilt and shame. When he lingered too long watching her, she stiffened again and another wall of shipping forms presented itself for his perusal.

"I'll call you if anything changes," he said.

~

On the drive back to the stone house, Sebastian sorted through the bizarre encounter. If Ila was trying to prevent him from sensing her thoughts by thinking of trivial matters, then it meant she knew to be careful around him. He didn't like the timing of her behavior and William's presence. Sebastian decided to talk to Chaza about it since she had more experience with Ila.

When he returned to the stone house, he found Chaza pouring water into a large bowl of ice at the kitchen sink. She'd just got Luke to sleep and wanted to take the ice water upstairs to place cool compresses on Meg's and Alec's foreheads. If their fevers spiked any higher, she suggested packing them in ice.

"They're strong," Sebastian said and took the bowl from Chaza. "They'll pull through this."

"I hope so."

"Come on, let's check on them," he said. "Afterward, I want to talk to you about Ila. She's not sick, but there's something else troubling me."

Meg and Alec were still sick and feverish, but Sebastian determined they weren't getting any worse. "The next few hours should tell us a lot about the direction this illness will go," he told her.

Back downstairs, Chaza checked on Luke again to find him still sleeping, and still cool to the touch. Sighing with relief, she patted his back and quietly left his bedroom to join Sebastian.

"You wanted to talk to me about Ila?"

"Physically, she's fine," Sebastian said. "But there's *something* definitely wrong with her."

"What do you mean?"

"Ila was in the stables when I got there. When she saw me, she looked at me as though she'd never seen me before. I sensed her comparing me to Alec and Tavis and then she switched her thoughts to meaningless things, like paperwork. You and I both know that's an excellent strategy to keep certain thoughts private."

"I've never found Ila to be particularly strong-minded." Chaza grimaced. "I don't mean that in a bad way, I just seriously doubt she could pull that off. Maybe she really was concerned about the paperwork. Ila's high-strung, she obsesses over stuff like that."

"Then why did it seem like she didn't know me? It wasn't until I told her that

I'd just come from checking on Meg and Alec that she appeared to realize who I was. I tested her, too. I mentioned the time Tavis and I first met her, but I changed the factual events and she didn't correct me. Chaza, I don't think she remembers ever meeting me before today."

"She's an odd-ball, always has been. My guess is that she was being socially polite by not correcting you."

"Tavis said Ila couldn't check on Meg and Alec herself because her stallion was injured. There was nothing wrong with him. In fact, when I went into the stables she was reassuring him that she wasn't going to put the foul-smelling medicine on him. The whole time I was talking to her, the horse walked around his stall without any problems."

"Well, that bit of news does bother me," Chaza said. "Ila has always fussed over Meg. Even if the horse was injured, it's not like Ila to send someone else to check on Meg, especially if she thought something was wrong."

"Don't forget, she didn't want Tavis or Jack coming over here either."

"Yeah, it seems like she wanted you to check on them. But why?"

"I'm wondering if there's a connection between Ila's behavior and William Davis being here."

It frustrated Chaza to consider the possibility, but the fact was that her daughter was upstairs, sickened by who knows what, and there had to be a reason for it. "All right, assuming there's a connection, why would Ila want *you* specifically to be the one to come here?"

Sebastian stood and went to the large bay window, scanning the landscape as far as he could see for any hint that something bad was about to happen. There was nothing—only the familiar scene of the oak tree, Meg's flowers, and the ocean beyond. He worried that if there was nothing occurring here, then something must be happening somewhere else.

He turned from the window, and Chaza saw fear in his eyes.

"What's wrong?" she asked.

"What if Ila wanted me away from my house?" Sebastian nearly knocked over every chair and table to get to the phone.

He hated the archaic communications on Gamma and struggled to dial the right number. Tavis answered on the first ring and, though he couldn't see her face, he knew it was her voice. Calm returned to him at hearing her barrage of questions.

"So you think they'll be okay? What about Luke? Why has it taken you so long to call me? I've been so worried… Jack's about ready to lock me in a closet."

Her anger was beautiful to Sebastian. "I'm sorry, Tavis. Chaza and I have been busy. They're doing better, and Luke doesn't seem to be suffering from whatever made them sick. How are you and Jack feeling?"

"We're fine," Tavis said. "Do you think it was something they ate?"

"It doesn't look like they cooked last night. What did you have at Ila's yesterday?"

"Meg made sandwiches to take with us, but all three of us ate them and Jack and I haven't had any problems."

"Did you have anything else before you left Ila's?"

"Just tea," she said. "Ila had already prepared it and wanted us to have some with her before we left. Alec wasn't there yet, so it can't have been that."

"How was Ila feeling yesterday?"

"Fine, but she was really stressed out about the forms she had to fill out. That was all she seemed to think about."

"Thank you, Tavis. I'll let you know how Meg and Alec are doing throughout the day."

"Is she okay?" Chaza asked when Sebastian set the phone down.

"Yes."

"Do you still think Ila was trying to get you away from your house?"

"Yes, I do," he said and returned to the bay window to think.

He stared at Luke's swing blowing back and forth in the wind for a while. His gaze moved up the massive tree trunk and he marveled at its gnarled twists, knots, and numerous cavities. A small yellow bird flew in, hovering alongside several branches before landing on one of the limbs higher up. Sebastian watched the bird preen its feathers until it took off again. On the trunk of the tree, behind where the bird had perched, he saw it—the answer staring right at him.

It was a camera; so small and insignificant that it could be overlooked as a normally occurring tree knot. Yet, there was no mistaking what it was meant to observe; it faced the front and side of the house and the forest behind it. William watched who came and went from the stone house; the only question was, for how long?

Sebastian turned to Chaza and more of the clues fell into place. So perfectly, in fact, that he would've been impressed if it had involved anyone else other than the people he cared about.

"I just spotted a camera on that tree," he said and took a seat in the chair opposite the sofa Chaza sat on. "When you came here the other day to talk to Meg, where you cloaked?"

Her eyes widened and he had his answer. Still, she said, "No."

"He saw you, I'm sure of it. William wants to know who you are now." He leaned back in the chair. "Ila must be helping him. It wasn't me William wanted out of the house, it's you."

"But—"

"No, Chaza," he stopped her attempt to defend Ila. "You're wrong about her. She's helping William, she served them tea just before they left her house yesterday. Ila was alone with the babies, she probably got their DNA samples. There's only one other person William would want to get a sample from next… you."

"I'm sorry." Chaza averted her eyes to the floor. "I should've been more careful."

"Don't, I can't handle humility from you." He got up and sat next to her on the sofa, putting his arm around her shoulder. "You can't have known Ila would do that to Meg, regardless as to who she's aligned with."

Chaza was disgusted, and it still seemed impossible to have been so wrong about Ila. Shoving Sebastian away, she stood and walked toward the front door. A hint of light emanated from all around her and it worried Sebastian.

"Hey," he called to her, "where are you going?"

"Where do you think I'm going?"

"You can't do that."

"Oh, yes I can." She turned to face him. "I want to see Ila for myself, I have to know."

"Not right now, Chaza," he said, pleading. "I need your help here. We need to check on Meg and Alec again, and we need to start trying to get them to take some fluids."

She abandoned the attempt to leave, but anger still etched her expression. "Why hasn't Luke become sick?"

"Either it isn't contagious, or Ila inoculated the babies." He saw how close she was to changing her mind about not leaving. "Will you stay and help me?"

"Yes." Her voice was filled with miserable defeat.

"Don't worry, they'll all be home soon."

After a few hours, Meg and Alec began to feel better; enough to take some of the broth Chaza had made for them and they wanted as much water as Sebastian would bring to them. By late evening, they were both starving for something more than just broth and they came downstairs to eat.

"Do you need for us to stay longer?" Chaza asked them.

"I think we're gonna be fine now," Meg said and looked at Alec.

"I feel a whole lot better." Alec nodded, then turned to Chaza and Sebastian. "You've both been a great help, I don't know what we would've done without you. Thank you for coming over."

"You're very welcome," Chaza said. "Call us if you need anything, we'll come right back."

"We will," Meg said.

~

"Drive by her house," Chaza said when Sebastian drove away from the stone house.

"I don't think that's a good idea."

"You don't have to stop, just drive by. Okay?"

Sebastian went in the direction of Ila's house and as he drove past it, Chaza noted how all the blinds and curtains had been drawn. This wasn't like Ila; she was notorious for displaying the entire front of her house for all the islanders to bear witness to her magnificent décor.

He sensed Chaza's disappointment when he continued driving on. "Another time," Sebastian said.

After parking the cart in front of his house, Sebastian walked with Chaza into hers to inspect her belongings. He followed her as she made her way through the house, searching for differences.

When nothing seemed astray in the kitchen, Chaza went to the only other obvious place—the bathroom. She stared silently at her hairbrush for what seemed an eternity to Sebastian. He looked at it and saw that what few hairs remained stuck out in all directions as if someone had cleaned it, but stopped halfway through the task. Several long individual strands trailed down the front of the counter to add more of a glaring carelessness—indicating the person was in a hurry.

"It appears you were right," Chaza said, still staring at the brush.

"Until I have more time to think about what this means, let's keep this to ourselves," he said. "By that, I mean I don't want Tavis knowing."

23

And So It Begins

Sebastian went home, defeated after discovering the brush had been tampered with. The time had come for him to give the threatening problem the consideration it required, and to come up with a plan that would ensure the safety of those most important to him. This would have to wait a little while longer, though. Exhausted from the long day, he collapsed onto his bed and fell asleep within seconds of his head meeting the pillow.

The rain began to fall in the middle of the night; the gentle kind that lulls and comforts you. For those still awake, the whispering rain calls on you to give in to the drowsy pull of your eyelids. For those already asleep, it takes you to a deeper, more peaceful, slumber—to the place where reality doesn't matter for an unencumbered moment. And thus it softly rained for a while, before the clouds became more determined to empty themselves onto Gamma, growing more punishing as the night marched forward to dawn.

When the darkness of night gave way to the light of a new day, it was still raining. Normally, the sun would cast beautiful rays of sunlight all over the island, refracting light in the dewdrops that had collected on leaves and flower petals. There was no such brilliant display this morning, only grey, and it matched Sebastian's somber mood as he sat in a chair on his back porch.

Shielded from the downpour by the porch roof, he watched the rain fall. He wondered if his dark emotions produced the rain, or if it was Alec's inattentiveness while recovering from his illness. Either way, he welcomed the inclement weather. It kept Tavis inside her house, delaying the moment he'd have to put on a brave face and pretend like nothing was wrong.

There was a lot wrong, however, and Sebastian felt trapped. It wouldn't be long before William had the test results; he'd know more about Chaza, and that Meg was her daughter.

Movement near the trees got Sebastian's attention. He searched for the source of what dared to disturb his meditation and saw Chaza. He wondered where she'd been off to before she noticed him on the porch. Then it occurred to him exactly where she had intended to go. Instead, she came over and sat in the chair next to him.

He said, "You could've asked to borrow an umbrella."

Chaza's quip was instant. "You could've offered to drive me there."

"Let's go. I wouldn't mind seeing what there is to discover myself."

~

Sebastian took the forest footpaths to avoid being seen by anyone, though it was unlikely given the early morning hour and unpleasant weather. When they neared Ila's house, they came across a cart parked in the woods.

"Think it's William's?" Chaza asked when Sebastian slowed down to inspect it.

"Yes."

He drove to a denser part of the forest and cloaked the cart before beginning the trek through the trees to Ila's house. The rain came down harder with every step that brought them closer, pelting the umbrella they shared.

They approached the back of Ila's house. Without having to discuss the matter, they cloaked themselves, walked up the back stairs, and paused by the door to listen for potential conversation. Hearing nothing, Sebastian opened the door.

Stepping inside the eerily quiet house, Chaza followed Sebastian down the hallway toward the bedrooms. They passed Meg's old bedroom first and continued on to Ila's. Rounding the doorway entrance, they witnessed Ila's head resting on William's chest, his arm wrapped around her. Both were asleep and their clothes were strewn about all over the floor—empty wineglasses sat on the nightstand.

Sebastian had seen enough and he turned away, but Chaza tugged on his arm and silently told him to wait. He relented and followed her back to Ila's kitchen as she searched for her own confirmation.

She found it in the trashcan under the sink. Underneath an empty wine bottle and several wet teabags were three empty vials—seals broken on each. Chaza pocketed them and motioned to Sebastian that they could leave now.

Hatred emanated from Sebastian as they passed by Ila's bedroom doorway again. Once they reached the cart and had traveled a good distance away, Chaza pulled the empty vials from her pocket to examine them.

"I recognize the two that have pink residue as being a typical vaccine that's given to infants. Without the proper equipment, I can only guess at what was in the clear vial."

Sebastian brought the cart to a stop. "Proper equipment isn't necessary to confirm the obvious."

Chaza frowned at him. "I don't like what this place is doing to you. You seem… dark."

"Kind of like how you look?" He gave a disgusted nod toward the vials still in her hands. "While you're holding the proof that Ila deliberately made Meg sick?"

Chaza deflated at his words; he was right. The woman whose hands she put the life of her child in had not only failed to protect her, but took risks with her life. This kind of betrayal could turn saints into unrecognizable creatures hell-bent on revenge. She threw the vials away from her and watched them bounce along the forest floor before coming to a stop in a rain puddle.

"I mentioned to you before what living here can do to someone, even us," she said. "You've been here too long, you need to go home before it's too late."

"It's time for everyone to go home, the sooner the better. It won't be easy considering how closely we're being watched now."

An awkward silence descended on them as they each remembered a previous conversation about the transportation dilemma. Chaza spoke first: "I feel we're about to have a disagreement."

"Maybe not," he said. "Do you still have your amulet?"

She broke eye contact with him, turning away to stare off at the falling rain.

Sebastian's purpose for inquiring about her amulet was that when two are placed together to form a diamond, they could be used as a communication device to their home, no matter where they were.

There was too much shame and guilt for her to look at him or answer his question with words. Instead, she allowed Sebastian access to a memory—knowing and hating that it would answer him.

Sebastian understood immediately what she meant to do. The initial feeling of reception and comforting warmth—euphoric in nature—graced him as she opened her mind. It surprised him. Even before the problems began in their marriage, Chaza was always guarded and private with her thoughts and memories.

"Another rare glimpse, are you sure?" he asked; a hint of playfulness colored his tone.

"Please, Sebastian, before I change my mind."

Since she wouldn't look at him, Sebastian reached for her hand and closed his eyes. At first, she made to pull away, but relaxed and allowed him to lace his fingers into hers. What he saw first was what he'd seen before, Chaza looking back one more time at the sleeping Ila holding the newborn Meg in the cave before running off. Her new intent was to show him what happened after she had left the cave.

She raced through the darkened forests at an unnatural speed—she was somewhere between her light and physical form. The canvas bag slung over her shoulder occasionally slammed into her back when she would jump over any fallen limbs laying on the path. There was pain, but it never slowed her pace.

She reached Mors Cliff and sat at the very tip to look out over the moonlit water of the ocean. At one point she glanced down the jagged, rocky cliff and Sebastian saw its violence through her eyes. Even though it was Chaza's memory, Sebastian still hated the damn cliff and had to resist the urge to pull himself out of her memories.

After a minute or so, Chaza brought the canvas bag around and set it in her lap; she unzipped it and pulled out her amulet. Similar to his, the only differences were the gems—instead of sapphires, Chaza's were emeralds.

Chaza lifted the amulet up in front of her and Sebastian suffered through her tears of sorrow and regret. She held the amulet still higher, until it was level with the moon. When the light shown through the emeralds, a bit of happiness return to her at seeing their home. Sebastian knew the look of the smile he felt on her face and how it shared a moment with one last tear.

And then she flung the amulet far away from her and into the waves below. She lay down, closed her eyes, and willed sleep to find her and end this horrible day. The memory ended here. Chaza erected the wall of privacy as quickly as she'd removed it, and Sebastian was shut out again.

Releasing her hand, he said, "Well, there goes that idea."

"I'm sorry," she whispered, still refusing to meet his gaze.

"Why'd you do it?"

"I had resigned myself to never seeing my home again. Keeping it would only be a painful reminder," she said. "I'm so sorry."

Sebastian was among the few who'd ever seen Chaza cry, he'd seen her tears plenty of times during her miscarriages. They stung him then, they stung him still. Though her head was turned away from him, he knew the tears were rolling down her cheeks.

"Chaza, please don't cry." He couldn't stand her pain anymore. Hoping she'd allow him, he pulled her into a hug and said, "You'll cause a star to die."

She wiped her cheeks dry, and finally faced him. "Still telling children's tales?" Chaza braved a smile after sitting up straight in her seat.

"I wish you and Tavis would believe me." Sebastian put a hand to his chest and feigned a wounded pride, causing Chaza to chuckle.

It was a short-lived reprieve of their worries. Sebastian sighed and said, "I've been lying to Tavis about the reality of our not having enough pods to get everyone home."

"What are you going to tell her now?"

"My plan is to keep lying to her, at least until the last minute." To finally admit it sounded strange and scary to him. "I want to discuss it with Alec first, because I'm hoping he'll help with Tavis when it's time to send her home. Knowing how she is, it might be best if she left first."

"Don't plan on her cooperating with you," Chaza said. "I assume you mean to tell her you'll be leaving last, she may fight you on it."

He turned the cart on, saying as he drove away, "I'll do whatever I have to do to get her and everyone else safely back home."

After a few silent minutes, Chaza chanced a delicate question. "Is it a boy or a girl?"

"A boy."

Chaza thought it would hurt to hear Kyrie carried another child of Sebastian's, but it didn't. They were facing something much bigger. All of their children depended on them to get them back to a home where the basic right of choice reigned for all to enjoy.

"Well then, I'll do whatever I have to do to help you get *everyone* home, lies and all if necessary," she said and saw he was close to tears. "Oh, no you don't, remember all those stars you're so fond of. And don't you dare say thank you, I'll kick you as hard as I can if you do."

~

When they returned to the newcomer houses, the rain had subsided and the first few rays of sunshine found a way through the dissipating clouds to reach the ground. The break in the rain had brought Tavis out of the house. She had Lani in her arms and Jack held a frog up to them; he must have said something funny, as Tavis was laughing.

"What have you got there, Jack?" Sebastian asked.

"A Mountain Chicken." Jack turned the huge frog toward Sebastian. "I found it out back by the koi pond."

Sebastian was amused at first, but then he looked into Jack's eyes and saw that he was completely serious. "Jack, surely you know that's not a chicken."

Jack chuckled. "The scientific name is Leptodactylus fallax, Mountain Chicken is a common name," he said and handed the frog to Sebastian.

"Ah, common names." Sebastian examined the creature. "I wasn't aware you knew so much about amphibians."

"I was fascinated with them when I was growing up. I used to drive my mother crazy because I'd always try sneaking them into the house."

It took both hands to hold onto the frog, who seemed like he'd had enough of being held captive. "I think he wants to be free again," Sebastian said. "Perhaps he was on his way to meet a female companion."

"It's possible," Jack said. "I should put him back where I found him. These frogs almost went extinct, but conservationists stepped in and now their population has rebounded."

"I'll do it."

Sebastian went around the back of the house and held the frog to the ground. He eased his grip, but the frog stayed near Sebastian's hands—it made him smile.

"Don't grow complacent, Mountain Chicken, just because you've been denied your freedom. Go now."

As though the frog understood, it leapt away from his hands, bounding off toward the forest. Sebastian watched it go for a while. When he stood to leave, he found Jack standing close by. Jack's worried expression was full of unspoken questions, as though he'd watched and listened to the entire releasing of the frog. Sebastian found it odd that he hadn't been aware of his presence.

"Did it upset you that I caught the frog?" Jack asked, concerned Sebastian found it offensive. "I only wanted to show it to Tavis and Lani, I didn't intend to keep it."

"Even if the thought to keep the frog had crossed your mind, you wouldn't have been able to do it... not for long. You're not a little boy anymore, Jack. You're a man, and a very special one at that. Taking away the liberty of another being would be unacceptable to you now."

"We're not just talking about the frog anymore, are we?"

"No."

"Are you worried about your freedom?"

"I'm worried about *our* freedom." Sebastian glanced at the koi swimming around in the pond. "Now's not the time to talk about it."

"Maybe you should make time."

"I wish I could, but Tavis might sense it and I can't have that right now. I will tell you this, William Davis is a bigger threat than we realized. It's more important than ever that you don't let Tavis and Lani out of your sight."

"You're gonna have to tell me more eventually."

"I know. I have to figure some things out first. Will you trust me, Jack?"

It was a giant step for both of them and it softened Jack's reserve. "I trust you, because I know how much you love Tavis," he said, humbled by Sebastian's need of his understanding.

Though Sebastian was relieved, the urge to be playful proved impossible to resist. With a straight face, Sabastian said, "I'm glad you finally realized that I love Tavis more than you do."

It took a moment, but Jack sorted out the switch to their silently agreed upon quarrelsome nature. "You're nuts, and wrong," he said. "*I* love her more, just like she loves me more than she loves you."

Sebastian smiled as Jack turned away; he was at peace that he could depend on him to keep Tavis and Lani safe. He knew Jack loved them, that he was devoted to them, and would prefer death over allowing anything to happen to either one of them.

It was Tavis that Sebastian worried about. If she knew the full impact of what their immediate future held, she'd stop at nothing to prevent it from happening. What he needed was to talk to Alec, to tell him how to handle Tavis should he not be able to do it himself.

~

"Hello?" Alec answered the phone.

"Alec, how are you and Meg feeling?"

"Much better, almost back to normal."

Sebastian got right to the point. "I need to talk to you about something."

Several seconds passed before Alec responded. "Okay, I'm listening."

"Not on the phone." It disappointed him that Alec had resurrected his usual aloofness. "I need to talk to you in person."

"I'm not leaving Meg alone right now."

"And you shouldn't. I'm thinking we could get together this evening. I, Chaza, Jack, Tavis, and Lani could come over to your house for dinner. You and I can talk while we're fishing. Chaza will be there to watch over everyone."

"Have you already talked it over with Chaza?"

Sebastian laughed to himself; it still amazed him that Alec had grown to trust Chaza more than his own father. "She knows that you and I need to talk, and she agrees that it's important. I wanted to run the plan by you first before I told everyone else, in case you and Meg weren't quite well enough."

"Well," Alec considered lying, but was interrupted.

"Please don't insult me by trying to lie. This can't wait any longer, we're running out of time. You have others depending on you to make the right decisions, you can't keep avoiding it."

Alec wanted to call Sebastian all sorts of names and then hang up the phone, but something deep inside of him nagged to be liberated. He couldn't suppress the overwhelming feeling that everything he considered to be most precious in his life, and beyond even that, depended solely on his next response.

"I'll get the fishing gear ready after I tell Meg we're having company over."

Sebastian wanted to thank Alec, but felt it was inappropriate. "I'll tell the others our plans."

~

It was late afternoon when everyone showed up at the stone house. The entire drive over, Sebastian thought about how he was going to handle excluding Jack from his conversation with Alec. Ultimately, he decided to deal with it when the time came.

While Jack was preoccupied with looking at the painting of the horses Meg had started on, Sebastian turned to Alec. "Let me help you get the fishing gear ready."

Once they were in the barn, Sebastian said to him, "There are a couple of things I need to say to you, but first I want you to know I discovered a surveillance camera on the oak tree. It's pointed at your house and I think it's been there for a while."

Alec groaned and contemplated whether or not to make it obvious to William that he knew about the camera the next time he walked by it. "All right, what else?"

"Not now, I can hear Jack coming out. Find an excuse for Jack to leave while we're fishing so I can talk to you privately."

"There you are," Jack said as he walked into the barn. "You guys ready to bet on who catches the biggest fish?"

"I'll bet you five seashells that Sebastian catches the biggest fish, but releases it because he wants to set it free," Alec said, keeping the mood light. He saw them exchange a glance and wondered what he was missing. "What?"

"Nothing." Jack laughed. "Sebastian had a moment with a frog earlier today."

Alec laughed, too. The image of Sebastian holding a frog was too much to successfully stifle the laughter.

"Okay, that's quite enough fun at my expense," Sebastian said, but smiled.

The trio headed to the beach and settled on a nearby spot for surf fishing. Soon Alec said, "Oops, we forgot the tackle box with the hooks. Jack, would you mind getting it?"

"No problem," Jack said and trotted off.

Alec turned to Sebastian. "Tell me before he gets back."

"I want you to know where the transportation is hidden. There are three pods buried at the base of the footpath that leads up to the cave. It's enough to get you all home. Each pod can hold two adults and a small child. I'm telling you about this because I'm counting on you to get everyone in them when the time comes."

"I never said I was willing to leave, remember?"

"Of course you're leaving, staying here isn't an option."

"It's my decision, Sebastian."

There wasn't enough time to argue with Alec, he dove right in to relaying the facts. "William has collected the DNA samples from Luke and Lani that he's been so desperate to get. He got one from Chaza as well, he'll know she's Meg's mother soon."

"How'd he get them?" Alec asked, angry at the thought of William being anywhere near Luke.

"He did it with Ila's help. I don't know what they've done to her, but she's helping them. She's responsible for making both of you sick to get Chaza out of the house. William took hair samples from Chaza's brush while we were here yesterday."

"Why do you need my help?" Alec asked. "What exactly am I supposed to do?"

"If William finds a way to detain me, I'll need for you to get everyone in the pods and leave. By everyone, I mean Kyrie and I hope Chaza as well."

"Why aren't you asking Tavis to do this? Doesn't she know more about these *pods?*"

"I can't ask her, I can't even tell her about my plan." Sebastian sighed. "Do the math Alec, there aren't enough pods to get us all home. I want Chaza to go home, and Kyrie's carrying your brother."

A darkness flashed in Alec's eyes at the reminder of his mother's pregnancy. "Then why don't *you* leave? Maybe everything will go back to normal if you weren't here. Did you ever consider that?"

It was clear to Sebastian, Alec lacked too much information to make a rational decision. He advanced toward Alec, his hand mere inches from his shoulder when he saw Alec's eyes widen. He followed the direction of Alec's gaze and found Jack standing behind him; and he wasn't carrying a tackle box—he had never left.

"That's the second time today you've snuck up on me without my detecting your presence," Sebastian said to Jack. "I'm beginning to wonder why that is."

"What were you about to do to Alec? The same thing you were gonna do to me when *I* thought about not leaving here?" Jack stepped closer to them.

"Not exactly," Sebastian said. "I was only going to absorb the conversation."

Jack's eyes narrowed at the comment. Sebastian had planned to absorb every memory Jack had of Tavis. Unlike with Alec, there would've been no second chances, no do-overs, only complete oblivion. It made Jack feel unequal.

"You're wrong, Jack." Sebastian easily read his thoughts. "I did give you a second chance, because I trusted you and I still do. More than you know."

His expression softened, but there was still worry in his frown. "Please don't do that to Alec. I heard everything you said and if you'll allow it, maybe I can help."

"How?"

"By confirming a lot of what you said. First of all, there are detailed files of every person on Gamma, and on Delta. DNA profiling is probably page two of everyone's file. I'm sure William has already seen Chaza through the cameras and discovered there's no file on her. They'll do whatever it takes to get that profile. Usually, the island physician handles collecting samples. I don't suppose Chaza's ever gone to Dr. Patrick, has she?"

Sebastian snorted. "Of course not."

"Tavis won't allow him anywhere near Lani." Jack then asked Alec, "Has he seen Luke?"

"No, Chaza warned me not to let him examine Luke."

"Then they'd have to use other methods to get testable samples," Jack said. "I was there and I can confirm that Ila seemed a little different. She was nice to me, didn't snarl at me once."

"Yeah." Alec gave it some thought. "She was nice to me, too. And she forgot Meg and Luke were coming over."

"Did you ever hear Ila's name mentioned at the research station?" Sebastian asked.

"No, they don't discuss that sort of thing around research employees," Jack said. "Maintenance workers hear a lot of stuff, though, and they're bad about gossiping. Also, some things are obvious. The scientific team has departments, one of them is the psychology division, but maintenance employees call it the fruitcake factory."

Sebastian blank-stared at Jack. "The what?"

"On the surface, they're responsible for the sociology of the islands. Beneath the surface, their work involves mind control through the use of brainwashing and advanced levels of hypnosis. When Tavis showed me your memory modification abilities, it made me think of how badly they'd want that trait for themselves. It makes their techniques look like parlor tricks."

"Do you think they've done that to Ila?" Sebastian asked, sounding horrified, but only because he was already sure of the answer.

"It's a possibility."

"Chaza and I suspected Ila was involved somehow in Meg's illness, so we cloaked ourselves and went into her house early this morning. We found her and William asleep in her bed. Chaza discovered three empty vials in the trashcan, two of which had remnants of a pink liquid she thinks were vaccines given to the babies to prevent them from getting sick."

"They were… *together*?" Alec asked.

"Yes, Alec. They were naked. I think that eliminates a friendly sleepover."

"Chaza's right about the pink vials being infant vaccines," Jack said. "I had to take the same thing. It tastes sweet so the infants will consume it." When Sebastian and Alec frowned at him, he mumbled, "I'm not a big fan of needles."

"There was a clear vial, also empty. Any ideas on what that was?"

"I'm only guessing, but something William didn't want the babies to catch."

"I went over to her house to check on her because she didn't answer the phone. I found her in the stables." Sebastian shook his head. "The stallion wasn't injured and she didn't know who I was until I mentioned Alec and Meg's names."

"Sounds like something's been done to her," Jack said. "There's one way to find out for sure."

"How?" Sebastian and Alec asked in unison.

"Island physicians keep two sets of files on each inhabitant. One is the medical chart kept at the office in the town center. The other is what I heard were called the *classified* files. Those would have the more sensitive information like DNA profiles, family tree, and who knows what else. Dr. Patrick probably keeps them under lock and key at his own house. If we could find a way to break in, we could look at Ila's file."

"Damn, you're smart!" Sebastian said.

"I'll do it," Alec said. "I make the order deliveries, no one questions why I'm at any particular house, whether they're home or not. I'm not sure how I'll get to the files if they're locked up, though."

"I can show you how to pick a lock," Jack said. Again, they frowned at him. "What? I did mention I grew up in East America."

"You'll have to be careful, Alec."

"That's not a problem for me," Alec said, eliciting a proud smile from Sebastian.

"Anything else you happened to have observed during your employment?" Sebastian asked Jack.

"Yeah, management meets with the East American military and a handful of politicians several times a year." Jack shrugged. "Unfortunately, not even maintenance workers can overhear what goes on in those meetings, the walls and doors are soundproof."

"That surprises me the least at this point," Sebastian muttered.

"If you don't mind, I'd like to ask *you* a few questions," Jack said.

"Go ahead."

"I heard what you said about the transportation. I assume the pods have weight limitations, is that right?"

"That's correct."

"There're only three?"

"Also correct."

"So, that's Tavis, myself, and Lani in one pod. Alec, Meg, and Luke go in the second pod. You want Kyrie in the third because—" Jack paused, not wanting to cause more tension between Alec and Sebastian. When he saw they were waiting for him to continue, he said, "She's pregnant, and you said you wanted Chaza to go."

Sebastian nodded. "That's what I want."

"But that would leave you here."

"Right."

"The islanders will freak out about so many disappearing at once. There's no way to prevent the chaos, management will probably destroy the island when they discover we've escaped… and if you're stranded here…"

"And now you know why I can't ask for Tavis' help." Sebastian turned away from them. "I can't ask for Chaza's help either. She knows the circumstances and she won't leave me here to die alone, but it's time for her to go home. She's been here far too long."

Jack turned away as well. Only Alec stood still, looking at both of their backs, but he felt something, too. He hesitated before he put his hand on Sebastian's shoulder.

"I'm sorry for doubting you," Alec said. "It doesn't matter who you are or where you came from, if you're willing to sacrifice yourself for us, then you're clearly a worthier person than all the ones you're trying to save."

Sebastian faced him. When Alec saw the raw emotion in Sebastian's eyes, tears threatened to well up in his own.

"No, none of that, a star dies with every tear," Sebastian said.

Alec had never heard this before and it made him smile.

"There, that's better."

"You have my support," Jack said. "I'll help you in every way I can."

"You have my support, too," Alec said.

"With the both of you working together, I know you'll get it done. However, Jack, I'm worried Tavis will sense these thoughts and memories from you."

"I can help him with that," Alec said. "I'll cloak his thoughts from Tavis. I cloaked my mother's and Meg's from both you and Tavis."

"You certainly did." Sebastian chuckled. "If Jack will allow it, I see no reason why it wouldn't work."

"It's not necessary, but if it'll make you feel better, then go ahead."

Sebastian was intrigued by Jack's confidence. "Why don't you think it's necessary?"

"Because I've noticed that I can keep thoughts private from her," Jack said. When Sebastian's eyebrows arched, he added, "Nothing important, just stuff like surprises for her and Lani."

"You're assimilating so quickly." Sebastian's brow knitted in concentration. "It's like you were one of us already."

"Well, that's not possible. I know where I was born and raised." Jack fidgeted under their scrutiny.

"Why hasn't William confronted you yet?" Alec asked. "With all the cameras around here, he has to have seen you by now."

"I don't know." Jack shrugged. "I've wondered about that myself."

"Think I'll find a file on you?" Alec asked, an edge of suspicion in his voice.

Jack thought it over. "I'm beginning to think you might. If you do, I want to know everything that's in it."

"I'll tell you if I find anything." Alec nodded, then grinned. "Come here, I want to give you a hug."

All three of them laughed as Alec embraced Jack. Though somewhat awkward for them, he successfully shielded Jack's thoughts. When Alec released him, Jack looked around as though he expected to feel different.

"That didn't hurt at all, did it?" Alec teased. "No needle required."

"Whatever. You both realize, I hope, that we haven't caught dinner."

"I'll do it, follow me and grab them as I pull them out," Sebastian said.

He waded out into a calm area of the surf and Jack and Alec stood by the water's edge, waiting to see what Sebastian was trying to accomplish. One by one, he pulled fish from the water, tossing them onto the beach for Alec and Jack to secure into a cooler of ice.

"That's all we need," Jack called out for Sebastian to stop.

"All the times we've gone fishing together, I thought you were horrible at it. How'd you do that?" Alec asked.

"It's easy enough to convince the fish to come to me, but it doesn't come without a price. I took them without really giving them a choice, some of them may be quite young still. Let's make sure they didn't die for nothing."

After a dinner in which Alec and Jack ate every morsel of fish off their plates, even eating the remnants of what Meg and Tavis didn't finish, Alec attended an impromptu lock-picking class.

Jack explained: "Basically, you need to push all the pins up inside the lock with this wire. Once you've done that, use the tension wrench to turn the doorknob."

Alec tried it a few times and soon got the hang of it. "Okay, that takes care of the back door. I've been in Dr. Patrick's house before, he has a basement, but the door was always shut. Will I be able to pick it open?"

"Shouldn't be any different than the back door, I hope. Just see what you can find, and don't get caught."

~

Later in the evening, Alec told Meg everything that had taken place on the beach with Jack and Sebastian. Then he waited for her to share her thoughts about Ila. The rain had started again, tapping against their bedroom window sills.

Meg was wrapped in Alec's arms with her back nestled against his chest. She'd interlaced her fingers with his and thought about how much she liked the way it felt and how sad she would be if anything were to happen to him.

"Promise me you'll be careful when you go to Dr. Patrick's tomorrow," she said. "Can you cloak yourself?"

"I did it a few times when I was a teenager." He hoped she wouldn't ask why. "It takes a lot of concentration and I think it must get easier the more you do it. Don't worry, I'll be careful." Alec leaned over and kissed her cheek. "How're you feeling about Ila?"

"I knew something was different about her the minute I walked in the door, but I ignored it because she's the woman who raised me and I didn't think she was capable of deceiving me."

"Are you gonna be okay when you see her again?"

"I'm definitely not having tea with her again, or letting her baby-sit Luke," Meg said. "It's not her fault, though, she's being controlled by William and the rest of that evil group he's a part of. I don't know which Ila is the real one, but I do know the woman who raised me loved me very much and would never hurt me. Obviously, the Ila we're dealing with now isn't that woman."

"Does that make you sad, or upset… angry? Tell me."

"What it makes me is curious about how *you* feel." There was pronounced determination in her voice. "You seem more willing to help Sebastian, does that mean you're willing to go now?"

"It isn't easy for me," he said after a moment. "This is the only home I've ever known. There's still a part of me that doesn't want to leave, but it's starting to look like we may not have a choice."

Meg understood his turmoil. "I know what this is doing to you and there's a part of me that feels exactly like you do. But there's another side of me that wants to leave, I want to go home. I need to go."

"I did feel something when I looked inside that amulet, like I wanted to be there," he said, a note of sadness in his voice. "I'm just having a hard time with being able to let go of this place first."

"I know you better than anyone. You just haven't been through enough of what it'll take to make you want to leave here yet, but you will. I'm begging you, Alec, please don't put it off for much longer."

~

Early the next morning, Alec dropped Meg and Luke off at Tavis and Jack's house before going to work. When he walked in through the back entrance of the store, Kyrie was surprised to see him.

"Are you well enough to work today?" she asked, eyeing him carefully in case he intended to lie to her.

"I'm fine, I promise. So is Meg. Whatever made us sick was short-lived." He went to the utility cart, already loaded with the deliveries. "Where to first?"

"Where do you think?" Kyrie rolled her eyes. "They've already started calling about their orders. For my sanity, please deliver the packages to the elderly residents first."

Alec had just hopped into the driver's seat when the phone started ringing. He laughed and said, "I'll drive as fast as I can."

As he neared the cluster of homes where the island's elderly lived, Alec grew more nervous. His plan was to park in the center of the houses and make the individual deliveries by walking back and forth from the cart to their homes. It was after the third delivery when Alec saw Dr. Patrick leaving his house to go to the medical office for the day.

"Dr. Patrick, wait a minute," Alec called to him.

He turned and saw Alec sprinting over with his packages. "Oh, thank you, Alec. You can give those to me, I'll take them to work with me."

When he left, Alec hurried through the rest of the deliveries before going to Dr. Patrick's back yard. He concentrated all of his efforts into cloaking himself, but still his heart pounded as he walked up the back stairs.

He was making a mockery of his lock-picking prowess, fumbling until he forced himself to calm down and focus on what Jack had taught him. When the fifth and final pin was pushed up, he rotated the tension wrench and the doorknob turned with it. Once inside, he looked at the basement door, situated to the right of the back door.

The lock on this door was identical to the other and he set to work on it. To his surprise, the pins were already in the up position. He removed the tension wrench and wire to test the doorknob.

"How about that, not even locked," he muttered.

It was a narrow staircase and when reaching the bottom, Alec found the room was no bigger than a spacious office. Along two of the walls was one file cabinet after the other. Against the third wall was a long desk with the usual office supplies set in their typical places and several open folders lined up side-by-side. The fourth wall, the one with the doorway Alec still stood in, had nothing but a small table with a telephone on it.

Alec moved over to the desk and scanned the open folders. At the top of the first, the name Luke Arcana Ellison was written out with his date of birth underneath. In the blanks under parent information was the word, *Pending*, and below it was a photograph of Luke in his swing.

The next page was titled, *DNA Profile*, but all it had was a sticky note in the center. In Dr. Patrick's handwriting, it read, *Sample sent to lab*, and was dated the day Meg and Luke were at Ila's house. There were no more pages in Luke's folder, so Alec moved on to Lani's. Besides the name and date of birth, it was the same as Luke's folder, with the same sticky note.

On the last folder, where a name should be, was: *Unknown female*. The next page had the same sticky note, but was dated the next day following Luke and Lani's. It appeared that Sebastian and Chaza were right about what happened.

Alec set his anger aside and turned to look at the file cabinets. On the front of each cabinet was a label with two letters, indicating its contents alphabetically. He went to the first one labeled, *A-B*, and pulled out Sebastian's folder. It had his name, but no date of birth. Instead of parents, there was a listing for children, where Alec and Tavis' names were listed. Below that was a picture of Sebastian driving his cart. The next three pages consisted of his DNA profile with notes and symbols written in the margins that Alec didn't understand. Beyond these were notes about Sebastian's arrival with Tavis—they were surprisingly accurate.

Putting it back, he pulled Tavis', and its DNA profile had the same markings in the margins. He went for Arcana next and pulled Ila's folder, noticing right away that it was much thicker than the others.

As she'd been born on Gamma, her parents' names were listed. However, the notes indicated they were sent away for noncompliance. Listed for children was only one word, *Infertile*. Alec's eyes widened at the revelation, but he continued reading. Her DNA profile was more of the same, but it was the additional notes pages that created the thickness of the folder. He confirmed that Ila had been trained to work for management since she was a young child.

On the last page, written in fresh ink and dated the day before Meg and Luke were at Ila's house, was, *Per William Davis, initialize switch and resume informant status*. Alec stuffed the folder back and pulled Meg's.

For her father, Joseph Arcana Sterling was listed with, *See vault file*, written after his name. The space for her mother was blank; under children it was still blank. Meg's DNA profile pages were like the rest and Alec was getting frustrated that he couldn't understand them. After putting the folder back, he closed the cabinet drawer and went next to the cabinet labeled, *E-F*.

He pulled both his and his mother's out in the effort to save time, worried he'd been in the basement for too long already. In his own file, under father's name, William Davis and the line going through it was of older ink, and Sebastian Abbott had replaced it in a newer pen. The DNA profile pages were just as lengthy and strangely marked as the rest he'd seen.

Kyrie's folder listed her children as Alec, and Tavis' name had been recently penned. On the additional notes page was: *Not an acceptable candidate for training*. He wondered if it had anything to do with the top note reading, *See vault file*. He looked around the room for a safe, but found no such vault.

Putting the folders back, he went to the cabinet labeled, *C-D*, to search for Jack's folder. Though not as large as Ila's, it was still thicker than everyone else's; at the very top were those words again, *See vault file*. The more he read of Jack's folder, the wider Alec's eyes became—astonished by the information he already began wishing he hadn't seen. He was on the last page of the additional notes when a door slammed from somewhere above him.

Fast as he could, with the sound of shoes clomping on the floor overhead, Alec stuffed the folder back into the cabinet. He cloaked himself and backed up against the wall near the table with the telephone.

The footsteps came down the basement stairwell and Alec hoped his cloaking abilities were good enough to avoid detection. Dr. Patrick entered the room and went over to the desk to gather the folders awaiting lab results. As he was about to leave, the phone rang, startling both he and Alec.

Dr. Patrick picked up the phone and stared in the direction he thought he heard a sound come from. "Hello?" he said into the phone.

"Yes, William, I have them. When I get back to the office I'll print the results. After I make my notes I'll go over them with you." Dr. Patrick hung the phone up and continued to stare at the wall Alec was pressed up against. "Is someone there?" he called out, his eyes slightly narrowed.

Alec held his breath, terrified he was about to get caught, but then Dr. Patrick shrugged and walked back upstairs. Alec didn't uncloak himself until he heard the front door open and close. Still, he waited another minute or so before attempting to leave.

Once he was back in the utility cart, Alec returned to the store to get the rest of the orders—deciding to get them all delivered by the end of the day. As he made his way all over the island, he thought about what he'd discovered. It was bad enough learning Ila's true history, but what he'd found out about Jack stunned him. Alec had no idea how to tell him, or how Jack would handle the news.

When the deliveries were done, Alec returned the utility cart back to the store. Kyrie had already closed it up for the day and had left. He got in his own cart and headed for the newcomer houses, unable to put it off any longer.

He knew they were all probably waiting for him, wanting to know what he found out. The closer he got, the more he dreaded it, as he still had no idea what to say to Jack.

Meg was waiting on the porch steps when he pulled up. "You could've called me to let me know you were okay. I've been worried all day."

"I'm sorry, I wanted to get all the deliveries done today so I wouldn't have to go in tomorrow."

"Well, you're here, so I assume you were careful."

"Yeah. I was worried for a minute when Dr. Patrick came back to get something, but he didn't see me. Is everyone inside?"

"Yes, we've all been worried." Meg grimaced. "I thought Sebastian was about to lose his mind."

"Let's go in. I'd rather only have to say it all once."

~

Everyone was relieved to see Alec when he came inside. He told them about the folders he found on Dr. Patrick's desk. "So, you and Chaza were right, they got samples from Luke, Lani, and you, too." He looked at Chaza. "Your name's unknown female."

"Did you find a file on Ila?" Sebastian asked.

"Yep, a huge one, and it's just like Jack described. They've been training her since she was a child, using hypnosis to switch her back and forth as they needed her to gather information for them. Dr. Patrick puts dates on everything and on her last notes page it said that William wanted her switched back to informant… the day before Meg and Luke went over."

"Well, that explains her odd behavior," Meg said.

"Were there DNA profiles on everyone?" Jack asked.

"In all but the three on the desk. There were a lot of markings and notes on them that didn't make any sense to me. They also know Tavis and I are siblings and that we're your children with Kyrie," Alec said to Sebastian. "In my mother's notes, it said she wasn't an acceptable candidate for training and something about seeing a vault file."

Sebastian only nodded at the information, but was intrigued by the reference to vault notes. He wondered why some information was kept separately from an already classified location. Also, he was curious about the DNA profile notations Alec mentioned.

"I think they may have the results of the tests." After telling them about Dr. Patrick coming back to retrieve the folders on the desk, Alec added, "He told William on the phone that he'd meet with him later to go over them once he made his notes."

"Did you find a file on me?" Jack asked; the question Alec had been dreading.

"Yeah, they had one." Alec shielded his thoughts from everyone. "You want to go outside with me so I can talk to you about it?" He refused to break eye contact with Jack, preferring not to acknowledge the new tension in the room.

"All right."

Jack frowned as he stood and led Alec out the back door to the garden—the only place free from the camera's watchful gaze.

"I'm worried, Alec." Jack laughed nervously. "Did you find something bad in my file?"

"I read some stuff that could upset you and I've been thinking about it all day. I even thought about saying I didn't find one on you, but I decided to let you choose." Alec shrugged. "You tell me, do you want to know what I found?"

Jack sensed Alec's heavy burden and ultimate resolve to let him be in charge of what he wanted to know—it was both daunting and frightening. He sat down on the stones edging the koi pond. Finally, he asked, "Would *you* want to know?"

It was an easy question in Alec's opinion. "No."

"Okay." Jack stood, feeling better despite the fact that he'd normally hate having information kept from him. "I trust you, I don't want to know."

"Wait," Alec said when Jack started walking back toward the house. "That's just how I feel now. Tomorrow, I could have a different opinion."

"Then I'll ask you again tomorrow."

"Hold on, I want to ask you something before we go inside."

"Go ahead."

"Did you really consider not going to Tavis' home?"

"Briefly. Whatever stupid idea I had at the time wasn't worth losing Tavis over. Besides, she and Lani are my family now. Why are you asking, are you having trouble with leaving?"

Alec shook his head and offered a forced smile. "Nah, I'm good."

When they went back inside, everyone had already decided that they should part ways before William grew suspicious of why they'd all gathered together. Sebastian walked with Alec and Meg to their cart and helped get Luke secured in the carrier. He put his hand on Alec's shoulder to stop him from taking off right away.

"I'll need to see you tomorrow," Sebastian said. "I want you to show me the memory of what you found in the folders. I'm particularly interested in the DNA profiles because I need to know more about what's going on here."

"Sure, come over tomorrow."

~

In the middle of the night, Alec gave up on trying to fall asleep. He'd been so tired, but every time he closed his eyes, he kept seeing Jack's file. He checked to see if Meg was awake; her steady breathing told him her quest for sleep had been more successful.

Alec slipped out from under the covers, pulled on a pair of sweatpants, and went downstairs. For a while he sat on the sofa, but felt caged, so he went outside. He headed over to the farther side of the oak tree, out of the camera's view, and settled down on the grass. It amazed him how much more relaxed he was watching the waves crash against the beach in the moonlight.

Twenty or so minutes later, he heard the front door open and close. Meg settled down beside him and put her arm under his. Alec thought she might ask him why he was out here so late in the night, but she didn't—she sat quietly with him, listening to the same waves. The wind picked up and the chill in it caused her to shiver, but still she remained silent. Meg understood the broody side of his nature and he counted himself lucky to have her.

"I want to show you something." Alec broke the silence. "Something I found in those files."

When she nodded, he showed her the memory of being in Dr. Patrick's basement and everything he'd seen in all the folders. Then he shared the memory of his talk with Jack by the pond.

"I'm glad Jack made the choice he did," Meg said.

"You don't think I should *ever* tell him?"

"I can't answer that, I'm only saying he shouldn't know right now."

They sat here for a little while longer until Alec yawned. "I think I can sleep now. Let's go back inside," he said in what Meg referred to as *Yawnese*.

~

Noon the next day, Sebastian came over—alone. When Alec questioned why Chaza wasn't with him, Sebastian smiled and reassured him he'd update her when he went back.

"Do you want me to just show you now?" Alec wondered if he was going to have to hold Sebastian, and wasn't very keen on the idea.

"Not yet." Sebastian laughed at Alec's thoughts. "I want to show *you* something first. Bring your amulet to me."

Alec left the kitchen to retrieve the amulet from the fireplace mantel. After placing it on the table, he sat back down next to Sebastian.

"This was my amulet before I had Tavis give it to you on your birthday. There are others, everyone has one where we come from. Each is unique in its own way, tailor-made for each individual, or sometimes they're handed down from one generation to the next. You've already seen one thing it can do, it showed you our home, but it can do other things. When there are two of them, they can be connected to communicate with our home. Look at the bottom."

Alec picked the amulet up and turned it over, eyeing the indentation in the shape of a perfect circle. In the better light, he saw there were tiny markings etched into the bottom of the circle. "What's this part for?"

"For this," Sebastian said and removed his necklace. "I want to give this to you as well."

Sebastian held the pendant up to Alec, showing him that it had similar markings, and placed it flat against the indentation. When the two pieces connected the sapphires immediately lit up.

"As long as you have this key, you don't have to have any other source of light to communicate with your amulet. Keep this necklace with you at all times, especially while you're here." Sebastian smiled at how enthralled Alec was with the sapphires. "The key is also a translator, as long as you're wearing it, you can understand most languages."

"What do you mean by I can communicate with it?"

"You can communicate what you saw in Dr. Patrick's basement to the amulet, it's like showing someone a memory. The amulet will store the memory for you with exact clarity, and it'll be much more precise than if you tried relating it to me yourself. We have vast libraries at our home, but they're not like the libraries here. One of the purposes of these amulets is to record accurate historical accounts for future generations."

"Cool!"

Assuming *cool* meant that Alec was pleased, Sebastian said, "It is. Go ahead, think about what you saw and focus on concentrating the images into the amulet."

Alec turned his attention back to the amulet. There was a feeling of warmth and comfort, and he didn't feel awkward at all trying to communicate with the amulet. It felt natural to him, more so than trying to share this large of a memory with another person.

The memory of being in the basement flowed from Alec at an accelerated speed and he began to worry it was happening too quickly—having previously decided where he wanted to stop. He caught a flash of a folder with Jack's name on it and he abruptly turned his head away to focus on something else.

"Why did you stop, Alec?"

"That was all there was."

"No, that wasn't all. What about Jack's folder? Why didn't you show me?"

"Because I haven't shown it to him. I gave him a choice and he chose not to see it."

"I'm not Jack."

"I feel like I'd be betraying his trust."

"He didn't say you couldn't tell someone else. Have you already done so?"

"Yeah… Meg knows."

"I don't want to die on this island wondering if I made the right decision allowing Tavis and Jack to choose each other. In a lot of ways, I helped influence their relationship to grow. I took a chance because I thought there was something special about Jack. I'm hoping that wasn't a mistake."

"It wasn't. Fine! You want to know? I'll show you." Alec clutched the amulet again and allowed the rest of the memory to fall into place.

Sebastian was silent for a bit after seeing Jack's folder, and he stared out of the kitchen window at the forest trees swaying in the wind.

Alec worried when the silence stretched on for too long. "Well?"

"I can see why you gave Jack a choice." Sebastian looked at Alec. "What did Meg say about it?"

"She was glad he chose not to know."

"I agree, I don't think Jack should know about this right now. It does explain a lot about him, though. Things that were beginning to confuse both myself and Chaza."

"What do the markings mean on the DNA pages?" Alec asked.

"They're notes on certain genetic traits, the ones the scientists and management want to cultivate."

"But what does it all mean?"

"It means they know a lot more about us than I thought they did," Sebastian said. "It means, for the first time, I'm scared we might not be able to get away. I need to talk to Chaza, she needs to see this, and she and I need to plan out the escape. Are you still having problems with leaving?"

Alec just stared at him.

Sebastian stood. He wanted to yell at Alec, shake some sense into him. Instead, he pointed at the necklace. "Put that on and don't let it out of your sight, it's also the key to the homing pods."

Nodding, Alec put it around his neck and picked up the darkened amulet before following Sebastian out of the kitchen.

"Goodbye, Meg. Wish I had more time to visit, but I need to talk to Chaza," Sebastian said when he came into the front room. He leaned over the playpen to pat Luke on the back, and then he left.

"I suppose you heard everything?" Alec asked Meg.

"I did," she said without looking up from the book she'd been reading.

24

Acquisition

Sebastian traversed Gamma to the newcomer houses and went to Chaza to show her what he learned from Alec.

"I think Jack's already suspecting it," Chaza said. "I agree with you, it won't be good for him to know about this right now."

"It's time to start planning their escape," Sebastian said.

"It's not just leaving now? You think it's come to trying to *escape*?"

"There are cameras everywhere, what do you think?"

"Once the pods are in motion, nothing can stop them. You know that."

"But we have to be able to put them in motion."

"Where's your key?" Chaza frowned at his chest.

"I gave it to Alec." Sebastian saw the doubt on her face. "I know he'll do the right thing, I have to trust him. Where's yours?"

"I put it in a safe place."

He stared hard at her, waiting.

"I have a garden in one of the forests and I put it there a long time ago. It was a painful reminder as well. Besides, I had the language sorted out within a week."

"You should give it to Meg."

"What would be the point? My amulet's gone."

"It doesn't matter, I think Meg would like to have something that belonged to you."

"*Belonged*?" she questioned. "In case I die, she'll have something to remember me by?"

"Something like that," Sebastian mumbled, wishing he'd been more careful with his words. "She'll need it when she gets there."

Chaza switched subjects, preferring not to dwell on her own demise. "It appears they know quite a bit about DNA, especially ours."

"Some of their accuracy surprised me."

"They don't have it all figured out yet. I mean, they know more than I gave them credit for. That much was obvious based on their notations. How do you think they've been able to figure out so much?"

"I've been thinking about that, too. They're very intelligent, and evolving more so all the time." He sighed. "Maybe it's just natural advancements in their medical knowledge and discoveries."

"So, you think it's a natural progression?"

"What are you trying to say, Chaza?"

"Do you think it's possible they had help from the Dissenters?"

"That was a long time ago. I doubt it."

He didn't sound all that convinced to her, but she knew it was a sensitive subject for him and thought better of pushing the issue. Even more delicate was the fact that Chaza knew more than he thought she did about his secrets.

"What about the Ancients?" she asked.

"Absolutely not!" Sebastian was horrified at the question. "How could you think that about your own people?"

"Okay, I know, you're right." Chaza shrugged off the creeping shame. "I just thought I'd suggest it since I mentioned your ancestors."

"There's another possibility." Sebastian went over to the window and looked up at the sky. "You've been on this island a long time, have you ever seen him here?"

"I saw something once, but I think it was a natural occurrence. As much as I'd like to pin it on the last Lucusan, I have to admit he wouldn't do anything like that. It's not in his nature." Chaza shook her head, trying to clear her thoughts. "Hypothesizing the causes of their advancements is pointless, what I want to know is what their next move will be. More importantly, when?"

"I don't think they'll do anything unless they suspect an attempt to leave, but they are calculating. William may choose not to wait before exerting his control."

"We need to convince everyone to leave immediately," Chaza said, her tone heavy with new urgency. "William doesn't seem like the type to wait for long."

"I need to plan the timing of their departure." His gaze shifted to the camera pointed at the newcomer houses. "I'll have to talk to Tavis, and I'm gonna have to keep lying to her, there's no other way. Brace yourself for more bad weather."

Soon as Sebastian said the words, clouds formed over Gamma. The sunlight diminished and an ugly grey replaced it. When lightning streaked across the sky, Sebastian left—returning to his house to prepare himself to lie to Tavis.

~

In the surveillance room of the bunkers, William cursed at the renewed rain. It had finally stopped raining after days of it, only to return, rendering the camera views useless. He'd been watching Sebastian make his rounds to everyone and it made him nervous—he picked up the phone and called Dr. Patrick.

"Are you ready to go over the results with me yet?" William barked, irritated by the lack of progress. "You had all night to look at them."

"Yes, I—"

"Good, I'll meet you at your house in twenty minutes."

When Dr. Patrick arrived home, he found William was already there and sitting on the front room sofa with a bored expression on his face. "I didn't know you had a key," he said.

"Of course I do," William said. "You didn't think I was gonna huddle on your porch while your neighbors stared at me through the curtains, did you?"

"Yeah, what's with all this rain? It's getting ridiculous."

"I have no idea, but it's annoying the hell out of me." William pointed at the folders Dr. Patrick pulled from his briefcase. "Are those the results?"

"I'm sorry, it took longer than I expected. There was a lot to sort through." Dr. Patrick sat next to William and spread the files out on the coffee table. "Turns out our unknown female is Margaret Arcana's biological mother, and both their genetic markers are most similar to Jack Cavanaugh's."

"I can't say that surprises me," William said. "What about Luke and Lani?"

"Their parents are who we assumed. They express the same traits as Sebastian and that woman. Do we know her name yet?"

"No, but I hope to soon. I'm bringing Sebastian and this woman in to not only question them, but to make sure the rest stay put. My thinking is they won't leave without Sebastian's instructions."

"How do you intend to capture them?"

"Like I said before, bait," William said. "I'm hoping to get them to come to me willingly."

"What's the bait?"

"Tavis Abbott. Do you have any chloroform?"

"Yes, why?"

"I plan to abduct Tavis and leave a note for Sebastian, instructing him to bring both himself and that woman to me in exchange for releasing her." William nodded slowly and took a deep breath. "I'll need to incapacitate her somehow."

"When do you plan to do it?"

"Probably tomorrow night. I need to talk to Eldridge tonight, he's gonna help me watch them while we have them in the holding cell."

Dr. Patrick got up and went into his office to retrieve the chloroform. He handed the bottle to William with a warning: "You won't need much of this, just a small amount on a cloth over her mouth and nose. She may struggle for a moment, but will quickly succumb to the fumes."

"Okay." William pocketed the bottle.

"I'd prefer you to sedate her properly after she passes out from the chloroform. You'll find sedatives in the drug cabinet in the bunker's physician's office. The dosage is on the bottle and the syringes are in the supply closet. If you have any questions, you're to call me immediately."

"Yes, sir."

"I'm sorry, are you a doctor?"

"Fine, I'll call you if I run into trouble." William stood to leave, but pointed at the files. "Put those away before someone sees them."

"I should tell you something." Dr. Patrick gathered the folders. "When you called me the first time about the results, I heard a sound... like a gasp. I didn't see anyone there, but I know what I heard. Alec was in the area at the time, you may want to check the recorded video."

"I'll do that, thanks for letting me know."

~

When William returned to the surveillance room, he reviewed the footage from the previous morning. He watched Alec make the usual deliveries and then he simply disappeared, even though the utility cart was still parked in the center of the houses. After a while, Alec reappeared and drove away—right after Dr. Patrick left.

William figured it was more than likely that all of them knew about the classified files by now. There was no point in putting it off any longer; he picked up the phone and called Eldridge.

"It's time. When do you think you can be here?"

"Do you have a plan?" Eldridge asked.

"I do. Can you be here in the next day or so?"

"I'll start packing tonight."

William thought Eldridge sounded almost excited about his new menial task as a prison warden. "I take it you've already received a report on the test results?"

"I have, and we'll talk more about it when I see you," Eldridge said and hung up.

The rain continued to fall, sometimes in sheets. William gave up on seeing anything more through the cameras and busied himself instead with preparing the containment area. He hoped he'd thought of everything they'd need—he wanted Sebastian and this woman to be comfortable. In the grand scheme of things, they were among the ones who made it all possible.

~

Evening came and Sebastian decided it was time to talk to Tavis. There was no use in excluding Jack, so he went over to their house in the pouring rain to discuss his plans with both of them. Before knocking on their door, he took a moment to steady his nerves. Withholding information from Tavis was one thing, but to purposely deceive her wouldn't be an easy thing for him to do.

Tavis was surprised to see him. "Is everything okay?"

"Everything's fine, I just wanted to talk to you and Jack." Sebastian stepped inside and saw Jack sitting on the front room sofa holding Lani.

"About what?" Tavis asked, shutting the door.

"About leaving."

She nodded. "When?"

"Possibly the night after next. I want to spend tomorrow preparing Kyrie to leave."

"But what about—" Tavis started, but he cut her off.

"That problem has been solved. I used Chaza's amulet with mine to send for another pod, it's hidden with the others. I gave Alec my key and instructed him to get you, Jack, and Lani out first. After that, he'll get Kyrie and Chaza into another and send them off. Then I'll take the key and send Alec, Meg, and Luke on. I'll leave last."

"When did you get another homing pod?" She watched her father with a keen eye, ready to detect any falsehood.

"Today, during the storms," he said with a straight face.

"I don't feel comfortable with you leaving last."

"I knew you'd feel that way, but I hope you understand this plan is better for all of us. Alec has no experience with these pods, especially with cloaking them, that's why I should go last."

"You could let Jack and I go last."

"Absolutely not!" he shouted. "This is how I've planned it and you'll do as I say."

It had been long enough since last hearing his imperious tone that she'd forgotten how powerful he could be. Humbled, Tavis said, "Okay, I understand. I've been worried about how we're gonna handle this situation, that's all. I'm sorry." She averted her eyes to the rug under her feet.

Jack had remained quiet during their conversation, but at her submissive response, his body instinctively postured to defend her. Sebastian was quick to pick up on it and while Tavis continued staring at the rug, he shot Jack a look that told him he'd better steer clear of interfering. Jack obeyed the silent warning, even though he hated doing it—assuming Sebastian had a purpose in forcing Tavis' acquiescence.

"No, I'm the one who should apologize. I shouldn't have shouted at you. I know all of this seems sudden, but it's important that we leave soon. Also, since I'm who William's constantly watching, he won't know you're all gone until it's too late." Sebastian softened his tone. "Spend tomorrow however way you choose and gather whatever you may want to bring home."

She offered a grin and said, "I will."

Sebastian left, feeling better about his plan to get Tavis off the island first. He was about to get into his cart when Jack stopped him.

"Was that the truth? Did you really get another pod?"

Sebastian glanced around, searching for Tavis.

Jack said, "Don't worry, I told her I wanted to ask you about infant safety seats in the homing pod."

"No, I lied to her. Tavis thinking I'll be right behind her will be the only way she'll leave. I'm counting on you to make sure that happens. Alec has a key to the pods, Tavis has the other, if for some reason..." He looked up and knew Jack had sensed his doubt in Alec. "Whatever happens, get them all off this cruel oppressive planet."

~

Sebastian drove to Kyrie's house and watched her from the safety of night's darkness. She was turning off all the lights in the house before going to bed and he settled back into the cart's seat to wait for her to fall asleep. Half an hour later, he crept up the back stairs and let himself inside.

He found her sleeping and he fought the urge to join her. From the shadows of her bedroom he waited for her to go into a deeper sleep before approaching. When it became more torture than he could stand, Sebastian stepped forward and kneeled by the bed to listen to her breathing.

It was slow and steady, so he slipped his hand under the sheet. He pulled her nightgown up, just enough to place his palm flat against her abdomen—ignoring the impulse to remove the gown altogether. His hand trembled and he lifted it for a moment to compose himself. He closed his eyes and returned his hand to her abdomen while concentrating all of his energy into detecting his son.

'Ah, there you are.' Sebastian found the baby's heartbeat and it made him smile. It was a beautiful sound and he imagined what the child would look like as a grown man. The baby began to move and kick, responding to Sebastian's thoughts.

'Yes, you're very strong, but don't kick too much because you'll wake your mother,' Sebastian communicated and the baby settled back down in his small, protective world.

A realization penetrated Sebastian's mind—he'd never get to see his son be born; he'd never get to hold him or see him grow into a man. He reassured him then: *'Your brother and sister will help your mother take care of you. Remember always that I love you, not even death will change that.'*

Sebastian shifted his focus to visualize his son's environment. Kyrie was doing well physically and he determined she would have no problems carrying the child to term. Again, sadness washed over him knowing he wouldn't be there.

"You're an excellent mother, Kyrie, raise him as well as you did Alec," Sebastian whispered.

Though he'd been avoiding it up to now, Sebastian inhaled Kyrie's scent. Since she was carrying their child, her scent was all the more aromatic to him. He recognized the trouble he was having initiating the point of leaving her. With great effort, he grasped the hem of her nightgown and pulled it back down over her thighs.

It bothered him that as soon as he removed his hand, he'd no longer be touching her skin and he dared to linger a bit longer. He went to look at her face again and what he saw shocked him—her eyes were open and she'd been watching him. Frozen, he had no idea how to fix the unexpected situation.

Kyrie saw the fear in his eyes and she wanted to make it go away; she put her hand on his cheek and smiled at him. Her fingers went to his lips—knowing he was about to offer some weak excuse for why he was in her bedroom, tugging at her nightgown, and that he would leave immediately.

"Don't leave," she said, her voice so soft that it was almost silent.

Her touch on his face was so wonderful to him and his eyelids fluttered closed. He felt the bed move as she sat up and placed a feather-light kiss on his forehead. "Stay with me," she said in a breath, and he opened his eyes.

The bed sheet had slipped down around her waist and exposed her shoulders. When she shivered at the cool air, his instinct to protect her from anything, even a chill, overpowered his resolve to leave. He pulled her to him to give her warmth and when his chest met with hers, his previous notions to leave dissolved into the abyss of everything she was.

Sebastian gripped the back of Kyrie's head and his lips went to hers as he guided her body down onto her bed. Though it took all his strength, he forced himself to be gentle with her and to take his time. He wanted it to last for as long as what time would grant him.

In the middle of the night, Kyrie lifted her head up from where it rested on his chest. The look in her eyes was heartbreaking for him, as was her voice when she asked, "You aren't leaving yet, are you?"

"No." He chuckled. "I have no desire to leave right now." Sebastian pulled her head back down to his chest and twirled her hair between his fingers.

"I'm gonna give him your name."

"What?" Sebastian asked.

"Our son, I'm going to name him Sebastian."

"You know?" He was astonished.

"Of course I know," she said. "I've been pregnant before. Did you really think I wouldn't know my own body? Also, it's getting harder to hide it. I dare not leave the house without wearing a baggy sweatshirt."

"What else do you know?"

"Everything. Whatever Chaza tried to do, it didn't work. By mid-afternoon that day I had remembered all of it, but I was in a much better frame of mind about the situation. I just decided to keep quiet."

"She did warn me it might not work." Sebastian shook his head. "How could I not know you still remembered?"

"Because you were avoiding me." Kyrie gave him a good pinch. "And it seems that no one's paying attention to me right now, so I've been able to go about peacefully."

"It wasn't easy for me to stay away from you."

"Good."

"How do you know it's a boy?"

"I woke up the minute you touched me, I heard you talking to him."

"You heard my thoughts?" Sebastian asked, smiling and curious.

"Some. Can you hear mine?"

"Some." He laughed.

"You want me to go to your home, don't you?" Kyrie trailed her fingers down Sebastian's side, circling around at his upper thigh, then back up again, causing him to shudder at the sensation.

"Yes, but not right now," he said, growling playfully and pulling her body over his own.

~

They were both exhausted when morning came and they allowed themselves a lazy start to the day. "You won't be coming with me, will you?" Kyrie asked, the question seemed to choke her. She set the fork down on her plate, eggs that he'd cooked for her uneaten.

Sebastian leaned over the kitchen island they sat at and picked up her fork. "There'll be none of that," he chastised and held the fork with eggs up to her mouth. "Open up, there's someone who needs for you to eat properly."

Their eyes locked as she opened her mouth. He slipped the eggs in past her lips and smiled when she started chewing.

"That's a good girl, have another bite."

"Oh, give me my fork. I can feed myself." Kyrie took her fork and consumed the rest of the eggs. "Guess I was hungry." She looked up and saw him watching her—a profound sadness marked his expression.

"No, I won't be coming with you. If you were listening to my thoughts last night, then you already know that. I wanted to check on you and the baby, I wanted to tell you both goodbye."

"There's no other way?" she asked.

"I'm sorry, but no. I want you to know, you and our son will be very well cared for. I want you to raise him in my house, it'll be your home when you get there. Alec, Meg, and Luke will be there. Tavis, Jack, and Lani will be there for you, too."

"This is so hard."

"I know. It won't be long, maybe tomorrow. There've been developments." Sebastian was still reluctant to tell her about William. "I've asked Alec to handle getting everyone into the pods if I'm not able to see to it myself. The pods will get all of you home safely."

Kyrie frowned. "How did Alec respond?"

"I'm not… too worried." Sebastian offered an encouraging smile. "I know he'll do what's best for his family. I also asked him to make Tavis go first. I had to lie to her about how many pods we had. She can't know, Kyrie. She won't leave if she knew the truth."

"You two are very close," Kyrie said, acknowledging it aloud.

"We are. I want *you* to be close to her now. She's gonna need your help and support, especially at first. Please tell her how much I love her and how hard it was for me to do this. Tell her how sorry I am that I lied to her." Tears sprang to his eyes, it was agony for him to think about how hurt Tavis was going to be.

Kyrie stood from the chair and put her arms around him, and he rested his head onto her shoulder. Though he was quiet, she knew he was crying. His body would tremble occasionally and her robe's collar became saturated with his tears.

"You don't have to worry about that." Kyrie's voice was soft with compassion. "I'll be there for our daughter, and I'll do everything I can to make her realize that what you did was out of love for her."

"Thank you." Sebastian pulled himself together. "It means everything to me knowing that you both will finally have the relationship you should've always had. I'm so sorry I took that away from you. Can you ever forgive me for what I did?"

She hadn't been prepared to hear him apologize for taking her daughter away at birth. It had never dawned on Kyrie that he owed her an apology, but he was giving Tavis back to her now and she was grateful for it.

"I forgive you."

He cupped her face in his hands. "Are you really going to name him after me?"

"I really am."

~

It was late afternoon when Sebastian left and returned to his house, feeling sour at having to leave Kyrie and their unborn child. When he pulled up in front of the house, Tavis and Jack had also just returned from their afternoon at the waterfall lake, as it was where they wanted their last memories of Gamma to occur.

"Where've you been?" Tavis asked when he got out of the cart.

"Kyrie's," he said. "I explained everything to her and she knows to be ready when it's time to go."

"So, it went well?"

"Yes, and she's very ready to leave."

"I know you're relieved about it," Tavis said and hugged him. "Would you like to join us for dinner?"

Sebastian was about to decline the offer, but thought better of it. He wanted to spend as much time as possible with them, especially Tavis. "I'd love to." A smile spread across his face. "Who's cooking?"

Tavis rolled her eyes at him. "What if I said I was, would you still have dinner with us?"

"Yes, I'd still have dinner with you… and I'd eat every last horrible bite."

She laughed. "Don't worry, Jack doesn't like my cooking either. I'm sure he'll come up with something we'll all enjoy. I'm about to get Lani from Chaza's, so I'll ask her to join us, too."

Their dinner together was intimate and perfect, everything Sebastian wanted. They enjoyed each other's company with good food and wine, he only wished the hour would stop growing so late. However, it was obvious how worn out Tavis and Jack were from their day of swimming when they started yawning and leaning against each other as though to stay propped up.

"We should let them get some sleep, Sebastian," Chaza said. "Before they fall asleep at the table."

"I hadn't realized how tired I was until I ate," Tavis said.

"Me, too." Jack covered a wayward belch with his linen when he stood. "We haven't been swimming in a while, I guess it wore us out." He winked at Tavis.

Sebastian walked Chaza to her house, and then returned to his own. Soon as he saw his bedroom, he started yawning as well. He turned all the lights off and crawled into bed; the sheets felt great, but he remembered how much better Kyrie's arms felt. He denied his sudden desire to get up and go to her, forcing himself to settle for the much needed sleep.

~

While William waited for the lights to go off in each of the houses, he got ready to put his plan into motion. He wrote the letter to Sebastian first, then he changed into dark clothing in case anyone would be wandering around the island late at night.

He went to the physician's office and prepared two syringes, one with the appropriate dose of a sedative, the other with the reversal agent. After slipping the sedative it into his pocket, he set the other syringe on his bedside table. Before leaving the bedroom, William attached one end of the timecuffs to the bed's railing and left the other end open.

Pocketing the chloroform and a handkerchief, as well as another set of timecuffs, he grabbed a blanket from the end of the bed and draped it over his shoulder. When he returned to the surveillance room, he opened the top drawer of the desk and picked up a gun. Once he inserted the magazine, he frowned at it, and with a sigh, tucked it into his jacket pocket. He had decided to take the gun with him only as a precaution in case his plan went horribly wrong.

William turned to the monitors again to check the status of the houses; the lights were still off and all was quiet. He poured himself a scotch, downed it to steady his nerves, and left the bunkers through the cave.

When he arrived at his destination, he hid the cart in the trees across the lane from the houses. William chose to enter Jack and Tavis' house through the front door, as the bedrooms were located toward the back of the house and he didn't want to risk making any noises that could wake them.

The door was locked, but William planned for this and had brought a master key. A master key was made for the houses on each of the islands from the very beginning and it was the first time William had to use it on Gamma. The only other times master keys were used happened on Alpha and Beta, and both times it was right before the end—he hoped the damn keys weren't cursed.

He crept down the hallway, first looking into their bedroom and found Jack and Tavis asleep. He slipped into Lani's room and she was also sleeping. A check of the closet revealed plenty of room for him to hide in. After he poured a small amount of chloroform onto the handkerchief, he went to the baby monitor and slowly began to tap on it.

His idea was to give it light taps at first and graduate the volume and frequency in the hopes that Tavis would wake up to check on Lani. He was prepared to knock Jack out if he was the one who woke up instead.

He increased the tempo of the tapping. Occasionally, he tapped against the monitor a little harder and would lean over to make sure it hadn't disturbed Lani. He finally heard footsteps and he dashed back to the closet, hiding himself and hoping it would be Tavis. As the footsteps drew closer, William held his breath and kept the handkerchief in his right hand.

Through the slats in the closet door, William saw it was a woman's figure that came into the room. When she bent over Lani's crib, he came out from his hiding place and grabbed her from behind, shoving the handkerchief over her mouth and nose.

Immediately, Tavis fought against him—her sounds muffled at first, but grew louder. He whispered into her ear, sending her a clear message, "I have a gun. I'll shoot Jack if you wake him up."

Tavis stopped struggling. Soon after, he felt her body relaxing, succumbing to the chloroform until she fell limply against his chest. He took the syringe from his pocket and injected the sedative into Tavis' arm. Once he hoisted her unconscious form over his shoulder, he looked one more time in their bedroom and saw that Jack hadn't moved.

Upon exiting the house, William took Tavis to the cart and secured her in the back seat with the timecuffs. He covered her with the blanket and ran over to Sebastian's house to slip the note under the front door. On the way back to the cart he pulled the gun out, fearing it possible that someone would wake and discover the abduction before he had a chance to get out of the area. It wasn't until he was almost back to the cave that he realized how easy it had been. William turned around to look at her, making sure he wasn't dreaming.

After parking in the usual spot, William scooped Tavis up and walked up the cliff with her slung over his shoulder. He carried her into the physician's living quarters, laid her out on the bed, and attached one end of the timecuffs to her wrist and the other to the wrought iron scrollwork on the headboard.

Tavis moaned a little in her sleep, and for a moment William was afraid she was about to wake up, but she continued sleeping. He sat on the bed beside her and examined her face for the first time in person—Ila was right, Tavis was exquisitely beautiful.

The satin, ivory nightgown she wore had inched up to the top of her thighs. William tugged the hem line down as far as the gown would allow and trailed his finger along her leg until he reached her knee. Shaking off the primitive urge to continue perusing her body, he pulled the blanket over her. Not only for her comfort and propriety, but for his own sanity.

With one last look at her, he brushed his thumb lightly across her lips and there was an instinctive response from her to the sensation. Her lips parted as though she expected a kiss and even through the blanket, he saw she'd arched her back receptively. William groaned and forced himself out of the room.

"Jack's a lucky man," William mumbled to himself and headed back to the surveillance room.

Interestingly, a glance at the monitors revealed nothing had changed; the houses were as he left them. All that was needed to change the stillness was a phone call. William went to the steel doors that led to the holding cell and opened them, revealing another set of doors—the prison bars, which he opened with a set of keys he kept in his pocket. Once activating the time lock, the key to the cell doors would be a secondary locking option. William decided to wait until the prisoners arrived before activating it.

For all it lacked in liberty, it made up for in niceties.

The first room was the living room. To the left was the kitchen, and toward the back of the narrow apartment were the bedrooms. The area was quite large, at 1150 square feet it was rather spacious. It had three bedrooms, each with its own bathroom. It had all the amenities for decent living conditions, except there were no windows to allow the sunlight in, there was no door that led to a backyard, and no front door leading to a front porch where beyond there was freedom.

Not only was the wall's core made of the cave's naturally occurring stone, but reinforced concrete had been added to it with a soundproof wall interior. Absolutely nothing was getting in or out of the area—it was complete isolation for any occupant.

Earlier, William had stocked the refrigerator and cabinets with food. He did his best to provide the necessary things, like clothing and bathroom supplies. Whatever else may be needed, he'd have to get from the bunker's supply store or request from Digamma.

William exited the holding cell, leaving both sets of doors open, and sat at the desk to call Sebastian. The phone rang several times before he answered—sounding sleepy, but worried at the late night phone call.

"Check your front door, I believe there's a letter for you."

"Who is this?" Sebastian asked, confused by the unusual request.

"William Davis," he said and hung up the phone. He leaned back in the chair and watched the lamplight illuminate Sebastian's house.

~

Sebastian hung up the phone and reached for the lamp on his bedside table. Slowly, he stood from the bed while trying to make sense of the phone call and went to the front room. He found a sheet of paper near the door, a handwritten letter.

Sebastian,

I have your daughter. If you want me to let Tavis go, then come to the cave and bring Margaret Arcana's mother with you. Try not to wake Jack up when you check to see if Tavis is really gone. It would be a shame to torture such a beautiful woman.

William Davis

The letter fluttered from Sebastian's hand, coming to a rest on the floor again. He didn't want to believe the letter, but it was all too obvious what was happening. After getting dressed and turning off all the lights in the house, he left and went over to Tavis'.

The inside of their house was still and quiet; Sebastian cloaked himself and silently walked down the hallway. Jack slept, alone. Lani was asleep in her own room. He looked around and saw an empty syringe on the floor by Lani's crib. It horrified him, he'd failed to protect his own child. He leaned over Lani's crib, placed his hands on her head, and concentrated all of his efforts into putting her into a deeper sleep.

Sebastian went back to where Jack was with the intention of doing the same to him, but paused in the doorway to consider the feasibility of the attempt. Ultimately, he decided it wasn't worth the risk and hoped Jack wouldn't wake anytime soon since Lani would sleep deeply for at least an hour or so. He hoped Tavis would be back by then.

As he left the house, Sebastian uncloaked himself. There was no point in hiding anymore, and he wanted William to see that he was complying with his demands. He headed over to Chaza's house and by the time he reached her bedroom, she was already awake. Worried about the time, he shared the memory without bothering to prepare her for it.

Chaza stared at him blankly for a moment, scared by what it all meant and at what they were about to do. Honestly, she was terrified of what awaited Sebastian and herself. For a brief second, Chaza imagined snatching the necklace off of Alec's neck and dragging Meg and Luke to a pod—leaving the wretched island forever. Though it was rare for Sebastian to see Chaza's thoughts, he did see this one. The absolute disappointment, mixed with his already established agony, showed in his eyes and Chaza realized he'd seen the thought.

"I'm just scared, I'd never really do that," she said. "Please don't fault me, I'm not as strong as you."

"Will you go with me, despite your fears?" he asked, his voice flat.

"I will, but only if we tell Alec and Meg first."

She was insuring the safety of Meg and Luke by making the demand and Sebastian could hardly blame her.

"Of course. I think it would be wise anyway," he said.

~

"What's wrong?" Alec asked when he opened the door and saw Sebastian and Chaza standing there.

He put his arm up to prevent Meg from stepping past him. She frowned and pushed it away.

"What now?" she asked them.

"We need to tell you something, but we don't have a lot of time," Chaza said, making her way inside.

Chaza explained what had happened while Sebastian stood by silently. He figured William wouldn't be happy with them for informing Alec and Meg before coming to the cave. All Sebastian could do was hope it wouldn't cause William to refuse Tavis' release.

"He could be lying!" Alec shouted at Sebastian. "What if he has no intention of letting her go? All three of you could be captured."

"What choice do I have, Alec?"

Realization of the hopelessness reverberated throughout Alec's thoughts and it brought a chill to everyone. "I guess there isn't one," he said.

"I've already talked to Kyrie," Sebastian said to him. "She knows to be waiting for you to tell her when it's time to leave. Don't fail her, or your brother, and don't do anything until Tavis has been freed. After that, I urge you not to wait."

Sebastian and Chaza left the stone house and drove to the path that led up to the cave. Neither of them spoke as they trekked up the cliff and upon entering the cave, they noticed several changes. The old beach blanket was gone, as were the empty wine bottles; the unopened ones had been crated and placed in the far corner. At the top of the cave wall, above the steel door, a camera had been installed. Sebastian figured William watched them at this very moment.

They went to the steel door and discovered yet another difference. A new locking mechanism had been put on the door, along with a handle to open it from either side as long as you knew the code to punch into the keypad.

Chaza laughed at it. "What a joke! Why don't I just—"

The rest of her words were cut off by Sebastian's silent warning.

"Right," she said.

They stood in front of the door, wondering what they should do. Knocking seemed inappropriate, but Sebastian was about to anyway when the door opened. William stood there, smiling at them as though they were all great friends. Sebastian stifled his revulsion so it wouldn't show on his face.

"So glad you could make it. Please, come in." William opened the door wider and after they came inside, he shut it behind them. "It's so good to finally meet you," he said to Sebastian.

"Can't say I feel the same."

William ignored him and turned to Chaza. "It's very nice to meet you as well. I'm afraid to admit that I don't know your name. I only know you're Meg's mother."

"Chaza," she said. When William waited for her to go on, she added, "Abbott."

"Chaza *Abbott*? Are you any relation to this gentleman?" William motioned toward Sebastian.

She looked at Sebastian, hoping to get an idea as to whether or not she should answer truthfully. He nodded. "Yes, Sebastian's my husband."

"Husband?" William laughed. "Oh! What a delightful drama we have here."

"Where's Tavis?" Sebastian was irritated with the false friendliness.

"She's here, safe and sleeping. I gave her a sedative to keep her asleep. I assure you, I don't want to cause her any stress. Follow me and I'll show you she's fine, and that all she needs is the reversal agent."

They followed William through the loft and down the narrow stairwell to the corridor. He led them to the surveillance room and Chaza finally got a look at what was beyond the steel doors. It was clear to her that it was about to be her new home. Sebastian eyed the monitors; most of them were off, except for the newcomer houses and the stone house.

"Keeping an eye on things, are you?" Sebastian asked.

"Did you expect any less? I have to say, I'm disappointed you went to Alec before you came here. I hope that doesn't lead to any trouble."

"It won't. I just felt like he should be aware that Chaza and I might be" –Sebastian glanced at the prison bars– "away for a little while."

"I assume you didn't disturb Jack?" William asked, not so subtly.

"Considering his parentage, I was afraid to attempt putting him into a deeper sleep as I had done to Lani. So, if you don't mind, can we let Tavis go before he wakes up?"

"Yes, that's right." William shook his head disdainfully. "Alec did some snooping. I guess Jack's true history is common knowledge now. Tell me, how did he react?"

"He doesn't know, Alec gave him a choice and Jack decided against knowing."

"That's probably for the best, for all of us," William said. "Let's do this, shall we? Now, as you've mentioned, we're working in a tight time frame. If you wouldn't mind stepping into that area, I'll show you that Tavis is fine." He pointed to the holding cell.

Sebastian guided Chaza through both sets of doorways, but went no farther than the front room. William had followed them through the first entrance, then stopped at the barred doors to pull them together, locking Sebastian and Chaza inside. He returned to the desk and typed in a command on the keyboard.

"Turn around and you'll see a screen on the front room wall," William said.

Sebastian spun around and saw a much larger version of the surveillance room monitors affixed to the wall, directly in front of the sofa. An image popped up of Tavis asleep on a bed with a blanket pulled up to her chin—Sebastian determined she appeared unharmed.

'Do you recognize that room?' Sebastian asked Chaza silently.

'It's the physician's living quarters here in the bunkers.'

"As you can see, Tavis is perfectly fine." William looked at the wall clock. "It'll be a few more minutes before her timecuffs open. In the meantime, I'd like to tell you how lovely she—"

The rest of William's goading statement was cut off by two simultaneous events: the pulling back of his head by some unknown arm; and the feel of cold metal against his throat.

Sebastian and Chaza turned their attention to the scuffle and saw Jack standing behind William holding a large kitchen knife to his neck. Emanating from all around Jack was raw power and dominance as he hovered over William.

"I believe you took someone from me and I want her back. Where's my wife?" Jack snarled into William's ear. The knife cut into William's neck a little as he struggled and a small trickle of blood appeared. It rolled down his neck and absorbed into the collar of his shirt.

"She's in the physician's bedroom," Chaza blurted out. "He said the timecuffs are about to unlock."

Both Jack and William looked up at Sebastian and Chaza. Their fingers were curled around the bars, watching the new proceedings with caution.

"She's right," William said. "Tavis' timecuffs will be unlocking soon. You'll only have three minutes to open them before they reset."

"How do I know you're not lying?" Jack asked, maintaining the knife to William's throat.

"You don't, but I have who I want now." William gestured in the direction of Sebastian and Chaza. "Besides, I can always take her again, whenever I want. However, all I want is for you to take her home… she's rather distracting." There was a sickening smile on William's face as he stared hard at Sebastian.

Jack's eyes narrowed at the rakish comment and the expression of angry, raw power morphed into savage retribution. His knuckles whited over the knife handle and he tugged William's head farther back, the neck stretched taut for a deeper cut.

"No, Jack!" Sebastian yelled from his prison. "Don't do it!"

"Why not?" Jack snapped. "He's scum."

"Because you made promises, Jack. You told Tavis you'd never hurt her again." Sebastian hoped he hadn't overstepped his boundaries by mentioning private matters between Jack and Tavis. Even if he had, it was worth it to keep Jack from possibly killing William. "You're gonna have to trust me, if you kill him, it'll hurt Tavis."

Jack couldn't imagine Tavis would've told her father how callous, even cruel, he'd been to her when she refused to tell him where she and Sebastian came from. It was more likely that Sebastian had sensed it and chose not to confront Jack. It occurred to Jack that Sebastian had trusted him for a long time, and he decided it was time to give some of it back.

He eased his grip on the knife. His mind raced, knowing he had to hurry to free Tavis from the timecuffs. "Release them," he said, using the knife blade to point to Sebastian and Chaza.

"I can't," William said. "Their lock is on a timer as well. I believe we have no less than seven hours before it's even an option to open those bars,"

Sebastian worried about the dwindling seconds. "Go, Jack, get Tavis out of here."

Though it disgusted him to do it, Jack released his hold on William. With one last look at Sebastian and Chaza, he rushed out of the surveillance room.

William jumped to his feet and slammed shut the steel door to the corridor. He went to the monitor and saw Jack removing the timecuff from Tavis' wrist while Sebastian and Chaza watched from their own screen.

After snatching the blanket off of Tavis, Jack unlatched the timecuffs from the bed, slipping them in his pocket. He tucked the knife under his belt and scooped her up into his arms. When walking back through the corridor, he noticed the steel door to the surveillance room was shut, but ignored it—his only goal was to get Tavis out of the horrible place.

Soon as Jack left the cave with Tavis, William scrambled to find a padlock and chain from the supply cabinet. When he found them, he opened the steel door and raced up to the loft, securing the cave door with a good old-fashioned lock and key.

While they waited for their warden to return, Sebastian said to Chaza, "I'm pretty sure Jack can cloak himself. I've suspected it for a while now."

"I'm just happy he got her out of here without resorting to violence." She turned to look at their new living space and let go a loud sigh.

"I don't think he would've done it," Sebastian said. Chaza raised a cynical eyebrow at him and he grimaced at the truthful reality. Nodding, he added, "I'm glad we were able to intervene."

Chaza looked around again; she already felt caged. "What are we gonna do?"

"We're going to behave like good little prisoners until I see they're escaping." He pointed at the screen on the wall. "You know he's gonna try using that to drive us crazy so we'll talk. He's smart in some ways, but mostly William's just a lucky idiot."

~

Jack half-ran, half-stumbled down the cliff until he reached the cart. He laid Tavis down in the back seat and quickly examined her still sleeping form to make sure she hadn't been harmed in the ordeal. Not seeing any signs of physical trauma, he jumped into the driver's seat and sped off toward the stone house.

Meg and Alec were waiting for Jack's return. Not even an hour had passed since Sebastian and Chaza had left. They'd only just begun to discuss what they should do next when Jack walked into their house from the back door and showed them the note he'd found on Sebastian's floor.

After he'd passed Lani off to Meg, he insisted he was going to get Tavis himself. Alec dared not reason with him, having sensed Jack's urgency and determination. However, when Jack came out of their kitchen with their biggest knife, Alec tried to stop him.

Jack then turned to Alec with a challenging and formidable look, silencing Alec's attempts to argue. "If it was Meg, what would you do?" he asked, his voice teetering on sinister.

"The same as you. Cloak yourself first, I already know you can."

A crooked smile spread across Jack's face. He'd been able to cloak himself for a while now and was glad someone else finally knew it. In the time it took to take a breath, Jack had vanished seamlessly in front of Alec.

Still, Alec worried and wasn't comfortable until he heard the cart pull up in front of the stone house. Meg was on her feet, too, and they went to the door to see Jack carrying Tavis' limp form in his arms.

Jack saw their panicked expressions and set their fears to rest. "She's been sedated, but other than that she's fine."

Alec bolted over to Tavis anyway, wanting to see for himself that she was okay. Besides the fact that she was barely dressed, she looked like she was only sleeping. "Let's get her to the spare bedroom and see if we can wake her up," Alec said.

"No!" Jack said. "I mean, let's put her in there, but I'd prefer to let her sleep."

Jack set Tavis on the bed, covered her with a thick quilt, and shut off the light. When he returned to the front room, where Meg and Alec waited for him, he relayed what had happened. He didn't enjoy telling either one of them the full weight of their new problems, but he sat in the chair opposite them and dove right in—none too delicately.

"William's keeping Sebastian and Chaza prisoners in a confinement cell of the bunkers," Jack said. Both he and Alec looked at Meg, who tried unsuccessfully to keep her chin from trembling. Jack grimaced, but continued. "He abducted Tavis as bait to get them to come to him. He even said that they were who he really wanted."

Again, they looked at Meg. She recognized how they were being with her; like she was a fragile ornament. Though she realized how she must look—quivering chin and teary-eyed expression—she refused to be coddled by either of them.

"William's holding them because he thinks no one will leave without them," she said exactly what they were already thinking. "What he doesn't know is that Sebastian has already decided we're to leave despite the fact he won't be joining us."

"Yeah, Meg, but Tavis doesn't know that," Jack said.

"I know, and I have no intention of ruining Sebastian's plans," Meg said, wiping the tears from her cheeks. "What about you, Jack? Alec still has issues with leaving, do you?"

Jack frowned and glanced at Alec, unsure of how to respond. All Alec did was avert his eyes away from both of them.

"I hate this whole thing more than you know," Jack said to Meg, giving up on Alec saying anything. "But I'm very ready to get my family the hell off this island."

Meg nodded and smiled a little. "I'll help you with Tavis when she wakes up. We'll find a way to make this work." She kept nodding, simply to keep from crying. "It's what Sebastian and Chaza wanted. They didn't hand themselves over for nothing."

Alec suddenly felt alone without Meg by his side. He sensed she'd chosen a side—one he wasn't willing to join yet. He clutched the key dangling from the chain around his neck and found comfort in the fact that no one was leaving until he was ready.

25

What It Took

Tavis didn't wake up until mid-morning. The first sight to greet her was Jack hovering over her, wearing a worried, though conservative, expression. She looked around at the unfamiliar surroundings and tried to piece together the timeline that would bring her to waking up in the stone house. The last thing she remembered was checking on Lani and then having to struggle against something. A thought, or some memory, competed for first place in the swirling mass of events racing through her mind.

The words, *'I'll shoot Jack if you wake him up'*, kept repeating and she tried to place a face to them through the hazy fog still confusing her. A face emerged, and it was the man she'd seen on the lane leering at her—William Davis. Tavis' eyes widened.

"Where's Lani?" She lunged from the bed, pushing past him and scanning the room for their daughter.

"She's fine, she's with Meg." Jack took a step toward her, but paused when she moved away. There was a wild look in her eyes that he'd never seen before and he averted his own to hide the anger it caused him. He composed himself and reached for her again; she allowed it this time. "Lani's in the front room with Luke, and Meg's having fun encouraging her to crawl. Luke's got a bit of a head start." Jack offered a reassuring smile.

"I want to see her," she said, staring at Jack's chest.

"I need to talk to you first." Since she didn't protest, he continued. "William kidnapped you in the middle of the night. I woke up and couldn't find you, so I went over to Sebastian's and found a note on the floor. It said for him and Chaza to come to the bunkers in exchange for releasing you. I brought Lani here and went to get you myself. When I found you, you were sedated and timecuffed to a bed."

Tavis looked up at him, confused. "I don't remember any of that."

He hated to ask his next question. "Is it possible...? I mean, do you think...?" It was difficult for him to form the words. "Did William *hurt* you in any way?"

She glanced down at her scantily clad body and understood what he meant. However, she knew her body and was sure William hadn't harmed her. "No, he didn't."

Jack sighed his relief and pulled Tavis into his embrace. "There's something else I have to tell you."

Her eyes closed for a moment. "He took them prisoner, didn't he?"

"Yes."

"He used me for leverage to make them go to him?"

"Yes."

"I'm not worried," she said, surprising him.

"You're not?"

"There's no prison that can hold my father, certainly not with Chaza there, too. When he wants to leave, he will. He's just trying to keep us all safe."

"I hadn't thought of that, but you're probably right." Jack nodded. "Come on, let's go see our daughter. Meg and Alec have been worried about you, they want to know you're okay. Meg left some clothes for you, they're on the dresser."

Jack waited by the door for Tavis to change clothes. It drove him to the brink of madness imagining William seeing her in the dainty nightgown she wore—laying her down on the bed he was clearly using for his own. William's words replayed again in Jack's thoughts, *'...she's rather distracting'*. When she was completely undressed, he had to look away, hating that William may have stolen a look for himself while she was unconscious.

~

Meg was sitting on the rug with Luke and Lani when Tavis and Jack entered the front room.

"Tavis." Meg looked up at her. "How're you feeling?"

"Fine." After sitting next to her on the rug, Tavis saw the worry in Meg's eyes—it wasn't solely for Tavis' well-being. "Please, Meg, don't worry. My father will keep Chaza safe and he'll bring her back soon."

"I hope you're right." Meg let out a weary sigh. "Alec's having trouble with everything."

"What kind of trouble?"

"Ever since Jack brought you back and told us William was keeping Sebastian and Chaza prisoner, he's been mostly quiet. He's keeping his thoughts to himself, I'm not really sure what's bothering him."

"He's just worried about your safety."

"Maybe." Meg nodded.

"Where is he?" Tavis glanced around the room.

"He went for a walk on the beach," she said. "What are you and Jack gonna do? You can stay here if you think it would be safer." Meg looked from Tavis to Jack.

They considered her proposal, but decided to go back to their own house. "Let me see how I feel after tonight." Tavis spotted the necklace Meg wore. "Is that Chaza's key?"

"Yes, she gave it to me yesterday before you two left to go to the lake." Meg lifted the pendant and looked at it.

"What about her amulet?" A small part of Tavis was afraid that Sebastian had lied to her about getting another pod. Short of unearthing the pods for a total count, communication with someone from her home would confirm the truth—or expose a lie she desperately hoped wasn't the case.

Meg recalled the conversation she'd overheard between Sebastian and Alec.

Above all, she could feel Jack's silent warning to tread cautiously. "She didn't mention anything to me about it. Is it important?"

"If we had two, we could communicate with others from our home. I wouldn't mind talking to them right now."

"You can talk to them when you get back home."

"Of course." Tavis took a deep calming breath. "Let's just hope they get out of there soon so we can leave."

"I need to talk to Alec." Jack stood. "I want to check on a few things before we go back to our house, and I'd prefer it if Alec stayed in here with you while I'm gone."

"Where are you going?" Tavis asked.

"To see if Kyrie has any locks that William might not have a key to. If she does, I'm gonna change the locks on all our doors."

"Kyrie doesn't know who William really is." Tavis' shoulders slumped a little. "I assume she doesn't know about what happened last night either."

"Then it's time she found out." Jack was impatient with all the secrecy.

"He's probably still on the beach," Meg said to Jack before Tavis argued with him. "We'll be fine here. I'm sure William's preoccupied at the moment."

~

Jack sat on the sand next to Alec and said, "I want you to stay with them while I go ask Kyrie if she has any locks that William doesn't already have a key for."

Alec glanced at Jack before returning his attention back to the ocean, staring at an unusual dark spot well off-shore. "My mom isn't aware of who William really is," he said mildly, but with clear rejection of Jack's idea.

"Maybe it's time for Kyrie to know the facts," Jack said, not bothering to keep the contempt from his tone.

"Is that so? Think it's time for *everyone* to know all the facts?"

Before he could respond, Jack caught glimpses of a folder bearing his name with brief, but indiscernible, flashes of data about himself. Alec hurled the images at him in a taunting way, and in the misguided attempt to alleviate his dark mood.

"You know what?" Jack maintained a careful guard of his temper. "Go ahead, show me. Let's just be done with it. Let me see what you found out about me."

Finally, Alec gave Jack his full attention. He stopped watching the distant waves, as they no longer seemed important. He'd been hasty and overstepped his boundaries with Jack, and now he had to deal with the consequences.

"No, I'm not showing you."

It was a challenge in Jack's opinion. "Show me or I'll force it out of you!" Jack gripped Alec's arm in the effort to make him understand that he was ready to know, and that Alec didn't have an option anymore.

Alec looked down at Jack's vice-like hold, then met his eyes again. "I suppose you could force it out of me if you wanted to." His voice was cold and mean-spirited. "I'll save you the trouble. Here ya' go, take a look."

Jack was inundated with images from the classified folder, almost as if Alec was throwing rocks at him. His mind had to make sense and order of the images without Alec's help. When it was over, Alec went back to watching the waves again, as though he hadn't just changed someone's life completely. Jack was stunned by the things he'd learned and his body tingled from the disturbing knowledge.

"Thank you for showing me that… so compassionately, Alec."

Alec refused to look at him.

Jack released Alec's arm, stood, and stared down at him. For the longest time, there was nothing but silence, save the wind and waves. Finally, Jack spoke and there was nothing but pity in his voice. "I have no idea why Sebastian puts such faith in you. All I see is a coward."

Alec was on his feet at the insult, glaring into Jack's eyes. "Apparently, he has more faith in me than he does in you," he spat, grabbing the chain and key and flaunting it in front of Jack's face.

"A mistake I hope he never realizes, or me for that matter. What's wrong with you? Are you waiting for William to snatch up Meg in the middle of the night? Neither she nor Luke deserves to suffer from your uncertainty. If you're not man enough to do what's right for your family, then give the key to me, because I am."

"Didn't you mention you had an errand to take care of?" Alec snarled and pushed Jack away from him before storming off to the stone house.

Jack waited until he saw Alec enter the house. Just before the front door closed, a bolt of lightning lit up the sky. He hoped a bit of anger would do Alec some good.

~

"How are you, Kyrie?" Jack asked when he entered the general store.

"I'm doing well, Jack." Kyrie smiled at him from her desk. "How're you? And Tavis and Lani?"

Jack sat in one of the chairs facing the desk. "We're doing fine" –he shrugged– "now."

"Did you two have a spat?"

"No, but I need to talk to you about some things you're not aware of."

Kyrie didn't like his expression. A crease had formed on his forehead and he seemed genuinely worried about her. "Is everyone okay?"

"Yes, Tavis and Lani are at Meg and Alec's house right now. Late last night, Tavis was abducted from our house while I was asleep, but she's fine now. I got her back."

"Who took her?"

"William Davis." Jack waited for the inevitable reaction.

"William?" Kyrie frowned.

"You need to know something about William. He's always been a member of management. In fact, he's second in command, answering only to Eldridge Stone. When you were married to him, he was only pretending to be an islander."

"Oh." She slumped back into her seat, trying to absorb what he'd told her.

Kyrie had seen the name E. Stone before on many of the signed and dated forms over the years, but never William's. "Are you sure? Why would he take Tavis?"

"Because he wanted to detain Sebastian and Chaza, which he did. He used Tavis as bait to make Sebastian come to him willingly. He's holding them in the bunkers."

"He didn't hurt Tavis, did he?" Kyrie's eyes narrowed; the thought of William anywhere near Tavis made her stomach lurch.

"No!" Jack said. "I'd like to make sure he can't try taking her, or anyone else, again. Do you have any locks here that don't have a master key?"

"I sure do." She smiled, almost wickedly, and sat up straight. "It used to be that alcohol wasn't allowed here. Of course, that was a joke. Some newcomers came in already knowing how to make wine from whatever fruit was available. It was my idea to use the native grapes, but since it wasn't allowed, we had to hide the barrels from the tattle-telling do-gooders. Joseph Arcana rigged locks for me so that the only keys that fit were the ones he made, and I still have them all."

"Were you and Joseph *good* friends?"

"Just friends," she said. "We sort of felt connected since we both came from Beta."

"You were born on Beta?"

"Yes, but I don't remember much about it. I was brought here when I was a child. A good thing, too, since Beta was destroyed."

"You know about that?"

"Sounds like you know quite a few things yourself," she said. "Feel free to spill all."

"Well, I know a bit." Jack let out a nervous sigh. "Ila isn't who you think she is. She's working with William, helping him do things like get DNA samples from Luke, Lani, and Chaza."

"I already knew that about Ila, but I thought they had decided to leave her alone so she could raise Meg properly."

"They did, until recently." Jack crossed his arms to keep his hands from fidgeting. "Ila isn't Meg's real mother, Chaza is. She gave Meg to Ila at birth and altered her memories so Ila would remember giving birth."

Kyrie's eyes widened. "Who's Meg's father?"

Jack guessed at what worried her. "No, not Sebastian. Joseph's her father, he and Chaza had a brief affair."

After the initial shock, her eyebrows raised at the new information. "I certainly didn't know about any of that." Kyrie gave Jack a stern look. "I'm sure I don't need to tell you, but it's in all our best interests if Ila never learns of this."

"I agree." Jack snorted. A moment later, he found an alternate way to fidget, leg bouncing.

"Is there something else you want to say?"

"It's about me. There's another island, Delta. I was born there, but I was taken away from my birth parents as a baby and given to a couple who raised me on the mainland. I just found out today."

Jack crossed his ankles to keep his legs still. It was hard for him—discovering his whole life had been a lie, and there was still more he needed to tell Kyrie.

Seeing how upset he was, Kyrie asked softly, "How did you find out?"

"Alec told me."

"Alec? How would he know that?"

"He broke into Dr. Patrick's basement and read it in the classified files." Jack saw she was still confused. "Classified files are kept at the physician's house. They contain information on the inhabitants that are considered too sensitive to keep in the medical office."

"I can't believe Alec did that. He could've been caught."

"We had to know about Ila. In her folder, it said they'd turned her back to an informant per William's request the day before Meg and Alec got sick. They had new folders ready for Luke, Lani, and Chaza, waiting for the DNA test results."

"How is it that you know so much about these things?"

It bothered Jack that she eyed him with suspicion. "Because I was a researcher on Digamma before I ran off from my job with Michelle to hide here."

"You were a researcher?" Kyrie laughed, relieved. "You had me worried for a minute. I thought you were gonna say you were with management, or one of those scientists. Don't researchers have about as much clout as a maintenance worker? What did you research?"

"The weather, that's what I studied in college," Jack mumbled.

"The weather?" Kyrie snorted and her laughter renewed. "You must have been so bored!"

He scowled at her candor, but soon grinned. "Yeah, I got bored."

Kyrie opened the top drawer of her desk and pulled out a set of keys. "My advice is to act normal, you don't want to arouse the suspicions of the islanders. Also, I've noticed some new cameras. Is William watching us?"

"Yep."

"Then be careful about what you do and when you do it, we don't want to give him reasons to watch us more. If we're to leave here, it would be better if he was paying less attention to us. Obviously, that's Sebastian's thinking."

"Are you really okay with leaving?" He thought about her pregnancy and risked adding, "Both of you?"

She stared at him for a moment, then sighed. "I guess if *you* know, then Alec must know I'm pregnant." There was just a hint of a question to the statement.

"He knows," Jack said and saw her disappointment. "I don't get the impression he's very happy about it. I think he assumes Sebastian took advantage of you."

Kyrie chuckled at this. "That's not how I remember it happening. If anything, it was the other way around." She waved her arm elegantly through the air to dismiss the subject. "How's Alec handling everything else?"

"Not very well, I'm afraid."

"I figured that. He's just scared to trust it. It's easier for Alec to be suspicious of an idea than to accept it completely." Kyrie contemplated what she should do. "I'll probably have to go to him."

"I think that's a good idea."

"Timing's everything. If I go too soon, he won't listen to anything I have to say. In the meantime, let's go find those locks."

~

Jack took all the locks Kyrie found, more than he needed, and changed the ones on the doors of his, Kyrie's, and the stone house. When he finished with the last door, he handed the key to Alec.

Alec attempted small talk with Jack. "So she had locks, huh?"

"Yes. I changed the locks on her doors, too."

"Did you tell her about what happened?"

Jack nodded.

"How'd she take it?"

"Better than you," Jack said and went to find Tavis and Lani. Feeling better about everyone's security, even if only temporary, he wanted to take his family to their own house.

Alec had wanted to apologize for his earlier behavior, but it seemed Jack was more interested in leaving. When they were gone, Alec found a disappointed look on Meg's face and it made him even angrier.

"Lock the door behind me," he said. "I'll use the key when I get back."

"Where are you going?" Meg asked, puzzled by his renewed grumpiness.

"I just need to clear my head." He tried to sound calm for her. "Maybe I'll go see my mom at the store. I'll be back later."

He hopped into the cart and drove off toward the town center. When he got to the store, it was already closed for the day. He got out of the cart anyway and headed for the café. Soon as he opened the glass doors, the thrumming white noise coming from all the islanders who'd come to have dinner here instead of cooking at home hinted at attainable calm. Alec fed off of their simple relaxation and turned toward the bar.

"Hello, Alec. How's it going today?" James asked.

"Not bad, but it'll go a lot better after a beer."

James smiled as he placed a perfectly poured beer on a napkin in front of Alec. He asked with a wink, "Having a tiff with Meg?"

"Something like that," Alec said.

The early dinner crowd came and left. Alec continued to sit at the bar, kicking back several more beers while the wait staff readied the café for the late-evening dinner parties. When they began to trickle in, he enjoyed guessing at the circumstances of what brought them here. Some were older folks who dined at the café almost every night, others came to celebrate a special occasion.

From afar, Alec joined in on: seven birthdays, two anniversaries, four 'I'm-pregnant!' surprise announcements, and one adulterous affair in a booth set back in the café's darkest corner. Then there were the nervous first dates, where each tried to impress the other and hoped they were succeeding at it.

"Would you like to order something from the menu?" James asked, interrupting Alec's people watching.

He turned to find James holding the dinner menu up. Alec half-peered, half-squinted into James' eyes. Though it was a hazy peek at his motivations, Alec sensed James was worried that he'd had too much to drink and should probably eat, or go home. "No, I'm good. I'm leaving after I finish this beer."

When Alec left the café, he found that walking took concentrated effort. He drove by his mom's house first to make sure all was well, but stayed in the cart as he didn't want to risk a potential lecture from her. She was in the kitchen putting her dinner plate away, and she was wearing her bathrobe. For the first time he could see the small rounding of her abdomen.

Alec continued on his way to the stone house. Driving took enormous effort as well, but he managed to make it back without running into any trees. However, the wood fence around their house wasn't so lucky when the front of the cart bumped it and knocked it over.

"Oops," Alec said and hiccupped at the same time; he chuckled.

After surveying the damage, he headed toward the barn to get the toolbox, but stopped when a strange light grabbed his attention. He went to the other side of the oak tree and squinted at the source of the light. It came from somewhere on the water, the same place he'd noticed a dark spot earlier in the day. Though small, he guessed it wasn't all that far out. Even with his drunken, fuzzy vision, Alec could make out that the light was green and would turn off and on intermittently.

Shrugging, he dismissed it as strange, but unimportant. He also decided against fixing the fence and staggered up the front steps. Since he couldn't remember if he had the new key or not, he knocked on the door.

"Meg," he called out. "It's me, Alec, your husband." The door remained closed and Alec frowned at it. "Meg?" he called louder.

Without warning, the front door swung open, causing Alec to sway with it until he caught himself from falling at Meg's feet.

She stared at him for a moment, then shouted, "Where've you been? I've been worried sick about you."

"The café," he said, trying unsuccessfully to keep from slurring his words.

"You're drunk!"

"Iamnot!" He started swaying again and his stomach protested its emptiness.

Meg reached out and grabbed Alec's arm, pulling him inside and out of the camera's view. She slammed the door shut and glared at him. "I'm getting Luke ready for bed. There's food on the kitchen table and I highly suggest you eat it."

Alec shuffled to the kitchen and ate everything on his plate, then consumed a second helping. He was still hammered, but now full and sleepy. When Meg came in, she found him slumped over the table with his head cradled in his crossed arms, snoring loudly. She sighed, forced him awake again, and helped him upstairs to their bedroom.

~

In the middle of the night, Meg was startled awake by Alec. She turned the bedside lamp on and discovered he was still asleep. Sweat had formed on his forehead and he mumbled incoherently. When she shook his shoulder, his eyelids popped open. His eyes were wild at first, but soon focused on her face and then his expression softened.

He frowned, trying to remember details of the dream and got out of bed to go to the window facing the ocean. He scanned the darkened surface and found the flickering light.

"Hey, come here. Do you see a light out there, over the water?"

Meg looked to where he pointed and saw a green light. "Yeah, I see it. What about it?"

"I've never seen anything like that before," he whispered.

"It's probably nothing." Meg shifted her gaze to him. "I shook you awake because you were having a nightmare, do you remember what it was?"

"A little, it was about that light." He pointed at it again. "I was on the beach and I had a feeling like I was supposed to know what that light was, but I couldn't figure it out and I had no way of getting to it. I even tried diving into the waves to swim out to it, but they were so strong and kept throwing me back onto the beach. I kept running up and down the shoreline trying to find a way to get out there… I think that's when you woke me up."

"That explains why you were thrashing around all over the bed." She chuckled. "If we're done gazing out of the window, can we go back to bed?"

"Yeah, my head's pounding," Alec said and offered her a smile.

It was Luke who woke them next in the early morning light. The sound of him babbling to himself came in through the baby monitor, filling their bedroom and making them laugh. Meg rounded the bottom of the stairs to get Luke from his crib, but Alec came to a stop.

"Aren't you coming?" Meg asked at the doorway to Luke's room.

"I'll meet you in the kitchen," he said, eyeing the sheet of paper in front of their door.

He bent down to pick it up and went to the kitchen to scan it quickly. The top half was dominated by a picture of Sebastian and Chaza standing in a living room area, looking at a huge screen affixed to one of the walls. He could just make out the image; it was of him from last night, when he'd left the café.

The bottom half of the page contained another image of Chaza and Sebastian sitting at a kitchen table. They were both focused on eating what looked like salads, and he saw the bars that kept them prisoners—it was a dismally oppressive scene.

Between the two pictures, in the center of the page, were the handwritten words: *As you can see, they're fine. If everyone behaves, Sebastian and Chaza will continue to be well cared for.*

It had been signed by William Davis and Eldridge Stone.

He stuffed the letter in his robe pocket when Meg came into the kitchen. "You want some tea?" he asked when she sat with Luke at the table.

"I'd love some."

After preparing her tea, Alec took Luke from her so she could enjoy it without him constantly trying to reach out for the teacup. "We're going out to the barn to check for eggs," he said. "I have deliveries to take care of today, would you mind staying at Tavis' while I work?"

"Sure, I'd planned on going over there anyway."

While in the barn, Alec shoved the letter into his toolbox. The last thing he wanted was for Meg to see it, but then it occurred to him that Jack and Tavis may have also gotten one. He left the barn, hoping she was upstairs getting ready so he could call Jack and warn him. Halfway to the front door, he came to an abrupt stop. Though it wasn't as obvious as it was at night, Alec saw the glint of something green flashing over the water.

He squinted over Luke's head, trying to make out the source of the light, but it was too far out. The best he could tell was that it came from a small boat.

Thankfully, Meg had already gone upstairs. He picked up the phone and was relieved when it was Jack who answered. "Hey, Jack, I need for you to check on something. See if you got a letter by your front door."

"Hold on." When Jack came back to the phone, he confirmed Alec's suspicion. "Yeah, we got one. I assume you did, too?"

"Yes, I found it first and hid it. Has Tavis seen it?"

"No, she's in the shower."

"Good, get rid of it. I don't want them to see it," Alec said. When Jack didn't respond, he grew irritated. "Is that a problem for you?"

"I'd prefer not to keep any more secrets, Alec."

"Oh, really?" It was all Alec could do not to yell. "So, you'd rather give this lovely update to Tavis. I'm sure her day will be all the better for seeing her father reduced to being a prisoner. By the way, Meg and Luke are coming over while I'm working. I hope you're in the mood to handle Meg's and Tavis' distress all day."

"Alec, please calm down. I'm not gonna show it to Tavis. I agree with you, it'll upset her. Besides, it's just William taunting us and she doesn't need that right now. I only wanted you to know where I stand as far as keeping anything important from Tavis."

"Okay, I get it." Alec forced himself to relax. "Sorry, this whole situation is bothering me a lot."

"I know it is," Jack said, trying to be understanding. "We'll see you in a little while."

~

After dropping Meg and Luke off, Alec drove to the town center. When he saw the store was open, he sat in the cart and pondered whether or not he wanted to face his mother yet. Deciding against it, he drove off toward Alaret Beach.

He parked the cart in a thick stand of trees, away from the prying cameras, and walked the rest of the way to the beach. Once settled down amid a patch of sea oats, Alec studied the flashing light. At times, he would get up and go chest deep into the water to get a closer look at the source.

Mid-way through the day, he grew thirsty and was forced to go to the stone house. When he opened the front door, he found another letter. There was only one image this time: Sebastian and Chaza were seated on a sofa, watching the screen, and on it was Alec driving away from the general store just a few hours earlier. Underneath the picture was yet another handwritten comment from William: *Why not? Everyone needs an occasional day off.*

Rage began building up in Alec's bloodstream, flooding his thoughts with hatred. "Damn you!" he said, tearing the letter in half.

Part of him wanted to set it on fire in front of the camera pointed at his house, but he stuffed the pieces in his pocket instead and went to the kitchen. As the water was only quenching his thirst, Alec opened a bottle of wine and poured it into the teacup Meg had used earlier.

When the teacup became little more than a formality, Alec drank directly from the bottle and opened another when he'd emptied it. Unfortunately, it was the last bottle in the cabinet, but he knew where he could get more. He could almost imagine the next letter's picture—him in the cave, retrieving as much of the old wine as he could carry.

~

With great effort, Alec lugged the crate of wine bottles down the cliff. While he'd been up in the cave, he looked into the camera and smiled, bowing in a ridiculous curtsy. Standing straight again, he threw the empty bottle he'd brought with him against the cave wall. He laughed as the bottle shattered into pieces and came to rest on the cave floor in hundreds of shards.

Alec had also looked out at the flashing light when he'd reached the top of the cliff, but it still looked the same, only a slightly better vantage point that had confirmed it was a small boat.

After getting the crate of wine bottles to the barn, he put the crumpled pieces of the second letter with the first in the toolbox. As he drank from a newly opened wine bottle, he contemplated the flashing light; it was driving him crazy.

He ran back outside and settled down on the other side of the oak tree to resume his study of the strange apparition. The flashing had ceased for the moment, but he could still make out the shape of the boat. At times, he saw the kind of movement that only a person standing in a small watercraft could make.

When the third bottle was empty, Alec forced himself to stand. It was late afternoon now and he wanted to get Meg and Luke, fearing Meg may call the store and find out he hadn't really gone to work.

She said nothing when he showed up. Instead, she gathered up Luke and told Tavis they would see each other tomorrow. It wasn't until later, while they were in bed, that she asked, "How was work?"

"Fine," he lied. "I still have more work to do, though. Is Tavis coming over here tomorrow?"

"That's the plan."

Meg woke up again in the middle of the night by Alec having another nightmare. This time, she didn't have to wake him as he'd already gotten out of bed and was rushing to the window.

"Another nightmare?" she asked and pushed the covers aside to join him.

"Same as the last one. I'm running back and forth along the beach, trying to find out what the light is."

She glanced in the direction Alec's eyes were fixed on and saw the same green light she'd seen the previous night. Positioning herself between Alec and the window, she took his hands into hers and looked up at him.

"Alec, I agree that light out there is weird, but I don't think it concerns us. We have other things we need to focus on right now."

"I think it does concern us," he said in a soft whisper, still looking out of the window over her head.

"There's nothing we can do about it, please just let it go." The desperation in her voice drew his eyes to hers and he saw how scared she was. He felt like it was his responsibility to chase away her fears, but he couldn't.

"I'm sorry, Meg, I can't let it go. I feel like it's trying to reach me somehow."

Disappointment overshadowed the fear in her expression, but he was powerless to try easing her frustration. She released his hands and went back to bed.

~

When Alec woke the next morning, Meg and Luke were already gone. He looked out the window and saw that she'd taken the cart; he had a feeling she wasn't planning on returning right away. His eyes drifted toward the ocean; the light was still there and he could just make out the tiny speck of the boat floating on the water.

He searched for the clothes he'd worn the previous day. Not bothering to brush his teeth or shower, Alec got dressed and went downstairs to call Meg.

"I thought they were coming over here today," Alec said when Tavis handed the phone to Meg.

"I changed my mind," she said.

He heard the underlying annoyance in her tone.

"Besides, I figured you'd like to be alone with your flashing light."

"Meg, please don't be like this."

"How am I supposed to be when you're obsessing over a stupid light instead of focusing on more important matters?"

"I think this is important, too. I can tell there's someone on that boat and it seems like they're trying to tell me something."

"I'm trying really hard to be patient with you, but what you're saying right now sounds crazy. If this person wanted to talk to you, why wouldn't they just come to you?"

"Maybe I'm supposed to go to him," Alec said, but it was more like he was answering his own questions. "I think that's why he's out there."

Worried now, Meg said, "That sounds dangerous to me. You don't know who this person is, or what they want." When he didn't respond, she asked, "What are you planning to do, Alec?"

"Well…" He was nervous, but resolved. "I'm gonna go out there and find out what he wants."

"What if I said I don't want you to do that?"

"I'd say I'm sorry we disagree, but I'm gonna do it anyway."

She was silent for a moment, then asked, "When do you plan to go out there?"

"I'm not sure." He hadn't planned that far yet. "I'll probably ask Frank if I can borrow his rowboat, but since you took the cart I'll have to walk to his house."

"Maybe you should walk to the general store first. You can use the utility cart, and maybe help your mother. Yes, Alec, I know you didn't really go to work yesterday."

"I'm sorry I lied to you."

"Do whatever you feel you need to do and let me know when you're ready to be my husband again, and Luke's father again. In the meantime, we'll be staying at Kyrie's, I've already talked to her about it. Goodbye, Alec."

Meg hung up, and Alec stood in the kitchen, still holding the phone in his hand. Slowly, he placed it back on the base, feeling numb. The walls of the stone house seemed to lean at wrong angles, as though they meant to close in on him and capture him—for what purpose he had no intention to discover.

He ran out of the house as though it was on fire and didn't stop until he reached the barn. Standing in the doorway, listening to the hens cluck their objections to his sudden appearance, he stared back at the stone house. Imagining Meg and Luke gone from there made it ugly to him. Alec turned away from it, picked up a half-empty wine bottle, and finished it off, but it wasn't enough. He opened another and began the long walk to the town center.

Alec drove away quietly from the general store in the utility cart, ignoring his guilt for not telling Kyrie he was taking it. He didn't want to face her—he couldn't. If he saw disappointment in her eyes, he'd crumble for sure.

On the way to Frank's, he stopped by his mother's house—it was the barn he was interested in. He went inside to retrieve the most recently bottled wines. Frank had a fondness for Gamma-produced wine, Kyrie's in particular, and Alec planned to bribe him with it for the rowboat. After snatching several bottles off the table, he was about to leave when he spotted some unfamiliar bottles tucked away at the back.

The shape and size of them were different from the wine bottles and he leaned over to examine one of them. The label indicated it was rum, some Caribbean import, a rarity on the island. He set all but one of the wine bottles back down, trading them for the rum, and left for Frank's.

~

Frank opened the door, beaming. "Alec! How are you? It's been a while. How are Meg and Luke?"

Alec stood on the front porch, holding a wine and rum bottle behind his back. "We're doing great, Frank. I brought a surprise for you."

"You did? Come inside and show me what you brought." Frank was intrigued, but mostly because he hadn't had a visit from Alec in a long time and he'd always liked him.

Once inside, Alec pulled the bottles around and held them up for Frank's inspection. Frank nodded with a grin when he saw Kyrie's wine. When he saw the rum, his eyebrows arched.

"Rum? I haven't seen a bottle of rum in years. Where'd you get… never mind, I don't want to know!"

"I hope you approve," Alec said.

"I more than approve." Mischievous excitement gleamed in his eyes. "I say we give it a taste."

Frank went to the kitchen and pulled two glasses from the cabinet while Alec sat at the table and opened the rum bottle. After Frank joined him and poured them each a glass, he treated Alec to stories of his youth when he and his friends used to try making their own rum.

"None of it was very good," he said. "Of course, we drank it anyway."

It was getting late so Alec shifted the conversation to his reason for being there. "I was hoping you'd let me borrow your rowboat. I wanted to take it out, if you don't mind, that is."

"You don't mean tonight, not after this rum? I'd hate for Meg to come pounding on my door."

"No, I wanted to take it home tonight and use it early in the morning," Alec lied.

"Sure. I'll help you get it hitched to the cart when you leave." Frank scrutinized Alec. "Are you sure everything's okay with you? You look terrible."

"Everything's fine. I've been working a lot lately for my mom. Guess I need a haircut, huh?"

"You need to shave, too, unless you're trying to grow a beard."

Alec rubbed his face and chin and found several days' worth of growth there. "Yeah, I guess I do need to shave. Maybe that's why Meg's been looking at me funny." He laughed and refilled their glasses. "I have another bottle of rum for you out in the cart, if you're interested."

"I'm always interested in another bottle of rum," Frank said.

They polished off the rum and went outside to hitch the rowboat to the utility cart. Alec grabbed a second bottle and handed it to Frank. "Thank you for letting me borrow the boat," he said and got in the cart.

Frank stood near the driver's side and stared down into Alec's eyes. It seemed like he was making one final judgment before saying anything. "You know something, Alec?"

"What, Frank?" Even though the rum had numbed his senses, he still knew what Frank was about to say.

"Before Lena died, she tried to tell me you were no good. She especially wanted me to do whatever I could to keep you away from Meg."

"Why didn't you?" Alec braved.

"Because I felt she was wrong about you." Frank swayed a little. "Please, Alec, don't let it be that *I* was the one wrong."

A chill went through Alec's body. He remembered all too well how Lena viewed him just before she died and it shamed him knowing how things were between him and Meg right now. It also made him more determined than ever to discover the reason for the strange apparition signaling to him.

"I swear to you, Frank, you weren't wrong."

"All right then, off you go." Frank smiled and clapped the roof of the cart.

~

Alec pulled up at the south end of Alaret Beach with rowboat in tow, well out of sight of the cameras. He was surprised by how late in the day it was and checked to see if the mysterious boat was still out there. It was—still flashing the green light that taunted and beckoned him.

He headed down the beach toward the stone house, wondering if Meg had changed her mind and would be there waiting for him. When he reached the top of the hill overlooking their home, the cart wasn't in the driveway. He briefly considered going inside, but the stone house without Meg made him sick to his stomach—and he imagined the house wasn't happy about it either. As there was nothing inside he wanted, he turned and went back to the utility cart.

For a while, he sat in the driver's seat, staring out at the light. Eventually, he reached into the back seat and fished around for the last bottle of rum. He opened it and took a long draw from it, hoping to quell the growing hunger pains that reminded him he hadn't eaten since yesterday. When he'd drank over half the bottle, his eyelids grew heavy and, though he didn't intend to, he fell asleep.

Another nightmare that had become too intense was what jolted him awake. Though similar to the previous ones, where he ran up and down the beach, it differed in that the boat was closer to shore and he could almost see what the person looked like. It was a much older man, even older than Frank, but he didn't behave so very old and seemed to be laughing at Alec. Each time Alec heard it, he'd stopped running, thinking the old man laughed cruelly. However, the laughter turned out to be more encouraging than mean-spirited and it made Alec start running again; trying to find a way to get to him.

It became a cycle that kept repeating itself until the old man pointed at something on the beach. When Alec turned his head, he found Meg chained to the oak tree—that was no longer by their house, but in the middle of the beach. The majestic oak appeared dead; there were no more rich green leaves and it looked more like it belonged in an eroded maritime forest. Beneath the tree, where it should have been growing out of the sand, was the rug that adorned their front room floor. The decayed roots either splayed out over the rug, or had punched through it in the vain attempt to find life-sustaining water.

Meg was trying to scream, but her mouth had been gagged by an old filthy piece of tattered cloth. All around her were brilliant, iridescent colors and orbs that reminded him of the ones they'd encountered in the forest. Only in the dream, there were also dark masses coming in from everywhere—threatening to take over the beautiful lights, one by one.

Alec had an overwhelming sense that he was supposed to stop them from taking over and consuming the luminous ones before Meg disappeared forever with the last shining light. When there were only half of the beautiful lights left, he turned to the old man to question if this was what he was supposed to do. The old man simply nodded that Alec should make a decision soon, or risk losing Meg to the darkness. Then he began to retreat, taking the still unexplained flashing green light with him.

For a brief second, Alec contemplated going after the old man before he got too far away from shore. His gaze returned to Meg, discovering there were only a few lights left and that he'd wasted too much time and that he may not be able to save her. The pain and disappointment in her eyes as she stared at him was more than he could stand; he ran toward her. The terror of thinking he might not make it in time is what forced Alec awake.

He leapt from the cart, still clutching the rum bottle in his hand, and sighed with relief that it had all just been a dream. The sunlight was completely gone now, and only the light from the moon allowed Alec to survey his surroundings. His stomach lurched again in protest of its emptiness and all it received was more of the rum.

Looking out over the water, zeroing in on the familiar sight of the green light for the last time on land, Alec made the decision to end the mentally torturous affair. He capped the rum bottle and put it in the rowboat before getting back into the cart to ease it into the ocean. After he unhitched it, he parked the cart near the sea oats and ran back to the boat to settle in.

His muscles complained when he began rowing, but he ignored the pain, pausing only long enough to finish off the last of the rum. He threw the empty bottle to the farther end of the rowboat and fixed his eyes on his intended destination.

What seemed a lifetime passed, but he'd only gotten halfway to the other boat, so he stopped to stretch his tired arms and to glance back at the shoreline. The beach looked so far away now. Part of him longed to be on it again, but that would mean he'd still be looking out over the ocean, trying to understand what the green light was for. There was no way for him to accept that defeat; he gripped the oars and pushed on.

Sweat formed on his forehead and stung when it rolled down into his eyes, blurring his vision. Using his shirt to wipe his eyes, he persevered, continuing to row toward the light. When his hands began to sting, he looked at his palms and saw blood appearing from the newly formed blisters that had already burst—still he kept rowing, even when the blood fell in droplets to the bottom of the rowboat.

When the burning became unbearable, Alec removed his t-shirt and ripped it into two pieces to wrap around his hands. Taking the oars up again, he locked his eyes on the target. He was close enough now that he could see more details of the boat. It was more like a canoe, and incredibly long—at least fifteen feet by Alec's estimates and each end curled up ornately. The man standing in the center of the canoe was facing Alec, waiting for him to finish closing the distance between them.

Though his arms were aching, Alec pushed through; he was almost there and nothing was going to stop him. When he finally reached the canoe, he released the oars and collapsed backward onto the bottom of the rowboat. Not only were his hands and arms in agony, the muscles in his back convulsed, adding a searing pain that forced him to remain motionless. His breathing was out of control, his heart raced from the effort to get here, and he was thirstier than he'd ever been in his life.

In this supine position, Alec studied the figure of the man looming over him while his breathing and heart rate returned to normal. The man was tall, somewhat titanic, and he towered over Alec's prostrate form, wearing a knowing and discriminating grin. His white hair was long, cascading down his shoulders and ending just below his chest. The wise, observant appearance on his face indicated that he was old, almost ancient, but there were few lines to prove it.

His clothes were simple and earth colored. Everything about him was neat and tidy; unlike Alec, who was sweaty and disgusting from several days' worth of not caring what he looked like. There was something familiar about the man, something Alec felt he should know, but couldn't quite remember.

Alec's eyes drifted down the man's arm, examining the unusually long walking stick gripped in his left hand. It was made of wood and there were carvings etched into it that reminded him of the symbols on his amulet, but it was hard to tell for sure in the moonlight. At the very top of the cane, faceted by intricate braids of what looked like thin roots, was an enormous stone. It was clear, like glass, but it refracted so much of the moonlight that it dazzled Alec's eyes.

The man broke the silence between them: "Hello, Alec. It certainly took you long enough to come to me. I was beginning to doubt you ever would." His voice was as monumental as his stature.

"You could have just come to me," Alec brazenly said.

"I'd rather not soil the bottoms of my shoes with the filth of that island."

"How do you know my name?" Alec asked, frowning at the man's austerity. "I'm sure I've never met you before."

"I know everything about you, Alec Ellison."

Alec snorted. "You, too?"

"Are you done resting? I'd prefer it if you stood like a man when you're addressing me."

Though Alec couldn't believe the stranger would speak to him in such a condescending way, he did what he was told and stood to face him. "Better?"

"Much better," he said. "Even though I'm being addressed by a man who looks and smells like dung. However, I'll try to ignore the stench."

"Oh, pardon me." Alec scowled at the old man and his slew of insults. "I did just row all the way out here to find out why a complete stranger was flashing lights at my house."

"And it only took three days of drinking, neglecting your family, and lying to make it happen."

The words were like a hard slap in the face to Alec, and his pride wouldn't allow him to listen to another insult. "You know what? You're absolutely right. I should learn to listen to my wife more often. You and I have wasted enough of each other's time, I'll be on my way now."

Alec sat back down in the rowboat and picked the oars up, his hands stung in defiance. After turning the rowboat around to face the island, he'd not yet gotten but a few feet away from the canoe when a glowing green light flooded the water around him. With fear of the unknown, Alec slowly turned his head toward the man again, the only possible source of the light.

His left hand still clutched the cane as before, but in his right hand he held an amulet. It rested in his palm and his fingers curled up around the base to keep it secured. Alec recognized it as identical to his own, but with the exception that instead of sapphires, its gems were emeralds. His gaze returned to the man's dark, almost black eyes; a knowing smile was spreading across the ancient face.

"Where did you get that?" Alec asked in a hoarse whisper, nodding toward the amulet. He dropped the oars again and stood.

"That's none of your concern."

Alec had long grown weary of him. If the man didn't want to give the information willingly, then Alec was more than happy to extract it from him. Soon as he began to concentrate his efforts to probe the man's thoughts and memories, laughter burst forth from him.

"Don't bother, you're wasting your time… and mine. Your abilities don't work on me," he said, but was clearly amused.

The failure of his feeble attempt to gain information angered Alec. "I think it's time you told me what the hell it is you want from me."

"I came here to give you a message."

"All right, let's hear it."

"Leave," the old man barked. "Tell your father it's time to go. Gamma's about to be destroyed, one way or the other. If the East American military can't get it done, my people will. Either way, it's gone, and Delta will be next."

"As much as I'd like to relay your message, I'm afraid it's not possible. The man you're referring to is being held prisoner."

"The man I'm referring to is your father, and you should respect that fact and behave in a more humble way to the man who gave you breath."

"I prefer to credit my mother for that."

"Kyrie's credited for each day you made it to the next until you became a man, it's Sebastian who put breath in your lungs." The man appraised Alec from head to toe. It seemed like he meant to agree—or not—with some preconceived conclusion. "I fear your ego has clouded your better judgment. Tell me, did Sebastian leave you with any important tasks?"

Alec hated having to admit it, but figured lying was probably useless against this man. "He wants me to get some people home, where he thinks they should be."

"And what do you think?"

"I'm worried about the people we'll leave behind," Alec muttered, feeling the horrible reality of their fate more than ever.

"That's a rather large burden you're trying to shoulder. It's not only the ones on Gamma, but the ones on Alpha, on Beta, and all the ones on all the lands from recent to ancient times that you'd truly be worrying about. You can't save the ones who have already died, you can only save the ones who haven't yet lived."

Tears brimmed in Alec's eyes and spilled onto his cheeks, and he hated them. He felt vulnerable in a helpless sense. "But why can't I find a way to save *all* of them?"

For the first time since Alec began talking to this strange man, he saw a gentleness warm his expression. Yet, it was mixed with profound sadness when he said, "Because they're already dead, Alec."

Despair and hopelessness overpowered Alec's previous determinations; he sobbed like a child in front of a man he knew nothing about. After a while, despite the gamut of his raw emotions, he asked, "Why do you care so much about what happens to me?"

"I don't want you to die here. You're important to me." He lifted Chaza's amulet in the air between them. "You'll find this only if you need it. However, I warn you now, finding it will mean you are in grave danger and close to death."

"I don't know if I can do it." The face of everyone Alec cared about flashed through his thoughts.

"It was predicted to me, in what *you* would consider to be a long time ago, that you'd be a great protector and survivor, but I don't think you feel it yet. It's time for you to prove it to yourself. The reason why I care so much is because my blood runs through your veins, don't waste it on this planet."

The man lifted his walking stick and tapped the end of it against the edge of the rowboat. Upon contact, the huge diamond sprang to life, emitting and scattering a bright light, momentarily blinding Alec before it went dark again. There was an odd sensation of electricity coursing from the boat to his body, and then he heard a cracking sound. Where the man's cane had touched the boat, a visible fracture had formed and continued to split it in half—water began rushing in.

Alec teetered from the new instability of the sinking rowboat and fell off the side into the ocean, where he watched the two segments sink beneath the water. Panic crushed his chest while he tried to keep his head above the water. Spitting seawater out of his mouth, Alec looked at the old man again, seeing the knowing smile had returned as he sat down in the canoe and took up the oars.

"Your hands are still bleeding, by the way. If you attract any sharks, try to *talk* to them and convince them not to tear you to shreds." The man laughed. "If you make it to shore, tell my granddaughter I said goodbye."

Confused, Alec's mind raced to think of who his granddaughter could be. Dismissing the request, he turned toward the island and grimaced. The shoreline may well have been a million miles away, but he had no choice but to prepare himself mentally to start the long swim back.

After twenty minutes of the forward crawl style of swimming, and given his atrocious physical state, Alec had to periodically switch to swimming the backstroke. Though he still made distance this way, the disadvantage was that he couldn't see which direction he was going. Eventually, he noticed that when he rolled over to backstroke, he spent more time resting than swimming.

Forward crawl swimming took a toll on his already exhausted muscles. He began looking forward to floating aimlessly on his back when he started experiencing cramps in his arms and legs. Another thing he noticed was that he no longer made a decent amount of distance to the shore when he returned to forward swimming. At some point, he stopped checking his progress, fearing disappointment would make him give up.

The muscle cramps happened more often, forcing him to take longer rests between swimming. He knew it was an indication that he was dehydrated and he laughed at the irony of all the undrinkable water surrounding him.

Facing skyward, during one of his resting intervals, Alec watched the stars flickering in the night sky above him. He wondered if the sky looked the same where Sebastian came from. While he pondered the thought, something brushed against his leg. Though he didn't have to look to confirm it, he did anyway and saw three fins circling the water around him.

"So, this is it, huh?" Alec asked the sharks. "You've come to eat me. Well, I'm glad it's now and not when I was almost there."

The sharks kept circling, but ceased nudging him. "What the hell are you waiting for? Let's get this over with," Alec yelled into the air, slamming his fists against the surface of the water.

Still, they only circled. Alec remembered when Sebastian gathered the fish by the beach and that he'd said he had convinced them to come to him. He wondered if he could convince the sharks to leave him alone.

"I was kind of hoping that I wouldn't be part of your next meal," Alec said, somewhat sheepishly as he had no idea how to convince a shark not to eat him. The barbs the old man tossed at him about his stench and appearance came to mind. "I probably wouldn't taste very good anyway."

A memory replayed in his mind, of Meg telling him on her birthday to make sure he fed the sharks first before she would agree to swim with him in the ocean. He had laughed then, and it made him laugh again while he kept a watchful eye on the fins circling around him.

"If you don't mind, I'd be grateful if you found somewhere else to hunt for food," Alec said, determined to give it a final attempt. Quickly as they'd arrived, the fins submerged beneath the water and left him alone.

"Damn!" he shouted. "Unbelievable!" Alec rolled over and began swimming again in earnest, certain he wasn't going to give those sharks a chance to change their minds.

He swam for as long as he could, even through the next wave of muscle cramps, before allowing himself to rest again. Each time he rested, it became harder to stay afloat. Staring at the twinkling stars helped for a while, but eventually they started shifting and moving in patterns that Alec knew were impossible. At one point, he thought he saw an outline of Meg's face.

"I'm hallucinating now," he told himself.

His body had had enough of the abuse from the last few days and he knew it was close to giving up entirely. He thought his mind was next when he saw the stars shift again to form the pattern of a spider.

The memory of the little birthday-girl Meg, sitting on her bedroom floor, serving tea to her doll came to life in his eyes. Her innocent face, that crazy and wonderful hair, her beautiful green eyes looking at him as he stood in her doorway. The tree. Alec flinched in the water at the memory of the stone hitting her head.

He chased the memory away and forced himself to continue swimming some more. At the next moment of resting, he tried avoiding the stars, but there was nothing else to look at. They shifted again and this time he saw Meg's face as it appeared to him when they were together for the first time in the cave. He liked this memory and it gave him strength enough to swim again.

Alec almost looked forward to his next rest. He looked up at the stars, hoping for another good memory and saw Meg's happy face while they were being married and she pledged her vows to him till the end of their days. Deciding today wasn't to be the end, he forged ahead to get back to her.

Next, the stars showed Alec the night of Luke's birth. At first, Meg's face was contorted in pain, but then the stars shifted again to show three new faces—him and Meg looking proudly at their newborn son. Alec smiled up at the vision and if his arms weren't so tired, he would've tried to reach up and touch all three of them.

He trudged through the pain and water again. Some part of him wanted to look toward the island to determine how close he was, but a larger part refused to allow it for fear of seeing how little progress he'd made. Alec swam for the longest time yet before relenting to another rest. He rolled over onto his back, gliding his arms slowly through the water in the effort to stay afloat and waited to see what memory formed next.

The stars aligned to form Meg's face again and she was smiling down at him. A streak of lightning flashed over the sky and the sound of rolling thunder followed it. Somewhere nearby there was a thunderstorm and Alec wondered if it was trying to make its way to him. He silently wished it would; he'd welcome the rain as he could no longer remember what fresh water tasted like.

Meg's face began to fade while Alec dreamt of water and he refocused his thoughts to bring her image back. Her smile became clear again, but changed when another flash of lightning filled the night sky and ripped through the memory of her beautiful face. The smile vanished and a frown replaced it—representing a failure in expectations written in her eyes and he knew he was the author. The once hopeful look became defeated, leaving Alec as the sole victor. He wanted to make it right again, but doubted he'd ever get the chance.

Another flash of lightning passed over the sky, erasing Meg's face from his eyes, and he groaned at the start of rolling over to swim once more. It was harder than before and his arms felt like lead. He was vaguely aware that they didn't work in a coordinated way anymore and he felt like he needed to rest again already. Accepting that he wasn't going to make it, Alec allowed himself to finally look at the shoreline.

From the moonlight, he saw the sea oats at the bottom of the cliff swaying in the ocean breeze. He looked in the direction of the stone house and he could just make out the gigantic oak tree. It occurred to him that it couldn't be possible for the tree to be that massive, given the age of the island.

But the house shouldn't be there either, he thought.

For a moment he imagined he saw the ghostly figure of a woman standing on the beach and he assumed he was about to see another memory of Meg. Not wanting to see the painful look of disappointment again, and he especially didn't want to see her tears, Alec turned his eyes away from the apparition.

"Of course, so close… I almost made it." Alec mused over how well he was able to make out the details of Alaret Beach. "I love you, Margaret Arcana. I'm sorry I didn't just take us home. I'm sorry I couldn't make it back… the ocean owns me now."

He couldn't lift his arms anymore, so he rolled onto his back again, floating for as long as he could. Before closing his eyes, he fixated on the image that he wanted to be the last thing he thought of. He remembered their first kiss, or rather the kiss of their shadows, but it had been so real to him.

The encounter had had a profound effect on him in so many ways. It was the day that he'd given back a tiny piece of her true self, and she chose to dance. Of all the things Meg could've done, she decided to have fun with the miniscule remnant of her rightful identity—she even surprised the thief by giving him a kiss from her shadow.

He'd sworn many times to always protect her, and it had scared him that he may have to protect her from himself. But on that day—and in that moment of their playful shadows—he was happy thinking they could be together without any repercussions. He'd felt a rare peacefulness then that he still carried with him to this day.

With this beautiful memory of happy shadows, a warm tranquility relaxed his tired body and he welcomed the end to the struggle.

And then eyelids closed over the bluest of eyes, and Alec slipped beneath the whitecaps.

26

Today Is a Good Day to Fight

After Meg had hung up with Alec, she explained everything to Tavis and Jack and told them that Alec was determined to row out to whoever it was flashing a light at him. To keep from bad-mouthing Alec, Jack took Lani and Luke outside to the garden so they could look at the koi swimming in the pond.

"He'll be fine," Tavis said. "Alec just needs to satisfy his curiosity."

Meg saw the facade of confidence Tavis tried holding up and thought it looked a little shaky. "I know how close you and Sebastian are. How are you coping with everything?"

"Not very well at all." Tavis' confession came in a barely audible whisper. Her blue eyes became bluer as the tears formed. "I don't know how much longer I can take it. I'm trying so hard to hide it from Jack, but I can't stand the thought of my father having his freedom denied."

"I shouldn't have brought it up." At seeing the facade crumble, Meg pulled Tavis into her arms. "You've been doing such a great job of being brave for us. You said Sebastian could walk out of there whenever he wants and I think you're right. Don't lose faith in him."

"Thank you, Meg. I just needed to say it, I feel better now."

"I like being able to help you, don't wait so long next time."

"You really are amazing. I don't know what you see in Alec."

The hurt look in Meg's eyes shamed Tavis.

"I didn't mean that in a bad way. Alec's my brother, you have to know how important that is to me."

"I know Alec's…" Unable to come up with the perfect description, Meg settled on a good enough one. "Difficult. Part of the reason he's like that is because he spent so much of his life knowing he was different, and that I was, too. He was afraid of what that could mean. Right now, everything he feared seems to be happening."

"He won't have to be scared anymore when we go home."

"Yeah, but everything's happening so fast… *too* fast. There's no time to develop a trust of it. He'd just have to take a leap of faith into the unknown and that's not an easy thing for him to do. What's worse is that he's been taking a whole lot of leaps lately."

"He saw our home through the amulet" –Tavis shrugged– "and he seemed to like it."

"Liking something and trusting it doesn't always go hand in hand. There's also another problem."

"What?"

Meg stared hard at Tavis. Not in a mean or an incredulous way, but more in the way of trying to figure out how and why someone doesn't see and understand the obvious. The expression on Tavis' face was one of blissful ignorance and Meg couldn't fault her for this, she hadn't grown up on Gamma.

"Do you love your home? I mean, the place where you grew up and all the people you know there?" Meg asked.

"Of course I do, I miss everything about it."

"Alec and I are gonna miss this place because we grew up here. Not only that, but you know what will likely happen to Gamma when we leave."

Tavis sighed. "They'll destroy it like it never mattered."

Though she already knew this, it was still difficult to hear. Meg composed herself before continuing. "The way you say it sounds like you're referring to Gamma in the most general of terms, but there are people here, Tavis. Don't you understand that? They're all gonna die. Imagine how hard that is for Alec to accept, how hard it is for *me*. Think about the people you've gotten to know since you've been here, and then think about what's going to happen to them."

So many faces flashed in Meg's mind. There was Frank, laughing and always happy except for when Lena died. She thought of all the people she went to school with, and her teachers. The faces of all the children and the babies tormented her; and even Ila, the woman who'd raised her. All of them were going to die because a few chose to leave. The totality of it all overwhelmed Meg and her stomach churned, sending her on a race to the bathroom with Tavis following after her.

"Please forgive me," Tavis said as Meg fell to her knees and bent over the toilet.

Tavis held a handful of blonde curls in one hand and patted Meg's back with the other.

When Meg was over the bout of nausea she rinsed her mouth, flushed the toilet, and leaned back against the tub, waiting for the last of the queasiness to pass. Once Tavis settled down beside her on the floor, Meg asked, "Forgive you for what?"

Before Tavis could answer, Jack appeared in the doorway and frowned at them.

"Can you give us a minute, please?" Tavis asked.

"Sure," he said, but was still frowning as he pulled the door closed.

When his footsteps retreated, Tavis answered Meg. "For failing to know what this was doing to you and Alec. For being too stupid to acknowledge the loss of life when we leave."

"Don't say that again, you're not stupid."

"You're right, though, and I hate that everyone will die and that we're all going to be safe at home." Tavis buried her face in her hands.

Meg hadn't expected another tearful response from Tavis; she was always a sea of calm—so reserved and collected. She put her arm around Tavis' shoulder, bringing her head to her chest. At the contact, the silent tears became audible sobs and Meg heard Jack's footsteps advancing back toward the bathroom. She half-expected the door to burst open, but he only knocked.

"Do either of you need anything?"

"No. We're fine, Jack, thank you," Meg said. When his footsteps hadn't retreated, she nudged Tavis and whispered, "Answer him before he breaks the door down."

"We'll be out in a minute."

"Okay," Jack finally said at hearing Tavis' voice.

"Sensitive guy, huh?" Meg teased, hoping to lighten Tavis' mood.

"Yeah." A tiny smile returned to Tavis' face. She wiped the tears away from her cheeks with her long graceful fingers.

"Good." Meg grinned and shook her head. "No more crying, you'll make stars die."

Chuckling, Tavis asked, "Where did you hear that?"

"Alec said it to me once."

"That's something my father says all the time. It's a kind of story told to children to make them stop crying. He must've said it to Alec. It made me happy to hear you say it."

"You gonna be okay?"

"For now. What about you? Is your stomach still bothering you?"

"Oh, I'll be fine in a few months." Meg raised an eyebrow at Tavis.

Tavis' eyes widened. "Are you really?"

"Yep, pregnant again."

"Does Alec know?"

"Not yet. I was gonna tell him the other night, but he came home late, and drunk. I'll tell him later."

"May I?" Tavis held her hand near Meg's abdomen. "I'm not sure how good I am with this kind of medical knowledge, but I've watched my father do it lots of times. Maybe I can see how the baby's doing."

Meg nodded and Tavis wasted no time slipping her hand under Meg's shirt, flattening her palm on her belly. It was strange to Meg, having Tavis touch her in such an intimate way. She had to stifle her giggles to keep from breaking Tavis' concentration, and it wasn't long before Meg put her hand over her mouth to keep from outright laughing.

"Meg, I know you're trying not to laugh, but could you try a little harder? I've never done this on someone else before and your thoughts are getting in the way. Think about the baby instead, maybe that'll help."

"Okay, okay."

A moment later, Tavis leaned back. "Meg!"

"What? Is something wrong?"

"Nothing's wrong," Tavis said. "With either of them."

"What?" Meg asked again.

"Twins, Meg! You're pregnant with twins… identical, I think." Tavis' energy was electrifying. "Alec's gonna be so happy. Two of them, he'll certainly have his hands full, that's for sure. I found out something else, too. Do you want to know?"

"Boys or girls?" Meg couldn't believe her own pluralized question.

"Girls!" Tavis stood, pulling Meg up with her. "Can we tell Jack?" She already had her hand on the doorknob.

"Wait!" Meg bellowed. "I need to digest this for a minute."

"Oh, I'm sorry." Tavis forced herself to calm down. "Of course, you want to keep it private."

"No." Meg sighed. "You're just happy and excited for me. I only wanted… I mean" –she grimaced– "are you sure?"

Tavis nodded. "I'm very sure. There's no mistaking what I just heard, unless you're having more than two and I missed a heartbeat."

"Hush, don't even say such things. Giving birth to Luke was hard enough." She saw how excited Tavis still was—her eyes bright and hopeful again—and it was so much better than seeing her cry. "Okay, we can tell Jack, now."

When Tavis opened the door, Jack was standing at the threshold. "Were you listening to our conversation?"

"Yes, and I feel bad about it now." He wore a guilty smile as he swayed back and forth with Lani sleeping in his arms. "Congratulations, Meg."

"Thank you, Jack."

~

Later in the evening, Jack and Tavis insisted they drive Meg and Luke to Kyrie's house instead of letting her drive there alone in the dark. After they left, Kyrie helped Meg put Luke to bed in Alec's old bedroom, walling him away from falling off the edges with all the extra pillows they could find in the house. They tiptoed out of the bedroom, eased the door shut, and went to the kitchen.

"What would you like for dinner?" Kyrie asked while pouring a glass of wine for Meg, noticeably omitting one for herself.

Meg laughed when Kyrie put it in front of her. "I can't have any either."

"Why not?"

"For the same reason you're not."

"Really? You're pregnant?"

"Yes. I've been suspecting it for about a week and your daughter confirmed it this morning." She eyed Kyrie. "Are you okay with me calling Tavis your daughter?"

"Why wouldn't I be? She *is* my daughter, and I'm looking forward to having a proper relationship with her." Kyrie banished the wineglass to the kitchen counter. "I'm curious, how did Tavis confirm it?"

"By putting her hand on my abdomen and tickling the hell out of me."

"Sebastian did the same thing to me." Kyrie reflected on this and chuckled. "I guess they don't have the ticklish gene. Was she able to find out anything? About the baby, I mean?"

"She sure did! Apparently, I'm to have a litter."

"Excuse me, what?"

"According to Tavis, I'm pregnant with identical twin girls."

"Oh." Kyrie stood back a little to take in the full view of Meg, as though there would be some kind of sign hanging from her neck that would confirm it. "You know, Tavis is probably right about that?"

"I know. You should've seen her, she was so excited about it."

"Aren't you?"

"Of course I am," Meg said. "I just hate that everyone except Alec knows now."

Before Kyrie could comment, there was a knock at the door. Meg's eyes lit up, thinking it was Alec, but Kyrie knew better. She grabbed Meg's arm and led her to the hallway.

"It's Ila," Kyrie whispered. "She's taken to dropping by every other evening lately. If you don't care to see her, then I suggest you go check on Luke and stay there until I get her to leave."

Meg bolted down the hall, hiding herself away with Luke. She had absolutely no desire to see Ila right now and hoped Kyrie would be able to get rid of her quickly.

After a long twenty minutes, Kyrie poked her head in. "She's gone now."

Back in the kitchen, Meg asked, "Why's she coming over so much?"

"She's reporting anything suspicious to William." Kyrie opened the refrigerator. "She keeps asking if I've seen you."

Meg joined her and they stared at the refrigerator shelves, hoping some food item would volunteer for dinner on its own. "How about sandwiches? I don't feel like eating anything too elaborate."

"Sounds good to me."

They were munching away on curried turkey salad sandwiches, sharing a great big bowl of salty potato chips set in the middle of the table, and glass after glass of lemonade, when Meg broached the Ila-dilemma. "I should stop putting it off. At some point, I'm gonna have to visit her."

"I hate saying it, but it might be wise. I've been running interference for you and Alec by reminding her that you're still newlyweds. That seems to be working, but she's getting agitated. If you don't trust going to her house, then invite her to yours… while Alec's there, of course."

At the mention of Alec and their house, Meg lost her appetite and put the rest of her sandwich down. She looked at the glass of wine sitting on the kitchen counter and longed to down the whole thing, though she knew the very smell of it would send her running to the bathroom. Looking at it reminded her of how Alec had spent the last three days in various states of drunkenness and it saddened her.

Kyrie sensed the shift in Meg's mood. "I think it's time for you to tell me what's going on with Alec."

The enormity of having to explain it all again after having already done so with Tavis and Jack earlier seemed exhausting. An idea came to Meg and she asked, "I'm wondering if it's possible for me to just *show* you."

"Yes, Meg, you can just show me."

"Really? How does that work, can I show whatever I want to whoever I want?"

"No, not just anyone," Kyrie said. "It takes a certain kind of distinctiveness to see the thoughts of another person. If you wanted to say something to, Frank Doscher for example, you'd have to use spoken words."

"But you said that I could show you, rather than tell you. Does that mean you're different, too?" Meg asked and watched carefully for Kyrie's outward response.

Kyrie knew Meg was scrutinizing her and it made her respect Meg's intuitiveness all the more. "Yes. That means I'm different, too."

"Oh." Meg nodded while still frowning. "So I can just show you what's been happening with Alec, right?"

"Right." Kyrie smiled to encourage her. When Meg stood, Kyrie stopped her. "Contact isn't necessary, just remember everything clearly and make sure you want me to see it all."

Meg sat back down again and pulled all of the memories from the past few days to the forefront of her mind. She remembered first how worried Alec was over Tavis until Jack brought her back, but that his mood had already darkened—enough to make him choose solitude instead of waiting with her and Jack for Tavis to wake up.

She recalled the next few days and what appeared to be Alec's meltdown: his nightmares, the preference to escape their problems through a haze of semi- to complete inebriation, and him obsessing over a light coming from a fixed point on the ocean. The words, *'I can tell there's someone on that boat'*, and, *'I'm supposed to go to him'*, kept repeating in Meg's memories. They ended with her disappointment when Alec told her he was going to row out to the man to find out what he wanted.

When the memories dissolved, she waited for Kyrie's opinion. Instead, she found her staring blankly at the massive painting behind Meg. The old wood-framed painting had hung on the dining room wall for as long as Meg could remember. She'd never paid much attention to it before, but since she had created a few of her own, she viewed it in a different way now.

It was bordered in tiny intricate patterns and symbols that were strangely familiar to her. They were painted in such a way that, from a distance, it appeared as braided rope tied in a series of nautical knots. Inside the border was a typical open ocean scene, with one important exception: in the center was an old canoe, the kind that Meg had only ever seen in history books. Inside the canoe, stood a man of appreciable age.

Meg moved closer to the painting, examining every detail, quizzing every brush stroke involved in making a creation of this magnitude. At one point, she even touched her fingertips against the ridges of the dried paint and it brought a sense of wonder to her knowing it was painted so long ago.

Her attention was drawn to the main subject again, the man standing in the ancient canoe. For a moment, Meg thought she heard his name, but she hadn't been expecting it and couldn't quite catch it clearly enough. There were a few fine age lines on the man's face, and with his reddish skin tone and wise expression, it brought to her mind a feeling of something inexplicably wonderful. In one hand, he held a cane of sorts that was beautiful and decorative; in his other, he held a pyramidal object.

Her eyes widened as she examined the pyramid. It was an amulet, like Alec's, but instead of sapphires, there were green gems that she recognized as emeralds. She felt herself wanting to snatch the amulet from out of the painting. As a substitute, Meg brought her fingertips to it and touched the painted amulet with loving affection.

She closed her eyes and inhaled deeply to calm the unexplainable tide of emotions that had forced themselves into her consciousness. Removing her hand, she opened her eyes again and took a step back. She was about to turn to Kyrie when something else in the scene got her attention. Lost and barely visible among the waves was the figure of a man floating on his back, staring up at the stars the artist had thought to add to the painting.

Following the swimmer's gaze to the stars, Meg saw they had been painted to resemble the face of a woman. "Oh, my God," she said. "That's my face."

A chill went down her spine and her eyes fell to the floating figure. Meg gasped when she realized who was floundering in the water, and who was on the cusp of giving up the fight to stay afloat.

Panicking, Meg turned to Kyrie, but found an empty chair. She scanned the room for her. "Kyrie?"

"I'm here, Meg. We have to go," Kyrie said, rushing back from the hallway with Luke in her arms. Meg remained rooted to the floor near the painting, watching Kyrie struggle to the door with Luke, who was awake now from all the excitement. "Dammit, Meg, snap out of it. We have to save Alec."

Not only had Kyrie gotten Luke, she'd also managed to change clothes, forcing Meg to wonder how long she'd been lost in the painting. "Okay," she said, taking Luke from Kyrie's arms.

Though dark, Kyrie feared it was possible that William watched them through the camera aimed at her house. She hoped it would appear as though she was merely driving Meg and Luke home since their cart was still parked by the newcomer houses.

"I'm gonna take you and Luke to your house, don't forget to lock the door because Alec won't be there."

"Where are you going after you drop us off?" Meg asked.

"To find Alec."

"Is he in trouble?"

"You saw the painting, Meg. What do you think?"

As they approached the stone house, Meg's anxiety magnified when she saw that there was not a single light on in it.

"NO!" Kyrie shouted when Meg nearly jumped from the still moving cart.

"I have to find him," Meg said, pleading. "Something's wrong, I can feel it."

Kyrie grabbed Meg's wrist, preventing her from getting out. "You'll take Luke and go inside that house right now and wait for me to bring Alec back. Make sure to have plenty of water and warm soup ready for him."

Meg's eyes appeared feral and it seemed to Kyrie that she was contemplating wrestling her arm free and running off into the night. She dug her nails into Meg's wrist, figuring pain would get her attention—it did.

"You're hurting me." Meg stared at Kyrie in disbelief.

"You'll feel much more pain than this if you don't let me bring Alec back to you," she spat, her eyes narrowed. "Go, now! We're wasting time, there'll be no saving him if I don't go to him now." She released Meg's wrist, hoping her warning was enough to force Meg's submission.

Slowly, Meg stood and reached into the back seat to retrieve Luke, not once taking her eyes off Kyrie. "Fine, we'll go inside, but you better bring him back to me… alive."

As Meg turned to make her way up the steps to the house, Kyrie sped off toward the south end of Alaret Beach. She found the store's utility cart hidden in the sea oats, with a now empty boat trailer attached to it.

She parked her cart beside it, got out, and raced down the beach in search of Alec. A few clouds had formed, periodically blocking the light from the moon, impeding her ability to see much of anything in the water or on the beach. There was no infamous flashing green light anymore; she knew the deed was done. All that was left was for Alec to have made it back, but she couldn't find him anywhere.

"ALEC!" She listened for any sound that may lead her to him, but there was nothing save the wind and waves. "ALEC," she called again—still nothing.

Kyrie ran to the water. An incoming wave hit her at full crest and brought her to her knees. The saltwater splashed into her eyes, blurring her vision. She pounded her fists on the surface of the water and screamed out again.

"Why?" She choked on the saltwater that continued to slam against her. "Why did you have to do this? He would've left."

Kyrie cast a hateful look at the ocean and forced herself to stand again. Though it couldn't possibly help, she wiped her eyes with the back of her hands in the effort to see clearly again. She refused to give up and was about to call out for Alec again when she spotted a glimpse of something green glinting on the dark horizon.

She stared hard at the spot, wondering if she would see it again. It flashed green several more times and there was no mistaking it, it was a message filled with hope and that she shouldn't give up.

She tread the water faster, but in no particular plan or direction. Her only goal was finding Alec no matter how long it took. The sheer magnitude of the task was daunting and the lack of light wasn't helping her to remain hopeful of finding him alive. Tears streamed down her cheeks when the muscles in her legs fatigued from the ordeal.

Each time despair pushed down on her shoulders, Kyrie shook it off, forcing it away—she'd rather die on this beach than go back to Meg alone. She trudged farther out into the water until she was chest deep, not caring about what predators lurked in the ocean at night.

While Kyrie squinted, trying to find any kind of shape that resembled a person floating in the water, there came a flutter in her abdomen. It was the first time she'd felt him move in response to her emotions.

She put her hands on her belly; her tears fell and mixed with the salt of the ocean. "I can feel you moving, and you're scared, too. I wish you could help me find your brother."

As the words escaped past her lips, the wind picked up speed, forcing the clouds to part and allow the moonlight to cascade over the whitecaps of the waves. She could see with clear perfection and she scanned the surface of the water.

And then she saw him, barely twenty feet away in front of her—Kyrie found her son just as he slipped beneath the waves. "Oh, no you don't!" She dove headlong into the next incoming wave, not coming up for air until she felt what could only be Alec's arms.

Refusing to look at him while trudging through the water back to the shoreline, fearing she'd discover he wasn't breathing, Kyrie focused on maintaining her grip on his wrist. It was easy to reach the beach, but her real struggles began when she had to drag him without benefit of the buoyant water that she'd so desperately wanted to get him out of.

It seemed to take forever, but Kyrie pulled Alec far enough away from the punishing waves to redirect her focus solely on his health. She put her ear to his nose to listen and feel for any sign that he was still breathing, but heard nothing, and felt nothing. She repositioned to his chest—there was no sound there either.

"No, Alec." Kyrie shook his shoulders without moving her head from his chest, but still there was nothing. "Oh, please, please, Alec."

Kyrie's panic twisted into anger, thinking she'd finally found her son only to find him dead. It seemed too cruel to her. "NO!" she yelled, refusing to accept it. She sat up and started pounding on his chest, pausing only to force air into his lungs.

The moon appeared to swell in size, giving her more light and courage to keep fighting for Alec's life. Kyrie thought an eternity had passed before relenting to check for signs that he was breathing. She listened, but the only stir of air came from the wind.

"DAMMIT, ALEC!" Kyrie pounded again on his chest, more violently than before. She took a deep breath of air and impaled it into Alec's lungs; she saw the effort expand his chest—still he didn't move.

A mournful wail escaped her when her mind wrapped around the fact that Alec may be lost forever. "Why won't you come back? How am I going to tell Meg I couldn't save you?" Her body convulsed with her sobs and she collapsed on top of him.

She eventually sat up straight again and looked down into her son's lifeless face. The chain and key on his chest gleamed in the moonlight. "You were going to be a father again, twin girls." Beaten and desolate now, she reached out to retrieve the chain from Alec, but was startled backward when he lunged forward, expelling seawater through his mouth and nostrils.

"Alec?" She scrambled back to him, helping him roll to his side so he wouldn't inhale the seawater again.

After a painful minute of continued retching, Alec took the first precious breath of air he'd been denied since slipping beneath the waves. A few more torturous minutes passed before he was able to sit up and look at his surroundings.

"You're alive." Kyrie pulled him to her, still crying, but they were happy, thankful tears now. "I'd given up hope."

"Don't cry, Mom." He hated seeing her so weary. "I'm sorry… I've been so stupid. I think that man tried to kill me."

"You mean John Paul?" Kyrie sniffed and leaned back. "He didn't want you to die, he just wanted you to come close to it. It's about becoming a man."

Alec stared at her, shocked. "You know that crazy man?"

"He's my grandfather, your great-grandfather."

"Well, your grandfather told me to tell you goodbye." He tried to stand, but every muscle in his body seized in agony, causing him to wince and recline back onto the sand. "Just tell me where Meg is first, before I try to move again."

"She and Luke are at the stone house, waiting for me to bring you back."

He was anxious to see Meg; wanted to touch her face, to kiss her again, and to beg her forgiveness. "Is she still mad at me?" Alec wondered aloud, his voice cracking.

"No." Kyrie stood and held her hands down for Alec to take. "Right now, she only wants you to be with her, so let me help you walk back."

Alec gripped her hands and got to his feet. "Ugh, I don't think there's a spot on my body that doesn't hurt." He moaned as he limped along, inching his way forward to the stone house. "I shouldn't be leaning on you like this."

She looked up at him. "Your brother and I are doing just fine." Going further, Kyrie added, "I've decided to name him Sebastian."

A semblance of a smile curved his lips. "That's a fine enough name, I'll look forward to picking on my younger brother all the more."

He continued to lean on her while he hobbled along the beach and thought about how wonderful it was going to feel to lie down in his bed and close his eyes. Some part of him knew that he could finally sleep again without the tormenting dreams. His stomach reminded him that he hadn't eaten in days and Kyrie heard the rumbling.

"I told Meg to have warm soup waiting for you."

"Oh, that sounds like heaven," came his breathy thought of warm soup.

It was a sluggish walk home and still Alec grew weaker from the effort. "I need water," he said as though it would magically appear before him.

"We're almost there," she said to encourage him. To keep him focused, she asked, "Tell me what happened out there."

Alec sighed as he recalled the conversation he had with John Paul. "In some ways he was very cryptic, and in other ways he was *very* straight forward about what he wanted to say to me."

"Maddening, isn't it?" Kyrie chortled, remembering her own conversations with her grandfather when she was a little girl.

"He wants us to leave Gamma because it's gonna be destroyed, either by the military or by his own people." Alec frowned, trying to remember bits and pieces of the conversation. "Actually, he wanted me to tell Sebastian, but I told him management had detained him. He said it was my job to get everyone out of here if my… Sebastian couldn't."

"He knows about Sebastian being here?"

"It seemed to me he knew about everything." Alec snorted, then grimaced at how even this hurt. "He didn't know about Sebastian being imprisoned, but he didn't seem fazed by it either." He thought of another part of their conversation. "I told him I wanted to find a way to keep all the people here from dying and he said I couldn't do that because they were already dead." The words choked him and once again, simply breathing was a strenuous chore and air became a precious commodity.

"I know that was hard for you to hear, but he's right." Kyrie pushed aside her own dread over the senseless loss of life. "I hate it, too."

"How did you know where to find me?"

"That old painting in the dining room."

Alec recalled the painting she referred to. He stared at it often when he was a child, especially at meal times while waiting for Kyrie to bring his plate to the table. As a young boy, he found the individual subject matters rather curious—the way the man floated in the water and stared up at the strangely aligned stars while an old man in a beautiful canoe stood by watching. The painting as a whole always made him feel scared and vulnerable. By the time he was a teenager, he no longer paid attention to it.

"Where did you get it?"

"From John Paul," Kyrie said. "He gave it to me just before I came here from Beta."

"You were a child when you came here, right?"

"Yes, and you already know that." She leveled a scolding look at him. "Since you took it upon yourself to read everyone's files in Dr. Patrick's house."

"Guess Jack told you about that," Alec muttered.

"He also told me how worried he is about you. Jack's afraid that you're having trouble accepting many of the issues we're *all* facing."

A sudden pang of guilt crushed Alec. "I'm so ashamed of myself for the way I treated Jack, I was horrible to him." It wasn't just Jack, he'd been reckless with everyone. "And look at what I've done to you and Meg. She's worried, I can feel it. And you, in your condition, dragging a grown man back to his wife and son."

"Okay, that's enough," she said, her voice soft and soothing. "All that matters is that you're alive and safe. You can make amends later. Besides, you can look up now."

Alec lifted his head, which he'd purposely kept aimed at the ground during their trek up the beach. They stood near the oak tree and he'd never been happier to see it so firmly rooted in the ground—alive and vibrant, so unlike the way it looked in the dream. He eyed the stone house and saw the lights on inside. Goose bumps formed on his skin at knowing Meg and Luke were in there, and that she waited for him.

As much as he wanted to find out whether or not he could run to them, he had to say something to his mother first. "Thank you for giving me life, twice. I swear to you right here, right now, you'll not have to do it a third time."

Kyrie frowned at him. "I'll give you however many lives you need. There is no limit, Alec."

"I'm ready," Alec said, nodding. "I know what my responsibilities are now." He lifted the pendant up from his chest. "This is more than just a key to the pods, it's the key to all our futures." His eyes met hers, then went to the lit up windows of the stone house where his family waited for him. "I'm ready to get everyone home."

It sapped the last of Alec's strength to climb the few steps to the front door, but he made it on his own. Kyrie was right behind him, ready to help him at any sign of trouble. He was about to put his knuckles to the door when it swung open. Meg's eyes widened at the sight of him—expressing both her relief and horror—but she regained her composure quickly.

"Get in here, both of you."

Once they entered, Meg slammed the door shut and locked it. She ushered Alec to the couch and then threw herself into his embrace. Kyrie left to get water and soup for Alec, and to allow them a moment alone.

"Meg, please don't—"

"Don't you dare tell me not to cry!" Meg pulled away and glared at him. "I thought you were dead, I felt it."

"I'm sorry." His voice was hoarse and it broke her heart to see how he tried to hide his tears by looking down. "If you'll forgive me one more time, I'll spend the rest of my life trying to make it up to you."

The last few days had been rough on Alec—his appalling appearance was beyond dreadful. All that remained of his clothing was a filthy pair of shorts, sporting new rips and holes, and there was sand all over him. In his hair, which was a tangled mess of a long overdue haircut, were bits of seaweed and small splinters of driftwood. The stubble he'd needed to shave a good week previously had become a fledgling beard and the stench coming from him was almost unbearable to Meg. Her eyes scanned his body and she noticed he'd lost weight as well.

When her eyes met his again, she saw the purity of an innocence still intact there, that which only Meg recognized and understood. However, she detected something else, a hint that he'd aged from his ordeal—there was a maturity about him that wasn't there before. Also reflected in his blue eyes was a sincere and desperate plea for her forgiveness.

"I forgive you, I love you, and you owe me nothing." Meg smiled and picked up the pendant resting on his chest. "Except for a ride home."

Kyrie returned, carrying a tray with a bowl of the soup Meg had prepared, a pitcher of water, and a glass. Alec caught the soup's aroma before Kyrie had reached him and his hands trembled at the thought of being able to finally have something to drink and eat. All he could see was the tray coming closer to him and if he weren't in such pain, he would've gotten up from the couch to get it faster.

Meg and Kyrie sat in the chairs opposite the couch and watched in awe as Alec emptied two glasses of water before turning his attention to the bowl of soup, oblivious to their presence now. When the spoonfuls proved to be too slow in providing the soup, he picked the bowl up and slurped directly from it.

At the sight of the ravenous display, Meg jumped to her feet. "I'll get him some more."

"Better just bring the pot," Kyrie said, not taking her eyes off of Alec, who suddenly had a bottom of a bowl for a face. "And the ladle."

When Meg returned with the pot and ladle on another serving tray, Alec had already gulped down a third glass of water and was looking around for more food to eat. He was about to get up and search for it himself.

"Here," Meg blurted. "I brought more soup."

Alec stared, lips parted, at the large pot of soup. Fearing he was about to snatch the still warm pot off of the tray, Meg placed it on the couch next to him and backed away so he could help himself to however much he wanted.

They continued gawking at him as he ate the soup from the pot with the ladle, their mouths hung open at the spectacle. After dropping the ladle in the empty soup pot, Alec drained another glass of water and reclined against the soft back of the sofa. Bits of noodles clung to his stubbly face and water dripped from his chin onto his chest.

He said, "That was the best soup I've ever had in my life." He moaned, patted his full belly, and then let out a loud burp.

"How about having the best shower you've ever had?" Kyrie asked, seeing the sleepy look drift over Alec's eyes.

He moaned again, more like an attempted groan, at the thought of having to get up. Though a shower sounded nice to him, sleeping sounded better. His eyelids were already forcing their will onto him. "Later," he mumbled as his head fell forward.

"Let him sleep." Meg scrunched up her nose. "I'll clean the couch tomorrow."

Meg covered him with a blanket, and Kyrie helped her carry the dishes to the kitchen. Once all had been cleared away, Meg turned to Kyrie. "No arguing, you're spending the rest of the night here. You can sleep in the spare bedroom and help me keep an eye on Alec."

"I was hoping you'd say that, I'm so exhausted." Kyrie flung the dish towel onto the counter and yawned.

"Off to bed with you," Meg said.

~

Sleep wouldn't come to Meg while she lay in the bed upstairs alone, so she gathered some pillows and blankets and slept on the floor near the couch. In the morning, Kyrie nudged her awake and when her eyes opened, she saw Kyrie holding Luke and motioning for her to be quiet so as not to wake Alec.

Seeing that he hadn't moved positions the entire night, Meg followed Kyrie to the kitchen. Awaiting on the table was an assortment of breakfast dishes, Meg's full teapot, and Luke's empty dishes.

"I've already fed Luke and got him ready for the day," Kyrie said.

"How long have you been awake?" Meg asked in awe, amazed by Kyrie's talent to get things done in a timely manner.

"About an hour and a half." Kyrie chuckled. "I move quickly."

Meg sat down to her tea and Kyrie took the seat next to her. After a few minutes, Meg said, trying not to become an emotional mess, "Thank you for bringing him back."

Kyrie looked at Meg, saw her trembling chin, and averted her eyes to Luke to keep from becoming her own emotional mess. "I have to tell you, Meg, I didn't think I was gonna be able to. When I found him, he wasn't breathing, and he didn't have a heartbeat. I did everything I could, but nothing worked. Not until I started to take the key off of him. Suddenly, he started breathing, and it was like giving birth to him all over again."

"You're the most amazing woman I know, Kyrie," Meg said before changing the subject. "Now, how much longer do you think your son will sleep?"

Smiling, thankful for Meg's directive, she said, "I wouldn't guess much longer." Kyrie laughed, remembering the soup event. "I bet hunger will be what wakes him."

"Are you opening the store today?"

"Maybe later. All I care about is seeing how he's doing after he wakes up—"

A horrible moaning came from the front room. They rushed to Alec and saw him trying to sit up on the couch. When he managed to pull himself into a sitting position, he looked up and gave them a pained smile.

"Every muscle I have is sore, and I'm so hungry I could eat this couch."

Meg helped him to his feet and the first thing Alec wanted to do besides eat was to kiss the top of Luke's head. The second Alec's face drew near to Luke, that baby's scent wafted through his nostrils, giving him a sense of ease that he wasn't dreaming.

His face took on a pained expression again and he flattened his hands on his abdomen. "I'm starving. Somebody, please feed me."

While Meg frantically prepared more food, Kyrie stared at Alec as he chose to forgo utensils and scooped scrambled eggs into his mouth with filthy fingers. She resisted the urge to chastise him, knowing how hungry he was.

Instead, Kyrie focused her attention on Luke and occasionally offered Meg suggestions on what to cook next. When his belly was full again, Kyrie took control. She stood, handed Luke to Meg, and turned to Alec.

"Okay, you," she said, lording over him. "I don't care how sore you are, or how tired you are after eating again, you will get up from that chair and go straight to the bathroom to clean yourself. I let it go last night, but I can't take one more second of suffering through the war you've waged against anything that smells remotely decent."

Alec's lips parted in a surprised *O* shape at her harsh words. There were bits of egg stuck to the stubble on his chin, further incensing her. Kyrie tugged at Alec's arm to help him stand from the chair and led him to the downstairs bathroom.

"You're not thinking of washing me yourself, are you?" Alec attempted joking with her.

"Certainly not!"

"Fine! I get it, I'm obviously gross right now. I'll fix it."

He shut the bathroom door with a little more force than necessary, annoyed at being treated like an unruly child refusing to take a bath. It wasn't until he turned to the mirror above the sink that he saw what his mother and Meg had been looking at.

Alec was shocked at the image reflecting back at him. Not only was he thoroughly filthy, he was almost unrecognizable to himself. It had been a week since he'd last shaved; he touched his fingertips to his cheeks and chin and noticed how gaunt his hands and face looked. The saltwater had plastered his hair in random directions. In some places it was dried flat against his head, but mostly it stuck out in odd spikes of various lengths and when he touched them, they felt crispy.

His eyes were still their usual blue color, but they were edged with dark circles. He went over to the shower and turned the water on. While waiting for it the heat up, he peeled his shorts off. They, too, felt crispy and were full of sand, as was every crevice of his body. Alec wondered where his shoes were and figured they must have come off while trying to swim to shore. After grabbing a washcloth from the closet, he stepped into the steamy shower.

At first, coming into contact with water again made him cringe and he experienced flashes of his own drowning. In a panic, he snatched at the shower curtain, feeling like he had to stay above the water. Alec forced himself to calm down and waited for his heartbeat to return to normal before beginning the long arduous process of cleaning the layers of grime from his body.

When he reemerged from the shower, Alec saw someone had discreetly placed his razor and shaving cream on the sink counter. While he toweled off, he considered whether it was his mother, Meg, or a collaboration of the two who decided to make the shaving equipment delivery. Either way, it made him laugh and he wiped away the fog from the mirror to see what they found so offensive about a growing beard.

Though his face was finally clean, the long stubble gave the appearance it was still dirty. It wouldn't be so bad if the beard grew evenly. Instead, there were several patches where the growth was sparse, or completely absent. Laughing again at what he imagined was their horror of his patchy beard, Alec picked up the shaving cream and lathered it onto his face.

When he was finished returning himself back to the Alec that Meg and Kyrie approved of, he started to walk out of the bathroom, but realized that in their obsession to rid him of dirt and beard, they'd forgotten to bring him something to wear. Briefly, he considered walking out as he was, but figured they wouldn't find it as amusing as he would. He grabbed a dry towel from the closet and wrapped it around his waist before joining them in the front room.

Meg had removed all the blankets and pillows from the couch and floor; she'd even cleaned the sand from both places while Alec had been in the shower. He waltzed in, clad only in a towel, and plopped down in the wing-back chair opposite the sofa Meg and Kyrie sat on.

"Oops," Meg said. "I forgot clothes."

"Of course, you're the one who snuck in to bring me my razor."

"I'm the one who told her to do it," Kyrie said. "If you're curious which one of us hated your horrible attempt at a beard, it was both of us... and probably me more than Meg."

"I doubt it," Meg said definitively.

~

Dressed in clean clothes again, Alec walked with Kyrie down the beach to her cart and promised to bring the utility cart to the store later. When he returned to the stone house, he helped Meg get Luke down for a nap so he could talk to her about everything that happened and how much it had changed him. He also had an idea he wanted to discuss with her.

Alec took the amulet off the mantel and placed it on the coffee table before joining Meg on the sofa. She cuddled up to him and rested her head against his chest.

For a long time, Alec stroked her hair, twirling the blonde curls in his fingers, saying nothing at all while wave after wave of emotions flooded his thoughts. Not only was he recalling every memory from his experience, he relived every thought and feeling he had while he desperately tried swimming back to shore. At times, it overwhelmed him and tears sprang to his eyes—he allowed them to fall rather than fight them and he gave Meg full access to all of it.

Her every muscle tensed when he recalled the moment his body had given up and he sank beneath the waves. He felt the physical pain again when he could no longer hold his breath and was forced to breathe the ocean water. As his life slipped away, and with his last thoughts being of Meg, they both saw an explosion of all the memories Alec had ever had. They shattered in a brilliant display of light and color and cascaded into the abyss of the watery world around him, and then there was nothing. No light, no color, there was only black—and only silence.

"Why did you show me that?" Meg asked.

"Because I didn't want to hide it from you." He wiped the tears from his face. "I hope I'll never have to show you something so awful again."

"Yeah, that'd be great." She stared at her trembling hands.

"I want you to know I'm ready to leave. I know what I have to do and I accept it now. Sebastian wants me to get us all home, John Paul told me to get us all away from here, and I won't rest until we're off this island."

Meg was relieved to hear his acceptance. She looked down at the necklace Chaza had given her and picked the pendant up, twirling it around in her fingers as she reflected on her own thoughts. She knew it was a key, like Alec's, and she'd recently begun to think that she may be the one who'd have to get them all home. Alec saw wisps of her recent determinations.

"You don't have to worry about that now. I hate that I made you think you'd have to do it on your own."

"Don't worry, I wouldn't have left you." She smiled a little. "I would've waited until you were passed out drunk and then get Jack to drag you to one of the pods."

He chuckled, but turned serious again. "I have an idea about how I want to get everyone home." Alec paused, nervous that Meg would reject his idea. He blurted it out quickly while he had the nerve. "When I send my mom home, I want to send Luke and Lani with her."

Her body went rigid. Alec kept a steely gaze on the amulet and readied himself for her attack of his plan. Minutes passed by and the only sound to be heard came from the clock on the fireplace mantel. He was about to ask her if she'd understood him when she took a deep breath.

"No," she said.

"Why?"

"Because we have to think about Sebastian and Chaza, they need to get home, too."

"Meg, there's never been enough transportation to get everyone home. You know that already." Alec tilted her chin up to look into her eyes. "Is there something you need to tell me?"

She was confused at first, but the expectant look on his face clarified his meaning. "You know?"

"My mom mentioned it when she thought she couldn't save me," Alec said. "Listen to me, I'm happy about it and it makes me all the more determined to get everyone who can be saved out of here. I have no idea if Sebastian and Chaza are able to escape from William, but even if they could, it doesn't change the fact that there are only three pods. I think that's why Sebastian's staying there, to allow us to get away."

"And Chaza's not gonna let him stay behind, not alone," Meg said, mostly to herself. Her gaze drifted toward the coffee table and rested on Alec's amulet. She remembered what John Paul held in his hand from Alec's memories. "He had Chaza's amulet. If we can get it and use it with yours, we can communicate with them and get another pod."

Alec hated crushing her new hope. "Meg, if you'll remember what John Paul said… whoever finds it will be in real danger of dying. I don't want us getting anywhere near close to that option."

Her shoulders slackened as she realized the impact of what it meant; John Paul probably didn't think Sebastian and Chaza had a chance in hell of escaping. "Funny how he gets to keep on living, though, while everyone else is sacrificing themselves for others."

"We can always hope to save them," Alec said, though he had no idea how to make it happen.

She stood from the couch and picked up the amulet. After handing it to him, she said, "You need to put this in a safer place, its intrinsic value just increased, in my opinion. As far as Luke and Lani are concerned, I've decided to trust your plan, but understand me now when I say it'll almost kill me to watch my son leave without me."

"It won't be easy for me either."

"I hope you realize that you still need to try convincing Tavis and Jack to send Lani ahead of them. Jack more so than Tavis, and you know I'm right." Meg laughed sardonically. "To tell you the truth, I have no idea how we're gonna convince Tavis to leave the island while Sebastian's still being held prisoner."

"By lying to her," Alec said.

"That's what I thought."

"What would you have me do, Meg?"

Meg thought of how close Tavis and Sebastian were, she thought of odd memories that plagued her from time to time, and she had to fight the threat of fresh tears. "I'd have you do exactly that, lie to Tavis. I'll help you in every way that I can."

He set the amulet down and stood up to take her hands. "So, you'll help me convince them?"

"I want Luke to have a better life, whether I'm there to see it or not." Meg nodded and squeezed his hands. "It's *our* plan now, we'll make this work."

"Thank you," Alec whispered and wrapped his arms around her.

A feeling of warmth and peacefulness bridged them—their bond complete now. The potential sacrifice of their own lives, that which they'd agreed together to make, perfected a bond that would normally take a lifetime to create; an achievement both rare and fixed in time. Its only imperfection was its crucible. Though their futures held much heartache, there would always be this ionic unity between them in the stone house of Gamma.

~

Appearing dazed, Tavis and Jack stared at Meg and Alec as the two couples sat across from each other at the dining room table. They'd just finished listening to what happened to Alec when he rowed out to John Paul, and then Alec told them his idea to send Kyrie away first with Luke and Lani. The silence coming from them seemed to go on forever before Jack stood.

"Hell no." Jack hovered over all three of them—prepared for any argument thrown at him.

"Jack, please listen before you reject the plan entirely," Meg said.

"My mom's pregnancy is starting to show," Alec said. "I'm afraid of what William Davis may do if he finds out."

"Then send Kyrie home, we don't have to send our children with her. They can leave with us."

"I say we send them with her now, while it's still easy. We have no idea how long this thing with Chaza and Sebastian is gonna take."

"Why can't we all just go at once?" Jack asked.

Alec and Meg turned their gaze to Tavis. They were unsure of how to respond without exposing Sebastian's lie.

Tavis felt their heavy stares and she searched for why they were all watching her. The truth was evident, even in Jack's eyes—there were only three pods.

"He lied to me, didn't he?" Tavis asked all of them.

Jack sat back down. "He did it so you wouldn't be upset. There isn't a fourth pod."

"I'd like to talk to Alec alone," she said calmly. "Will you go outside with me?"

"Okay." Alec nodded, but was confused.

He and Tavis stood from their chairs and went outside to Jack's garden. Alec waited for Tavis to speak, having no idea what she wanted to talk to him about. She went over to the koi pond and watched the water cascade down the rocks into the pool. After a quiet minute or so, she turned to face Alec.

"I really want to trust you right now." She sat on one of the rocks edging the pond. "My father put a lot of faith in you, more than anyone else has. I want to trust you because you're my brother and because our father trusts you."

"I'm sorry it took me so long to trust him." He didn't hide his shame from her.

"Before I agree to your plan, and that doesn't mean Jack will," Tavis warned, "I want to see the memory of your encounter with John Paul."

Alec was surprised that this was all Tavis needed to agree to his plan. "Sure, whatever you want." He started to focus his mind so Tavis could see his memories.

"No, Alec, I want to see them clearly." She held her hands out.

He sat beside her and waited for her to make contact with him first. Instead of taking his hands, as he thought she would do, she wrapped her arms around his shoulders and hugged him to her. There was no instant barrage of intrusion into Alec's mind, she was simply hugging her brother for the first time. Though it was awkward at first, Alec reciprocated Tavis' need for comfort from him. Not only did he give it, he greedily accepted the comfort she offered him in return.

Slowly, he allowed the still fresh memories of his moments with John Paul to flow to Tavis. Alec thought she'd pull away at the moment he began his impossible quest to swim back to the island, but she continued to hold onto him. He allowed her to see every detail, even when their mother fished him out of the waves and tried to force air into his lungs. Tavis watched when Alec returned to the living, after Kyrie thought him gone forever. Then she pulled away to look at him.

"I'm so glad you came back. You could've chosen that black nothingness. It would've been so much easier to do, but you didn't accept that, you chose to fight against it instead. That had to have been the hardest thing you've ever done in your life."

"It wasn't easy, and I've never felt that kind of pain before," he said. "But the hardest thing I'll ever do hasn't happened yet. That'll be when I send my son away from here without me… and having to suffer with Meg when we let him go."

"I'll agree to your plan. I can't speak for Jack, though. He already appears to be against it, but I'll talk to him about it. I wouldn't say it's *easier* for me to accept sending Lani without me, it's just that I know where she'll be going and it's so much better than this place."

"If what I saw in that amulet is anything close to the truth, then I believe you. I trust you, Tavis."

"I'm glad you brought that up," she said, shifting her focus. "You were right about John Paul having Chaza's amulet. I don't know how he got a hold of it, but if we manage to get it ourselves then we can solve our problem. There'll be a way for our father and Chaza to get back home."

"Sebastian told me they can be used to communicate with our home."

Tavis smiled at him. "I like hearing you call it your home."

"I feel like it's my fault for wasting so much time to finally accept it, we could've all been gone by now."

"That's not true." She sighed. "There was never enough transportation, too many things have changed."

"John Paul didn't tell me how I was gonna find it."

"He said you'd find it if lives depended on it." There was resoluteness in Tavis' tone. "Their lives do depend on it. They can't stay caged up like they are for very long, it'll kill them. I don't know why they haven't left yet, I know they could if they wanted to."

"He's staying there for us, Tavis. They're hoping to give us a chance to escape. Sebastian wants us to leave, he already accepted that he wouldn't be able to go with us."

"We need that other amulet," she said, determined. "I can't leave him here. Just like you fought against that black nothingness, I have to fight to find a way to save him."

"I know, and I'm gonna do whatever it takes to try saving them, too," he said. "That's why I want to get our children home first. We may have a better chance at fighting if we're not constantly worrying about their safety."

"Hide your amulet in a safe place."

He smiled. "I already have."

27

No Liberty

Chaza woke up before Sebastian did. If it weren't for the huge ornate grandfather clock bonging in the front room of their windowless prison, she wouldn't have the slightest clue if it was day or night. Usually, it was Sebastian who was up first, but he had stayed awake almost the entire night watching the screen William had provided for them. Sebastian had been spending more and more time watching it, looking for signs that any of them had left the island. He grew more frustrated with each passing day they were all still there.

She and Sebastian had reverted back to their nonverbal language. The only times they spoke aloud were when they knew they couldn't be overheard, or when addressing Eldridge or William. They'd also taken to sleeping in the same bedroom after Sebastian insisted on it, telling her he was afraid they weren't above trying to torture either of them for information.

After many long, boring days and nights of being there, it was obvious what Eldridge and William most wanted by their line of questioning—they wanted to know where their transportation was hidden. Soon after their captivity, Eldridge arrived. He smiled when he saw they were successfully imprisoned and there was a horrible greediness in his eyes. Sebastian was repulsed by both Eldridge and William and would turn away from them every time he saw them.

Their individual guarding styles were different. William constantly goaded them, almost like he wanted to know more than just the whereabouts of their transportation. He wanted to know intimate knowledge, such as: where they were from, how were they able to keep their home hidden and undetectable, and what was it like there. They rarely answered his questions and their continued silence irritated William more with each passing day.

Eldridge's guarding technique differed wildly from William's, as Chaza heard when she entered the front room. The sound of his snoring was amplified by the underground nature of their environment.

She could easily tell whose shift it was to stand guard by the tell-tale sounds of Eldridge's snoring. If their goal was to drive her to insanity, then they'd found the perfect way to do it. Before going to the kitchen, Chaza looked past the bars to see him slumped back against the oversized desk chair, deep in sleep. His mouth was open and a bit of drool ran down his chin. She turned away from the bars, disgusted, and decided she wasn't hungry after all—a simple cup of tea would do. When Chaza brought her teacup to the dining table, William entered the surveillance room to start his shift.

At seeing and hearing Eldridge asleep, William was also disgusted. William's eyes met Chaza's briefly, and then she changed seats and turned her back to him.

"Wake up!" William barked.

Eldridge's eyelids popped open at the vigorous shaking of the desk chair. "Oh, good, you're here, I'm exhausted. I'll see you in ten hours."

"You mean, in *eight* hours?" William corrected, backing away so Eldridge could pass by him.

"Right, see you in eight hours." Eldridge peeked over at the prison and saw Chaza's back facing them. "You know, it seems they're rather secured. I don't think we have to worry so much about them escaping," he whispered, fearing Chaza would hear him.

"We'll always have to worry about them trying to escape," William said loudly, wanting Chaza to hear him.

Winking, Eldridge said, "Quite right, William."

When Eldridge left, William sat in the chair and cringed at how warm it still was. "How are you this morning, Chaza?" he asked, imbuing a false chipper tone to his greeting. "Is Sebastian still sleeping?"

She ignored his question at first, but couldn't help voicing the snide remark that came to mind. "No, he stepped out for a moment to take the dog for a walk," she said without turning around.

"I had no idea you were so funny, Chaza." William chuckled. "Did you make enough tea for me?"

Chaza snorted. "And I had no idea *you* were so funny, William. Make your own damn tea."

William had a good laugh at her quip, it was seldom that Chaza ever spoke. When a question was directed at them, it was usually Sebastian who answered it. In fact, it was the first time she was out in the visible area without Sebastian. William wondered if he'd have any luck with her during Sebastian's absence. He got up from the chair and went over to the cell doors to reset the timelock.

He and Eldridge had agreed to reset the timelock at each shift change so that neither one of them had the option of being able to open the cell doors during their own shift. The scientists had strongly recommended the procedure, fearing potential influences the detainees may have on the guards.

Chaza could feel his presence still lingering at the bars and figured William wanted to take advantage of the rare private opportunity. She waited for him to speak, knowing the fool had no idea why it was that Sebastian always spoke in her stead. In fact, Chaza found herself hoping Sebastian slept a little longer so she could have some fun with William.

"I'm curious about something," William said. At her continued silence, he pressed on. "I know you've been hiding on Gamma for a long time, and I know Meg's your daughter, but that you gave her away at birth. So I was wondering, how did Sebastian feel when he found out about your… fling with Joseph?"

She finally turned in her chair to look at him. "How did you feel when your wife gave birth to not one, but two, of Sebastian's children?"

"It stung a little, and by the way, she's my *ex*-wife."

"At least you were kind to her at the end. I'm sure it brought her immense joy getting divorced from you, and *by the way*, I'd say it stung more than just a little."

"Fine. I can admit it, it bothered me a lot."

"Luckily, you had Ila to comfort you."

It surprised William that Chaza knew about his relationship with Ila. He assumed Sebastian knew as well and that they'd already discovered Ila's status. "I should've realized you'd know about that. How long have you known?"

Chaza refused to answer the question and it irritated him, but he forced a pleasant calm in his tone. "I know how much Meg means to you," he said with as much compassion as he was capable of faking. "And I know you don't want anything to happen to her. Neither do I. I can guarantee you she'll be safe here, all you have to do is tell me where the transportation is hidden."

"I'm not gonna tell you, William. You're wasting your time."

"You're making a mistake."

"That's not how I see it."

"Is that so?" William was losing his patience and it showed in his narrowing eyes, but he retained the careful control of his voice. "How about I give you a different way of looking at it then? The East American military is hounding me daily. They want the location of your transportation immediately. I told them to give me time to find out, but they're getting restless. They're not opposed to digging up this entire island themselves to find it."

A flicker of fear formed in Chaza's eyes and William saw it. Seizing the rare moment that enabled him to glimpse into her most basic of thoughts, coupled with the fact that she was alone, William figured it was the perfect time to plant doubt in her mind.

"I can tell you don't like the idea of them coming here." A timely, though overly-done and cheesy, arch of his eyebrow formed for her perusal. "I feel the same way."

Chaza stood and made her way over to William, only the steel bars separated them. She was indeed concerned about the level of East America's involvement. If true, then their situation had become all the more dangerous. Knowing full well that William was doing his best to persuade her to reconsider her alliance, and with his utmost attempt at charming her, Chaza decided to give him a lesson on how to use natural charm worth gloating about.

"Have they been threatening to come here?" she asked, imbuing a shyness that did not exist in her composition.

"Yes, they call me or Eldridge constantly for updates. So far, we've been able to put them off, but they're annoyed with our lack of progress."

She put her hands just below his on the bars. "What if they're already tired of waiting? They could already be planning to come here."

Sliding her hands upward, closer to his, she waited for the right moment to make contact. She had several goals in mind, but the most important one was finding out if he was being truthful about the extent of the military's involvement. For once, she needed William to know how concerned she really was. She allowed that worry to show in her eyes when she looked into his, hoping he'd snatch up a perceived opportunity to feed off her fears. Though it disgusted her, she even batted her eyelashes.

William gazed into her troubled eyes and fell headlong into a sense that he was winning. "Of course they're tired of waiting, sweetheart. I have no doubts they've already planned out their next phase if I don't deliver the whereabouts of the transportation soon."

His ego was unmatched by any that Chaza had ever encountered and she doubted if she could keep up the ruse if he called her one more pet name. She had to fight hard against the instinct to recoil away from him to continue with what she'd started. While he stared into her eyes, thinking he may have won a chance at her giving him the information he wanted, she made the first contact she'd wanted by just barely touching his fingers with her own.

To keep him distracted, she asked, "What would they do if they came here?"

"Whatever's necessary to keep anyone from leaving. I have no power over them and I wouldn't be able to stop them from doing whatever they needed to do to seize your transportation."

Chaza's fingers had inched a delicate path toward William's wrists while he talked. Her touch was feather light and she flooded him with a sense of calm when her fingertips found his pulse. "Does it bother you that the military can come here and trump your authority?"

He started to feel tired and wished he'd spent his time off from guarding asleep instead of going to Ila's. He realized that Chaza had just asked him another question and he focused hard on trying to remember what it was. "Um, right." William frowned and shook his head. "Yeah, it bothers me. Management never wanted their involvement in the first place."

"Why were they allowed to get involved?"

Though it struck William as odd to be so forthcoming with his answers, he had an overwhelming sense that he could trust Chaza. "It was the only way we could have the nuclear devices. We were cryptic with our explanations of the purpose for the islands at first, but the government forced us to have scientists on board. *Their* scientists, and it didn't take them long before they told them what we were really doing."

"You mean experimenting with genetics and cultivating desirable traits, like slower aging?"

"That's old news." William snorted. "Every government already has that gene figured out and more than half the world's population express the trait. Naturally, the wealthy have the option to fix any of their own… the poor have to rely on a genetic luck of the draw. Our goal was to experiment with lesser known traits."

"What other traits?" Chaza lowered her voice to a whisper, coaxing William to a calm that would give their conversation a dream-like quality. She divided her concentration between keeping him in this condition and getting more information.

"I kind of like that cloaking ability, but it's so hard to pinpoint on the genome. The scientists have it narrowed down to the most probable location at the DNA level, but we've had very little to compare it to until recently." He winked at her. "We compared the small amount of knowledge we got from Alpha and Beta with what we were getting from Gamma and Delta and we discovered something had changed. It wasn't until we got Sebastian's DNA results that we realized he'd been part of the reason for that mysterious change and that he'd been here before… solved the mystery of who Alec's father was at least."

"You mentioned something had changed."

"Well, Alec's DNA was proof of it. Oh, and so was Meg's." William was so relaxed now, he sounded somewhat intoxicated. "Two different DNA profiles show up that we can't find *both* parents for. Clearly, foreign DNA somehow managed to make its way onto Gamma. We'd been used to seeing a certain set of anomalies and then something new comes along, but just as fascinating, and now we even have some combinations. The scientists are working day and night trying to make sense of it, but I already know why."

Chaza was astounded at how much William knew, and at how much she didn't know. Her intellect wanted to study the new information, but his last statement forced her continued quizzing.

"Why do you think you already know?" she asked.

"My father spent his young adult life traveling, mostly to the remote corners of the world, and I grew up listening to his adventures. He often told me about this one island he encountered and the things he said sounded like pure fantasy, but I was a child and was mesmerized by his descriptions. When he died, I found his journals and maps, and they reminded me again of the stories he told me.

"I decided to see that island for myself. The morning after high school graduation, I took his maps and set off to find it. It took me a year to locate it, but when I did, the things I found there amazed me. They showed me things, impossible things. Those people were so different than anyone I'd ever encountered. It took me another year to leave that place, partly because I didn't want to leave, and partly because I couldn't. The weather was always producing tropical systems that made sailing impossible and I knew they were somehow responsible for it.

"During my time there, I began to have all kinds of ideas. I'd inherited my father's holdings in the company he started with Eldridge, perfecting and developing small-scale land development. The result of that start-up business led to what we have today, island creation in large bodies of water. I started to imagine taking some of these people and introducing them to other people, those more like me, because even with their incredible abilities they were still living in a simple and primitive way."

"They agreed to come with you?" Chaza asked.

"There was never an *agreement*. The ideas I had were solely my own, or so I thought. Almost as soon as I started visualizing taking some of them to a newly created island, they began treating me differently. The older ones avoided me, except for one. Every time I entered one of their buildings, the adults would leave, but that older man didn't. He never said anything to me, just watched me like he was my babysitter, so I ignored him.

"The only ones who wouldn't scurry away when I came around were the children. That's when it became obvious to me what was happening with the adults, they'd sensed what I'd been planning and they were clearly not interested in moving. No problem, if the adults weren't interested, then I'd select some of their children to take with me.

"I could only take a few of them since my sailboat was only big enough to handle myself and maybe ten others. The weather cleared, and to this day I still don't know if they were the ones responsible for that. More and more of the adults were going out on fishing excursions, especially at night, except for the one man who never spoke or even interfered when I talked to the children.

"Since I'd already taken to living on my sailboat again, the adults didn't notice that I was spending my days getting it ready to leave. In fact, it appeared as though they were hoping I'd leave soon. During their absence, I gathered as much food and supplies as I thought I could get away with to feed a group of ten children. I was so obsessed, I didn't care if there was enough food and water for myself.

"The night of their annual celebration came, marking a day shy of how long I'd been there. I had arrived the day after their last one and I knew the adults would celebrate all night and sleep all day afterward. I planned it all out, I'd go to the celebration, stick to the back of the crowd, and in the morning I'd convince the children to go on an adventure with me.

"Halfway through the celebration, everyone left to follow a man who'd given a long speech in some language I wasn't familiar with and I went along with them. They walked to the center of their island and went down a narrow cave entrance. The end of the tunnel opened up to a giant chasm that contained only one object. It was a huge aircraft of some kind, one I'd never seen before, or since."

Chaza briefly saw the image in William's memory and thought she recognized it, though she hadn't seen one in a long time. But then the vision was interrupted by the old man who kept a vigil over William. He'd stepped in front of William and blocked the view—it was John Paul. The entire memory dissolved when William started speaking again.

"I felt like a party crasher, the uninvited and unwanted, so I went back to my boat and waited. When morning came, I made my way to the heart of the island and saw some children left to entertain themselves while their parents slept. It was easy enough to talk to them, but still I was terrified I'd get caught. I went to a group of the older ones, thinking they'd be the easiest ones to convince, but only one would agree and told me she could get nine more to go with her.

"I told her to hurry and meet me at my boat because I was leaving with or without them. By the time I reached the end of the dock, the girl was already there with the other children. I couldn't believe my eyes, and I didn't care how they got there before me, I was too happy thinking my plan had worked. I rushed toward them, refusing to look back at the island, and ushered them onto my boat. Then I turned to untie it from the dock and that was when I saw him, the same old man who'd been watching me.

"I froze immediately, feeling sure he was about to do something to wake the islanders. Instead, all he did was walk past me and got on the boat. He stood in front of the children and stared at me while I still held the rope in my hands, waiting for the wrath of the entire island to advance on me. I chanced a look at the beach, but nothing was happening there, not a soul to be seen, so I looked back at the old man. The only thing he said to me was, 'Go.'

"I didn't hesitate. I finished untying the boat, we set sail, and I haven't been back to that island since. It wasn't an easy trip getting back. I hadn't amassed as much food as I thought I had, so we let the children have it all. Not long after we arrived, I integrated them into the Alpha population.

"They're all dead now, Alpha was destroyed," Chaza said.

"No, I wouldn't allow it. I relocated the ten to Beta, the old man was the only one who managed to escape. I never saw him again. Want to know something interesting about him?"

"Yes."

"He was the father of the oldest girl I'd first talked to about getting nine other children. He's also Kyrie's grandfather."

"The oldest girl was Kyrie's mother? Where is she now?"

William yawned, then said, "Dead. She refused to leave Beta, but she did allow me to move Kyrie to Gamma. So, there you have it, the history of how I started these islands."

Chaza released her hold on William's wrists and took a step back, watching him to see how well he'd recover from her influence. He blinked a few times and the glassy, languid look in his eyes cleared. When his vision refocused onto her, a knowing smile spread across his face and she reciprocated it.

"You didn't need to do that," he said. "I would've told you anyway."

"I'll remember that next time."

"Where's the transportation hidden?"

"I'm afraid I can't tell you that."

"I can think of a few ways to convince you to be more forthcoming with information."

The smile on Chaza's face vanished. She knew what his subtle threat alluded to. Leaning forward, bracing her hands against the bars once more, she said, "Touch her, and I'll kill you."

"Your threats are empty, Chaza. We already know you lack the violent gene, so you aren't capable of killing me."

"Wrong, William. It's not that we're physically incapable, it's that we chose to eliminate the idea of it. And, if you were half as smart as your scientific team, you'd know that we don't *lack* the violent gene, it's merely turned off. Given the right set of environmental circumstances, that gene can be expressed again. Did you think Jack was only trying to give you a shave?"

William's smile left his face as quickly as Chaza's had. Given her abilities—just the ones he was aware of—he inwardly cringed at the multitude of ways she could kill him if she were telling the truth about her capacity for violence.

"You're making a mistake, you have to tell me where the transportation is," he said. "You know I have no intentions of hurting Meg, it's *my* threats that are empty."

"I think you'd hurt her if it meant getting what you want, abducting Tavis in the middle of the night is proof of that." It was getting harder for Chaza to control her temper. "You don't think it's hurting Meg that I'm being held against my will?"

"What's going on in here?" Sebastian asked when he came into the front room. "Why are you talking to him, Chaza?"

"William was just giving me a little history lesson," Chaza said and walked away.

William sneered at Sebastian for the interruption and returned to his desk. He didn't speak to either one of them for the remainder of his shift and when Eldridge returned to take over, William was more than happy to leave.

~

Later, Chaza led Sebastian to the bedroom and shared the conversation she'd had with William.

"That's very interesting," Sebastian said, frowning and fidgeting.

"Don't," she said.

"What?"

"I'm not gonna fight with you, but I'm done with pretending that I don't know about the plans you made with John Paul. I know the extent of your involvement. I know you schemed with him since before even Alpha. I've always known."

He wanted to keep lying to her, but her eyes narrowed in what he took as a warning not to dare. "How did you find out?"

"You're so diligent about handing your amulet over to the librarians. You should've known I'd learn about it through Edmund."

"I'm sorry, Chaza. I was scared to tell you. If you would've rejected my ideas back then, I probably wouldn't have gone through with it and—"

"Stop it, Sebastian. It's done, it's over. I'm glad you made the choices you did. We finally had children, just not with each other." Chaza offered an understanding smile. "And I'm not sorry about it, not anymore."

Worried he'd dwell on the matter, Chaza retrieved her robe and a book. "I'm going to read and have a bath, a long one. I can't stand listening to Eldridge's snoring."

"I know what you mean," Sebastian said, thankful to her for the dismissal. "I'll see you in a few hours?"

"Well, I certainly don't have any other plans."

~

The scent of a mushroom and onion omelet wafted through the bars and reached Eldridge's nostrils.

"That smells wonderful, Sebastian."

"Forgive me if I don't offer you a taste."

"No worries, I ate before my shift. How are you feeling today?"

"As well as can be expected, Eldridge."

Sebastian looked over his shoulder at the screen in the front room; it was off. Eldridge wasn't as bent as William was at showing the prisoners the daily events taking place on the island. Their difference in tactics was what set the two apart in wisdom. William used the screen as a form of torture for Sebastian. Eldridge's vast experience brought with it a wiser approach—he had no intention of allowing Sebastian to pick apart potential meanings from his clan.

"Life goes on as usual," Eldridge said, noticing Sebastian's glance at the screen.

"Too bad I'm not there to see it for myself." He scarfed the omelet, afraid he'd lose his appetite.

"You could be, all you have to do is tell me where the transportation is."

"We both know I'll never tell you."

"Fine, but it *will* be found, one way or the other," Eldridge said. "It would be a shame, though, if the military came here to find it. I assure you, they'll excavate the whole island."

Sebastian had grown weary of the threats, and he cared very little about the East American government, or their military. All he cared about was seeing some kind of a sign that the escape was under way. During William's shifts, when Sebastian was allowed to see the screen, all he saw was that they were still here.

"I found out some interesting history today about how and why all the islands were created. It's intriguing how William found those people and decided to experiment with genetics, don't you think?" Sebastian's tone was smug and he took great delight in seeing Eldridge's demeanor ice over.

"William has a loose tongue. Well, since you know that bit of history, do you have any questions for me?" Eldridge asked, his smile back into smarmy position now.

Sebastian had been about to get up and take his plate to the kitchen, but couldn't resist the open invitation to gain more knowledge of the events through Eldridge's perspective. "I'd like to know more about what went wrong on the first two islands that were destroyed."

Eldridge kicked his feet up on the desk and leaned back in the desk chair. By his estimates, Sebastian was asking to know more about a lengthy topic.

"I assume you already know the chaos on Alpha got out of control, which was why the decision was made to destroy it. After all, there were three other islands. What we discovered was whenever you take away people's basic right to choose certain paths in their lives, such as choosing who they want to be with, and being forbidden to leave the island, it never works out… they'll rebel against it. There was a mixture of people on Alpha, some with certain desirable genetic differences that set them apart and we wanted to cultivate it with the people William showed up with, and I can't tell you enough how unique they were.

"Eventually, we put a few ordinary people in with the population as well, thinking it would be healthy to do so. Because we had a goal in mind, we set strict controls on who could be with who, obviously we wanted the ones with unique traits to have offspring. Unfortunately, the inability to choose for themselves led to the uprising. It got out of control, people were trying to escape, and one of them was successful. Most of the population refused to cooperate in any way at all, so I ordered its destruction.

"William wanted to relocate the people he'd brought with him from Alpha to Beta. Clearly, I allowed it because of what our goal was. The destruction of Alpha was hideous and that was how the East American government became more involved with our operations. On Beta, we took a different approach. At first, we let everyone make their own choices, but not enough of them were choosing the right partners. We began to interfere again and the same thing started to happen. Slowly, and they were sneaky about it this time, resistance formed, leading up to a full blown rebellion with some of them trying to escape in crudely built rafts.

"When they started setting fires, the military came in to stop them, but they were so much smarter than what we had dealt with on Alpha. The military couldn't bring order back, so they recommended implementing the nuclear devices, what we refer to as the End Plan.

"Again, William wanted to relocate the original ten, and by then, their children as well. Only one of them refused to go, Kyrie's mother. My stipulation was that we split them up between Gamma and Delta. At the time, I suspected they may have been influencing some of the rebellions from the very beginning. After they were relocated, Beta was destroyed, quickly and seamlessly this time.

"We spread the ones we spared from Beta among the already thriving populations on Gamma and Delta. On both islands, a population was building with the desirable genetic traits we were looking for, thanks to our newly enforced scientific team. As before, we allowed some conventional people to live on the islands, mostly just to have a larger society. With the scientists' help, we developed departments of sociologists, medical personnel, and researchers. The physicians made sure the ordinary population was sterile, that way we wouldn't be pressed to interfere with their daily lives as much.

"The sociologists and psychiatrists recommended we introduce naturally aging people to the islands since patriarchs were necessary to any population. Apparently, they help to keep cooler heads among the younger islanders. They were right, we haven't had another uprising since. So far, all of our efforts seem to be successful. We only interfere from behind the scenes now and only in subtle ways, it's more like we influence certain situations to achieve the same results. I'd say it's all working out very nicely. That is, as long as all of our hard work doesn't manage to find a way to escape."

"When did you find out I became interested in Gamma?" Sebastian asked.

"With the birth of Alec, of course!" Eldridge let go a hearty laugh. "The scientists keep strict DNA profiles on every inhabitant. Not only did we discover that someone had infiltrated Gamma, we also discovered some amazing new things in the DNA he left behind… and they match yours, Sebastian."

Sebastian suppressed the urge to yank the bars open and strangle the pompous man so callously referring to Alec as nothing more than DNA. "Tell me more about the original eleven people that William brought back. Are they still alive?"

"*Nine* of the original people," Eldridge corrected, "Remember, Kyrie's mother chose to go down with Beta and one escaped from Alpha. During the relocation from Beta, five of them vanished, we assumed they escaped. That left only four of the originals, plus Kyrie, and a few others of their children. William decided he only wanted Kyrie and one other to go to Gamma. The rest went to Delta."

"How does Jack relate to Delta and those people?"

Eldridge was surprised by the question at first, but then remembered Alec's stent at snooping the classified files. "Jack is the child of two of the originals who were relocated to Delta. The two had paired off while living on Beta and gave birth to Jack on Delta. When we took their infant from them, they refused to have more children."

"So, they're still alive?"

"Alive and well, but still refusing to reproduce. A shame really, Jack's DNA profile is quite remarkable. The scientists have been discussing harvesting his mother's eggs and going the surrogacy route."

Sebastian got up and went over to the bars; he stared straight into Eldridge's eyes. "These are living, breathing people, Eldridge. They aren't property, or some kind of a possession that you can control or dictate how and where they live their lives. You're denying them their basic right of liberty."

"Liberty?" Disgusted, Eldridge snorted. "There is no liberty! There's no such thing, everybody is owned by something or someone."

"You're wrong," Sebastian spat.

"Am I?" Eldridge's confidence grew visibly, twinkling in his eyes and oozing from his words and tone, as he appeared to be enjoying the shift in their conversation. "I'm a businessman, I make business decisions. Not unlike yourself, Sebastian."

"I am nothing like you."

"Is that so? Did Kyrie give you her full permission and cooperation all those years ago to be a surrogate mother to your children? Did she agree to let you take her daughter away? Did you discuss it with her when you returned here to retrieve Alec? Or is it more like you made a businessman's decision and denied her the basic right of choice and liberty to achieve your own goals?"

Eldridge laughed when he saw the look of horror on Sebastian's face. "I can see it's a sensitive subject for you. Sometimes business can get rather ugly. Let me explain how I see this situation. These islands and everything on it belong to the Stone Davis Corporation. We answer to ourselves, our investors, and the East American government. All of the people you're trying to take away were born here. In a business sense, I have more right to them than you do, and that makes you nothing more than a common thief trying to steal someone else's hard work. I'm afraid I can't let you do that."

"These people have the right to make their own choices, no matter what you and I think or want. You're right, though, I've made a few unethical decisions in the pursuit of my own agendas and I'll pay for it. Will you?"

"I certainly hope not, it's bad for business," Eldridge said coldly.

Sebastian had to close his eyes and take a deep breath to steady his calm before looking at Eldridge again. "I have one more question."

"I'm listening."

"What's in the vault?"

"For one thing, all of Roland Davis' journals, for another" –Eldridge winked– "everything I'm not going to tell you about. I *will* disclose one juicy bit of information, but it has to stay just between you and me. I wouldn't want William to know."

"Fine," Sebastian said, though it sickened him to agree with Eldridge on any matter.

"When William told me Kyrie was pregnant… the first time." Eldridge smiled knowingly at Sebastian before continuing. "I knew something was going on. It wasn't possible for him to be the father, I personally saw to it that our physicians made him infertile. The way he was behaving, he would've had the entire island expressing only *his* DNA."

"He doesn't know he's sterile?"

"Of course not!" Eldridge winked again. "And let's keep it that way."

Sebastian shoved away from the bars. Rage of the likes he'd never experienced before built up inside of him as he stomped out of the living room. After slamming the bedroom door shut, he could still hear Eldridge's laughter. He walked back out again to talk to Chaza.

"They have to get off this island," Sebastian said to her when he burst through the bathroom door.

She'd only just finished her bath and had put her robe on when Sebastian came in with his declaration. "I thought you said you weren't going to engage in conversation with Eldridge," she said, assuming he was upset over whatever that vile man had said to him.

"*We* weren't supposed to talk to either one of them," Sebastian reminded her. "I couldn't stop myself from quizzing Eldridge after what you showed me."

Frowning at him, Chaza said, "I'm beginning to regret having shown you."

"I don't know how long they plan to keep us imprisoned, but you know what will happen if it goes on for much longer."

Sebastian's voice was desperate and pleading—which was rare for him and overwhelming for Chaza.

"We'll begin to suffer. The lack of liberty will change us, Chaza, I don't want that primitive part of us surfacing. Why are they taking so long to leave?"

"They're hoping they can save us," she said.

~

Sebastian immersed himself into watching the screen when it was William's turn to guard them. As usual, William turned the screen on, selecting which camera view he thought held the most promise for torturing Sebastian. Tonight, it was Kyrie's house.

After a long while of watching Sebastian stare at the screen, on which nothing at all happened, William decided to add some excitement to the quiet room.

"I wanted to show you Kyrie's house tonight… apparently there's been some new developments."

Both Chaza and Sebastian knew what William was about to say to them. Fed up with William's taunting, Sebastian chose to acknowledge it first. "No congratulations are necessary, William. Kyrie told me she was gonna name him after me, isn't that nice?" He turned to look at the shock on William's face and it brought him a sick pleasure to see it.

Not one to accept being bested, William turned his attention to Chaza. "How do you feel about Sebastian's future namesake?"

Sebastian stood from the couch, ready to put an end to the torture once and for all. Chaza's hand restrained him.

'Let it go, ignore him,' she said silently.

He sat back down. *'I could stop his heart, Chaza.'*

'No, you can't do that.'

'Yes, I can do that.'

Sebastian's ill-guarded thoughts were full of new hope and determination, and it scared her.

'No, Sebastian. They'd know what you had done when you get back home, they'll send you away.'

He looked into her eyes and saw she still held hope that he'd make it back to their home.

Chaza sensed his pity for her and she felt stupid for having created it. *'If it comes to that,'* she said, glaring at him, *'I'll be the one who kills him, not you.'*

Regretting his harsh words, he patted the top of her hand and leaned closer to whisper aloud, "I shouldn't have said that, I'm just frustrated right now."

Sebastian glanced over his shoulder toward the surveillance room and saw that William had returned to his desk, appearing as though trying to find a camera angle that held more entertainment value.

William settled on the view of the stone house and sent it to the front room screen. He stood and went over to where he kept his overpriced scotch and poured himself a glass.

Sebastian gave the screen his full attention just in time to see Alec and Meg speeding off in the cart. And it was raining.

Hoping to keep William distracted, Sebastian nodded to Chaza, got up from the couch, and rushed to the bars. "I could use one of those," Sebastian said, pointing at the glass in William's hand.

Bemused by the uncharacteristic way that Sebastian addressed him, William smiled and wondered what new round of banter awaited them. "Do you drink scotch?"

"I will if you pour me a glass."

William laughed softly and returned to the cabinet to pour a second glass. When he turned toward him again, Sebastian had already placed one of the dining room chairs in front of the cell bars and was sitting in it. William handed Sebastian the scotch through the bars and rolled one of the desk chairs over to join him.

"You must be getting bored," William said.

Sebastian sighed. "Well, I am running out of reading material."

"How about a toast?" William raised his glass. "To your new—"

"Don't." Sebastian's interruption of William's toast came with clear unspoken warning—there were to be no more comments about Kyrie's pregnancy.

Deciding to back down, William said, "Okay, to our health then."

They clinked their glasses together and each took a generous gulp of the scotch. The strength of it surprised Sebastian, making his eyes water. "I see why you asked me if I drank scotch."

"Sorry," William said, chuckling. "I should've warned you."

The smoky notes were pleasant enough. "It's good though, I like it."

"Scotch was my father's favorite."

"Chaza mentioned to me that you inherited your father's business. I assume he's no longer living?"

"I'm quite sure she mentioned our entire conversation," William said. "My father was a geological engineer and he came up with the idea that forced land formation was not only possible, but very profitable. He used hotspots in the oceans to create volcanic activity, which eventually leads to the formation of a land mass. You can tweak the process a little to make the land mass more inhabitable by shipping in soil and vegetation that's been genetically engineered to achieve faster results.

"In the blink of an eye, you have a pristine piece of real estate… lush and green and worth a fortune. Brilliant as he was, my father had an adventurous streak, he wanted to be there to witness the initial land formations. On one such occasion, he miscalculated how far away the observation platform should be. After his death I inherited his half of the business, but I didn't have to do anything. Eldridge was and still is the second half, the brainy-business side, of our enterprise.

"The next island creation caused the same kind of unusually large explosion and took out a nearby containership. The company was forced to take on more of a controlled way of creating the land masses, which basically came down to getting and scheduling approval from the nearest government. I guess you could say that's how East America first learned about the Stone Davis Corporation. Eldridge formed a loose association with them because of their lax protocols."

"What made you decide to use your father's islands to start a population of people with unique abilities?" Sebastian asked. "Why didn't you take them to the mainland and let the government maintain their population?"

"I got the idea from my father's journals. He was the one who came up with the idea of a unique population of people after he discovered that island. He wrote about taking some of them to one of his created islands since they were new and held no residual memories. His journal entries went on and on about how damning residual memories were.

"I wasn't exactly sure what that was supposed to mean, but when I started having the same ideas of creating a better and stronger race of people, I viewed the created islands as an excellent place to start because I own them, and there was already small populations on them. Based on the rest of his journal rants, I realized that my reasons were very different from his."

Their glasses were empty, so William went to get the bottle of scotch. While William's back was turned, Sebastian looked over his shoulder to view the screen. Alec's cart was still gone and the rain was beginning to obscure the camera's view. Sebastian felt the first stirrings of hopefulness that they'd started their escape. His gaze drifted to the couch and he noticed Chaza had left the room.

"More?" William asked.

Sebastian turned his attention back to William, who was holding the bottle of scotch up. "Please," he said and held his glass up between the bars. "Your father was right about residual memories. By creating new land, you can eliminate that possibility. I wouldn't mind taking a look at his journals, it sounds like he was a smart man."

"He was, but also impulsive," William said. "Hence why he's dead. I get as far away as I can when an island is created. As for his journals, Eldridge keeps them in a vault on Digamma. I'm sure he'd work out a deal with you, a sort of exchange of information."

Ignoring the hint, Sebastian asked, "You said your reasons for starting a population of unique people were different from your father's. May I ask what they were?"

"Actually, they were mine and Eldridge's. When I showed up with those kids and that old man, I pitched my idea to Eldridge. I even let him read my father's journals to convince him. A week later, he came back to me, agreeing to give my idea a chance. We decided to use our islands instead of selling them, and the fact that they're surrounded by a large body of water made for the perfect isolation."

Raising his eyebrows, Sebastian asked, "You mean, to prevent escape and to keep outsiders away?"

"Well, an open ocean full of hungry predators does make for an excellent and free fence." He grinned at Sebastian. "Although, it didn't keep out *all* outsiders."

"What were you hoping to accomplish?"

"Personally, I wanted a new project and those people fascinated me like they did my father. I just wanted to be king of my own little world of people who could do amazing things. Of course, Eldridge saw the potential for money. He came up with the idea to work out the genetic engineering aspect of it all... patent it and sell the knowledge for billions, maybe trillions! I let him take care of the investment side of the new venture since he already had the experience, and taste, for it. His idea was to sell it to the rich, but then we got involved with the East American government and it's looking more and more like they own us now."

"What exactly are they hoping to gain?" Sebastian drained the rest of his scotch and held the empty glass out for William to refill.

William topped off both their glasses. "Right now, they desperately want to get their hands on your transportation."

"You've already told me that, repeatedly," Sebastian said. "What else do they want?"

William's eyes narrowed at Sebastian, and he considered the wisdom of telling him what the government really hoped to achieve. "Why not?" William said aloud, convincing himself that it no longer mattered what Sebastian knew.

"They want an army," William said and rolled his eyes as though the trite answer should've already been obvious. "Not just any army, but one filled with soldiers who have the ability to vanish before the enemy's eyes. They want soldiers who can manipulate the thoughts and memories of enemy soldiers so that they go back to their own leaders with false information. They want medical personnel with your advanced knowledge for the purpose of saving, or ending, any life they wish. Personally, I think they want to take back West America. Most of all, they want to know more about what we haven't discovered yet, like how you're able to hide wherever you came from. How *are* you able to hide your home from our technology?"

Sebastian couldn't help but chuckle. "By way of the things you haven't discovered about us yet."

"The president of East America called me himself earlier today," William said in a strangely calm voice. "He said if I or Eldridge don't deliver your transportation within forty-eight hours, he'll give the orders to the military to uncover it themselves." A defeated sigh escaped him. "They already have a naval ship positioned nearby."

While William poured the last of the scotch into each of their glasses, Sebastian glanced at the screen. He could just make out the shape of Alec's cart parked in front of the stone house again through the increasing onslaught of rain.

"Guess that means they'd better hurry," Sebastian said, no longer caring what William thought.

William laughed heartily at Sebastian's words and said, "I guess they'd better!"

28

Today Is a Good Day to Die

Alec had influenced the weather patterns on Gamma his entire life. He was so adept at it that creating tonight's storm was as easy for him as merely preferring that it rain.

It was a befitting finale for Alec's last night on Gamma—and also portentous.

When he opened the front door, he found Meg tucking something into Luke's tiny pants pocket.

"It's my pearl engagement ring," she said. "I want Luke to take it home with him."

"Is there enough room in his bag to put one more thing?"

"Yeah, I think so."

Alec turned toward the wall and pulled the painting of him and Luke from its hook. Flipping it over, he removed the canvas from the frame and after rolling it up, put it away in the bag. He sat on the couch next to Meg and pulled Luke onto his lap.

"You listen to my mom until we get there. Okay Luke?" Alec said to him. "I promise we'll hurry and be with you again real soon."

Hugging Luke close to him, Alec put his arm around Meg's shoulder and pulled them both to his chest. It took a while for him to release them and when he did, he wiped the tears away from his eyes and said, "We should go, it's getting late."

~

When they pulled up to Kyrie's house, Jack's cart was already there. "I guess Jack hasn't changed his mind," Meg said in a soft whisper.

Alec heard the disappointment in her voice. "Are you having second thoughts?" After a minute of her silence, he added, "Meg, I need to know now. We won't go through with this unless you're completely sure about it."

Meg blank-stared at Alec while considering his question. Up until now, she'd been more willing and accepting to leave than he'd been, but she had imagined leaving together as a family. Separating herself from Luke was becoming harder the closer she got to having to do it.

"Meg? Talk to me."

She looked at Luke. He'd fallen asleep in his carrier in the back seat and he looked so peaceful—so oblivious to the turmoil. Alec reached for her hand.

Without taking her eyes off of Luke, she said, "I don't want Luke having the kind of childhood you had, always worrying about what being different means. I want him to turn out as happy as Tavis is. I don't want him to feel like he has to hide himself, or hide anyone else for that matter."

She paused, feeling the sudden tension in Alec's hand, and she turned to look into his eyes.

"I haven't changed my mind, you and I both know he won't be happy here. As glad as I am to be alive, that you're alive, it was wrong of Sebastian and Chaza to come here and add more to the injustice of what shouldn't be happening in the first place. I hope John Paul does destroy every island management makes, what's going on here is atrocious."

Alec tried to pull her closer, but she resisted. "Meg—"

"No, Alec, let me finish. When we get to our home, I want to make them all understand what has happened here. I want to put a stop to this. I may not know everything about what went on there, but I do know what happened here and if our people hadn't interfered, then people like William Davis wouldn't have been able to destroy lives."

"She's right," Tavis said, startling them.

Tavis stood in front of their cart, holding an umbrella over her head. "Though I owe my life to my father's involvement in Gamma, in many ways he added to the travesty that's taking place here. Our council has been against it for a long time now. The only one still keeping a vigil over Gamma is our father, and lately he's been keeping it a secret."

Alec nodded and took a deep breath. "Where's Jack?"

"Inside with Lani and Kyrie."

"Has anything changed?"

"No, he's resolved to send Lani home, but it's still upsetting him."

"Maybe it would help if you took Luke inside first," Alec said to Meg. "You know, seeing Luke and knowing he'll be going with Lani. I'll go inside in a minute, I want to talk to Tavis about the transportation."

When Meg went inside with Luke, Alec motioned for Tavis to sit in the cart with him. "You okay?"

"I'm doing better than Jack, but it's easier for me, I know where Luke and Lani are going. I'm happy for them." Tavis smiled at him. "You'll see what I mean when you get there. You're gonna love it, Alec."

"I want to ask you about the pod. Are you absolutely sure it's safe?"

Tavis considered how best to reassure him of the pod's safety. Then it occurred to her to share with him the first time they 'almost' met. "Do you fancy turtle eggs?"

"What?" He frowned at her.

"Hermit crabs are funny little critters, aren't they? Seems like they never want to be seen." Tavis stared at him with wide, expectant eyes.

"What are you talking about?" Alec sat up straight and put one foot on the ground, ready to go inside if necessary.

"Let's get that pearl." She smiled and leaned in closer to him.

Alec began to think something was seriously wrong with Tavis and was about to go inside to get Jack. He got out of the cart and took a few steps, but stopped at recognizing her words. He turned to her. "Wait—"

"Right," she said, nodding. "I heard that conversation between you and Frank. I was a watcher for a little while when I got old enough. Of course, I didn't know I was watching my brother at the time, not until the night we came here." Tavis rolled her eyes. "I have to confess, you and I both were watching Jack that day by the docks. How I got back and forth from here to our home was by way of the homing pods. To answer your question, they're more than safe, they're infallible to any obstruction that I'm aware of."

He sighed with relief before giving her a stern look. "You scared me, Tavis, I thought you'd lost your mind." After a good chuckle, he went back over to her. "So, that was you? I thought I saw someone else before Frank showed up. Wow, so you had to bury the pod every time you came here?"

"No, Alec." Tavis scoffed at the idea. "They're waterproof, too. I hid it in the lake during my watcher assignments."

They went inside to find Kyrie and Jack already immersed in conversation at the dining room table while Meg sat with Luke on the sofa, listening to them.

"Do you think this is how our parents felt when they had to let us go?" Jack asked Kyrie. His bloodshot eyes and the dark circles beneath them suggested he hadn't had a decent night's sleep since Alec first proposed sending Luke and Lani with Kyrie.

"Probably." Kyrie glanced at Alec before continuing. "I was very young when it happened to me, but I still remember some of it. My mother told me I had to go to another island and that a boat would be there soon to take me and a few others away. She told me she wouldn't be coming with me and that it may be a while before we saw each other again.

"When it was time for me to leave, I walked through the forests alone to the dock where the boat was. I saw my grandfather ahead of me and I was so happy to see him because it had been a while since he'd last visited us. I ran to him and jumped up to hug him.

"I asked him if he would walk with me to the boat. He told me he couldn't because he wasn't supposed to be on the island and that it would upset some people if they saw him. Then he put a rolled-up piece of canvas into my bag. He said it was a painting and that I was to keep it safe for him. He warned me not to ever let it out of my sight, and I never did. It's hanging on the wall behind you."

Jack swung around to see the painting. After a few minutes of taking in the main subject matters, he stood and went closer to it as Meg had done.

From her own experience of studying the painting, Meg knew Jack was scrutinizing the painted rope knots bordering the scene.

"Did he say anything else to you about this painting?" he asked.

"Only that I was to always keep it with me because it would be useful one day." She glanced at Alec again. "And it was."

When Jack turned around, his eyes met Tavis' briefly before he sat back down. Alec noticed the unspoken exchange between them, and at first it made him angry that they chose to keep their thoughts private. Deciding he'd come too far to allow something that was probably nothing more than Jack checking to see if Tavis worried about his resolve, Alec let it go.

Alec started to walk over to Meg, but Tavis stopped him. "Wait, we need to work out a few things before we get started tonight. How experienced are you at cloaking an object?"

"I do all right with it," he said, embarrassed. Alec spent his whole life hiding—to have his abilities questioned, with all eyes on him, made him uncomfortable.

Tavis went to the kitchen and took a big red apple from the fruit bowl. She placed it on the coffee table and turned to Alec. "Cloak this apple," she said.

He stared at her, wanting to know why she tested him.

"When we send the pod off, we'll need to cloak it collectively until we can't see it any longer. Once it gets to a certain altitude, it'll seem to disappear because time will be shifting the pod away from us and the island. When our home begins to receive the first signals from it, the pod will be shifted instantly into their time.

"To anyone inside the pod, the process appears to take less than ten minutes. When the pod arrives at its docking station at our aerodrome, there'll be people waiting for them. Kyrie, Luke, and Lani will be ushered to a quarantine area where our physicians will examine them. After they're cleared medically, they'll work out where Kyrie wants to live. They'll show her everything she needs to know."

Alec turned his attention to the apple and it was cloaked as soon as he wanted it to be. When Tavis nodded her approval, the sphere surrounding it dissolved.

She turned to Meg, hating to ask, "Do you think you can do that?"

All eyes fell on the apple, except for Meg's and Tavis'. They continued to maintain eye contact. Not only did the apple vanish, but Meg did it while trying to gain access to Tavis' thoughts—knowing there was an undercurrent of secrecy occurring between her and Jack. Tavis recognized the intrusion and steadied herself. She turned her eyes to the table and smiled at the cloaked apple; the iridescent sphere was familiar to her.

"Just like Chaza's." Tavis returned her gaze to Meg. *'Jack and I have made a decision. We're gonna try to save them. Please, help us,'* she said silently and shielded the thought from Alec as soon as it was recognizable in Meg's eyes.

"Excellent," Tavis said. She picked the apple up and walked to the other side of the front room. "Now for the hard part, Alec. I'm going to throw this apple to the couch and I want you to cloak it while it's in motion."

"Wait!" Meg shouted. "Let me move first." She stood, still holding Luke, and joined Kyrie and Jack at the dining table.

"Ready?" Tavis asked.

He nodded and stared intently at the apple in her hand. When she tossed it, his attempt to cloak it in midair failed.

"Dammit," he grumbled.

"Cloaking the moving pod won't be as difficult as this. By the time it's moving as fast as the apple is, our cloaking won't be necessary anymore. All we need to do is cloak it from the cameras and any islanders who may be outside."

Alec retrieved the apple from the couch and handed it back to Tavis. "Throw it again."

On the third attempt, he successfully cloaked it while still in motion. "Yes!" Alec shouted, punching the air in front of him.

"What is it with men and winning?" Tavis asked, shooting an exasperated look at Jack while retrieving the apple from the couch.

"Can you do it?" Alec asked her.

Tavis' eyebrows raised at the challenge. With a grin, she tossed the apple up above their heads. Just when gravity was ready to reclaim the apple, Alec darted away to avoid being hit by it. Instead, a sphere formed around it, seeming to freeze the apple in midair a foot above Tavis' head. Amazed by the sight, Alec looked around at the eerily quiet room. It was the clock on the fireplace mantel that got his attention. The second hand barely moved, but when it did, it ticked backward once for every three seconds it moved forward. Or maybe, he considered, it ticked in place; it was hard for him to settle on any one perception.

"Unbelievable!" Alec said when the sphere dissolved, sending the apple down to the Tavis' waiting hand. He looked at the clock again and saw the second hand moving at normal speed.

"Any more doubts?" Tavis asked with a smile.

"Not a single one." He smiled back at her. "Just a million questions we don't have time to answer."

"Meg's turn," Tavis said.

Alec went to the table and took Luke from her arms. Instead of sitting down, he handed Luke to Kyrie and followed Meg over to Tavis. On the first attempt, the apple was cloaked soon as it left Tavis' hand, but they glared at Alec.

"Why did you do that, Alec?" Meg asked.

"I would know if it wasn't Meg who cloaked it, hers looks different than yours," Tavis said. "Please, Alec, let Meg try to do it on her own."

"Sorry," he mumbled and took a few steps back.

On Meg's first *true* attempt, she cloaked the moving apple, but cloaked herself with it. Meg looked at Tavis for approval. "Well?"

"You cloaked it, and yourself." Tavis chuckled. "But that's okay, I'm just glad you can cloak a moving target."

"What about Jack?" Alec asked. "Have you tested him yet?"

"Yes. Turns out he can do it even better than I can."

Alec turned toward Jack. "Mind showing me?"

"Sure, I'd love to." Jack, finally smiling, got up and put Lani into Alec's arms. "Hold her for a minute?"

"Throw it," Jack said to Tavis without breaking eye contact with Alec.

Tavis sent the apple sailing across the room, directly at Jack's head. Alec had a brief glimpse of Jack's arm reaching out to catch it before not being able to recall anything else happening.

"That's enough, Jack." Kyrie looked back at the motionless Tavis, Meg, and Alec.

"I'm almost done." He took one last bite of the apple and placed it in Alec's arms, where Lani had been. After returning back to the table with Lani, he allowed the sphere to dissolve.

"Eww, gross!" Alec dropped the apple core to the floor and turned at the sound of Tavis laughing.

"Jack, was that really necessary?" Tavis asked.

Alec looked at Jack, who was seated again at the table with Lani back in his arms. "How'd you do that?"

"He manipulated time," Tavis answered for Jack. "I hope he doesn't do it again" –she shot him a Sebastian-worthy glower– "because too much of that won't go unnoticed. Anyone on this island with any sense of time could notice that something strange is happening."

"I won't do it again," Jack said. "I just wanted to convince Alec."

"You could've just cloaked the apple," Alec muttered. He went to the kitchen to wash his hands before joining everyone already seated around the table.

"I've planned out how we're gonna get there," Tavis said. "We'll go to the stone house and enter through the front in case William's watching, but leave out the back door. Then, we'll cloak ourselves while we walk to where the pods are buried. It'll be raining, so we'll use towels to keep Luke and Lani dry."

Everyone nodded that they understood and agreed with her plan.

~

Meg grabbed a stack of towels from the downstairs bathroom closet as they passed through the hallway of the stone house and handed several to Tavis. Once the babies were shrouded, and everyone had cloaked themselves, they opened the back door. Alec walked in front, while Jack stayed to the back of the line they'd formed.

When they arrived at the base of the cliff, Alec allowed the rain to slow to a soft mist, then his was the first shovel to strike ground.

Jack watched him remove several loads of wet sand before he turned to Tavis with a knowing smile. "Together?"

"Together," she said.

Tavis turned to Kyrie and put Lani in her arms. They looked at each other briefly before Tavis walked away. She took one of the shovels from Jack and they began helping Alec dig the dirt away from the pod.

"I feel like I should be helping," Meg said to Alec.

"No, Meg," he said. "Stay by my mom. She can't hold Luke and Lani at the same time and neither one of you should be digging anyway."

Jack, Alec, and Tavis dug as fast as they could and it was Alec's shovel that first hit something solid. The digging stopped so Tavis could inspect the area.

"That's it," she said. "We need to keep going until I can reach the door switch."

After another few minutes of digging, Tavis held her arms up to stop Alec and Jack from going any farther. "That should be good enough."

She climbed down into the hole and felt around for the switch. Some of the dirt came in from the top of the hole and fell into her hair. Tavis couldn't have cared less, if she could just find the button, she could easily get the pod out of the ground. She grew more agitated as her feet became encased in the falling sand—and then her fingers made contact.

Her eyes closed at the familiar feeling, it seemed like such a long time ago since her fingers had last touched the switch. She rested her forehead against the side of the pod, sighing with relief—it was like finding an old friend.

"Jack," Tavis called.

"Yeah?"

"I'm gonna activate it. The programmed goal of these pods is to be free of all obstacles before preparing for take-off. At the moment, the obstacle is a lot of dirt. When I activate it, it'll remove itself from the ground… which means the dirt's gonna fall back in on me." Tavis paused to address Jack's inevitable rejection.

"How about you let me turn it on?"

"No, Jack. I'm lighter than either you or Alec. As soon as you see the pod lights come on, I want you to start pulling me out of here. Okay?"

Tavis could hear Jack and Alec arguing in whispered voices while more dirt fell in on top of her. *'Please, Jack, don't argue. Trust me,'* she pleaded silently. The whispering came to an abrupt stop and she glanced up to see Jack's face looking down at her.

"Give me your free hand," he said.

She gripped Jack's hand and pressed the button. The pod lit up, and soon the thrumming sounds of hydraulic machinery sprang to life, fracturing the still silence around them. As Tavis had warned, the pod began to vibrate, freeing itself from the earthen tomb encasing it. More and more wet sand started falling in on Tavis, forcing her to look away from Jack to keep it out of her eyes. She let her body go limp at feeling him tug at her arm—she winced when he yanked harder and more frantically to get her out as the pod began lifting above ground level to search for a suitable launching site.

They all watched in horror as the pod settled on an open area of Alaret Beach. Without discussion, they all raced toward it. Once the pod was cloaked, Alec, Jack, and Tavis collapsed against its side, exhausted.

"I forgot about that," Tavis said, trying to catch her breath. "If given the option, pods will seek a solid foundation to take off from."

"I'm glad it didn't go any farther," Alec said.

Tavis stood and shook as much dirt off as she could from her clothes and shoes. She turned to the pod and pressed a second button on the side of the door. It opened from the top and came to a rest on the ground, forming a ramp to enter the pod.

She stepped inside for a few minutes, then reemerged, saying, "Everything's functioning properly."

While she'd been inside the pod, Jack had retrieved Lani from Kyrie and was swaying back and forth with her. He hummed the ancient lullaby to her exactly as it was meant to sound.

"For Jack's sake, we're gonna go in with Kyrie first," Tavis said to Alec and Meg. "When we come out, you two can take Luke inside… and take as much time as you need."

When Alec and Meg nodded, Tavis turned to Kyrie and slipped her hand into hers. "Ready?"

Jack followed Tavis and Kyrie into the pod, still humming to Lani. When they were inside, Tavis led Kyrie to the seating area of the pod. It wasn't a large space, as it was designed to hold only one or two people, but it was comfortable. Kyrie looked around at the circular interior and appeared intimidated by the lights of the console.

Tavis knelt in front of her. "Don't worry, the pod is programmed to do all of the work. I want you to be okay with this, do you have any questions?"

"No. I'm ready to leave, but I do want to say a few things to you," Kyrie said. "You better make it back to me. We've lost too much time and I want my daughter back."

A lump formed in Tavis' throat and she bowed her head. Kyrie cupped her face and made her look up again. "Just get back as soon as you can. I want to say one more thing, I know what you and Jack are planning to do and I'll help you."

"You do?" Tavis' eyes widened. "You will?"

"Thank you, Kyrie," Jack said from behind Tavis. "Keep them in here long enough for us to get another pod out."

Jack came forward and placed Lani in her arms before kneeling down alongside Tavis. He kissed Lani's forehead and then looked up into Kyrie's eyes.

He spoke to her silently, in a language so ancient that Tavis could only understand its barest meaning.

'No matter what happens, keep Lani safe… you raise her… you love her.'

'I swear it,' Kyrie said.

Tavis looked back and forth between Jack and Kyrie as they made their silent exchange. She was confused and wanted to question them both, but time ran short, forcing her to stand instead. There was still work to be done while Alec and Meg had their time with Kyrie.

"Let's go, Jack."

~

Alec and Meg were mesmerized by the pod's interior, neither of them had ever seen anything like it. Aside from the sand that had been deposited on the floor, everything inside was pristine and flawless.

"Guess they forgot to put in windows," Alec said.

Kyrie laughed. "I have a feeling that's for good reason."

"How'd it go with Jack and Tavis?" Meg asked.

"Not bad," Kyrie said. "They're both ready to get Lani home."

"So are we," Alec said. "I'm worried about you, though. Are you sure you want to do this?"

"Yes, Alec, I'm very sure." Kyrie looked up at him. "I don't belong here, I didn't belong on Beta either. Where I'm going, that's where I want to be. It's where you and I both belong, and it's where Meg and Luke belong."

Meg turned her focus to Luke. He'd heard his name and was reaching out his hand toward Kyrie. "I'll see you soon," Meg whispered into his ear, kissed his cheek, and sat him next to Kyrie. She stepped back so Alec could talk to him.

"Remember what we talked about, you listen to my mom." Alec fought back against the emotions that threatened to make him pick Luke up again. Leaning over Luke, he put his arms around Kyrie. "I love you, Mom. Take care of yourself and Luke until we get there."

When Alec stood up, Meg bent down and hugged Kyrie. "We'll see you soon, too."

Tavis peered into the pod entrance. Kyrie spotted her first and when their eyes met, Tavis nodded.

Looking back at Alec and Meg, Kyrie said, "Let's do this."

"Alec," Tavis called out. "Before you leave the pod, go to the console. You'll find a small circular indentation in the center, that's where you press the key into. Only once, though, because you'll have to do it again on the secondary initialization switch."

She waited to see if he understood her instructions, but he stared at her with a blank expression. Smiling at her own mistake, realizing Alec wouldn't know the terminology of the pod's mechanisms, Tavis clarified: "Use the key once inside, using the key a second time on the outside will send the pod off."

"Oh," he said. "We'll be out in a minute."

"I'll wait for you outside," Meg said to him. With one more glance at Kyrie and Luke, she turned and left the pod.

Alec went to the console and found the circular indentation. He pulled the chain off over his head and placed the key into the switch, pressing downward. More lights lit up in rows along the console and he heard the muted clicking sounds of the pod readying itself for take-off.

He started to walk back to Kyrie, who'd been watching the procedure, but she stopped him. "Go," she said. "We'll see each other soon."

When he came out, Tavis closed the door. As it shut, she maintained eye contact with Kyrie until the door closed completely. She then turned to Alec. "Use the key again, here." Tavis pointed to the secondary switch. "Then we'll all need to concentrate on cloaking it, it won't take long."

Meg and Jack stepped closer. When Alec pressed the key to the switch, the pod sprang to life and lifted off the beach a few feet and hovered there. A few seconds passed of it staying in this position; he looked to Tavis for an explanation.

"It's mapping trajectories and calculating potential flight paths." She smiled when he tilted his head and frowned. "It's deciding on the best exit."

"Oh," he said and nodded.

The four of them fell silent, focusing all of their energy onto hiding the pod.

It became enshrouded in the densest sphere that Alec had yet to see. He heard the barely audible clicking sound increase in intensity until it reached a frequency resembling a person whistling.

Then it came to an abrupt dead-silent stop. Instantly, the pod was ten feet in the air above them. Alec blinked several times; he couldn't believe how fast it had moved. It hovered at this higher elevation for another minute before shooting off toward the sky at an equal pace. What was once a large round pod that he could stand in, was no more than a pinpoint in the sky. When his eyes strained to keep the pod in sight, it vanished against the background of stars.

Alec noticed it wasn't raining anymore. Thinking of the cameras, clouds formed again at his command as he turned to the others. The three of them were looking at him with odd expressions on their faces and he wondered if something may have gone wrong with the pod.

Sensing his worry, Tavis came to stand in front of him. "It went very well, they may even be home already. The rain isn't necessary right now."

The clouds broke apart and she looked up at the pristine sky—she laughed softly. "You really are exceptionally gifted with that, even better than our father, in my opinion."

Alec smiled at Tavis before turning his attention to Meg, wanting to make sure she was coping well with Luke being gone. He found her still looking somewhat nervous, but dismissed it as her probably being worried for his own sake.

"I'm fine," he said and wrapped his arms around her.

Her body was tense and no matter how tight he hugged her to him, she seemed unable to relax. "Are you okay?" Alec whispered to her.

"I will be, when you forgive me."

"What's wrong?" Alec pulled back to look into her eyes. "Forgive you for what?"

Meg glanced at an area behind him and he followed her gaze to find Tavis and Jack standing beside another unearthed pod. His hands left Meg's shoulders, surprised by the unexpected sight. He walked over to the pod and saw that Tavis and Jack had already begun refilling the holes.

"Why did you do that?" Alec shouted at them. "William might see it. How the hell are we supposed to hide it by morning?" He grabbed his shovel, determined to undo the damage.

"We're not going to rebury it. You and Meg are leaving in it," Tavis said.

"What?" Alec groaned, frustrated and tired. He looked at their faces, each expressed unwavering resolve.

"Meg's pregnant, she shouldn't be here," Jack said. "You know it isn't safe."

Alec considered Jack's logic. "You're right, but it should be Meg and Tavis who go next. You and I can stay here and find a way to get Sebastian and Chaza away from William."

"I'm not leaving here without him," Tavis said, her eyes set in fiery determination. "Jack's already chosen to agree with me and Meg on this."

"No. Sebastian wanted Tavis to go home first," Alec said to Jack, hoping it would have a more profound effect. He refused to look at Meg, knowing she'd aligned herself with them. Already feeling the rejection, he turned his back on all of them and began digging again to rebury the pod.

Tavis and Jack turned to Meg; though she hated it, she nodded her permission and entered the pod to wait for Alec. Jack looked at Tavis, who also nodded, then turned her back on what he was about to do.

Jack closed in on Alec and put his hand on his shoulder. Alec turned to see who was touching him, and who was undoubtedly about to try arguing with him.

"I hope you're here to help me."

"We may not be capable of killing, but I am capable of this." Jack leaned back, balled his fist, and swung it forward as hard as he could, making contact with Alec's jaw.

The force of the blow threw Alec backward and sent the shovel somersaulting through the air until it came to rest at the base of the footpath. Scared, Jack rushed to Alec's side, fearing he'd hit him too hard. He was breathing, but unconscious.

"He's out, Tavis," Jack called to her, grabbing Alec's ankles. "Help me drag him."

Tavis secured her hands under Alec's shoulders and they dragged him inside the pod, then she collapsed onto the floor and refused to look at anyone. Jack pulled the timecuffs out of his pocket and set the timer to release in ten minutes. After securing Alec's wrist to the bench, where Meg sat silent and watching, Jack stood and turned to Tavis.

"We need to hurry," he said. "I set the timecuffs for ten minutes because I don't want him showing up restrained." Jack leaned over Alec again and removed the chain from him, putting it over his own head after pressing it into the console switch.

There wasn't much time and there were a few things Tavis needed to tell Meg. "Alec will be fine… maybe mad, but he'll get over it. I doubt our council will approve sending another pod, not until they see and talk to my father first. I'm hoping we'll find Chaza's amulet. Where did Alec put his?"

"On the left side of the fireplace, you'll find some of the stones are loose," she said. "He hid it behind them."

Tavis dropped a shoulder bag on the seat beside Meg. "These are Chaza's hand-written journals, probably an account of her time here. Once you're settled in, give them to our historians, they'll know what they are and what to do with them."

Meg's gaze shifted from Tavis to the zipped shoulder bag. Her fingers twitched, wanting to open it, but she controlled the urge. "Yes, of course I will," she said softly, appearing to answer the bag instead of Tavis.

"We have to go now."

"You won't have much time, William's gonna notice we're gone," Meg said. "Stay at the stone house tonight, wear some of our clothes tomorrow… with hats. It might buy you a day or so. Just hurry and be careful."

"Come on," Jack urged Tavis. "We need to send them off, and we still have to finish putting the sand back."

"Jack's right," Meg said. "And I'd rather not risk Alec coming to while we're still here." She glanced at Jack and grimaced.

Tavis hugged Meg, kissed her cheek, gave her a reassuring nod, and exited the pod with Jack. When the door was shut, Jack pressed the key into the switch. Soon as it began calculating a flight path, they cloaked it. Once it was gone, they resumed the grueling task of putting the ground back as it had been. Exhausted, they returned to the stone house.

After a long shower of scrubbing off sand, mud, and sweat, they went to the spare bedroom and crawled under the sheets. Jack pulled Tavis to him and ran his fingers through her still wet hair. He worried about her as she hadn't said much since sending Alec and Meg away. "Are you okay?"

"I'm fine. I just miss them already, and I'm so sleepy. Are you okay?"

"I'll be fine, and I'm sleepy, too. Let's try to get some rest, we have a lot to do."

~

When Tavis woke in the early afternoon, her body ached from all the digging. She turned to wake Jack up, but he was gone. "Jack?"

"I'm in the front room. Come here, I want to show you something."

Jack had pushed the furniture against the walls and had rolled up the large rug. He sat on the floor, staring at it, occasionally touching his fingers to some particular spot and would mumble to himself.

"What are you doing?"

"I want you to look at this," Jack said, not taking his eyes away from the floor as she sat next to him and looked at the spot he pointed to. "What do you make of it?"

Tavis leaned over to study the markings, then backed off again to follow the linear pattern of faded symbols etched on the stone floor. She saw they were part of a large border, creating a rectangle that was almost the entire length of the front room. There was something familiar about it.

"How'd you discover this?" she asked.

"I first noticed it when Ila insisted on Meg and Alec giving us all a tour. I'd forgotten about it until I saw these same markings again at Kyrie's house, in a border around that painting."

"Get the amulet."

Jack went to the fireplace and searched for the loose stones. When he found them, he removed them one by one until there was a pocket of space where Alec had placed the amulet. He handed it to Tavis and she set it on the floor near the border to compare the symbols on the amulet with those etched in the stone.

"Some of these are the same," she said. "But how can that be?"

He sat next to her, watching while she compared the symbols. "Is it important?"

"Wish I knew, I should've studied it more." Tavis frowned and shrugged. "I considered it to be a frivolous subject, guess I was wrong."

"Tavis, I have no idea what you're talking about."

She looked at Jack. "This is an extremely ancient language and it's difficult to understand, even with my key. There's only a few people, most of which are equally ancient by the way, who know how to read and write it very well. I've only heard it spoken a few times in my life, and one of those times was tonight."

He continued to stare at her, wearing a blank expression, as though waiting for the punchline.

"When you and Kyrie were speaking it silently."

"What?" he asked.

His confusion was enough for her to surmise that he really didn't understand what the symbols were, or that he'd spoken it silently with Kyrie. "When you were talking to Kyrie in the pod, you were both using this same language. I could hear it in both your thoughts."

"I wasn't aware that I was speaking to her any differently than I have been with you," he said.

"I don't understand how you and Kyrie are able to speak in this language. I could barely understand it, and I certainly don't know how to read it. I'm wondering if you might be able to."

Jack glanced at the markings and grew more curious about them. He took the amulet, compared it with the symbols in the etched border, and became more involved with one particular spot. After half an hour of watching him mutter incoherent whatnot before inching farther down the border, Tavis' stomach started to growl. As Jack had only progressed about a foot along, it was clear to her that it would take him a while.

"I'm going to the kitchen to find something to eat," she said.

Jack said nothing, only stared hard at one symbol, like it held promise of being understood.

She made two sandwiches and took one to Jack, setting the plate near him inside the border. He was still engrossed, but at least he'd scooted another two feet along, and so she went to the kitchen with her lunch to let him concentrate.

When she was finished eating, she went upstairs to find clothes they could change into. She picked out items that were typical attire for Meg and Alec and went through every drawer until she found hats they could wear if they needed to go outside.

Tavis had turned to go back downstairs when she spotted the bassinet in the corner of the bedroom. She went over and picked up Luke's soft blanket, bringing it to her face to feel it against her cheek and to inhale its scent. It smelled like Luke, but it was a painful reminder that Lani wasn't with her. After putting it back, she went downstairs and saw that Jack had made it to the other side of the border—the sandwich still untouched on the plate.

She took the clothes to the spare bedroom, got dressed, and set Alec's clothes on the bed for Jack to change into later. The unmade bed invited her to get more rest while she could and soon Tavis fell asleep wishing she had one of Lani's blankets to hold.

~

When she woke again, Jack was standing over her, smiling. He'd changed into the clothes she left for him and was eating the last of the sandwich. She sat up and swung her legs over the side of the bed, noticing there wasn't much light left coming in through the windows.

"How long have I been asleep?"

"Several hours, at least," Jack said. "It's almost night again. Come with me to the front room, I finished looking over the markings."

Tavis followed Jack to the center of the rectangular border. He delved right in to explaining the little bit that he'd learned from analyzing the symbols.

"First, you were right about the symbols being the same as the ones on the amulet, most of them anyway. Makes me wonder if Sebastian might know how to read this language."

"It's possible," she said. "Do you?"

"The markings on the floor are mostly just two or three sentiments, but they're repeated over and over again to create this giant rectangle."

"But do you know what they mean?"

"I can't translate it exactly, all I can tell you are the thoughts and feelings I got when I studied them. A few of the symbols seem to be a condensed version of an ancient history of people, but none that I've ever read about. Other markings express things about truth and power and that if you were truly worthy, on some level I couldn't make out, then you'd find sanctuary here if your life depended on it.

"There was something else, saving a worthy life meant saving a future life and that would continue the ancient history of the people. The markings end with the retelling of the history, then the patterns repeat themselves to form this border. At each of the four corners, there's another symbol. The best I could make of them was that they mention a different but dependent history, almost like it's about a different race of people. I don't know, it's rather confusing. I can understand why you didn't want to study it."

"What do you think it means by *sanctuary*?"

"I have no idea," Jack said.

Tavis was about to suggest using Sebastian's key to gain access to the amulet's stored memories, when they heard muffled voices and shouting from somewhere near the stone house. They strained to listen, ready to run if necessary, but the sounds continued to be carried in by the ocean breezes and were indiscernible. Jack turned the lamp off and went to the large bay window that overlooked Alaret Beach. Tavis sat on the bench and searched for the source of the voices.

Scouring the beach was a group of at least thirty men dressed in beige uniforms. They were poking the sand with long metal rods, marching forward in a coordinated line—and heading in their direction.

"Who are those people?" Tavis asked, looking up at Jack.

It took him a moment to answer, but when he did, worry and fear defined his tone and expression. "The East American military."

"What are they doing here?"

"Searching for the pods, I'm guessing."

"We can't let them find it, Jack," Tavis whispered. The thought of anyone here getting their hands on their technology almost made her sick and panic surged in her chest.

"We won't."

Jack picked the amulet up, shoved it back into the fireplace wall, and lined the stones back to cover the hole. He grabbed Tavis' hand and they hustled to the back door, cloaking themselves before opening it. At the bottom of the stairs, Jack grabbed two shovels and they ran to where the last pod was buried. Frantically, they dug the sand away until Tavis stopped to check if they'd reached the pod's external switch.

"We can press it twice from the outside, it'll pulsate until it's free enough of the sand."

Jack frowned. "Won't it leave if you press it twice?"

"Yes."

The frown on his face vanished, as he understood what Tavis meant to do. "I want you to get in it. Please, Tavis, go home. I promise you, I won't rest until I save Sebastian and Chaza. I'll find a way to get all three of us back to you."

"No, Jack. I'm not leaving you here."

Jack's shoulders slumped in defeat. There was no point in arguing with her and he wouldn't be able to knock her out like he'd done to Alec. Instead, he looked deep into her eyes, searching for any fear she may have of staying. He found nothing but bold determination, and even sensed that Tavis was considering whether or not she'd be capable of knocking him unconscious.

"Together?" Jack asked, and a delicate smile formed on his face.

"Together."

Tavis had already removed her necklace, the key gripped tight in her hand and poised over the secondary initialization switch. When Jack nodded, she pressed it in, twice, without taking her eyes off of Jack's.

"Start cloaking it with me," she said.

The pod began to vibrate and then shook with such force that they had to back away from it. Since it had been activated to leave, there was no need for it to relocate to a second area and it calculated an exit strategy while it freed itself from the sand. They focused all their concentration onto cloaking the pod from the military presence still on the beach.

Once all calculations were complete, the clicking sounds came to an abrupt halt. Tavis sighed with relief at its silence, and it shot off skyward in a blur, disappearing from their view. As a precaution, they remained motionless, waiting for any sign that the men had detected the pod leaving. All they heard were the casual conversations that had first gotten their attention at the stone house, only much closer now.

They threw as much sand back into the hole as they could and ran off to a dense part of the forest. It wasn't long before they discovered where William kept his cart parked. Jack's lip curled in disgust as he recalled the night William had abducted Tavis—he glared at the timecuffs still in the back seat. After pocketing them, Jack spotted the keys dangling in the ignition and a wicked smile spread over his face at the thought of stealing William's transportation.

He sat in the driver's seat. "Care for a ride, beautiful?"

"Jack! What if he sees us?"

Jack snorted. "Ask me if I care what he thinks."

Tavis rolled her eyes and got into the passenger seat. They took only the footpaths and parked in the woods behind the newcomer houses. Jack reached for Tavis' hand before she got out. "I want to say something before we go inside."

"What is it?" Tavis asked, concerned by his sudden pensive tone.

"I don't know how all of this is gonna turn out. I hope we all get home safely, but if we don't, I want to…" Jack had trouble forming the words he wanted to say to her.

She recognized the pain he was in. Tavis started to put her finger to his lips to shush him, but he caught her hand in midair and kissed it instead.

"Let me finish, please."

"Okay."

"I want to thank you for all the changes you've made in my life. Even if we die on Gamma tonight, my life has been so much better because you've been a part of it. You've helped me to become a better person. If I die, I'll die knowing that I've made all the right decisions. I have no regrets. I want to thank you for Lani, too. I've enjoyed being her father more than I could ever express with words. Thank you for giving all of this to me. I love you, Tavis Abbott."

She pulled Jack to her and hugged her arms around his neck. "To say you're welcome is nowhere near honorable enough, you're so much worthier than that. I love you, too, Jack Cavanaugh."

They held on to each other until rain began to fall; softly at first, but then increasing in intensity. Jack leaned back and asked, "Are you doing that?"

"No, are you?"

"Nope. Maybe it's naturally occurring, for once." Jack got out of the cart and held his hand out for Tavis to take. "Let's go inside, we should make it look like we're still around. In a little while, we'll go back to the stone house and work out a plan to free Sebastian and Chaza."

Once they were inside their house, Jack headed for Lani's bedroom, as Tavis knew he would. "Grab her blanket, I want to take it with us."

Tavis went to the front room and looked at the waterfall painting hanging on the wall. If there was any chance of getting back, she'd love to take it with her. She reached up and grasped the frame in her hands. Just as she removed it from the hook, an arm snaked around her neck and a cold metal object was pressed to her temple.

"Where is she?" A female's voice hissed into Tavis' ear.

The frame fell to the floor and banged the wall.

"What was that?" Jack called from the hallway. When he stepped into the front room, he saw Ila had a gun pointed at Tavis' head. Lani's blanket fell from his hand while his mind raced to find a way of getting Tavis away from Ila.

"What are you doing, Ila?" Jack asked calmly.

"Stay where you are." Ila shuffled backward with Tavis to the wide open front door while keeping an eye on Jack. "Tell me where Meg is and I'll leave."

"Meg's fine," Jack said.

"Where is she?"

"Meg and Alec left. She's happy now. Please, Ila, put the gun down."

"She's gone?" Ila shrieked.

"Yes, they left the island."

"You and your stupid father did this." Ila shook Tavis. "Everything was fine until you came here."

Jack took a step toward them, but Ila saw the motion and pressed the barrel of the gun more firmly against Tavis' temple. He considered cloaking Tavis, but since Ila had her arm around her neck, it would be useless. To see if she was capable of firing the gun, Jack tried sensing her thoughts. Though it was like being in a zoo, there was one prevailing thought above the fray—not only was she capable, Ila was on the verge of doing it out of revenge.

"Ila, please, listen to me. It's not Tavis' fault. It's mine. If you want to shoot someone, then shoot—" His plea was cut off by the sound of gunfire.

Jack roared in anger, thinking Ila had shot her. However, instead of Tavis falling to the floor, Ila collapsed into a heap in front of the open door. The gun she'd been holding hit the floor and skidded to a stop near Jack. He snatched it up and ran to Tavis, who stood over Ila's lifeless form. A look of horror framed Tavis' face as she watched a pool of blood form on the floor by Ila's head. When Jack got to the front door, he saw William running away. He aimed the gun near William and fired a bullet into the ground beside him.

"Stop running or I'll shoot again, and this time I *will* aim to hit you."

Jack's warning brought William to a halt and he turned around to face him.

"Put the gun on the ground, William."

William considered the wisdom of relinquishing his weapon, but decided to risk it after remembering Sebastian's words to Jack when he rescued Tavis. He knew Tavis wouldn't let Jack kill him.

"Fine, I'll put it down." William leaned over slowly and dropped the gun on the ground. When he stood back up, he said, "I shot Ila because I was positive she was about to kill Tavis."

"She *was* about to shoot her, because you destroyed Ila's mind. Did you give her the gun, too?"

"She stole it from me while I was sleeping."

"You should be more careful who you sleep with. Why's the military here?"

"You know about that, huh? Why else would they be here, Jack? They want the transportation that Sebastian and Tavis came here in."

"Walk over to Sebastian's porch and sit down."

William frowned at the strange request, but did it, thinking they were only wanting to get away without him seeing which direction they went. Once he was seated on the top step of the porch, Jack walked over to him while Tavis waited nearby. Staring at William, Jack reached into his pocket and brandished the timecuffs, smiling menacingly.

He didn't try to stop Jack from attaching the cuff on his wrist, or when he locked the other end to the porch railing. William knew the maximum length of time they were capable of—at most, he'd be stuck on the porch for two hours.

"I'm so glad I nicked these timecuffs, they're so useful," Jack said. "Don't get me wrong, I really hate that you used them on my wife, but since I stole the first pair I've enjoyed their convenience. Like... when I cuffed Alec to the seat in the pod last night, just before Tavis and I sent him and Meg off." Jack reveled in watching the smug smile vanish from William's face.

"They left?" William asked, a scared desperate pleading laced his voice.

"They did, right after Kyrie left with Luke and Lani. Unfortunately, Tavis and I had to send the third, *and last*, pod away about an hour ago because the military was getting too close to finding it."

"But that's why they're here, Jack, to find them. Are you telling me there's none left?" William clambered to his feet, but could move no farther and he shook his arm in protest. "How long did you set these for?"

"For the maximum length," Jack said casually and looked at his own wrist, scrutinizing a nonexistent watch. "I'd say you have about an hour and fifty-five minutes before they unlock."

William yanked at the railing, looking for any weakness in the structure so he could free himself. Jack laughed at the futile attempt and turned away to join Tavis.

"Wait!" William yelled when he saw Jack leaving. "You don't understand, they have the technology now to detect when any vessel that produces even the slightest trace of an electrical signal is entering or leaving the island."

Jack faced William, worried it was possible. "You're lying."

"Not about this, I swear. They may not be able to stop it, not *her* transportation." William motioned in Tavis' direction. "But they do know when it enters or leaves. Don't you understand what I'm telling you? However many came in, they already know about. So they know when they're all gone, too. Cultivating DNA is secondary to them, and there's still enough on Delta to keep that goal intact. It's the transportation they want from Gamma."

"What are they planning?" Jack asked, his fear growing exponentially.

"Hmm, I wonder." William laughed in a way that sounded like he was parting company with his sanity. "They also have that almighty button... bye-bye island... we're all dead!"

"I thought management was in charge of making that decision."

"We're a lying bunch of shits, Jack. Management hasn't been in charge of that decision since Alpha. Once the East American government got involved, they took over that decision-making policy." William sat back down. "If what you said is true about sending off the last of the transportation, then it's just a matter of time. We're toast. I'll see you in hell."

Jack turned his back to William again and went to Tavis. He saw in her eyes that she'd heard everything. "We have to get to that cave," he said.

~

Driving as fast as the cart was capable of going, Jack nearly overturned it when he swerved to an abrupt stop at the bottom of the cliff. They ran to the top and upon entering the cave, they saw the steel door was already open. Tavis looked at Jack and he shrugged.

"Maybe William left here in a hurry to get to us," he said. "Stay behind me, Eldridge could still be in here."

They crept past the doorway and listened for any sound of movement that wasn't their own. Jack kept a grip on the gun, prepared to use it—if only to scare Eldridge. When they entered the loft, they found it in complete disarray; as though someone had been in a race to leave. Drawers were left open with clothes still dangling over the sides while others were strewn about the floor. Along the far wall, papers were shuffled all over the desk and the file cabinet had been emptied of all its folders.

"Looks like Eldridge was in a hurry to get out of here, too," Jack said.

Tavis followed Jack down the stairwell to the main corridor. As they passed under the archway, they heard the familiar hum of the electronic equipment coming from the surveillance room, but nothing else. They made their way down the hallway, occasionally pausing to listen for unusual noises. At the doorway to the surveillance room, Jack chanced a peek and found it empty.

"Is he in there?" Tavis whispered.

"No," he said, still surveying the scene from the corridor.

She walked around him without a word and marched into the surveillance room; he followed after her. Jack would've preferred to check out the entire area first, worried about what state Sebastian and Chaza could be in, but she apparently wasn't about to entertain his compassionate chivalry.

At noting the chaos of this room as well, his eyes scanned the surfaces for details. He found the phone on the floor, the desk chair had been pushed back against the wall, and the file cabinets here had also been rummaged through.

Jack's gaze went to the monitors on the farther desk and wall; he saw William on one of them—still cuffed to Sebastian's porch railing. He was swaying from side to side and would stop for a moment to run his fingers through his hair, as though frustrated, then would return to his swaying. His mouth was moving, like he was talking to someone, but there was no one there that Jack could see.

"I think William's losing his mind," Jack said. When Tavis failed to offer a comment, he looked up and saw her walking back out of the detainment area.

"They're not here," she said.

"Did you open the cell doors?"

"No, they were already open. Where do you think they are?"

"Maybe they went to the stone house," Jack said, relieved they'd gotten away.

He turned his attention back to the monitors and searched for the one dedicated to the stone house. Seeing nothing there, he scanned the rest and his gaze fell to the one of the ocean side cave entrance to the bunkers. Eldridge was tossing the last of the items he chose to take with him down into a boat, including his satchel that had been stuffed with folders from the file cabinets.

Eldridge almost lost his footing several times during his hasty descent down the staircase. Soon as Eldridge reached the boat, he started it and turned it around, coming close to crashing into the cave wall as he made his way to the rocky exit. Eldridge was fleeing the island.

"Why's he leaving so fast?" Tavis asked.

"There's only one thing that could make him run like that." Jack pointed at the screen of the cave they'd just seen Eldridge vacate from. "William was telling the truth, they're about to destroy Gamma. We have to get out of here."

They bolted out of the surveillance room, taking the stairs to the loft two at a time. Both of them skidded to a halt at the top of the cliff and covered their ears as two military helicopters flew overhead. On the beach below were three military amphibious vehicles just entering the water. Jack's gaze followed the direction they were headed for and saw the lights of a naval ship anchored well off-shore.

"They're all abandoning the island." Jack was shocked at the final realization and another wave of panic hit him. "They'll probably detonate the nuclear devices after they move the ship to a safe distance, we don't have a lot of time. Hopefully, Sebastian and Chaza are at the stone house."

Jack and Tavis ran, and didn't stop until they reached the stone house. They were out of breath, and their hearts pounded, when they burst through the front door. Other than the sounds of their breathing, the house was silent. Refusing to give up, Tavis searched every room for any sign that they'd been here, but found nothing. She returned to the front room, hoping Jack had better luck.

"They're not outside either," he said.

He went to the fireplace and removed the loose stones, throwing them haphazardly in any direction—he had no intention of replacing them again. Once he reached the pocket of space, he yanked the amulet out and swung around to Tavis. The hopeless expression Jack found in her eyes was a crushing blow to him.

"He thinks we left," Tavis said. "He must have seen something on that screen in their cell, or he noticed the time variations. Either way, he thinks we've all left now and there's no time left to find them."

Tavis fell into a crumpled heap on the floor. Jack was by her side in an instant; he couldn't stand seeing her so defeated. He pulled her into his arms and could feel her body convulsing from her silent crying. As he did with Lani, he rocked back and forth, humming to Tavis the same lullaby—the same she'd heard countless times from Sebastian when she was a child and it had its intended calming effect on her.

"We have to try finding a way to get off this island," Jack said when he stopped humming.

"It's too late, we'll never make it," she said. "Even if we did, we'll just drown at sea."

"I think we should try anyway."

"No, Jack. Just hold me, please."

Jack wanted to argue with her, he wanted to try to save them, but she was right—they'd never swim out far enough in time to avoid the blast field. Even if they did, he doubted that drowning would be their end. He lay down on the floor, pulling Tavis with him and tucked his knees behind hers. Her body relaxed against his and peacefulness came over her, not just from their contact, but also from his acceptance of their fate.

"I love you so much, Jack."

"I love you, too, Tavis."

"Will it hurt?"

"No," he said.

"Together?"

"Together."

"Always," they said in unison.

He set the amulet down just as the floor began to rumble underneath them, slowly at first. They were facing the fireplace and it seemed to be suffering the brunt of the increasing tremors as some of the stones began to shake loose, creating an uneven appearance. Tavis squeezed Jack's hand, clutching it close to her chest. They were in the center of the rectangle, and the stones with the symbols began to shake loose as well, pushing upward from the rest of the floor.

One of the marked stones tumbled away from the rest. A green light emitted out of the resultant hole, casting a beautiful emerald glow throughout the dark room. Tavis lifted her head at the sight of it. Jack lifted his, too, amazed at how much light poured in to the room from beneath the floor.

"Do you think…?" Jack was too afraid to ask.

"It has to be!"

Jack scrambled over to it and without considering the wisdom of sticking his hand into a hole of unknown origin, he plunged his arm in up to his elbow. His fingers snatched at anything that felt like a solid object and the rough edges of the stones scratched and cut into his arm. At last, his fingers brushed against something cold and metal. Jack screamed in pain as he pushed harder against the stones, trying to get a grip around the bottom of the amulet. The stones continued digging into his skin and he could feel blood running down his arm. The amulet became harder to grasp, slick with his blood, and his screams of pain turned into screams of frustration.

"Jack, let me try."

"No!" he shouted. "Your arm isn't long enough to reach it."

Enough blood flowed from his wounds to begin acting as a lubricant and he was getting close to being able to wrap his fingers around the bottom of the amulet. He let go one more guttural scream of painful determination to push the rest of his arm past the rugged stones, and then grabbed it. In doing so, the skin on his arm tore, leaving behind a gaping wound he knew to be significant.

"I have it, get the other one."

"Here." Tavis scooted closer to him and held Sebastian's amulet near the hole, waiting for Jack to bring Chaza's up.

Jack took a deep breath, knowing he'd have to pull his arm up against the same stones that had cut him. Clutching the amulet tight in his hand, he yanked upward as fast as he could. The explosion of pain, as the gash in his arm ripped open even more, was beyond any he'd ever experienced before.

When he maneuvered Chaza's amulet out of the hole, the emeralds were shining bright, even through the trickles of Jack's blood. He fell backward onto the floor, dizzy and nauseous from the pain. Soon as Chaza's amulet neared Sebastian's, the sapphires sprang to life, flooding the room in beautiful colors of blue and green.

"You do it," Jack said, still trying to get his breathing under control.

Tavis took Chaza's amulet from his hand and connected it to Sebastian's to form a diamond. There was an instant change; the beams of light became more organized and merged together to create a focal point in front of them.

Another change occurring was that the entire floor beneath them began to shake more than it had been, causing more of the etched stones to protrude away from the rest of the floor. Ignoring it, Tavis kept her eyes locked on the center point of the amulets' converged beams. Before she saw his face, Tavis heard Alec's voice permeate throughout the room.

"Tavis?" Alec called.

"Yes, Alec, I'm here, with Jack," she said, happy and relieved to see his face again.

"An empty pod showed up a few weeks ago. What happened?" Alec asked.

Awed by the image's clarity, Jack sat up to look at Alec. Jack explained, "The East American military showed up, they were looking for the last pod. We didn't have a choice."

There was a long pause in which all three of them had the same thought—why did they choose to send it empty? Alec didn't have to ask, he knew the reason.

"Are Sebastian and Chaza with you?"

"No, they left the bunkers. I don't know where they are." Tavis' voice quavered. "I'm pretty sure they think we *all* left."

"What do you want me to do? Can I convince them to send more pods?" Alec's expression took on a desperate pleading.

Neither Jack nor Tavis wanted to tell Alec what was really happening. Tavis was considering the prospects of another pod arriving in time to escape when the floor shook more violently, jostling tables and chairs and overturning lamps. It was too late. She looked at Jack and saw the same thought expressed in his eyes. They both turned back to Alec and saw his face was beginning to fade.

"Alec!" Tavis shrieked. "Please, if you can still hear me… please, tell Lani about us. Tell her how much we love her."

The last image they saw of Alec was of him standing up, appearing alarmed. They heard him ask before he disappeared, "What's happening? What is that—?"

Though his image was gone, the lights coming from the amulets were still shining and they began to swirl and merge in ways that Tavis had never witnessed before. Not only was the floor beneath them becoming more unstable; parts of the walls, fireplace, and ceiling were breaking loose and falling down around them. Tavis turned with the intent to bury her face into Jack's chest—if their end was coming, she had no desire to watch it.

Just as she was about to lean against him, her lips parted in shock and her eyes widened with fear.

Jack swung around to see the cause of her distress and found that not only had all of the etched stones completely upended themselves from the floor, but an enormous curved wall was breaking through the rest of the floor. It continued to emerge, continued to devour the structural integrity of the stone house, and as it neared the position directly over their heads, it scraped the ceiling, causing it to crumble even more.

The strange wall kept going and as it passed over them, the floor lifted under them. It dismantled itself, flinging the stones outward into the front room, some bouncing off what was left of the walls. The last few stones beneath them gave way and Jack and Tavis fell to a new floor. They heard a tremendous crash as the ceiling finally collapsed, bringing with it the furniture on the second floor—but they were protected by the strange metal wall that was close to connecting to another emerging wall coming up from the floor.

The gun that Jack had tucked into his back pocket flew out and hit the fireplace with such force that what remained of it fell into a heap. Jack and Tavis saw one last glimpse of what used to be the stone house becoming nothing more than a pile of rocks before the curved walls sealed them off entirely. They looked around at the new room they were in and neither one of them recognized it, nor could they explain it.

They dislodged themselves from one another and stood to examine their new surroundings. The thunderous sounds of the stone house falling apart had ceased, and they spotted several glass portals circling their new protective room. The windows were domed, projecting outward from the walls so that they could see beyond and below them. Both of them ran to the nearest portal, but it was small and they struggled with each other to see outside. Jack scrambled to the next one over and stared out, watching as they slowly lifted upward, away from the rubble.

As they broke free from the last of what was once a beautiful and mysterious stone house, they saw the night sky and the vast ocean beyond Alaret Beach. Still, they ascended higher above the pile of stones, and then above the trees. Jack looked over at Tavis to see if she knew what was going on, but she was immersed in watching the island through the domed window.

Both of her hands were on the glass as she looked down at the island. Jack had a strange feeling that he'd seen the image before and was trying to figure it out when he saw her expression change to something akin to crippling loss. But he also felt they were beginning to ascend higher and faster, and his attention snapped back to his own portal.

Jack looked down on Gamma, and though it was night, he could still see the highest peaks that were visible in the moonlight. They were passing over the island's mountainous area, a place he'd yet to explore. Due to its morbid history, he never really cared to. He heard a whimper coming from Tavis and he turned to find tears streaming down her face—one after the other. Her fingers were opening and closing against the glass of the domed window, as though she'd claw her way out if she could, and her gaze was fixed on one single point on the island.

"Tavis, what's wrong?" Jack went to her. She looked so incredibly sad, like she'd never know happiness again. No answer came, so he looked over her head to see what garnered her attention.

And then he saw them, too, just as they leapt from the highest point on Gamma—Mors Cliff. Joined together by holding hands, Sebastian and Chaza appeared to be flying for a brief second before freefalling to the turbulent surf of the ocean that was illuminated by the pearly glow of moonlit sea spray.

Tavis let go a mournful wail. Jack turned her around and pulled her head down onto his chest just in time. He didn't want her to see them plunging into the waves; he wished he hadn't seen it.

It occurred to Jack why he'd had a strange familiar feeling when he saw Tavis in the domed window a moment ago. The day he met her, when he and Michelle had arrived on Gamma and he had shook Tavis' hand, he'd seen a series of expressions and emotions on her face in what seemed to be a montage of memories. What had disturbed him most was the image of Tavis suffering from grievous sadness while looking out of a domed window and realizing the truth of something—it was the sad reality that she'd failed to save her father.

'I'm sorry we couldn't save him,' Jack said to her silently.

Whatever transportation they were in accelerated its pace and the window Jack still looked through lit up in a brilliant, blinding light. It flooded the interior of the pod and Tavis swung around to find what caused it. Through the portal, they saw a giant ball of white and orange light racing and mushrooming outward and up toward the sky.

The night sky turned into instant day by the explosion—Gamma was being destroyed. The sight of the pluming mushroom cloud could almost be described as magnificent if it weren't for the destruction of so many lives.

'Except for one,' Tavis shared the thought with Jack, a perverse satisfaction that was rare for her.

"I agree." Jack verbally acknowledged her thought. "I think it's the best kind of justice that William went down with Gamma. I only wish Eldridge hadn't managed to scurry away like the rat he is."

The pod seemed to have slowed its motion once it got far enough away from the blast field of the nuclear explosion, but Jack saw another problem heading in their direction. It was a dark circular ring racing outward from the plume—the shock wave of the blast, and every bit as destructive.

"Tavis, why isn't this pod moving anymore? Do you know if it can withstand a shock wave of that magnitude?" Jack asked, becoming increasingly more alarmed.

"I don't know… I mean, it looks a little like ours… it feels like it moves like ours." Tavis' eyes widened at the sight of the black ring racing toward them. "This isn't one of our pods. I've never seen one like this before."

They started to close their eyes when the shock wave was almost to them, but then they saw something else coming straight at them with even greater speed. It was at least three times the size of the pod they were in and the bottom of it was opening at the same time that it barreled toward them. It was like a race between the new object and the shock wave—they thought it didn't matter which one got to them first, their pod would surely be destroyed by either one. At the last second, just before impact, Jack and Tavis closed their eyes and braced themselves, hoping their demise would be quick.

After what seemed like hours, in which nothing at all happened, Tavis and Jack opened their eyes to complete darkness.

Tavis remembered her words to Alec about the blackness, and that accepting it was easier than fighting against it; she wondered if she was experiencing her own blackness. She felt the glass of the domed window first, and then turned around to where she last remembered Jack standing. A relieved sigh escaped her when her hands found his chest.

"Tavis?"

"I'm here."

"Do your pods go dark like this?"

"No."

"What's happening?"

"I don't know."

29

The Ancients

Tavis and Jack clung to each other in the darkness. Ideas formed in their minds as to what was happening to them and they each sensed the other's possibilities. Jack kept going back to one singular theme.

"We're not dead," she said.

"How do you know we're not?"

"Because we're having a casual conversation about its possibility?"

"Oh. Yeah, I suppose you're right." He fumbled blindly to find her face and then pulled her close for a kiss—with more passion than she'd expected. "Yep, you're right, we're definitely not dead."

"Jack, stop it." Tavis worried he'd lost too much blood.

"My arm's really starting to hurt."

"Leave it wrapped, it'll help slow the bleeding." Tavis brushed away his hand from tugging at the shirt he'd taken off to use as a bandage. It had only been a temporary fix. She knew he'd need medical attention soon, or risk bleeding out. "Where are the amulets?"

"On the floor, somewhere in here."

They dropped to their hands and knees, feeling around in the dark for the amulets. Disoriented, they kept bumping in to each other. They decided to work strategically, starting against one wall and hunting in linear rows. Jack found the first amulet, and based on the fact that it felt somewhat dirty, he figured it must be Chaza's—covered with his dried blood.

"I found it!" Tavis shouted. "Hand me the other one."

He was groping around for Tavis' hand when a sudden noise, coupled with a new blinding light, scared them into dropping both amulets. She clutched at Jack and he positioned himself in front of her, not knowing what to expect when the door fully opened. Their eyes adjusted to the new light filtering in and they saw a man enter the pod. He stopped and stared at them as they cowered on the floor.

"Who are you?" Jack asked.

The figure laughed and took a few cautious steps closer before stopping again. Jack considered retrieving one of the amulets to use in self-defense.

"That won't be necessary," the figure said of Jack's thoughts.

"I'm still waiting for you to tell me who you are."

A set of orange lights along the base of the pod floor lit up. It was enough for

Jack and Tavis to better see the man who stood in front of them. He was uncommonly tall, a narrow build, and had white hair that fell past his shoulders.

"John Paul," Tavis whispered.

"Very good, Tavis. I suppose Alec showed me to you?" he asked and she nodded.

"What?" Jack yelled. "You're the lunatic who tried to kill Alec?"

"Alec was never in any real danger of dying."

"Oh, really?" Jack scrambled to his feet. "I guess drowning doesn't count as dying!"

"Kyrie had all the information she needed to save him."

Jack stood straight as he could, attempting to level out their height difference. "She wouldn't have had to if you didn't force him to swim an impossible distance."

"Alec needed the experience to accept some very important realities about his life."

"Well, if you're thinking of sending Tavis and I out for a dip, you can forget it."

"No, I believe Sebastian already taught you a few things about acceptance." John Paul laughed. "Enough banter. If you wouldn't mind, Jack, I'd like to see my great-granddaughter… if she'll agree to come out from behind you."

Jack's uninjured arm tensed when she tried to move.

"It's okay," she said to reassure Jack.

She went to John Paul and he looked deep into her eyes. His delicate seeking and learning of her life's every thought and memory ended with his warm smile fading. Her most recent memory turned his expression to one of compassion.

"Your heart is heavy with sadness from the loss you've suffered," he said. "You can't let it consume you this way, Tavis. That's not what he had in mind when he made his choice. Don't dishonor Sebastian's sacrifice by holding on to your grief."

Tears welled in her eyes and she hated them. She went to wipe them away, but John Paul caught her hands.

"No, child. Let them fall, and let them be the last."

Tavis' eyelids closed and the tears fell. They rolled down her cheeks and when she opened her eyes again, John Paul wiped them away himself. She felt stronger and a little more hopeful.

The warm smile returned to his face.

"Where are we?" she asked.

"My home. You and Jack found the amulet I hid in the floor of the sanctuary. Soon as the pod was free of Gamma, we came for you."

"The *sanctuary*?" Jack asked. "The symbols on the floor mentioned—"

"You were able to read them?" John Paul asked. "I'm impressed, considering where you grew up."

"What's that supposed to mean?"

"How about we go meet our people, Jack? You need medical attention, you've lost a lot of blood."

"Are there physicians here?"

"The very finest."

They exited the pod and stepped into an expansive cave of such enormity that Tavis and Jack felt like tiny specks standing in the middle of it.

"Seriously?" Jack groaned. "More caves?"

"Think of it as a nice place to park," John Paul said, motioning behind them.

There were two different pods. The biggest one sat atop stone columns that were intricately carved with the same symbols Jack had studied for hours. The bottom of the larger pod had a door beneath that opened downward, hence why it sat on the columns. Inside the wide opening was the smaller pod that had burst through the floor of the stone house.

"Where are we now?" Jack asked. "Delta?"

"No, a similar fate awaits Delta," John Paul said and a frown formed on Jack's face. "Don't worry, none of our people will die on Delta. Your parents have already been safely removed."

"Where are they?"

"They're here, and very anxious to see you."

Jack was suddenly excited to follow John Paul up the narrow stairway. When they reached the top, it opened to a landscape that reminded him of being on Gamma again. The main square was busy and bustling with people who paid no attention to them until they saw Tavis—they stopped what they were doing to look at her. Jack sensed some of their thoughts, particularly among the children. They knew who she was and who she wasn't, and they all seemed fascinated by her.

"Why are they so curious about Tavis?" Jack asked.

"I'll tell you about that later, after your arm has healed," John Paul said.

"That could take a while."

"No it won't."

"He's right." Tavis spoke up before Jack argued with him. "They're the ones who shared their medical knowledge with my ancestors."

John Paul walked up the steps of a stone building and greeted a man who'd been standing in the doorway watching them approach. Jack's eyes widened at the sight of him. He was perhaps the largest man Jack had ever seen and he hadn't a single hair on his head, or on his face for that matter, save his eyebrows and eyelashes.

"This is Galen," John Paul introduced. "He's the best physician you'll ever meet."

"Hello, Jack, and Tavis. It's a pleasure to meet you," Galen said and, like John Paul had done, perused their every thought and memory.

Jack felt the intrusion, unlike any Tavis had ever treated him to. He tried shielding his thoughts from Galen, but it had no effect. "It's nice to meet you, too, Galen," Jack said, extending his right hand.

Galen looked at Jack's offered hand and instead of shaking it, said, "Yes, I see you have a bad wound there on your arm. Shall we go inside and take care of it?"

"Of course, thank you." Jack dropped his hand back down to his side.

"I'll come back after Galen's finished," John Paul said and vanished like he was never there.

~

Jack and Tavis followed Galen into a room that looked like any other typical medical office, but it was spare in the way of extensive medical equipment. After he had Jack lay down on an examination table, he filled a basin with water, to which he then added a few liquid ingredients of various colors.

Galen picked the entire basin up as if it weighed no more than a glass of water and placed it on a table next to Jack, wheeling it parallel to the wounded arm. Once he removed the bloodied shirt Jack had used as a bandage, he assessed the mangled gash.

"It's pretty bad. What's worse is that it's saturated with the filth of Gamma. I'm going to put your arm in this basin to remove the impurities before I heal it. Don't worry, there won't be any needles."

Jack frowned and mumbled, "Did you get that when you were assaulting my thoughts outside?"

"Yes."

Galen guided Jack's arm down into the basin while Tavis stood next to him, fascinated, watching the procedure as she'd done countless times with her father. She loomed closer when he swirled circles in the water with his gigantic hands, leaning in closer still when he would pause to check the progress. Each time he stopped, she tried to decipher what he muttered.

"Are you interested in becoming a physician?" Galen asked.

"I've been thinking about it a lot lately. I just worry that I won't be very good at it. I couldn't even understand what you were saying when you swirled the water," Tavis said, embarrassed to admit it.

Smiling, Galen said, "You couldn't understand me because I was speaking in my own language, and it's a good thing you don't understand it very well. What I was saying was…" He appraised Tavis' innocent expression. "Let's just say I was aggressively complaining about how Gamma's filth doesn't want to detach from the wound."

"Oh."

"Jack may have understood what I said." Galen glanced at his face. "If I didn't have him fully relaxed at the moment."

Tavis looked at Jack; his eyes were half-closed and his mouth was half-open. He was immersed in a state of tranquil peacefulness, paying no attention to either one of them. She'd seen Sebastian use this technique many times and the people always had this same checked-out, goofy expression. Tavis chuckled and considered showing him the memory later.

"You try it." Galen moved his hands aside in the basin. "Maybe you'll have better success since you spent time on Gamma."

Unsure of what he meant, but eager to try and maybe learn a thing or two from the best physician to ever exist on any planet, Tavis plopped her hands into the basin. She swirled her hands around in circles, and then Galen guided them to show her the proper slanted-figure-eight technique. She got the hang of it quickly and soon he allowed Tavis to do it on her own.

All of the residual memories of the island were in the debris embedded in Jack's wound and seemed reluctant to let go. Since Tavis shared memories of Gamma with Jack, especially the memories that led to the wound's creation, she was able to coax the filth out. Her eyes lit up when the gash was clean and fresh blood flowed again.

"Excellent, Tavis," Galen said. "That was so much faster than I would've been able to accomplish. I've never set physical foot on Gamma. It may have taken me hours to clean it. Now that it's a fresh wound again, I can show you how to heal it."

Tavis took the towel Galen offered her to dry her hands and then he lifted Jack's arm and placed it on another towel resting by his side. After removing the basin to a nearby counter, Galen returned with a tray. On it were several bottles containing liquids of various colors and a clear sterile container protecting several layers of the opaque, tissue-thin sheets used to cover wounds.

"I love the way these work," Tavis said.

"Show me the order of the liquids."

Tavis grabbed the bottle with the clear liquid and held it up. "To use as a final cleaning agent, right?"

"Correct." He motioned for her to apply it, and when she poured the substance on the open wound, it ran clear. "What color would it have turned if there were still impurities in the wound?"

"Black."

Galen nodded and Tavis picked up a second bottle containing a blue liquid.

"To stop the flow of blood," she said.

"Very good."

She poured just enough to the ragged edges of the cut and the blood immediately stopped flowing. Tavis took the final bottle containing a white liquid and said, "Adhesive, for the strips."

He nodded again and waited for her to begin. Not expecting that he'd want her to apply the strips, she took a moment to focus on the many times she'd seen Sebastian perform the procedure. Her confidence restored, Tavis scanned the tray and frowned.

"Are you missing something?" Galen quizzed.

"Applicators."

"Correct again. Why can't it be applied directly to the wound?"

"Because it only appears as a free-flowing liquid in glass. Once I apply it to his skin, it will sit there as an iridescent bead that needs to be spread out. If I use my fingers, I won't be able to apply the strips."

Galen retrieved the applicators and handed them to Tavis. After doling out the exact amount of adhesive, she opened the sterile container and applied long strips of the healing film, knowing precisely how many were necessary to achieve the maximum speed of healing time. When the last strip was in place, the process began. They watched briefly before turning away in mutual disgust.

Underneath the strips was a bubbling of fluid and skin in various degrees of forming new layers. The sight of it was bad enough, but the fizzing, crackling, and gurgling sounds were close to intolerable. "Yuck!" Tavis croaked.

"I know. It's a gruesome process, which is why we always relax the patient first. Too bad we can't relax ourselves while we wait."

"How long do you think it'll take?"

"Not long." He glanced over his shoulder at the progress. "While we're waiting, I want to tell you how impressed I am with your medical knowledge. You were obviously paying attention to your father. In my opinion, you possess a natural talent for healing and you should pursue it."

"Thank you, Galen."

"I taught a few courses to Sebastian."

"I've heard him mention you before. He has… had a lot of respect for you." It hurt Tavis to speak of her father in the past tense.

Galen refused to let her think this way. "He's a good man. I know he's proud of you." He smiled at her. "You know what else? I also taught Chaza, when she and Sebastian were in medical school."

"Wow, you must be really old."

"Very." After advising her on which were the best medical courses to take first, Galen glanced at Jack's arm. "Back to our lessons."

He assisted Tavis with removing the healing strips, but stopped when all but the last one remained. Explaining to her his favorite technique, which was considered unorthodox by most physicians, Galen insisted it prevented scar tissue from forming.

"Just rip it off quickly and with as much force as you can."

"Um…" Tavis was reluctant to question Galen's method, but felt she had to. "Won't that be painful for him?"

"Without a doubt, and it'll bring him out of his tranquil state instantaneously. By ripping off the last strip, you'll also remove the skin's natural tendency to form a scar."

She didn't move, could only stare at Jack's peaceful face.

"If you truly want to be a physician, you'll have to accept this part."

"Okay." She sighed.

Gripping the edge of the last strip, Tavis braced herself and yanked upward—Galen caught her before she fell over backward. Jack's reaction was instant and explosive; the peaceful look vanished and he sat up, screaming at the sudden introduction of pain. His eyes were everywhere, searching for the source and ready to fight, then locked onto them like they were strangers.

Galen protected both he and Tavis in a cloaked sphere as a precaution. He knew the delicate balance taking place in Jack's mind all too well and waited until he saw the calm form in his eyes. When Jack remembered where he was, Galen dissolved the sphere.

"That really hurt," Jack said, his expression pitiful now.

"Can we check your arm to see if the wound healed properly?" Galen asked.

Jack lifted his arm to inspect it himself. "Whoa, that's amazing!"

Tavis and Galen joined him and declared it a success. All that remained of what had been a gaping hole was a pale pink line in the center of a hairless patch. Galen assured Jack the hair would grow back.

"Thank you, Galen," Jack said, briefly glancing at Galen's hairless head.

"Don't thank me, Tavis was your doctor. She's decided to follow in her father's footsteps."

"Really?" Jack smiled at her. "I think that's a wonderful idea. I'll help you in every way I can." He couldn't help himself. "Except being a guinea pig."

~

John Paul returned to take them to a vacant house that had been prepared for them. Along the way, he said that it had been decided among the Ancients to host a celebratory dinner the following night in their honor.

"You'll find everything you need here," John Paul said. "Clothes, water, soap, shampoo, and yes, I'm hinting at visiting the shower right away… you're both filthy and smell horrible. Most importantly, get some sleep. I'll see you tomorrow."

Once clean again, they lay down on the blissfully soft bed. Tired as they were, Jack knew there was something important keeping Tavis from falling asleep. She cradled Sebastian's amulet and Jack had purposely held onto Chaza's. He knew what she wanted to do, but he waited for her to broach the subject first.

"Jack?"

"I'd prefer not to," he said. "Not right now."

"Why?"

"If I see them right now, it'll make me want to leave immediately, to be with Lani again. I'm already struggling with it. I want to meet my real parents. Please, tell me you understand."

"I do," she said. "I want you to meet them, and I want to meet them, too."

"I want to ask you something before we go to sleep."

"Okay."

"You're so reserved with your thoughts sometimes, and it's so hard for me to know what you're going through when you do that. How are you coping with what happened?"

It wasn't easy for Tavis to think about her father's death long enough to find a way to express her feelings over it. She decided to go with the thoughts that kept haunting her.

"It's difficult to imagine him gone, and I hate that Meg lost Chaza just when they were beginning to build a relationship. I hate that Alec never got the chance to know our father like I did. More than anything, I hate that he and I will never have our conversations again. But, I know he sacrificed his life to spare mine and I have to keep remembering that every time I get angry and sad."

Jack caressed her cheek. "I know that wasn't easy for you to say. I want you to always talk to me about these things. Don't keep it all shielded from me. I want to help you get through this and anything else that bothers you."

~

Mercifully, they slept in a dreamless state and when they were awoken by a knock at the door the next morning, they were well-rested and ready to start the day.

"It's probably John Paul checking to see if we smell any better."

"I'll get it," Tavis said.

She opened the door to find that it wasn't John Paul, but a woman holding a breakfast tray—her face and smile was kind and loving. There was something vaguely familiar about the shape of her mouth. Tavis smiled back and continued to study her, and then she figured it out. It was Jack's mother.

When the woman sensed that Tavis had sorted out who she was, she said, "Not yet, have breakfast first. I'll come back in a little while."

Tavis nodded and took the tray from her. Returning to Jack, she placed it on the bed and sat down. "Hungry?"

"Starving," he said.

Jack inhaled his food and looked at her plate to see if there was anything she didn't want. When his lips started parting every time she took a bite of her omelet, Tavis took one last forkful for herself and pushed her plate forward for Jack to have.

"Are you sure?" He was practically drooling in anticipation, his fork already advancing.

"Go ahead. You're hungrier than normal because of the healing process. It took a lot of energy for your body to heal that quickly. For the next few days you'll feel like you're starving all the time."

He ate the rest of her omelet and licked both plates clean. "I'm still hungry."

Patting his back, she said, "I know. Let's get dressed and see if we can find more food for you."

Once they were dressed, a knock sounded at the door. This time, Jack got to it first with Tavis right behind him. He opened the door wide and saw a woman standing there. When their eyes met, a shining white light emanated briefly from her. Tavis moved from around Jack so she could see both of their expressions.

Jack had seen the display of light before it vanished and he scrutinized the woman more fully. She was as tall as he was and had a slender but sturdy build. Her hair was kept in a pixie cut and of a vibrant color that reminded Jack of the late autumn days of his childhood when the trees had come to rest for the approaching winter months. He remembered the weekends, joyfully free of school for two days only to be told to rake all of the fallen leaves from the front yard by his mother because his boredom was driving her crazy.

"You're my mother, aren't you?" Jack asked her, but he already knew that the woman standing in front of him was so much more to him than the mother he'd known in Charleston.

"Yes," she said, and some of the light he'd witnessed before flowed from her again until she made the conscious effort to make it stop.

His arms were around her in an instant, holding on to her as though afraid she, too, would vanish. She hugged him back and they spoke silently and rapidly in the ancient language that Tavis struggled with. Sensing the thoughts and emotions of the conversation became Tavis' next best way of translating. They spoke of painful separations, of their happiness to be reunited, and an explanation of how she and Jack's father were able to leave Delta with John Paul's help.

"He likes making people swim, doesn't he?" Jack leaned back to view her again.

"John Paul refuses to ever step foot on any of those islands again. Your father and I were more than happy to swim out to him." She turned her attention to Tavis. "Jack, would you please introduce me, *properly*. We did meet earlier when I brought your breakfast."

"This is my wife, Tavis Abbott. Her mother is Kyrie Ellison."

"Hello, Tavis. My name's Mabel. You're John Paul's great-granddaughter, and Sebastian Abbott's daughter," Mabel said, and looked at Tavis with that same captivated expression as everyone else did.

Though still curious about the strange fascination, Jack let it go to address his growling stomach. "I'm starving," he said, unable to find a more delicate way to express his hunger.

Mabel laughed. "Come on, let's go to my house, there's food there."

Jack took Tavis' hand and followed after Mabel. When they arrived, they sat at the table and consumed everything she put in front of them. Mabel watched them, amazed at how hungry they both were.

"I understand why Jack's so hungry, but why are you?" Mabel asked Tavis. "Is it possible you're—?"

Tavis tried giving a silent warning look to Mabel, but Jack saw it.

"Possible you're what?" he asked.

Neither one of them said anything, nor gave any indication that they were going to. Jack tried sensing Tavis' thoughts, but she guarded them vehemently. He turned to Mabel, only to find he'd have better luck rooting it out of Tavis. He replayed their words in his mind and soon deduced the only logical explanation.

"How long have you known?" Jack asked her, subduing his anger.

Tavis sighed, there was no point in trying to hide it anymore. "Not long, just a few days… or so."

"Why didn't you tell me?"

"Because of everything that was going on at the time. Which only got worse, if you'll recall."

Given everything that had happened, he could hardly blame her for putting it off. However, he did have a nagging feeling that he would've tried harder to convince her to leave in the last pod had he known.

"I'm not angry." His curiosity refused to be ignored. "Do you know if Lani's to have a brother or a sister?"

She smiled. "It's still early, but I think a brother."

~

Mabel took Jack and Tavis outside to show them around the island. When she reached the old docks, she related the story of when William came and took ten children and John Paul. Jack stared at the pilings, trying to imagine what it must've been like and wondered what John Paul had been thinking to willingly go with William.

"Will I get to meet my father soon?"

"Tonight, at the dinner," she said. "He's helping to get everything ready. Isaac wants it to be perfect."

Tavis suggested a nap when they returned to the house in the effort to ignore Jack's already renewed hunger. Several hours later, he leapt from the bed, hoping it was a sandwich knocking on the door. When he opened it, the man standing next to Mabel may just as well have been the man Jack saw any time he looked in a mirror.

They smiled at each other.

"Isaac?" Jack whispered.

"Yes." He pulled Jack into his embrace. "I'm so glad they kept your name. I decided to name you Jack. I didn't think I'd ever see you again."

Hugging him tight, Jack experienced a feeling of being complete and whole again. Once he released his father, he said, "Come inside and meet Tavis."

"It's nice to meet you, Tavis," Isaac said.

"I'm happy to meet you, too." She couldn't keep from staring. "It's crazy how much you and Jack look alike."

Isaac appraised Jack and winked at Tavis. "I'll take that as a compliment, that's a good-looking son I have there." He slipped his arm around Mabel's waist—so much like Jack was keen to do with Tavis. "I hope you're both hungry, there's a huge feast waiting for us."

"Oh, I could definitely eat." Jack snorted.

The four of them went to the main square where Tavis and Jack had first emerged from the cave. A long table had been set up to accommodate a large number of people. There were easily fifty chairs lined up along each side of the table, with people either already sitting down, or standing behind their chairs engaged in conversation.

John Paul stood at the head of the table and motioned for Tavis and Jack to sit on either side of him. Isaac sat next to Jack, and Mabel took the seat next to Tavis. Once the five of them were settled into their seats, John Paul motioned for everyone else to take their seats before he spoke.

"We're all gathered here to share our gratitude that Mabel and Isaac are with us again. There are still a few others on Delta, but they're being removed at this moment and will be with us soon. We're also here to celebrate the successful rescue of our guests, Jack and Tavis, as well as the others who escaped Gamma before it was destroyed and are now safe at my great-granddaughter's home." John Paul turned to Tavis and smiled before continuing. "While we give thanks for those who made it to safety, I ask that we also remember Sebastian and Chaza Abbott and the sacrifices they made to ensure the lives of so many others."

There was a moment of silence at the conclusion of John Paul's speech. Then everyone, except for Tavis, Jack, and his parents, stood up collectively with their heads bowed and their eyes closed. One at a time, starting with John Paul, then with Galen seated next to Isaac, they emitted a glowing white light. It was soft at first, but grew in such intensity that it was almost impossible to look at. Jack was forced to look at the next person in line, who was instantly beginning their own process of lighting up.

The process repeated itself down the line of people standing on one side of the table, then up again with the last person standing next to Mabel. For a few seconds, they were no longer people, but beacons of light and energy, reminding Jack of the lighthouses that dotted the coastline of East America. He thought them beautiful.

Though they all lit up as separate individuals, their light faded all at once. It took only seconds for them to return to their previous forms. Then they sat back down in their chairs and waited for John Paul to speak.

"Let's eat," he said.

Everyone began to serve themselves from the platters of food, except for Jack and Tavis. He met her gaze and saw that, though mystified by the experience, she seemed to have a better understanding of it than he had. When he tried finding answers in her thoughts, he discovered they were unusually well-shielded. Her eyes lingered on John Paul, hinting he was responsible, and Jack looked to find him watching and waiting.

"What was that?" Jack asked him.

"I know you have questions, and though Tavis could answer some of them, *I'll* be the one who shares the knowledge of our people with you. You'll have to be patient, Jack. For now, I'd prefer you quiet your growling stomach because it's driving everyone around you crazy."

Rather than argue, Jack did as John Paul commanded. While giving in to his body's demands to consume the food in front of him, he watched the people occasionally glance at Tavis. He analyzed their expressions when they watched her. They seemed awed by the simple fact that she was sitting among them and there was deep admiration mixed with extreme curiosity in their eyes. He found himself watching her differently, too, as though he could almost understand why they kept looking at her.

~

The hour grew late and everyone came to the front of the table to say their good-nights to them. Eventually, all that was left was John Paul, Tavis, Jack, his parents, and Galen.

John Paul and Galen shared a silent exchange, then Galen nodded and left. Only the five of them remained at the table now. John Paul appeared to be arriving at some decision as his pensive eyes met each of theirs. He stood from his chair and turned to Mabel and Isaac.

"Stay with Tavis until Jack and I are done talking."

"Of course," Mabel said.

Jack got to his feet and weighed the usefulness of arguing. As much as he wanted to learn from John Paul, the ordeal he'd been through on Gamma had a more influential pull on his decision to allow Tavis to be away from him on an even stranger island.

John Paul quickly dismissed Jack's thoughts. "There is no Gamma anymore. There's no William Davis who will come in the dead of the night to abduct Tavis. Our people are merely curious about Tavis, they would never harm her. They love her, and the child she's carrying. Your parents are staying with her so she's not inundated with too many visitors."

He was still torn, reluctant to let Tavis out of his sight.

She went to him and took his hands into hers. "*Not* together this time. Go with John Paul and listen to what he has to say, you'll be glad you did. I'll be getting to know your parents in the meantime."

"You're sure?"

"I'm sure."

Tavis smiled and let go of his hands. Jack watched his parents escort her away and when they were almost out of his line of vision, his legs seemed to move of their own accord to follow them. It was John Paul's hand on his shoulder that stopped Jack from going.

"I admire that about you, you've assimilated toward Tavis' people," John Paul said. "All of them are like that, they'd sooner fall on the proverbial sword than risk the life of another. That's one of the reasons our people are so curious about her. She represents a race of people who, by universal standards, shouldn't exist."

"Well, she's your great-granddaughter." Jack frowned. "Isn't she part us?"

"Maybe a little," he said, shrugging. "It's rare, though. She's still very young, but I'm guessing she's more like her own people… like the Abbotts."

John Paul leaned over the table and gathered several rolls, wrapping them neatly in a cloth napkin. After tucking the bundle in his jacket pocket, he scrutinized Jack and then made another bundle. "I'd rather not be interrupted by your inevitable hunger pains."

"Actually, I'm stuffed."

"We're walking to the beach." John Paul handed the second bundle to Jack. "I bet you'll be reaching for those rolls by the time we get there."

When they got to the beach by the old docks, John Paul sat down on the sand. Jack sat next to him and followed his gaze to the shoreline where several wooden poles jutted up from the water.

"You're very stubborn," John Paul said at the first sound of Jack's grumbling stomach. "Would you please eat some of the rolls we brought with us?"

Jack groaned, but pulled the bundled rolls out of his jacket pocket. "How long is this gonna last?" he asked between mouthfuls of bread.

"Another day or so."

Jack pointed to the pilings. "What happened to the docks?"

"They were dismantled after I left with William."

"Why the hell would you help William?"

"Oh, there were many grand schemes and ideas floating around in lots of heads back then. William's were self-serving, of course. Mine? I thought that perhaps mixing some of our people with some of who he had in mind could be the very thing that could save this planet. But things went horribly wrong and I came to regret having brought my daughter to Alpha. Though I'm glad we were able to help Sebastian's people, I'd been hoping for more. I wanted bigger and better things to come from my sacrifice."

"So we're not the same as Tavis' people?"

"Not exactly. I'll get into that later. First, I want to thank you for all you've done for Tavis and the others. Also, I'm glad you decided to stay here for a bit before going to Tavis' home."

"Is this island your home?"

"Only when we're here, and only in this moment. We take it with us everywhere we go. I think this has been the longest time it's ever been in this ocean."

John Paul's eyes swept across the night sky, unseeing, as though reflecting.

"How long has it been?" Jack was almost afraid to ask.

"Hmm, let me think." John Paul did a few calculations in the sand with his finger. Mumbling to himself about the figure not being right, he erased it with a swipe of his hand and started over again. "Guess that was right. Apparently, we've been here for the last seven centuries… this time."

Jack shook his head and chuckled. "Is that why I keep hearing the word *ancient* being tossed around?"

"Actually, most here are descendants of descendants of descendants of the Ancients. Oh, and by the way, that term came from Tavis' people. There are very few original Ancients left, and yes, I'm one of them." John Paul erased the figures in the sand and sighed. "I was wrong about my ideas. Trying to integrate our people with those on this planet isn't the answer. I can see that now. Bettering a civilization comes from within, not by external influences."

Jack said, "There are way too many people on this planet like William Davis and Eldridge Stone that would exploit certain aspects of what we can do. Don't even get me started on what the East American government would do, they'd have no intention of creating a nobler kind of existence. Seriously? What were you thinking?"

"Well, Jack, I was hoping for the best. Unfortunately, you're right, the small number of good people are outnumbered by the kind who have the most power. The only solution to it would probably involve a great deal of violence, one way or the other."

The conversation paused when a ghost crab exited its burrow and tossed out a clod of dirt atop Jack's foot.

"What did you mean by Tavis' people shouldn't exist by universal standards?" Jack asked, preferring to steer the conversation away from violence. "Is there something wrong with them?"

"No, they're pretty close to perfect in a roundabout sense." John Paul shot Jack a scathing look. "Surely, you've noticed that by now."

John Paul chuckled at Jack's scowl and refusal to comment. It was a daunting amount of information he wanted Jack to know and he relied on what he was exceptionally gifted at to begin—telling accurate accounts of history.

"When we, *Ancients*" –John Paul smirked– "first came to this solar system, we found two planets that contained life forms, and one that was already dead. Interestingly, it was Earth we came to first because it was so easy to find. Once we entered the atmosphere, we discovered why. There was nothing but simple life forms existing here, what you know to be the earliest of the hunter-gatherers. We studied them a bit and concluded they'd undergone a rare evolutionary process and, if lucky, would continue to do so barring any planetary disasters.

"We left them to seek out the other planet. It wasn't easy, which intrigued us as we knew it was somewhere in this solar system even though we couldn't see it. Whatever life forms existed there were well-evolved as they'd figured out how to manipulate time to always be either ahead, or behind, actual time. It didn't scare us at all, as we already possessed the knowledge and were better at it since we're able to manipulate time in a much bigger sense than by mere hours or days.

"Finally, we found it and confirmed that the planet was using cloaking technology. Our only question was, *why* were they using it? We had to ask ourselves if we would be imposing on a planet that may not want visitors. Being nomads at the time, we roamed, we explored, learning more from every solar system we visited. I don't think it's possible for us to ignore our curiosity. So, we entered their atmosphere and what we found both amazed and confounded us."

John Paul stopped speaking, reliving the memories and marveling at them all over again. After several long minutes of silence, Jack interrupted his reverie.

"Were they upset at being found?"

"No. Turned out they weren't even aware that their manipulations with time had built up on itself to produce the cloaking effect. They used it for controlling their weather patterns. The only thing that upset them was how we looked when we landed and exited our ship."

Jack appraised John Paul's appearance and decided that, although he appeared somewhat eccentric, there was nothing particularly disturbing about him. "You're a bit of a period piece, but I don't think you look creepy."

"This isn't how we looked then," John Paul said. "We looked like what you saw at dinner tonight, our light forms. Though we thought we were rather tame for the light and energy we're capable of, they were shocked by our appearance. Their language had evolved to the point of thought and memory perception. It was due to that fortunate common ground that we were able to sort each other out and understand one another."

"How did they get past the way you looked… as lights, I mean?" Jack asked.

"They told us right away that we were impossible to look at and wanted to know if we could take on an organic form. It was an easy enough task for us, so we did it for their sake. Some of us have retained their original appearances since that day, and some of us have changed many times over. I've had more than you'd care to know, but I have kept this form since we settled on this planet over seven hundred years ago. I took up cause with the Native Americans and I haven't cared to change appearances yet."

"For every one of my questions you answer, at least three more pop up," Jack grumbled.

"I know, I can hear them all as they form in your head. It's distracting." John Paul leaned back on his elbows and admired the stars. "You keep going back to one question in particular, though. Why do we find Tavis and her people so fascinating? Why do *you* find her so fascinating, Jack? What drew you to her in the first place?"

"Um…" Jack glanced at John Paul, unsure if he should answer what first came to mind.

"Besides that," John Paul said.

Jack thought of every memory he had of Tavis, going back to the day they met. Though he had no idea how or why, it was like the memories started even before then. "Everything about her. I knew there was this tension between us when we met, but Tavis seemed more at peace with it than I was. The only way I could deal with it was to try avoiding her. She, on the other hand, was always calm, always patient, like she was waiting for me."

"Waiting for you to do what?"

"To choose her." Jack let out a sigh. "More patiently than I was."

"Exactly! You were drawn to her complete lack of torrential chaos, that which rules like a supreme god over this entire universe and everything in it… except for the people on Tavis' planet. Even at the molecular level, violence is an everyday natural occurrence. Unfortunately, this same idea of violence can also drive many higher life forms to act in despicable ways. Tavis and her people aren't like us."

"*Us*? Are you saying I'm violent?"

"All life is violent, it's inevitable and it's fundamental for life to begin in the first place." John Paul sensed Jack's preference to dismiss the notion. "Are you going to deny it? What about East and West America? What about the execution of your adoptive parents? The destruction of life and land everywhere, all the time? What about you, have you ever contemplated violent acts?"

"That's enough," Jack said, raising his voice.

"Tavis and her ancestors defy that universal law. We sensed it as soon as we landed on their planet. It was different than the other places we'd been to. They knew we were curious about them and that we had no intention of harming them.

"We were roamers of the galaxy, but what we really wanted was to find a place to rest again and then we found a planet that would have us. And we'd yet to be truly welcomed on any planet by this point. They were already fairly advanced, but there was still so much they could stand to learn and we shared our knowledge with them. We lived among them for so long, they came to *adopt* us as their own ancestors.

"They were like sponges, eager to learn anything and everything. We educated them, and eventually we shared our ancient history, and it made them very sad. It also worried them that the same thing could happen here. Over time, they wanted to know more about what lay beyond this solar system.

"Our roaming nature got the better of us and we took off again to explore, but we came back periodically. Each time we returned to this solar system, we always checked on Earth first. On one such visit, we discovered a catastrophic event had taken place, the one referred to as the Toba catastrophe. The early hunter-gatherers had almost been wiped out… *almost*. The small population that remained bore a striking similarity to our friends and we wondered if the event wasn't so natural after all.

"We left Earth and discovered that it was much more difficult to pinpoint our friends' planet this time. It upset us because we'd decided to stay with them permanently. Our inevitable end was coming down to mere generations and we understood that our days of roaming were over..."

"Obviously, you found them," Jack said when John Paul appeared lost in his thoughts.

"Yes, but it took a while. As always, they were happy to see us and we were relieved. Right away, we noticed some other changes... besides the new complete and purposeful cloaking of their planet. Though there was never a huge population there to begin with, it seemed to have dwindled to half of what it had been. Also, there seemed a melancholy about them.

"We questioned what had happened to Earth and they explained that they'd influenced a super-volcano to erupt, hoping it would destroy the life forms we'd warned them about. They had listened to our premonitions of what they could eventually evolve into and it clearly scared them, enough to try causing their extinction. It bothered us that not only was the act their first attempt at intentionally creating violence, but that we were the ones who had caused it."

"Are you kidding me?" Jack shouted. "Tavis' ancestors were the ones responsible for that?"

John Paul raised an eyebrow at Jack. "It was *your* ancestors who taught them how to do it, and scared them enough to think they had to."

"They could've just continued cloaking their planet," Jack muttered. "They didn't have to create global chaos on other planets."

"Don't judge them," John Paul said. "They also told us that they'd suffered for their single act of violence. Though, by universal standards, they were merely trying to prevent the evolution of unimaginable creatures with supreme intelligence. They'd also been divided, not all of them wanted to do it. The ones who pushed the issue left and never came back, and that explained what had happened to their population."

"Where'd they go?"

"More on that later," John Paul said. "First, I want to talk about the ones who didn't leave. It was agonizing for them to have been part of a plan to destroy other living beings over potentialities. That was when they decided to do whatever it took to remove any and all tendency for violence from their civilization. They begged us to help them.

"Again, they employed all of the medical knowledge we shared with them to make that happen. They worked on suppressing the potential for violence at the molecular level, through their DNA. We warned them to be careful, but they were determined to stay a peaceful race of beings.

"We reminded them that violence comes in many forms, not just in destruction. We explained that a certain amount of violence and chaos was necessary for the basic building blocks of all creation. They wouldn't listen, and after they achieved their goals, our warnings became a reality. They'd grown so complacent that their already small population dwindled further. Why do you think that happened, Jack?"

Jack understood the conversation had come full circle from the first mention of violence. He thought about what John Paul was so obviously waiting for him to say. "Because even the act of choosing and loving someone is built on necessary turbulent emotions. More than that, the creation of a new life has no hope of beginning without the combined forces of disorder." Jack smirked at John Paul. "It's written in every high school science textbook."

"It's true, though." John Paul sighed, sounding tired. "By removing their tendency for violence in the destructive sense, they annihilated their passion to forge new generations. Fewer and fewer children were being born. By the time they heeded our warning, they feared it may be too late."

"Is that when they came up with the idea of viewing Earth as a potential source of increasing their population?"

"Not quite, that decision would come much later, from Sebastian's grandparents. They suspected that the ones who left, Dissenters they called them, probably went to Earth. The idea was to try convincing them to return home. In the meantime, an interesting development had occurred between two of our people. They formed a close bond with one another in their organic forms, they were Chaza's great-grandparents."

Jack frowned. "I don't understand."

"We weren't aware that we could reproduce in our assimilated forms. The birth of Chaza's grandfather was proof that it was possible. It was a happy discovery for everyone and new bonds formed. Eventually, a few of our people formed bonds with some of theirs, but not very many. It seemed a good many of our people chose among ourselves. Though it was disappointing, they never faulted us for our choices because they were, and still are, unbending with their notion of liberty… everyone is free to make their own choices."

"I've noticed that about them." Jack recalled the memory of Sebastian looming over him with the threat of absorbing his memories of Tavis if he refused to leave Gamma. "But I've also noticed it isn't always adhered to."

"I disagree," John Paul said. "I clearly see the choices Sebastian offered you. I said they were strict with the code of free will, I didn't say they were stupid. Based on your foolish behavior, he gave you the option to choose between two paths that *you* created, not the other way around. If I'm confusing you, just ask yourself what you would do if Lani were in the same situation."

Jack imagined Lani as a grown woman, married to a man who refused to give her ideas a chance, who refused to even listen to her needs. It surprised him how much he disliked a hypothetical man.

"I see your point," Jack admitted begrudgingly. "Tavis' people are perfect saints, and we're all unworthy, ignorant mules."

Laughing softly at Jack's wit, John Paul said, "Oh, Jack, I'm gonna miss you."

"What do you mean?"

"Later," he said and handed Jack the bundle of rolls. "Here, eat another roll, you're getting grumpy again. Don't eat them all, we still have more to discuss. I'd like to tell you how I came to be involved with William Davis' islands."

"You have no idea how much I want to know."

"I, Galen, and Sebastian had formed a close friendship. Sebastian was always coming at us with all kinds of ideas, most of which were medical discoveries he'd found. One day he came to us, upset about some calculations he'd come across. Before their deaths, his parents had determined that their race would become extinct in the next millennia at their current growth.

"Galen looked over the calculations and found them to be correct, but over-inflated as they'd left out certain variables. Basically, it came down to the necessity of a population boom to avoid extinction *within* the millennia, not after. As you can imagine, Sebastian was distraught, and so were we. We'd known about their predicament for a long time, but to have a conclusive end date staring us right in the face was disturbing.

"We hatched a plan that day. Sebastian had several ideas he wanted to try. He wondered if we moved some of our people to Earth for a while, then introduced some of his people, maybe the isolated environment of this island would have an effect. A few years passed and only one bond had formed from the experiment.

"Sebastian grew wearier. He and Chaza had married by this point, but it turned out they were unable to have children and it caused a strain in their relationship. He came to me privately one day with an idea he wanted to get my opinion on.

"He guessed the residual memories of this island were responsible for our people choosing only among themselves. What he wanted was for me to explore the other lands on this planet, those already populated, and see what I thought about trying our experiment where none of our people had common ground. Of course I was interested, exploring is in my nature. So, I agreed and took Galen with me.

"We were gone for a long time, and we became entrenched in the warring saga that was taking place on the North American continent. Galen and I picked a side, can you guess which one?" John Paul pivoted his body around so Jack could view him fully.

"Hmm, this is a tough one, John Paul," Jack said, feigning ignorance. "I'm gonna take a guess and say you sided with West America."

"Naturally," John Paul said. "The oppression they suffered for centuries was ghastly and unbearable to me. Sebastian's request would have to wait."

"Wow, I just realized how all of my schools' history books were full of…" Jack caught himself before he finished the vulgar remark. "I mean, how inaccurate they were."

"You grew up in East America, of course they were full of *inaccuracies*."

"Do you know how sore the East American government still is over that loss?" Jack asked. "How much they want all that land back?"

"It won't happen, I made sure of it. The rest of this world is watching that situation too closely for East America to use brute force to seize West America. Hence, their involvement with the Stone Davis Corporation. They need to find a sneakier way of making it happen."

"How did Sebastian get involved?"

"When Galen and I finally came back to this island, we found a very irate Sebastian." John Paul shared the memory of Sebastian's expression with Jack.

"Oh! I've seen that look a few times," he said of the image of Sebastian's angry appearance when John Paul and Galen walked out of the aircraft in the cave.

"I imagine you have." John Paul chuckled. "He was angry that we'd taken so long. After he calmed down, we explained what we'd done for West America and he was impressed, but he was appalled that they'd been so oppressed in the first place. You see, Jack, they cannot fathom such an oppressed state of beings and I sometimes wonder if they truly understand the concept of the quest for power. I had to share memories of their history with Sebastian for him to even get an idea of what it must be like. The way he reacted, you'd think I was trying to kill him. Obviously, we didn't mention the other injustices that plague this world. I don't think he could've taken it.

"Then he wanted to know something that's always been a sensitive subject for his people. You should know, it still is. He asked if we'd found the ones who left during the Dissention. It hurt me and Galen to consider telling him the reality of the situation, the Dissenters were everywhere. They were who repopulated Earth, and are now the very ones who understand power and crave it. So I lied and told him we couldn't be certain.

"Galen mentioned how far the people on this planet had advanced on a technological level. Sebastian became hopeful again, wondering if we'd somehow missed them during our preoccupation with West America. He flat out asked Galen if it was possible for them to have advanced so quickly. Galen isn't very good at lying, he said no. The hope in Sebastian's eyes made me cringe, I knew what he thought. He found hope where I found disaster, in the sad reality of having to consider that Earth may still be their best chance at a future.

"Sebastian was excited by the prospect that his ancestors had formed a new population here and he went back to his home to discuss the matter with his council. They, too, were enthralled with the idea that they could potentially restore their people to their rightful home. The council allowed Sebastian to explore this planet further to find who would want to come home.

"Understand, it took me only a few minutes to relay these events, but when Sebastian returned, many years had passed." John Paul waited for Jack to confirm that he understood the time variations.

"The cloaking of their planet, right?"

"Right," John Paul said, but doubted Jack fully grasped his meaning. "During the years Sebastian was gone, Roland Davis had come and gone. Then William showed up, and he was enchanted by us.

"I took on the task of monitoring William and I became just as interested in him as he was in us. The thoughts that went through his mind were both impressive and oppressive, but it was his father's legacy that captured my attention. Brand new land, created by someone who had no clue as to who his ancestors really were, and I began looking to William's thoughts as a way that I could maybe help Sebastian and his people. I felt it was worth a try.

"I discussed it with our people and we all agreed to try, but only if we used the stone houses as a sanctuary—"

"Wait, *you* didn't make those stone houses?"

"No," John Paul said. "It doesn't matter how they came to be, they worked to our advantage. Where was I before you rudely interrupted?"

"Handing innocent children over to William," Jack grumbled.

Ignoring him, John Paul continued. "I knew William was getting restless, and I'd hoped Sebastian would show up again so I could tell him about my idea. Then William decided not to wait any longer, he was leaving, even if empty-handed. If it was to happen, I'd have to go through with it on my own. I didn't even inform our people of the change of plans. When they discovered the children were gone, it angered them. They moved the island, destroyed the docks, and refused to allow another person to come here after my betrayal.

"I took my own daughter with me in the hopes they'd forgive me one day. Eventually, I sent Galen to inform Sebastian of what had occurred, and to keep quiet about it until I had a chance to see if my idea would work out. I also told Galen to only mention Eldridge Stone's name. Sebastian didn't know who William Davis really was because I didn't want him knowing."

"Why?"

"Just before the relocation from Beta, I called on someone I know and begged him to show me a little of what was to happen on Gamma. He showed me enough that I allowed the transfer. He gave me that painting, saying Kyrie would need it one day. And then I told Galen to have Sebastian take over the monitoring of Gamma, and more importantly, to watch over my granddaughter, Kyrie."

"Who did you call on? How did he know what would happen?" Jack asked, frowning and frustrated at his inability to make sense of John Paul's explanations.

"I guess you could say he's one of our people, or more like he's *from* our people. He's an anomaly that's difficult to explain, Jack, and I'm not going to try tonight. If you truly want to know more, go to the libraries when you get to Tavis' home. All the information is there."

"Okay," Jack said, hearing the finality in John Paul's tone. "Was Kyrie the only one of us who was transferred to Gamma?"

"Just her and Joseph Arcana. William added the Sterling."

Jack was floored by the revelation. "What? He was one of our people?"

"Yes," John Paul said. "Joseph aged at an accelerated rate and had reached the end of his short life span. Toward the end, he was forgetting most of who he really was."

"They said he died in a boating accident."

"Not true. His last day came and I was there because we all felt it coming. I didn't want him to go through it alone, and I also had to worry about the two other islanders on the fishing boat."

"How'd he die?"

"He remembered who he was at the end and he saw me waiting for him in my canoe. Joseph realized what was happening to him, so he jumped off the side of the boat and swam over to me. We went beneath the waves together and I stayed with him until his light extinguished. When it was over, I altered the memories of the two men on the fishing boat to reflect Joseph's *accident*. By then, the events involving Sebastian and Kyrie had already taken place."

"Did you know about Joseph and Chaza, that they had Meg together?"

"Not until recently," he said. "Eat the rest of your rolls, your hunger is distracting me again."

Laughing at the random request, Jack complied. After finishing off the last roll, he asked, "Do you think Chaza knew who he was?"

"I can't speak for Chaza, but I find it hard to imagine she didn't have some idea."

A movement got Jack's attention. A figure had come out from behind the trees at the farther end of the beach and came toward them. John Paul looked over his shoulder to see what Jack stared at.

"Galen," he said softly.

"Is something wrong? Tavis?"

"Tavis is fine. Galen's here out of friendship. He and I go way back."

When Galen reached them, he nodded a greeting to both of them, but otherwise remained silent and took a position several feet back from them.

"Why's he here?" Jack whispered.

"I've already told you, he's here because he's my closest friend."

Jack shifted his gaze to John Paul. The moonlight fell on his face and Jack could see every line etched there clearly. It could've only been an illusion, but it seemed that John Paul emitted a bit of his own light.

"We've talked about many things," John Paul said. "And I hope I've answered most of your questions. If there's more you want to know, then it's up to you to ask me now."

Again, Jack looked at Galen, who stood like a sentinel with his eyes fixed over the ocean—he also emitted a small amount of his own brilliant light. The sheer size of Galen awed Jack and he wondered what the rest of the world must have thought about him during their explorations of Earth.

"Too much, isn't it?" John Paul asked of Jack's thoughts and he, too, looked back at Galen. "He thinks people want to see someone big and strong in their physicians."

"What kind of people are you that you can look like whatever you want?" Jack asked, there was a note of fear in his voice, knowing he was one of them. "You can appear as normal people one minute, then turn into a brilliant orb of light the next. I suppose you could look like a tree if you wanted to?"

John Paul frowned. "Do you normally prefer to talk to trees?"

"It was an example," Jack mumbled.

"If I really wanted to, and pined away long enough for it, and if it were in my best interest, I suppose I could take on the characteristics of a tree. I don't imagine it would be very practical, though," he said, contemplating life as a tree.

"What do you look like normally?"

"The shape and appearance of what remains of the original Ancients is the light you've already witnessed. Every once in a while, the people on this planet have seen us in that light form and we've been called many things because of those occurrences. My favorites are ghosts and haints, spirits, souls, angels, and even gods. I especially like the god references. Galen likes being called an angel."

They laughed at the idea of someone as large as Galen being referred to as an angel. When Jack imagined the size of the wings it would take to paint a portrait of a biblical Galen-angel, all three of them burst out into a new fit of laughter.

"But we've also been called demons, Satan, hallucinations, and witches. Obviously, those are my least favorites. Lately, particularly among the East American government, we're called elf*s*."

"You mean elves?" Jack clarified.

"No. I mean ELFs, extraterrestrial life forms."

"Oh, right."

In a gentle voice, John Paul asked, "You're worried you have the potential to appear in that light form because you're a direct descendant of us, aren't you?"

"Yes." Jack finally admitted it. "I don't know why, but it scares me to think I'm capable of looking like that. It seems beautiful to me, but it also seems so powerful… almost in a destructive sense."

"It is both beautiful and destructive, all at the same time. You shouldn't be afraid of it, though, it's what you're made of. It's what everything and everyone is made of. However, you're very young and inexperienced. I doubt you'd be able to present yourself in a light form on your own. Go ahead, give it a try."

Jack fidgeted at the unexpected command. He hadn't the slightest clue how to begin changing his form to that of a light. Simply hoping it would happen didn't make it so.

"See? You were worried over nothing. If you really want to know how it feels, I could probably help you. I think I have enough left in me to do that."

"Okay." Jack closed his eyes, afraid it would hurt, and inched his hands forward in the direction of John Paul. What he heard was laughter coming from John Paul and Galen. Jack opened one eye to peek at what they found so funny.

"What the hell are you doing?" John Paul asked, still chuckling.

His hands were almost touching John Paul's face. "Well, I'm sorry! It's not like I've done this before." He brought his arms back to his sides.

"I know you haven't, I shouldn't have laughed. We're sitting close enough together that contact isn't necessary. I know that's how Tavis' people do much of their transferences." John Paul shook his head. "Honestly, as much as they like to make physical contact with one another, I'm amazed their population declined."

Jack heard Galen snickering behind them and it made him laugh, too. "Yeah, good point."

"You ready?" John Paul appraised Jack's demeanor.

Nodding, though somewhat nervous, Jack said, "I'm ready."

John Paul burst into a brilliant white light, forcing Jack to avert his eyes to the side of him. The conversation turned from spoken words to thoughts, and he sensed John Paul urging Galen to join them to help encourage Jack's light to emerge. Galen had already shed his human form by the time he flanked Jack's right side and their warmth and benevolence encompassed him—continuing further until it reached every cell in his body.

A sensation of freedom came over him as his body let go of its physical form, the only form he'd ever known. Jack felt himself exploding into a new kind of existence, his previous self not gone or destroyed, only expressed in a different way—one full of light. It didn't hurt, nor did it feel any better or worse, it was simply another way of being and he was no longer afraid of it.

Jack initiated the next flow of thoughts: *'Is this how we looked where we come from?'*

'It's how we came to look,' John Paul said in the ancient language. *'Our solar system was much older than this one and it came time for it to die, but some of us fought against it. We bounced from planet to planet as our star entered its first stage of death. When our star entered its white phase, it had a profound effect on us. It changed us on a molecular level, one that mirrored our white star. We left our dying solar system, searching for others like ours, but we were unable to find any that had survivors. It seems we're the first of our kind.'*

'So, there's no home to go back to for our people?' Jack asked.

'No, but our planet was very much like Tavis' and our people were quite similar. We lived in mutual peace and nonviolence, but we did so at a cooperative level. We understood the universal necessity of chaos and violence that's required for any life form to begin. Unlike Tavis' ancestors, we didn't try to change DNA to reflect our already agreed upon decision to live without war. In my opinion, our way is better. After all, our solar system died of old age, not by war and the endless quest for dominance.'

When John Paul finished speaking, his light faded and he returned to his physical form; then Galen and Jack instantly resumed theirs. Jack noticed it felt just as normal to return to his body as it was to become a sphere of light.

"Thank you for that," he said to Galen and John Paul.

"There's no need to thank us," Galen said. "This is part of who you are, you should be proud and express it any time you want to."

"I will, Galen."

Turning back to John Paul, Jack was surprised to find him still emanating a small amount of light beyond his physical form. He studied his face and discovered John Paul appeared much older than he had at dinner, and his eyes were closed, as though taking a nap.

"What's wrong with him?" Jack asked Galen.

"He's dying, Jack. John Paul is older than all of us combined, a rarity, even for us."

Jack was at a loss, but asked the first question that came to mind, "How long does he have?"

"Not long. That's why I'm here, to be with him at the end. We've all known his light was close to its end for a while and he's done everything possible to help get everyone off of Gamma and Delta. He was also determined to be the one to answer all of your questions tonight. He used the last of his energy to correct the time variations between this planet and Tavis'."

"Why?"

"For you, so that you and Tavis don't go home to find Lani grown up," Galen said. "Cloaking is nothing more than manipulating time in various amounts depending on what you're cloaking and what your goal is. At the moment, Tavis' home is ahead of this planet, but it changes often. They've been cutting it close for a long time, for Sebastian's and our sake, but they're getting nervous with all the incoming people and no explanation from Sebastian."

Jack got to his feet and went toward the shoreline, not wanting to disturb John Paul's resting. He felt Galen's presence before seeing his giant form join him.

"Don't be upset," Galen said. "It was his gift to you and you should accept it graciously, don't sully it with unworthy feelings of guilt."

"I'm sorry. I just wasn't prepared for this being my last… Dammit, my only, moment with him. I'd hoped for more time."

"He gave you more *time*, just not in the way you were thinking of."

"Tavis knew about the time difference, didn't she?" Jack nodded, reflecting. "That's why she wanted to contact them last night with the amulets."

"Tavis would be very well aware of the time variations. If she didn't warn you, it was because she knew you had something important to do. Please, don't blame her. I'm sure she didn't relish the idea of missing out on her daughter's childhood so that you could get answers to all of your questions."

"I'm not mad at anyone," Jack said. "I just wish…"

"I know, I wish he had more time as well. John Paul is my closest friend, I'll miss him very much."

Jack turned to see if John Paul was still resting. Not only was he still there, but a line of people had shown up and bordered the tree line in front of the beach. Some faces he recognized from the gathering at dinner, others he was seeing for the first time, and there were several children standing among the adults. His gaze searched the wall of people until he found his parents and Tavis. Behind them was the very same pod that saved him and Tavis from being destroyed with Gamma—he understood it was there to take them away.

Everyone's eyes were focused on John Paul, as he continued to rest peacefully on the beach. Jack's eyes met with Tavis' before she, too, turned her attention to her great-grandfather. A stillness fell over the island; the wind barely caressed the trees behind the procession of people who stood to celebrate John Paul's life, and the waves crashed against the beach at a slower tempo.

The dim light around John Paul began to pulsate in a steady rhythm, growing brighter with each pulse. Jack panicked, thinking these were the last few seconds, and he ran, desperately trying to reach him before he was gone forever. He was shocked that Galen had somehow gotten there first, pulling John Paul into a sitting position.

When John Paul's eyes opened, he looked around and saw his people lined up on the beach. A warm smile of pride curved his lips.

Turning his attention to Galen, who waited patiently to fulfill any request, John Paul asked, "You will take me?"

"Nothing in this world could stop me," Galen said.

John Paul faced Jack and hoped that he'd helped him find conclusion with his origins, and more importantly, his future. "Tavis' home is your home now, just like it has been our home since we arrived to this solar system."

"Galen's gonna take you to the ocean, isn't he? Like you took Joseph? I want to be with you, too."

Galen scooped John Paul up in his massive arms and walked toward the water. Jack followed them, feeling as small and helpless as John Paul looked in Galen's arms. Galen came to a stop and exchanged a private thought with John Paul.

"Are you sure?" Galen asked.

"If you'll help me," John Paul said. "He won't settle until he's seen it. Please, Galen, let me stand."

Though he hesitated, Galen placed John Paul down on his feet.

"I'm sorry, Jack, but you can't come with us. I know what's tormenting you, I can see it so clearly in your thoughts. You want to see where your people came from, you want to know the history."

"Yes, I do." Jack struggled to keep his raw emotions from ripping him apart. "I want you to show me what it was like, and I want to see what happened to our people."

A powerful explosion of images burst forth in Jack's mind. He knew they were memories of a world that no longer existed, but it didn't matter to him—he needed to see it. Through Galen and John Paul's combined memories, Jack saw a landscape similar to any and all that he'd ever seen on Earth, full of trees and plants, but with slight variations.

The trees were as tall as the ones edging the westernmost border of West America, the sequoias and giant redwoods, they were either enormous or gargantuan. Some of them had buttress roots so large, Jack imagined he could stand in their cavernous recesses without touching the top. The tree roots were covered in a carpet of green moss that appeared so soft, he wished he could reach out and touch it.

'These are the biggest trees I've ever seen in my life.'

'Because we never chopped them down like they do here on Earth. Our buildings were made of stone,' John Paul explained. *'You'll find similar forests and buildings in Tavis' home.'*

A repeated sound kept pulling at Jack's attention and the vision he saw through John Paul's memories traveled up the massive tree trunk in front of him until it reached the first branch. There perched a butterfly—of the most colossal proportions—on what appeared to be a huge nest made of large sticks, some were even small tree limbs. The wingspan of the creature was easily Jack's height and its body was enormous; its colors were dazzling in their luster and brilliance. The light filtering in through the tree canopy turned the colors Jack thought were blue at first to purple. At other times, the wings looked pink; yet he knew the colors he perceived were only substitutes.

'Oh, I get it now,' Jack said, finally understanding the confusing display of colors. *'You could see in the ultraviolet spectrum.'*

'Yes, but not the ones who were born in this solar system,' Galen said.

Jack heard the sound again that had gotten his attention before and he looked at the giant butterfly, discovering it had made the sound. It had a musical quality, and was being reciprocated from somewhere far off, becoming louder as it drew closer. Directly overhead, an even bigger butterfly came into view carrying a mass of vines bearing lush green leaves the size of a dining room table. The duet continued until the second butterfly landed on the other side of the nest. Together, the two butterflies worked to place the vines inside of the structure. When they were finished, the first butterfly took off silently, leaving the larger one in charge of guarding the contents of the nest.

'What's it doing?'

'Feeding its young,' John Paul said. *'There are two larvae in the nest and they need constant feeding. Their parents go back and forth in turns to bring more leaves.'*

'Your butterflies built nests? They sang… like birds?'

'Yes. There are just as many differences as there are similarities with the animals among closely related solar systems.'

John Paul's voice became livelier as he recalled and shared the memories he was fond of.

Wanting to know more about John Paul's interests, Jack asked, *'Were there birds there, like the kind we have here?'*

'Oh, yes,' John Paul said. *'Though they're very tiny compared to the avian life here, ours were more like hummingbirds. They were also fewer in number, but they lived for hundreds of years. They didn't live fast and die hard like they do on Earth because they didn't have to contend with predators, both natural and unnatural, nor did they suffer destruction of their habitat. Pay attention to the memory, you're about to see one.'*

Turning his attention back to the scene, Jack was simultaneously met with something darting back and forth in front of his face. A hand, John Paul's, reached out and waited patiently for the bird to land. Jack could feel its tiny feet landing on his forefinger. Its feathers were mostly grey, but it had a blue crest on its head and blue tail feathers that fanned out occasionally to reveal yet another color Jack couldn't quite decipher.

The bird looked at John Paul, as though waiting for something. Another hand came into view, holding a white flower with petals that were comprised of fringes, somewhat like a tassel. At the tip of each fringe was a different color; some of which Jack could define, the rest were repeated substitutes for what he couldn't.

As the exquisite bloom inched closer to its beak, the tiny bird grew more excited, flicking its wings and emitting sounds that resembled glass harps. It greedily lapped up the nectar from the center of the flower—almost disappearing inside of it—and when finished with the treat, took off again in a blur of grey and blue.

'That was the cutest thing ever,' Jack said, wishing the bird would come back.

The memory changed to a group of massive stone buildings. It was early evening by Jack's estimate, based on the dwindling sunlight. An extremely tall woman—she was easily six foot sans shoes—stepped out from a courtyard carrying a basket of what looked like fruit. Her hair was the same unique reddish-orange color of Mabel's and if it hadn't been braided and coiled to form the several intricate coifs spaced down her back, it would have trailed in a magnificent train far behind her. She turned to the person whose memory Jack was experiencing and he gasped at the vision of her.

'Beautiful, isn't she?' Galen proudly asked Jack.

"What I'm seeing, beautiful isn't a good enough word," Jack mused aloud, clinging to the vision. "I don't even know what the right word is."

As the woman smiled at Galen, Jack studied every inch of her, looking for differences and similarities between his own form and hers. She had the same physique, but was taller and her skin was the color of highly polished ivory, except for her lips—which were close to resembling holly berries in winter. The color of her eyes were violet, most likely of the same ultra-violet spectrum he was unable to see.

She seemed to glide rather than walk toward Galen. When she was just a few feet away, Jack took instant notice of the way she was dressed. The fibers of the fabric encasing her body from neck to ankle consisted of the sheerest imaginable, causing Jack to look away from the memory.

'Who was that?' Jack cleared his throat, thankful the memory was changing again.

'That was my sister,' Galen said. *'She didn't make it to the ship in time when we had to leave. I still miss her to this day.'*

The next memory began before Jack could say anything about Galen's loss. It started with an aerial view that continued to climb higher in elevation. The scene below was of the same stone buildings, but Galen's sister was no longer there, and the sunlight was unusually bright.

As the structures grew smaller, the trees in mass came into view. There were huge expanses of forests, densely covered with the very trees Jack had seen up close only moments ago. Though he wouldn't have thought it possible, it looked even more beautiful than it did on the ground. There was no time to fully appreciate it, as the vantage point of the memory accelerated quickly, becoming more of a satellite view of the planet below. Blue-green oceans covered most of the planet's surface, with fluffy white clouds partially obscuring both land and water.

The land formations had been engineered to form neat bands surrounding the planet; three in total encompassing it. Each band was connected by diagonal swaths of pristine forests in which there were no manmade structures except a narrow corridor of cleared pathway abutting the left-most edge of each forest. It was how they traveled on the surface to each circular land mass to visit with other populations.

Jack noted the lack of massive cities made of concrete that he was so used to seeing on Earth's satellite images. Soon as he turned from the memory to question it, John Paul was already answering.

'Collectively, we decided at the beginning of our epoch to refrain from over-populating

our planet. We decided to work with our planet, instead of against it,' he said and continued with the memory.

The vantage point had reached a high enough altitude that Jack could see more of the space the planet inhabited. Little by little, the planet and its moon became smaller and the rest of the solar system came into view. In the background of the aqua colored planet, on a black canvas of open space, there was not one, but two suns. The biggest star seemed entirely too close, while the farther, smaller one appeared to be a destructive annoyance to the larger one.

The memory flashed to the interior of a vessel filled with people who were still tall, but seemed greatly reduced of a physical form in a healthy sense, appearing more spindly-like now. A familiar glow was beginning to emanate from all around them. The scene returned to the window, allowing the view of the planet, and it was being bombarded by one asteroid after another. Their planet was being destroyed by the forces of the two merging stars. It broke Jack's heart, right alongside Galen's and John Paul's to relive it again so that he could learn what happened to his people.

Shifting further along in a series of blurred images, he saw they'd taken refuge on a desolate, lifeless planet, but still within their own solar system. Each day, they watched from their temporary place of rest as their main star puffed up and devoured everything around it. They traveled to the very edge of their solar system and, after landing on a large but stable asteroid, they foolishly watched its death. Though they should've left long before, it proved difficult to leave the only home they'd ever known. When the star shed the last of its outer layers, it exploded in a spectacular array of light and energy.

John Paul said, *'We knew the blast produced a shock wave and that we'd all die when it reached us, but we had given up by then and welcomed an end to our constant state of fear and isolation.'*

'But you didn't all die.' Jack watched the wave of energy barrel toward the ship. Though it was only a memory, he still closed his eyes at the last second before impact.

He couldn't see it, but he could feel it when the ship was struck. There was immediate upheaval as they were blasted from the asteroid's surface. It was eerily quiet; no whimpering, screaming, or crying—only silence. Jack knew there had been some kind of an energy field that had passed through the walls of the ship; he'd felt it through the memory.

'Open your eyes, Jack.' John Paul waited for him to see how they didn't all die. *'Look at what we became.'*

Jack opened his mind again to see what John Paul wanted him to discover. He no longer saw physical forms, not even in their weakened state. They were all the brilliant orbs of light and Jack sensed their own astonishment at how they all looked to each other. Toward the back of the ship, a brilliant stream of beautiful colors shifted behind the bright white orbs. It was different from the others and Jack hoped for a better look, but the memory faded away and once again he was standing in front of Galen and John Paul by the ocean.

John Paul put his hand on Jack's shoulder and smiled warmly. "We all became remnants of our dying star. We were flung out of our solar system and forced to roam the galaxy. We've seen many things in other solar systems, but we've yet to find anyone like ourselves… like what we became."

"Why did you stop searching?"

"Just like the stars that made us, we original Ancients are also burning out." John Paul laughed at his own comparison. "Thankfully, for anyone nearby, we don't die quite so explosively. However, there is quite a bit of energy involved and that's why we take our dying to the deepest trenches of the ocean. I hope you understand now why you can't go with us."

Grimacing, Jack asked, "Will it hurt? Are you gonna suffer?"

"Not sure, exactly. I haven't ever died before." John Paul's attempt to make Jack laugh was unsuccessful. He knew what Jack really wanted to know. "Don't worry, only the original Ancients die in this manner. We're still learning how the subsequent generations of our assimilated forms live and die, particularly those like Joseph. Galen is studying a potential correlation—"

"Hold on a minute." Jack frowned. "What about Chaza? Can she take on a light form?"

"I don't know what to say about that situation." John Paul eyed Jack, wondering if it was wise to say any more. "Listen to me carefully, Jack. I'm not so sure, and neither are you, that Chaza is dead. Since none of us can be sure of that finality, you are not to give Tavis false hope that her father may still be alive. Do you understand me?"

Jack was shocked by the unexpected possibility, but he had no intention of mentioning it to Tavis. Not unless there was more to go on than mere speculation. "I understand. I promise you, I'll shield this thought from her."

"Any more questions?" John Paul asked.

"Why did you choose to stay with Tavis' ancestors? You said you roamed all over our galaxy. Why'd you choose to end your days in this solar system?"

"When we finally pinpointed the exact location of the hidden planet, Domum, we were astounded by what we saw. They had terraformed their planet in the same design we'd formed ours. It was like being home again. We were tired, and if the people there would have us, then we wouldn't die alone. Had they not accepted us, I think we would've sat in their atmosphere, pining away for a millennia."

"Did our planet have a name?" Jack asked.

"Archilochus." John Paul smiled again. "You're going to like Domum very much, I suspect."

"Yeah, but are there any giant butterflies there?"

Laughing anew at Jack's jokes, John Paul said, "None that I've seen, but you'll discover many things there that will be both new and familiar to you."

John Paul swayed a little as an incoming wave washed over his feet. Galen's hands shot out to support him. "It's time," he said.

"I have to go with Galen now, and it's time for you and Tavis to go home." John Paul turned with Galen to begin their ocean journey.

"Wait!" Jack scrambled to catch up to them. The waves were beginning to increase to their normal speed and frequency again. He struggled both physically and emotionally. "Come with us to Domum. You said they have oceans there, too."

"There isn't enough time," John Paul said. "And if ever a planet needs some of what made us what we are, it's certainly Earth."

Jack's eyes stung, not just from the salt of the splashing waves, but from agonizing guilt mixed with gratitude. John Paul had saved his and Tavis' lives, and he'd spent the last of his life giving them time. Jack couldn't hold them back any longer, the tears welled and spilled onto his cheeks. He couldn't find the right words to express how thankful he was for all that John Paul had done.

"Ah, how befitting," John Paul said, his voice a bare whisper. "Here are your tears, and a star is dying."

Jack stared into John Paul's eyes and said, "Thank you."

"You're welcome. Take care of my great-granddaughter."

Galen and John Paul submerged beneath the waves. Their spheres of light formed and lingered briefly, then shot off at an incredible speed to deeper water. Jack continued to stand there, staring out over the water, wondering which ocean it was—he hadn't thought to ask anyone.

Then he floated on his back awhile and stared at the night sky, marveling at all the stars. Knowing he had to leave soon, he wanted to have this miniscule moment to take in his surroundings one last time. There was no helping it, no matter how bad things were on Earth, it was still the place where he was born.

It was still the same sky he grew up staring at. Thus far, Earth contained his only history. No one waiting back on the beach, not even Tavis, could understand what he was experiencing. He was saying goodbye to the only home he'd ever known and there was no reason to think he would ever return.

Jack remembered what John Paul had said about Chaza. If it was possible that she somehow survived, then it was more than likely that Sebastian did as well. He thought of the multitude of ways they could've survived, especially given Chaza's abilities.

'If there's even the slightest glimmer of hope they made it, I swear on everything I know, I'll bring them home,' Jack muttered to himself in the Archilochun language. He did so with purpose, as he had every intention of keeping his promise to John Paul and not fill Tavis' mind with potential false hope. *'If they live, I will find them.'*

He closed his eyes and shielded these thoughts and ideas—hiding them away from not only Tavis, but from Meg and Alec, too. Jack locked them away in his memories, keeping only a fragment; a skeleton of a thought he shielded so well that he was already losing track of it when he left the water.

As he approached the beach, Jack saw that everyone had left except for Tavis and his parents. Tavis handed him a towel and he dried off his body. As he wrapped it around his waist, he said, "They're gone now."

"Galen will stay with him until the very end," Mabel said. "John Paul will have his closest friend with him."

Tavis hugged her arms around Jack's waist and rested her head on his chest. She could smell the saltwater still clinging to his skin—organic, like fish and seaweed.

"Are you ready to go now?" Tavis asked him.

"Yes. Thank you for being patient with me." Jack held her tight, tucking the top of her head under his chin. The warmth of her body and hair soothed his chilled skin. "How about you, are you ready to go home?"

She leaned back, laughing. "Very much."

"I'm looking forward to seeing my new home."

"Your parents want to talk to you about something."

He turned to them and felt an overwhelming sense of appreciation that he couldn't define. Maybe it was the mere fact that they were here, supporting Tavis while Jack spent time with John Paul.

"We've already discussed this with Tavis, but we wanted to make sure you were okay with our plans," Isaac said. "Your mother and I would like to go with you to Domum, for two reasons. First, the pod isn't like the homing pods, it's not programmed to travel back and forth between only two locations. It needs to be piloted and at some point, it will need to be returned here. The second reason is more of a selfish one, I hate to admit."

Jack waited for Isaac to give the second reason, but his father seemed hesitant to finish. Instead, Jack turned to his mother for an explanation. Though smiling, Mabel gave Isaac a stern look for his sudden silence.

"What your father is somehow unable to say is that he'd like to be with you when you see Domum for the first time. He's excited by the prospect of being able to explore it with you. We'd also like to meet Lani and stay long enough to welcome your son. To be honest, we don't ever want to come back here."

Absolutely nothing would make Jack happier than to have his entire family with him while he endeavored to discover his new home. Yet, there was something else pulling at his thoughts—like he might be forgetting something important.

A wisp of a memory flashed through his mind—a cliff, a few spoken words, and silent memories of possibility echoed in this thoughts. He remembered enough of it to shove it away again to just below the surface.

"I want that, too," Jack said.

Isaac perked up. "Shall we get going then?"

"Soon. I'd like to change clothes first. Do we have enough time for that?"

"Of course," Mabel said. "I'll wait with Tavis in the pod while you and Isaac go. You'll find dry clothes in the house you stayed in last night."

Mabel ushered Tavis toward the pod, dropping Tavis' shoulder bag on the sand as she chattered on about how much Jack was going to love seeing some object he didn't quite catch the name of.

Just as they entered the pod, Mabel turned to Jack and winked at him, then nodded at the shoulder bag. "Find some food while you're there, your stomach's growling again."

His mother had just given him the items, and the time he needed to hide those items, and he wasn't about to waste the opportunity. "We need to hurry," Jack said to Isaac and snatched up the shoulder bag.

Isaac rushed to keep up with Jack as he raced through the island forest to reach the entrance of the massive cave. Jack nearly tripped down the narrow staircase leading to the bottom of the cave, but Isaac grabbed his arm, saving him from a graceless fall.

When they arrived at the center of the cave, Jack scanned the entire surface, hoping to confirm what he suspected. They stood on a narrow strip of cave floor that led to the larger ship, still perched on the stone columns. Jack studied the deep pools of water surrounding them and settled on one singular question.

"Is this a naturally occurring underwater cave?"

Grinning first, Isaac said, "It is. Any time this island is moved, it's always situated over a cave like this so that we can hide our ship. It just so happens to be the perfect kind of hiding place."

Jack smiled and nodded at his father, and then rummaged through the shoulder bag for the two amulets. After removing the towel from around his waist, he took an amulet into each of his hands and dove into the water. He swam alongside the underwater portion of the cave wall, looking for the best place to put them. There were many ledges and alcoves to pick from, as well as several rock formations that jutted outward from the wall.

One in particular snagged Jack's attention. It had the odd shape of a frog that appeared to be about to leap forward and he remembered the day he showed Sebastian the Mountain Chicken he'd found.

It was as good a place as any, and Jack placed the amulets side by side under what would be its belly if it was a real frog. There was a faint glow coming from the amulets since they were placed so close together, giving the underwater alcove a ghostly haunted look of loneliness.

Feeling his lungs beginning to protest the lack of oxygen, Jack took Sebastian's chain and key off and hung it around the rock frog's neck. When he reemerged at the surface, his father held out the towel for him.

"Did you find a spot?"

"I think so." Jack had to trust his choice. "If they're alive, and if they manage to find this cave, then at least they'll have some way of communicating with us."

"You've done the best you can, Jack. I just wish we could leave the island in this spot for longer. We used to be able to, but it's unwise these days… and there's been talk of leaving Earth permanently."

~

When they reached the house, Jack changed clothes quickly and scarfed down two apples on the way back to the pod—they only made him hungrier. "They're all gonna think I'm a gluttonous pig!"

"Probably, but once they give you a medical exam, they'll understand why," Isaac said.

Jack grimaced at the reminder. "They're not gonna stick probes anywhere, I hope."

"Of course not, they have machines for that."

"What?" Jack stopped just short of the pod entrance.

"I'm kidding you." Isaac laughed at the horrified look on Jack's face. "The exam is to make sure you aren't carrying any foreign bacteria or viruses. Which you're not, Galen would've discovered it if you were."

As a distraction, Isaac insisted Tavis help him pilot the pod so she wouldn't notice the missing shoulder bag. He said there was no excuse for why she didn't know how to operate a non-homing pod at her age. "I knew how to fly this pod by the time I was knee-high to a grasshopper," he told her. "Besides, think of how much fun you'll have teaching Jack how to pilot."

Tavis frowned at the idea. "Nah, you can teach him yourself later."

"Hey! I heard that," Jack said.

She settled into the seat next to Isaac at the control desk while Jack sat next to Mabel by one of the domed windows. He watched as the pod lifted off the beach, there was no commotion as before when it came up through the floor of the stone house. The pod idled momentarily before beginning its ascent skyward. The full view of the island took shape and Jack noted its simplistic tropical design. It was nothing like Gamma's large size and mountainous terrain.

It became a speck in a vast ocean as they ascended to an even higher altitude, then it disappeared altogether. For a while, all Jack saw was the enormous ocean. Finally, the larger landmasses came into view and he recognized one of them right away.

"East America," he whispered. "We were in the Atlantic Ocean."

"The Archilochun Island has settled in every one of the oceans on this planet, several times over," Mabel said.

All of East and West America formed in his window. He saw the ongoing efforts of West America to separate itself from the East by changing the flow of their rivers, hoping to one day be separated by a wide sea. It had to be John Paul who devised this plan for them and it made Jack smile and hope that West America continued to maintain their independence.

As their speed accelerated, the planet began to look more like a blue marble with swirls of white, green, and brown, surrounded by black space. It was so wondrous looking at it like this; like nothing but peaceful things lived there—beautiful, but deadly in so many ways. Though he would miss some of the beauty, he was happy to be leaving it.

Just like the island, Earth became a speck as they traveled farther away from it. For another while, there was nothing to see but black empty space. Jack was vaguely aware of Isaac and Tavis' voices in the background, but he wasn't listening to their actual words. He was too immersed in escalating fear as he remained glued to a window that offered nothing of a landscape beyond black nothingness. Aside from the pod, Jack felt homeless.

A hand brushed against his back. "We're almost there," his mother whispered, as though she'd sensed his anxiety and wanted to quell it.

"I'll show you how to land another time," Isaac said to Tavis, as she hadn't been able to sit still for five minutes straight.

"I'm sorry. It's just that we're almost there, and I was hoping to be with Jack when he sees Domum."

"Go be with him. I'm sure he wants you there, too."

Tavis sprang out of the chair and joined Jack at the window. Jack put his arm around Tavis after she sat in the seat Mabel had graciously vacated. He was thankful she was with him—he needed to feel her excitement. Right away she started fidgeting, unable to sit still here either. It brought a smile back to his lips.

Jack's mood fed off of her spirited energy and he grew anxious to see the planet, too.

The pod slowly veered to the right and Domum came into view—his jaw dropped at the sight of it. He'd just seen Earth only moments before from the same distance, and now he was looking at another planet that bore a striking similarity—and no one on Earth knew about it; save a few he doubted would ever get the chance to find it.

"John Paul was right," Jack said. "It does look like Archilochus."

"I can't wait for you to see it all."

The turquoise ocean planet was banded in neat rings of land formations, connected by diagonal land bridges, and all was blanketed in large tracts of forests, dotted with lakes and rivers. Beautiful white clouds swirled around parts of the planet, giving it a familiar marbled appearance.

"They know we're coming," Tavis said. "Isaac sent them a message."

"I hope they have the good sense to have Lani there."

"I'm sure Meg and Alec will see to it personally."

Jack turned to stone at the mention of Meg and Alec. "We're gonna have to tell them about…"

"I know," she said. "We'll tell them together."

"Together."

30

Epilogue

Jack stood from his desk chair in the communications office of Princeps' Administration Building. He should've left ten minutes earlier and if he didn't hurry it up, he'd be late for Lani's birthday celebration—which Tavis had spent a considerable amount of time planning to perfection. He was halfway down the hallway when he realized he'd left Lani's gifts on his desk.

Turning around, he trotted back to his office. Months ago, he'd asked Galen to find a few books Jack remembered reading as a child, and he wanted to read them to Lani. There were plenty of books on Domum, but they were mostly academic, or of a historical nature. Books of whimsy and folly were few and far between.

When his hand reached out to open the door, Jack could've sworn he heard someone talking inside his office. He frowned and eased the door open.

"Hello? Is anyone there?" a man's voice asked.

The hairs on the back of Jack's neck stood up and he peered around the door to where the message receiving base was. As the lights were off, the brightest light in the room now came from the image projected from the base.

Animating from it was a man's burly face with a full thick beard, and whose wet hair needed a trim by no less than a year. His hologram face looked around the dark room, searching for signs that anyone may still be there while droplets of water fell from the scruffy beard. Jack came out a little farther from behind the door, mesmerized by the image.

The man's gaze shifted to Jack's figure and he squinted to get a better look.

"Who's there?" The bearded man called out in a familiar commanding way. "Come closer so I can see who you are."

Step by slow step, Jack inched nearer, causing the man to squint all the more. A knowing look evolved in the man's eyes, and what little could be seen of his mouth through his shaggy beard spread into a smile.

"Jack? Is that you? I can't tell you enough how good your face looks right now."

Jack bounded across the room and fell to his knees. He was eye to eye with the ridiculous-looking man and there was no mistaking whose blue eyes looked back at him. Jack's body shook with emotion and profound relief.

"You made it, Sebastian… you're alive." Jack barely recognized his own voice as it trembled with his body. He pulled himself together when the infamous chastising expression began to form on Sebastian's face. It was one Jack hadn't seen in a long time, and he realized now how much he'd missed it.

"I can't tell *you* enough how awful your face looks," Jack said, laughing, even though his eyes glistened with tears.

Sebastian's eyebrows raised at the playful insult. "Find a way to get us the hell out of here and I'll make it pretty for you again. How's that for a plan?"

"Yes, sir. I like that plan very much."

31

Acknowledgments

Props go to Anna Ashley, who was integral to GAMMA's inception... and its every iteration. She pulled no punches – hitting hard, but hitting true. Her charming badassery is legend. Without her, there would be no story to tell, and that is why this book is dedicated to her. She is my crux and crucible.

Others I would like to acknowledge and give thanks to:

Pamela Mather. She, too, is a blessing and I don't know what I did to deserve such an angel. (I'll dedicate the next one to you!) Propwash Gary, for all the technical jargon and mumbo jumbo. Google and YouTube, for everything – seriously, I really don't think I could've done it without you. (Maybe I'll dedicate one to you some day!) The powers that be, for not banging down my door after some of those Google and YouTube searches. I should probably thank all my neighbors, and also apologize, for putting up with all my shushing of: them, their children, and that one very loud barking dog, whose name is synonymous with 'Pancakes'. A small army of early readers: your opinions – the good, the bad, and the in-between – were invaluable to me. You each deserve an award for molding the path I took. I dedicate a great and vast swath of this acknowledgements page to you, because you educated me on the important points to ponder, and I am forever grateful. Acknowledgements also need to be given to *GAMMA*'s inspiration generators: Lieber, Abrams, Lindelof, and Cuse. Yes, I was a hopeless *LOST*ie, one who imagined yet another island, *and in this place I found a book.*

...And last, but never least:

Mom,

I still think about you all the time, still miss you every day, and still love you always. I know you're in a better place, but I sure would love it if you were still here with me. Until we meet again, I'll credit my every breath and endeavor to you in this world.

32

About the Author

M. Susanne Wiggins respectfully misbehaves in downtown Charleston, South Carolina, living vicariously through the historic city's bounty of diverse tourists and residents, and their many tales, adventures, and stories. They are, without a doubt, the workhorses of her imagination. Without them, and the vibrant snapshots of their lives, she says, "I am but an empty page. They've earned a standing ovation, and my undying gratitude, because there's a little bit of each of them in everything I write."